# His Other Wife

By Umm Zakiyyah

**HIS OTHER WIFE**
A Novel
By Umm Zakiyyah



ISBN: 978-1-942985-00-6
Library of Congress Control Number: 2015958572

All characters and events in this book are fictional.
Any resemblance to real persons or incidents is coincidental.

Order information at ummzakiyyah.com/store

Verses from Qur'an adapted from Saheeh International, Darussalam, and Yusuf Ali translations.

Published by Al-Walaa Publications
Camp Springs, Maryland USA

## AUTHOR'S NOTE

This book gives a glimpse into the fictional lives of Muslims who are striving to hold themselves, their lives, and their faith together after having suffered emotional, spiritual, and sexual abuse. As such, some sensitive subjects and experiences will be highlighted, albeit lightly. In this vein, all reflections, quotes, and journal entries mentioned herein are devised by me for the purposes of this literary work unless otherwise noted, whether in reference to a popular saying or to a specific author or expert.

The self-help book *YOU CAN BE A BETTER PERSON!* that is referenced in the latter part of the novel is completely fictional, as are the quotes from it. However, the books *Trail of Broken Wings* by Sejal Badani and *No Time To Say Goodbye* by Carla Fine are real, as is the organization Words Heal Inc: Sadie Peterson Delaney Literary Collaborative that provides resources for bibliotherapy, the use of books in healing and therapy.

The term "groupie" as referenced in fictional conversations in the novel was borrowed from the context used in the Facebook post by coach Megan Wyatt:

> Seeking Islamic knowledge isn't about being a "groupie." It's about seeking *'ilm* [knowledge] to bring you closer to Allah, and deeper into living your purpose. And for growth to happen, people often need to leave their 'group' to expand their knowledge. People often panic when they see people doing this, assuming they are somehow going astray. Beneath the panic is a hidden fear that one is afraid if they were to leave their group, they would go astray. So holding on to a "groupie identity" becomes a means of feeling certain. But a true seeker, one who is sincere about knowing God and living their purpose must not be one caught up in titles and labels, and rather, be moving with a heart that is always saying "Guide me [O Allah], and I will follow You." *La ilaha il Allah* is our purpose - find it wherever you must to actualize it.

Anyone interested in participating in affiliate programs or projects dedicated to community outreach and/or promoting literature and organizations for those facing spiritual and emotional crises can contact info@findingpeaceproject.org.

## ACKNOWLEDGEMENTS

I thank all of my UZ readers and members of His Other Wife Discussion Group for their support and feedback. I thank my developmental editor Jamilah El-Amin at jelaminedits@gmail.com for her time and dedication to this project. I also thank my daughter Fareedah for her honest critique of the original short story series.

I send a special thanks to my business consultant, KI Creative Studios at kicreativestudios.com, for their phenomenal work. This project wouldn't have been possible without you.

And as always, after God Himself, I owe my greatest thanks and appreciation to everyone who has remembered me in their private and public supplications to the One who holds with Him all good. A heartfelt thanks to you all.

Last and definitely not least, I thank you, the reader, for taking this journey with me.

May each of you be granted the greatest success in this world and the highest success in the Hereafter.

# GLOSSARY OF ARABIC TERMS

***Abi:*** "my father"
***adhkaar:*** recitation of remembrance of God or mentioning His Names (plural of *dhikr*)
***akhi:*** "my brother"
**Allah:** the Arabic term for "God"
***Allahu'alam:*** "God knows best"
***alhamdulillah:*** expression of praise to God
***'aqeedah:*** foundational religious beliefs
***'aqeeqah:*** celebration after the birth of a baby
***as-salaamu'alaikum:*** the Muslim greeting of peace, often followed by *wa-rahmatullaahi* and *wa-barakaatuh*
***astaghfirullah:*** "I seek God's forgiveness"
***a'oodhubillaah:*** "I seek refuge in God"
***ayah:*** part or verse of the Qur'an
***bai'ah:*** vow/pledge of loyalty and obedience
***bi'idhnillah:*** "with the help of God"
***bismillaah:*** "in the name of God"
***daff:*** hand drum
***da'wah:*** any teaching about Islam
***dhikr:*** recitation of remembrance of God
***du'aa:*** informal prayer or supplication to God
***dunya:*** the life of this world (as opposed to the Hereafter)
***emaan:*** faith or belief in God and Islam
***fatwa:*** religious ruling
***fitnah:*** a trial, tribulation, problem, or something that causes great difficulty to face or overcome
***habeebti:*** "my love"
**hadith:** statement of Prophet Muhammad
***halaal* or *halal:*** permissible, allowed
***haraam:*** forbidden, sinful
***hifdh:*** memorization of the Qur'an
***inshaaAllah*** or ***insha'Allah:*** God-willing or if God wills
***Istikhaarah:*** formal prayer and supplication performed when trying to make a decision
***Jannah:*** Paradise
***jilbaab:*** outer garment for Muslim women that resembles a large, loose dress (also "abaya")
***Jumu'ah:*** congregational Friday prayer services
***khimaar:*** cloth head cover worn by Muslim women, often referred to as hijab
***kufi:*** skullcap
***kufr:*** disbelief in Islam
***maashaaAllah*** or ***mashaAllah:*** "It was God's will," said in admiration or acceptance of something
***madhhab:*** an Islamic school of thought
***madhloom:*** one who has been wronged or oppressed
***mahr:*** dowry (marriage gift) given to the woman upon marriage
**masjid:** mosque
***mimbar:*** pulpit
***mus-haf:*** an all-Arabic Qur'an (Muslim holy book)
***musallaa:*** prayer area
***naseehah:*** sincere advice
***nasheed:*** Islamic song
***nikaah:*** marriage contract or ceremony
***niqaab:*** face veil
***qadr:*** fate or predestination
***qiblah:*** the direction of Makkah, faced during formal prayer
***Qiyaam al-Layl:*** voluntary night prayer (also *Taraweeh*)
**Qur'an:** Muslim holy book
***Salaah:*** formal, obligatory prayer, of which there are five: *Fajr*, *Dhuhr*, *Asr*, *Maghrib*, and *'Ishaa*
***sallallaahu'alayhi wa sallam:*** "May peace and blessings be upon him."
***seerah:*** biography
***shahaadah* or *shahādah:*** formal testimony recited to mark one's entry into Islam
***Shaytaan* (plural: *shayateen*)** Satan or demon
***shirk:*** worshipping other than God; giving God attributes of creation or vice versa
***shuyookh:*** plural for "sheikh"
***surah or soorah:*** a chapter of the Qur'an
***subhaanAllah:*** expression of glorification of God; often said in surprise, dismay, or deep reflection
***Sunnah:*** life example of Prophet Muhammad; also: voluntary prayer
***tab'an:*** "of course" or "naturally"
***tafseer* or *tafsir:*** explanation of the meaning of Qur'an
***taqwaa:*** God-consciousness or sincere piety
***tawakkul:*** complete trust in God
***thawb:*** Arab-style male robe
***ukhti:*** "my sister"
***Ummi:*** "my mother"
***wa'alaiku mus-salaam:*** the Muslim greeting of peace and response to *As-salaamu'alaikum,* often followed by *wa-rahmatullaahi* and *wa-barakaatuh*
***waleemah* or *walimah:*** wedding celebration
***wali:*** a woman's marriage guardian; also: ally of Allah or sincere, pious worshipper with whom God is greatly pleased (plural: *awliyaa'*)
***wallah, wallaahi,* or *wallahi:*** a term used to make an oath in God's name
***zina:*** fornication or adultery

*For the struggling men and women. You know who you are.*

*"Marriage is not the end of the rainbow, and divorce is not the end of the world."*

—from the journal of Umm Zakiyyah

# 1
# His Other Wife

In the foyer of her apartment, Aliyah tilted her head to the side and unfastened the decorative hijab pin that secured the plum chiffon fabric in place. As the *khimaar* loosened itself from her head, she exhaled and kicked off her flats, relieved to be home. She set the scarf pin on the front table next to her cell phone then casually tapped her forefinger on the mobile screen to log in to her voicemail.

Aliyah frowned in disappointment as she realized that the single message that had been left on her phone while she was at work all day was from her uncle. Disinterested, she put the voicemail on speakerphone as she pulled the loosened cloth from her head then ran a palm over the braids plaited to her scalp in cornrows. Holding her *khimaar*, she scooped up the phone with her free hand and headed to the couch as her uncle's eager voice projected from the mobile.

"…So give me a call, Aliyah. I think this may be the one." Aliyah rolled her eyes as she let the chiffon cloth fall to the floor table in front of the couch then stabbed at her phone to delete the message before pressing the red icon to end the call.

She appreciated her uncle's enthusiasm in fulfilling his role as her marriage guardian, but she wasn't ready to get married. Her uncle had converted to Islam when she was in high school and had been influential in her own decision to become Muslim, and for that, she would always be grateful. Her parents practically disowned her after she left the church, and Benjamin was the closest thing to a father she'd had since accepting Islam in college. But for the past eight months Aliyah was becoming increasingly annoyed with her uncle.

But Aliyah couldn't ask her uncle to stop looking for a husband for her. Benjamin was wrestling a guilty conscience more than he was feeding his enthusiasm as her *wali*. It wasn't his fault that Aliyah was divorced. She wished he could understand that. If there was anyone to blame for her marriage falling apart, it was Aliyah herself. She was the one who'd eagerly introduced Matthew to her uncle and begged him to support the marriage. She'd foolishly believed that if she did everything right, everything would turn out all right.

Matthew was one of the good guys, Aliyah couldn't deny that. But she should have been less naïve about the nuances of the spiritual growth of a new Muslim. Matthew had been Muslim only a year when they'd met, and Aliyah had been Muslim for eight. It wasn't until they were living together as husband and wife that the seven years between their Islamic experiences felt like light years.

Aliyah tossed her cell phone on a sofa cushion then collapsed onto the couch herself. She leaned her head back in exhaustion and stared at the ceiling of her apartment. *I need a new job*, she thought to herself. She liked teaching algebra and computer science at the local college, but the money simply was not enough.

She fought a tinge of guilt as she recalled being penniless and jobless and begging God to send her any form of provision. In the end, it was her best friend,

Deanna, who came through for her by asking her husband to put in a good word for Aliyah at the college where he worked. Aliyah was ecstatic when she was notified that she was hired for the position. It had been hard to believe she was a bona fide college professor now. And it didn't hurt that the masjid was only a five-minute drive from the campus, so she was able to relax in the women's prayer area during her lunch break and planning periods if she didn't have any student appointments.

The shrilling of the home phone sent Aliyah's heart racing, and she sat up quickly and opened her eyes. Aliyah hadn't realized she had fallen asleep. The house was dark except for a glow of light coming from the kitchen. The phone shrilled again, and Aliyah groaned as she pushed herself off the couch and walked over to where the cordless sat on a wall table near the front door.

"Hello?"

"Girl, open the door."

Aliyah hung up without replying, and true to character, Deanna was pounding on the front door before Aliyah could even unbolt it and pull it open.

"Are you deaf?" Deanna said as she stepped into the foyer carrying a half-full paper grocery bag. "I've been standing outside that door for at least ten minutes."

Deanna must have come from one of her workshops, Aliyah guessed based on the tailored crimson pantsuit and matching stilettos that she wore. Deanna's flushed cheeks suggested agitation that had been incited by something other than Aliyah, but Aliyah knew Deanna wouldn't mention whatever it was. Deanna's façade of strength was impenetrable.

"I'm sorry, Deeja," Aliyah said as she closed the door and locked it. "I was knocked out."

Deanna rolled her eyes as she handed the paper bag to Aliyah then readjusted the straps of her designer handbag on her shoulder. "Put the ice cream in the freezer before it melts, and you might want to heat up the gyros in the microwave."

Aliyah's eyes widened, and a smile spread across her face as she peered into the bag. "You brought gyros?"

"Yes, against my better judgment," Deanna said as she kicked off her heels. "You know that bread has too many carbs."

"I love you, Deeja!" Aliyah sang out as she made her way to the kitchen and Deanna invited herself into the living room.

"Yeah, yeah, whatever. Where's the remote?"

"It's probably on the couch somewhere," Aliyah called out from the kitchen. A minute later she returned to the living room with the gyros on a glass serving plate, a stack of paper napkins next to them.

"I saw his other wife," Deanna said as she stretched out her legs and flexed each foot from where she sat on the couch.

Aliyah felt nauseated as she set the plate on the floor table in front of Deanna then pushed aside the *khimaar* that was lying there. "How do you know it was her?"

Deanna pointed the remote toward the television to turn down the volume. "It was her." She set down the remote then reached for a gyro. "She was with Matt," she said as she folded her legs under her as she often did to get comfortable.

"May Allah bless their marriage," Aliyah muttered as she lifted a gyro from the plate then sat down next to Deanna on the couch.

Deanna's hand froze inches from her mouth as she glared at Aliyah. "No, Ally. That is not the correct response to this news."

"Deanna Janice Bivens," Aliyah said, purposefully using the authoritative tone that Deanna's mother often used when she referred to Deanna by her full name, "yes it is the correct response. Now let's eat."

"You know what your problem is?" Deanna said thoughtfully, setting down her gyro. "You're too nice. That's why people run all over you. I'm not saying you have to wish harm on that girl, but you don't have to pray for her marriage. She stole your husband, for goodness sake."

"She didn't steal my husband." Aliyah took a generous bite of her gyro, her eyes on the television screen as she savored the taste of soft bread, seasoned lamb, raw onions, and cream sauce.

"Oh, I'm sorry. I forgot," Deanna said sarcastically. "You *gave* him to her." She picked up her gyro again and took a bite, a disturbed expression on her face as she stared at the TV, her cheeks bulging slightly as she chewed.

Aliyah lifted the remote from next to Deanna and turned up the volume, but it was difficult to pay attention to what the detective actress was saying to the police officer.

"Even when we were in college," Deanna said, raising her voice over the television, "you always wanted to make everyone happy. But there's only one woman who can make a man happy, and that's his wife."

Aliyah remained silent until she finished her gyro. "She is his wife," she said as she lifted a napkin from the plate and wiped her hands and mouth.

"And she was also his *second* wife."

Aliyah gritted her teeth. "Deeja, let's not go there."

"Ally, please. You know I'm right. You practically became the poster child for women supporting polygamy, and that was a terrible mistake. You don't let some woman convince you it's your Islamic duty to share your husband."

"I suggested polygamy, she didn't," Aliyah said, voice clipped. "Anyway, what does it matter now? I've been divorced for over a year. Leave it alone."

"No, I can't," Deanna said. "I'm really bothered that you didn't take my advice."

"Why do you think you have the answer to everything? You may be a marriage counselor, but that doesn't make you an expert on marriage."

"Do you even hear yourself? Of course that makes me an expert on marriage. This is my area of expertise. I did my doctorate thesis on—"

"Yes, I know, as you've said a million times. But every marriage isn't salvageable, Deeja."

"See, Ally, this is what pisses me off, your defeatist attitude. Do you know why I've been married for eleven years and why Jacob and I would never even think about divorce?"

"Um, let's see..." Aliyah said sarcastically. "Could it be because of Allah's *qadr* maybe?"

"This is why you should spend less time in the masjid. You think it's okay to hide behind religion so you can blame all your mistakes on some divine plan. God helps those who help themselves."

"I'm just trying to—"

"Stop trying, Ally, and *do*," Deanna interjected, annoyance in her tone. "I don't sit around saying I'm *trying* to stay married. I stay married. I don't sit around saying I don't want my husband to marry another wife. I make sure I'm the only wife he'll ever want. If you think proactively, then you won't react to life. You'll make life happen."

Aliyah rolled her eyes. "And how do I do that? Do tell."

"First of all, you have to quit being so cynical. You look way better than Matt's new wife. There's no way he would've chosen her over you without you egging him on. If you would've just—"

Aliyah raised a palm to Deanna. "Deeja, just stop, please. I can't stand all this *if only if*. I don't believe in that. You can call me a religious fanatic if you want, but I believe it was Allah's plan that I'm not married to Matt anymore. I did everything I could to save my marriage."

"Except listen to your best friend."

Aliyah's eyes widened. "I can't believe you're saying that. I did listen to you. I just—"

"Then how did Matt end up marrying that tramp while you were still married to him?"

"Like I said, Deeja. I listened to you, but I just had a different point of view."

"Then you didn't listen to me. You can't just *hear* me. You have to listen. The way to keep a man from marrying someone else is you keep the subject of divorce and polygamy out of your marriage. Jacob would never marry another woman because I don't give him any reason to."

"Jacob would never marry another woman, Deeja, because he doesn't want to. You said yourself that he believes it's part of Islam to respect the laws of the land and that he just doesn't think polygamy is worth the headache."

"Yes, but the main reason he'll never do it is because I make sure I'm good enough for him. I take care of myself. I give him sex every night. I pamper him. I—"

"I, I, I," Aliyah said as she pointed the remote forward and powered off the television. "Dr. Deanna Bivens, the I-specialist."

"I know you think I'm arrogant, but—"

"Overly confident is what crosses my mind. But I don't think *arrogant* is too far off the mark."

"—I know what I'm talking about. I've counseled dozens of couples, Ally, so I'm not talking out the side of my neck. There really is something to putting in the work to make a marriage last. When a married person cheats, there's always a reason, a preventable reason."

"Matt didn't cheat."

"He didn't have to. You gave him permission to betray you right in front of your face. With your approval."

"That's not how I define supporting polygyny."

"You can try to put an Islamic stamp on this if you want. But the bottom line is that your marriage was in trouble and instead of proving how much *you* were worth, you supported the very thing that was tearing apart your marriage."

Aliyah felt exhausted all of a sudden. "Look, Deeja, I don't feel like fighting about this anymore. What's done is done. I can't rewrite the past."

"I'm not bringing this up to open old wounds. I just don't feel comfortable helping you find a new husband until I'm sure you understand what marriage means."

Aliyah felt herself getting upset again, but she remained composed. "I didn't ask you to help me find a new husband."

"You don't have to, Ally. I'm your friend, so I'll do whatever I can to help you whether you ask me or not. But the first step is learning what it means to be a woman."

Aliyah clenched her jaw. "And now you're an expert on the female sex?"

The chiming of a phone came from next to Deanna. Deanna turned and reached into her handbag and withdrew her cell phone. "That's Jacob," Deanna said apologetically after looking at the screen. She returned the phone to her purse and stood, pulling the straps over her shoulder. "Sorry I couldn't stay long. I just wanted to give you something decent to eat. I figured you're starving yourself up in here."

"Thanks for stopping by," Aliyah said in as cordial a voice as she could manage. She stood and followed her friend to the door.

Deanna drew Aliyah into a hug and kissed her on the cheek. "I love you," Deanna said as she opened the front door.

"I love you too," Aliyah said. "*As-salaamu'alaikum.*"

Aliyah closed the door as the sound of Deanna's footsteps faded in the apartment hallway. As she turned the bolt to lock the door, Aliyah realized she hadn't prayed *Maghrib*, the sunset prayer. She glanced at the clock and sighed. It was already time for *'Ishaa*. She had to get better at praying on time.

After completing her prayers, Aliyah sat on the carpeted floor of the living room, her body heavy in exhaustion. *I don't know how much more I can take from Deanna.* The plea had come from a deep place inside, and Aliyah frowned at their implication. Was she really thinking of giving up her best friend?

"You need to be more like me," Deanna often said to Aliyah.

Maybe Deanna was right. Aliyah needed to have more confidence in herself. If Aliyah were more like Deanna, perhaps Aliyah would still be married to Matthew. Aliyah couldn't deny that a part of her envied the relationship that Deanna had with Jacob. It was obvious that Jacob absolutely adored his wife. Aliyah would often overhear Jacob talking about Deanna at work. Occasionally, when Deanna was assigned to conduct a marriage workshop, she and Jacob would facilitate the workshop together, and the chemistry and connection between them was undeniable. Once, when Aliyah and Matthew had attended one of the workshops, they had left in awe and were full of determination to implement some of the marriage-saving strategies Deanna and Jacob had discussed.

But as inspiring as Deanna was as a speaker and marriage counselor, she was becoming more and more difficult to deal with as a friend. In college, Aliyah and Deanna had bonded like long-lost sisters being reunited for the first time. They had so much in common then. They were both new Muslims struggling with difficult families. They were both academics with big dreams and high hopes. They both wanted to run their own businesses *and* be dedicated wives and mothers. And most importantly, they both were determined to make Islam the foundation and focus of their lives.

On the soft carpet of her living room, Aliyah murmured the Arabic phrases of glorification and praise of God, as was the prophetic custom after obligatory prayer. Her gaze was on the upturned palm of her right hand, where she was using her thumb to enumerate the recitation of *dhikr*. But her conflicted feelings about her friendship with Deanna were distracting her from the remembrance of Allah.

*Could what Deanna and I have even be called a friendship?* Aliyah wondered. In college perhaps, she considered thoughtfully. But even back then, when all seemed to be going well for their lives and friendship, Deanna had been the anchor of their relationship. At the time, Aliyah saw this as an immense blessing. She had been suffering from bouts of depression after her parents told her to never call or visit the family again "if you insist on being part of that Osama bin Laden religion." Aliyah had been very close to her family and had never imagined that the all-encompassing Christian love her parents talked so much about would not be extended to their now-Muslim daughter.

During this difficult time, Deanna's presence alone was enough to cheer Aliyah up. Deanna would cook for her, accompany her to Islamic events, give her surprise parties, treat her to a day at the spa, and even sleep on the floor in Aliyah's dorm room if Aliyah was having a particularly bad day.

Sometimes Aliyah had felt like a burden to Deanna, but Deanna would always reassure Aliyah that she was happy to be there for her and earn so many blessings. "You're my sister, girl. I love you. If you're happy, I'm happy."

But Aliyah was often racked with guilt because she just couldn't muster the same enthusiasm for impetuous fun, or for Deanna's presence. There were times she really did want to be alone. Even when she was a child, Aliyah hated crowds. Attending church on Christmas and Easter often stressed her out because there were just too many people in one room, and Aliyah didn't know what to do with herself. So when Deanna would plan sudden trips to the mall or announce that they were going to some relaxing retreat for the weekend, Aliyah would often feel suffocated with anxiety. In college, there were even times that Deanna's presence itself was suffocating.

But Aliyah was never able to bring herself to talk to Deanna fully and honestly about her feelings, though there were moments that she tried. Whenever the thought came to her, she felt like an ingrate. *I mean, what kind of person gets upset when her best friend is going out of her way to be nice and helpful?*

"Shut up, girl. You know you love me." That had been Deanna's response when Aliyah had, shortly after the divorce, mustered up the courage to tell Deanna that her unannounced visits, incessant phone calls, and constant "constructive criticism" were becoming too much to bear.

"I just need some time alone," Aliyah had said.

"That's what got you into this mess in the first place," Deanna had responded flippantly, a playful grin on her face. "You spending time alone while you let your husband sleep with another woman." Then she pulled Aliyah into a tight hug and said, "Let's go shopping. That will make you feel better."

But it didn't make Aliyah feel better. And Aliyah had come back home with three department-store bags full of clothes and accessories that she didn't want or need.

"I think you're jealous of me," Deanna had told Aliyah last week after they had another big argument over the "real reason" Aliyah was no longer married. As always, Deanna insisted that it was because Aliyah wasn't more like she was and because Aliyah had been open to letting Matthew marry another wife. Agitated and sick of Deanna's constant holier-than-thou nitpicking, Aliyah had said, "Maybe your marriage isn't so great. You don't know everything. For all you know, Jacob could be looking for another wife right now. I would if I were him. I can't imagine living with your nagging every day."

Aliyah immediately regretted the comment after she'd said it. But at the time, she felt justified. Couldn't Deanna just leave well enough alone already? *Okay, fine, your marriage is great. Your husband loves you and doesn't want another wife. But that's from Allah, not you. So shut up already.*

"I'm sorry," Aliyah had said, dropping her head in shame. "I shouldn't have said that."

"It's okay," Deanna had replied, reaching out and squeezing Aliyah's hands warmly. "I forgive you. I know it's hard to have a friend like me."

Aliyah had coughed laughter, nodding in agreement. Tears stung her eyes as she realized that Deanna was finally understanding the heart-wrenching struggle it was for Aliyah to maintain their friendship.

"It would be hard for me too if my friend had the life I could never have," Deanna had added before pecking Aliyah on the cheek with a kiss.

The shrilling of the home phone interrupted Aliyah's thoughts, and she immediately stood and walked over to the cordless. She glanced at the caller identification display and sighed when she saw the name *Nelson, Benjamin.*

"*As-salaamu'alikum*, Uncle Ben," Aliyah said as if exhaling into the phone. She didn't feel like talking about marriage right then, but she couldn't keep avoiding her uncle. Besides, after the tense visit with Deanna, she relished the opportunity to hear from someone who actually believed she had all she needed to be happy and make someone else happy on top of that. She was tired of being Matt's "other wife," the wife he didn't choose after he married another woman—with her support.

"*Wa'alaiku-mus-salaam wa rahmatullaahi wa barakaatuh*, my beloved niece," Benjamin practically sang through the receiver.

Aliyah burst out laughing. Benjamin's mood was always upbeat whenever he felt he'd finally found "the one," the man who was Aliyah's long-lost soul mate, the man for whom (by some divine order) Matthew had only been Aliyah's boot camp in preparation for "the real deal."

"Who is it this time?" Aliyah said, an expectant smile lingering on her face.

"Hey," Benjamin said playfully, "that's no attitude to have before I announce who your Prince Charming is."

"You say that every time."

"This time is different. I really think this is the one."

Aliyah chuckled. "And you say that every time too."

"Well," Benjamin said guiltily, laughter in his voice, "this one called me a couple of weeks ago and asked that I give him a chance to prove he's the one for you. But I didn't want to tell you until I was sure he was worthy."

"Does he have a green card?" Aliyah asked jokingly.

"Yes."

"A job?"

"Yes," Benjamin said, "and a successful side business." Aliyah could practically hear her uncle beaming in triumph.

"That actually makes money?"

"Yes, lots of it."

Aliyah was unable to temper the growing curiosity. "And he called you, not the other way around?"

"Yes, he called me." Benjamin chuckled self-consciously. "Truth be told, if I would've known he was looking, I would've called him myself. He's definitely the kind of man I think would see how special you are and never take that for granted."

"Do I know him?"

"Yes, I think you do."

Aliyah furrowed her brows as she searched her mind for who this could be. "How? From the masjid?"

Benjamin was silent momentarily. "Look, Aliyah," he said, his voice more serious. "Before you give your answer, just think about it, okay?"

"Uncle Ben," Aliyah said, her voice stern and cautious. "Don't tell me this is another one of those perverted she-could-be-my-second-wife brothers."

"Aliyah, don't say that."

"Uncle Ben!" Aliyah should have known better than to get her hopes up. She had made it abundantly clear that she was not entertaining the proposal of any married men. She was not interested in another Matt-style disaster. She didn't want to marry someone and wonder whether or not she would be the woman he dumped in the end.

"It's Jacob."

It took several seconds before Aliyah registered her uncle's words.

"*What*?"

"I know it's unexpected, Aliyah," Benjamin said, apology in his tone. "But he and I have been talking almost every day, and I really think this could work if—"

Aliyah felt faint all of a sudden, and her heart raced in confusion and shock. "Let's not talk about this anymore," she said, almost choking on her words.

"But, Aliyah, he's really seri—"

"*As-salaamu'alaikum*, Uncle Ben," Aliyah said through gritted teeth before pulling the phone away from her ear and disconnecting the call.

## 2
## Her Secret Admirer

"There are five ingredients to a successful marriage," Deanna said as she stepped from behind the podium to make herself more fully visible to the audience. "Selflessness, trust, honesty, intimacy, and confidence." She casually slipped her hands into the pockets of her wide-leg black pants, conscious of the intrigue that her powerful words and exotic appearance inspired in the audience. "You might be thinking to yourself: But she forgot to mention love. She forgot to mention communication. She forgot to mention friendship." Deanna smiled and shook her head, the cloth of her rust colored hijab moving with her. She had chosen the color because it was subtle enough to exude humility and bold enough to accentuate her light creamy brown complexion. "No, I didn't forget any of these things. Love can never be an *ingredient* to a successful marriage." She lifted her hands as if to ward off an attack. "I know, I know. You want the moderators to forcibly remove me from this marriage conference."

There were ripples of laughter throughout the auditorium.

"But an ingredient is what you put into something for a desired result," she said. "And love is not something you put into a marriage. You either bring love with you before you tie the knot, or it blossoms as a natural result of a successful marriage."

She walked toward the other end of the stage. "And as for communication and friendship. Communication in itself isn't an ingredient to a successful marriage. It's a natural result of selflessness, trust, and honesty. Without selflessness, trust, and honesty, communication is not helpful; it's harmful. And as for friendship," she said, "that too is a natural result of selflessness, trust, and honesty."

She nodded her head toward the large projector screen that displayed the cover of her bestselling marriage advice book, *You Can Have Him All To Yourself.* "And as I discuss in the chapter entitled 'Confidence Is Sexy,' having confidence in yourself and your self-worth not only makes you more physically attractive, it is also a lifesaver, a marriage lifesaver. Because that confidence you feel translates into confidence in your marriage and confidence in your spouse. And guess what? That confidence is contagious. And it serves as one of the most formidable forces protecting you or your spouse from even considering divorce." She smiled then added, "Or cheating."

There was a roar of applause as Deanna descended the steps on the side of the stage, and a surge of pride rose in her chest as she realized that she had effortlessly wowed the audience once again.

***

Aliyah brought her hands together in applause then glanced at her wristwatch. She wondered if it would be rude to leave the convention center right then. Weeks before her uncle Benjamin had called to tell her that Jacob, Deanna's husband of eleven years, had expressed interest in marrying her, Aliyah had reluctantly agreed to come to the *Don't Get Lost in Love* marriage conference. Her best friend—Dr. Deanna Bivens, Ph.D.—was an invited speaker and facilitator for several sessions and had insisted that Aliyah attend.

"I don't see the point," Aliyah had told Deanna when she'd first mentioned it. "I'm divorced."

"That's all the more reason you should come," Deanna had said. "It can help you understand your mistakes better."

*You mean* you *can help me understand my mistakes better*, Aliyah had wanted to say. But she'd held her tongue. There was no use arguing with Deanna. It never ended well, at least not when Aliyah appeared to have a mind of her own.

"There you are!"

Aliyah's shoulders jerked in surprise as Deanna's smiling face appeared in front of her. Aliyah had no idea how Deanna was able to single her out in such a large crowd.

"Let's go get something to eat," Deanna said, tugging on Aliyah's hand. "I'm famished."

"I'm kind of tired actually," Aliyah said as she stood, Deanna still tugging on her hand. "I wanted to go home and get some work d—"

"Oh, girl please," Deanna said, cutting Aliyah off mid-sentence. "You promised me that we'd spend this whole weekend together."

Aliyah furrowed her brows. On the stage, the moderator was announcing the next speaker. "I said I'd try to come to some of your sessions if I wasn't busy," Aliyah said in a hushed tone, leaning into Deanna.

"I have one more session tonight," Deanna said as she looped her arm through Aliyah's and started walking toward the auditorium exit.

Aliyah felt a bout of anxiety overcome her. "What time?"

"Nine o'clock," Deanna said. "But don't worry, I'm free until then."

Aliyah's eyes widened. "That's in two and half hours, Deeja. I can't—"

"Thank you so much for that," an older woman said, leaning into the aisle as Deanna and Aliyah passed. "It was really eye-opening."

"Thank *you*," Deanna said, halting her steps and turning to face the woman, a broad smile on her face. "People like you are the reason I work so hard."

"Well, it's much appreciated," the woman said. "Truly. It's so inspirational to see young people taking marriage seriously. Sessions like these should be mandatory for young couples. They take marriage so lightly these days."

"I *know*. Don't they?" Deanna side-eyed Aliyah.

"You all have a good evening," the woman said as the next speaker took the podium.

"You too," Deanna replied, beaming, and Aliyah sensed a hint of triumph in Deanna's gait as they exited the auditorium.

"That's a sign from Allah," Deanna said when they were in the conference hall lobby area.

Aliyah was distracted by thoughts of how to get out of having dinner with Deanna and attending another session. "What?"

"That woman," Deanna said. "I think Allah sent her so that you'll take me more seriously."

"Or maybe He sent her so you'll be grateful for the blessings He's given you in your work," Aliyah said. "Everything isn't about proving me wrong."

"I'm not trying to prove you wrong, Ally. There's no point in wasting time on something like that."

"Well, it seems all you have time for these days."

"Ally, I don't need to prove you wrong. There's nothing to prove. You're wrong, and that's clear, even to you. The only thing you need to do is stop being so committed to failure."

Aliyah swallowed the anger building in her chest. She turned away from Deanna and pretended to study the conference schedule on a large vinyl sign hanging from the ceiling.

"I paid for you to come here so you can learn something," Deanna said, "not to prove you wrong. I don't want to see you throw away another marriage."

*Hmph,* Aliyah thought. *Another marriage.* Aliyah hadn't even met anyone she wanted to marry, so how could she throw away a marriage that didn't exist? *"It's Jacob,"* Benjamin had said to her a week ago. *"He asked that I give him a chance to prove he's the one for you."*

Aliyah shifted in guilty discomfort at the memory. Maybe she'd misunderstood her uncle. It was impossible that he could've been talking about Deanna's husband. Jacob and Deanna were a power couple. They were invincible. They loved each other. Jacob would never want to marry anyone else. He did marriage workshops with Deanna. He'd even written the introduction to her book *You Can Have Him All To Yourself.* Why would he do that if he knew Deanna wouldn't have *him* all to herself?

This was all one big misunderstanding, Aliyah realized. It had to be. Her uncle must have confused Jacob with someone else. Or maybe Aliyah herself had misheard. Whoever this "Prince Charming" was who Benjamin believed was "the one," it wasn't Jacob, at least not Deanna's Jacob.

"It's Jacob," Deanna said.

Aliyah's heart nearly leaped from her chest as she turned around, wide-eyed, to meet Deanna's gaze.

"It's Jacob," Deanna said again, grinning as she grabbed Aliyah's hand and pulled her forward, walking swiftly toward the glass doors leading outside. "I knew it all along."

"You did?" Aliyah asked, stumbling over her words—and her legs—as she stared dumbly at Deanna. The cool February air drifted toward them as Deanna opened the door and they stepped into the darkening evening and bustling atmosphere of downtown Washington, D.C.

"*As-salaamu'alikum,* sweet cake!" Deanna called out as she bounded toward a small crowd gathered on the wide sidewalk near a streetlight. "I knew it! I knew it!" Deanna shouted, laughter in her voice as she released Aliyah and rushed toward the crowd. Deanna laughed as she embraced a man in the crowd, and they kissed briefly on the lips.

"*Wa'alaiku-mus-salaam*, honey," Jacob said coolly, a knowing grin on his face.

Deanna glanced back and gestured for Aliyah to come join them. "It's Jacob," Deanna said, a smile still plastered to her face. "He said he couldn't make it to the conference. But he just wanted to surprise me. I *knew* it," she said again, brushing his cheek with a kiss.

The pounding in Aliyah's heart was deafening as she took a cautious step back. Her mouth opened to protest, but her tongue wouldn't move. Even in that confusing moment, she noticed him looking at her. Not Jacob, but a man next to him. The man had a closely trimmed beard and wore a business suit that did little to conceal his athletic build. There was an air of familiarity about him that Aliyah couldn't place.

"Jacob, man, who's that?" the man said in a low voice, clamping Jacob's shoulder as he nodded his head discreetly in Aliyah's direction.

"Did you guys eat yet?" Deanna asked, distracting Jacob's attention away from the man.

"We were just about to walk to this *halaal* restaurant down the street." Jacob's tone was so nonchalant that Aliyah wondered if he even noticed that she was standing less than ten feet away. Or maybe he was behaving normally because it made no difference to him that Aliyah was nearby—because the thought of marrying Aliyah as a second wife had never crossed his mind.

Aliyah had purposely avoided Jacob at work all week, even going as far as to skip a mandatory faculty meeting out of fear he might be there. It was the first time she'd ever done anything like that. She normally took her job responsibilities seriously, especially since she no longer benefited from Matt's income. Though Matt had custody of their now four-year-old son, Aliyah still had to factor in basic expenses for Ibrahim for when he came to visit; and she could barely pay basic expenses for herself. So she couldn't afford to slack at work. In the six months since she started working at the local college, she had never missed a single day, even when she was ill enough to stay home. But on Thursday, two days ago, she had told her supervisor that she was too unwell to attend the faculty meeting.

"That's perfect," Deanna said, turning to Aliyah. "We were just about to eat too."

"*MashaAllah*," Jacob said, looking toward Aliyah for the first time. "Then come join us. But we should start walking now. It'll probably be really crowded because of the conference."

Aliyah immediately lowered her gaze. But she couldn't help feeling self-conscious all of a sudden. In her mind's eye, she reviewed how she'd looked when she left home earlier that day. She'd selected one of her business-casual cream and black blouse-skirt ensembles because she liked the way it complemented her gentle brown complexion. Inadvertently, she reached up and smoothed down the soft fabric of her cream hijab and made sure the black-studded scarf pin was still in place. But she couldn't tell if her eyeliner, mascara, and frosted lip-gloss were undisturbed.

*What is your problem? Astaghfirullah,* Aliyah scolded herself, asking God's forgiveness. She had no business worrying about her appearance in front of her best friend's husband. Besides, most likely, she had misunderstood what her uncle was talking about. She hadn't even given Benjamin a chance to explain himself before ending the call. But now she wondered what her uncle was trying to say before she'd hung up on him.

As Jacob had mentioned, the restaurant was crowded due to the overflow from the marriage conference, but the receptionist who greeted them said the wait for a table shouldn't be more than thirty minutes. Aliyah felt the familiar tightening in her chest as she stood huddled with the group inside the restaurant near the entrance. She really should have found some excuse to go home. She wouldn't be able to enjoy her food if she had to be surrounded by so many people, especially while sitting at a table with a bunch of strangers—and Jacob.

Aliyah glanced in the direction of Jacob and saw him laughing at something one of the other men said, Deanna at his arm laughing too. Aliyah looked away. A sense of loneliness weighed on her, and she found herself wondering what Matthew was doing right then. But the image of Nikki, his new wife, came to mind, souring any chance of reminiscing. Rage burned her chest, and she muttered a *du'aa* to calm herself. The supplication helped quell her anger, but sadness settled in its place.

Aliyah should have known that Nikki and Matt had known each other long before Nikki suddenly appeared, eager to learn about Islam. Matt had asked Aliyah to talk to Nikki and answer any of her questions, and being the naïve, trusting wife that she was, Aliyah enthusiastically fell into "help the clueless non-Muslim" mode. It wasn't until months after talking on the phone with Nikki and occasionally inviting her over that Nikki casually mentioned that Matt had been her boyfriend in the last two years of high school and throughout most of college. Nikki had broken up with Matt mainly because she feared a long-distance relationship wouldn't work, so she'd suggested that they date other people to avoid feeling like they were tied down. When Nikki tracked Matt down years later, he was on the verge of converting to Islam, which was an immediate turnoff for her. So once again, they lost touch—until she reappeared after Matt married Aliyah, now suddenly interested in Islam herself.

"Excuse me," the receptionist said, approaching the group, "we have a table for eight ready now."

*Wow,* Aliyah thought to herself. Were they really that many? A surge of apprehension rose inside of her, and pain pulsated at her temples as she wondered where she would sit. But it turned out that Aliyah didn't have to worry about that.

"Come on, girl," Deanna said, almost yanking Aliyah forward as she made her way to the front of the group. "Let's get the best seats."

"The best seats" ended up being at one end of two tables pushed together near a window. Aliyah breathed a sigh of relief as she settled in a seat directly opposite Deanna. Moments like these she really appreciated her best friend. Even as a child, Aliyah was never good at speaking up for herself and saying what she wanted. As an adult, the only time she felt completely comfortable speaking her mind was when she was in front of a classroom. It wasn't the worst trait in the world, but at times it was debilitating. And, tonight, had it not been for Deanna's proactive move to get to the table first and ensure that they weren't sandwiched between anyone, Aliyah would probably have suffered an anxiety attack before the meal was over.

"*As-salaamu'alaikum*, sister. I don't think I've met you before."

Aliyah was fumbling with her menu when she had the odd sensation that someone was looking at her. She looked up to find the man from earlier sitting diagonally across from her next to Jacob, who was sitting next to Deanna (which put Jacob almost directly across from Aliyah). Instinctively, Aliyah glanced to her left to see who was sitting next to her. She recognized the woman immediately. Aliyah couldn't recall the woman's name, but she was definitely one of Aliyah's Facebook friends. The woman's profile picture frequently appeared in Aliyah's newsfeed.

"Jacob," the man said, "is this Brother Benyameen's niece, the one you were telling me about?"

Taken aback, Aliyah creased her forehead as she looked at the man. Was he talking about her? Muslims often referred to her uncle as Benyameen, the Arabic translation for the name Benjamin.

"Yes, it is," Jacob said, a proud smile on his face. But his eyes were skimming the menu he was holding.

Aliyah felt a soft kick to her shin under the table, and she immediately glared at Deanna. *What?* Aliyah mouthed. In response, Deanna wore a wide smile and jerked her head in the man's direction. *What?* Aliyah mouthed again, this time with an exaggerated look of confusion on her face. *That's him*, Deanna mouthed back. *That's who?* Aliyah replied. But Deanna just chuckled quietly and rolled her eyes. She picked up her menu and raised it high enough to block the lower part of her face, a clear hint that, whoever this man was, Aliyah was supposed to impress him tonight.

"Your name is Aliyah, right?" the man said.

Feeling awkward and put on the spot, Aliyah cheeks burned in embarrassment, but she managed a noncommittal nod. "Yes," she mumbled.

"Brother Benyameen talks about you all the time," the man said.

“Aliyah,” Jacob said, an apologetic smile creasing one corner of his mouth, “this is my brother, Larry. He took his *shahaadah* a few months ago.”

Aliyah realized then why the man seemed so familiar. He and Jacob resembled each other. And Aliyah may have even met Larry in passing years ago, before he was Muslim.

“But the brothers call me Ya’qoob,” Larry said quickly. Aliyah sensed the brother’s need to feel affirmation as a Muslim. In a way, it reminded her of Matthew, and a tinge of sadness pinched her. If there was one thing a new Muslim should never do, it was eagerly seek other Muslims’ approval.

“That’s because they keep confusing you with me,” Jacob said, humor in his tone.

Aliyah couldn’t keep from smiling. It was kind of funny, Larry thinking that the Arabic translation of Jacob was a “Muslim name” the brothers had given him.

A thought came to Aliyah suddenly. “Are you married?” she said, her tone a combination of hope and humor as she looked at Larry. It was an aha moment for Aliyah. Maybe it was Larry whom her uncle had been talking about when he’d referred to a brother “Jacob” interested in marrying her. Benjamin knew Jacob and Deanna, but he wasn’t close enough to them to easily distinguish Jacob from Larry. They did favor each other significantly. Even their voices sounded similar. And if Larry referred to himself as “Ya’qoob” whenever he called Benjamin, it was unlikely that her uncle would know it wasn’t Deanna’s husband he was talking to, but Deanna’s brother-in-law. So maybe Larry was the married brother looking for another wife—hence Aliyah’s sudden question.

The deafening silence at the table made Aliyah realize her faux pas. The sister next to her side-eyed her and contorted her face in disapproval.

*Married ladies! First rule of thumb: Dump your single girl friends! Ijs.*

Aliyah cringed. *Juwayriah bint Abdullah.* The sister’s name came to her just then. *Oh my God*, Aliyah thought to herself. The sister next to her was the one who’d posted that “rule of thumb” Facebook status a few months ago, sparking one of the longest and most heated social media debates in Aliyah’s online friend list.

Aliyah had expected Juwayriah to un-friend her after posting that controversial point of view (since, technically speaking, Aliyah was now single), and Aliyah remembered being surprised that the Juwayriah didn’t. But maybe that rule of thumb only applied in real life interactions, Aliyah figured.

“No,” Larry said, embarrassed laughter in his tone. Aliyah sensed that Larry was flattered by her question, naturally oblivious to the fact that the inquiry was not motivated by any personal interest in him. “But I hope to be soon,” he added, his gaze resting on her long enough to make her shift uncomfortably in her seat.

The flirtatious glint in his eye was unmistakable, and Aliyah was mortified for Larry. Someone really should have taught him about the social etiquette of lowering his gaze. Aliyah was all for letting new Muslims take the baby steps they needed to embrace the Islamic faith at their own pace, but gawking at females was one of the first things Aliyah felt male converts needed to curtail. It really was unbecoming, especially on a man who otherwise appeared levelheaded and intelligent.

"Are you all ready to order?" a perky voice said, interrupting Aliyah's thoughts.

"Yes, we are," Jacob said quickly, apparently in an effort to shift the focus to something other than Aliyah's social blunder and Larry's naiveté.

"Let's talk some time," Larry said, the side of his mouth twitching in a grin.

Aliyah met his gaze briefly, surprised to feel her own eyes glinting flirtatiously. "Yes, let's," she said in a low voice.

# 3
# The Other Woman

Aliyah turned to the left then to the right as she surveyed her appearance in the full-length mirror affixed to the door of her bedroom. *Not bad*, she thought to herself, an almost imperceptive grin forming on her lips. She had feared that the dark chocolate business suit wouldn't compliment her skin tone, but the silk ivory pearl-button blouse and matching georgette hijab brought out her brown complexion as well as the rich color of the tailored blazer and pants. *O Allah,* she silently supplicated, *You have made my physical constitution good, so make my character good also.*

As she drove to work Thursday morning, Aliyah's thoughts drifted to Larry. In the two weeks since they'd met at the *halaal* restaurant during the weekend of the marriage conference, Aliyah and Larry had spoken nearly every day. "Call me Ya'qoob," he'd told her during their first conversation. "I like that name."

"It's your brother's name," Aliyah said humorously, "only in Arabic."

"I know," Larry said, a tinge of sadness and humor in his tone. "It kind of grew on me." Larry told Aliyah that after a brother in the masjid first addressed him by that name, he'd researched its origin and came across the story of Prophet Ya'qoob in the Qur'an. "He went through so much, yet he remained patient," Larry said reflectively. "I could use that sort of inspiration in a name."

"I can understand that," Aliyah had replied. "I think we should find inspiration wherever we can."

"Did you know that in the Qur'an, the name Israel is actually another name for Jacob, the Prophet Ya'qoob?" Larry had childlike excitement in his voice. "The children of Israel are descendants of Jacob."

"Really?" Aliyah said, interest piqued. But she was more impressed with Larry's knowledge and spiritual motivation than with the information itself. "No, I didn't know that."

The chiming of her cell phone interrupted her thoughts. She glanced to where her cell phone lay in the compartment next to the driver's seat, and she was surprised to see a photo of Matthew appear on the screen. Though she and Matthew communicated regularly regarding their son Ibrahim, it was unlike Matthew to call early in the morning when they were both due at work. Aliyah's heart constricted in trepidation. Had something happened to Ibrahim?

"*As-salaamu'alaikum*," Aliyah said after accepting the call on speakerphone so she could use both hands to steer the car. "Is everything okay?" She was raising her voice so loudly that it verged on yelling, which was a bad habit of hers whenever she used the speakerphone option.

"*Wa'alaiku-mus-salaam*," a soft female voice replied.

Aliyah drew her eyebrows together. "Who's this?"

"This is Nicole."

Oh. Nikki. But why was Matthew's wife calling her? Aliyah and Nikki would sometimes see each other in passing whenever Aliyah came to pick up Ibrahim, but they hadn't spoken at length since Aliyah's divorce. *Oh my God,* Aliyah thought suddenly. Had something happened to Matt *and* Ibrahim?

"What's going on?" Aliyah asked. "What happened?"

"Everything's fine." There was a touch of haughtiness in Nikki's tone, as if amused by Aliyah's panic. "I'm just using Matt's phone because mine isn't working."

"Oh, okay…" Aliyah was unsure what to say.

"I know you're probably on your way to work," Nikki said, "so I won't take too much of your time." She drew in a deep breath, and Aliyah sensed that Nikki was preparing to say something offensive. "When my phone is fixed, I'll text you my number. That way you can communicate directly with me from now on."

"Excuse me?" Aliyah said, confused.

"It's not appropriate for you and Matt to be talking to each other since you're no longer married," Nikki said. "So if you have any questions or concerns about Ibrahim, call me."

*What the—?* A surge of rage lit Aliyah's chest. The mere sound of her son's name on this woman's tongue was enough to make Aliyah want to go through the phone. Was this woman actually saying that Aliyah had to talk to *her* for anything related to her own son?

"Thank you for letting me know." Aliyah spoke through clenched teeth, but she made her best effort to sound cordial. "But I'm walking into my office now," she lied. "So we'll have to talk later." Aliyah stabbed the end-call button, and her body shivered in fury as she steered the car onto the exit toward the local college.

*Now* I'm *the other woman?* Aliyah thought, irate. Had Nikki lost her mind? Had Matt?

*It's not appropriate for you and Matt to be talking to each other since you're no longer married.*

The words resonated in Aliyah's mind in time with the angry thumping in her chest. *Oh, but it was appropriate for* you *to talk my husband while we were married,* she said to Nikki in her head. *And you didn't even have a child to talk about!*

A sharp pain sliced through Aliyah's temples as she pulled her car into a parking space in the lot reserved for faculty and staff. She turned off the ignition and took a moment to breathe in and out so she could gather her composure. The last thing she wanted was to come into work with a nasty attitude. She was only six and a half months into the standard one-year probation that all new employees went through, so she couldn't afford a bad day. The money wasn't much, but it did pay the bills, even if only barely. She was divorced, technically a single mother, so she didn't often allow herself the indulgence of imagining a better job.

But right then she imagined a better life. Aliyah wished she didn't get upset so easily. Now she would have to spend half the day trying to calm down and focus on work.

Had Nikki purposely called at this time so she could unnerve Aliyah before work? Aliyah imagined that Matt must have told Nikki about Aliyah's hypersensitivity and anxiety attacks if she had to deal with confrontation. Sometimes it drove Matt nuts that he couldn't get a decent argument out of Aliyah. "What's wrong with you?" he'd said to her once. "Don't you ever get mad?" But Aliyah's anger came out in small bursts, usually in snarky remarks, but she'd immediately apologize afterwards and do all she could to smooth things over. In retrospect, that's probably why she'd pushed the idea of Matt taking Nikki as a second wife. It helped Aliyah avoid a confrontation with Matt or Nikki, because it had been clear Matt was really drawn toward Nikki and Nikki toward him. With polygyny, everybody could be happy. Or so she'd thought.

Nikki knew that Aliyah was overly accommodating. Was that why she'd timed her call right before Aliyah went into work? Nikki must have known that Aliyah wouldn't have time to discuss the issue, thus forcing Aliyah to comply—or to at least be duly informed without opportunity for a fuss. But Nikki's phone call could have waited until that evening. Ibrahim was at Matt and Nikki's house right then, so what was the point?

"That girl is jealous of you," Deanna often warned. "Watch your back."

Aliyah would laugh in response. "Jealous of *me*? For what?"

"What do you mean *for what*?" Deanna would say. "You're smart, educated, *and* good-looking, *mashaAllah*. But all she has is her looks. Barely."

Aliyah would listen only halfheartedly whenever Deanna talked like that. Nikki had majored in fashion design in college and had never pursued a degree after her bachelor's, but Aliyah didn't feel that made Nikki any less intelligent or less educated than she was. Yes, Aliyah knew that having a dual bachelor's in mathematics and computer science, a master's in education, and an unfinished doctorate in mathematics made people think of her as "smart" and "educated," but Aliyah's definitions of those terms weren't so simple. A person's worth couldn't be summed up on a piece of paper or resumé. If it could, then why did Matt choose Nikki over Aliyah? Why wasn't Matt so impressed with Aliyah's "papers" and accomplishments?

"He was intimidated by you," Deanna often said. "Most men need to feel superior to their wives. In everything," she added.

"Then why was he helping pay for my doctorate, Deeja?"

"And why did he *stop* paying for it? Long before divorce was even a topic of discussion?" Deanna said. "That's what you *should* be asking."

"He didn't have to pay for it in the first place," Aliyah said.

"Of course not," Deanna said. "That's the point. It was a control thing with him. He was supportive as long as you were indebted to him. But as soon as it looked like you were actually about to get that Ph.D., he put a stop to it. Fast. And he had the nerve to say you shouldn't get a loan to pay for it yourself because you needed to focus on being a mother."

"He was right," Aliyah said. "After I had Ibrahim, it was hard juggling classes and research while I took care of him. And Matt saw how stressed I was. He was just looking out for me."

Deanna groaned, laughter in her voice. "One day you're going to realize that some people only help you so they can control the outcome."

Aliyah entered the math and science building and swiped her badge. "Good morning, Professor Thomas," she heard someone say. Aliyah glanced over her shoulder and saw her supervisor.

"Good morning, Dr. Warren," Aliyah replied, a wide smile on her face as she greeted the woman. Aliyah hoped there were no traces of her earlier fury.

"Will you be able to make it to today's faculty meeting?"

Aliyah's face became enflamed with mortification as she recalled trying to avoid Deanna's husband by telling Dr. Warren she was too unwell to attend a meeting. "Yes, I will be," Aliyah said, probably too enthusiastically.

Dr. Warren nodded. "Good. Enjoy your day."

"You too," Aliyah called after her.

Aliyah felt the vibration of her phone just as she unlocked her office door and pushed it open. She had turned off the ringer before getting out the car, as she routinely did before signing in to work. She hoped it wasn't Nikki again. Aliyah doubted she could handle the stress right then.

Aliyah pulled the straps of her handbag from her shoulder, set the bag on her desk, then unsnapped the compartment for her mobile phone. When she withdrew the phone, she saw that it was text message that had come through. She unlocked the phone and saw Larry's name on the display.

*Salaamz. I hope you enjoy your day at work. I miss talking to you already :)*

A smile pulled at Aliyah's lips as she put the phone back into her bag. She would text Larry later. She didn't want him to think she was sitting around waiting to hear from him. But she couldn't deny the flattery nestling inside her. It really did lift her spirits to read his message. It wiped away some of the lingering aggravation she'd felt after talking to Nikki. She doubted the aggravation would ever be completely gone, at least not until she spoke to Matt and addressed this stupid "you can't talk to your son's father" rule. But for now, she appreciated Larry's small kindness. It was just what she needed to get through the day.

"I need your advice." It was Aliyah's lunch break, and she'd decided to use the free moment to call Deanna about the conversation she'd had with Nikki earlier. Before calling Deanna, Aliyah had placed a sign on her office door saying she would return in an hour. She then closed the door and locked it, hoping no one would realize she was inside. She usually worked through her lunch hour and made herself available to help her supervisor or other administrators with anything they needed. It had become such a habit of Aliyah's that sometimes an administrator would approach her early in the morning and ask if she could do something for them "during lunch." But today Aliyah was too distracted and upset to care about impressing her superiors. She needed perspective. "I hope I'm not catching you at a bad time," Aliyah said hesitantly.

"If it's you calling," Deanna said, her cheerful mood detectable in her voice, "no time is a bad time."

Aliyah chuckled self-consciously. "*MashaAllah.*"

In that moment, Aliyah realized just how grateful she was that it wasn't Deanna's husband, Jacob, who'd called her uncle about marrying her as a second wife. It was Larry (who often called himself "Ya'qoob") who'd called Benjamin. And because the discussion of marriage had been through phone calls alone, Benjamin never realized that it was Larry he'd been talking to the whole time. Aliyah had never spoken to Benjamin himself about the mix-up, but she was able to talk to Larry about it, who'd confirmed that he indeed had been calling her uncle Benjamin about marrying her.

"Nikki called me this morning," Aliyah said, anxiety tightening in her chest as she blurted this out. "And she said I can't talk to Matt about Ibrahim anymore. She said I have to talk to her, but I—"

"What!" Deanna said before Aliyah could finish her sentence. "Are you at your office now?"

"Yes," Aliyah said. "It's my lunch break, so I can't talk long."

"Don't worry, *ukhti*," Deanna said. "I'm coming."

"No, no, it's okay." Aliyah's heart raced in panic as she realized that Deanna intended to come to the college. Aliyah's department had a strict no-visitors policy for faculty and staff during work hours, and Aliyah did not want to violate it. Occasionally, some of her colleagues would have family and friends visit, but these employees had tenure *and* the supervisor's good graces. "I'm not allowed to have—"

"Girl, forget those people," Deanna said. "I know about that stupid no-visitors rule. Jacob told me about it when they started it a few years ago, but that doesn't faze me. I'm not going to let these people tell me I can't be there for my best friend when she needs me."

"Deanna, no, really." Aliyah's voice was a plea. "I can talk to you when I get home. It's not a problem. I don't want anyone to come here. They don't even know I'm in my office. So we could just..." Aliyah's voice trailed as she realized that Deanna was actually listening to her without interrupting. "...meet for dinner or something? Or even tomorrow, if that's better for you?"

When Deanna didn't respond, Aliyah pulled the phone from her ear and saw the standard mobile display. Her heart dropped. There was no indication that a call was in session. She should have known. Deanna had hung up already. Aliyah groaned and shook her head as she redialed Deanna.

Deanna answered after the first ring. "Don't worry, Ally-pooh," she said before Aliyah could even give salaams. "I'm not letting that school tell us what to do."

“But Deanna,” Aliyah said hesitantly, not wanting to offend her friend, “I could get in trouble.”

“Girl, shut up. They don’t own you,” Deanna said. “Don’t forget I’m the one who got you that job, so I can come up there any time I want. Now let me drive.”

Aliyah pulled the phone from her ear to see if the call was still active, and the call ended just as she did. Aliyah sighed as she set the phone on her desk and leaned back in her chair. Experiences like these were what kept Aliyah from confiding in Deanna more. Deanna rarely saw the world from anyone else’s vantage point.

Once, a few years ago, Deanna had made plans to spend a whole Saturday with Aliyah without even informing Aliyah beforehand. Deanna had bought the two of them tickets to a movie and planned to spend the rest of the afternoon and evening at an outlet mall taking advantage of closeout sales. But Aliyah and Matt had already made plans themselves and had even arranged for Matt’s parents to babysit Ibrahim while they were out. About an hour before Aliyah and Matt were scheduled to leave, Deanna showed up at their house. “Girl, get dressed,” Deanna had said when Aliyah opened the door. “We’re having a girls day out.” Taken aback, Aliyah didn’t know what to say. “But…” she had stammered, “Matt wants to spend time with me today.” Aliyah’s voice was pained, and she apologized with her eyes. “That’s perfect!” Deanna had replied, stepping inside the house and closing the door behind her. “I don’t mind if he joins us,” she said.

A loud knock along with the sound of a key being turned in the door interrupted Aliyah’s thoughts. She immediately jumped to her feet, worried that the custodial staff were doing their cleaning rounds. Though Aliyah was sure her presence wouldn’t make any difference to them, it was still embarrassing to imagine anyone realizing she was in her office when the sign on her door suggested she was not. The door opened just as Aliyah started to turn the handle herself.

“*As-salaamu’alikum*, my Aliyah-pooh!” Deanna called out cheerfully, stepping inside the office. Patches of red colored Deanna’s yellowish brown cheeks as she smiled.

Aliyah quickly pushed the door closed and locked it. “How did you get here so fast?”

“I was dropping off some of my business cards at the masjid,” Deanna said. She chuckled and rolled her eyes. “You know those Muslims could use some *serious* help in their marriages.”

Aliyah started to ask Deanna how she had gotten a key to her office, but Aliyah remembered Deanna removing the original from Aliyah’s key ring shortly after Aliyah was hired at the college. At the time, Aliyah was cleaning out the office and setting up, and Deanna was helping. Though it had made Aliyah uncomfortable that Deanna would go through her purse and make a copy of the office key without asking, Aliyah told herself that Deanna was only trying to be helpful. Deanna having her own key made it easy for her to come and go when Aliyah couldn’t be in the office herself while setting up. Ironically, it was during this time that Aliyah was told about the no-visitors rule. Thankfully, it had been

Jacob, the head of the math department, who had told her. But he assured her that for the time being, it wasn't an issue. No one would think Deanna was there because of Aliyah, he'd told her. At the time, the staff knew Deanna only as Jacob's wife.

"No offense," Deanna said.

Aliyah creased her forehead. "What?"

"Never mind." Deanna waved her hand dismissively as she settled in one of the student chairs in front of Aliyah's desk. "Tell me about this Nikki wench."

Aliyah was uncomfortable with Deanna's derogatory reference to Matt's wife. It treaded too closely to backbiting for her tastes, but she knew there was no use saying this to Deanna. In the past, whenever Aliyah had asked Deanna not to backbite, Deanna had rolled her eyes and said, "Girl, nobody's backbiting. I don't know what those masjid fanatics are putting in your head."

Aliyah decided to focus on the problem at hand, so she settled in her desk chair and explained to Deanna what had happened. "…and now she's saying it's not appropriate for me and Matt to talk anymore," Aliyah finished.

"I told you she's jealous of you," Deanna said.

Aliyah suppressed a groan. That was beside the point. She didn't need Deanna to psychoanalyze Nikki. Aliyah wanted practical advice on how to deal with the situation.

"No she's not." Aliyah was surprised by the exhausted brusqueness in her tone. Maybe it was Deanna's insistence on coming to the office against Aliyah's protests that was making Aliyah irritable. But whatever it was, Aliyah wasn't in the mood for Dr. Deanna Bivens, the know-it-all. She wanted Deeja, the friend.

"Look, Aliyah," Deanna said, her tone soft with empathy. Her expression was thoughtful as she leaned forward, her hands clasped on her lap. Deanna looked down for a moment, as if trying to find the right words for what she needed to say, and Aliyah got the feeling that Deanna was in therapist mode. "I don't blame Nikki just like I don't blame you."

Aliyah nodded, listening, though she was unsure what Deanna meant.

"Nikki looks at you like you look at me."

Aliyah moved her head in the beginning of a nod then stopped. "What's that supposed to mean?"

Deanna drew in a deep breath and exhaled, apology in that sound. "Like I said, Aliyah. I don't blame you. But with you it's normal jealousy, but with Nikki, her jealousy is out of control."

"Jealousy?" Aliyah said, her eyebrows drawn together.

"It's okay, Aliyah," Deanna said, waving her head. "I can excuse your jealousy. But Nikki's is inexcusable. She's using it to—"

"Are you joking?" Aliyah coughed laughter. "Do you really think I'm *jealous* of you?" Of course, this wasn't the first time Deanna had mentioned Aliyah's alleged jealousy, but it was the first time that Aliyah realized that Deanna actually meant it.

Deanna sighed and stood, lifting her handbag and pulling the straps over her shoulder. "I didn't mention that to offend you, Ally. I just mentioned it so you can understand better where Nikki is coming from. It's natural to feel jealous of someone who has a lot more going for them than you do. But it's not natural to let jealousy cloud your judgment. You don't let jealousy interfere with your interactions with me, so maybe you can help Nikki do the same with you."

Aliyah's offense nearly choked her, her words caught in her throat.

"I'm really happy to be here for you," Deanna said, her hand on the door handle as she turned to Aliyah. Deanna's lips formed a thin line, suggesting that she was troubled by something. "But next time, just keep in mind, I'm not always able to drop everything and come comfort you at a moment's notice. Some things you'll have to work through on your own," she added. "But I'll do what I can because I love you."

Aliyah went through the rest of day as if in a daze. She felt as if she had been punched in the stomach. At some moments, Aliyah felt like she was going to throw up; at other moments, as if she would break down crying. She sat through the math faculty meeting with a polite close-lipped smile plastered to her face. She nodded when the other faculty members nodded, laughed when they laughed, and jotted down notes when they jotted down notes. But all she could think about was how humiliated she felt. She didn't know whose audacity offended her more, Nikki's or Deanna's.

After the meeting, Aliyah sat in her office staring off into the distance. She couldn't bring herself to go home yet. She needed a moment to pull herself together. A lump developed in her throat as she realized how pathetic her life was. No, she wasn't jealous of Deanna, at least not consciously, but Aliyah couldn't deny that, like Deanna had said, Deanna had a lot more going for her than Aliyah did. If nothing else, Deanna knew how to keep a husband. Even if it had turned out that it was Jacob and not Larry who had called Benjamin about marrying Aliyah, at least Jacob would have been seeking another wife, not a divorce. And that spoke volumes. Aliyah had supported Matt marrying another wife, and still he'd divorced her.

"*As-salaamu'alaikum.*"

Aliyah's shoulders jerked in surprise at the sound of a man's voice. She looked up and saw her department head standing in the open doorway. "Oh. *Wa'alaikumus-salaam*, Dr. Bivens," Aliyah said to Jacob.

"I'm sorry to come unannounced," he said.

"Is everything okay?" Aliyah was worried that someone had seen Deanna at Aliyah's office during lunch break.

"Yes, everything's fine," Jacob said. "It's not about work. Larry called me."

*Oh. Thank God.* Aliyah sighed in relief.

"He said he's spoken to your uncle about marrying you."

Aliyah smiled beside herself. Jacob's words reminded her that she wasn't without hope after all. Maybe Larry was indeed "the one," as her uncle so ardently believed. "Yes, he told me," Aliyah said.

"But he said you thought it was me who had called your uncle." Jacob had a troubled expression on his face, but a confused smile creased one corner of his mouth.

Aliyah's heart thumped in embarrassment, and her eyes widened in apology. "I'm sorry, Jacob," she said, professional etiquette dropping from her tone. "I didn't meant to…" Her voice trailed as she realized that there were no words that could excuse her behavior. It had been completely irresponsible for her to say that to Larry. She could have left the topic alone after Larry had replied to her inquiry saying yes he had been in touch with Benjamin. But she had been so relieved that she'd laughed out loud and said to Larry, "Oh my God. You won't believe what my uncle thought…" Then she told Larry point-for-point details about the conversation she and her uncle had had before she and Larry met in person at the restaurant.

"No, no, no," Jacob said, shaking his head. "It's okay. But I just wanted to make sure you didn't mention your uncle's phone call to Deanna."

"No, of course not," Aliyah said quickly. "I wouldn't do anything like that."

"Good." Jacob exhaled in relief. "I told Larry I'm really happy for him and that I completely support the marriage. If that's what you want, of course," Jacob added tentatively, as if waiting for Aliyah's confirmation.

"I'm definitely considering it," Aliyah said.

"I'm sorry about the confusion," Jacob said.

Aliyah laughed self-consciously. "No, *I'm* sorry. I shouldn't have assumed. I should've known that you wouldn't do anything like that."

Jacob's forehead was creased as he regarded Aliyah briefly before averting his gaze. "Aliyah, are you saying you…" Confusion was in his voice as if he'd lost his train of thought. "No, Aliyah," he said finally, shaking his head. "What I'm saying is, it *was* me. But I told Larry I had spoken to your uncle before I knew he was interested in you. When my brother started calling your uncle, Benjamin and I spoke, and I told him that it was better if Larry married you."

Inadvertently, Aliyah's jaw dropped. She was at a loss for words.

Just then Aliyah recalled Larry's silence on the phone after she had laughed and told him about her uncle saying it was Jacob who had called about marrying her. Aliyah had assumed it was male jealousy that had kept Larry from laughing too. But now she realized it was because her detailed story had made him privy to information he'd never known before.

"But I just wanted to apologize," Jacob said. "Larry is really bothered by all of this. So I wanted to clear the air and let you know it was just a momentary lapse in judgment. I was going through a lot at the time, and I just thought if…" He shook his head, as if willing the thoughts from his mind. "Never mind. It was a stupid idea, and I should've never entertained the thought. I'm really sorry."

“It’s okay,” Aliyah said, surprised that she’d found her voice. “We all make mistakes.”

Jacob’s expression held a tinge of sadness, and Aliyah sensed that her words had offended him somehow. “Yeah,” he said, chuckling to himself. “We certainly do.”

# 4
# Her Best Friend's Husband

Jacob and Deanna first met when Jacob was a Ph.D. candidate preparing to defend his thesis and Deanna was a second year doctorate student at the same university. Jacob had been sitting alone at a table in the food court when he heard a chair being pulled out across from him. He looked up from the soft drink in his hand and the array of open books in front of him to find a woman smiling down at him. The first things he noticed about her were her eyes and her hijab. Her eyes were a rich brown, the kind that makes you do a double take because you might have missed them at first glance. The hijab she wore was a burnt red, a detail that stood out to him because it was his mother's favorite color and because it brought the color of Deanna's cheeks.

"*As-salaamu'alaikum*, Mr. Jacob Bivens," the woman said, setting down her food tray as she lowered herself into the seat she had pulled out for herself. "I'm Deanna Michaels. I remember you from your lecture at MSA career day."

Jacob smiled, flattered that he had made an impression at the Career Day Symposium sponsored by the Muslim Student Association about a month ago. "*Wa'alaiku-mus-salaam.* I'm glad you enjoyed it."

"I didn't say I enjoyed it," Deanna said, humorous sarcasm in her tone. "I said I remember you."

Jacob chuckled self-consciously and nodded. "Sorry about that."

"Are you coming to the dinner tonight?" Deanna looked at him in between putting forkfuls of lasagna into her mouth.

"Dinner?"

"The MSA is having a dinner tonight. Well, it's actually more like a cocktail party," Deanna said, "but without the cocktails."

"This is the first I've heard of it."

"You should come," she said. "You need a break from all that studying."

It struck Jacob how the woman was speaking to him as if they'd known each other for years. He didn't know whether to be flattered or offended. He'd never liked forward women. Before he became Muslim, there were times that he reveled in the attention he received from assertive females, but that was only when he had selfish motives. As early as middle school, he'd known that the woman he finally settled down with had to be not only educated and intelligent, but also humble and reserved.

Which was probably why he was still single. He was beginning to wonder if such a woman even existed. "What time does it start?" Jacob asked.

Deanna couldn't keep from grinning triumphantly. "Six thirty," she said. "In the MSA room."

Jacob nodded. "If I don't get too bogged down," he said noncommittally, "I'll see if I can stop by." But internally, he knew he had no intention of coming. He wasn't a fan of religious-based clubs, though he occasionally felt obligated to accept invitations to speak.

"Give me your number."

For a second, Jacob thought he'd misheard, and an uncertain smile lingered on his face. "What?"

"Give me your cell phone number." She spoke as if it were the most natural request in the world. "I know you won't turn down the chance to spend more time with me." Her lips twitched in a flirtatious grin. "This is a once-in-a-lifetime opportunity. I could be your future wife."

Jacob laughed out loud. He liked this woman already. He wasn't one to laugh easily, but Deanna's confidence and not-so-subtle hints touched a part of him that he didn't know was there. "I'll give you my number if you give me yours," he said, mirroring her flirtatiousness.

"Deal," she said then opened her purse and withdrew her phone. "I'll give you a missed call."

When Jacob arrived at the MSA dinner, his attention was immediately drawn to the far corner of the room. A woman was leaning against a wall reading a book, oblivious to all the commotion and chatter around her. Her expression was one of thoughtful intrigue, as if the words on the page offered a perspective she had never considered before. *Educated and intelligent*, he found himself thinking. *And humble and reserved.*

He wondered if she, like he, had been convinced to come to this event though she desired to be elsewhere. The thought humored him, and he smiled to himself, as if he and she were of a single mind. He walked toward her, but before he was close enough to introduce himself, he heard someone yelling his name.

He turned to see Deanna bounding toward him with all the confidence of an old friend. "*As-salaamu'alikum*, Jacob. You came!" She was no longer wearing the burnt red hijab, and for some reason, this disappointed him. The shimmering gold cloth that she now wore struck him as excessive and gaudy. *"It's too much,"* he heard his mother's voice in his head. *"If you want to make a statement, make it with your mouth shut."*

Jacob's mother was a fashion connoisseur who ran a small but renowned public relations company known for its witty, often figurative advice about physical appearance and social image. She often made analogies between being mouthy and annoying, and wearing loud "look-at-me" clothes. As a teenager, Jacob was often frustrated and embarrassed by his mother's comments about people's wardrobes and behavior, especially when she was quoted in a newspaper or magazine or was being interviewed on local television. But as he grew older and became directly involved with the company, he began to understand the significance of what he'd previously interpreted as hypercritical and nitpicky.

"*Wa'alaiku-mus-salaam*," Jacob said to Deanna, forcing a smile. He tried to keep from looking across the room at the woman leaning against the wall, but his gaze kept lingering in that direction.

"You must be hungry," Deanna said. "Let me get you something." A grin played at her lips. "But don't worry, Jacob. I'll find us a quiet place to sit down and enjoy each other's company while we eat."

Jacob offered a tightlipped smile that faded after Deanna turned around and headed toward the buffet tables. He found it unsettling the way Deanna was already referring to him by his first name. He was a respected adjunct professor at the university, so he was accustomed to being referred to as either *Professor* or *Mr.* before his last name. Amongst Muslims, the respectful title *Brother* was used if anyone referred to him by his first name alone. Only close friends and family called him "Jacob."

Jacob glanced over to where he'd seen the woman reading a book, and he was disappointed to find that she was no longer there. He looked around the room, hoping she hadn't left without him noticing. He scanned the faces of the crowd, and after a few minutes, he spotted her at one of the buffet tables, a paper plate in one hand and a large serving spoon in the other. He watched as she carefully tilted the spoon, a pile of spinach spilling onto the plate. Her mouth spread into a full-teeth smile, and she tossed her head back in laughter. And though it was the most irrational thing to do, he smiled too, as if it were he making her laugh. He glanced next to her and saw that it was Deanna who had been saying something to her.

"There you are," Deanna said a few minutes later, handing him a plate of food while holding another close to herself.

He surveyed the plate's contents and nodded approvingly though he wasn't fond of most of the food items on the plate. That was another thing he didn't like about forward women. They behaved as if they knew exactly what you wanted; and they rarely, if ever, asked you yourself. It was while he was in undergrad that he learned that many women saw it as a sign of being "a real woman" to know exactly what a man wants and be able to give it to him without instructions, feedback, or advice. *"That's dumb,"* he'd said to a woman he was dating at the time. *"What does reading someone's mind have to do with anything?"* She'd responded, *"It's about connection, not telepathy. If you're soul mates, you don't have to say anything. You just know things."* Incidentally, their relationship crumbled because she felt he prioritized his studies over spending time with her. *Of course I do*, he'd thought to himself at the time. *I'm a college student, for goodness sake.* But for her, his reaction was apparently a sign that their telepathic soul mate signals were out of sync. That was one of the last relationships he'd had before studying Islam. Sometimes he wondered if his internal frustration with women was what sparked him to search for deeper meaning in life. Maybe it wasn't a humble and reserved "perfect woman" he was looking for, but a meaningful connection with a deeper part of himself.

"It's quieter out in the hall," Deanna said, her voice jolting him back to present tense. She was already walking toward the door before he had a chance to reply. She glanced back only once—to make sure he was following—before disappearing into the hall herself.

Jacob halted his steps. A part of him was tempted to stay right where he was. Maybe he could find a place in the MSA room to sit comfortably (preferably near the woman he'd seen earlier) and eat alone. But he knew it would be rude to stay inside the main room if the woman who'd invited him wanted to sit in the hall. As Jacob walked out into the hall himself, it was like *déjà vu*. Following a girl out of a room when he knew he didn't like her reminded him of his experiences at his fraternity's parties. It was unsettling to have that same feeling as a Muslim.

"So where are you from originally?" Deanna asked in between mouthfuls of food after he joined her on a couch in the hall lobby. As Deanna had predicted, the lobby area was much quieter than the MSA room, but right then, Jacob didn't care about the quiet. His mind kept wandering back to the woman he had seen reading a book.

Jacob answered the questions as affably as he could, but he made sure that his answers were as brief as politely possible. He hated that he couldn't get the other woman out of his head, and he mentally debated making up an excuse to go back into the room.

"We have a lot in common," Deanna said after they had been talking for about fifteen minutes. "We should keep in touch. I'm sure you'd like to see me again."

Jacob chuckled, again surprised by how easily he laughed with Deanna. And he couldn't deny that he did want to see her again. Her charisma was contagious, and her physical beauty made it difficult to tear his eyes away from her. He even had to fight the urge to touch her, which was a rare struggle in his interactions with Muslim women. Maybe there was something to their meeting after all.

"Who was that sister with the book?" Jacob said when he sensed it was safe to ask.

"What sister?" Deanna voice was tight, and Jacob sensed that she didn't appreciate the question.

"You were talking to her when you were getting our plates," Jacob said, hoping he sounded casual. "She had on a green hijab."

"Oh, you mean Aliyah?" Deanna contorted her face. "She *would* be reading a book when everybody else was socializing. She has zero people skills."

"So you know her?"

"I'm her best friend. Probably her *only* friend," Deanna added, rolling her eyes. "She's so high maintenance."

Jacob furrowed his brows in confusion. He knew what the term *high maintenance* meant when a man was talking about a woman, but this was the first time he'd heard it from a woman talking about another woman. "What do you mean? She's materialistic?"

"No, not at all," Deanna said, a glint of humor in her eyes as if enjoying a private joke. "She buys her clothes from Wal-Mart. *And* her shoes." Deanna wrinkled her nose. "Can you imagine?"

Jacob didn't know what to say. He shopped at Wal-Mart himself from time to time. As a grad student, he had no choice but to be frugal. But his mother, who was a stickler for quality designer brands, had bought most of his wardrobe and all of his shoes, so he was rarely faced with the need to buy anything for himself. But his mother could afford to have expensive tastes. He imagined Deanna's friend couldn't. Oddly, that made him like her more. He respected a person who was levelheaded enough to live according to his means, and he found this quality especially appealing in a woman.

"She's high maintenance *emotionally*," Deanna said, shaking her head. "She's been Muslim for eight years, and she still has a strained relationship with her family. To me, that's just pathetic. If you can't find a way to have a good relationship with your own parents, then that says a lot about your Islam."

Jacob pulled his head back in surprise. "I don't agree with that. Some parents give their children a really hard time after they become Muslim. My mother refused to speak to me for a whole year."

"But you're both speaking now, aren't you?"

"Yes, but I—"

"That's my point. With Aliyah, everything is melodramatic. It's like she can't tie her shoelaces without my support. I swear, sometimes I feel like I'm stuck in a codependent relationship or something. It's so exhausting."

"Is it really that bad?" Jacob wondered if he had completely misjudged the woman. To him, she'd appeared quite self-sufficient and sensible.

Deanna fixed her gaze on Jacob with her eyebrows raised. "You can't *begin* to imagine what I go through with that girl. I feel sorry for her fiancé."

"She's engaged?" Jacob hadn't meant to sound so disappointed, but he couldn't help it.

Deanna averted her gaze and shrugged. "Pretty much," she said. "If the poor guy agrees to marry her after he learns she needs to be spoon-fed basic life skills."

It wasn't until years into his marriage to Deanna that Jacob realized that Deanna had been lying to him that day. Not only had she embellished her description of Aliyah so that Jacob would think Aliyah was a mental case, but Deanna also had concocted the whole story about the fiancé.

"Girl, you have to be proactive," he'd overhead Deanna say on the phone one day as he was sitting in their home office grading midterm exams. He had no idea who was on the other line, and he was only half listening as he got up to close the door to drown out the conversation.

"Let me tell you how I snagged Jacob," he heard her say just as he started to close the door. Interest piqued, he halted the motion. He heard her giggle. "He didn't know what hit him," she said. The door to their bedroom across the hall was closed, but as usual, Deanna's voice was loud. Even her whispers were often intelligible. But she wasn't whispering today.

"Did I ever tell you he was interested in another sister when I met him?" There was a brief pause as Deanna listened to whoever was on the other line, then a burst of laughter sounded through the house. "I know, right? By any means necessary, girl. That's my motto when you see a man you want." A knot of apprehension tightened in Jacob's stomach as he sensed he was about to hear something he didn't like.

"But let me tell you," Deanna said, laughter in her voice. "I fixed that sister up *real* quick. People had been talking about this new Muslim brother looking for a wife, and I'm not playing when I tell you I made sure that sister hooked up with *him*, not Jacob. I didn't want that new brother for myself because I'd heard he was still getting over some old girlfriend of his. And you know, *I'm* not about to be somebody's rebound. Those relationships never worked in the *dunya*, so I sure as hell wasn't about to marry into it as a Muslim. Men always end up going back to their girlfriend. And I'm not about to be cheated on, divorced, or co-wifed if I can help it. And anyway," Deanna said jokingly, "I needed a *real* man. And that new *shahaadah* brother just wasn't it."

Jacob slowly closed the door to their home office and walked over to where his iPod was connected to a stereo system. He powered on the iPod then turned up the volume. The bass from the first song on his playlist thumped in the room, drowning out his wife's voice across the hall. Deanna was talking about how she had intentionally misled Jacob into believing that the woman he wanted to marry was already engaged to someone else, and the news disturbed Jacob more than he could stomach right then. Jacob sat on his leather swivel chair and turned himself until he was looking out the window behind his desk.

Aliyah and Matthew. The thought still left a bitter taste in his mouth. When he'd first met Matt in person months after the MSA dinner, Deanna had introduced him as Aliyah's fiancé. Even at that moment, Jacob knew something was amiss. Matt just didn't seem like Aliyah's type. Though Matt appeared to be doing well for himself, Jacob sensed that the brother wasn't ready for marriage, and definitely not to someone like Aliyah. Matt barely seemed ready to be fully Muslim. But Jacob had fought these thoughts, assuming they were coming from jealousy.

Looking out the window in his home office, Jacob clenched his jaw. It had been a stupid decision to come to Deanna's apartment for dinner about six months after they'd met. He knew it was a bad idea before he even agreed to it, but there was something about Deanna that made it difficult to stay away from her for long. In retrospect, he probably desired her more than he could rationally admit to himself as a young practicing Muslim. But at the time, he kept telling himself that their frequent conversations, which often included sexual innuendos, were inspired by their need to determine if they should get married. Besides, they would not be alone, he'd told himself as he stood outside Deanna's apartment door. Deanna had said it would be a double date. Aliyah and Matt would be there too. Except that they weren't. Jacob knew that less than five minutes into his visit. And still he stayed.

The truth was, in the pit of his stomach, he knew exactly what he wanted that night. But he wouldn't let his mind believe it. When he'd accepted Islam, Jacob had vowed to remain celibate until marriage. He had grown tired of the meaningless relationships and one-night-stands. They had left him feeling empty and filthy inside. Even as a Christian, he knew that was no way to live. Sex was supposed to be something special shared between two people who loved each other, not a casual encounter after a drink or a celebrated conquest after a party.

When Jacob fell into that same sin with Deanna, he was ravaged with guilt. During that time, Jacob would wake up every morning feeling nauseated, dreading even looking at himself in the mirror. He tried to remind himself of Allah's mercy, but he just couldn't bring himself to believe he deserved forgiveness. But still, Jacob spent night after night in prayer, begging Allah to forgive him.

"The only solution is for us to get married," Deanna had said to him on the phone about a month later.

Jacob had recoiled at the thought. If there was one thing this experience had clarified for him, it was that he definitely didn't want Deanna as a wife. It didn't escape him that not once did Deanna say she regretted what had happened between them. It left him wondering if she'd planned the whole thing. No, he certainly couldn't deny his own culpability in their sin. But he seemed to be the only one with a heavy heart about the whole ordeal.

"Marriage isn't a solution," he told Deanna. "If anything, it'll bring more problems."

"Raising a child without a father brings more problems." Her voice was tight in offense. "And I'm sure you don't want something like that for your child."

Jacob's heart dropped. He was immediately reminded of his high school girlfriend telling him she was pregnant. Even years later, he was still unable to forgive himself for convincing her to get an abortion. After that experience, he carried protection with him everywhere. He didn't want a repeat of that agonizing ordeal. But naturally, he'd stop carrying contraceptives after he became Muslim.

A week after they spoke, upon his suggestion, Deanna went to a clinic for a pregnancy test. When she called him and said that it had come back positive, he felt as if the world was caving in on him. It was painfully ironic that he was faced with this predicament as a Muslim, and for a sin that he'd fallen into only once after his *shahaadah.*

Jacob reluctantly agreed to marry Deanna in a private ceremony at the local masjid. But just weeks after the marriage, Deanna rented out a hall at a five-star hotel and hosted a wedding party with more than three hundred guests. She said she wouldn't be able to dance so hard once the pregnancy was further along. But it turned out that the pregnancy would never progress further along. She lost the baby about a week after the *waleemah.*

But as Jacob sat in his home office chair, his wife's words to her friend replayed in his mind. *By any means necessary, girl. That's my motto when you see a man you want.* An angry knot tightened in his chest as he wondered if the pregnancy itself was one of Deanna's "snag Jacob" routines. ...If there had been a pregnancy in the first place.

***

Aliyah watched as Jacob turned to leave her office after apologizing for calling her uncle to ask if he could marry her. She sensed that there was a lot Jacob wasn't saying, but she knew it wasn't her place to ask. He appeared to be under a lot of stress, and Aliyah's heart went out to him. She felt horrible for thinking it, but she wondered how he handled living with Deanna. Aliyah imagined he had to be a really patient brother. Or maybe he and Deanna were so compatible that he didn't need patience to deal with her. They certainly interacted easily whenever they did marriage workshops together.

Aliyah was walking toward her car in the faculty and staff lot when she heard someone behind her. She turned and saw Jacob walking toward his car, which apparently was in the same row as hers. She lifted a hand in a polite wave then turned back around.

"Aliyah," Jacob called out, prompting Aliyah to turn around again. He broke into a jog to catch up with her. "Can I ask a favor?"

She immediately felt on guard. But she reminded herself that he had apologized about the marriage inquiry, so this had to be about something else. "Sure," she said with more assurance than she felt.

"Deanna and I…" He looked away from Aliyah and pursed his lips, apparently trying to gather his thoughts. "Well, it hasn't been easy."

Aliyah averted her gaze. She didn't like where this was heading. She felt like she was betraying her best friend by just listening to him.

"I was just wondering if you could talk to her some time," he said, "you know, about some of the things you've studied about Islamic marriage in your classes. Maybe just a few things about the role of the husband as the leader of the household."

Aliyah shook her head, apologizing in that gesture, her expression pained. "I'm sorry, Jacob, but I don't think it's my place."

"I'm not asking you to come outright and say she's not a good wife or anything. And I'm not saying she isn't," Jacob said quickly. "Because she's a really good sister, *mashaAllah*. It's just that I don't think she'd listen to anyone else."

Aliyah lifted her palm as if to ward off any further details. "Jacob, I really don't think Deanna would listen to anything I say. And I don't mean that sarcastically. I mean that seriously." She coughed laughter, but it was due to discomfort at the irony of the conversation, not anything humorous. "There's nothing I could say about marriage that Deanna would listen to."

"But as her best friend, you know what to say. She has a lot of respect for you."

"I don't think so," Aliyah said apologetically. "Honestly."

"Can you at least give it a try?"

"Okay, *insha'Allah*," Aliyah said, mainly because the conversation was making her uncomfortable. She didn't want to talk about this anymore. "I'll see what I can do."

"*JazaakAllaahukhairan,*" Jacob said, a smile of grateful relief spreading on his face. "I really appreciate it. Truly."

"*As-salaamu'alaikum,*" Aliyah said, turning and walking toward her car again.

"*Wa'alaiku-mus-salaam,*" Jacob called out in response.

In her car, Aliyah exhaled and leaned back on the headrest. *Oh my God*, she thought to herself. *What just happened?*

# 5
## The Toxic Friend

"People don't give you room to be human," the man said to the interviewer. "That's one reason I never asked for help. But I don't blame my friends and family," he said. "They had no idea what I was going through. But if I'm honest, I didn't fully know myself. The problem with being a mentor to troubled youth is that you're always expected to have it all together, so your whole life ends up becoming one big inspirational pep-talk session. And then you wake up and find that you're both mentor and troubled soul to your own life. But that's a really lonely existence."

"Mommy."

At the sound of her son's voice, Aliyah pointed the remote toward the television and powered off the screen. "I'm right here, sweetie," she said from where she was sitting on the couch in the living room. Traces of sleep were still on Ibrahim's face as he squinted at his mother. Aliyah opened her arms wide, and a grin tugged at one side of Ibrahim's mouth as his padded feet moved swiftly toward her. He wrapped his arms around her as he situated himself on her lap and nuzzled his head at her neck. Aliyah couldn't keep from smiling as she held him close.

"I'm hungry," Ibrahim moaned.

"Alrighty, cookie monster," Aliyah teased as she tickled him with one hand, setting off a spurt of giggles and body wriggling. "Then get off my lap."

"No…" he whined playfully, clinging to her neck.

She smiled and shook her head as she stood, still holding him close. He wrapped his pajama-covered legs around her, and she could almost feel him smiling in triumph as she walked toward the kitchen with one of her arms holding him securely in place.

"You're almost five," she said as she opened the refrigerator, Ibrahim's arms and legs still locked around her. "I can't keep carrying you around."

"Mmmm," he protested.

"Okay," she said, laughter in her voice. "But you know the rules."

He nodded in agreement, as he always did when she gave in to his desire to be carried.

"No oatmeal," she said. "And—"

"—no grits!" he sang out before she could finish.

Laughter bubbled in her stomach, but Aliyah suppressed it with a grin as she removed a half-gallon of milk from the refrigerator and set it on the kitchen table. The no-oatmeal, no-grits rule was originally one she'd made for herself when Ibrahim was still an infant and she was experimenting with attachment parenting. After meeting a few women in the masjid who were vocal supporters of the method, Aliyah fell in love with the concept of keeping her son physically close to her as much as possible, and she immediately went out and bought a cloth sling for her son. When she finally got the hang of how to secure Ibrahim in the elongated cloth and tie it around her at the same time, she was surprised by how comforting and freeing it was. Not only did she have free use of her hands to do whatever she needed to do throughout the day, but she also was able to carry her son around at the same time. With the sling, she never had to worry about choosing between tending to her son and doing work or chores.

However, she hadn't been able to bring herself to cook or bake while Ibrahim was secured against her in the cloth sling. She was afraid she might accidentally burn him or cause a fire if the cloth touched the hot stove. When she'd asked for advice from the sisters in the masjid, they told her to simply adjust the sling with Ibrahim on her back if she needed extra precaution. She tried the back sling for only a few hours before she gave up and readjusted her son to the front. It was probably the most irrational feeling in the world, but Aliyah just couldn't bear being unable to look down at her son and see that he was all right. After that day, she made a rule for herself. *If you're carrying Ibrahim, you can't use the oven or the stove.* Eventually, it became the rule for Ibrahim himself if he wanted her to hold him.

A loud pounding on the front door followed by the repetitive chiming of the doorbell interrupted Aliyah's thoughts. Instinctively, she glanced at the small analog clock on the stove.

"Mommy, who's that?" Ibrahim asked as Aliyah leaned forward to set down a ceramic bowl and a box of cereal on the kitchen table. Ibrahim released himself from his mother's arms and slid into the chair next to his breakfast.

"I don't know," Aliyah said honestly. It was shortly after nine o'clock Saturday morning. She had no idea who would be visiting at this time, especially banging and ringing with so much impatient urgency. Eyebrows drawn together in confusion, Aliyah walked out the kitchen. "Wash your hands first!" she called out over her shoulder as she passed through the living room, heading toward the front door. She heard a rush of water from the kitchen sink as the pounding and doorbell ringing ceased. But before she could look through the peephole and ask who it was, the pounding and ringing picked up again.

"Who is it?" she yelled just as she got to the door.

"Aliyah!" she heard a slightly muffled voice yell. "I'm going to kill you."

Aliyah recognized the voice at once. Groaning in annoyance, she didn't even bother looking outside before she unbolted the door and pulled it open. And sure enough, Deanna stood in the doorway, looking peeved as usual.

"Girl, you know you ain't got nothing important enough going on in your life to make you too good to answer your phone." Deanna shoved past Aliyah and slipped off her shoes in the foyer, not bothering to ask if it was okay to come inside.

Aliyah started to say that after Matt and Nikki had dropped off Ibrahim last night, she had turned off her cell and home phone so that she and Ibrahim could spend time together uninterrupted this weekend. But she was stunned to silence as she saw Younus and Thawab trailing behind their mother, bulging knapsacks on their backs and lunchboxes in their hands.

"Deanna," Aliyah said, trying to maintain her calm, "what are you d—"

"*As-salaamu'alaikum*, Aunty Aliyah," Younus said, his polite tone and innocent expression disarming Aliyah. He shrugged off his knapsack then set it next to his lunchbox on the foyer floor. He then kneeled and pulled off his shoes with such casual familiarity that you'd think he lived there. As usual, Thawab followed the motions of his brother, setting down his knapsack and lunchbox then kneeling and taking off his shoes too.

"Say salaams to Aunty," Younus whispered to Thawab. Obediently, Thawab looked up at Aliyah and gave her salaams then looked back toward his brother for approval. Younus nodded, and a shadow of a smile flashed on Thawab's face.

The scene touched a soft spot in Aliyah. She often marveled at how mature Younus was for his age. At eight years old, he was already a little man. Thawab was only five, so it would be years before he could appreciate the blessing he had in his big brother. Aliyah smiled beside herself. She imagined Younus would grow up to be like his father: helpful, patient, and paternal. Younus and Jacob already had noticeable similarities, in appearance and mannerisms.

"May-I-use-your-bathroom-please-Aunty," Thawab said in the voice he used when he was making a conscious effort to be polite to elders.

Aliyah nodded. "Yes you may, munchkin," she said, her tone soft with compassion. As she watched Thawab hurry to the bathroom, she couldn't bring herself to voice her annoyance with Deanna for having stopped by unannounced. She would have to talk to Deanna later, when the children were not in earshot. She didn't want Younus or Thawab to think she was upset or annoyed with them.

"Boy," Deanna's voice thundered, "get up off your lazy behind and see if your brother needs help."

Aliyah cringed. She hated when Deanna spoke to her children like that. Younus was so well behaved and mild-mannered that Aliyah couldn't imagine that a harsh tone like that could ever be justified with him. But she kept her thoughts to herself. Just as Deanna was the expert on marriage, she was also the expert on childrearing. Aliyah was a "pushover" and Ibrahim was "spoiled" according to Dr. Deanna Bivens, Ph.D. "You need to take some parenting classes," Deanna often said. "You have no idea what you're doing."

"Can I get the salaams at least?" Deanna said after Younus went to check on his brother. Her expression conveyed annoyance as she walked over to the couch and sat down. "You have zero social skills."

"The general custom," Aliyah said, her voice purposefully didactic and condescending, "in America *and* Islam, is for the person entering the home to greet those already there." She gave Deanna a tightlipped smile. "So *wa'alaiku mus salaam wa rahmatullaah*, Deeja."

Deanna laughed and waved her hand dismissively. "Girl, come here," she said, patting the place on the couch next to her. "I need your advice on something."

*That's new,* Aliyah thought to herself. She couldn't imagine any topic troubling Deanna enough that it would require her input. But she would address

Deanna's dilemma later. Instead of sitting next to Deanna, Aliyah stood in front of the couch, arms crossed. "Are you all planning to stay the whole day?"

Deanna wrinkled her nose as if Aliyah had said something disgusting. "Are you crazy?" Deanna said. "I have too many things to do. I'm already running behind schedule as it is, thanks to you. But I *cannot* coddle you today. If you got issues, girl, then you're on your own, at least for the next twenty-four hours."

The comment stung, but Aliyah willed herself to ignore it. She needed to have thicker skin with Deanna, but it was becoming more and more difficult to withstand the constant subtle and direct insults. She knew Deanna only meant it as friendly teasing, at least Aliyah kept telling herself that she did. But it didn't feel like friendly teasing. Aliyah hated herself for being so sensitive, but it was becoming really stressful to be around Deanna.

The inspiration Aliyah had once received from Deanna's blunt, "no nonsense" advice was now replaced with anxiety and apprehension. Even years ago, when Aliyah was less secure about her perspective on life, Aliyah sometimes had a difficult time withstanding Deanna's frankness and insensitivity. The most trying period of their friendship had been when Aliyah was indecisive about marrying Matt, and Deanna kept telling Aliyah that she needed to "stop being so arrogant." Deanna kept saying, "Matt is a good Muslim, and that's all that matters." When Aliyah said she didn't feel any spark or connection with Matt, Deanna had said, "Get over yourself. If you're half the Muslim you say we all should be, then you'd have faith that Allah will work everything out. But if a good Muslim wants to marry you, you marry him. Period."

Incidentally, Aliyah received the same advice from the local imam, who convinced her that "true believers marry for the sake of Allah, not for their *nafs*." The imam's words affected Aliyah so deeply that it made her reflect on her selfishness in wanting a love marriage and not a purely Islamic one. So shortly thereafter, she agreed to marry Matt, putting her trust in Allah that everything would turn out all right. She even managed to convince herself that she was excited to get married, so she'd eagerly introduced Matt to Benjamin in hopes of getting her uncle's approval. But now that Aliyah was divorced, Deanna insisted that the marriage had fallen apart because Aliyah didn't know how to keep a husband. "No woman in her right mind lets her husband marry another wife," Deanna often said.

Aliyah imagined that anyone else would be grateful to have Dr. Deanna Bivens, a renowned relationship guru, as a close friend. But right then, Aliyah didn't feel grateful. She felt used. "Then what are the lunchboxes and backpacks for?" Aliyah said to Deanna, gesturing a hand toward the now cluttered foyer.

"I said *I'm* not staying." Deanna narrowed her eyes, as if finding it difficult to comprehend Aliyah's ignorance. "I came by to drop off the boys."

A flash of rage swept through Aliyah. "No," she said, heart pounding so forcefully that she could already feel her voice shaking. "No, Deeja. I'm busy today. I can't."

"Can you just shut up and sit down?" Deanna said irritably. "I need your advice."

"No, Deeja." Aliyah felt the anxiety and frustration building. Deanna was, again, dismissing her protests, ignoring her concerns, and operating on only what Deanna wanted. "You don't need my advice. You need to *listen* to me."

"*Listen* to you?" Deanna pulled her face into a look of distaste. "That's all I do, night and day. In fact, ever since we met, that's all I've ever done, listen to you and help you. I helped you get a husband. I helped you get a job. I help pay your bills. I listen every time you stress over your stupid, childish problems. But when will you listen to *me*?"

Aliyah's eyes widened in shock and hurt. Deanna's words cut deep. Over the years, Aliyah had never asked anything from Deanna except for occasional advice. Everything else (and often against Aliyah's refusals and protests) Deanna had offered—and *insisted on*—completely on her own. Aliyah hadn't even been interested in marriage when Deanna introduced her to Matt. Aliyah had already been looking for a job when Deanna asked Jacob to speak to the college about hiring her. Aliyah had been quietly (though stressfully) living paycheck to paycheck whenever Deanna surprised her with a handwritten check. And though Aliyah couldn't deny turning to Deanna for reassurance and advice whenever she was stressed, Aliyah thought that was what friends do. Besides, Deanna herself would repeatedly tell Aliyah that she would always be there for her. Why then was Deanna throwing all this back in Aliyah's face?

*One day you're going to realize that some people only help you so they can control the outcome.* The words, which had been spoken by Deanna to Aliyah in an earlier conversation about Matt, took on a sudden, terrifying meaning in present tense. Aliyah shook the troubling thoughts from her head and sought refuge in Allah from *Shaytaan*. What was wrong with her? When had she begun to think so negatively of people?

No matter how irritating Deanna could be, she had a big heart and had helped Aliyah more than Aliyah could count. And for that, Aliyah owed Deanna a great deal. Aliyah didn't have the money or resources to benefit Deanna's lifestyle in any significant way, and she certainly wasn't as knowledgeable about life and marriage as Deanna was. So what was so wrong with babysitting Deanna's children at a moment's notice? What was so wrong with being overly accommodating to someone who had done so much for her? What was so wrong with being thankful for the blessing she had in Deanna instead of being constantly annoyed?

Aliyah opened her mouth to apologize, but she saw Younus and Thawab return to the living room, their eyes full of confusion and concern as they saw the mothers' upset expressions.

"Hey!" Ibrahim said, excitement in his voice as he entered the living room and saw Younus and Thawab.

"Hey, man," Younus said, a grin spreading on his face upon seeing Ibrahim.

“Take Younus and Thawab to your room,” Aliyah said. “Now, please,” she added in as soft a tone as she could manage.

“Yes!” Ibrahim called out then ran out the living room. Younus and Thawab followed, no less eager as they walked swiftly behind him.

Aliyah felt heavyhearted as she saw how giddy Ibrahim was once he realized Younus and Thawab had come over. Maybe she was blind and self-centered, as Deanna often said. She had wanted Ibrahim all to herself for the weekend, but why hadn’t she considered inviting Younus and Thawab over to play with him? Was this “spending quality time” priority really about Ibrahim’s needs? Or was it about allaying Aliyah’s guilt as the divorced, part-time mother?

“I’m really stressed about all this marriage stuff,” Deanna said after the boys disappeared into Ibrahim’s room.

Aliyah was immediately reminded of the brief conversation she’d had with Jacob a couple of days before, when he alluded to marital problems between him and Deanna. The mere reminder incited a headache. Aliyah felt horrible for being privy to what Deanna would certainly see as vicious betrayal for Aliyah having even listened to Jacob’s concerns. *“I was just wondering if you could talk to her some time,”* Jacob had said, *“you know, about some of the things you’ve studied about Islamic marriage in your classes. Maybe just a few things about the role of the husband as the leader of the household.”*

*And I agreed,* Aliyah thought regretfully. At the time, it was her way of ending the conversation and getting in her car and going home. But now she wondered if Allah would hold her accountable for making that promise. In one of her Islamic studies classes, Aliyah had learned that getting advice was the right of every Muslim, and that any agreement made, even if only verbal, was a type of *amaanah,* a sacred trust that must be fulfilled. But Aliyah didn’t want to get involved in advising Deanna about marriage. It wasn’t her place. But perhaps Deanna’s sudden visit that morning was Allah giving Aliyah a way out. She could listen to Deanna’s concerns while casually throwing in a comment about the rights of the husband in Islam.

“Tell me what I should do,” Deanna said.

“Did you already talk to Jacob about your concerns?” Aliyah said as she sat down on the couch a comfortable distance from Deanna.

Deanna waved her hand dismissively. “Girl, I had to train Jacob on the basics of marriage counseling before we did workshops together. He doesn’t know anything. Anyway, I need the perspective of someone who can relate to what I’m trying to do.”

Taken aback that Deanna had that much respect for her point of view, Aliyah was at a loss for words. *“There’s nothing I could say about marriage that Deanna would listen to,”* Aliyah had said to Jacob. At that moment, Aliyah wished she could take those words back. She should have never said anything like that about Deanna, especially to Deanna’s husband. Guilt gnawed at Aliyah, and she wondered if her words had counted as backbiting, or worse, slander.

*Astaghfirullah*, she said silently, seeking Allah's forgiveness. "What is it you're trying to do?" Aliyah asked.

"It's kind of complicated actually…" Deanna appeared to be trying to gather her thoughts. "I know marriage is supposed to be really inspiring, but I'm starting to wonder if I'm going about all this the wrong way."

Aliyah nodded, but the guilt kept eating at her. How was it that she had misjudged Deanna so terribly? Was it as Deanna had said, that Aliyah had never taken a moment to actually listen to Deanna, even as Deanna listened to her all the time? *Oh my God*, Aliyah thought. *Am I that self-absorbed?*

"Be patient with yourself," Aliyah heard herself saying to Deanna. "Marriage isn't easy for anyone. It's only natural that you'll do some things wrong. Nobody's the perfect wife."

Deanna met Aliyah's gaze with her eyebrows raised, and for a moment, Aliyah thought Deanna was reflecting on what she had said. "*What*?"

The harsh tone of Deanna's voice flustered Aliyah. Had she said something wrong? "I'm just saying," Aliyah said hurriedly, "I know it's hard respecting a man as the leader of the household, especially coming from the *dunya* where everything's fifty-fifty."

"You mean it was hard for *you*?" Deanna's face was contorted as she stabbed a forefinger in the air toward Aliyah.

"No, I mean, I…" Aliyah's thoughts became jumbled as Deanna glared at her. "…I was just thinking, I know everyone struggles in their marriage, so you and Jacob can—"

"Me and Jacob?" Deanna interjected challengingly. "What's *that* supposed to mean?"

"You said you're really stressed about this marriage stuff," Aliyah said weakly. But Deanna's icy glare was unmoving, as if waiting for further explanation. "So this is just my advice on what you and Jacob can—"

"Are you out of your mind?"

Aliyah shook her head. "Wh…."

"When I said I'm stressed about this marriage stuff," Deanna said indignantly, "I was talking about a new workshop idea I'm considering."

*Oh.*

"And the only reason I'm asking your advice is because you represent my ideal client," Deanna said, a sneer in her voice. "You're divorced. You're depressed. You're broke." Deanna enumerated her points with the forefinger of one hand pressing each finger on the other. "You have no marriage prospects. And you have no idea how to fix your relationship problems on your own. So my workshop idea is to help people like you."

Aliyah stared at Deanna, speechless in shock and offense.

"That's why I need your advice." Deanna wrinkled her nose as she regarded Aliyah. "A marriage workshop is supposed to be inspirational, so I was hoping you could tell me if I'm on the right track."

An hour later Aliyah found herself mindlessly yanking the vacuum cleaner back and forth on the living room carpet. It was all she could do to quiet the fury in her chest. Ibrahim was still in his room with Younus and Thawab, and Deanna was out doing God-knows-what to save the world of pathetic divorced women like Aliyah.

*"Well, it hasn't been easy,"* Jacob had said a couple of days ago when he'd asked Aliyah's help in advising Deanna.

*Well, it hasn't been easy for me either!* Aliyah thought in frustration.

***

Deeja Marriage Guru: *It's cute when people with zero counseling credentials and zero success in their relationships try to offer experienced, married folks advice! LOL #nicetry #DontQuitYourDayJob #ijs*

Juwayriah bint Abdullah and 159 others like this. 62 comments.

It was early Sunday morning and Aliyah was sitting on her bed with her laptop balanced on her folded legs in front of her. She had finished praying *Fajr* a half hour ago and had decided to log into her Facebook account before taking a short nap until Ibrahim—and Younus and Thawab—woke up. Aliyah should have known that when Deanna had dropped off her sons Saturday morning, it was going to be an all-day affair. Deanna didn't do things halfway. If she was going to get free babysitting, she was going to milk the opportunity dry.

But Deanna leaving her sons overnight without prior agreement was something new. This certainly was not the first time that Deanna had dropped off her sons or left them in Aliyah's care without asking first, but previously, Aliyah had viewed this casualness as evidence of their close bond. "You're practically family," Deanna would often say, and Aliyah had naively been flattered. But as Aliyah sat in front of her laptop with Deanna's latest Facebook status at the top of her newsfeed—posted last night at 11:58 pm, when Aliyah had been on the verge of a headache after trying to get Deanna's sons to go to sleep—Aliyah felt nauseated.

It was at this moment that Aliyah realized that her friendship with Deanna was not based on the mutual bonds of friendship and compassion, but on the toxic bonds of manipulation and control. Aliyah could never have dropped off Ibrahim at Deanna's without calling first, and most certainly not last minute on the day-of. Even if she'd called a week in advance, Deanna most likely would have still refused.

"I don't do babysitting," Aliyah had overheard Deanna say to someone once. At the time, Aliyah had thought nothing of it. She had assumed Deanna had meant she didn't babysit as a hobby or profession. Aliyah herself didn't "do babysitting," but since she considered Deanna her best friend and an "aunty" to her son, Aliyah was usually more than happy to babysit for Deanna if she needed it. But before this moment, Aliyah hadn't realized that this sisterly, selfless relationship was uncannily tilted in only one person's favor, Deanna's.

Aliyah had naively assumed that Deanna's help with getting the college post, Deanna's periodic monetary "*sadaqah*," and Deanna's eagerness to continuously "drop everything" and be by Aliyah's side to offer comfort and advice was coming from a place of genuine love, compassion, and mutual respect. But now that the cloud of helplessness was being lifted from Aliyah's outlook on life, she was beginning to understand why being in Deanna's presence continuously inspired anxiety and apprehension.

Aliyah was anxious and apprehensive around Deanna because Aliyah had experienced this all before —in her relationship with her mother and her eldest sister. After more than ten years of Aliyah being Muslim and continuously reaching out to her family via phone calls, postcards, and emails, they refused to speak to her because her mother and sister (the unofficial heads of household) felt that her Islamic faith and hijab "embarrassed the family." Though they attended church at least once a month and often spoke of the importance of Christian love and compassion, they weren't religious people; so their contempt for Aliyah's religious choice was genuinely rooted in social image and reputation. Before they had cut off ties with her completely, they obstinately maintained that Aliyah had no right to a lifestyle that they didn't approve of "after all we've done for you."

*One day you're going to realize that some people only help you so they can control the outcome.*

*Yes, Deanna,* Aliyah thought to herself as she closed her laptop, *and that "one day" is now.*

# 6
# The Perfect Man

"Thank you all for coming tonight," Jacob said as he stood in front of the conference room in the math and science building Monday night. "Twice a year we host an information session about our scholarship and internship programs for high school students interested in pursuing math or science as a major. Our department offers academic as well as financial-need based awards." He lifted the small remote and aimed it toward the projector screen. "As you can see, each summer we host a one-on-one internship mentoring program for qualified high school juniors and seniors who show exceptional promise in the fields of mathematics and science. This mentoring program, entitled One Plus One *Equals Won*, I personally founded, and I continue to work as project manager in training mentors and occasionally working directly with interns. The program also—"

"I wouldn't mind him mentoring *me*," a female high school student whispered suggestively to her friend, who giggled and nodded in agreement before saying, "Mm hm. Where do we sign up?"

Instinctively, Aliyah, who was sitting in the last two rows reserved for math and science faculty, looked at the girls in front of her. But she could make out only the backs of their heads.

"...So if you have any questions," Jacob said, "you can talk to me or any of my colleagues who are wearing the green One Plus One badge. You'll also find more information in the packet that we've given each of—"

"*I* have a question," whispered the girl with a butterfly clip holding her ponytail in place. "Is he married or single?"

"I don't care if he's married or single," whispered back the girl with a mass of synthetic braids spilling over the back of her chair.

"I know, right?" said the butterfly-clip girl.

The synthetic-braids girl snickered, and they both nodded emphatically. "And you know what?" said the synthetic-braids girl, a hint of humorous sarcasm in her tone. "I'm no longer undecided. Whatever he majored in, *I'm* majoring in."

"I'm with you on th—"

"Shhhh." The shushing sound was so insistent that Aliyah assumed it must have come from one of the high school teachers present, but she couldn't be sure. But it silenced the girls right away, and they immediately straightened themselves in their seats and remained quiet.

As she listened to the rest of the program, Aliyah found herself wondering how old the girls in front of her were. Sixteen? Seventeen? Eighteen? Jacob was in his thirties, probably pushing forty. Aliyah wondered if that mattered to them. Or perhaps his actual age hadn't crossed their minds. Dressed in black slacks and a short-sleeved shirt that revealed his well-toned arms, Jacob did look younger than his age.

A ripple of laughter sounded throughout the room, and Aliyah saw Jacob chuckling to himself, his expression indicating that he had just said something humorous. Most of the high school students were laughing, the butterfly-clip and synthetic-braids girls laughing more heartily than everyone else. A smile crept onto Aliyah's face as she glanced around her, as if that gesture would reveal to her what Jacob had said.

"Again, thank you," Jacob said, nodding his head politely before gathering and stacking the papers that were scattered on a table next to him. There was a roar of applause as he returned to his seat in the first row.

***

"*As-salaamu'alaikum.*"

Aliyah turned from where she stood surveying the refreshment table and found Jacob standing behind her. The presentation segment had ended forty minutes ago, and now the guests were eating, milling around, or stopping by the information tables set up along the peripheral of the conference room.

"*Wa'aliku mus salaam,*" Aliyah said, a smile forming on her face. "That was a really good presentation, *mashaAllah.*"

"You should join us," Jacob said before taking a sip from the paper cup he was holding.

Aliyah furrowed her brows and shook her head. "Join what?"

"One Plus One."

"Your mentoring program?"

A shadow of a grin played at Jacob's mouth. "I wouldn't call it *my* mentoring program."

Aliyah chuckled self-consciously. "I'm sorry. I meant—"

"Dr. Bivens," a middle-aged woman with graying hair said as she stepped between Aliyah and Jacob. Aliyah stepped back as the woman grabbed hold of Jacob's free hand and squeezed it affectionately. "Thank you so much for that. Your work with this program is absolutely amazing. I follow you on Twitter, and I just think you are—"

Feeling awkward, Aliyah stepped out of earshot and resumed surveying the refreshment table. She spotted some soft fruit pastries that looked appetizing and walked down to the end of the table to get herself a plate then served herself two pastries, quieting the voice in her head that said they were unhealthy. She sat in one of the many empty seats and set the paper plate next to her as she opened her handbag and removed her iPad. After powering it on, she tapped the icon for her downloaded books and selected the eBook she had begun reading a week before. She then lifted a pastry in one hand and nibbled on it while holding the iPad with the other. To avoid ruining the iPad screen, she set the iPad on her lap whenever she needed to scroll down and avoid touching the screen with sticky fingers of her other hand.

"I love that head cloth."

Aliyah looked up and saw the middle-aged woman from minutes before pausing as she passed. The woman squeezed Aliyah's shoulder compassionately.

"It looks beautiful on you," the woman said.

"Thank you," Aliyah said as the woman walked toward the exit. Self-consciously, Aliyah ran a hand over the soft fabric of the sea green hijab she was wearing. The *khimaar* was one of her favorites, and she wore it so often that some of the threads were loose. But she would find new ways of folding it so that she could keep wearing it whenever she wanted.

"I hate that," Jacob said, settling in a chair a couple of seats away from Aliyah.

"What?"

"When women are all touchy-feely."

Aliyah chuckled. "I always wondered how Muslim brothers handled that."

"We don't," Jacob said, peering briefly into his paper cup before drinking the last bit of juice. "We deal with it. We don't have a choice."

"It's a good thing non-Muslim men don't feel so comfortable touching Muslim women."

"You think so?" Jacob said, intrigued. "What about during interviews or introductions?"

Aliyah nodded thoughtfully. "Except for that, I suppose. But I usually just tell them I don't shake hands with men."

"Does it work?" Jacob said doubtfully.

Aliyah lifted a shoulder in a shrug. "Not always honestly. Sometimes they take my hand before I can say anything. But when they extend their hand, I always feel horrible for not shaking it."

Jacob was silent momentarily. "Do you think it's wrong? Shaking hands with the opposite sex?"

"Yes," Aliyah said. "But I'm not sure I'd call it *haraam*. More like inappropriate."

"That makes sense."

"What about you? Do you think it's *haraam*?"

"I think *haraam* is a pretty serious word," Jacob said. "When I think of something forbidden, I think of what Allah forbids in the Qur'an specifically. I'm not comfortable putting that label on anything else."

Aliyah nodded, unsure what to say. She couldn't help feeling that the casual conversation itself was "not quite *haraam*, but inappropriate." Before Jacob had admitted that he actually called her uncle Benjamin about marrying her as a second wife, Aliyah thought nothing of occasionally conversing with Jacob at work. But now, everything felt wrong. She wondered what had motivated Jacob to make that phone call to her uncle, or series of phone calls, apparently. For someone like Jacob to actively pursue polygyny, he had to have good reason to believe that it was both possible and worth the risk.

Aliyah hoped she had never unintentionally given Jacob the impression that she was attracted to him. The mere possibility petrified her. Was it possible that a fleeting concern for her appearance had translated into a detectable change in behavior? *O Allah*, she thought, *forgive me.*

Naturally, Aliyah was aware of Jacob's attractiveness; it was impossible not to be. But she noticed the attractiveness of many men she saw and interacted with each day. That didn't mean she was attracted to them, did it?

"So do you think you'll join our mentoring program?" Jacob said.

Aliyah kept her eyes on the iPad balanced on her lap as she scrolled down the screen using her left forefinger. She shook her head, partially eaten pastry in her other hand. "I'm not sure I'd be a good fit."

"Dr. Warren asked me why you hadn't signed up."

"She did?" Aliyah's eyes widened, hopeful, as she looked at Jacob. Aliyah was surprised that her supervisor believed that she could be considered for a mentoring position.

Jacob chuckled, shaking his head as he looked down, as if enjoying a private joke. "The students really like you, Aliyah," he said, looking in her direction again, smiling with his eyes. "You know that?"

Aliyah averted her gaze as she took a bite from the pastry in her hand. She never knew how to take compliments. She shook her head. "Don't believe everything you hear," she joked weakly, her left hand scrolling the iPad again though she wasn't sure what she was looking for.

"I'm not only saying that because you're a family friend," Jacob said, the word *family* calming Aliyah's nerves a bit. "I mean it. You're one of our best first-year professors."

A nervous smile tugged at her lips. "*MashaAllah*," she muttered gratefully. "Thanks for telling me."

"I'm your department head," he said, laughter in his voice. "It's my job to tell you."

Aliyah chuckled self-consciously. "I suppose that's true."

"And I'll tell you in more detail when we have our evaluation meeting in a few weeks, *insha'Allah*."

"I hate evaluation meetings," she said. *That was unnecessary*, she told herself, uncomfortable with the seamless honesty of her words. She should not be speaking to him like he was a good friend.

"Tell me about it," he agreed, shaking his head.

Aliyah laughed beside herself. "But you have tenure."

"I mean I hate doing evaluations," he said. "I don't like sitting people down and telling them their faults. I wish there was another way to get the point across."

"You handled our first meetings pretty well, *mashaAllah*," Aliyah said. "I was doing a lot of things wrong, but the way you explained it felt more like helpful suggestions than listing my faults."

"That's good to know," Jacob said, his eyes thoughtful and distant. "It's just that with some professors, there really isn't much positivity to cushion the helpful suggestions with."

"Are you serious?" Aliyah said, humor in her voice. "Are some of us *that* bad?"

"You don't want to know," Jacob said, a sad smile on his face. "Sometimes I hate this job."

"But you're so good at it." Aliyah cringed at her words. *Why did you say that?*

Jacob chuckled self-consciously. "I'm glad you think so. Knowing that makes it a whole lot easier to come to work each day."

Aliyah couldn't tell if he was joking or serious, but she willed herself not to ask. She finished the last bit of pastry and wiped her hands with a napkin before shutting down her iPad.

"You heading out now?"

"Yes," Aliyah said, apologizing in her tone. "I have some things to do before I go to sleep."

"How's my brother Larry treating you?" Jacob said, brotherly teasing in his tone.

Aliyah smiled in thoughtful reflection. "Good, *mashaAllah*. I really like him."

Awkward silence lingered as Aliyah opened her handbag and slipped the iPad inside.

"He was always pretty levelheaded," Jacob said sincerely. "I always knew he'd do something great one day."

"Something great?" Aliyah said quizzically as she glanced at Jacob.

"No, I didn't mean it like that," Jacob said quickly.

Aliyah creased her forehead, confused. "Mean it like what?"

Jacob's expression conveyed mortification. "I'm sorry. I thought you thought I was talking about..."

Cheeks aflame, Aliyah looked away, realizing that he thought that she'd misunderstood "something great" to be in reference to marrying her. She pulled the straps of her purse over her shoulder as she stood, giving Jacob a polite tightlipped smile. "*As-salaamu'alaikum*, Dr. Bivens," she said before walking sideways to the end of the row of chairs.

"*Wa'aliku mus salaam*, Professor Thomas," she heard Jacob say, sounding subdued, as she headed toward the exit.

***

"Will you marry me?"

It was Saturday afternoon, and Aliyah sat in a mall restaurant booth next to Ibrahim, who was kicking his legs gleefully and moving his head from side to side as he licked from an ice cream cone. She kept softly patting Ibrahim's thighs to get him to sit still, but Ibrahim remained oblivious. Several seconds passed before Aliyah registered the question. Larry sat opposite her and was leaning forward on his elbows, a hesitant smile on his face.

"What?" Aliyah couldn't keep the laughter out of her voice. She glanced self-consciously at her son, hoping he hadn't heard. He was still swaying his head to the music in his head, his attention on devouring the last bit of vanilla swirled atop the sugar cone.

"I'm serious," Larry said, embarrassed humor in his voice. "Marry me."

Aliyah laughed again. "We barely know each other."

"What more do you want to know?"

"Let's talk about this later," she said, voice lowered. She discreetly nodded her head in the direction of Ibrahim.

"Okay," he said, a smile lingering on his face. "But for me, there's nothing more to talk about. I'll wait for your answer."

As Aliyah drove home from the mall, Ibrahim in his "big boy car seat" in the back, her instinct was to call Deanna to see what she thought of Larry's proposal. But Aliyah stopped herself, remembering Deanna's passive-aggressive Facebook status a week ago. *It's cute when people with zero counseling credentials and zero success in their relationships try to offer experienced, married folks advice! LOL.* Sadness overwhelmed Aliyah until her heart felt heavy.

After Deanna had picked up her sons from Aliyah's apartment last Sunday afternoon, Aliyah programmed the numbers to Deanna's home and mobile to go directly to voicemail, and she blocked the texting option for Deanna. It was probably the most cowardly way to deal with what was bothering her, but Aliyah couldn't bear the thought of hearing Deanna's voice after reading that status. Of course, Deanna could simply show up at Aliyah's front door as she always did whenever she felt like it, but Aliyah figured she could pretend not to be home. Or better yet, she could make it a point to actually *not* be home at the times that Deanna was most likely to stop by. Incidentally, that was why she'd agreed to meet Larry at the mall that afternoon.

For the past two weeks, Larry had been asking if he could go on a "*halaal* date" with Aliyah. When he'd first used the term in a conversation, she thought he was joking. But when Larry told her he'd already spoken to her uncle Benjamin and got his approval, Aliyah realized that Larry had given this a lot of thought. "Is there even such a thing?" she'd asked humorously. "I looked it up," Larry had said. "Some scholars say it's okay as long as we're not alone or in a secluded place."

At the time Aliyah wasn't interested in going on a "*halaal* date" with Larry, but she found it interesting that any scholar would approve of the arrangement. Most of the fatwas she'd come across on the topic of male-female interaction were impossibly rigid. She was often left wondering what the scholars expected converts to Islam to do since practically everything, from talking on the phone to going on a chaperoned date, was considered *haraam*.

"They said it's allowed only if you don't have Muslim family," Larry had told her when she shared her skepticism. She'd nodded thoughtfully in response, impressed that there were actually scholars who took into account a reality outside the confines of worn pages of books written centuries ago. "But they don't call it *halaal* dating," Larry added. "That's my terminology."

After leaving the mall, Aliyah slowed the car as she pulled into the parking lot of her apartment complex. She pulled into a parking space in front of her building and turned off the ignition. As she turned her shoulders to unbuckle her seat belt, she caught sight of a familiar vehicle parked a few spaces down. Aliyah's heart constricted in panic. Was that Deanna's car? Aliyah debated getting out to check so she could leave if it was Deanna. But what if Deanna saw her?

"Look, Mommy!" Ibrahim called from the backseat. "It's Younus and Thawab."

Instinctively, Aliyah refastened her seat belt, turned the key in the ignition, and looked in the rearview mirror as she backed out of the parking space. She didn't even bother looking in the direction of Ibrahim's pointing finger. She wanted to be able to tell the truth when Deanna asked what happened. "I didn't see you," Aliyah could say, and that was true. She'd only seen Deanna's car.

Aliyah fumbled for her phone in the compartment next to her, and between glancing at the screen and at the road and back at the screen, she scrolled down to *Larry Bivens* in her address book.

"*As-salaamu'alaikum*," he answered on the first ring.

"*Wa'aliku-mus-salaam*," she said, her voice shaky. "Can I ask you a favor?"

***

An hour later, Aliyah held Ibrahim's hand as she pressed the doorbell of the massive brick suburban home that her navigation system had directed her to. Larry had warned Aliyah that she'd probably be bored and uncomfortable, but she assured him that sitting amongst a bunch of strangers at his aunt's house was much more preferable than being a prisoner in her own home next to Deanna.

The door opened, and the scent of potpourri and cigarettes drifted in Aliyah's direction. A woman with tired eyes and a kind face stood in the doorway, her features reminding Aliyah of the late Coretta Scott King, widow of Dr. Martin Luther King, Jr. "Are you Larry's girlfriend?" the woman said in the hoarse tone that Aliyah associated with lifetime smokers.

"Yes, ma'am," Aliyah said, hesitating only briefly as she processed the word *girlfriend* in connection with herself.

"Come on in, sweetheart," the woman said, opening the door wide and stepping aside. "Larry said he invited a friend." The woman looked to be in her mid-fifties, and Aliyah assumed she must be the aunt who owned the home.

Aliyah stepped into the foyer and instinctively glanced around, taking in her surroundings as she held Ibrahim's hand. A sparkling chandelier hung high on the ceiling above her head, and an oak-framed mirror hung on one side of the foyer.

"Is this your little boy?" the woman said, smiling and kneeling in front of Ibrahim, her voice the high-pitched tone adults often adopted in front of children.

"Yes, ma'am. His name is Ibrahim." Ibrahim clung to Aliyah shyly, eyeing the woman skeptically. Aliyah kneeled in front of him until she was at eye level. "Say hi, sweetie."

"Hi, Ibrahim. My name is Mrs. Johnson," the woman told him. "Mrs. Sadie Johnson."

"Hi," he mumbled, a shadow of confusion and discomfort in his eyes.

Sadie laughed heartily as she stood. "I'll take your coats," she said.

"Should we take off our shoes?" Aliyah asked as she unbuttoned Ibrahim's jacket and slid it off his arms. She then stood and peeled off her own jacket as her eyes scanned the plush oatmeal carpet beyond the marbled ceramic tiles where they were standing.

"If you like," the woman said as she reached out to take the jackets from Aliyah.

Aliyah slipped off her shoes and instructed Ibrahim to do the same. She then straightened the shoes against the wall under the framed mirror near the front door. "Is this okay?" Aliyah gestured her hand toward the two pairs of shoes neatly aligned.

"Yes, that's fine."

Aliyah was relieved when she saw Larry's face amongst the men and women sitting on couches and chairs in the living room. He stood and smiled when Aliyah and Ibrahim entered. Seeing Larry walk toward her, Aliyah's heart softened toward him. He looked handsome in the long-sleeved polo shirt and khaki pants. It was same outfit that he'd worn to their "*halaal* date" at the mall, but for some reason, the outfit looked more distinguished on him now. He walked toward her with an expression of pleasure that suggested that they hadn't seen each other in a long time. Aliyah snickered. "Long time no see."

"I know," he said, chuckling.

"The children are downstairs playing with the Wii," Sadie said.

"Can Ibrahim play with the other children?" Larry asked Aliyah.

Aliyah hesitated, apprehensive. She wasn't prepared to part with her son at a stranger's house. "Um… What game is it?"

"Larry, honey, take your girlfriend downstairs and show her the playroom," Sadie said. "Maybe Ibrahim will find something he likes."

Aliyah and Ibrahim followed Larry down a long flight of carpeted steps, and the noise level rose as they descended. The playroom was an expansive room with dark hardwood floors and video game consoles, boxes of toys, and three wide-screen monitors along the walls. There were about ten children downstairs, engrossed in their own games. They didn't even glance up when Larry, Aliyah, and Ibrahim walked in.

"Yes!" Ibrahim yelled as he let go of Aliyah's hand and ran to a box of cars and action figures.

"*MashaAllah*," Aliyah said. "This really is a playroom."

Larry smiled, a sense of pride on his face. "Aunt Sadie has been blessed."

"Yes, I see that." Aliyah crossed her arms as she surveyed the room again. She nodded her approval as she saw Ibrahim toying with a remote control until the car on the floor started moving. "What does your aunt do?"

"She's CEO of my mother's PR firm," Larry said.

Aliyah felt a sense of pride for their family. It was always motivating to hear success stories of racial minorities in America. "*MashaAllah*, they've done really well," she said. Aliyah wondered what his mother's house looked like, but she knew it wasn't polite to ask.

"It's a family business actually," Larry said. "Jacob is the head consultant for PR and fashion, and I'm financial consultant for most of our clients. We all own a percentage of the business."

"And your mother founded it?" Aliyah said, admiration in her tone.

"Yes. But it started off really small. My mom says it took a lot of sweat and blood to get to this point. But she's been in business for about forty years now."

"Forty years? *MashaAllah.* I need to get some tips from her."

"She'd love to talk to you, I'm sure," Larry said.

Aliyah shook her head, self-conscious. She hadn't meant it literally. "I'll wait till I get myself together enough to know what I want to do. Right now, I'm just trying to survive."

The boisterous noise of games and a zooming car filled the silence between them for some time.

"If you ever need anything," Larry said tentatively, "just let me know. I don't mind doing what I can."

Anxiety twisted in Aliyah's chest as she was reminded of Deanna saying the same thing to her. "No," she said, folding her arms until her fists were under her armpits. "I'm fine."

A tense silence followed, and Aliyah realized that she had spoken brusquely. She sighed in self-reproach. "Larry, I'm sorry," she said. "It's just that I can't accept any more help right now. I have to figure out how to do this on my own."

A shadow of concern passed over Larry's face as he looked at Aliyah, perplexed. "What happened?"

Aliyah drew in a deep breath, her gaze distant as she exhaled. "I'm just realizing that most help comes with strings attached."

"I don't intend to take advantage of you," Larry said, his tone soft and empathetic.

Aliyah coughed laughter and rolled her eyes to the ceiling. "People usually don't *intend* harm, Larry," she said. "They just do it naturally." Aliyah blinked, embarrassed that tears stung her eyes. "It's like second nature to some people."

"Let me get you something to drink," Larry said before turning and taking the stairs two at a time out the basement.

As her vision blurred, Aliyah realized that she was trembling and her eyes were filling. Not wanting Ibrahim to see her like this, Aliyah turned and hurried up the stairs herself. Tears slipped from her eyes with each step, and self-conscious, she quickly wiped them away. At the top of the stairs, Aliyah's heart raced as she glanced beyond the spacious kitchen for any sign of a room where she could shut herself inside. She walked back and forth, hoping no one would see her before she could lock herself inside a bathroom or empty room.

"The bathroom is the second door on the left," someone said.

Aliyah glanced behind her and saw Larry holding two paper cups filled with water. "I'll wait for you out here," he said.

In the bathroom, Aliyah leaned against the door, and her shoulders shook as she dropped her head and covered her face, letting herself cry. *"You should be ashamed of yourself,"* her mother's voice said, "*embarrassing the family like that.*" Aliyah sobbed and hiccupped, her breath catching intermittently. *"That's just like Aliyah,"* Deanna's voice said, *"crying like some pitiful child. I swear, it makes me sick."* Then her sister, *"Ignore her. She just wants attention."*

"Do you feel a bit better?" Larry asked after Aliyah emerged from the bathroom, her face moist from splashing water on it and dabbing it with a hand towel.

Aliyah shrugged, an embarrassed smile tugging at her lips. "Yes, thank you. Sorry about that."

"It's okay," Larry said as he handed her a cup of water. "I have my moments too."

Aliyah laughed as she accepted the cup and took a sip. "I have a hard time believing that."

"Maybe not with tears," Larry said. "But I definitely have my moments."

"What could possibly stress out a Bivens?" Aliyah teased.

"The same things that stress out a Smith, a Thomas, or a Ya'qoob."

Aliyah nodded. "Well," she said after taking another sip of water, "at least your family respects your decision to be Muslim."

"That's true." Larry nodded thoughtfully. "But it's not easy for them. They're devout Christians."

"Well, supposedly, my family is Christian too, but they barely believe in God," Aliyah said with a thoughtful frown. "But they act like I broke the eleventh commandment."

Larry raised an eyebrow, a humored expression on his face. "The eleventh commandment?"

"Thou shall not wear clothes that hath not appeared in fashion magazines."

Larry tossed his head back in laughter, and Aliyah couldn't keep from grinning herself. "I assume you mean hijab," he said after he gathered his composure.

"What was your first clue?" Aliyah said, a smirk on her face.

Larry set down his cup of water then crossed his arms and leaned against the island counter in the middle of the kitchen, an affectionate expression on his face. "What's going on with you and my sister-in-law?"

Aliyah drew her eyebrows together. "Your sister-in-law?"

"Deanna."

*Oh.* In the warm, friendly atmosphere of the home of Larry's aunt, Aliyah had forgotten that Deanna had any connection to Larry's relatives. Aliyah started to reply then realized that her responses might offend Larry. After all, Deanna was technically family. "Just some friendship kinks to work out."

Larry snorted, a smirk on his face. "I doubt that."

Aliyah creased her forehead, a smile playing at her lips. "Why?"

"She shows up at your home, and you call *me*."

"What's that supposed to mean?"

"You don't call me for anything."

Aliyah didn't know what to say to that, so she averted her gaze and drank the last bit of water in her cup.

"So what's going on with Deanna? Is she making an Excel sheet of your faults and her solutions?"

Aliyah burst out laughing. It took several seconds to pull herself together. "Pretty much," she said.

Larry shook his head. "I swear, I have no idea what Jacob sees in that woman."

Aliyah frowned. "Don't say that."

"It's true."

"Yeah, but don't say it," Aliyah said, her tone subdued. "It's not right. It's backbiting."

"I'm not saying she's a bad person," Larry said. "I'm just saying I don't understand their relationship."

"But you don't have to understand it, Larry," Aliyah said. "You're not in it."

Larry nodded reflectively. "It's just that sometimes I worry about my brother. He seems stressed all the time."

"He seems fine to me," Aliyah said, hoping to change the subject. "He's actually pretty inspirational, to be honest."

Larry was silent, a sad smile on his face as if enjoying a private joke. "So have you ever talked to Deanna about what's bothering you?"

"Do you mean have I ever talked to her about it, or has she ever listened?" Aliyah said, bitter humor in her voice as she rolled her eyes.

"Both I suppose."

"Yes and no."

"Yes and no to both questions?"

"Yes, I've talked to her about it," Aliyah said. "And no she's never listened."

"Whenever Deanna decides something," Larry said, "it's like the whole world has to fall in line."

Aliyah's eyebrows rose in surprise. "You sound like you're speaking from experience."

"I am," Larry said with a grunt. "She's the reason I accepted Islam months ago."

"That's good, *mashaAllah*," Aliyah said, impressed. "I'm really happy to hear that."

He shook his head. "No," he said. "It's not good."

Aliyah contorted her face in disapproval. "Larry, becoming Muslim is a good thing. If she helped you make that decision, then—"

"I didn't say she helped me," he said. "I said she's the reason I accepted Islam months ago. If it weren't for her, I probably would've converted sooner."

Aliyah closed her mouth, his words cutting her off mid-thought. "What happened?" she said after a moment of awkward silence.

"Every time I saw her, she always had something offensive to say about me not being Muslim. She would even send me these long texts and emails with proofs about the Qur'an and contradictions in the Bible. It got to the point that I filtered all her emails to a folder labeled W-T-F."

"*SubhaanAllah*," Aliyah said. "Are you serious?"

"What made it so bad is she was always smiling when she spoke about religion. But, in my opinion, it wasn't from kindness," he said. "It was condescending. It was like she was talking to some helpless puppy she needed to save instead of a grown man with a mind of his own." He shook his head, clearly still disturbed by the memory. "And she always inserted these smiley emoticons into everything she emailed or texted me. I guess she thought smiley faces would make the message seem lighthearted and sincere. But it came off as snarky and sarcastic. At least to me," he added with a shrug.

Aliyah was silent as she digested what Larry was saying. Ironically, hearing his experience made Aliyah feel better. At least she knew she wasn't alone. Sometimes she feared she was imagining things when she felt disrespected by Deanna. *But she's so nice*, Aliyah kept telling herself. And seeing Deanna's wide, full-teeth smile almost always disarmed Aliyah.

There was something magnetic and charismatic about Deanna. She had that way about her. You couldn't help feeling like you were in the presence of greatness when you were around her. Perhaps that was why she was so successful as a marriage counselor and speaker. You couldn't sit in the audience opposite her and *not* get inspired.

"Well…" Aliyah said. "She's always smiling when she tells me she'll be there for me." She frowned thoughtfully. "But then she turns around and calls me selfish and arrogant for asking for advice or accepting her help. She takes credit for almost every good thing that's ever happened to me," Aliyah vented. "My marriage to Matt, my job at the college, my—"

"Your job at the college?" Larry interjected, amused. "She took credit for *that*? She doesn't even work there."

"I know, but she did help me get the job," Aliyah said, feeling obligated to clarify the truth. "She asked Jacob to talk to the administration on my behalf."

"You're joking?" Larry shook his head, amusement on his face.

"No, I'm serious." Aliyah sighed thoughtfully. "She's not a bad person, Larry. It's just that—"

"She didn't ask Jacob to help you get that job," Larry said. "I did."

Aliyah furrowed her brows as she regarded Larry. "What do you mean? You and I didn't even know each other at that time."

"I know," Larry said. "It was only recently that I found out that you were the Muslim woman who started working with Jacob. But when he asked my advice, I told him he should talk to the college on your behalf."

"But Deanna said…"

"I don't know what Deanna told you," Larry said, a hint of a smirk on his face, "but when she found out about the job, she was angry with Jacob for going behind her back."

Aliyah's face twisted in confusion. "Going behind her back?"

"To help you get a job at the college without asking her first," he said. Aliyah stared at Larry, a blank expression on her face. "It was all they fought about for a long time," he said. "I got sick of hearing the arguments whenever I came over. I couldn't understand what was so wrong with a Muslim man helping a divorced Muslim woman in need of work. What was the woman supposed to do? That's what I kept asking Deanna. Be homeless?"

"But that doesn't make any sense…"

"It makes sense," Larry said frankly. "One thing I learned in the *dunya* is that you can't help an ex-girlfriend without your current girlfriend giving you hell."

"*Girlfriend*?" Aliyah recoiled. "I barely knew Jacob before he married Deanna."

"I'm sorry," Larry said sincerely. "I meant, you can't help a woman you wanted to marry without upsetting your wife."

Aliyah brought a hand to her mouth. "You told Deanna about Jacob's phone call?" A second later she realized that the question made no sense. They were talking about what happened more than six months ago, long before Jacob's phone call to Benjamin.

"No," Larry said, shaking his head. "I'm talking about when he wanted to marry you before he married Deanna."

Aliyah drew her eyebrows together. "I think you're confusing his phone call to my uncle with me getting the job at the college," she said. "Those were at least six months apart."

Larry was silent as he studied Aliyah momentarily as if realizing something all of a sudden. "I think you're right," he said noncommittally. "I think I'm confusing those things."

Aliyah nodded. But something about the way Larry averted his eyes as he spoke left her with the lingering feeling that he was not telling her something.

# 7
# When a Man Loves a Woman

"Marriage isn't hard work," Deanna said, a bright smile on her face as she sat opposite the talk show host. "It's work, yes, but not hard work. It's only hard work for people who don't understand what marriage means."

"So," the interviewer said, puzzlement on her face, "are you saying that all the experts and married couples are wrong when they say marriage is hard work?"

"No," Deanna said. "I'm saying they are ignorant of the meaning of marriage. Or they have bad marriages."

"That's a really provocative statement." The interviewer shifted in her seat then leaned forward. "So tell me, is this point of view based on your professional opinion, or your religion?"

"Both, actually," Deanna said, pride in her voice. "Islam teaches us that God is the foundation of all our relationships, so when you understand this, life isn't so difficult, and everything begins to fall in line. Only people without a proper understanding of God and the sacred bond of marriage have serious problems in their lives and marriages."

"But what about divorce? Certainly, people of your faith experience this problem like everyone else."

"Yes, they do," Deanna said, frowning briefly. "But only the Muslims who are ignorant and take marriage lightly. If they were really following their faith and valuing their relationships, they wouldn't be in th—"

Jacob turned and walked toward the kitchenette around the corner, mentally shutting out Deanna's voice. He needed a shot of coffee before he joined his wife on the set. It was a few minutes past 7:30 on Sunday morning, and he was already regretting getting out of bed. He had agreed to this interview weeks ago, but he was beginning to wonder if it would be wrong to back out right then.

In the kitchenette, Jacob removed the glass pot of coffee from the hot plate and filled an insulated paper cup. *Only people without a proper understanding of God and the sacred bond of marriage have serious problems in their lives and marriages.* Jacob clenched his jaw in annoyance. How could Deanna say something so recklessly stupid? He hated when Muslims touted the "Islam will solve all your problems" line. It was such a load of bull. Maybe Islam offered the best spiritual guidelines when facing the inevitable problems in life and marriage, but it certainly didn't guarantee that the more serious problems of life and marriage would skip you. And, heck, marriage *is* hard work, he thought to himself, even if you have a proper understanding of God and the sacred marriage bond.

Then again, Deanna might be on to something, he considered. Maybe Jacob was one of the ones stuck in a bad marriage.

Jacob stirred sugar and cream into his coffee and carried it back to the set. As he waited behind the cameras for the cue to sit on the couch next to Deanna, he mentally planned the most strategic way to offset the absurdity his wife was sharing with the world about Islam and marriage.

"How could you do something like that?" Deanna said an hour later, glaring at him from the passenger seat as he drove back home. "That was so disrespectful. We're a team. You don't undermine my advice in public. If you disagree with me, you do it privately."

"I didn't undermine your advice," Jacob replied, surprised by the sense of calm he felt after having spoken his mind instead of parroting the lines that he knew Deanna expected of him. "I offered a different perspective."

"You can offer a different perspective when we're alone."

"Not when you're offering yours in the public."

"But *I'm* the marriage expert," Deanna said, fury lacing her words. "How do you think that makes me look to have my own husband saying I'm wrong?"

"Truthfully?" Jacob glanced toward his wife then back at the road as he guided the car along the interstate. "I think it makes you look like a human being instead of a self-righteous know-it-all. And," he said before she could cut in, "it also makes Muslims look like human beings instead of self-righteous know-it-alls."

Jacob could almost taste the disgust in Deanna's glare, but he refused to back down. The mere thought of her audacity infuriated him. "You have no right to speak on behalf of Allah and Islam when you share your views on marriage," he said, narrowing his eyes toward the road in front of him. "It's one thing to say 'In my professional opinion,' but it's another entirely to say that the people who aren't Muslim or who have serious relationship struggles are effectively godless, ignorant, or doomed to bad marriages. You do *not* have that right."

"I have an obligation to speak the truth," Deanna retorted. "And if you find that too difficult to be a part of…" She sniffed haughtily. "…then you can go back to focusing on fashion fads and mathematical formulas. I, on the other hand, have a higher purpose in life."

"You'd do well to make your primary purpose keeping your mouth shut from time to time," Jacob spat, the fire of anger flaring inside him. "You have no idea how many lives you're ruining every time you open it." Jacob huffed, tired of politely listening to all of his wife's holier-than-thou rants. For years he'd assumed she was the expert on marital life, but he'd recently begun to realize that she was an expert on only marital theory.

The car swerved as Jacob's head jerked to the side with the sting of Deanna's slap. Car horns sounded as he quickly regained control of the vehicle and steered the car back into the center of its lane. Pain pulsated from his cheek and he gritted his teeth to calm the conflagration of rage sweeping through him. He willed himself not to look in Deanna's direction or to even acknowledge her violent outburst. Over the years, he'd learned that giving even the slightest attention to her slaps, hits, punches, or kicks, even if only in argument or protest, only fueled her enragement. So he'd learned to go inside himself until her fit of anger passed.

He knew the routine. She rarely apologized with words, but she would pour out her apology in the minutest of details in preparing his favorite meal, in the touch of perfume on her clothes, and in the alluring, sensual smile and coquettish words as she coaxed him into the blind passion of sexual intimacy that lasted late into night. He hated himself for looking forward to it, but it was difficult not to relish in that pleasurable release. But as he guided the car onto the exit toward their home, there was an unfamiliar surge of resistance that unleashed a heartfelt determination in two words. *No more*.

Jacob had no idea where this wave of strength was coming from, but it reminded him of the determination he'd felt after he accepted Islam and his mother refused to speak to him. During that time, his mother threatened to fire him from the PR firm and to remove his partial ownership in the corporation if he insisted on remaining Muslim. *No more*, he'd told himself at the time, sparking his determination to get a doctorate in mathematics so that he could stand on his own two feet without his mother's support. He was not his father, he'd told himself at the time. He was not going to allow the sway of a woman's social and financial status to be a constant tool in her emotional manipulation of him, even if that woman was his own mother. He refused to voluntarily subject himself to emasculation at that hands of anyone, man or woman.

But had he been blindsided from the emotional manipulation in his own marriage? Had his wife's marital "expertise" and Islamic identity served as blinders to the possibility that he was living merely another version of his father's existence? The thought terrified him. Perhaps Jacob himself was like Deanna, imagining that a proper belief in God and a strong educational background protected him from the humiliating existence of "other people."

Or maybe he was, as Deanna often said in a fit of anger, a "poor excuse for a husband" who was lucky that someone as beautiful, intelligent, and prominent as Deanna even looked his way and agreed to marry him.

***

*"Oooooh. It looks like Larry finally got over Jasmine!"*

Laughter still echoed in Aliyah's mind as she pulled the covers over her head Sunday morning shortly after praying *Fajr*, trying to make up for her restlessness the night before. She had to work tomorrow morning, and though she still had a full day ahead of her before she had to worry about that, Ibrahim was staying with her until that evening. So she wouldn't be able to sleep as much as she'd like, especially if she couldn't stop thinking about this "Jasmine" person.

"Who's Jasmine?" Aliyah had asked Larry on the phone last night. A week had passed since she'd visited his aunt's house, but no matter how hard she tried to push his family's teasing out of her mind, she couldn't. After talking to her uncle Benjamin, Aliyah was on the verge of accepting Larry's marriage proposal. But she was beginning to fear that she was about to repeat the same mistake she'd made with Matthew. Had she known that Matt was still getting over an ex-girlfriend, perhaps she would have never married him. The soul's attachment to false beliefs might be completely erased upon accepting Islam, but the heart's attachment to former relationships certainly were not.

"She's my ex-girlfriend," Larry had told her nonchalantly. "My family is constantly making bets that I'll never move on."

"Oh…" There was a litany of questions storming Aliyah's mind after hearing Larry's response, but she had been unable to articulate a single one. But even if she had been able to think of a sensible response, it was no use. Seconds later, Larry had already moved on to another topic.

"Have you thought any more about what we talked about?" he'd said.

"About what?" Aliyah said, distracted by thoughts of Jasmine.

"Marrying me," Larry said.

"Oh, well, I…" *There you go again,* Aliyah had thought to herself. Why did she find it so hard to express herself to Larry? Did she think he wouldn't understand her doubts and fears? "…have to think about it."

Larry chuckled. "That's what you said last week."

"Larry," Aliyah had said, exhaling her apology, "I just came from a really bad marriage. It's not easy to just pick up and start all over again. I have a four-year-old son. I have my…" Aliyah's words trailed as she realized that nothing she said after mention of Ibrahim would make any sense to Larry. She didn't even fully understand the apprehension herself. She was about to mention her job at the college and her strained relationship with her family. But what they had to do with her reluctance to marry again, she had no idea. Or perhaps they were merely the excuses she'd used so often to get out of other things that she now imagined they would somehow allow her to wriggle out of this.

"I don't mind being a stepfather to Ibrahim," Larry said. "I have a pretty big extended family, and I take care of my young cousins all the time. In fact, I grew up helping my aunts and uncles with their children."

That's beside the point, Aliyah thought to herself. It wasn't Larry's adjustment to change that she was most worried about. It was Ibrahim's. He'd been through so much already. First there was the divorce, something he was just beginning to make sense of (and with understandable difficulty). Then there was the thrusting of a strange woman into his father's life in a role that his mother had once fulfilled. And now, the prospect of his own mother remarrying? Aliyah couldn't stomach the thought.

Though Aliyah was wrestling the idea of accepting Larry's proposal, she didn't know if she had the heart to put her needs above her son's. The only normalcy Ibrahim seemed to have in his life right then was spending weekends with Aliyah without distractions. Aliyah imagined that, to Ibrahim, their time together wasn't much different from what he'd grown accustomed to whenever Matt was gone to work all day or away on a business trip while he and Aliyah were still married. Though Ibrahim would occasionally ask why she wasn't "coming home" with him,

Aliyah sensed that her no longer being in their "home" was not as confusing as another woman being there instead.

But Aliyah didn't have the energy to explain all of this to Larry.

"Mommy. Mommy."

Aliyah's eyes fluttered open as she felt rhythmic patting on her shoulder. As the grogginess of sleep wore off, Aliyah saw Ibrahim leaning into her face, his pupils moving from side to side as if searching for signs of life. "Mmm," Aliyah moaned as she looked at him through squinted eyes.

"I'm hungry."

"I know, sweetie," she said apologetically, scratchiness in her voice. "Go wash your hands and wait for me in the kitchen. Mommy's coming now."

***

Deeja Marriage Guru: *Sometimes the people closest to you are the ones you can't trust. Watch your back. #realtalk* (a few seconds ago)

Groaning, Aliyah sat up and tossed her mobile phone on the crumpled comforter of her bed as she swung her legs around until her bare feet rested on the carpeted floor. It was probably a bad idea to check her email and Facebook account before going to the bathroom and preparing Ibrahim's breakfast, but it had become a daily routine of hers.

Maybe she should unfollow Deanna, Aliyah considered as she lathered her hands with soap then held her hands under the stream of water from her bathroom faucet.

For the past few days, Aliyah had toyed with the idea of unfriending Deanna on Facebook, but she ultimately decided against it because it would defeat the purpose of preventing anxiety and avoiding confrontation. It would likely be only a matter of time before Deanna realized that Aliyah had unfriended her, and Aliyah knew that Deanna would leap on the opportunity to make her life miserable as a result. Deanna's passive aggressive statuses would quickly become openly hostile, perhaps even stopping short of only mentioning Aliyah by name. Deanna had certainly done no less to other sisters who'd made the inauspicious choice of crossing her. Aliyah shuddered to think that the same could happen to her.

What Aliyah really wanted was Deanna out of her life completely. She was tempted to block Deanna on social media, but the idea made her nervous. Deanna was so well known for her marriage workshops and relationship advice blogs and books that she was used to being the one whom people flocked to for the mere honor of being associated with her. Deanna had so many friends and followers online that she no longer could accept Facebook friend requests. So, naturally, Deanna was used to being the one to unfriend, block, or unfollow someone. At times, it appeared as if she took pride in this prerogative. *Don't bring your BS on my page. I'll unfriend you real quick. #watchyourself*

Aliyah remembered being bothered by that status, posted more than a year ago. Because it was posted on the heels of a longwinded online debate about the high divorce rate amongst American Muslims, it had given the impression that anyone who disagreed with Deanna's point of view was not only speaking "BS" but would be duly punished for it by Deanna unfriending them.

"People might misinterpret that," Aliyah had told Deanna. "It sounds like you don't welcome legitimate disagreement, and that people should view it as a privilege to be on your friend list. As a respected marriage counselor, you don't want to give that impression."

But as usual, Aliyah's point of view was lost on Deanna because, allegedly, it wasn't based on knowledge or experience. Aliyah didn't have a degree in marriage counseling, Deanna pointed out, and had Aliyah not been still married at that time, she was sure that her divorce would have been used as further evidence against her. "You should stick to math and science," Deanna had told her in condescension. "You don't have a good feel for social interactions."

Despite Deanna's incorrigible arrogance, a part of Aliyah admired Deanna's strength and determination. In private conversations with Aliyah and in some of her blogs and interviews, Deanna spoke of how she was inspired to go into marriage counseling after witnessing an aunt of hers endure domestic violence for years.

"My uncle was an alcoholic," Deanna had said in an interview once. "So maybe he wasn't always aware of the harm he inflicted on his wife and family, but that didn't make it any less pernicious. Abuse is abuse," she said, "no matter what context it happens in. And the only way to deal with abuse is to educate yourself and get out."

Deanna then added, "But I choose the proactive approach. I'll never allow myself to be abused because I know better. I wish I could have helped my aunt, but I was too young and naïve at the time. But what gives me solace is knowing that I'm saving women just like my aunt each day. The best protection against abuse is prevention, and this is the message I implore my patients and readers to pay attention to."

*Sometimes the people closest to you are the ones you can't trust. Watch your back. #realtalk*

As Aliyah stood in front of the stove pouring dry oats into boiling water while Ibrahim sat at the kitchen table waiting for his oatmeal, she saw Deanna's status from a different perspective. Maybe it had nothing to do with Deanna taking a jab at Aliyah or any other person in Deanna's close circle. Maybe it was just Deanna's way of telling women to be careful about letting someone close to them harm them by using their trust as an inroad and a weapon. And that was definitely "real talk."

Aliyah didn't know how it felt to be in an abusive relationship, but she definitely knew how it felt to have her trust used as a weapon against her. Till today, the knowledge that Matt and Nikki had known each other long before

Aliyah was in the picture was still a sore spot for Aliyah. The mere reminder made her stomach churn.

How could she have been so naïve as to welcome Nikki into her social circle and even her own home without asking a single question about why Matt was so keen on Aliyah teaching her about Islam? It should have struck Aliyah as odd that Matt cared so much about the woman's soul given that he wasn't actively involved in any Islamic work himself. But being the trusting person that Aliyah was, she'd assumed the best—when she would have done better to "watch her back," as Deanna suggested. Then perhaps she would still be married to Matt today.

***

When Jacob had arrived to work early Monday morning, he was hoping to catch up on some work that he had fallen behind on. So when he heard a soft knock at his office door forty-five minutes before his official clock-in time for work, he couldn't help feeling annoyed. A part of him was tempted to ignore the interruption. But whoever it was knew he was inside, possibly due to the thin rectangle of light glowing beneath his door, so there was nothing to do but get up, unlock the door, and see what they wanted. Jacob put on an expression of forced cordiality as he pulled open the door. If it was Dr. Warren, he didn't want her to think she was unwelcomed.

"*As-salaamu'alaikum*, Dr. Bivens," she said tentatively, apologizing with her eyes and soft tone.

The sight of Aliyah was so unexpected and pleasantly surprising that Jacob's spirits lifted immediately. A smile spread on his face before he even realized it. "*Wa'alaiku mus-salaam*, Professor Thomas," he said, unable to keep the happiness out of his voice. "What can I do for you?"

"I'm sorry for interrupting," Aliyah said. "I saw you walking ahead of me to the building, so I knew you had come early too."

"It's okay," Jacob said, opening the door wide and stepping back so that Aliyah could come in. "Take a seat." He propped the door open with the door stopper, as he customarily did whenever he was meeting with a woman. "You're always welcome."

"Thank you," she said, averting her gaze as she sat on the edge of a chair opposite his desk, as if anticipating that she wouldn't stay long.

For some reason the prospect of her leaving so soon dampened his spirits slightly, but he still wore a smile as he settled in his office chair. "What's on your mind?"

"I was thinking to maybe sign up for One Plus One *Equals Won*." She was fiddling with the straps of her purse on her lap, unable to look at him directly, and in that moment, jealousy enveloped Jacob so completely that he recoiled at the thought of his brother marrying her.

*"Pray for me, bro. I asked Aliyah to marry me,"* Larry had said to him a few days ago. *"I will, man,"* Jacob had said. *"I'm really happy for you."* And Jacob

was happy for Larry. Or at least he'd thought he was. But now that Aliyah sat opposite him in flesh, Jacob couldn't quell his desire to have Aliyah for himself. It was a selfish thought, but he couldn't help thinking that Larry didn't deserve Aliyah. What had Larry done to justify having someone like Aliyah as a wife?

Jacob immediately sought refuge from *Shaytaan*, the accursed devil, and silently asked forgiveness for his vain thoughts. If Larry didn't deserve Aliyah, Jacob reasoned in self-reproach, then Jacob certainly didn't. At least Larry was able to offer Aliyah some semblance of normalcy in her life. But what about Jacob?

The most Jacob could offer Aliyah was the miserable lot of the "second wife." And Aliyah deserved much better than that. Yet Jacob couldn't come close to being able to offer her even half of what she deserved. Besides, she didn't want Jacob as a husband in any case. For all intents and purposes, Aliyah had already made that abundantly clear. *"It's okay,"* she'd said after he told her about his "momentary lapse in judgment" in calling her uncle to ask about her. *"We all make mistakes."*

Jacob grunted. *A mistake.* That's what the culmination of all his years of unrequited longing and regret had amounted to. A forgivable "mistake." The realization cut him so deep that he had a difficult time focusing on what Aliyah was saying to him in his office that morning as she sat opposite him. But he found himself looking at Aliyah and taking in her breathtaking beauty while comprehending none of the words she spoke.

"—give me your point of view, if you don't mind," Jacob heard Aliyah say, looking up at him for the first time, a question in her eyes.

Her words jarred him back to reality, and he immediately averted his gaze. "I think you'd be a great fit," he said quickly. "We'd be honored to have you in our program."

Aliyah looked confused momentarily. "Thank you," she said hesitantly. "But I'm also asking about Jasmine." She lowered her eyes, an embarrassed expression on her face. "You know…" she said. "…in case I have anything to worry about."

Jacob drew his eyebrows together. "Jasmine? Is she a current or former student?"

Aliyah shook her head. "No, I mean, Larry's Jasmine," she said. "His ex-girlfriend."

"Oh, Jasmine," Jacob said, his eyebrows rising in sudden realization. "Yes, I remember her. Why do you ask?"

"Last weekend I went to your aunt's house and—"

"Oh yeah," Jacob said, smiling, "my aunt and mother wouldn't stop talking about you when I saw them a couple of days ago."

"—some of the family said…" Aliyah appeared to lose her train of thought as she registered what Jacob had just said, a shadow of concern passing over her face. "What do you mean?"

"No, no, no," Jacob said, chuckling and apologizing in his tone. "It wasn't anything bad. They couldn't stop talking about you because they really like you."

"Oh… *MashaAllah,*" Aliyah said, the smallest hint of a smile appearing on one side of her mouth. "I really like them too." A shadow of concern passed over her face as her thoughts seemed to shift. "But they kept joking about this Jasmine person and saying they were happy Larry was finally moving on." She frowned as she glanced at Jacob. "Do you know anything about that? Are he and Jasmine still in touch or anything?"

Jacob immediately felt uncomfortable. He knew what Aliyah was asking, but he didn't feel he had a right to divulge that information. Larry and Jasmine's relationship had been serious for many years, but Larry's interest in religion had driven a wedge between them. Jasmine was a self-proclaimed agnostic, but she held such a strong contempt for religion that it bordered on anti-theism. However, as Larry's inclination toward Islam grew, Jasmine's contempt for religion appeared to wane, but only to the point of obligatory respect.

Ultimately, the biggest point of contention between Larry and Jasmine was Larry's desire to have a life partner who believed in God while Jasmine felt that love, not a person's religion, should matter most in a romantic commitment. They eventually broke up officially shortly before Larry became Muslim. But Jasmine was still a Facebook friend of Larry's though they rarely communicated except for the occasional "like" or commenting on the other's status.

From what Jacob could tell, Larry and Jasmine were still "friends" in the loose, meaningless definition of the term. But based on what Jacob knew from his own past relationships, a man remaining casual "friends" with a former girlfriend was an indication that he had moved on. Or it was a sign that he still had strong feelings for her and was holding on to the hope that they would get back together one day. In all honesty, Jacob believed that the latter was more plausible, at least from a male point of view. And given the complex history between Jasmine and Larry, Jacob had a difficult time believing that Larry was completely over Jasmine despite Larry's apparent sincere dedication and commitment to Islam.

*"Those feelings don't just go away,"* Benjamin had said to Jacob during a phone conversation in which Jacob told him about how strongly he'd felt drawn to Aliyah twelve years ago at the MSA dinner. *"You can deny them all you want. But when a man loves a woman..."* Benjamin paused and made a "hmph" sound. *"...I'm telling you, man, there are only two ways to deal with that. Leave her alone completely, or marry her immediately. There are no safe compromises."*

At the time, it was so unsettling for Jacob to hear the term *love* used to describe his feelings toward Aliyah that he was almost offended. But it took some time for Jacob to come to terms with the fact that it wasn't the word *love* that disturbed him most, but the fact that it really didn't matter what term was most apt in his situation. He'd never have Aliyah for himself anyway, so what difference did it make?

***

Aliyah left Jacob's office more confused than when she'd arrived. She hated thinking that Larry and Jacob were hiding something from her, but the feeling kept gnawing at her. There was something amiss about this whole Larry-Jacob ordeal, but she couldn't put her finger on it.

It had been difficult enough divulging her concerns to Jacob. But Aliyah really didn't know where else to turn. She had considered calling her uncle, but she realized that would do little good since he didn't know Larry well enough to tell her what she needed to hear. The only person who could allay her fears about having another Matt-experience was either Larry himself or someone close enough to him to be privy to his interactions (or lack thereof) with his ex-girlfriend. Aliyah had loathed the idea of asking Jacob about a deeply personal matter concerning his brother, but after careful thought and *du'aa*, Aliyah accepted that it was her best option. Of course, she could call Deanna. But besides the fact that there was little Deanna would likely know about her brother-in-law, Aliyah no longer trusted Deanna to be honest and impartial in what she said to Aliyah.

Aliyah had no idea why Deanna seemed to despise her so much, but if what Larry had said about it actually being Jacob and not Deanna who had initiated the idea of Aliyah working at the college, Aliyah could understand Deanna having some level of resentment toward Aliyah. A part of Aliyah wanted to apologize to Deanna for unintentionally being a source of stress in her marriage.

But even if Aliyah decided to reopen the channels of communication with Deanna, there was really no context to make such an apology. At best, what Larry had told her was hearsay, and at worst, it was grossly incorrect. Of course, Larry had no reason to lie to Aliyah about who had suggested the idea of Aliyah working at the college; but it was possible that Larry himself had misunderstood his role in the ordeal. Perhaps it had been Deanna's idea initially and Jacob had merely asked Larry's advice to see what he thought of the idea.

But why would Deanna be so upset with Jacob about a proposition that she herself had suggested? Or maybe Larry had misunderstood that too. It was possible that Deanna and Jacob had been arguing about something else and the topic of Aliyah's job had been brought up somehow, leading Larry to believe that the argument was about the job itself.

The vibrating of Aliyah's phone interrupted her thoughts as she walked into her office and set her handbag on her desk. She withdrew the phone from her purse and saw a notification for a Facebook message. *Girl, I hope you don't think you're avoiding me. I keep getting your voicemail. Call me back. Now.*

A headache pulsated at Aliyah's temples as she walked around her desk and settled into her office chair. She turned off her phone's Wi-Fi connection then drew in a breath and exhaled slowly. Whether she liked it or not, Aliyah needed to have a long talk with Deanna, sooner rather than later.

# 8
## Why He Stayed

"I have a slightly different perspective from my wife," Jacob had said as he and Deanna sat opposite the talk show host. "I don't think a belief in God and understanding the sacredness of the marriage bond can prevent major problems in life or marriage. Problems, whether relatively insignificant or monumental, are natural parts of life; so no one is exempt from them."

Jacob had sensed Deanna tense up at his words, so he put his hand on hers and squeezed affectionately. "So in that respect," he continued, "marriage can be viewed as hard work. Thus, both points of view have validity. It just boils down to how each married couple or relationship expert defines 'hard work.'"

He looked at his wife compassionately and smiled. "I do, however, mirror my wife's sentiments in that a couple's lack of faith or trivializing the importance of marriage can exacerbate existing problems," he said, feeling the heat of the lamps blazing on them.

"But I don't believe divorce is necessarily a symptom of that," he added, turning his attention back to the host while still holding Deanna's hand. "Divorce in itself isn't a sign of anything except that a marriage has ended. It is in answering the question *Why?* that we determine whether or not a deeper, preventable problem existed," he explained. "Because, in practical reality, it is possible that the marriage ended simply because the man and woman were not compatible, or because one spouse was abusive or because they were both a harm to each other."

When Jacob and Deanna had stopped by his aunt's house to pick up their sons after leaving the television studio Sunday morning, Deanna stayed in the car. She sat taut in the passenger seat with her arms folded over her chest and her body pushed against the door, her head turned stiffly away from him, looking out the window. Jacob walked up the pathway leading to the front door, the rage in his chest simmering only slightly as the side of his face throbbed in pain as it recovered from the sting of Deanna's slap.

"A real man *never* hits a woman." Throughout Jacob's youth, the oft-repeated words of his father remained etched in his mind, and by adulthood they had settled firmly in his heart. Before he was Muslim, it had been a source of pride for Jacob that he had never lifted a hand toward a woman, even if the extent of their relationship was only a drunken one-night stand. But there had been one girlfriend with whom it took all his will power not to strike.

Like Deanna, this girlfriend would slap, hit, punch, and kick him whenever it suited her; and during arguments she would throw anything from a wooden coat hanger to a steel iron. Once, when he had not ducked his head fast enough during his girlfriend's fit of anger, the side of his forehead was sliced so deeply that it required six stitches and left a scar that remained till today. After that incident, Jacob experienced so much anxiety in his girlfriend's presence that he'd do all he could to appease her and acquiesce to whatever she wanted so that he could avoid another explosive episode. But it was to no avail. His breaking point was when she wrapped her thin fingers around his neck and nearly choked the life out of him because, despite his massive strength, he'd stood in a confused stupor, unwilling to lift his hands to even ward off the attack.

*No more*, he'd said to himself that day so many years ago. Then he walked out of that woman's life and never looked back.

Younus's innocent chatter and Thawab's childish enthusiasm upon seeing their father at the door sapped the last bit of simmering rage from Jacob's chest. His sons made all the pain and heartache worth it.

There had been many times over the years that Jacob contemplated divorce, but he couldn't stomach the idea of his sons having a broken home. But as a wide smile spread on Jacob's face as he held Thawab's hand and listened to Younus describe his victories on the Wii, he wondered if he was giving his sons a broken father instead.

***

"Can you believe that?" Deanna's face was contorted in disgust as she gestured a hand toward the video from where she sat on her couch with her legs tucked under her. Because the show was recorded and aired two weeks ago, Deanna was able to obtain a DVD of the interview from the television station. "It's so disrespectful."

Juwayriah frowned thoughtfully as she lifted a shoulder in a shrug from where she sat next to Deanna a Wednesday afternoon. "It's actually not that bad, Deeja. The way you made it sound..." She coughed laughter. "...I thought the brother cursed you out on the air or something." She shrugged again. "Chill. It's not a big deal."

"Are you joking?" Deanna glowered at Juwayriah. "It would've been better if he *had* cursed me out. Then at least it would be clear who's in the wrong here. But with the underhanded way he attacked me, he made me look like some ignorant, emotional idiot. And I'm the marriage expert, not him. So it's *my* reputation on the line."

"To be honest, Deeja," Juwayriah said, "I think you're overreacting. He made some good points, *mashaAllah*."

"So you're siding with *him*?" Deanna's eyes widened in hurt and offense. "I thought we were friends."

"We are, girl," Juwayriah said. "And I definitely don't agree with what he did. But all I'm saying is it's not as bad as you think. People won't see it as him undermining you." She grunted humorously. "If anything, they'll admire you more for being married to someone who thinks differently yet you're still able to be a power couple, *mashaAllah*."

A smile twitched at Deanna's lips despite the taut frown on her face. "You think so?"

"Girl, yes."

"But don't you think it's bad *da'wah*?" Deanna said, a shadow of disappointment on her face. "As Muslims, we're supposed to be the example."

Juwayriah furrowed her brows. "What do you mean?"

"Jacob sat there and basically told the world that Islam doesn't solve all your problems."

Juwayriah shrugged nonchalantly. "It doesn't."

Deanna narrowed her eyes in shock. "Please tell me you're joking."

"Girl, Muslims have problems like everybody else."

"No they don't."

Juwayriah's expression was of amusement. "Please tell me *you're* joking."

"If we're no different from anybody else, then what's the point of being Muslim?"

"I didn't say we're no different. I said we have problems too."

"That's an oxymoron, girl." Deanna snapped her hand at the wrist and rolled her eyes, dismissing her friend's words. "I don't know *what* you're talking about."

"Muslims believe in Allah properly and acknowledge all His messengers," Juwayriah said. "That's the only difference between a Muslim and anyone else."

"But that belief makes you a better person," Deanna said. "If it doesn't, then you're not really Muslim."

"Islam might make you a better person, Deeja. But it doesn't make you a perfect person. People have problems, no matter what their religion is." Juwayriah contorted her face in annoyance. "That's all I'm saying."

Deanna looked at her friend pointedly. "So you're telling me you have the same problems you had before you reverted?"

"I didn't convert to Islam," Juwayriah said. "My parents did." She waved her hand. "And even if I was a revert, what problems I still have is irrelevant."

"If you really accepted Islam, then you wouldn't have those same problems."

"You know what I like most about Islam?" Juwayriah asked rhetorically. "The promise of mercy and forgiveness. And the way I see it, if we didn't have problems, then we wouldn't need Allah's forgiveness."

"I'm not talking about sins," Deanna said. "I'm talking about serious problems like depression, suicide, and bad marriages. Real Muslims don't have problems like that."

An amused grin lingered on Juwayriah's face as she glanced at her wristwatch and stood. "Girl, I have to go," she said. "But I think you should talk to Jacob if what he did is bothering you so much."

"I already talked to him." Deanna grunted. "But you know how men are. They can't take advice from anyone except another man."

"Mm hm," Juwayriah said, nodding emphatically as she walked toward the front door. "That is so true."

"But I tell you what always works." A mischievous grin creased one corner of Deanna's mouth as she got up and walked to the foyer where Juwayriah was putting on her shoes. "Sex deprivation."

Juwayriah tossed her head back in laughter then lifted a hand to Deanna, who lifted her own so they could slap hands. "Don't I know it," Juwayriah said, laughter in her voice. "That's how you beat *them* lightly."

Deanna twisted her lips to the side thoughtfully. "I don't know about the lightly part," she said, humor in her tone. "When I deny him, I do it *hard*."

Juwayriah shook her head, smiling reflectively. "I hear you. That's definitely their kryptonite."

"And after that trick he pulled during our interview," Deanna said, "I'm going to have to step up my game. I usually give him sex every night." She grunted, indignant. "But desperate times require desperate measures."

"Good luck with that," Juwayriah said, laughter in her voice. "'Cause I'm not even going to lie. I need it as much as my husband does, so..." A playful smirk formed on her face as she purposely left her thoughts unfinished.

Deanna laughed. "I know what you mean. But when he thinks he can disrespect me like that..." She huffed. "...I can do without. Trust me."

"All right, girl," Juwayriah said, her tone exhausted as she drew Deanna into a quick hug. "Let me go pick up these kids before the school starts blowing up my phone."

"Thanks for stopping by," Deanna said as she released Juwayriah's embrace. "It's good to have someone I can come to for advice." Deanna sighed as she reached past Juwayriah and opened the front door. "I'm usually talking to people like Aliyah all day."

Juwayriah rolled her eyes to the ceiling and shook her head. "I already told you about that girl, didn't I? It's nice you want to be a good Samaritan and all, but she's not on your level."

"I know," Deanna said, sighing, a sad smile on her face. "It's just that I feel so sorry for her. When we met in college, she was so depressed after her family disowned her."

"Well, she's a grown woman now," Juwayriah said. "She can survive without you."

"I feel obligated to help her."

"Help her what?" Juwayriah twisted her face in disapproval. "You got too many things going for you to waste your time with someone like her." She stepped onto the front porch and glanced back to narrow her eyes at Deanna. "You know what I say about single and divorced women."

A humorous smile formed on Deanna's face. "Yes, I do."

"Drop them, girl. All of them." Juwayriah lifted a hand in a wave as she walked away from the house, her back to Deanna. "They can never be your friends."

"*As-salaamu'alaikum*, girl," Deanna called out, laughter in her voice as Juwayriah approached her car.

"*Wa'alaiku-mus-salaam, ukhti*," Juwayriah called back in response as she opened the driver's side door. "*Insha'Allah*, I'll see you soon."

***

Aliyah's heart dropped as she pulled the bundle of postcards from the manila envelope that was in her mailbox after returning from work Wednesday evening. Her name and address were written on the envelope in familiar bubbly handwriting, but there was no return address. Her head throbbed in time with the pounding in her chest as she steadied her breathing. With trembling hands, she put the postcards back into the envelope then walked toward the stairs leading to her apartment.

Her hands were still shaky when she slipped the key into the lock and pushed open her front door. She mindlessly muttered the prophetic supplication for entering the home as she closed the door behind her and locked it. She walked over to the couch and let it receive the force of her body weight as she fell against it.

Though there was a small voice in her head telling her not to, Aliyah removed the bundle from the envelope again and yanked off the rubber band. Like a poker player examining a deck of cards, she spread the postcards into a fan in front of her. Then pressing her lips together to gather the nerve, she randomly pulled at the postcards one at a time and scanned the short, heartfelt words she had written to her mother, father, and siblings over the years.

*Cassie,* Aliyah wrote to her eldest sister Cassandra, *remember when we went to the state fair and you won that ugly teddy bear? When I saw this picture of a raggedy bear, I laughed and remembered how mad you were when they handed you that beat-up prize after you won all those games! LOL. Missing you loads. XOXO Ally.*

Aliyah sat for a full hour sifting through the cards and reading each one as she got choked up, but she fought the tears.

*You should pray*, said a voice in Aliyah's head.

Aliyah set the fan of postcards on the couch and dragged herself to the hall bathroom for *wudhoo'*. Aliyah's mind kept wandering as she rubbed water on her hands, face, and arms during the ritual ablution in preparation for formal prayer.

Minutes later Aliyah stood in the living room with her hands folded over her chest, her body facing the holy city of Makkah. "*Alhamdulillaahi rabbil'aalameen,*" Aliyah muttered what meant, *All praise is due to God, the Creator, Owner, and Manager of the worlds.*

*Daddy, remember when you and I would go to church together when no one else felt like going? I can't thank you enough for making me put God before everything. I don't know why, but when I saw this picture of the Taj Mahal, I thought of the time you told me, "Ally, sweetheart, God is GREAT!" I love you, Daddy. I miss you sooooooo much. With my warmest love and prayers. Your "little girl", Ally.*

"*...Eeyaaka na'budu wa iyaaka nasta'een.*" *[O Allah!] You Alone do we worship, and to You Alone do we turn for help and assistance.*

*Happy birthday, Mommy! I think this picture of a cake made out of cucumbers, carrots, peppers, and spinach says it all. I admit, I still indulge a bit ☺, but underneath all these bulky, strange-looking clothes, I'm still (as you would say) "giving men a heart attack!" LOL. I wish I could give you a BIG HUG right now. Thanks for being the best Mom ever. Still striving to be half the woman you are...*

Aliyah's shoulders shook and tears filled her eyes. She felt utterly helpless in showing proper gratitude for all the blessings in her life—and in showing sustained fortitude in traversing the severe trials that her religious path had brought her.

*"Ehdi nas siraatal mus taqeem..." Guide us on the Straight Path... the path of those who have earned Your favor, not [the path] of those who have earned Your wrath, nor of those who have gone astray.*

*...I miss you guys! I hope to see you all soon. Love, Ally.*

***

Thursday morning Jacob sat in his car in the driveway of his home and called in sick at the time he normally left for work. After exchanging a few words of apology to Dr. Warren and listening to her concerned voice tell him to get better soon, he ended the call. He stared thoughtfully out the driver's side window before turning the key in the ignition and entering into the car's navigation system the address he'd found online the night before.

It probably wasn't a good idea to make the one and a half-hour drive to the next city without calling first. But he had no idea what he would say to the receptionist when the young man answered. Jacob was having a hard time articulating to himself exactly what he needed right then, but there remained within him an overwhelming urgency that this couldn't wait another day.

Jacob connected his iPod cord to the auxiliary port and tapped the Qur'an icon after powering on the device. He imagined he'd probably need some upbeat music to keep him awake during the drive back home, but right then, he needed to hear the empowering Words of Allah. After selecting the option for Arabic recitation followed by English translation, Jacob glanced in his rearview mirror and pulled out of his driveway as the soothing recitation of *Surah Al-Hashr* filled the car.

*"...And be not like those who forgot Allah, and He caused them to forget their own selves,"* the measured, deep voice of the translator said. *"Those are the defiantly disobedient. Not equal are the dwellers of the Fire and the dwellers of Paradise. It is the dwellers of Paradise who will be successful."*

"O Allah," Jacob whispered in prayer, "give me patience during this difficulty, protect me from being amongst those who forget You, and, O Allah, write me down amongst the successful."

*"Had we sent down this Qur'an on a mountain, you would certainly have seen it humbling itself and cleaving asunder for fear of Allah..."*

As his car crawled along the interstate in rush-hour traffic, Jacob remembered reading the Qur'an for the first time as a Christian. It had been like the sudden awakening of a spirit that had lain dormant inside him for too long. Jacob had no idea what he'd expected, but it definitely wasn't what he experienced. He'd always been somewhat of a skeptic, especially regarding things that could not be easily proven with tangible evidence. But his skepticism was often tempered in religious matters. When doubts had clouded his mind about the veracity of Jesus being both God and the son of God, there was a sense of reluctance in speaking his thoughts out loud. Even as he'd drifted from religiosity itself, there remained within him the tacit acceptance that human intellect did not have the capacity to comprehend the infinite power, wisdom, and reality of God…

*"…He is Allah, other than Whom none has the right to be worshipped except Him, the All-Knower of the unseen and the seen. He is the Most Beneficent, the Most Merciful…"*

Deanna was probably right, Jacob reflected. If he understood and practiced Islam as he should, perhaps he wouldn't be so racked with confusion and despondency right then. There were times that he was left in awe of his wife's spirit. Where she got the motivation to keep smiling and moving forward even in the dimmest of circumstances he couldn't fathom. Other than dealing with Jacob himself, nothing seemed to unnerve her or cause her to waver.

*Maybe she'll be better off without me,* Jacob thought sadly.

*"…[He is] the King, the Holy, the One free from all defects, the Giver of security, the Watcher over His creatures, the All-Mighty, the Compeller, the Supreme…"*

Jacob flinched, anger stabbing his chest as he recalled Deanna slapping him after the television interview. It wasn't the first time that she'd attacked him, but for some reason, this time, he found it difficult to suppress the simultaneous feelings of shame, guilt, and resentment. He clenched his jaw in indignant satisfaction as he imagined striking her back. But he quickly stopped himself. *A real man* never *hits a woman.*

*"…Glory be to Allah! [High is He] above all that they attribute to Him."*

***

"…So I just really need some time alone now," Aliyah said as she stood in the doorway of her home late Thursday evening. She frowned apologetically and averted her gaze from the look of shock and offense on Deanna's face. "It's nothing personal, Deeja," Aliyah said. "I just have a lot going on right now, and I can't handle anything else."

"But I'm your best friend, Ally-pooh," Deanna said, her high-pitched chipper voice only thinly masking her annoyance as she stood on the welcome mat outside Aliyah's door. "I'm here for you."

"I know you are, Deeja." Aliyah sighed as she met Deanna's gaze. "It's just that we don't always understand each other. Sometimes I feel like all I do is annoy you."

"You *are* annoying." Deanna's tone was soft and empathetic. "But I still care about you. You had me worried sick when I didn't hear from you."

"I'm fine, Deeja," Aliyah said, her voice clipped. It was difficult to withstand Deanna's underhanded insults right then. "Really."

"What are you so uptight about?" Deanna said, the compassion gone from her voice. "All I ever do is try to help you."

"I know," Aliyah nodded apologetically. "And I thank you for that. But, honestly, I don't think we're good for each other. I stress you out. You stress me out. I really don't see what either of us is gaining from this friendship."

"Blessings from Allah." Deanna spoke as if this should be obvious to Aliyah. "And that's enough for me."

"Then we can get blessings from afar," Aliyah said. "Keep me in your prayers, and I'll keep you in mine *insha'Allah*. But there are no hard feelings on my part. I just don't think I'm getting a lot of blessings if I cringe every time I see your name on my phone. It's like I already know what's coming, and I can't take it anymore. I have enough problems as it is, so—"

"Yes, you do," Deanna said flippantly.

"—it's best if we just part ways."

"What does that even mean?" Deanna lifted her upper lip in a sneer.

Aliyah willed herself to maintain her composure. Instead of responding directly, she smiled and started to close the door as she said, "Allah will make that clear to you, Deeja. *As-salaamu'alaikum wa-rahmatullaah*."

***

Jacob stepped off the elevator and walked toward the office suite bearing the name plaque "Dr. Melanie Goldstein, M.D. Office of Psychiatry." His eyes lingered on the name for a brief moment before he turned the door handle and stepped inside.

"Do you have an appointment?" said the young man who Jacob assumed was the Fredrick McDaniel listed as the receptionist and office assistant on the website.

"No, but I—"

"I'm sorry sir," Fredrick said. "But Dr. Goldstein doesn't take walk-ins." He tapped something into the computer then glanced at Jacob. "But we have an opening next Friday at ten o'clock. Does that work for you?"

"I'm actually an old friend," Jacob said, his voice sounding awkward and unconvincing even to his own ears. "And I was in the neighborhood, so I just wanted to say hello." Jacob forced a close-lipped smile. "Can you tell her Jacob Bivens is here?"

Fredrick regarded Jacob skeptically before pushing back his chair and walking through a door in the back. Jacob glanced around him and noticed several people seated in the waiting area of chairs bound together in single rows. Some of them looked up at him suspiciously then resumed reading their magazines, playing with their hands, or staring at the walls.

"Tiger!"

Jacob turned and saw Melanie holding the door open leading to what he assumed was her office. She was just as he remembered her, except that she had put on some weight, there were laugh lines next to her eyes, and her freckles seemed a bit faded.

"Hey, Annie," he said, exhaustion disrupting the playfulness in his voice as he used the nickname he had given her because of her resemblance to the character in the *Annie* movie. He walked toward the door, a hesitant smile on his face. "I hope this is not a bad time."

Fredrick settled back in his seat and eyed Melanie and Jacob curiously before resuming typing on the computer.

"As I always say," Melanie said, humor in her tone.

"Every time is a bad time," Jacob said in unison with her, unable to keep from laughing as he nodded, recalling her wicked sense of humor. "But it's up to us to change that."

The door closed behind them as he followed Melanie to the end of the hall. She stopped in front of an open door and gestured for Jacob to come inside. He stepped beyond the threshold and nodded approvingly at the large, spacious office bearing framed degrees and certificates, inspirational quotes, and paintings.

He gestured his head toward an acrylic painting of what looked like the lower half of a table with a girl sitting and eating. "I see you still like mystery."

"I have you to thank for that," she joked.

Jacob coughed laughter, but he got choked up instead. It still pained him that he had convinced Melanie to abort their child while they were an official couple in high school. Though he'd heard that she had three children now, he couldn't help wondering if the wound he'd inflicted would ever heal.

"Come here," she said affectionately as she pulled Jacob into an embrace.

He immediately lifted his hands as if in surrender in an effort to avoid participating in the hug. "I'm sorry. I…" he said, unsure how to explain his awkward predicament.

Melanie jerked her body away from him and brought a hand to her mouth. "Oh my God, Jacob. I totally forgot. I'm sorry."

"It's okay," he said, chuckling self-consciously. "It happens all the time."

"That must be so annoying though," she said sympathetically as she sat down on the long leather couch in front of her desk.

"I fear it annoys other people more than me," he said, a tinge of sad humor in his tone.

"Well, they'll just have to get over it then, won't they?" she said. "Living according to what you believe is more important than sparing people's feelings." Her words immediately reminded Jacob of having said something similar when they were in high school and Melanie's parents objected to their relationship because he wasn't Jewish. But Jacob had always suspected that their objection was due more to him not being White.

Seconds passed in awkward silence until Melanie patted the space on the sofa next to her. "Sit down. Tell me what's bothering you."

An embarrassed smile formed on his face as he sat down on the couch as far from Melanie as possible. "How do you know something's bothering me?"

"You live in another city, Tiger. And you're not the type of person to just stop by and say hello. I haven't seen you in over ten years." She rolled her eyes good-naturedly. "Besides, I *know* you. Don't forget that."

"Don't you have an appointment or something?"

"Yes," she said. "In twenty minutes, but I canceled them. I told them to reschedule."

Jacob's eyes widened apologetically. "I'm sorry. I didn't mean to…"

"Every time is a bad time, Tiger." She gave him a friendly tightlipped smile.

"Oh… well… thanks."

"Congratulations, by the way," Melanie said.

Jacob creased his forehead. "For what?"

"For being an inspiration to so many people."

"An inspiration?" Jacob said as if waiting for the punch line.

"Your marriage workshops, your interviews, your—"

"You've seen some of my interviews?" Jacob couldn't conceal the surprise in his voice.

"No," Melanie said. "I've seen *all* of them. I follow you on Facebook, Twitter, and Instagram. And," she said, raising a forefinger, "I get Google alerts for your name."

"Are you serious?" He coughed laughter. "That's insane."

She shrugged. "Maybe. Maybe not. But I call it caring about what's going on with you."

Jacob nodded. Though he hadn't gone as far as to follow Melanie on all her social networks, he did follow her on Twitter and occasionally Google her name when his curiosity got the better of him, so he couldn't blame her.

"I really like that last interview you did," she said. "The one with you and your wife. I'm really glad you made those points. The truth is, I get really annoyed when experts insult each other." She groaned and rolled her eyes to the ceiling. "And using religion to justify your opinion? I think that's my number one pet peeve in this field."

"So it happens in your religious community too?"

"Are you kidding me?" Melanie looked pointedly at him. "Show me a religious community it *doesn't* happen in."

Jacob nodded thoughtfully. "I thought it was mainly Muslims doing that."

Melanie laughed. "Please don't tell me *you're* falling for the Islamophobic propaganda. Like you said, everybody has problems."

Jacob laughed in agreement. "You have a point."

"Soooo…." Melanie said, her voice teetering between cautious and serious. "…let me be really honest with you. My wild guess is that there's a lot of trouble in the waters of your marriage, and you want my professional perspective."

Jacob grunted, surprised that it was still easy for him to be frank and honest with Melanie. "To put it lightly," he said, agreeing. But Jacob didn't mention that he'd chosen Melanie also because she was the only person he trusted to not misconstrue his and Deanna's marital struggles as some proof that Muslims weren't upstanding citizens, or to surreptitiously leak their marriage problems to the public. He and Deanna were well respected in both secular and Islamic circles, and he didn't want to take the chance that anyone would betray their confidentiality in an effort to ruin that respectable image. Unfortunately, the Muslim experts he knew had lives too deeply intertwined with his and Deanna's to trust their impartiality.

"In that last interview," Melanie said, shaking her head, "your wife looked like she was about to spit bullets when you gave a point of view different from hers. I felt like the only thing keeping those bullets in her mouth was that frozen smile on her face." She shook her head again. "And all I could think was, poor Jacob. He must be going through a lot."

"Well..." he said uncomfortably, "I wouldn't put it like that."

"I don't mean that judgmentally," she said sincerely. "Many of us are going through a lot, Tiger. I filed for divorce *twice* then backed out both times. So you're not getting any judgments from me. I might need to find a marriage counselor myself."

"I'm sorry to hear that."

She waved her hand dismissively. "Don't be. It's not your fault."

Silence filled the space between them for some time.

Jacob glanced at the clock on the wall. "Melanie," he said with a sigh, "I'm not even sure it was a good idea to come here, so I should probably just go."

"Okay, sure," she said, her tone unconvincing. "But let me say something first."

Jacob was silent as he gave a hesitant nod.

"Remember how I used to say you need to get in touch with your feelings more?"

A smile crawled on his face. "Yes, I do."

"Well, that's my advice. You avoid things too much, and you try too hard to put a positive spin on everything." She raised her hand as if anticipating a rebuttal. "I'm not saying you should think negatively of your marriage. All I'm saying is, being positive is only good when you're honest with yourself about the *whole* picture. You have to take a long, hard look at the good and the bad, and the positive and the negative. Otherwise, you're not being positive or optimistic. You're being willfully blind. It's like putting on blinders *after* you've already seen what's in front of you, then wondering what you keep bumping into and why you keep getting hurt."

On the drive back home, the bass of music thumped in his car speakers, and Jacob kept replaying Melanie's advice in his head. *You have to take a long, hard look at the good and the bad, and the positive and the negative.* As he tried to think of the bad circumstances in his life in a concrete way, his mind kept warding off the thoughts as if in self-protection.

Yes, Deanna had an explosive temper at times, but Jacob wasn't an angel himself. How then could he fault his wife for being flawed? Jacob's occasional frustration notwithstanding, her actions weren't hurting anyone. Deanna herself always tried to focus on the positive. How then could he allow himself to do anything differently?

***

Deeja Marriage Guru: *You know someone's Islam is a front when they line their pockets with your sadaqah, pretend to be needy so you'll help them get a job, and then drop you when they feel they can't use you anymore. #TiredOftheBS #ImTooThrough*

Juwayriah bint Abdullah and 29 others like this. 14 comments.

## 9
## He Broke Her

"You just need to work on your *mudood* and *ghunnah*," Reem said.

As Aliyah held the cordless phone to her ear Friday evening, she made a mental note of what her Qur'an teacher was saying about her recitation. Aliyah had begun studying *tajweed* with Reem a few years ago when Reem started the evening and weekend classes at the local masjid. But after Aliyah and Matt divorced, Aliyah was unable to attend regularly. It had been Reem's idea to resume classes via telephone, and initially, Aliyah refused. She did not want to inconvenience her Qur'an teacher. Besides, she had no way to compensate Reem for her time. It was one thing for Aliyah to accept Reem's offer for her to attend the regular group class without paying, but it was another thing entirely to accept a one-on-one class specifically catered to Aliyah's schedule and needs.

*"Let me clarify something, Aliyah,"* Reem had said to her about a year ago when Aliyah refused the offer for a third time. *"This is not something I do for everyone. As you know, my schedule is really busy. But you're one of my best students,* mashaAllah tabaarakAllah, *and I'd hate to lose you. So this is something I want to do for myself, honestly. I know you might not understand this right now, but, truthfully, it would be an honor if you allow me to teach you privately."*

"My *madd* counts are still off?" Aliyah's gaze was on the bundle of postcards on the floor table in front of the couch near where she stood.

"Only slightly," Reem said. "But you have a tendency to implement *ghunnah* in some of the *mudood* letters, especially at the end of an *ayah*."

"Make *du'aa* Allah helps me with that," Aliyah said, sighing in self-reproach. "It's a really bad habit of mine."

"It's a normal mistake, actually," Reem said. "Even some of the most famous reciters of Qur'an do it."

Aliyah nibbled at her lower lip, her mind distracted with thoughts of her family returning all the postcards she'd sent them. How was she supposed to fulfill the Islamic requirement to uphold family ties when her family refused to even speak to her or acknowledge her presence?

Aliyah was beginning to feel as if her world was caving in, and she wanted so badly to reach out to someone—anyone—who could help. But she had no idea where to turn. Her uncle Benjamin had always been a source of comfort and support over the years. Out of everyone, he understood Aliyah's predicament best. Though he was still married to his Christian wife (a sister of Aliyah's mother), Benjamin had experienced his own level of alienation because he was (allegedly) "forcing" his wife to stay married to him. As was the case with their view of Aliyah, that Ben's wife was a grown woman with a mind and life of her own was lost on them.

Despite his personal understanding of what she was going through, Aliyah felt that her uncle wasn't emotionally available to really *hear* her right then. He was so determined to get Aliyah remarried that she sometimes felt invisible to him. Aliyah had concerns that needed to be addressed and dreams she wanted to fulfill irrespective of whether or not she ever found "the one." Though Larry seemed nice enough and Aliyah was still contemplating marrying him, she just couldn't bring herself to be excited about the idea. Maybe she was still recovering from what she had gone through with Matt, but she was beginning to wonder if she wanted to remarry at all.

"How are you doing though, *habeebti*?" Reem said, her voice soft with compassion and empathy.

"I'm good, *alhamdulillaah*," Aliyah said, offering her standard response followed by praising God for His blessings.

"Are you sure everything's all right?" Reem said, concern in her voice. "You seem a bit distracted today."

*You know someone's Islam is a front when they line their pockets with your sadaqah, pretend to be needy so you'll help them get a job, and then drop you when they feel they can't use you anymore.* Aliyah gritted her teeth at the sudden reminder of Deanna's offensive Facebook status.

"I'm just tired," Aliyah said. But she felt a lump developing in her throat as she realized how emotionally exhausted she was. Maybe her Islam was a front. She wasn't feeling exactly spiritually motivated right then. She was even beginning to doubt that she had the ability to maintain her sanity much longer. She just felt so lonely. The sustained estrangement from her family, the unexpected divorce from Matt, and the eventual fallout with Deanna left Aliyah wondering if it was even realistic to have a companion or friend she could trust.

Aliyah wished she had the wherewithal to reach out to Reem and ask her perspective, but Aliyah just couldn't bring herself to admit her frailties to the one person besides her uncle who saw something special in her. But Aliyah hoped that she and Reem could become good friends one day. Aliyah imagined that there was so much she could benefit from her Qur'an teacher. Though Reem was a couple of years younger than Aliyah, Reem's knowledge of Islam and Qur'an made her seem like an elder.

"Okay…" Reem seemed hesitant to get off the phone, and Aliyah felt horrible for inciting concern in her teacher.

*Can't you have a relationship with at least one person without stressing them out?* Aliyah scolded herself.

When Aliyah finally hung up, she was overcome with sadness and frustration. What was it about her that made her so off-putting to people? First her family, then her husband, and now her best friend.

*You know someone's Islam is a front when they line their pockets with your sadaqah, pretend to be needy so you'll help them get a job, and then drop you when they feel they can't use you anymore.*

After more than ten years of friendship, that was Deanna's perspective of Aliyah? What had Aliyah done to make Deanna hate her so much?

***

*Hurt people hurt people.*

It was something Jacob's father would say often. *"Except when inflicting or suffering some egregious wrong, no one is completely wrongdoer or victim,"* he told Jacob. *"So be careful before you align yourself with anyone's cause. Things aren't always as they seem."*

But when Jacob heard the heartbreaking story of Janice Michaels, he couldn't fathom there being any explanation for her predicament except her having suffered egregious wrong. From childhood, Janice spent many afternoons and weekends in the church. The church was only a few blocks from her home, so whenever the bus dropped off her and her cousin Bailey after school, Janice (and sometimes Bailey) would often make the short trek to God's House of Worship. Usually Janice's father (who would later become a deacon), mother, and elder brother, Asher, would be at the church volunteering or facilitating one of the many activities that were always happening there: a youth group meeting, a clothes or food drive, a soup kitchen, choir practice, or merely dusting and cleaning the pews.

Bailey, who had lost his father to the war in Iraq and his mother (though still alive at the time) to drug addiction, lived with Janice's family off and on and gradually became like a second son to Janice's father and good friends with Asher. Bailey and Asher were around the same age, ten years older than Janice, so their interactions with Janice were primarily of obligatory tolerance and a mild annoyance. By eight years old, Janice had mastered the art of entertaining herself, so no one usually gave more than a passing shrug whenever she sifted through the donation boxes in the church basement and played dress-up with all the grown-up clothes and women's heels she'd find there.

"Child, take your butt to the bathroom and put on some proper clothes and wash that crap off your face." This is what her father would say if he lost patience after catching sight of her in layers of fake jewelry, oversized heels, and red lipstick, eye shadow, and foundation smeared childishly on her face. Janice would giggle and run along out of his sight, where she would resume her "pretty lady" walk in the shadows of an empty room as she held her mother's large purse (where she'd found the make-up) clamped closely to her side. Sometimes she would sing a popular song or hymn to herself as she swayed her small hips from side to side, imagining herself in front of flashing cameras and television crews eager to catch a glimpse of the famous, stunningly beautiful "Niecey Meesy," as she called herself in her pretend world.

"That's a stupid name," Bailey said to her once as they walked from the bus stop to the church during a particularly cold day in the winter, his hands stuffed firmly and deeply into the pockets of his wool-like polyester coat. The bottom of his face was ducked awkwardly behind the upturned collar, so his voice was muffled. He rarely wore a hat, earmuffs, scarf, or gloves; but Janice's mother was rather adamant that Janice herself never left the house during the winter except that she wore all of these items.

How Bailey was able to escape the tongue lashing of Mr. and Mrs. Michaels while he stayed in their house was a conundrum that Janice's young mind had never been able to decipher. Janice was equally perplexed as to why her parents would let her walk home or to church alone whenever Bailey was not staying with them but insisted that Bailey, whose high school was next to her elementary school, make sure Janice got home or to church safely whenever he was staying in their house. Asher couldn't see her home safely because he went to a magnet school for the gifted and talented in another part of the city. Ironically, he usually arrived to the church before Bailey or Janice.

"So. I don't care," Janice said, her voice muffled through her wool scarf as she turned up her head as much as she could manage with all the layers. "When I get famous, I'm going to be Niecey Meesy, and you're going to be sorry you ever said that. I won't even give you an autograph."

The sound of coughing and choking prompted Janice to stop in her snow-covered tracks and stare at Bailey in concern. *Is he dying?* she thought, petrified. "Are you okay?" she said, her breath white puffs beyond the wool fabric. Bailey kept coughing and choking and waving his hand desperately at her, and it was then that she saw the amusement in his eyes. He wasn't dying, she realized in mortification. He was laughing so hard that he couldn't contain himself.

"Your *autograph*?" he said after he gathered his composure as they approached the double doors of the church. "Do you really think someone named Niecey Meesy will be famous for anything except making a fool of herself?"

Tears stinging her eyes in offense, Janice marched ahead of him to the church, refusing to speak to him again that day. After waving a hello to her mother, father, and brother, she rushed to the basement where the donation bags and boxes were kept. She yanked off her hat, earmuffs, scarf, and gloves then huddled in a corner, where she sobbed and hiccupped as she thought of how stupid the name Niecey Meesy now sounded to even her own ears.

"It's okay, Niecey Meesy," she whispered to her alter ego. "We'll think of a better name. You'll see." She then wiped her face with her palms and stood with her hands on her hips. A look of determination was on her face as she surveyed the array of clutter. She was sure that somewhere inside the overstuffed bags and boxes of clothes, shoes, and weathered jewelry, there was an amazing outfit to match her new name (whatever it might be).

After more than an hour of rummaging around, she found a formal, heavily brocaded off-white sleeveless dress and a pair of heels that matched the dress perfectly except that they were soiled with dirt stains and the heel of one of them was missing. But she was filled with an air of personal satisfaction when she slipped them on and found that they were only slightly loose on her small feet. Proud of her discovery, she limped around in search of matching jewelry and was content when she found a bundle of chipped synthetic pearls and slipped them in loops around her neck.

"What are you doing?"

At the sound of a deep voice, Janice's body jerked in shock, and she halted her "pretty woman" limp-walk. Her hands slid cautiously from her hips, and she slowly turned around, knowing her father would punish her severely for disobeying his instructions to "leave those trashy clothes alone." Her shoulders sagged in relief and embarrassment when she saw that it was only Bailey. The look of amusement from earlier was still in his eyes and was now coupled with a sideways grin at his mouth. A tinge of self-incrimination pinched her as she recalled how he'd pointed out how stupid her stage name was. She could only imagine what he would think of her now after seeing her dressed like a pitiful person who probably could be named Niecey Meesy.

"I don't care what you think," she said, sniffing indignantly. She folded her bare arms across the empty puffy bust of the dress and turned her head away from him in a pout. "I can think of a better name, but I still won't give you my autograph when I'm famous."

Bailey chuckled. "I came to apologize," he said, his head tilted to the side as he approached her, studying her odd outfit.

"You did not," Janice said, her eyes crawling to the side, hoping he was serious.

"I did," he said, laughter in his voice. "I'm sorry. I don't think Niecey Meesy is a stupid name."

"Well, I do," she said firmly. "So I'm thinking of another one."

Bailey reached forward and lifted the string of synthetic pearls and let them slide through his large fingers. "What's all this?"

"I found it in a box. I'm going to put it back," she said quickly, defensive. "I know it's not mine."

"I didn't think you were stealing. It's just that I like how it makes you look. I think you might be really famous one day."

Janice's eyes widened as she looked at him, a broad grin spreading on her face. "You do?"

"Yes I do."

Janice averted her gaze and looked down at her lopsided stance. "But I have to fix my shoes."

"You don't have to fix anything," he said, pulling her into a tight embrace. "You're perfect just the way you are."

Janice smiled as he held her close and said nice things to her. She grew uncomfortable only when he squeezed her tighter and wouldn't let go, making her efforts to wriggle out of his grip futile…

The pain throbbed in her torso area as she lay alone on the floor of the basement, the back of her head against a worn plastic garbage bag overflowing with clothes that reeked of must and mildew. *"If you tell anybody about this,"*

Bailey had said as he brought his face so close to hers that she could smell food and cigarettes on his breath, *"I'll kill you."*

Janice's neck ached as she moved her head to look down at herself. Her first thought was panicked as she feared that she had ruined the dress. *Mommy and Daddy will be mad at me.* She pulled at the fabric bunched up at her waist, frantically trying to keep the glistening red smudges on her thighs from touching the beautiful dress. She forced herself to a standing position and carefully lifted the dress over her head and stuffed it back into a bag. She then gathered her clothes under her arms and hurried to the dilapidated basement bathroom. On shaky, aching legs, she stood in front of a filthy sink and held her palm under a stream of water then she rubbed her thighs clean.

Back upstairs, Janice found her mother, father, and Asher laughing together about something. She started to approach them to ask to go home, but she froze when she caught sight of Bailey just feet from them glaring at her. *"My father was in the war, and he trained me how to hurt people,"* Bailey had said to her. *"So if you say anything, I can kill your mother and father too. And it will be your fault."* Terrified, Janice backed out of the worship hall and sat quietly in the lobby of the church until it was time to go home.

***

It took Aliyah a full hour to calm her offense and frustration as Deanna's status kept resonating in her mind. *You know someone's Islam is a front when they line their pockets with your sadaqah, pretend to be needy so you'll help them get a job, and then drop you when they feel they can't use you anymore.* Aliyah certainly couldn't deny the litany of faults she saw in herself, but whatever Deanna didn't like about Aliyah, she had no right to question Aliyah's religious sincerity and faith in Allah.

Heart racing as she realized she was actually going to speak up for herself, Aliyah lifted her laptop from where it lay on the nightstand next to her bed. Balancing the laptop on folded legs, she opened it and connected to the Wi-Fi.

Aliyah rarely used Facebook except to share inspirational quotes, videos, and blogs or to post a link to an important news story. As a general rule, Aliyah stayed out of Facebook discussions because most of them seemed to serve no purpose except to offer a platform for complaining, exposing people's faults, bickering, and one-upping other commenters. In Aliyah's experience, even when someone offered a balanced, sensible perspective during a discussion, there was always someone who zeroed in on the tiniest contradiction (*It's* their, *not* there. *Learn how to spell, then come back and join the discussion*). When all else failed, some people went as far as to highlight a personal fault in the commenter that had nothing at all to do with the discussion.

Aliyah logged into her Facebook account, and her hand trembled as she opened the page of Deeja Marriage Guru.

*You make some interesting points,* Aliyah typed a comment under the offensive Facebook status. She willed herself to ignore the childish *LOL*'s and *Tell 'em, girl!* comments egging on Deanna's foolishness. Aliyah imagined that most of these commenters had no idea what or whom Deanna was referring to in her post. But Aliyah figured that Juwayriah knew exactly what Deanna was referring to, so it cut deep to see someone who knew her personally corroborating the character assassination (*I told you, girl! Some people are so uppity and fake, it's sickening*).

*But here's my question*, Aliyah typed. *If someone's Islam is a front, then doesn't that make them a munaafiq, a disbelieving hypocrite? Correct me if I'm wrong, but from what I understand, the Prophet, peace be upon him, forbade speaking about the state of anyone's heart (We aren't even supposed to speak confidently about our own), and this is even more so the case when we're saying someone's very submission to God (i.e. Islam) is just a mask they put on to take advantage of others. This is not only accusing a Muslim of disbelief, it's also accusing him/her of the worst form of disbelief: nifaaq (religious hypocrisy). In the Qur'an, Allah says these hypocrites (who pretend to be Muslim) will be in the lowest level of Hellfire. And to warn us against making such serious accusations against a fellow believer, the Prophet said, "Whoever says to his brother, 'O disbeliever,' then surely the disbelief falls back on one of them." So,* ***Deeja Marriage Guru****, are you saying the disbelief falls back on the person who "lined their pockets with your sadaqah," or on you?*

***

No one knew what was wrong with Janice when her previously honor roll grades slipped to near failing, and she did not utter a single word except when she was alone talking to herself, engrossed in an imaginary world that enabled her to laugh, dance, and sing in a delirium that incited deep worry in her family.

Her parents took her to doctors and psychiatrists, but no one knew what was wrong except that she was a "selective mute." It wasn't until she was thirteen years old and hadn't seen Bailey for three straight years that she told her mother in a runaway letter the details of what happened to her.

*I don't want anything bad to happen to you and Daddy*, she'd written. *So I'm going to go live somewhere else to keep you safe in case Bailey comes looking for me. I changed my name to be extra careful,* she wrote in the last lines of the letter. *My middle name is my first name now. But I'm only telling this to you, so please don't give away my secret. I'll come back when it's safer. Yours truly, Deanna.*

Janice had made it only a few miles down a main street before her parents found her and brought her back home.

***

*Oh my Lawd!* ***Deeja Marriage Guru****, please tell me you don't have bona fide religious zealots on your friend list! Who or *what* is Ally Thomas, and please save us from him/her/it!* (11 likes).

*Looks like you got yourself a potential client,* **Deeja Marriage Guru**. *Then again, you don't fix loony, do you? ROFL.* (7 likes)

*You can always count on at least one nutcase to sour a perfectly innocent discussion with some arrogant, sanctimonious quotes from God and scripture. #ImOut* (16 likes)

Deeja Marriage Guru: *Sorry about that folks! I've deleted the offensive comment. But now you see what kind of madness I have to deal with every day!!! :/ O Lord, give me the strength! #BePatientWithTheIgnorant #TakeTheHigherGround #BeTheBiggerPerson* (21 likes)

***

"That girl is crazy," Janice overheard her father saying to her mother in a heated argument the night they'd found the runaway letter and brought her back home. "There's no way anything like that happened to her. Bailey was a good kid. He wouldn't hurt anyone."

"But what about her falling grades and refusal to talk?" Janice's mother said, her voice a plea. "How do you explain that?"

"How do I explain anything she does? She's been living in an imaginary world since she could walk. We'd be crazy to believe anything that comes out of her mouth." He huffed. "And if it did happen, why did she wait so long to say anything? You saw how she was always walking around in those slutty clothes. The poor boy's been through so much, he probably thought she was seducing him."

***

"Unfortunately, most people view their spiritual life as separate from Facebook and other social media," Reem said from where she sat on the couch next to Aliyah Saturday afternoon. Ibrahim was in Aliyah's room watching a movie on her laptop so that Reem and Aliyah could talk privately without him overhearing.

Reem had called Aliyah an hour before saying that she was in the neighborhood and wanted to stop by Aliyah's before heading home. But as Aliyah listened to Reem talk about seeing the online discussion sparked by Deanna's Facebook status, Aliyah imagined that Reem had driven to Aliyah's neighborhood for the expressed purpose of checking on Aliyah.

"It's like we believe the angels stop writing for us once we log into our Facebook, Twitter, or Instagram accounts," Reem said, frowning, sadness in her tone.

"I can't believe no one challenged her." Aliyah shook her head, troubled. "How could dozens of Muslims read something like that and say absolutely nothing?"

"They probably didn't see anything wrong with it," Reem suggested.

“How is that even possible?” Aliyah’s eyes were narrowed in deep thought. “She practically called me a *kaafir*.”

“I don’t think she thought of it like that.”

“But it’s what she said.”

“It’s what she implied,” Reem corrected. “Had she been aware of the serious implications of her words, I don’t think she would’ve said it. Even in our angriest moments, most Muslims wouldn’t purposely call someone a disbeliever.”

Aliyah drew in a deep breath and exhaled. “Yeah, that’s true,” she said. “But that doesn’t make it right.”

“Well, I can’t disagree with that,” Reem said.

“But I’m sorry you had to go through that,” Reem said after an extended silence. “When I first saw Deanna’s status, I didn’t pay much attention to it because I’m so used to seeing those kinds of posts on her page. But when I saw your response, I grew really concerned.”

“You think I was wrong to post that comment?” Aliyah asked sincerely.

“I can’t say you were wrong,” Reem said tentatively. “I just don’t think it was wise, and Allah knows best.”

Aliyah nodded reflectively. “I can definitely see that now.” She sighed. “I just wish someone else would’ve spoken up.”

“People are scared, Aliyah. Facebook doesn’t exactly welcome righteousness, so no one wants to be the sacrificial lamb, so to speak.”

“But I’m talking about the Muslims. We have an obligation to speak up when something wrong happens.”

“I’m talking about the Muslims too,” Reem said. “Whether you’re Muslim or not, social media is terrifying when you’re the lone dissenting voice.”

Aliyah started to respond but was reminded of her own reluctance to participate in Facebook discussions. Over the years, Aliyah had seen dozens of posts and discussions that involved open wrong, but she’d said nothing. How then could she blame other Muslims for feeling the same wariness she felt?

“But I know how you feel,” Reem said. “A few years ago, Deanna posted a status that said something like, ‘Show me ONE real Muslim from Saudi Arabia. No offense to my Arab friends here, but you all know how MESSED UP your country is when it comes to women.’”

Aliyah wrinkled her nose. “I remember that.”

“Well, I don’t know if you remember the comment I posted in response. But like you, I was personally offended, so I mentioned some *ahadeeth* about the corruption of racism and nationalism and the *ayah* from *Al-Hujuraat* about Allah making us nations and tribes so that we can know each other.”

“Really? *MashaAllah*.”

“*MashaAllah*,” Reem said humbly. “But it didn’t go over well. She didn’t delete my comment, but she said something like, ‘You have some nerve coming on MY page talking about racism and nationalism while YOUR country is the most racist and nationalistic in the world. If you really care about fighting racism and nationalism, then go back to Saudi Arabia and fix that pathetic excuse for a so-called MUSLIM country.'"

"*SubhaanAllah*!" Aliyah brought a hand to her mouth. "Are you serious?"

"Unfortunately, yes. And like what just happened to you, no one said anything to challenge her." Reem shook her head, clearly still troubled by what had happened. "Can you imagine the backlash if I posted a status saying show me one real Muslim from America?"

Aliyah nodded her head sadly. "That's so true."

"That's why I said I don't think posting that comment was wise," Reem said. "I just don't see it bringing any good."

***

*Forgive, forgive, forgive.* Those were the words Janice's mother kept repeating over and over again. But at thirteen years old, Janice had no idea what *forgive* meant in this perplexing context. Janice was used to hearing the term in reference to God forgiving sins. Was her mother asking her to play God?

"Good Christians love their enemies," her mother would say whenever Janice would grow angry and start throwing and breaking things and yelling at the top of her lungs about how she hated her cousin Bailey. "So if you're showing any anger, then God is not happy with you."

It took a full year before Janice could understand and appreciate her mother's advice. "Put a smile on your face, and walk with your head high," her mother constantly advised. "You must walk with dignity. You are better than this. You are better than Bailey. You are better than the wicked and sinful. You are walking with the Lord."

By her junior year in high school, Janice's grades had shot up, and she was back on the honor roll. She was also on the Dean's List and was part of the National Honor Society. Whenever she remembered that fateful day in the church basement when she was eight years old, she would plaster a wide smile on her face, even if she was alone, and wrestle with her thoughts, repeating the mantra to herself: *You are better than this. You are better than the wicked and sinful. You are walking with the Lord.*

In her efforts to always be the "bigger person" and the "good Christian," Janice kept her anger and bitterness tucked away deep inside of her, convinced that only the sinful and wicked grew angry and refused to forgive those who had hurt them. She was determined to behave as if the tragic event had never happened. To stay focused, she threw herself into helping others and reading uplifting feminist literature about empowering women, and she vowed to never allow anyone to wrong or abuse her again. *I am better than them. I am better than the sinful and the wicked. I am walking with the Lord.*

The only sign that she had suffered anything that day was her insistence, at home and school and amongst friends, that she be called by her middle name Deanna instead of her first name Janice (But even that, she rationalized by telling herself that she liked the name Deanna more than Janice, but she gradually grew to prefer being called Deanna Janice). The only name that continued to give her anxiety and apprehension was the nickname Niecey.

But dating remained a problem for Janice. During her senior year in high school, her mother paid for Janice to make weekly visits to a therapist who specialized in sexual trauma. The therapist coached Janice on getting comfortable with her body and told her she should feel free to date.

"Don't force yourself to be intimate with anyone," the therapist told her. "But don't force yourself to resist either. Listen to your body, and listen to your heart," she advised. "During these times, it is your mind you will have to silence. Your psyche has recorded the trauma, so it will do everything it can to protect you from letting it happen again. But when you know you are safe, silence your mind, relax, and listen to what your body and heart are telling you."

Janice took these words to heart, as she did the therapist's advice to ignore the "misogynistic messages" about the shamefulness of the woman's body and the dirtiness of sex. *You were born in sin*, Janice had learned in the church. But even this the therapist advised Janice to cast aside for the purposes of healing. "That is a religious concept, not a practical one," the therapist said. "You were born faultless," the woman told Janice, "and you remain faultless unless you knowingly choose to harm yourself or others."

Incidentally, it was this concept that ultimately drew Janice to Islam. The Islamic concept of *fitrah* held that every person is born in a pure, faultless spiritual state with the natural inclination to live a life of obedience to God and worship of Him alone.

However, at the time, Janice was focused on enjoying the prom after having been asked by one of the most popular young men in the school. On prom night, Janice followed the advice of her therapist and allowed herself to submit to safe intimacy. But she returned home feeling a mixture of triumph (because she had overcome her anxiety about sexual intimacy) and emptiness (because it didn't seem to mean anything).

*Listen to your body, and listen to your heart,* she had told herself. It wasn't until months later that Janice realized the source of her hollowness. She had listened only to her body. Her heart had felt no love or connection with her prom date, so the physical intimacy had been merely a fulfillment of carnal desires, nothing more.

In college, Janice left behind the confusing world of men and immersed herself in spiritual study and personal development. When she happened upon an explanation of Islam in a book she had checked out at the college library, her whole world seemed to fall back into place.

But it wasn't until Deanna saw Professor Jacob Bivens at an MSA event during her doctorate studies that her heart stirred in desire for a deep relationship with a man. When he had come to her apartment about six months after they'd met, it was the advice of her high school therapist that she followed when Jacob openly flirted with her. *Listen to your body, and listen to your heart.* It wasn't until Deanna saw how guilt-ridden Jacob was that she realized, as a Muslim, she should have added the condition, *Listen to your soul.*

However, Deanna found it difficult to feel guilty because, deep inside, she didn't feel like she'd done anything wrong. The connection between her and Jacob wasn't like anything she'd experienced before (though her only intimate experiences had been Bailey's violent rape and the hollow, only vaguely fulfilling experience with her prom date). So she'd imagined that it was a sign from God that she felt whole and fulfilled with Jacob, without the least bit of fear, hesitation, or apprehension in giving herself to him. Nevertheless, upon careful reflection, she realized that she (and he) had indeed done something terribly wrong, thus prompting her proactive solution of getting married.

When they got married, Deanna wasn't entirely sure that she was pregnant. Many of the symptoms of pregnancy that she had read about in the waiting room of the clinic matched what she was feeling at the time. But she never went through with the actual pregnancy test. She had become overwhelmed with fear that she would lose Jacob if her pregnancy was unconfirmed. "Marriage isn't a solution," he'd told her, inciting in her a frenzied panic that she would lose the love of her life forever. "If anything, it'll bring more problems."

*"If you want something good to happen,"* her mother often said, *"you have to make it happen. Things don't just fall into your lap."* And "make good happen" was what Deanna was determined to do when she'd called Jacob back a week after their phone conversation and a day after her clinic appointment and told him that her pregnancy test had come back positive. She wasn't exactly lying, she'd rationalized. She might really be pregnant. Her bloating, nausea, and heightened emotional sensitivity were all the evidence she needed to convince herself that a life was indeed growing inside her.

***

"But I don't think you have to worry about her un-friending or blocking you or anything," Reem said.

Aliyah chuckled self-consciously. "Part of me wishes she would."

Reem smiled knowingly. "I felt the same after what happened to me. But I couldn't bring myself to un-friend or block her myself."

Aliyah creased her forehead. "Why? You had every right to."

"I know. But it felt wrong. I felt I should be patient with her." Reem seemed distracted by her thoughts for some time.

"I didn't always teach Qur'an," she said finally. "I didn't always *read* Qur'an. When I was a teenager, I was really rebellious and bad-tempered."

A perplexed smile formed at Aliyah's lips. "I can't picture that."

"Well, I can," Reem said sadly. "Sometimes I'm surprised I'm still alive."

Aliyah's eyebrows rose. "Still alive?"

Reem looked like she wanted to say more but withheld. "You know, Deanna wasn't totally wrong in what she said to me," Reem said finally. "We have a lot of problems in our country."

"Doesn't everybody?"

"Yes, but we take things overboard, especially when it comes to our lineage and tribes. But racism and nationalism are only half the issue," Reem said. "One thing I like about Americans is how honest you all are about your problems."

Aliyah averted her gaze, recalling her reluctance to open up to Reem.

***

*Women are like horses*, Deanna had read on a crude relationship blog shortly after she got married. *They are beasts running wild and showing off their beauty and prowess to the world, but with no one to really appreciate it. They have no idea where they're going or what they want until a man corners and captures them. It is only after a man tames and breaks them that they realize their full potential and worth. Then they spend the rest of their lives getting full satisfaction from being at a man's disposal. So they continuously serve him and await instructions on how to fulfill his needs.*

Deanna's stomach convulsed so severely after reading those words that she was huddled in a corner crying with her arms clutched over her stomach when Jacob came home from work. That was when she told Jacob the story of what her cousin Bailey had done to her when she was only eight years old.

"He broke me. He broke me," she kept moaning over and over as she rocked back and forth. "But I forgive him," she said finally, abruptly halting her rocking as she wiped her eyes and cheeks. A wide smile spread on her face before she said, "But I am better than him. I am better than the sinful and the wicked. I am walking with the Lord."

Mortified for having allowed herself to sink to the level of self-incrimination, Deanna vowed to always remain positive, proactive, and optimistic no matter what happened in her life or marriage. She made a promise to herself to always be the loving, confident, and sensually-satisfying wife that she'd read about in relationship books about how to maintain a long, happy, healthy marriage.

Upon reflecting on her own trauma and that of her aunt, Deanna became convinced that episodes like the one she'd suffered and deep depression like her aunt suffered were preventable. Thus, Deanna went on a mission to find preventative solutions to anger and depression, to seeking revenge, and to suffering rape or abuse.

Through her own personal determination to avoid giving in to weakness, rage, and depression, Deanna eventually came to despise the concept of the passive, helpless, abused woman. As early as high school, she viewed sad and dejected women with distaste. But she was determined to be a source of help to them whenever possible.

By graduate school, she loathed any theory or expert opinion that allowed women to waddle in melancholic grief over what could or should have been. *We are not helpless victims in a male-dominated world,* she wrote in her personal journal. *We are better than chauvinistic men. We are better than the sinful and the wicked. We are walking with the Lord.*

Deanna continually maintained that women had much more power than they realized, a message she couldn't seem to get across to her best friend, Aliyah, who stupidly imagined that there wasn't much she could do to improve her circumstances, particularly regarding her estranged family. "But you can empower yourself," she kept telling Aliyah. "We all have the ability to take control of our lives, circumstances, and marriages."

In her doctorate thesis, Deanna argued that a combination of authentic spirituality, confidence in oneself, and personal assertiveness (as well as knowledge of empirical evidence on the characteristics of generally happy couples in long-term relationships) equipped women with all they needed to protect themselves from harm, abuse, retaliation, depression, and divorce.

"It sounds like your thesis suggests that women should live in a constant state of suppression and denial," one of the professors said during the question-and-answer session of Deanna's first doctorate defense. "Evidence shows that this forced-happiness approach is merely a form of denial," the professor said. "And this leads to repressed anger, passive aggressiveness, or imagined grandiosity that makes people susceptible to narcissism and ultimately narcissistic personality disorder."

"They're just upset that I'm uncovering this groundbreaking research, and not them," Deanna had told Jacob. "I'm not going to let their jealousy deter me. There are too many women out there who've given up on themselves after suffering things like what my aunt and I went through. I'm determined to prove these arrogant so-called experts wrong."

***

"My family moved to America while I was still a child," Reem told Aliyah. "But the way we lived, we may as well have lived in the deserts of Arabia. Until middle school, I went to private Muslim schools, mostly with other Arabs, so I didn't really get exposed to American culture until high school. But I think the culture shock was too much for me."

"Is that why you rebelled?" Aliyah asked.

"No," Reem said. "But it's when I rebelled. A lot of things happened to me when I was a child," she said, her eyes distantly melancholic. "And I think it just got too much for me to keep holding inside. So I dyed my hair crazy colors. I wore a lot of dark make-up. I started smoking and drinking. And I kept company with a crowd I had no business being around." She shrugged. "I know some Americans might not consider that really risky behavior, but for a girl from a so-called good Arab family, it was really over the top."

Aliyah nodded. "My parents would've considered that over the top too."

"I might be looking at the world from my vantage point," Reem said thoughtfully, "but whenever I see someone like Deanna, it reminds me of myself during my rebellious stage. I wasn't mean-spirited by nature; at least I don't think I was. I just felt so pressured to be this perfect Arab girl that I couldn't take it any more. My family was constantly comparing Arabs to Americans to show how we were better. Yet no one spoke about all the bad things we did behind closed doors."

A shadow of anger passed over Reem's face. "It was almost like it was our Arab duty to have a double personality," Reem said, voice tight in upset. "All that mattered was that we upheld our family's honor and image. It didn't matter who we were on the inside, or if we were suffering in silence about anything. So in the Arab-Muslim community, I acted like a meek, perfect Muslim girl. But at school, I was crying out for attention. I think I wanted somebody to see through all my rebellion and say, 'I can tell something's wrong with you. How can I help?'"

***

*"Be wary of the one who uses his victim status as a shield against critical thought, dissenting views, or self-correction,"* Jacob's father said during a discussion in which he explained to Jacob why the work of Dr. Joy Degruy on post-traumatic slave syndrome should be lauded as the most important American research of our time. *"This victim mentality is fertile ground for oppression itself,"* Jacob's father said. *"No people were able to oppress another except that they blocked all paths to critical thinking, dissent, and self-reproach."*

It was these words that came to mind when Jacob pulled into the driveway of his home after returning from the brief visit to the office of Dr. Melanie Goldstein.

*Being positive is only good when you're honest with yourself about the* whole *picture,* he heard Melanie's voice in his head. *You have to take a long, hard look at the good and the bad, and the positive and the negative. Otherwise, you're not being positive or optimistic. You're being willfully blind. It's like putting on blinders* after *you've already seen what's in front of you, then wondering what you keep bumping into and why you keep getting hurt.*

It was true that during the rough spots in his marriage, Jacob often wondered what it was he kept bumping into and why he kept getting hurt. But he'd assumed this confusion was because he was the only one who ever believed there was a problem serious enough to be acknowledged, addressed, and fixed. Deanna's optimism and nonchalance often left him wondering if maybe he was the only one struggling in the relationship.

"I'm completely happy," Deanna often told him.

*Then why do you keep insulting and undermining me?* he wanted to ask. *Why do you keep physically attacking me?*

When the confusion and frustration got the better of him, Jacob would remind himself of the heartbreaking story of Janice Michaels and how he and she had eventually crossed paths. Then his relationship with Deanna Janice Michaels (turned Bivens) began to make sense, and he, once again, would feel a sense of purpose in being by her side.

*Hurt people hurt people.*

Was it possible that years of Jacob being racked with confusion and guilt boiled down to this simple explanation?

If so, who was the hurt person in the relationship? Jacob or Deanna?

Or were they both?

# 10
# He Wants To Marry Her

*Never argue with a stupid person. They will drag you down to their level and then beat you with experience.*

Aliyah did a double take then lifted one of the framed Mark Twain quotes from the store display. She turned the frame in her hand to see the price tag affixed to the back. *Was $12.99, Now $4.99*, the sticker said.

"You need self-affirmation," Reem had said a week ago when she visited Aliyah after seeing Aliyah's response to Deanna's Facebook status. "Perhaps you can write some notes to yourself in a journal," she suggested. "Or maybe you can hang some inspirational quotes on your wall where you can see them every day."

Aliyah doubted that the "Never argue with a stupid person" quote counted as self-affirmation or as what her Qur'an teacher had in mind when she'd made the suggestion, but Aliyah found the quote inspirational nonetheless. Had Aliyah realized how futile it was to argue with Deanna, she probably would not have publicly humiliated herself. Deanna had always been a difficult friend and never took well to even the slightest criticism (despite her constantly dishing it out to others). So Aliyah should not have been surprised by Deanna's public cockiness in not only deleting Aliyah's comment, but in also continuing the character assassination thereafter. But a part of Aliyah had really believed that she could appeal to Deanna's better senses. If nothing else could affect Deanna, then certainly reminders from Allah and the Prophet, peace be upon him, could. *I mean*, Aliyah had thought, *who could argue with the Lord of the Worlds?*

"Anyone can," Reem had told her. "In fact, that's what most of us do every day. Of course, we don't think of it like that. The technical term would be *self-justification* or *rationalizing*. But any way you look at it, when you're doing wrong and you insist on it and attack those who correct you, you're arguing with the Creator. But people use offensive terms and labels to shield themselves from rational thought," Reem said. "And that's what happened to you. Deanna and her friends basically called you a religious extremist so they didn't have to self-reflect. And in my case, Deanna ended up calling me a Wahhabi." Reem sighed and shook her head. "It's annoying, I know. But it's rare that you meet a person, Muslim or non-Muslim, who will leave off labels and name-calling and focus on basic right and wrong."

Aliyah turned the frame to the front and gazed at it a moment more before putting it back on the shelf.

"Oooooh," Larry said, appearing at Aliyah's side and picking up the framed quote. "I like this."

A smirk formed on Aliyah's face. "I do, too."

"Then I'll get it for you." Larry started to place it in the hand basket that he held, but Aliyah took the frame from him and put it back on the shelf.

"No thank you," she said humorously. "It's too un-romantic."

"Everyone needs a good laugh now and then."

"Trust me," Aliyah said, "this does not make me laugh."

"A good cry, then," he said with a shrug, but he left the frame on the shelf.

Aliyah laughed in agreement. "That would be more like it."

Larry was quiet as they walked toward the checkout. "This Nikki situation is really bothering you, huh?"

Oddly, Aliyah had momentarily forgotten about Nikki's phone call the night before, telling Aliyah that they wouldn't be bringing Ibrahim over that weekend. *"Matt and I want to spend more time with him,"* Nikki had said.

"You should talk to a lawyer," Larry said.

"I couldn't afford to *look* at a lawyer," Aliyah said. "And they know that." She shrugged. "Besides, what could I say? That his father wanted to take him to the space museum during the only time he's off work?"

"You give people too many excuses," Larry said after they had checked out and were walking toward his car in the parking lot, a bag in his hand.

Aliyah rolled her eyes, but she didn't respond. Deanna used to say the same thing to Aliyah, and Aliyah was growing tired of the criticism. Wasn't she supposed to make excuses for people?

"That's why I was happy when I saw you holding that quote," Larry said. "I know it's a small thing, but things like that can really help put things in perspective."

*Never argue with a stupid person. They will drag you down to their level and then beat you with experience.*

Aliyah couldn't deny that it did give her something to think about, especially after all she'd gone through with Deanna. But the truth was, it was Reem's words that stuck with her most. *People use offensive terms and labels to shield themselves from rational thought.*

If Aliyah sought inspiration in thinking of Deanna (or even Nikki) as "stupid," how was her behavior any different from what she was seeking reprieve from? Ultimately, snarky statements like Mark Twain's did little more than solve one problem by creating another. And perhaps the latter was worse than the former. Sure, you could avoid a host of pointless arguments by thinking of your opponent as a stupid person trying to drag you down to their level. But what did this do to your heart?

*No one who has even an atom's weight of pride will enter Paradise,* the Prophet had said, and more than anything, Aliyah wanted to enter Paradise. So she was not willing to compromise that opportunity if she could help it. She had enough faults as it is. What was the point of seeking self-affirmation by inciting pride?

"And it can also put arrogance in my heart," Aliyah said as she pulled the seat belt over her torso and clicked it closed.

Larry looked over at Aliyah, a grin on his face as he turned the key in the ignition. "Girl, you are way too uptight. The sky's not going to fall if you hang a Mark Twain quote on your wall."

The comment stung, but Aliyah remained silent and looked out the window as Larry pulled out of the store's parking lot. Maybe she was too uptight, she considered. *"You need to live a little,"* Deanna used to say. *"Laugh, go out, have some fun."* Perhaps that was why Aliyah had agreed to let Larry pick her up today instead of driving herself. But right then she wished she had her own car. She wanted to go home. She didn't feel like being stuck sitting in a restaurant booth across from Larry.

"I'm sorry," Larry said, his tone soft and regretful. "I didn't mean that offensively."

*Is there any other meaning to "way too uptight"?* Aliyah said in her head as she continued to look out the window. But she kept her thoughts to herself.

"The truth is," Larry said reflectively, "I really admire you. You make me want to be a better person."

Aliyah resisted rolling her eyes. How many times had she heard *that* before? Years ago she would have taken it as a compliment, but now it sounded condescending. *You're such a good person,* she translated in her head, *that it's annoying to be around you. Loosen up.*

"That's why I want to marry you," Larry said.

Aliyah's heart softened and a shadow of a smile formed on her face. But she couldn't fight the exhaustion she felt right then. His words, though pleasing to her ears, made her feel distant, as if Larry were a stranger and not Jacob's brother. But her face grew warm in flattery, and her heart fluttered in desire.

Internally, Aliyah groaned. She hated when sheer loneliness got the better of her. Moments like this, she was grateful for Islam. Because Aliyah and Larry were Muslim and unmarried, she was under no pressure to hold Larry's hand or be intimate with him in any way, and they would never be alone together because Islam didn't allow it. Thus, as long as she kept her impure thoughts to herself, the moment would likely pass without incident.

"Why would you want to marry someone who's uptight?" Aliyah asked. She knew that Larry might find the question offensive, but she really wanted to know. Larry's statement reminded her of Deanna. Aliyah couldn't fathom why Deanna wanted to be her friend if she found Aliyah so annoying and off-putting. Why not find a new friend? And in Larry's case, why not find someone else to marry?

Larry laughed. "You take me way too seriously. I like that."

Aliyah wrinkled her nose as she glanced at him. "You like that?"

"I like a challenge," Larry said with a shrug, grinning. "Most women I date practically throw themselves at me. I like it when women play hard to get."

Aliyah's stomach churned. This was not going well. If the car hadn't been in motion, she probably would have opened the door and walked out right then. Did Larry think this was all a game?

"I don't play hard to get," Aliyah said, surprised by her frankness. "If I like you, you know it. If I don't like you, you know it."

It wasn't until after lunch when Larry had dropped her off at her apartment that Aliyah realized her mistake. Her statement had been meant to clarify her honest approach to courtship, but it could be taken to mean that she didn't like Larry. *If I like you, you know it…*

Aliyah cringed at the thought. She immediately opened her handbag and fished for her phone. She needed to apologize and clarify what she'd meant. But holding her phone, hand suspended in front of her, she stopped herself.

*Maybe this is a good thing*, she considered.

For some time, she had been going back and forth about whether or not to marry Larry. Perhaps this was her way out.

*Oooooh. It looks like Larry finally got over Jasmine!*

At the reminder of Larry's family teasing, Aliyah lowered her hand and put the phone back in her purse. Up until now, the Jasmine question remained unanswered, and no matter how hard Aliyah tried, she couldn't bring herself to dismiss the possibility that Larry still had feelings for his ex-girlfriend.

But shouldn't she still call him and apologize? She didn't want him to think she disliked him. If it turned out that Jasmine was really out of the picture, then Aliyah might lose the opportunity to build a relationship with Larry.

*Just pray on it,* she told herself, *and see what happens.*

***

"One plus one equals won! One plus one equals won!"

Aliyah laughed and pumped her fist along with her colleagues as Jacob led the chant during the first orientation in preparation for the mentorship program in June, which was only a month away.

It had been a couple of months since Aliyah debated on whether or not to apologize to Larry for unintentionally implying that she didn't like him, but the status of their relationship hadn't improved much since then. The last time they'd spoken was more than a week ago when Aliyah openly expressed her concerns about marrying him while he had feelings for someone else.

"I'll probably always have feelings for any ex-girlfriend," Larry had told her. "But that has nothing to do with us."

"It has everything to do with us," Aliyah had said.

"What do you expect me to do?" Larry said. "Try to make myself hate her?"

"Of course not. I'm just not willing to marry you if you still care about her."

"I care about a lot of people."

"That's not what I mean, Larry, and you know it."

"Jazzy and I dated for years. My feelings aren't going to just disappear overnight."

"*Jazzy*?" Aliyah recoiled.

"I'm sorry," Larry said. "Jasmine, then."

"See, this is what I mean," Aliyah said. "You can't just say things to appease me. It has to come from you."

"It is coming from me. It was a slip of the tongue, that's all. I'm so used to calling her Jazzy that I forget to use her real name."

"Then call me back when your memory is better." Aliyah's tone was sarcastic. "I'm not doing this again."

"I'm not Matt," Larry said irritably. "I'm being completely upfront with you. I don't know what else to do. If I say I don't care about her, you'll think I'm a liar. And if I say the truth, you think I'm being unfair to you. This is why most men just tell women what they want to hear. It's so much easier and more productive."

In her office as she prepared to go home that evening, Aliyah wondered if she was being paranoid in her reaction to Larry's sentiments about Jasmine.

"He has a point," Reem had said when Aliyah had asked her advice a few days ago. "Moving on doesn't necessarily mean you stop caring about other people you've dated. It just means that in the part of your heart that matters most, there's room for someone else."

Aliyah sighed as she stacked some papers and rearranged them on the side of her desk. Aliyah herself couldn't deny that she still had "feelings" for her high school boyfriend. But the feelings were so miniscule that they hardly seemed to matter. At most, they amounted to little more than genuine respect and concern for him as a fellow human being. If she ever saw him on the street, Aliyah imagined that the run-in would inspire little more than an obligatory "How are you?" or a polite wave.

Was this what Larry had meant when he said he still cared about Jasmine?

"Thanks for joining us."

Aliyah looked up and saw Jacob standing in the doorway to her office, a basketball cradled under one arm, his briefcase in the other. Earlier that evening, Jacob had trained the One Plus One mentors on math and science drills to do with the high school students on the basketball court. He was still wearing a T-shirt and sweatpants.

Aliyah smiled self-consciously. "Thanks for selecting me."

"You came highly recommended," Jacob said, a smile on his face.

"Does that mean I still have a job?"

He laughed heartily. "Dr. Warren is preparing your formal contract and salary offer now."

Aliyah smiled to herself as she finished the last rearrangements on her desk. She still found it hard to believe that she was a bona fide college professor now. By fall term, she would qualify for tuition reimbursement to complete her unfinished doctorate in mathematics.

"Larry called me a couple of days ago."

"About what?" Aliyah said as she opened her purse to make sure her mobile and iPad were inside.

"He said you called off the engagement."

Aliyah sighed and shook her head. "I didn't call off anything. Besides, there was never an engagement in the first place."

Jacob stepped backwards into the hall as Aliyah turned off the light and pulled the door closed as she stepped into the hall herself. "So it's over between you two?" he said.

"I'm still trying to figure everything out." Aliyah turned the key in her office door to lock it. "But I don't want to string him along, so it's probably best to call it quits."

"Are you sure?" Jacob sounded skeptical.

"No. But that's what bothers me. If he's the right person, shouldn't I feel something?" she asked rhetorically. "Right now, he just seems like a really nice brother who'll make a good husband and father *insha'Allah*."

"Isn't that something?"

"Maybe," she said with a shrug. "But it's not enough. At least not for me. One thing I'm not doing again is marrying someone just because he's a good Muslim. Marriage should be built on more than that."

Jacob appeared reflective as he walked alongside Aliyah toward the elevators. "I know what you mean," he said. "People put too much emphasis on superficial Islamic qualities as if they're the be-all and end-all of everything. Life is more complex than that."

"Then again, maybe it's not," Aliyah said, her eyes lingering briefly on the wheeled gray garbage container that the custodial staff had pushed into the lobby during cleanup. "Maybe we just complicate the simplest things."

"Maybe," Jacob muttered as he stopped in front of the elevators near where one of their colleagues stood waiting, the down arrow already lit.

"Afternoon, Dr. Bivens," the man said, nodding a polite greeting to Jacob before his gaze lingered on Aliyah long enough to make her uncomfortable. "Professor Thomas," the man added with another nod, a smile in his eyes as he met Aliyah's gaze.

"Good afternoon, Dr. Stanley," Jacob said, his voice raised as if in annoyance, his close-lipped smile thinly veiling the grimace on his face.

Before Aliyah herself could reply to Dr. Stanley, the professor's mobile rang, and he immediately broke eye contact as he fished for the phone in his pocket. Putting the phone to his ear, Dr. Stanley quickly stepped away from the elevator and walked past the garbage container to take the call.

Aliyah did a double take as she saw a familiar frame atop the garbage, a crack spreading on the quote's glass encasement. "Isn't that yours?" she said to Jacob.

Jacob's line of vision followed her pointing finger. "It used to be," he said, chuckling self-consciously. "I'm trying to clean out my office before the summer internship starts."

"I like that quote," Aliyah said, stepping toward the garbage, wondering if it would be unhygienic and socially unacceptable to retrieve the frame and take it home. *Stop complaining. Be the change. Stop bickering. Be the bigger person. Stop criticizing. Be the better person. Stop settling for less than the best. Be YOU.* She imagined that this quote would be closer to the positive self-affirmation she was looking for when she'd considered buying the "Never argue with a stupid person" frame months ago.

"It's yours if you want it," he said as the elevator doors opened. "You'll need to get a new frame though."

Aliyah wrinkled her nose as she pulled it from the garbage pail and shook it free of trash. "That's not a problem," she said as she carried it away from her body, stepping into the elevator after him. Jacob and Aliyah nodded and mumbled a greeting to the three employees who were already inside.

As the elevator doors closed, Dr. Stanley came into view as he rushed toward them. He was still holding his mobile as he waved at them to open the doors. Instinctively, Aliyah reached for the button, but Jacob was already pressing it. When she heard a couple of employees snickering behind her, it took a moment before Aliyah noticed the smug grin on Jacob's face as the doors sealed shut just as Dr. Stanley reached the elevator.

"Sorry," Jacob muttered aloud, humor in his tone. "Wrong button." Aliyah chuckled and gave Jacob a curious look, but he merely responded with a shrug.

"You sure you don't want to keep it for yourself?" Aliyah said a few minutes later after they stepped off the elevator and were walking toward the exit leading to the faculty and staff parking lot. She was looking at the framed quote in her hand. "Sometimes I throw away things at the spur of the moment then regret it later."

"I don't think I'll regret it." The expression on Jacob's face suggested that he was enjoying a private joke. "I'm ready for a new perspective in life."

Aliyah creased her forehead as she looked at the quote again. "What's wrong with this perspective?"

Jacob shrugged. "Nothing, I suppose. I'm just starting to wonder if it inspires vanity more than it does motivation."

Aliyah pulled her head back in surprise and looked at Jacob quizzically. "Vanity?"

"Not for you," he said, clarifying. "For me."

Aliyah tilted her head sideways, considering the quote from a different perspective.

*Stop complaining. Be the change. Stop bickering. Be the bigger person. Stop criticizing. Be the better person. Stop settling for less than the best. Be YOU.*

"I guess it can be a bit negative, huh?" she said with a thoughtful nod. "Stop complaining. Stop bickering. I see what you mean."

"You see how it starts off with the assumption that you're seeing negativity in the people around you?" Jacob's tone conveyed relief that someone understood where he was coming from.

Aliyah smirked and pursed her lips in understanding. "Then it tells you that you're the solution."

"Not only *the* solution," Jacob said. "The bigger and *better* solution."

Aliyah laughed. "Oh my God, you're right."

Smiling with his eyes, Jacob shook his head. "I swear, Deanna made me feel like I was crazy for not wanting to keep that on my office wall."

At the mention of Deanna, Aliyah's spirit dampened slightly.

"With that quote in my head each day," Jacob said, shaking his head in reflection, "I felt like I was walking around telling myself I was better than everyone around me, while I was the only one with a negative outlook in the first place."

Aliyah was immediately reminded of the brief disagreement she'd had with Larry about the Mark Twain quote. *The sky's not going to fall if you hang a Mark Twain quote on your wall.* "I know what you mean," Aliyah said honestly. "You know that 'Never argue with a stupid person' quote?" she said, glancing at Jacob.

He grunted and shook his head knowingly. "Yes, and I hate it. I think it's sad that we rarely find inspiration except through focusing on negativity and insulting other people. There has to be a better way."

A thought came to Aliyah suddenly as she looked at the framed quote. "Did Deanna give this to you?"

"No, I bought it myself," Jacob said. "But she suggested I hang it in my office."

At home, Aliyah tossed the cracked frame in the trash. After the brief talk with Jacob, she kept hearing Deanna's voice in her head, so there was no way to interpret the words positively.

*Stop complaining. Be the change. Stop bickering. Be the bigger person. Stop criticizing. Be the better person. Stop settling for less than the best. Be YOU.*

Like Jacob had said, there had to be a better way.

***

Juwayriah bint Abdullah: *Married ladies! Hold on to your husbands. I ain't one to call a sister out, so... #NuffSaid #YouHaveBeenWarned*

Deeja Marriage Guru and 23 others like this. 57 comments.

"I guess this is about you?" Reem said as she turned her laptop toward Aliyah after they finished Qur'an class Thursday evening. Reem had started coming to Aliyah's apartment more frequently instead of doing the class on the phone, and Aliyah was grateful for that. It was much easier to study the Arabic rules in person.

Aliyah creased her forehead as she read the status. "I don't think so," she said doubtfully.

"Look at the tag," Reem said, her finger pointing to a comment by someone Aliyah had seen only in passing at the masjid.

***Reem Muhammad****, you need to stop using Qur'an to support home wreckers!* (17 likes)

Aliyah shook her head, still confused. “I don’t understand. What does this have to do with me?”

Reem looked like she was about to say something but withheld. “Maybe nothing,” she said finally.

“But why did the sister tag you?”

“Because I do *tafseer* classes about marriage, and some sisters feel I’m advocating polygamy.”

“Really?” Aliyah had heard of Reem’s classes that expounded on the meanings and lessons in the Qur’an, but she had never attended. “Why?”

“During my last class, I discussed *Surah Al-Nisaa*, *ayah* four.”

“Is that the verse that says, ‘One wife is best of you, if you only knew’?”

Reem smiled knowingly as she shook her head. “No, but it’s the *ayah* that’s mistranslated to mean that.”

Aliyah furrowed her brows. “Mistranslated? So it’s not in the Arabic?”

“It’s too much to go into right now,” Reem said as she closed her laptop. “But there are a lot of misconceptions about that *ayah*, and that’s just one of them. But I don’t advocate polygamy. From an Islamic perspective, the only thing any Muslim can advocate is marriage. How a man and woman live out their marriage is none of my business. So in my class, I just explain the meanings of Allah’s words and leave my personal perspective out of it.”

“Then what are the sisters so upset about?”

“*Allahu’alam*,” Reem said, acknowledging that God knows best, “but it seems they’re upset because I won’t condemn polygamy, or at least say that Allah favors monogamy.” She sighed. “During my last class, some sisters asked about the mention of orphans at the beginning of the *ayah* and how in another *ayah* Allah says men will never be able to do justice between their wives.”

“I always wondered about that,” Aliyah said. “It seems like men focus on marrying multiple wives and ignore the part about orphans and treating their wives fairly.”

“That might be true,” Reem said. “But that has nothing to do with what the Qur’an actually says. Based on the *tafseer*, if men were to focus on orphans, it’ll only mean they’ll marry orphan women. It doesn’t mean they won’t be involved in polygamy. The two have nothing to do with each other.”

“But doesn’t the Qur’an say that men will never be able to be just with their wives?”

“Yes, but if you look at the Qur’an and Sunnah as a whole, you’ll find that the emphasis is always on striving, not on perfection,” Reem said. “All I was saying in class is that we have to be careful not to use the Qur’an for our own purposes. If you don’t want to be in polygamy, just say that. That’s a right Allah gives you. But don’t say that our Creator says it’s wrong or not preferable.” Reem contorted her face and shook her head. “Who are we to make that claim?”

“But if men can’t ever be completely just in polygamy,” Aliyah said, “isn’t it a fair conclusion that one wife is best?”

Reem put her laptop in its bag and stood. “Let me ask you something,” she said as she adjusted the laptop bag strap on her shoulder and met Aliyah’s gaze. “Can you name one thing that you can guarantee you’ll be completely just with in front of Allah?”

Aliyah’s lips formed a thin line as she considered the question. “Guarantee?” she said doubtfully.

“Yes, guarantee.”

Aliyah was silent momentarily then shook her head. “No, I can’t, honestly.”

“Now think of all the blessings you have,” Reem said, “and think of all the things you’re still praying for. And since you can never guarantee you’ll be completely just with any of it, why do you accept the blessings you have, much less pray for more?”

Aliyah chuckled self-consciously. “I never thought about it like that.”

“I just find it interesting that it’s only polygamy that brings out our desire for human perfection,” Reem said. “But why not advocate for childless marriages since you’ll never be the perfect parent? Why not advocate for the lowest possible salary since you might overspend? Why not live in a small, furniture-less house and never buy brand names since they’re beyond your needs? We know we’re going to be asked about all of this on the Day of Judgment, but it doesn’t make us run the other way.”

Aliyah nodded thoughtfully but didn’t respond.

“All I’m saying is,” Reem said, “be honest with yourself. If men need to leave polygamy alone because they can’t be completely just, then we need to leave alone having children and nice things since we can’t be completely just either.”

“But don’t you think mistreating another human being is worse than something that can harm only you?”

“And don’t you think helping another human being is better than something that can benefit only you?” Reem countered.

Aliyah coughed laughter. “I don’t think the men of today care about helping women.”

Reem frowned. “Anyway, Allah didn’t say men will mistreat their wives,” she said. “He said they won’t be able to be fully just no matter how hard they try. And when you study the *tafseer*, this is mainly talking about what’s in a man’s heart, not his outward actions. The Prophet, *sallallaahu’alayhi wa sallam*, never mistreated his wives, but he loved Ayesha most.”

Aliyah nodded thoughtfully. “But can we really compare men of today to the Prophet, peace be upon him?”

Reem walked over to the foyer and slipped on her shoes. “Honestly,” she said, exhaustion in her tone, “I hate when people say that. When we think Islam favors monogamy over polygamy, we tell people to follow the Sunnah. But when we realize we’re wrong, we say it’s impossible to follow the Sunnah.”

A smile tugged at a corner of Aliyah’s mouth. “That’s so true. *Astaghfirullah*.”

"But I'm a woman," Reem said, "so I understand where the sisters are coming from. I wouldn't want my husband to marry another wife." She shrugged. "I even have a no-polygamy clause in my marriage contract."

Aliyah's eyes widened. "Really? I would've never guessed."

"I don't broadcast it," Reem said. "To be honest, I don't think it's anybody's business. But sometimes I'm tempted to mention it to make them understand that this isn't about what I personally advocate."

"Maybe you should tell them," Aliyah said. "I think it would be a good lesson."

Reem shook her head. "I want the focus of my class to be on the Qur'an, not me," she said. "Anyway, I'll probably just be called a hypocrite if they find out, and what good will that do? If we can't take our greatest lessons from the life of the Prophet and his companions, then our problems will never be solved no matter how much I share about myself."

Aliyah watched as Reem opened her purse and pulled out the folded black cloth she had placed there earlier. Reem shook the cloth to unfold it then tied the sides behind her head so that only her eyes were visible through a wide slit.

"Can I ask you a question?" Aliyah said.

"*Tafaddalee*," Reem said, agreeing.

"Why do you cover your face?"

"Because I believe Allah commands us to in the Qur'an."

Aliyah drew her eyebrows together. "So you think the Qur'an forbids women from uncovering their faces?"

"Everything that's *haraam* isn't explicitly mentioned in the Qur'an," Reem said. "But based on the Qur'an and Sunnah evidences together, yes I do. Unless women have an Islamic excuse to uncover."

Aliyah found that difficult to believe, but she didn't say anything. Instead she unlocked the door and opened it.

"Can I ask *you* something?" Reem said, humor in her tone. "What do you do to stay fit? You look good, *mashaAllah, barakAllaahufeek*. I need some tips."

Aliyah laughed self-consciously as she glanced down at herself. "*MashaAllah*," she said humbly. "I use workout DVDs."

"Can I join you some time, seriously? I'm really out of shape."

"If you want," Aliyah said noncommittally. "But I use music, so I'm not sure you'll feel comfortable."

"I don't mind the music," Reem said. "As long as it's not for passive listening, I don't think it's *haraam*."

Aliyah's eyebrows rose, curiosity piqued, but she didn't ask Reem to clarify. "Okay, just give me a call whenever you're free."

"Okay *insha'Allah*."

***

Aliyah woke early Monday morning with a heavy feeling in her chest. Her bedroom was dark except for the dim glow of a streetlight outside the window.

*"People don't give you room to be human,"* Jacob had said in the dream. Aliyah had sat opposite him, as if interviewing him on a television set, but they were sitting alone in her living room. As he spoke, there was a smile on his face, but Aliyah's heart ached for the pain she felt. It was as if his heart were in her chest, and she kept getting choked up with each word he spoke. *"That's one reason I never asked for help. But I don't blame my friends and family. They had no idea what I was going through. But if I'm honest, I didn't fully know myself. The problem with being a mentor to youth is that you're always expected to have it all together, so your whole life ends up becoming one big inspirational pep-talk session. And then you wake up and find that you're both mentor and troubled soul to your own life. But that's a really lonely existence."*

Aliyah lay awake in the darkness as sadness and concern gripped her, and a lump developed in her throat. It made no sense that she was on the verge of tears or that she felt a sudden urgency to know if Jacob was all right. But the feeling was so intense that she contemplated texting Larry to ask him to check on his brother, but Aliyah stopped herself. She and Larry weren't exactly on speaking terms though neither of them had called off the relationship officially.

Maybe Aliyah could text Jacob herself. But what would she say? Though she had Jacob's mobile saved in her phone in case she ever needed to call him or Dr. Warren if she couldn't come in to work, she had never actually dialed his number, and he had never dialed hers. So it made no sense for her to text him now, at almost four o'clock in the morning. Besides, they were both due at work in a few hours, so she could check on him at the college.

But what would Aliyah do until then?

*What is wrong with you?* Aliyah scolded herself. But no matter how illogical this all was in her head, Aliyah couldn't quiet the urge to know if Jacob was okay.

Facebook. The idea came to Aliyah suddenly. She could check Jacob's Facebook page to see if he had posted any recent statuses or updates. It wasn't perfect, but it might ease her heart until she had to leave for work.

Aliyah tossed her comforter to the side and reached for her phone on the nightstand. She waited impatiently for the Wi-Fi to connect then tapped the blue Facebook icon.

Deeja Marriage Guru: *Polygamy is just wrong. Unless you're a prophet, then there's NO EXCUSE for it. Brothers, take care of YOUR CURRENT WIFE. Sisters, GET YOUR OWN MAN. If you can't find a man, then you're just #SOL #ImDoneWithMyRant #ThenAgainMaybeNot #TiredofStupidity*

Juwayriah bint Abdullah and 235 others like this. 95 comments.

Aliyah was about to type in Jacob's name in the Facebook search when she saw Deanna's status at the top of her newsfeed. For some reason, reading the status made her feel even more panicky and concerned. Hands trembling, Aliyah scrolled down and saw three other statuses posted by Deanna in the last twenty-four hours.

*You can give some people the clothes off your back, and they'll still backstab you. Know who your real friends are. #BetrayalisReal* (38 likes. 10 comments.)

*I'm going to kill that b&*ch! For real! #WatchMe* (7 likes. 3 comments.)

*They're messing with the wrong person. #DeejaIsPissed* (9 likes. 11 comments.)

Heart pounding, Aliyah typed in Jacob's name until his Facebook ID came up. She quickly tapped his name until his page appeared on the screen.

*Reflecting on the blessings of Allah. Trying to stay positive. Life is a test. #selfreflect #selfcorrect*

Aliyah's heart constricted in concern. His last status was posted four days ago.

Aliyah nibbled on her lower lip as she disconnected the Wi-Fi and put her phone back on the nightstand. Something was wrong, and she had the gnawing feeling that this was all connected to her somehow.

Had Larry or Jacob told Deanna about Jacob's phone call to Aliyah's uncle months ago? The mere possibility incited throbbing at Aliyah's temples, and her legs grew weak. She wondered if she should call Deanna and explain everything. She didn't want Deanna to think she was going behind her back and discussing marriage with Jacob.

*"I guess this is about you?"* Reem had said when she showed Aliyah Juwayriah's Facebook status a few days ago. *Married ladies! Hold on to your husbands. I ain't one to call a sister out, so... #NuffSaid #YouHaveBeenWarned*

Aliyah went to the bathroom and performed *wudhoo'* to calm her racing thoughts and steady her breathing. As she rubbed the water of ablution on her hands, face, and arms, Aliyah felt as if her head was about to explode, and she had trouble fighting the tears.

*Here we go again*, she heard the voice of her sister Cassie in her head. *Drama. Queen.*

Aliyah didn't usually pray *Qiyaam al-Layl*, the night prayer before dawn, but she needed the spiritual connection and direction right then. *Our Lord, highly glorified is He,* the Prophet had taught, *descends every night to the lowest heaven, when only one third of the night remains. He says, "Who will call on Me, so that I will answer him? Who will ask of Me, so that I will give him? Who will seek My forgiveness so that I will forgive him?"*

Standing alone in her room dressed in the one-piece floral prayer garment Reem had given her as a gift, Aliyah cried to Allah and asked Him to protect her and keep her safe from harm in this world and in the Hereafter, and she asked Allah to protect Jacob and to ease his troubles and give him love, tranquility, and happiness in his marriage.

***

The college campus was quiet when Aliyah arrived an hour early. She had been unable to go back to sleep after she prayed *Fajr*, so she decided to come in to work. There were only a few cars scattered throughout the faculty and staff parking lot, but the sun shining above the horizon gave the morning a sense of calm that was a welcome contrast to what Aliyah had felt when she had woken up hours ago. Aliyah no longer felt an overwhelming concern for Jacob's well being, and she was left wondering if the dream was from *Shaytaan* or her subconscious. Praying *Qiyaam al-Layl* had helped tremendously in calming her nerves and quelling her fears, but there remained a lingering feeling that something was wrong.

It wasn't until she was reciting the morning *adhkaar* as she dressed for work that she'd realized that what Jacob was saying in the dream mirrored almost verbatim an interview with a famous youth mentor she had seen on television months ago. That was when Aliyah realized that most likely her paranoia was getting the best of her. Though she and Deanna were no longer friends, Aliyah often experienced anxiety as she wondered what type of revenge Deanna might take for Aliyah injuring her pride by ending the friendship. It was a relief to know that her concerns were most likely unwarranted. Aliyah just worried too much.

"Good morning, Professor Thomas," a kind voice said as Aliyah stepped off the elevator and swiped her badge to sign-in.

Aliyah turned and saw Dr. Warren carrying an insulated paper cup filled with coffee as she passed. "Good morning, Dr. Warren," Aliyah said, smiling and lifting a hand in greeting.

Dr. Warren entered her office and closed the door, and the hall grew quiet as Aliyah walked toward her office. Aliyah opened her purse and rummaged for her keys as she neared her door. Her keys jingled as she pulled their ring from her handbag. But she halted her steps as she saw that her office door was already ajar. Had Aliyah left the door unlocked the whole weekend?

Cautiously, Aliyah pushed the door open and peered inside.

"You have some nerve!"

The voice seemed to come out of nowhere, and Aliyah yelped as she lifted her hands to shield her face as she sensed someone coming toward her. A storm of fists landed on Aliyah's head and back before she could even process what was happening.

"You better stay away from my husband!"

It was then that Aliyah recognized Deanna's voice, and the familiar scent of Deanna's perfume tickled Aliyah's nostrils as Aliyah was yanked forward then thrown against the office door.

"You're just jealous that he married me instead of you! I couldn't let him marry someone like you. You wouldn't be able to take care of him. You were too pathetic to take care of yourself!"

Aliyah heard the sound of hurried footsteps approaching, but she registered it as only background noise. Deanna seemed distracted from Aliyah momentarily as she shoved at something near the door before coming back at Aliyah.

"Deeja, wait. Deeja, wait!" Aliyah said desperately, trying to grab hold of Deanna's arms. But Deanna pulled at Aliyah's head instead, ripping Aliyah's hijab from her head and causing the scarf pin to stab Aliyah beneath her chin. "I didn't know until later that Jacob called your uncle about marrying me! I didn't know, Deeja!"

"He called your *uncle* too?" Deanna recoiled, halting her assault briefly.

In the sudden silence, Aliyah realized that Deanna had had no idea about Benjamin's phone call. Then what was Deanna so upset about? But Aliyah didn't have time to ponder the question because seconds later Deanna was attacking her again.

"You and Bailey are not going to do this to me!" Deanna's body was yanked backwards, and her hands were forced behind her back. "You and Bailey are not going to do this to me!"

Deanna wrestled against the force holding her back as Aliyah was huddled next to her office desk watching the scene as if it were from a movie. *Who's Bailey?* Aliyah wondered, her thoughts foggy as her head pounded.

"Are you okay?"

Aliyah squinted her eyes and saw a blurry version of Dr. Warren kneeled beside her, a concerned expression on her face. Aliyah nodded. "Yes, I just need to..." She lost her train of thought momentarily. "…get ready f-f-for class…"

"No, we're going to take you to the college clinic to make sure you're—"

***

"She's fine," Aliyah heard a man's voice say. "She just needs to relax and stay off her feet for the rest of the day. It looks like she passed out from all of the commotion."

Aliyah's eyes fluttered open, and she saw a male nurse talking to Dr. Warren.

"Is Jacob okay?" Aliyah said when Dr. Warren met her gaze. "I didn't see him earlier."

Dr. Warren looked puzzled momentarily. "Dr. Bivens is fine," she said. "He sends his apologies. It appears his wife had a nervous breakdown. He says not to worry." Dr. Warren forced a smile and patted Aliyah's hand. "He's taking care of it."

Aliyah smiled weakly, her heart at ease now that she knew Jacob was okay. "That's good, *alhamdulillaah*," she said moments before she realized that her supervisor would have absolutely no idea what the Arabic phrase praising God meant.

Aliyah's smile faded as she realized that she was supposed to be preparing her students for their computer science final. *Oh no,* she thought, panicked. She could probably lose her job over this.

# 11
# The Crazy Muslim Woman

Jacob bent his knees and held the basketball above his head, poised for a jump shot as he narrowed his eyes and focused on the rim, the net blowing gently in the late Monday afternoon breeze. He released the ball and watched as it hit the backboard then whirled around the metal rim, dipping slightly toward the basket then falling lazily off to the side. The thudding of the bouncing ball on the court was like an apology, a hesitant rhythm out of time with the thumping in his chest. Thoughts incessant and muddled, Jacob walked toward the ball as it rolled to a stop in the grass of his backyard aligning the pavement, and he reached forward to pick it up and try the shot again.

"I'd definitely marry Aliyah," Jacob had said to Benjamin and Sayed as they chatted in the masjid lobby after *Jumu'ah* the Friday before Deanna's nervous breakdown. "If she would have me. And now that it looks like it might not work out between her and Larry, I might start making some extra prayers," Jacob said jokingly. "But my wife would kill me, so unless Aliyah agrees to be a secret second wife, I don't think I'll be so lucky."

It had been a week since Deanna had come to the college and attacked Aliyah, and Jacob still couldn't figure out how Deanna learned of that conversation after Friday prayers. Jacob's first guess was that Sayed had talked to his wife who taught Qur'an classes to the women in the community, many of whom were Deanna's friends. But according to Sayed, his wife wasn't friends with any of the students except for Aliyah, and of course Aliyah wouldn't have told Deanna even if the Qur'an teacher had told her. Was it possible that Benjamin had spoken to some brothers who might have told their wives? But that didn't make any sense because Benjamin, an elder whom many community members went to for advice and marital mediation, was Aliyah's uncle and was known for being prudent in not discussing Muslims' personal issues.

Jacob dribbled the ball as he ran up the court then released the ball in a layup. There was a banging noise against the rim before the basketball fell into the basket, yanking the net back and forth. Jacob stepped forward and caught the ball before it hit the ground, enjoying the fleeting satisfaction of making a good shot. He bounced the ball on the pavement and decided to try a few shots from the three-point range as his mind settled on the only plausible explanation for his predicament: Someone had overheard the conversation while passing through the masjid lobby after *Jumu'ah.* That person could easily have been the husband of one of Deanna's friends, or even Deanna herself or one of her friends.

When the sun was an orange glow at the horizon beyond the trees of his backyard, Jacob made one last three-point shot attempt then let the ball roll to a stop in the grass. Inside the house, he performed *wudhoo'* in the bathroom then called his sons from their room to join him for Maghrib prayer.

*"Allaahu'akbar! Allaahu'akbar!"* Younus raised his voice as he called the *adhaan* for prayer. *"Allaahu'akbar! Allaahu'akbar!"* Thawab stood next to his older brother and mimicked the young muezzin's words and motions.

The scene inspired a sad smile as Jacob wondered how his sons would adjust if he decided to divorce Deanna. They hadn't seen their mother for seven days, and they seemed to be taking it well. They had asked only once where she was, and when Jacob told them she was visiting her parents, they didn't ask again.

"Can I be the imam?" Younus asked after he finished the call to prayer.

"Of course," Jacob said, smiling.

A proud grin twitched at Younus's mouth as he stepped to the front of the living room as Jacob lined up next to Thawab.

"Can you do the *iqaamah*, little man?" Jacob said, rubbing Thawab's head playfully.

Thawab nodded his head emphatically then began the formal announcement that prayer was about to begin. *"Allaahu'akbar. Allaahu'akbar..."*

***

"What do you think?" the comedian talk show host said to the three guests at the roundtable discussion. "Is the crazy Muslim woman suffering from a lack of faith in God, or simply a bad marriage?"

"Based on Dr. D.J. Bivens's own expert opinion," one of the female guests said, "I think it's fair to say it's a bit of both. Sources say the so-called marriage guru was attacking her husband's mistress, so that counts for a bad marriage, don't you think?" The host and the other guests chuckled in agreement. "And since she couldn't keep her hands to herself like her peaceful religion teaches, that counts for godlessness, I think. Because, and I quote..." The guest smirked as she lifted a paper from the desk in front of her, a forefinger raised as she glanced at the camera then back at the paper. "... 'Only people without a proper understanding of God and the sacred bond of marriage have serious problems in their lives and marriages.'"

A roar of laughter sounded from the set. "But seriously, Will," the male guest said to the host, "I think this points to an underlying problem with religions in general. They teach holier-than-thou doctrines about God, peace, and love, but their followers turn out to be the most hypocritical, hateful human beings."

"Whoa," the host said, grinning. "Let's talk more about that after a short break." Humor was in his tone as he looked into the camera. "Don't go anywhere because we'll be right back with W-T-H. Will's Truth Hour."

Jacob groaned and lifted the remote toward the television as he stood and pressed the power button. His sons had fallen asleep, and though he dreaded the idea of walking into the college with all the judgmental eyes scrutinizing him, he had to go to work in the morning. So he needed to go to bed.

"Looking at this photo provided by the alleged mistress's family," the comedian had said earlier in the show as a picture of Aliyah appeared on the screen,

"I can understand the wife's rage. I mean, who's the lucky guy that gets a woman like *that*?"

The photo was of Aliyah wearing a long, strapless form-fitting dress, heels, and dangling earrings. She sported a short natural hairstyle as she smiled, her head turned slightly away from the camera as if laughing at something off-screen. Rage had swept through Jacob when he saw the picture. It was one thing for the media to drag him and his wife through the mud for the sake of entertainment, but it was another thing entirely to bring Aliyah into this, even if they never mentioned her by name.

As Jacob settled under the covers in his bedroom, his heart ached at the thought of what Aliyah must be going through right then. Through no fault of her own, she was being accused of having an affair with a married man while pre-Islam photos from her high school and early college years were being posted and shared on the Internet. Though he saw her at work each day, Jacob had been unable to work up the nerve to actually stop by her office and talk to her directly. He was too ashamed of himself. He was barely making it through the workday himself. For two whole days, the hashtags #CrazyMuslimWoman and #HotMuslimMistress were trending on Twitter, the former directed as his wife, the latter at Aliyah.

*And for what?* Jacob thought angrily. It wasn't like Jacob and Deanna were that well known in the media. Yes, Deanna had made a name for herself as a marriage counselor and relationship advice author, but neither she nor Jacob was famous by any stretch of the imagination. So the only thing that made this story newsworthy was that it involved practicing Muslims who were successful and well respected in their communities. Deanna's actions merely offered fodder for the Islamophobic media to have yet another field day with Muslims.

Jacob found it particularly bothersome that one of the guests on WTH was from the publishing company that had released Deanna's book, *You Can Have Him All To Yourself*, to which Jacob had written an introduction. This left Jacob wondering if all the media attention was being fueled by the publisher itself, perhaps in an underhanded attempt to increase book sales. "All attention is good attention," one of Deanna's agents had said after some bad reviews were posted online about the book.

"You can have him all to yourself, Dr. D.J.?" the host of WTH had taunted, intentionally making a pun with the title of Deanna's book. "I guess not."

Slowly, Jacob shut his eyes and recited *Ayat al-Kursy*, verse 255 in the second chapter of Qur'an, which was a prophetic custom before going to bed.

It was a blessing that final exams were starting, Jacob thought as he drifted to sleep. Soon no more classes would be in session, so he wouldn't have to face his students much longer.

***

"I'm really sorry about all this," Benjamin said as Aliyah sat across from him at the kitchen table in his home Friday evening, her expression distraught. "Val says your sister sold them the photos."

Aliyah nodded absently, but she didn't respond. For the past week, she felt as if she were walking in a daze. She had expected some passing mention of the incident in the local news since it had occurred on a college campus, but she would have never imagined that the story would gain national interest. And even so, wouldn't it be Deanna (or Deanna and Jacob) that would provide the media sensation? After all, it was Deanna who was constantly in front of cameras practically rubbing it in everyone's face that her religion and knowledge were superior to everyone else's. But Aliyah was a nobody, so what was so fascinating about her? But this was the age of social media, Aliyah reminded herself. So she shouldn't be surprised. The most insignificant events became newsworthy simply because they went viral online.

Aliyah drew in a deep breath and exhaled, trying to calm her agitation at the thought of her sister Cassandra sharing uncovered photos of her with the media. The news sites could not have paid more than a few hundred dollars for the pictures. The story simply wasn't worth more. And that hurt most. How could her own sister sell her out for such a paltry return? Cassie didn't need the money, so what was the point?

"Did Aunt Valerie say why she did it?" Aliyah said, finding her voice for the first time.

"You know Cassie," Benjamin said, exhaustion in his voice. "She does anything for attention."

Aliyah had never thought of her older sister in that way. Cassandra was constantly saying that Aliyah was the attention seeker. Cassandra had always been focused on her photography business more than anything else.

"Oh my God," Aliyah said, a realization coming to her just then. "Cassie took all those pictures."

Benjamin creased his forehead. "She did?"

"Yes. *SubhaanAllah.*" Aliyah shook her head as if everything suddenly made sense. "I thought it was strange that she picked only good photos of me."

"That's right," Benjamin said, nodding. "She has her own photography company now, doesn't she?"

*Photo credit: Cassie Studios,* Aliyah recalled the caption just then. It had been beneath every photo posted of her online. "Yes." Aliyah coughed laughter and folded her arms over her chest as she leaned back in her chair. "I can't believe this."

"That *is* something," Benjamin said. "I'm going to ask Val to sit down and talk to her."

Aliyah rolled her eyes. "Don't waste your time. Cassie doesn't have a moral compass unless it's gold-plated and can be sold on eBay."

Benjamin forced laughter, shaking his head. "May Allah guide her."

"And all of them," Aliyah added. "Ameen."

There was an extended silence.

"Have you spoken to any of them recently?" Benjamin said. "Your Mom, Dad, or anyone?"

Aliyah sighed, sadness overcoming her. "No. They refuse all my calls and won't let me visit." She decided against mentioning the returned postcards. "I don't know what else to do."

"Maybe you can go visit with Val one day."

The thought inspired anxiety. "They'll probably just keep us both locked out."

"Not if they don't know you're there."

Aliyah felt a headache coming on. "I don't know…"

"I know you have a lot going on, but I think your parents are worried about you."

Benjamin didn't say, *"…now that they think you're living as a mistress,"* but Aliyah understood his meaning. She imagined she herself would be worried if she were in her parents' shoes.

"They didn't know about the pictures until they saw them posted online," Benjamin said. "Val said they called her right away to ask what was going on."

*O Allah.* Aliyah slapped a hand to her forehead. "I pray she told them it was all a lie."

"She told them she didn't think it was true," Benjamin said. "And trust me, that holds more weight with them than telling them outright that it's a lie."

Aliyah nodded. She could understand that. After all, how could her aunt Valerie know whether or not the story was true? How could anybody, in fact?

Aliyah groaned. This was beyond humiliating. It took her last bit of energy to just wake up and get out of bed each day. She needed some time to clear her head, but she couldn't take off work and stay home like she wanted to. She was already on thin ice for allowing a non-employee to have a key to her office. The lock to her office had been changed, as had Jacob's, and the school had secured a restraining order against Deanna, but Aliyah knew the problem was far from over. She was already starting to wonder whether or not the college would renege on their full-time employment offer.

In the past, whenever Aliyah had gone through a difficult time at work or in her personal life, she sought refuge in the masjid. But with all the social media gossip about her and Jacob—in which many Muslims eagerly participated—she doubted she could ever show her face in the Muslim community again.

*Like I said before, and I'll say it again,* Juwayriah had posted online, *Married ladies! Dump your single girlfriends! And whatever you do, DON'T help them get a job working with your husband. That ain't charity. It's STUPIDITY. If they need work, pay their bus fare and send them to the Welfare office. That's charity! #MyTwoCents*

That was the last Facebook status Aliyah had seen before she deleted the Facebook and Messenger apps on her phone. She didn't want any more notifications about being tagged in someone's post or photo or receiving yet another message from some career-building media person or some sick, deranged man looking for a "relationship" or a second, third, or fourth wife. Aliyah was tempted to disable her Facebook account entirely, but she knew it would only make matters worse. People would definitely see it as a sign of guilt.

Several online groups were already dedicated to discussing the #CrazyMuslimWoman and #HotMuslimMistress saga, and some of Aliyah's Facebook "friends" actually tagged her to chime in. *What do YOU think?* was the most common discussion thread in Muslim circles, as if it made perfect Islamic sense to openly speculate on the guilt, chastity, and honor of someone just because the story was "in the news" or trending online. It was as if Aliyah wasn't their fellow Muslim sister, or even a fellow human being.

Even during past discussions involving well-known media personalities like Bill Cosby, Aliyah had never participated. It just felt wrong. It was one thing to discuss an issue (like how to handle cases of date rape or what the statute of limitation should be for certain crimes), but it was another thing entirely to publicly declare your "opinion" on whether or not someone was guilty or innocent, or lying or telling the truth. *Does Allah* ever *grant us that right?* Aliyah wondered. She thought not. But destroying people's honor had become so commonplace amongst Muslims that Aliyah was often left feeling that she should study more about her faith. Maybe there was a loophole for the soul's accountability in front of Allah that she was unaware of.

Aliyah's phone vibrated on the table in front of her, interrupting her thoughts. She reached for it and saw Nikki's name on the screen. Aliyah groaned as she refused the call then put the phone in her purse. She couldn't handle hearing the voice of Matt's wife right then. It was bad enough dealing with relentless judgment and negativity from strangers. She doubted she had the strength to withstand it from people she knew personally. It incited too much self-doubt.

"I better go," Aliyah said, standing as she looked at her wristwatch and pulled the straps of her handbag over her shoulder. "Nikki is probably dropping off Ibrahim now. I don't want to keep her waiting."

"Don't let Ibrahim watch television this weekend," Benjamin suggested, pushing his chair back and following his niece out the kitchen.

"I hope the story will be old news by then," Aliyah said as she walked through the living room toward the front door. Her reputation was ruined, that was for sure, she thought sadly. She hoped her son would be spared the agony of hearing horrible things about his mother. She had no idea how to get herself through this, and she was a grown woman. What could she possibly say to a boy who was almost five? "I mean, how long can the media spend on a nobody?" Aliyah said, frustrated. "I think my fifteen minutes of fame are up."

"They'll keep it going as long as people show interest," Benjamin said. "Unfortunately, turning a hijabi Muslim woman into eye candy can go a long way in today's world."

"Well, the good news is," Aliyah said, sad humor in her voice, "you don't have to worry about finding me a husband anymore. At this rate, no good brothers will want to marry me."

"I don't think that's true."

"I do," Aliyah said as she knelt to put on her shoes. "Who wants to marry a whore?"

"Aliyah, please don't talk about yourself like that."

"Well, that's what the media is saying."

"That doesn't mean you have to say it."

"Me not saying it doesn't stop it from being said." She shrugged, feeling choked up all of a sudden. "Even Muslims seem to agree on the whore part."

"It stops *you* from saying it," Benjamin said. "And that's all that matters."

Aliyah grunted as she stood upright, resisting the urge to break down. "If only that were true."

The look of sadness on her uncle's face made Aliyah wish she could take back the comment. She averted her gaze from him as she unlocked the door to let herself out.

"I'm praying for you, Ally," Benjamin said as she stepped out the door. "In all my prayers."

"Thank you," she muttered sincerely. "I really appreciate it."

"Keep your head up, pumpkin," she heard him say as she walked toward her car. "We'll get through this *insha'Allah.*"

Aliyah nodded, but she wasn't so sure. She was starting to wonder if it even mattered whether or not she got through this. What did she have to look forward to anyway?

In her car, she glanced at her phone and frowned when she saw that, other than Nikki, no one had called or texted. Or more precisely, Larry hadn't called or texted. Though it was probably a stupid idea, Aliyah had reached out to Larry several times that week, saying she was thinking about him and wanted to know if he wanted to get together some time. In the midst of the public character assassination, Aliyah had begun to appreciate the comfort she'd found in Larry, and she missed him terribly. If she could just hear his comforting and supportive voice, she imagined she could weather this storm. But he hadn't returned any of her calls, texts, or emails, and Aliyah was beginning to feel ashamed for reaching out to him at all.

*What did you expect?* she said to herself. *Larry probably thinks the rumors are true.*

The possibility that Larry himself would believe the lies cut deep, and Aliyah wondered if it were possible to feel any lonelier, more pathetic, or regretful than she felt right then.

***

*Crazy Muslim Woman Gate: Is There a Silver Lining?*

Jacob sat at the desk in his home office late Friday night, staring indecisively at the title of the article published on a popular Muslim blog. Younus and Thawab had gone to sleep a few hours before, and Deanna was still at her parents' house (as she had been since being released from the holding cell after Aliyah and the college declined to press charges, though both had secured restraining orders against her). This was Jacob's much-coveted quiet time, and he wondered if it was wise to spend it reading anything related to the source of his troubles. But this was a reputable Muslim site, he reasoned, so hopefully they had more integrity than the secular media (and the social media of Muslims on Facebook and Twitter). News sites and social media had spared nothing in making his wife look like a raving maniac, him like a sex-hungry Muslim man, and Aliyah like a sleazy seducer—and all of them "crazies" who represented "true Islam" or sullied its image (depending on the individual perspective).

*It is heartbreaking to learn that one of our respected Muslim personalities assaulted another Muslim and had to be, according to witnesses, physically restrained from harming her further,* the blog said. *Though I don't agree with the label "crazy" that the media has given our Muslim sister, I think this description brings to light a very important issue that the Muslim community has ignored for far too long: mental illness. I'm not saying that Dr. Deanna Janice Bivens is mentally ill, and I definitely don't want to speculate on the veracity of the rumors of any adulterous affair between Dr. Bivens's husband and his coworker, who was also Dr. Bivens's best friend. But regardless of whether or not either is the case, what Dr. Bivens did, coupled with her Facebook posts preceding the attack, was wrong and suggests that she was, at least temporarily, not in her best state of mind.*

Jacob grunted. This person is a genius, he thought in bitter sarcasm.

*It is unfortunate that our religious communities generally sweep psychological problems under the rug or view them as indicative of someone's lacking faith. However, the truth is, there are many reasons for psychological distress, whether short-term in the form of temporary depression or a nervous breakdown, or long-term in the form of clinical depression or lasting mental illness; and amongst the major factors contributing to psychological distress and disorders are unresolved personal problems and childhood abuse, especially when—*

Jacob exited the website and decided it probably wasn't the best idea to read the blog. It was difficult to be talked about in the third person, as if he and his wife weren't living, breathing human beings who deserved privacy and respect like everyone else.

*I definitely don't want to speculate on the veracity of the rumors of any adulterous affair*, the writer had said.

Then why mention it at all? Jacob wondered. Why couldn't you just focus on the "crazy Muslim woman" gate, as your title suggested? In all of this, it was only Deanna who was guilty of public wrongdoing, so it was understandable that her name would be mentioned. But why not leave Aliyah out of it? With all the media sites having a field day calling her Jacob's "whore" mistress, why couldn't at least one reputable Muslim source take the higher ground? Aliyah deserved at least that small kindness from fellow Muslims, didn't she?

Aliyah.

The thought of her made Jacob's chest constrict in anxiety. He wondered how she was holding up. He saw her in passing at work, but she wouldn't even look at him. And he couldn't blame her. He couldn't imagine what she thought of him now. She probably had no idea how any of this madness got started, and he didn't have the words or heart to tell her the truth.

*I wanted to marry you, Aliyah,* he could say. *And if you had accepted me, I would have rushed to marry you, even if it drove my wife crazy.*

In his mind's eye, Jacob saw Aliyah smiling, her head turned from the camera as she laughed at something Jacob was saying off-screen. Of course, he had never met Aliyah at the time the picture was taken, but he still liked to think of himself as the source of joy in her life, even back then.

But he could never say that out loud. It was bad enough that Larry was barely speaking to him in the midst of all this, and he didn't know what to tell his brother. Jacob didn't want Larry to know what he'd said to Benjamin and Sayed after *Jumu'ah* that day. Jacob was still holding on to the hope that the media fascination with the "crazy Muslim woman" would wear off soon so he could go on with his life.

But was that even possible? Jacob wondered. He hadn't called or spoken to Deanna in more than a week, and he didn't want to. Right then, he couldn't stomach the sight of her, much less the sound of her voice or her presence. How then could he resume life as usual, even if this public saga died down?

"She needs professional help," Benjamin had said after Jacob explained what had led his wife to physically assault Aliyah. Jacob hadn't wanted to divulge what happened to Deanna when she was eight years old, but the media had already leaked rumors about it (one of the only rumors that turned out to be actually true). Aliyah herself had already told her uncle that Deanna kept mentioning some "Bailey" person that day. So Jacob felt obligated to give Aliyah's uncle a full understanding of what was going on, especially since his family was being directly affected.

*Yes, I know she needs help,* Jacob had thought. He had said the same to Deanna herself on several occasions. "You can't keep all that stuff bottled up inside," he would say. "It will kill you."

"I'm fine," she'd snap. "You're the only one who can't seem to get over the past. Maybe *you* should get professional help."

"Then at least go to the masjid more often," he suggested, intentionally ignoring her insult. "Study Qur'an or *tafseer* or something."

"I don't need to study Qur'an," she'd say. "I'm living it."

Jacob pushed back his swivel chair and stood. He was worried about Deanna, this he couldn't deny, no matter how hard he tried to put his mind on other things. But he was at a loss for what to do. After more than eleven years of marriage, he was exhausted. He wanted to be a support for his wife during this difficult time, but like Deanna herself had said, he could use professional help himself. Months ago, it had been a desire for an expert perspective on his own troubles that had inspired him to make the one and a half-hour drive to see Dr. Melanie Goldstein.

Though Jacob had no childhood trauma that he was suppressing, he had years of marital trauma that he needed help understanding. He still cared about his wife and probably always would, but this recent incident sapped the last bit of marital patience from his chest. Yes, marriage was about support and compromise, but there was only so far the human heart could extend itself for someone else's sake. Jacob feared that he was at the end of his rope.

"I should've never married you!" Deanna had said the night before she attacked Aliyah. "You're nothing like I thought you were!"

Psychological distress or not, Deanna should not speak to her husband like that, Jacob felt. Had it been the first time or under different circumstances, Jacob probably could have overlooked the outburst. But how many verbal insults and physical threats was he supposed to take in the name of patience and compromise? She hung divorce over his head like a taunt, and he never knew whether she was speaking in anger or earnest. The slightest offense set her off. Meanwhile, she said and did things that, had they come from him, would be viewed as oppressive and abusive.

"I want to help other women," she often said in books and interviews.

Help them *what*? Jacob was often left wondering. *Manipulate and abuse their husbands before their husbands can manipulate and abuse them?*

But apparently his desire to marry Aliyah was the ultimate affront. Jacob understood how the prospect of polygyny could send any woman over the edge, but in his case, it hadn't even been a prospect. It had been a hypothetical. Deanna herself talked openly about men she would (hypothetically) marry if she weren't married to Jacob. And she'd say this to Jacob himself. At least Jacob had the decency to speak his thoughts aloud to friends, not to his wife. How did Deanna think it made him feel to hear his wife talk about desiring to marry one of his friends? Yet she goes ballistic after *hearing about* him having the same conversation?

"We like to see you all get jealous," Deanna had said once, explaining the psychology of women talking about other men to their husbands. "We need to know you appreciate what you have." She'd laughed then added, "We like to see you squirm."

Why then hadn't Deanna laughed it off when she learned of his thoughts about Aliyah? Why couldn't she view *her* jealousy and "squirming" as merely signs that she appreciated her husband? But that's how it always was with Deanna. She made the rules, and he had to play by them, even as they oddly and consistently leaned in her favor.

No, he couldn't live with Deanna another day, Jacob realized. Maybe he would never be able to marry Aliyah, the woman he'd wanted to marry all along, but that didn't mean he should live in misery for the rest of his life. He imagined that being single was better than remaining in this heart-wrenching marriage.

Jacob's only hesitation in going forward with a divorce was the thought of his sons being from a broken home. But, as he heard relationship experts say, *It's better to be from a broken home than in one.*

Then again, maybe this line of thinking was merely a trap of *Shaytaan*, Satan trying to destroy his life.

Jacob sighed and ran a hand over his face in confused exhaustion. It was time to get advice from Muslims he trusted then turn to Allah for guidance and direction through *Istikhaarah*, the prayer and supplication made when making a decision. Because he needed to make a decision.

***

"You should see this," Reem said Sunday evening as she sat on the couch in Aliyah's living room. Reem had stopped by earlier to teach Qur'an and exercise, and now she was chatting with Aliyah before heading home. Nikki had picked up Ibrahim a half hour before, so Aliyah was able to relax and spend time with Reem without feeling as if she had to divide her time between her friend and her son.

Aliyah's heart dropped in dread when Reem turned her laptop toward Aliyah. "What is it?" Aliyah said.

"Just read it."

Aliyah shook her head, already feeling the beginning of a headache. "I can't deal with any more surprises. If it's bad, just tell me."

"Then I'll read it to you," Reem said.

"Okay." Aliyah exhaled the word, wishing Reem would leave the public saga alone. Reem was Aliyah's only friend these days, and Aliyah didn't want the constant reminder of all she'd lost during the #CrazyMuslimWoman and #HotMuslimMistress drama.

"It's a status Nicole posted yesterday."

Aliyah clenched her jaw and crossed her arms over her chest. Aliyah knew that Nikki didn't like her, but as pathetic as it sounded, Aliyah was grateful that Nikki's disdain was at least due to an actual problem that had occurred between them. Why couldn't Nikki stay out of the public scrutiny on the unknown? Nikki had absolutely no idea what was going on, so couldn't she just keep her mouth shut?

"*I'm sure all of you have heard the rumors about my husband's ex-wife and Brother Jacob*," Reem read aloud.

Aliyah grunted and rolled her eyes, angry frustration building inside her.

"*And some of you have posted Facebook statuses about home wreckers and dumping single and divorced women as friends. You know who you are*," Reem continued. "*And though I hate getting involved in these stupid discussions, I have a few things I want to say. I haven't been Muslim long, but I must say I'm grateful that Allah chose Aliyah,* ***Ally Thomas****, to be the one who helped open my heart to His religion. I was going through a lot during the time we met, and she'll probably* *never know just how much she helped me face each day. Those phone calls, coffee dates, and woman-to-woman talks kept me from literally breaking down. I was suffering from depression, and seeing a text or email from her checking on me or sharing a verse from the Qur'an or hadith from the Prophet, peace be upon him, really lifted my spirits. She taught me the meaning of real sisterhood and love for the sake of Allah. And yes, she even welcomed me as a SECOND WIFE to her husband. You can think what you want about what happened between us, but I'm going to tell you what I KNOW happened: Allah brought Aliyah into my life because He wanted to show me the beauty of Islam. And, sorry if my words offend, but this is the truth: Sisters, after reading your posts and listening to your gossip and tale-carrying, I thank Allah I met that sister before I met any of you! I might have run away from Islam if I was exposed to your ugliness during that time. So as for all the gossip, slander, and foolishness you guys are spreading about our Muslim sister, I say this: Fear Allah! I swear by Allah, I only know good of that woman. And I would be honored if Allah blesses me with even half the knowledge, dignity, and faith she shows each day. And I pray that Allah blesses her in this life and the next for all the good she's done for me, her son, and yes, even MY HUSBAND, mashaAllah. And for those who still can't shut up about something you know NOTHING ABOUT, I leave you with the words of Allah in hopes that you have at least *some* concern about your souls on the Day of Judgment: 'Behold, you received it on your tongues, and said out of your mouths things of which you had no knowledge; and you thought it to be a light matter, while it was most serious in the sight of Allah' (24:15)."*

The tears slipped down Aliyah's cheeks, and she covered her face with her hands as her shoulders shook. *SubhaanAllah,* she thought, overcome with emotion. You really never knew where the blessings of Allah would come from.

## 12
## It's All Under Control

Deanna lay on her back staring at the ceiling in the guest bedroom of her parents' home on a Thursday evening, two weeks after the assault incident. The down comforter was gathered at the lower half of her body, and her fists were tucked under her arms, her jaw set in annoyance. A tray of food sat on the mahogany wood chest next to the king-size bed. She had managed to eat only a few bites before feeling nauseated. It was difficult to maintain an appetite amidst all the commotion in her head. She had thought she could pass time by watching television, but when she saw a photo of Aliyah, laughing and carefree, dressed in a revealing dress, natural hair cut and styled attractively, Deanna promptly powered off the television.

*Aliyah has some nerve*, Deanna thought indignantly, *shamelessly displaying herself like that in front of thousands of people—and in front of* my *husband.* It was clever though, Deanna admitted bitterly, giving the media alluring pictures like that. After that ruse, it was only natural that Aliyah would be labeled the "hot" mistress while Deanna was viewed as some nutcase.

At the thought of Jacob seeing those photos, Deanna's body was aflame in fury. Frustrated, Deanna kicked the covers from her legs. "Is this stupid A.C. even on?" she muttered aloud, glancing around the room.

*"You should apologize to her,"* suggested Deanna's aunt, of all people.

*"For what?"* Deanna had recoiled. *"She had that coming. She's lucky the security guard pulled me off of her."*

*"She was at work, baby. That was wrong."*

*"Well, she was* at work *flirting with my husband."*

*"You don't know that."*

*"And neither do you."*

*"I just remember when my husband used to accuse me of—"*

*"Do* not *compare me to that sorry excuse of a man."*

Deanna recalled her aunt's look of hurt and disappointment after she'd said that. *I should apologize to Aunt Stacy*, Deanna thought, her chest constricting in regret. She groaned in self-rebuke, annoyed that she had allowed Aliyah's antics to make her step out of character and disrespect her aunt. How long was she going to allow Aliyah to ruin her life? Deanna should have listened to Juwayriah and befriended only secure, married women who had their lives together.

*"I didn't know until later that Jacob called your uncle about marrying me! I didn't know, Deeja!"*

Deanna gritted her teeth. *Yeah right. Then where did he get the idea to call your uncle in the first place?* Men didn't just call a woman's marriage guardian unless the woman had already given him the go-ahead—and unless the man and woman had already spoken to each other about marriage.

But it was good that Aliyah had let that slip. If she hadn't, Deanna would never have known the extent of Aliyah's backstabbing. How dare Aliyah encourage Jacob to take her as a second wife behind Deanna's back. That was *low.*

*"It's nothing personal, Deeja,"* Aliyah had said when she cut off their friendship. *"I just have a lot going on right now, and I can't handle anything else."*

Deanna snorted. *I bet you do, trying to steal husbands and such. How* could *you handle anything else?*

Deanna should have known right then that something wasn't right. Now it made sense why Aliyah had kept avoiding her and refusing her calls. She could barely look Deanna in the face when she cut off their friendship. *No, it wasn't personal*, Deanna agreed. Because Aliyah ending the friendship had nothing to do with Deanna, and everything to do with Aliyah's guilty conscience.

*But I'm going to be the bigger person*, Deanna told herself.

*Forgive, forgive, forgive.* That's what Deanna's mother always advised, and maybe that's what Deanna needed to do to let go of the resentment that was eating at her.

*"By any means necessary, girl,"* Deanna would often say. *"That's my motto when you see a man you want."*

Trepidation gripped Deanna. What if her current predicament was a karma of sorts, coming back to haunt her for how she had convinced Jacob to marry her? *Allah created the world round,* Deanna had heard an imam say. *So whatever you throw out will come back to you.*

Deanna's stomach convulsed. What if Aliyah was now adopting that motto for herself?

"Just pray on it, baby," her mother had said earlier as she sat on the edge of the bed, petting Deanna's hair affectionately.

But Deanna had not prayed on it. In fact, she had not prayed at all since the ordeal. Because she was afraid that she didn't deserve any blessings from her Lord.

***

*Stress debilitates*, Jacob thought to himself as he sat on the soft prayer mat in his home office after performing *Istikhaarah* Thursday evening. He could hear the shouts, grunts, and stomps of excitement and frustration as Younus and Thawab played the Wii together. He had helped them with their homework earlier and allowed them a few games after dinner, but soon Jacob would have to tell them to go to bed because they had school in the morning. But right then, he needed to sit still and clear his head.

For the past week, he had spent extended time in self-reflection and sought advice from people he trusted regarding whether or not to divorce Deanna. It had been difficult to put aside his apprehension about others knowing what he was going through, but he was at a breaking point and could no longer suppress the pain and confusion he'd battled for so long. He'd reached out to Benjamin, the local imam, Dr. Melanie Goldstein, and even his own father; and everyone advised him similarly. Seek reconciliation and do marriage counseling.

But Jacob didn't want marriage counseling. And what was there to reconcile? Jacob wanted psychological and emotional freedom from the shackles of a suffocating, unhealthy relationship. Could arbitration or marriage counseling guarantee him that? *This isn't love,* he'd told himself. *This is laborious obligation.*

After learning of his wife's painful past, Jacob had felt obliged to be a source of protection and comfort for Deanna. From the moment she'd divulged what happened to her when she was eight years old, Jacob could see right through Deanna's bright smiles and claims of "I forgive him" and "I am walking with the Lord." Deanna hadn't forgiven Bailey (or her father) for what happened in the church basement so many years ago. And how could she? She had never allowed herself an honest assessment of what had happened in the first place.

Part of Jacob's determination to remain by Deanna's side was the desire to be a positive counter balance to how her parents, especially her father, had handled the trauma. Her father's dismissiveness and his ultimate blaming of Deanna herself was likely more traumatic than the rape itself. Though well-intentioned, her mother merely exacerbated Deanna's troubles through inciting guilt. *"Good Christians love their enemies,"* she'd told Deanna. *"So if you are showing any anger, then God is not happy with you."*

What does that even *mean*? Jacob had thought angrily. *Love is not word or a claim. It is an action-based reality that stems from a definite feeling in the heart, even if the word "love" is never used to describe it.* Even when he was a Christian himself, Jacob was often perplexed by the "love your enemies" message being used as a religious measuring stick for the goodness of a person. *Why would God ask us to* love *our enemies?* he wondered. Jacob imagined that to even attempt such a feat would result in some form of self-aggrandizing dishonesty within oneself or self-righteous contempt for the object of that "love."

When as an adult Jacob read in the Qur'an God's instructions to consistently strive for peace, justice, and mercy when interacting with one's enemies, what Jacob had learned as a Christian began to make sense. Perhaps the meaning of the original biblical concept had gotten lost in translations and rewrites over time, but the difference between the Christian concept of "love your enemies" and the Islamic concept of seeking peace, justice, and mercy was not insignificant. The former was rooted in a state of the heart while the latter was rooted in a person's behavior.

But only behavior was in one's control.

In Deanna seeking to do the impossible—force her heart to love what she (justifiably) loathed—she had incited a cycle of personal deception. Through believing that she was obligated to love her rapist, she had developed an inability to distinguish between love and contempt (because religious doctrine had effectively made them synonymous). Through following her mother's advice to "put a smile on your face, and walk with your head high" before ever giving herself permission to grieve and feel disgusted, Deanna had learned that external facades dictate internal realities.

But, in Jacob's view, the most destructive message Deanna had been given was, *You are better than this. You are better than the wicked and sinful. You are walking with the Lord.* As far as Jacob could surmise, Deanna's wholehearted belief in this mantra was the single most significant factor in destroying their marriage. It had incited such pathological arrogance that it permeated their every conversation and interaction. By her wide smile alone, Deanna reeked of incorrigible narcissism.

How then could any meaningful, lasting reconciliation take place?

Perhaps the "you are better" mantra had held considerable value at the time of the rape, but it was a harmful ideology to carry into other contexts. Without viewing this belief system as conditional upon her *own* adherence to non-wicked, non-sinful behavior, Deanna destructively believed that the wicked and sinful were always "the other"—and that in every context, it was she who was "walking with the Lord." This self-glorification led her to hold in contempt the very people she claimed to help: broken and abused women.

If a woman didn't stand up for herself like Deanna felt she should, if a woman didn't appear strong or courageous enough to leave a bad situation, if a woman appeared generally unhappy, broken, or troubled by her struggles in life; Deanna viewed her with condescending, unmerciful scorn, even as Deanna *claimed* to be full of love and concern…

Because, from eight years old, that was how Deanna had learned to treat herself.

Jacob sighed as he stood and walked over to his desk. He hesitated only briefly before picking up his phone and dialing his wife.

***

At the sound of the familiar ringtone, Deanna scrambled out of bed and rushed to the dresser to retrieve her phone. Even as her heart raced for fear of missing the call, Deanna smiled inwardly. She had known it would be only a matter of time before Jacob caved into loneliness and begged Deanna to come home. There had been moments that she was tempted to call him or drop by the house to check on him and the boys, but she'd resisted. She didn't want to give Jacob any reason to think she believed anything was her fault. By now he should be racked with guilt for sending her over the edge like that, and for allowing the college (and Aliyah) to secure a restraining order against her.

But she would forgive Jacob, Deanna decided as she put her ear to the phone and answered the call. That was the right thing to do. *Be the bigger person*, she told herself. A smirk crawled on her face as she softly said, "Hello?" She wanted him to hear the sensuality in her voice. She wanted him to hear an independent, confident woman who didn't need him, not a broken, helpless woman pining over him.

*"As-salaamu'alaikum,"* Jacob said.

*"Wa'alaiku-mus-salaam wa-rahmatullaah,"* Deanna sang, as if pleasantly surprised to hear from him.

"I wanted to talk to you about something," he said hesitantly. "Is now a good time?"

Deanna's lips twitched as she suppressed a smile, unable to contain her sense of triumph. *I'll give him a hard time*, she decided mischievously. *Then I'll put on something nice, drive back home, and slip into bed next to him.* "Um..." she said, feigning doubt. "...I'm in the middle of something, but—"

"Then I'll just call back la—"

"No, no," she said, perhaps too quickly. "It's okay. I can step away for a moment and talk to you, no problem." She sat on the bed and toyed with her hair as she held the phone to her ear. "What's on your mind, baby?"

"I want a divorce."

For a fleeting moment, Deanna felt faint. It was as if she were in the church basement and Jacob glared condescendingly at her while his words conveyed comfort and affection. In her mind's eye, Jacob smirked as he approached sneakily, giving her a once-over before holding her in a suffocating embrace.

"Baby," she said, laughing throatily, nervousness and panic pricking her all over. "You don't want a divorce. You just want to talk." She spoke as if convincing a young child. "You're upset, and you're not thinking straight." She laughed again and tugged at a lock of hair. "Forget Aliyah. Don't listen to her silly suggestions. She's not right for you. I am."

"This isn't about Aliyah. This is about us. I want a divorce," he said again, more resolute this time. "But Allah says reconciliation is best, so I'm calling to ask what is most comfortable for you. Marriage counseling or—"

Deanna laughed out loud, hoping in that sound that Jacob would see the ridiculousness of his words. "No, no, baby. *We* don't need marriage counseling. We work things out on our own."

She smirked as an idea came to her suddenly. "I'll tell you what," she said. "I'll come over now, then we can—"

"No," Jacob said so sternly that Deanna flinched. "I'm not interested in sexual manipulation. We need arbitration from our families, or we need a good marriage counselor. Which is it?"

The question hung in the air like a hard slap.

Deanna's chin trembled in fury and she lifted a side of her upper lip in a sneer, the passing silence a stubborn impasse.

"I'll take that as you trust my judgment," Jacob said after more than a minute passed. "*Insha'Allah*, I'll let you know what I decide. *As-salaamu'alaikum wa-rahmatullah.*"

The silence was more definite this time, and Deanna could barely breathe for the shock she felt right then.

*"I don't let that man worry me,"* her mother had said years ago when Deanna complained about how stubborn her father was. *"He can huff and puff and act like a slighted king if he wants. But* I *hold the keys to that kingdom. Yeah, I'll smile and play the good wife so he feels like a man. But when that door closes,"* she said, gesturing toward the bedroom, "I'm *the master."* Her mother laughed. *"And I'll tell you what. Once I'm done with him, he can't even remember what he was upset about."*

Deanna glanced at the clock on the wall then quickly opened the walk-in closet and wheeled out her luggage. She kneeled and unzipped the bag and yanked out several pieces of lingerie that she had stashed there.

***

Jacob's thoughts were distracted as he walked to Younus and Thawab's room. Even as Jacob opened the room door and told his sons to shut down the game, he sensed an urgency greater than school that made him insist that they go to bed right away. But it wasn't until he had prayed, taken a shower, and rubbed cologne on his chest that he was able to fully admit he was hoping Deanna would come home tonight.

His rational mind told him that now wasn't the time to give into carnal weakness, but physically, he yearned for his wife's body next to his. The chemistry between them was so compelling that at times he imagined that, based on intimacy alone, he could remain with Deanna forever. But Jacob hated the man he had become with her. Perpetual stress numbed him into inactivity, and he was morphing into only a shell of the man he used to be. He was beginning to feel as if he was trapped inside his own body.

Jacob climbed into bed and pulled the heavy covers over him, his thoughts muddled as he imagined the pleasurable release Deanna's arrival would bring.

*You know you love me*. In the space between sleep and wakefulness, Jacob heard Deanna's coquettish teasing. *So shut up about all that silly divorce talk. You know you can never live without me. Who would want you anyway?* A throaty laugh and playful wink. *I'll see to that. So don't mess with me, boy. I'll make your life hell. I'll take your sons from you, and you'll never see them again...*

At the sound of a door closing, Jacob jolted awake, sitting up in bed. Heart racing, his thoughts instinctively went to Younus and Thawab. Would Deanna stoop *that* low? The trepidation gripped him until his breath caught. Panicked, he threw the comforter from his body. Wearing only boxer shorts, he pulled the bedroom door open, the brass door handle banging against the wall as he rushed out. He was panting when he opened the door to his sons' room and found them sleeping peacefully, the covers pulled up to their shoulders. Jacob exhaled in a single breath, throwing his back against the doorway and rolling his eyes to the ceiling in exhausted gratefulness.

"*As-salaamu'alaikum*, baby."

The scent of Deanna's perfume tickled Jacob's nostrils, and the sound of her voice prickled his skin. Yet the lull of her presence alone sent his heart racing in desire before he even turned his head.

"Is everything okay?" Deanna said flirtatiously.

Jacob met her gaze just as her soft, long fingers cradled the closely cropped beard of his face. Before he could speak, she drew him into a passionate kiss. His shoulders fell, the tense agitation leaving as Deanna dropped her arms and massaged his lower back.

"It's okay," she whispered, her sweet breath warm against his face. "I forgive you. We don't have to talk about it anymore."

*Don't mess with me, boy. I'll make your life hell. I'll take your sons from you, and you'll never see them again...*

Jacob jerked his head back, and he gripped her arms and pulled them from his back. "No," he said, catching his breath as he stepped backwards. "We *will* talk about this. I want a divorce, and if you don't—"

Deanna stepped forward and slapped him hard, interrupting him midsentence. "Shut up, Jacob." She then pushed his chest in rebuke before kissing him again. "You're not leaving me." Her voice was soft and stern. "You wouldn't know what to do without me." She kissed him again, a sneer lingering on her face. "You think that pathetic excuse for a woman who just takes up earth space can ever do for you what I do? I did you a favor by telling her to marry Matt. She isn't good enough for you."

Jacob swatted Deanna's hand away and abruptly turned his back. As he walked toward their bedroom, he felt himself unraveling as fury and desire enveloped him at once. He yearned for Deanna in a maddening way, and he hated himself for it. No, Jacob had no problem enjoying the *halaal* intimacy of his wife that night, but if he gave in before she acknowledged the legitimacy of his concerns, he feared that he would fall back into the clutches of Deanna's physical and psychological manipulation. Like the bright smile she wore to deny her own pain, she imagined that sex would do the same for him; and he refused to be an accessory to her emotional crime against the soul.

*O Allah, give me strength*, he silently prayed as he heard Deanna's soft footsteps trailing behind him.

"If you want me," he said, his voice firm as Deanna closed the bedroom door and locked it, "then listen to me first."

Deanna smiled teasingly as she walked slowly toward him and slipped off her outer garment to reveal the lingerie she wore beneath.

Frustrated with her stubbornness and his own carnal weakness, Jacob walked past her, turned the lock and yanked open the bedroom door, then walked quickly down the hall. His head cleared with each heavy footfall upon the steps until he was at the sliding glass door next to the dining room. He unlocked it and slid it open, not caring that a peeping neighbor might see him dressed in only his boxers.

The pavement of the basketball court was cool beneath Jacob's bare feet, and the May night air was tolerably warm. He raised his eyes toward the sky as he drew in a breath and exhaled, confounded by the mixture of desire and contempt he held for his wife.

*I did you a favor by telling her to marry Matt. She isn't good enough for you.*

*Maybe Aliyah isn't good for me*, Jacob thought reflectively. It was entirely possible that his persistent desire to marry Aliyah merely represented his desperation to escape a toxic relationship. Perhaps Aliyah was merely symbolic of what he longed for in a wife. *Educated and intelligent. Humble and reserved.* No, this was not what he merely wanted in a wife. It was what he needed. Cocky and forward women had always annoyed him (at least outside the bedroom), and his tumultuous relationship with Deanna only confirmed that sentiment. If he were to maintain his sanity and thwart further emasculation, he needed to release himself from Deanna's claws.

*Men are the protectors and maintainers of women, because Allah has given the one more [strength] than the other, and because they support them from their means. Therefore, the righteous women are devoutly obedient, and guard in [the husband's] absence what Allah would have them guard.*

A sad smile formed on Jacob's face as he recalled reading that Qur'anic passage shortly after becoming Muslim. He had been so naïve at the time. He had actually imagined that all Muslim women embodied the meaning of that verse. It hadn't occurred to him that his experience with women as a Muslim wouldn't differ too greatly from his experiences with women as a Christian. He hadn't known that it might prove impossible to find any woman whose character and lifestyle reflected that of a righteous believing woman.

And he hadn't known that it might prove impossible to find within himself the character and lifestyle that reflected that of a righteous believing man.

The sound of the glass door being slid shut prompted Jacob to turn around and look toward the house. He saw Deanna, still in her black lingerie, glowering at him as she stood on the other side of the glass. The glow of the dining room light illuminated her fair caramel skin and incited a flicker of longing in Jacob. But the sight of her hand securing the lock, her angry glare unmoving, sapped any lingering desire from him.

***

Early Friday morning, Aliyah stood in front of the photocopy machine in the office supply room. She held a stack of exam papers in her hand as she hesitantly poked at buttons with her free hand. Her eyebrows were drawn together as she studied the changing icons on the glowing blue display. *Collated. Stapled. Two-sided.* For all her wits in math and science, Aliyah was continuously confounded by the department's high-tech copy machine. She bit her lower lip nervously as she keyed in 70 copies, wondering if she should calm her anxiousness to get this over with and just do one sample copy before risking facing the even more daunting task of interrupting a copy job in progress.

"Do you have a moment?"

Exams still in hand, Aliyah turned from where she stood and found Jacob in the doorway, a look of exhaustion and concern on his face.

"Is everything okay?" Aliyah said.

Jacob's lips formed a thin line in an effort to decide the best way to respond. "I don't know," he said. He exhaled as if in confession. "Dr. Warren wants to talk to both of us."

"When?" Aliyah's voice was etched in concern.

"In thirty minutes," he said. "But you and I need to meet before then, if that's okay."

Aliyah nodded as she glanced toward the copy machine, realizing she would have to photocopy the exams later. "Okay," she said, surprised that she found her voice with the apprehension she felt right then. She pressed cancel and followed Jacob out the supply room and down the hall leading to his office, exam papers still in her hand.

This was the moment that Aliyah had feared when she first began working at the college. After her probationary period had passed and she signed her full-time employment contract, she'd thought the worst was over. But now she wasn't so sure. A twinge of panic stabbed her chest as Jacob unlocked his office and pushed the door open, stepping to the side so that Aliyah could enter. Was she going to lose her job today? Where would she live? How would she take care of Ibrahim? Would she have to relinquish the little time she spent with her son?

"Please sit down," Jacob said, gesturing toward the seat opposite his desk as she walked past him and he secured the door stopper.

Aliyah lowered herself into the chair and set the stack of exams on her lap then nervously rested her hands atop.

"I won't take too much of your time," Jacob said as he pulled out his leather swivel chair and sat down.

Aliyah nodded, apprehensive.

"Firstly," he said, holding onto the handles of his chair as he moved himself closer to the desk, "how are you? I know a lot has been going on, and I apologize that we haven't been able to meet officially before now."

Aliyah felt a tinge of discomfort with the question. She had no idea how to respond. She was still at a loss regarding what exactly had triggered Deanna's vicious attack, and daily she battled the feeling of suffocating mortification every time she stepped into work. Since the incident, Aliyah had developed the habit of coming in at least thirty minutes early just to avoid the humiliation of withstanding the scrutinizing judgment and relentless whispers while she stood in line to swipe her badge.

"I'm okay, *alhamdulillah*," she said finally, deciding that was a safe response.

"That's good. That's good." Jacob nodded, but his expression suggested that his thoughts were elsewhere.

Aliyah's heart constricted, fearing that Dr. Warren had given Jacob the onerous task of telling her that her employment contract was being suspended prematurely. Yes, she was a full-time employee now, but she didn't have tenure. Aliyah imagined that allowing a non-employee a key to her office was serious enough grounds to let her go, especially since it had led to the school placing a restraining order against Deanna. Aliyah wouldn't be surprised if the president of the college himself had suggested firing her.

"Professor Thomas..." Jacob began. "No," he said, stopping himself as if self-rebuke. "Aliyah," he corrected, meeting her gaze pointedly. "I'm sorry for what happened here a couple of weeks ago, and I apologize for not apologizing sooner."

Aliyah furrowed her brows and shook her head. "It wasn't your fault. Deanna was probably upset because—"

"No," he interrupted, raising a palm to stop her. "It was my fault, and it *is* my fault."

"But Deanna is just—"

"Deanna is just my *wife*," he said. "So if she comes here and attacks anyone, *especially* you, it's my fault. There's no other way around it."

Aliyah started to say something but decided against it when she saw the serious look on Jacob's face.

"And I say especially you because there is a longstanding history of Deanna being upset that I ever wanted to marry you. And she's never forgiven me for talking to the college on your behalf." He frowned. "She remains convinced that you and I are planning to run off together and get married in secret."

Aliyah shook her head. "Is this because of that phone call you made?" Aliyah knew Jacob's phone call to her uncle had happened months after she was hired at the college, but Aliyah was beginning to wonder if Jacob had spoken his thoughts aloud before then.

Jacob shook his head. "No. This problem started twelve years ago when Deanna invited me to a campus dinner hosted by the MSA."

Aliyah nodded. "I remember that dinner. That was the night Deanna told me about Matt."

Jacob looked troubled by something, but he went on. "I didn't want to go to that dinner, but when I got there, I was glad I came. Even when I was a teenager, I had in my mind what I wanted in a wife. She would be educated and intelligent," I told myself, "yet humble and reserved." A shadow of sadness passed over his face. "But I'd begun to think she didn't exist."

Aliyah smiled in understanding as she recalled Deanna telling her something similar. Deanna had said that she had begun to think her soul mate didn't exist, but everything changed after talking to Jacob during the MSA dinner. *"Girl, with all the fireworks between us, we* had *to get married."* After all that had happened between Aliyah and Deanna, compounded by the stress that Jacob was under after the incident, it was comforting to hear Jacob allude to a softer, more romantic side of his relationship with Deanna.

"I know you're not interested in the entire backstory of my marriage," Jacob said apologetically, "but I've given this a lot of thought, and I think it's important for you to understand everything, especially since it has affected you directly."

Aliyah nodded. "It's okay. I appreciate the explanation."

"Well, when I got to the dinner," Jacob said, "I saw a woman leaning against a wall reading a book."

Aliyah looked at Jacob curiously. She didn't know that Deanna had been reading a book that night. Aliyah was usually the one who brought books everywhere while Deanna insisted that it was anti-social and rude to read while others were present.

"And my first thought was, *She's the one*," Jacob said. "I hadn't met her yet, and I didn't know her name. But when I looked at her, I saw my wife. *Educated and intelligent, yet humble and reserved*, I thought to myself. And all I did for the rest of the night was try to get closer to her so I could introduce myself. Even as I sat with Deanna in the hallway that night, all I could think about was the woman in the green hijab."

Aliyah averted her gaze as she got the odd sensation that this story wasn't going in the direction that she had expected.

"So I asked Deanna who the woman was, and she told me that she was her best friend Aliyah."

Aliyah narrowed her eyes in sudden understanding, recalling Larry alluding to Deanna being upset that Jacob had helped a woman he'd once wanted to marry. "So then…" Aliyah said, unable to give words to the question in her mind.

"I know this all might sound odd, especially since it happened so long ago," Jacob said. "But bear with me, and *insha'Allah*, you'll see how it's all connected to what's happening now."

Aliyah shook her head, forehead creased. "It's just... *SubhaanAllah*." She shook her head again. "I'm sorry. Go on."

"But when I asked about you, Deanna told me you were already engaged and that—"

"Engaged?" Aliyah said, taken aback.

"I know," Jacob said, a sad smile on his face as he shook his head. "I'm still trying to make sense of it all myself."

"But I don't get it. If you two had just met, why would she care what you thought of me?"

Jacob frowned thoughtfully. "Some people think of love as a finders-keepers territorial mission," he said. "In their world, not even the person they love has the right to refuse."

"But that is so…" Aliyah contorted her face as she searched for the right word. "…wrong."

"I agree," Jacob said. "But bear in mind that these are not conscious motives. My personal assessment of people of this mindset is that they're taught from young that humans are objects. Of course, they're not taught this outright, but the message is clear nonetheless."

"I read a book about that once," Aliyah said reflectively. "It was saying that unresolved trauma causes a lot of that."

Jacob nodded noncommittally. "That's possible."

Aliyah sensed that there was something about Deanna that Jacob was not saying, and she immediately grew concerned. Though her curiosity was piqued, she decided against speaking her thoughts aloud. She didn't want to put Jacob in the uncomfortable position of discussing more about his wife than he felt compelled to already. She imagined that this conversation alone was stressful and embarrassing for him.

"But Deanna didn't only say that you were engaged," Jacob said, returning to the backstory of his marriage. "For all intents and purposes she said that you were a helpless mental case who couldn't even tie your shoelaces without her support."

Aliyah's face twisted in offense. "*What*?"

"I know this is difficult to listen to," Jacob said, apology in his tone. "And trust me, it's difficult to tell. But I've given this a lot of thought, and I think it's only fair that you know what you're dealing with. If Deanna is physically attacking you for something that started twelve years ago, then most likely, this problem isn't going anywhere any time soon."

"What else did she say?" Aliyah's voice was tight in fury.

"That's the gist of it," Jacob said. "And I admit, I was a bit skeptical when she said it because it didn't match what I sensed from you. But I hadn't met you yet, and she'd known you for years. So I had no choice but to trust her judgment."

Aliyah rolled her eyes. "You had a choice," she said, surprised by her sudden frankness. "And I'm not talking about choosing Deanna over me because I didn't know you at that time." A voice in her head told her to calm down, but she was tired of keeping her feelings inside. Why did people feel that they could mistreat nice people, or let others do it on their behalf? "But you did *not* have to believe those lies about me. You didn't know Deanna either, so why did you believe her?"

"I'm sorry, Aliyah. I didn't mean—"

"Please, Jacob," Aliyah said, lifting her hand, "don't try to defend what you did. It was wrong. Yes, Deanna was wrong to slander me, but you were wrong to just sit there and soak it all in. And now you're saying you had no *choice* but to trust her?" Aliyah narrowed her eyes as she looked at Jacob. "Do you really believe that?

*"You have to teach people how to treat you,"* Aliyah's mother used to say whenever someone had bullied Aliyah and she chose to walk away. "*You keep on walking away and people will keep on bullying you.*" But Aliyah never understood that logic. No, Aliyah wasn't so naïve as to assume that she should *never* fight back. But she didn't understand the point of *always* fighting back. What was wrong

with avoiding confrontations? Every battle simply wasn't worth fighting. Besides, what was the point of fighting someone who was really battling their own ego and insecurity?

When Aliyah was in high school, classmates would constantly taunt her and pick fights, but Aliyah saw right through their twisted expressions, childish insults, and heartless bullying. When they called her conceited, they were really saying, *I see something admirable in you that I don't see in myself.* When they said she thought she was too good to hang out with them, they were really saying, *We'd love for you to join us and don't understand why you won't.* When they said she was "too nice," they were really saying, *It's frustrating that we can't find fault in you.* When they said she was a coward and a punk, they were really saying, *We hate that you won't stoop to our level and try to harm us like we harm you.*

On the rare occasions that Aliyah did speak up—for herself or someone else—she was called arrogant and judgmental. It seemed she could never win. Her silence was cowardice, and her fighting back was arrogance. Whenever she attended an event or visited someone's house, she'd hear later that something she said (or didn't say) was wrong, offensive, or self-righteous. It got to the point that social interactions, especially in large crowds, caused her so much stress and anxiety that she developed frequent headaches and heart palpitations at the thought of going anywhere. "*Focus on what* you're *supposed to be doing,*" her father used to say, so that's what Aliyah strove to do. But Aliyah had yet to develop a healthy coping strategy when she or someone else was slandered or wronged.

"I don't know what I believe anymore," Jacob said. "But looking back, perhaps I could have handled things differently."

"Perhaps?" Aliyah recoiled.

"Yes, perhaps," Jacob said firmly. "I don't fault you for being upset, and you have every right to be. But I'm not going to blame myself for assuming that a fellow Muslim was speaking truthfully, especially about her own best friend."

"You could have spoken up and stopped her."

"And you could have spoken up and stopped me from marrying her," he said defensively. "How can you expect me to see through Deanna after five minutes of talking to her when you couldn't even see through her after years of being her best friend?"

Aliyah didn't know what to say to that, but it was difficult to let go of her offense. It hurt that it was so easy to have your honor destroyed. Beyond the anxiety she battled in large gatherings, one reason Aliyah didn't socialize more was that many Muslims weren't too different from her high school classmates. They were constantly finding fault, assuming the worst, and rushing to pass judgment. If you didn't look like them, act like them, and think like them, then you enjoyed few (if any) rights of a fellow Muslim.

"But the purpose of this meeting is not to cast blame," Jacob said. "I can blame myself, and you can blame yourself. I can blame you, and you can blame me. But what good does that do? What's more important is that we're aware of the problem in front of us. I'm not even interested in blaming Deanna. Allah has recorded her deeds, and He has recorded ours. But the only deeds we're answering for are our own."

Jacob's words incited shame and regret in Aliyah, and she dropped her gaze to her folded hands.

"I asked to meet with you because, as Deanna's husband, I had the responsibility to protect and help her, and because I've failed in that, I was ill-equipped to protect and help you."

Aliyah frowned, her gaze thoughtful and distant.

"But, in a way, we're all to blame," Jacob said reflectively. "Muslim leadership, religious communities, and regular people like you and I. Whatever Deanna's issues are, they didn't happen overnight. Someone taught her that Islam solves all your problems, and that being strong and religious is mutually exclusive to feeling helpless and broken. Someone taught her that vulnerability is weakness, and that it's never okay to not be okay. And as long as *any* of us believes that, we have only one guarantee," Jacob said. "We'll *never* be okay."

***

*Whatever misfortune happens to you, is because of what your [own] hands have wrought. But He pardons [and forgives] much.*

This was the Qur'anic verse that came to mind as Deanna stood opposite her father Friday morning, her bundle of keys still in her hand after letting herself inside. Shortly before driving back to her parents' house, Deanna had given into the guilt gnawing at her conscience, and she'd forced herself to do at least *something* remotely spiritual. She had not prayed a single prayer in more than two weeks, so to quell her guilt, she decided to read something from the Qur'an. She had no idea if it was coincidence or a sign from God that she happened upon that verse, but she'd promptly closed the Qur'an, having had enough spiritual "inspiration" for one day.

"You know why this happened, right?" her father said, disappointment written on his face.

Deanna winced as she recalled waking up in the early hours of morning to find Jacob walking out of the master bathroom, his face and arms wet with the water of *wudhoo'*. The sight of him had been so unexpected that she almost screamed. She had thought he was still behind the house, perhaps tossing around a basketball or banging on the back door, or even sleeping on the pavement until she let him in. She had no idea how he had managed to get back inside. *Did he pick the lock?* she wondered. *If he did*, she thought, confounded, *the alarm system should have gone off.*

"No, I don't," Deanna said to her father, her voice clipped as she tried to control the annoyance she felt at his interrogation.

*"Then I divorce you."* Those were Jacob's first words after greeting Deanna with salaams and asking, for the umpteenth time, if she was willing to seek

arbitration or go to marriage counseling. *"We don't need marriage counseling,"* she'd retorted. *"You're the only one with a problem."*

"You know why this happened, right?" her father said again, as if daring her not to respond.

Deanna clamped her jaw closed in aggravation. She was thirty-six years old, but right then she felt like an eight-year-old child. Would her father ever treat her like a grown woman? During her youth, Deanna had admired her father's encompassing knowledge and unwavering strength. He knew *everything*, she used to muse. But now she had trouble maintaining a respectful countenance. She knew what he was hinting at, but she refused to take the bait.

"It's because you want to do things your way," he said, his voice rising. "I told you years ago not to get involved with those Muslims. But you didn't listen to me."

Deanna averted her gaze as if out of respect, but she was struggling to maintain her composure.

He shook his head knowingly, a troubled expression on his face. "But we love you," he said, his rough tone sounding odd with those words. "So you're always welcomed here."

Deanna nodded gratefully because that's what she was expected to do. But the truth was, she didn't need to be at her parents' home. She could return to her own house whenever she wanted. The school had a restraining order against her; her husband didn't. Jacob and Deanna were still married, despite Jacob's diarrhea of the mouth imagining that he could utter some religious incantation and suddenly end their lifetime commitment together. She had come home only because she needed time to herself and because she needed the company of people who loved and cared for her and because she needed to brainstorm on how to make Jacob regret that he'd ever uttered those words.

"But your mother and I are not going to repeat the mistakes we made when you were young," her father said. "We gave you far too much freedom, so now we're going to lay down some ground rules."

Internally, Deanna groaned.

"You're coming to church with us. *Every* Sunday," he added firmly. "And we're going to have some long talks about what it means to live an upright, God-fearing life."

"Dad," Deanna said, unable to keep quiet any longer, but she kept her voice controlled out of respect, "I already have a religion."

He snorted. "As we can all see."

Deanna knew that his sarcastic remark was in reference to the "crazy Muslim woman" saga that had only recently begun to die down, but she did not want to dignify his comment with a response.

"But what *we're* going to do," he said, "is remind you what real religion looks like, and that's at God's House of Worship."

Deanna's legs grew weak. It was at this church that her cousin Bailey had violated her when she was eight and he was eighteen. In her mind's eye, she saw

Bailey glaring at her in front of the pews. *"If you tell anybody about this,"* he'd said after he destroyed her innocence, *"I'll kill you."*

*"That girl is crazy,"* Deanna's father had said when she was thirteen and had written a letter detailing what Bailey did to her. *"There's no way anything like that happened to her. Bailey was a good kid. He wouldn't hurt anyone. And if it did happen, why did she wait so long to say anything? You saw how she was always walking around in those slutty clothes. The poor boy's been through so much, he probably thought she was seducing him."*

"Is that clear?" Deanna's father said pointedly, waiting for Deanna to meet his gaze.

Distracted by the anxiety she felt at going back to the church from which she'd sought escape for so long, Deanna shrugged in acquiescence, unable to find her voice.

*"When I get famous, I'm going to be Niecey Meesy..."* eight-year-old Deanna had said to her cousin after he'd said her stage name was stupid—and before he had morphed into the monster who attacked her. *"...and I won't even give you an autograph."*

Deanna's head snapped to the side, and she stumbled backward from the force of her father's slap. "Don't you *ever* shrug your shoulders at me," he said, his eyes menacing as he pointed a thick finger against her forehead. "When I address *you* with words, you address *me* with words. I. Am. Your. *Father*."

Deanna nodded dumbly. "I'm sorry, Dad," she said quickly. "I was just—"

"I don't care *what* you were *just* doing," he interrupted indignantly. "You speak to me like you know who I am. I brought you into this world, and I can take you out. Do you understand?"

"Yes, Dad," Deanna said, subdued, dropping her head in shame. "I'm sorry."

"You should be," he said, abruptly turning his back as he flipped his hand dismissively. "Now get out of my study."

***

"I think you both know why I asked you here," Dr. Warren said. She removed her reading glasses and set them on a manila folder on her desk. She leaned back in her chair and frowned thoughtfully. "Dr. Bivens, I have spoken to you at length about my concerns about any family coming to our offices during work hours, and you assured me that it's all under control. I hope this remains the case?"

"Yes, it does." Jacob spoke with humbled confidence from where he sat in the chair next to Aliyah opposite the department supervisor.

Dr. Warren looked toward Aliyah. "Professor Thomas, I'm confident that you are now fully aware of the serious repercussions of a non-employee holding a key to your office, even if the person is a close friend and family member of another employee."

Aliyah nodded. "Yes, and I apologize for that. It won't happen again."

*You did* not *have to believe those lies about me...You could have spoken up and stopped her.*

It was then that the realization came to Jacob. *Aliyah is right.* If nothing else, he could have challenged Deanna's perspective by offering a less incriminating perspective of his Muslim sister (even if he didn't know her).

*With Aliyah, everything is melodramatic. It's like she can't tie her shoelaces without my support. I swear, sometimes I feel like I'm stuck in a codependent relationship or something. It's so exhausting...I feel sorry for her fiancé.*

Was this unabashed character assassination what Jacob felt he'd had no choice but to believe? No one in his right mind would interpret those pernicious words as helpful information or sincere advice. Deanna hadn't even shared anything specific about Aliyah except that she had a "strained relationship" with her family. But even this neutral information Deanna managed to twist in the most defamatory way. *To me, that's just pathetic. If you can't find a way to have a good relationship with your own parents, then that says a lot about your Islam.*

*O Allah,* Jacob thought to himself. *How did I end up with someone like this as a wife?*

"However," Dr. Warren continued, "my reason for calling this meeting at a moment's notice is that it has just come to my attention that the incident that precipitated the trespass and assault two weeks ago was you two entering into a bigamous marital arrangement based on your religious customs."

Jacob sensed Aliyah's shock, but he willed himself to keep his gaze focused on Dr. Warren. Ten minutes before, he had divulged to Aliyah his conversation with Benjamin and Sayed on the Friday before Deanna's attack. *"I'd definitely marry Aliyah,"* Jacob had said that day. *"If she would have me. And now that it looks like it might not work out between her and Larry, I might start making some extra prayers. But my wife would kill me, so unless Aliyah agrees to be a secret second wife, I don't think I'll be so lucky."* By far, this had been the most self-incriminating part of his backstory, and he wished he didn't have to share it. But if he was going to be completely forthcoming, he had to share his part in what had happened, not only his wife's. *"But I was joking,"* he had assured Aliyah. *"It's something we brothers do all the time. I meant no disrespect, and I'm sorry you had to learn about it at all."*

"That is untrue," Jacob said to the department supervisor, voice firm. "But I take full responsibility for that misunderstanding. For some time, there have been a lot of misunderstandings regarding my relationship with Professor Thomas."

"Well," Dr. Warren said, "in either case, I want to be clear about something. As a general rule, I stay out of the private lives of the faculty and staff here. As you know, we have a strict policy against any romantic trysts within the same department, and especially between a tenured professor and a new employee, which we view as not too different from the romantic involvement of a professor with a student."

“We understand that.” As soon as he said it, Jacob sensed Aliyah cringing next to him. *You shouldn’t say “we,”* he mentally scolded himself. *It sounds like there’s something inappropriate going on.*

“Then let me be frank,” Dr. Warren said. “Our department, like most others at this institution, have for some time looked the other way when colleagues have carried out their romantic liaisons and extra marital affairs. This is because we don’t believe in policing the sexual lives of adults. In fact, as you know, Dr. Bivens,” she nodded toward Jacob, “as an atheist, I have strong opinions against mandated moral codes of any kind, especially those borrowed from religion. So I’m not a fan of our college’s intradepartmental policy against sexual relationships. However, I do understand the professional wisdom in establishing these codes.”

Dr. Warren leaned back in her seat, raising a forefinger to let Jacob and Aliyah know that she wasn’t finished. “But neither the school nor I can look the other way if any of these liaisons culminate into marriage, especially an illegal marriage. A state-recognized marriage itself would cast a wide net of suspicion on our entire department regarding what we allowed to go on here,” she said. “How much more the crime of bigamy?”

“I understand,” Jacob said, consciously leaving off the plural pronoun. “You don’t have to worry about that happening.”

“I hope you’re right,” Dr. Warren said, her eyes traveling between Jacob and Aliyah skeptically. “Because any evidence of a marriage taking place would be cause for the school to relieve you *both* of your positions, effective immediately. Despite your tenure,” she added, looking pointedly at Jacob. “So if you two ever do decide that you want to be more than mere colleagues, make sure that it doesn’t happen at work and that it doesn’t involve marriage.”

As Aliyah stood to leave, Jacob stepped toward Dr. Warren’s desk to ask her a question about the One Plus One mentorship program. It wasn’t an urgent or important question, but he wanted to allow Aliyah time to walk ahead of him to her office.

Minutes later, Jacob walked toward the lecture hall where he had scheduled a review session for a final exam, and his body was overcome with exhaustion. After Deanna locked him out of his house, he had waited several hours before attempting to come back inside. He didn’t want to arouse Deanna’s suspicions and risk her discovering that he kept a copy of the house key hidden away outside. Years ago, Deanna had locked him out of the house while he was taking out the garbage and wearing only a bathrobe. He’d rung the doorbell and banged on the door repeatedly while she haughtily ignored him and climbed into bed and slept for half the day.

Jacob clenched his teeth and shook his head, indignant. *This is no way to live.*

Even if Deanna agreed to arbitration or marriage counseling, could *he* continue to live with her?

## 13
## Reality Check

"Well, if you do accept his proposal, just know—"

"There is *no* proposal," Aliyah said irritably as she looked out the passenger window of Reem's car, her elbow propped on the seal.

"—that you won't be getting much community support," Reem finished.

"That's shocking," Aliyah said sarcastically. "You know, given the outpouring of support I received after my divorce."

The sound of snickering prompted Aliyah to turn her head, and she saw Reem's eyes narrowed humorously through the wide slit of her black face veil. A confused grin formed on one side of Aliyah's mouth. "What's so funny?"

"You," Reem said, nodding her head in Aliyah's direction. "Your sarcasm is killing me."

Aliyah shrugged, a grin still on her face. "A bitter sense of humor is therapeutic, believe it or not."

"Oh, trust me, I believe it," Reem said. "It's just funny, that's all."

"Well," Aliyah said, "I'm glad I make *someone* smile."

Reem was silent momentarily. "Don't say that," she said.

"I didn't mean it as self-pity," Aliyah said. "I'm really glad I have that effect on at least one person in the world."

"You make a lot of people smile."

"Now it's *my* turn to laugh."

"Why do you beat yourself up like that?" Reem said, concern in her tone as she glanced at Aliyah before turning her attention back to the road.

"I don't beat myself up," Aliyah said. "I'm just realistic."

"That's not realistic," Reem said. "It's cynical."

"Two sides of the same coin," Aliyah said, humor in her tone.

"I'm serious. You can't keep seeing the glass as half empty every time you think of yourself."

Aliyah shrugged. "I just haven't been feeling very optimistic lately."

"That's understandable. You've been through a lot," Reem said reflectively. "I don't know how you stay so strong, *mashaAllah, barakAllahufeek*."

"Strong?" Aliyah repeated, humored disbelief in her tone.

"Yes," Reem said firmly. "But everyone has a limit, and I think you're reaching yours."

Aliyah glanced out the passenger window again. *Is it* that *obvious?* she thought sadly.

"That's why you need to know what you're up against if you accept Jacob's pro—, I mean," Reem corrected, "if you ever marry Jacob."

"Like I said, there's no offer of marriage," Aliyah said, still looking out the window. "But if something like that did ever happen, don't worry, I'm aware of how Muslims treat their brothers and sisters who choose something they wouldn't." She snorted. "I got a crash course from Deanna."

"That doesn't bother you?"

"What?" Aliyah said, eyebrows furrowed as she turned to Reem. "That my best friend was stabbing me in the back for over ten years?"

"No." Reem shook her head. "That you have no support system if you get married."

Aliyah shrugged. "I never really thought about it, to be honest. I'm so used to hearing Muslims bash polygamy, I kind of drown it out. I wouldn't *dream* of them supporting me if I were in it." She grunted laughter. "I'd count it as a miracle if they touched my feet and shoulders when I lined up next to them in *Salaah*."

Reem chuckled. "Seriously?"

"Maybe not the prayer part," Aliyah said, a trace of humor in her voice. "But I wouldn't expect their support. At this point, I'm not sure I'd want it."

"Why not?" Reem sounded genuinely surprised.

Aliyah sighed, her eyes growing distant momentarily. "It's nice to have support, of course. But it's exhausting expecting good from people. It's so much easier to only expect good from Allah."

"But Allah created us as an *ummah* for a reason. We need each other. That's part of the good He's given us on earth."

"But I can't create an *ummah* by myself, Reem. If Muslims are going to ostracize me because my marriage looks different from theirs, what can I do about it? The way I see it, those aren't people I want in my life anyway. What if I start thinking like them? I don't want to view right and wrong through the lens of my personal insecurities. Allah can give His blessings to whomever He wants, however He wants, and I don't have a say in that, especially in someone else's life."

"*Astaghfirullah*," Reem said, her tone regretful. "May Allah forgive us. We're so arrogant and ungrateful."

"That, we are," Aliyah said pensively. "So, nope, I'm not expecting support from anyone for anything I do. After my family disowned me when I became Muslim, Deanna was the closest thing to a family I had." She rolled her eyes. "And you saw what happened with that."

"Your family *disowned* you?" Reem's voice was high-pitched in shock, her wide eyes going from the road to Aliyah then back to the road.

*Oh.* Aliyah had forgotten that she hadn't shared that information with her Qur'an teacher. "Yes, unfortunately," she said, surprised by the calmness of her voice. "They won't accept my calls, they won't let me visit, and they returned all the mail I sent them."

"*Laa hawla wa laa quwwata illaa billaah*," Reem uttered in dismay. *There is no movement or power except with God.*

"Don't sound so shocked," Aliyah said, embarrassed laughter in her voice. "I'm used to it. Life goes on."

"*Laa ilaaha illaAllah,*" Reem said, still in shock. "How can you survive without your family?"

Aliyah drew in a deep breath and exhaled. "I don't have a choice, that's how."

"*SubhaanAllah,*" Reem said as she guided the car into the parking lot outside the athletic complex. "I can't imagine how strong you have to be to deal with that. May Allah reward you with the highest level of Paradise."

"And you too, Reem," Aliyah said sincerely.

"But do me a favor," Aliyah said as Reem put the car in park and removed her keys from the ignition. "Can you stop talking to me about Jacob? I don't like it."

"I'm sorry," Reem said. "It's just that I'm worried about what would happen if you marry him."

Aliyah rolled her eyes as she unfastened her seat belt. "That's not going to happen, *insha'Allah.* I never want to put anyone through what Nikki put me through."

"I doubt Nikki was trying to break up your marriage."

"Whether she was trying to or not," Aliyah said, "she did."

Reem was quiet as she unfastened her seat belt and opened the driver side door. "You shouldn't say that," she muttered before she stepped out the car, Aliyah following suit. "Things happen, and they're not always anybody's fault."

"She could've told me that she was Matt's ex-girlfriend," Aliyah said after they closed their doors.

"Isn't that how you found out?" Reem pressed the button on her keychain to lock the car.

"Yes, but that was after I already let her into my life."

"You taught her about Islam," Reem said as they walked toward the building. "If that's the only good that came out of it, then that's a huge blessing, *mashaAllah.*"

Aliyah sighed. "That's true. It's just hard to see it that way. Right now, I can barely stand the thought of marriage, after what I went through."

"May Allah make it easy for you. I can only imagine. I hope you find someone that makes you happy."

"No, no, no," Aliyah said, shaking her head emphatically. "That is *not* something I hope for."

Reem's eyes widened, turning to Aliyah as they neared the front entrance. "Why not? Don't you want to be happy?"

"Yes," Aliyah said. "But not because of a man. What if I never get married again? I think I can still be happy."

Reem chuckled and shook her head. "You Americans."

"What?" Aliyah said, chuckling herself. "It's true. I don't need a man to be happy."

"We need companionship in this world," Reem said. "Allah didn't create us to live alone. That's why we have friends, neighbors, and family. Maybe it's not the only thing that makes us happy, but it's an important part of it."

Aliyah shrugged. "Important, maybe, but not essential."

***

*Jumu'ah*, the epiphany came to Jacob as he watched his sons run up and down the indoor basketball court taking turns dribbling a ball along with about fifteen other boys. About ten feet from Jacob stood Matthew, arms folded over his chest, eyes concentrating on Ibrahim. Next to Matthew was a woman dressed in wide-legged jeans, a long-sleeved T-shirt and hijab. Jacob assumed she must be Matt's new wife. *She seems nice*, Jacob found himself thinking after he greeted Matt with a perfunctory wave and salaams.

*How did I end up with someone like Deanna as a wife?* This question had haunted Jacob for the past month. It was only recently that he began to notice how strikingly different other Muslim women were from his wife. Their humble mannerisms, their easy smiles, the comfortable banter between them and their husbands. For years, these were interactions Jacob had associated with putting on a front. "We have to show people what a *real* relationship looks like," Deanna would often say, and Jacob had agreed.

Now, he wasn't so sure.

But it was difficult to extricate himself from this mentality because this was how he had been taught to think about Islam itself. Somehow the requirement to call others to worship God alone had turned into a marketing campaign that was more about optics than obligation. Personal struggles were unaddressed or outright denied if it meant risking presenting a "negative image" of Islam—and supporting open sin or wrongdoing was preferable to religious obligation if it meant presenting a "positive image" of Islam.

But Jacob was growing exhausted from living a life rooted in optics. Though it had been difficult for him to admit, part of the reason he felt stuck in his marriage was fear of looking bad in front of other Muslims—and fear of making Islam look bad. If he, the husband of a marriage guru and a source of marital inspiration himself, couldn't stay married, what did that suggest about his faith? It was his religious duty to stay married, he'd kept telling himself. If not for himself, then for his sons and other Muslims. "People look up to you," Jacob was often told, as if that alone laid in front of him the obvious course of action he should take when making a decision.

*O Allah, if You know this matter to be good for me regarding my religion, my life, and my welfare in the life to come; then ordain it for me, make it easy for me, and bless me in it...*

After praying the *Istikhaarah* prayer about whether or not to divorce Deanna, this was the part of the supplication that stayed with him. Up until a month ago, it had never occurred to Jacob to consider whether or not his marital decisions were about protecting his faith and soul. Everything had been about only one aspect of that prayer—his worldly life.

*Optics over obligation.*

During his doctorate studies, Jacob had been neglectful of *Jumu'ah*, the obligatory weekly congregational sermon and prayer, because he didn't feel comfortable being associated with most Muslims. At the time, not only did he have self-righteous convictions about religious-based clubs, he also had self-righteous convictions about religious-based gatherings. He would occasionally agree to speak at Muslim Student Association events because he felt he owed that to other Muslims, but he wouldn't participate in the MSA otherwise. Unfortunately, his attendance to the Friday prayer had been approached similarly. It was as if his occasional attendance was some sort of favor he owed to Islam and the Muslims.

*"You can't pick and choose how you worship Allah,"* a young undergrad student had said to Jacob. The way the student's voice was a mixture of concern and admonition had annoyed Jacob. *Who does he think he is?* Jacob had thought at the time. *I don't need a masjid to worship my Lord.*

How did he end up with someone like Deanna as a wife? Because at the time he married her, she was a reflection of Jacob himself. He'd arrogantly neglected the rights of Allah when it suited him, and she arrogantly neglected the rights of His servants when it suited her.

***

"Aunty! Aunty!" Younus eagerly waved with one hand while bouncing a basketball with the other. The shouts of his brother prompted Thawab to look toward the sidelines, and when he saw Aliyah, Thawab grinned shyly and waved too. At the sight of them, Aliyah grinned and lifted a hand in a wave, but she cringed at the prospect of seeing Deanna at the athletic complex. She quickly scanned the faces of the adults and exhaled in relief when she saw Jacob standing alone near Matt and Nikki.

"Mommy!" Ibrahim dropped his basketball and ran toward his mother, prompting one of the volunteers to rush on the court and grab the rolling ball before it obstructed the movement of the other boys.

Aliyah spread her arms wide and kneeled as Ibrahim met her with an enthusiastic embrace. "*As-salaamu'alaikum*, cookie monster," she said, brushing the top of his head with a kiss.

"Did you see me, Mommy?" Ibrahim said, breathless. "I was bouncing the ball and running fast!"

"Yes, I did see you," Aliyah said, still holding him close. "And I want to see more," she added as her gaze met that of the coach who was nodding his head in her direction as he held Ibrahim's basketball. "So you better go back out there." Ibrahim released Aliyah and rushed back to the court. A smile lingered on Aliyah's face as she watched him.

"That looks tough," Reem said good-naturedly after Ibrahim resumed running the length of the court, bouncing the ball at the same time.

"Have you ever played basketball before?" Aliyah asked.

"No," Reem said, shaking her head. "But I've shot around a few times. I prefer football, personally."

Aliyah's eyes widened. "Football?"

"Soccer, I mean," Reem said.

"Oh yeah," Aliyah said. "I forgot the rest of the world calls that football."

"*As-salaamu'alikum.*"

At the sound of someone behind her, Aliyah turned and found Nikki smiling at her.

"*Wa'alaiku-mus-salaam,*" Aliyah said, embracing Nikki briefly.

"Thanks for meeting us here," Nikki said. "Matt really wanted to take Ibrahim to his first basketball practice."

"It's no problem," Aliyah said sincerely. "I understand."

After Nikki defended her online, Aliyah's heart had softened to Matt and Nikki. Though Aliyah preferred to spend as much time with Ibrahim as possible, Aliyah didn't put up a fuss when Nikki asked if Aliyah could pick up Ibrahim from the athletic center Saturday morning. "You can drop by during the week any time," Nikki had added. "I don't mind. Matt works late most nights, so I could use the company, and I'm sure Ibrahim would be thrilled to see you." Aliyah had thanked Nikki and said, "I just might take you up on that."

"Anyway," Aliyah added with a grin, nodding her head toward her Qur'an teacher, "Reem wants to give me some tennis lessons."

"*As-salaamu'alaikum,*" Reem said, leaning forward and extending a gloved hand to greet Nikki.

"*Wa'alaiku-mus-salaam,*" Nikki said, a curious smile forming on her face as she shook Reem's hand. "You play tennis?"

"Yes, a bit," Reem said, releasing Nikki's hand. "I used to want to play professionally."

"Really?" Nikki sounded surprised.

"But I gave up that dream," Reem said humorously. "I'm not sure the world is ready for a *niqaabi* tennis champion."

Nikki chuckled and shook her head. "But that would be something, wouldn't it? Having a fully covered Muslim woman competing in professional tennis matches?"

"I would *love* that," Reem said, awe in her voice. "But it's not realistic."

"It is if you want it to be," Nikki said encouragingly.

Reem laughed. "*Insha'Allah.*"

"I think we left our rackets and balls in the car," Aliyah said, remembering just then.

"*SubhaanAllah.* I'll go get them." Reem swiftly turned and walked toward the exit.

"I admire women like that," Nikki said, her eyes following Reem. "Whenever I wear hijab, I feel like people are staring at me. I can't imagine how it feels to wear a face veil."

"I know what you mean," Aliyah said. "It took a long time for me to feel comfortable in hijab, and I still feel judged, especially at work. I definitely don't think *niqaab* is for me."

"Matt was saying that some scholars say it's obligatory."

Aliyah shrugged. "That's what Reem believes, but I don't agree with that."

Nikki nodded thoughtfully. "Does she have children?"

Aliyah furrowed her brows. "Reem?"

"Yes."

"Two. A boy and a girl."

"How old are they?"

"They're a year younger than Ibrahim."

"Both of them?"

"They're twins," Aliyah said.

"Four-year-old twins?" Nikki sucked in her breath. "That must be a handful."

"Her mother helps out a lot. She usually keeps them whenever Reem goes out."

"It must be nice to have help."

The sad reflection in Nikki's voice prompted Aliyah to glance down at Nikki's shirt. A knowing smile spread on Aliyah's face. "Are you pregnant?"

Nikki averted her gaze as an embarrassed grin toyed at one side of her mouth. She glanced cautiously behind her then lowered her voice. "Ten weeks. But Matt doesn't want anyone to know."

"*MashaAllah*," Aliyah said in congratulations. "This is your first, right?"

"Yes."

"How are you doing?"

"It's hard," Nikki said reflectively, exhaling her words. "I feel sick most days. I almost didn't come out today."

"How's your appetite?"

"I can't eat anything except white bread and potato chips." Nikki frowned. "It's a horrible diet, but I have to eat something."

"Just keep up with your prenatal vitamins, and you should be fine *insha'Allah*."

"I gag every time I take them, so it's a chore getting th—"

*"Isn't that that crazy Muslim chick?"*

Aliyah stiffened as she heard the loud whisper coming from a small crowd gathered near the court. She willed herself not to look in that direction.

*"Looks like it,"* another voice said. *"Or that whore mistress."*

*"Isn't it funny how they cover up like that? Like their stuff is all holy, but they get around like everybody else."*

Laughter. "*I bet they're—*"

"Are you here for a purpose, or just to harass people?" It took a few seconds before Aliyah registered that it was Nikki who was speaking, her face contorted as she looked toward the crowd. "Yes, I'm talking to you. I heard what you said about Muslim women, and I think it's ignorant and immature."

Aliyah glanced uncomfortably toward the small crowd then back at Nikki. "It's okay," Aliyah whispered, panic choking her as she placed a hand on Nikki's arm. "Just ignore them," Aliyah said.

"Is everything okay?" Matt said, appearing at Nikki's side suddenly, concern on his face as he looked at his wife.

"Everything's fine," Aliyah said quickly. "They were just—"

"No, it's *not* fine," Nikki said, glaring toward the crowd before rolling her eyes and turning away. "I'm sick of people's disrespect."

"What happened?" Matt said as he put his arm around Nikki's shoulders and led her away.

"These people were sitting there saying…" Nikki's voice faded as she walked with Matt toward the other side of the gym.

Cheeks aflame, Aliyah turned her back to the crowd and concentrated her attention on the boys on the basketball court, but it was difficult to stay focused. *Couldn't he at least give salaams?* Aliyah thought, offense stinging her. Here she was, coming to pick up *their* son—a day later on *his* request, and Matt was acting like she wasn't even standing there. Was it "inappropriate" to greet his son's mother?

"Sorry about that," Reem said, appearing at Aliyah's side, the straps of two tennis racket cases over her shoulder and a can of tennis balls in her hand.

*"I don't give a f—"* someone behind them said, and Aliyah winced at the profanity. *"She had no business talking to us like that. We weren't even talking to her."* Overcome with angry annoyance, Aliyah clenched her jaw, but she refused to turn around and give them the satisfaction of her acknowledgement.

Reem glanced curiously behind her. "What's their problem?"

"Who knows?" Aliyah shrugged nonchalantly and rolled her eyes, still facing forward. "You ready to play tennis?"

"My sister and my cousin are supposed to be coming too," Reem said as she handed Aliyah a tennis racket then readjusted the strap of her racket case on her shoulder.

"Are there enough courts?" Aliyah said, adjusting the strap on her shoulder.

"If there aren't," Reem said, "we can just play doubles."

Reem did a double take and nodded her head to the right. "Isn't that Jacob?"

Aliyah glanced hesitantly in Jacob's direction and found him still looking toward the court. "Yes. Younus and Thawab are part of the summer basketball league."

"*MashaAllah*," Reem said. "I saw them waving at you earlier."

The distant sound of rhythmic drumming interrupted Aliyah before she could respond, and Reem reached into an abaya pocket and withdrew her mobile phone.

"*Waynak?*" Reem said as she put the phone to her ear. "*Tayyib*."

Reem put the phone back in her pocket then gestured toward Aliyah as she walked toward the exit. "They're at the tennis courts waiting for us."

***

"Reem!"

Aliyah looked around to see where the voice was coming from, and two tennis courts down, she saw a woman dressed in shorts and a tank top waving her arm toward them as she held a tennis ball in her fist and a tennis racket in her other hand. Opposite the woman was another woman dressed similarly. Confused, Aliyah glanced toward Reem, who waved in response and started walking in the direction of the two women.

"Mashael, this is my friend Aliyah," Reem said once they were at the court and the women stood opposite them. "Aliyah, this is my sister Mashael and my cousin Nora."

"*As-salaamu'alaikum*," Aliyah said, reaching out her hand to greet the two women one after the other. Each leaned forward to touch cheeks with Aliyah as they shook her hand.

"*Wa'alaiku-mus-salaam*," Mashael and Nora said, both smiling widely. Up close, Aliyah could see the resemblance between Reem and her sister, and their cousin shared a similar olive complexion.

"My sister says you don't know how to play tennis," Mashael said, teasing Aliyah good-naturedly.

Aliyah laughed self-consciously and nodded. "It's true," she said. "But I'm hoping to learn."

"Reem's the tennis champ in our family, *mashaAllah*," Mashael said. "But we play okay."

"They play well too, *mashaAllah*," Reem said.

"Will you play in your *niqaab*?" Aliyah hadn't meant to speak her thoughts aloud, so she was relieved to see Reem smiling with her eyes in response.

"I know," Reem said, laughter in her voice. "It's a bit much, right?"

"Yes it is," Nora teased in lighthearted banter. "We're always telling her she's going to give people a heart attack dressed like that."

"I haven't had any problems, *alhamdulillah*," Reem said honestly. "As long as I have my ID, people are pretty accommodating."

Nora and Mashael shook their heads, knowing smiles on their faces. "I don't know how you do it," Nora said.

"You're American?" Mashael said, looking at Aliyah curiously.

"Yes," Aliyah said, finding the question awkward.

"I mean, originally?" Mashael clarified.

"Yes," Aliyah said.

"*MashaAllah*, so you converted?"

"Yes, *alhamdulillah*."

"*Wallah*," Mashael said, swearing by Allah, "you guys are much better Muslims than we are."

Nora nodded emphatically. "*Wallah*, it's true."

Aliyah frowned in discomfort. "I don't think so. We all have our challenges."

“Are we going to play tennis or what?” Reem said as she unzipped the racket case and pulled out her racket. “Or are you guys going to stand here chatting the whole time?”

***

Aliyah was tired and a bit agitated by the time Reem dropped off her and Ibrahim to the apartment that afternoon. Upon Reem’s urging, Aliyah had accepted a last-minute invitation to have lunch with Reem’s family. The visit was pleasant enough, so Aliyah knew her agitation wasn’t connected to the visit. Eating lunch at Reem’s house had actually been a blessing because now Aliyah didn’t have to prepare lunch for herself or Ibrahim. And with the extra plates Reem had made for them, Aliyah probably wouldn’t even have to prepare dinner.

Perhaps her annoyance was due to having been out all day without her car, Aliyah considered. She had agreed to ride with Reem only because she’d assumed she and Ibrahim would come home right after basketball practice.

*“Is everything okay?”*

As Aliyah put the plates of food in the refrigerator, in her mind’s eye, she saw Matt’s concerned expression a moment before he put an arm around Nikki. Aliyah gritted her teeth in offense.

“Can Younus and Thawab come over?” Ibrahim said, his small voice coming from behind her.

“No,” Aliyah snapped without turning around.

A moment later, Aliyah sighed, feeling bad for getting upset with her son. She closed the refrigerator and turned around, forcing a smile as she met Ibrahim’s confused gaze. “I’m sorry, Himy,” she said, using the affectionate abbreviated form of her son’s name. “Now isn’t a good time for Younus and Thawab to come over.”

“But they asked if they could,” Ibrahim whined.

“They’re welcome to come over another time,” Aliyah said sincerely. “But not now.”

“Then can I go over their house?”

Aliyah drew in a deep breath and exhaled. She wished there was some way to arrange a play date for the boys. “For now, you’ll see them every Saturday for basketball, *insha’Allah.*”

Ibrahim pouted. “But we can’t play the Wii there.”

“I know, Himy, and I’m sorry.” Aliyah’s heart ached as she watched her son walk out of the kitchen, shoulders slumped.

*Nobody cares about you.*

The realization came to Aliyah so suddenly that it was like a knife in her chest. Winded, Aliyah pulled out a chair and sat down, propping her elbows on the table as she held her forehead in her palms.

That was why she was so agitated. It wasn't that Matt should have given her salaams or asked if she was okay. It was that his ignoring her highlighted how insignificant—and alone—she actually was.

To her family, as long as Islam was part of her life, she wasn't part of theirs. To the Muslims, she simply wasn't part of their lives. As a single divorced woman, on a practical level, she was no one's responsibility. But on a theoretical level, she was everyone's responsibility.

*Men are the maintainers and protectors of women,* the Qur'an said.

But Aliyah was still grappling with what that verse was supposed to mean in *her* life. Was it in reference to only marriage? Or did it apply to other contexts? And had her belief in the latter incited offense that Matt had completely ignored her?

Aliyah sat up and folded her arms on the table in front of her as she gazed thoughtfully toward the floral centerpiece.

*Nobody cares about you.*

This time the realization was not as painful. It came to her as more matter-of-fact, more resolute. This was nothing to sulk about. It was merely something to keep in mind. She was in this world alone, and she'd have to learn to survive alone. As difficult as it was to accept, the united, loving *ummah* that she'd learned about in her Islamic classes was almost mythical in modern reality. There was no Muslim community looking out for her. There was no band of Muslim men (or women) rushing to her aid or making sure she was okay. They simply didn't care.

*Well, if you do accept his proposal, just know that you won't be getting much community support.*

Reem was right to warn Aliyah about the reality in which she lived. Reem herself faced that grim reality in her own life. Reem put her heart into teaching Qur'an to the community only to read Facebook statuses attacking her for doing just that. She dressed in the manner that she believed Allah instructed only to be constantly challenged and criticized because Muslims felt it was extreme. She tried hard to separate her culture from religion only to be accused of teaching an "Arab version" of Islam. How Reem, in the face of all that, kept coming back to the community day after day, Aliyah couldn't fathom. Aliyah herself was finding it difficult to even enter the masjid these days. Part of Aliyah had died after seeing how eagerly Muslims participated in online discussions tarnishing her name and honor.

But Reem had a husband and family who cared for her. Aliyah didn't. And that support system must certainly be a source of strength.

But who was Aliyah's source of strength?

*"Girl, you know I love you!"*

Sadness knotted in Aliyah's chest as she recalled Deanna's oft-repeated statement of affection.

*God, I miss her sometimes,* Aliyah thought sadly. Moments like these, she wondered if she'd made the right decision cutting off Deanna as a friend.

***

Deanna grunted as she pulled her car into the parking lot in front of Cassie Studios Saturday morning. *What happened to all that peace and love, and tolerance and reconciliation that Aliyah was always running off at the mouth about from her Islamic studies classes?* Deanna thought bitterly. *Good Muslims do not refuse to speak to each other for more than three days, so always seek reconciliation and make peace between people.* Aliyah was the one constantly mentioning that hadith. Deanna wasn't sure if she was remembering the wording correctly, but even if the wording of the prophetic statement was off, the principle remained. Aliyah was wrong. It was sinful for her to cut off their friendship and refuse to interact with Deanna.

Not that Deanna cared if they remained friends.

"It's okay if you miss your best friend," Deanna's mother had told her. "Losing a friend can make anybody upset." But Deanna had contorted her face. "*Miss* her? I'm just mad I didn't cut her off first."

Apparently, all that talk about "love for the sake of Allah" was just a front for Aliyah. It was a ploy to get Deanna to trust her, pamper her, pay her bills, and allow her to get close to Jacob. *How could I have been so blind?*

*Stop complaining,* Deanna thought in self-rebuke, abruptly halting her mental tirade as she brought her car to a stop in a parking space near the studio entrance. *I'm the better person in this situation*, she told herself. So she needed to act like it. She recalled the inspirational quote that her husband kept on his office wall. *Be the change. Stop bickering. Be the bigger person. Stop criticizing. Be the better person. Stop settling for less than the best. Be YOU.*

Empowered by these words, Deanna turned off the car and pulled the keys from the ignition before removing her designer shades and checking her appearance in the rearview mirror. A thin floral scarf hung loosely around her head and adorned the long, soft brown curls that framed her face. There was a flutter of concern as she realized that she hadn't shown her hair in public in more than ten years, but she quelled the discomfort by reminding herself that this was for a good cause. Besides, she was still wearing hijab, she rationalized, even if it didn't cover *all* of her hair. Something was better than nothing. She'd worry later about what to do during the photo shoot because she needed the photographer's input on that one.

But first she needed to explain to Cassie her purpose for making the appointment.

"May I help you?" the receptionist asked after the bells above the entrance chimed as Deanna stepped inside.

"Yes, you may." Deanna's mouth spread into a full-teeth smile as she walked toward the receptionist's desk. She pulled her large handbag over her shoulder and adjusted the straps. "I'd like to speak to Cassie Thomas-Daniels please."

The woman lifted an arched eyebrow as her eyes traced Deanna in a quick once-over. "You have to make a special appointment to speak to the owner."

"I have an appointment," Deanna said, maintaining her wide smile. "Cassie and I spoke on the phone last week."

"Your name?"

"Dr. Deanna Janice Bivens."

The woman's eyebrows rose in recognition. "You're the author of *You Can Have Him All To Yourself*?"

Deanna lifted her head in pride. "Yes, I am."

The woman nodded, the shadow of a smile on her face as she typed something into the laptop on the desk in front of her. "One moment please," she said before standing and walking down a hallway toward the back. "I'll tell Cassie you're here."

"Dr. D.J. Bivens," Cassie said once they were in her office. "It's an honor to meet you."

Deanna pursed her lips proudly as she sat down opposite Cassie's desk. "Thank you." She couldn't bring herself to say more than that because she didn't want to waste too much time on small talk. She reached into her purse and pulled out her smart phone, holding it in the air. "Do you mind if I record our meeting? I don't want to interrupt our conversation by writing notes."

A frown line creased Cassie's forehead, and in that moment Deanna was reminded of Aliyah. Cassie and her younger sister resembled each other significantly. Cassie had a thicker, fuller figure, but she shared Aliyah's smooth skin tone and sculpted facial features. Like Aliyah, Cassie kept her kinky curls natural and well kempt though Cassie had dyed hers brown. A flash of anger swept through Deanna as she thought of Jacob admiring this beauty. She had to stop Aliyah's madness, fast.

"I prefer not," Cassie said apologetically. "But I can make an audio file myself and send you the transcript," she offered.

"No problem," Deanna said, forcing a smile to hide her annoyance that even Cassie's voice intonations were similar to Aliyah's. She put the phone back into her purse.

After starting the audio file, Cassie said, "You mentioned on the phone that you wanted to do a special photo shoot for your marriage counseling business?"

"Yes," Deanna said tentatively. "But I want something more than that, mainly to counter the 'crazy Muslim woman' story."

"Well, that story is no longer trending, so I'm not sure if you'll be able to use your photos for that purpose."

"I don't plan to use them for that," Deanna said.

Cassie creased her forehead. "I'm sorry. I must have misunderstood. Tell me what you have in mind again."

"I want *you* to use them," Deanna said.

"Me?" Cassie furrowed her eyebrows in confusion.

"Your company provided the photos of Aliyah, right?"

"Aliyah?"

"Ally, your sister."

"Yes..." she said tentatively, her expression conveying skepticism.

"Now I want you to provide photos of me."

"I'm sorry. I think there's been a misunderstanding," Cassie said. "Cassie Studios doesn't work with the media. We do only photography."

"But you have contacts, don't you?" Deanna was on the verge of irritation. She had driven nearly two hours for this meeting.

"Yes, but—"

"Don't you want to make money?"

Cassie paused thoughtfully. "What do you mean?

Deanna smirked as she saw that she had Cassie's attention. "You and I have something in common, Cassie," Deanna said. "Ally has caused far too many problems in our lives."

Cassie glanced cautiously toward the audio recording. "I wouldn't say that."

Deanna waved her hand dismissively. "I know you don't want to admit it, and that's okay. But I'm here to offer you an opportunity to make money. A lot of money," she added. "I want to do a photo essay of the truth behind the 'crazy Muslim woman' story."

"You mean a visual memoir?"

"Yes, but one that puts Ally in her place."

Cassie shook her head, eyes narrowed in confusion. "Excuse me?"

"Ally needs a reality check." Deanna grunted. "And my husband does too."

"I'll tell you what I can do," Cassie said after a thoughtful pause. "You and I can create the photo essay. Then I'll share it with some of my media contacts. Depending on the angle we take, we might be able to spark renewed interest in the story."

"I already know my angle."

"What's that?"

"She's the crazy mistress. I'm the hot wife."

Cassie creased her forehead doubtfully. "Was Ally really your husband's mistress?"

"No, of course not," Deanna said, contorting her face. "I'd kill her if she was."

Cassie drew in a deep breath and exhaled. "I like your angle, but you don't want to expose yourself to a possible libel suit."

"Let me worry about that," Deanna said. "But for now, I need your advice on the best way to do the photo shoot."

"Visually speaking," Cassie said, "what is your overall goal for the shoot?"

"The same one that Ally had."

Cassie shook her head, confused. "I don't understand."

"To get my husband's attention," Deanna said. "And I want to do the same."

# 14
# Attractive Women Can't Be Broken

"All right," Aliyah said into the portable microphone as she lifted a hand to get the attention of the thirty youth gathered in the center of the conference room. The other One Plus One mentors stood staggered along the walls, observing Aliyah's group activity. Each mentor had been assigned the task of planning and facilitating an educational group activity for the "fun session" held every Friday morning for the duration of the internship program, and today the tables and chairs had been removed so that there was maximum range of motion for the activity. "Each of you should be holding a card in your hand," Aliyah continued. "It will say LAN 1, LAN 2, or LAN 3. Raise your hand if you do *not* have a card."

Aliyah surveyed the room then lowered her hand and pointed toward the flat carpet. "Okay, now look at the masking tape markings on the floor. Anyone who has a LAN 1 card should go to the area marked as number one. LAN 2 cards go to area two, and LAN 3 cards to area three." The interns surveyed the floor and moved themselves accordingly. A hint of a smile was on Aliyah's face as she saw them comparing cards to see who would be their group partners. She always found it heartwarming to see youth interacting with each other during group activities.

"On the back of each card are words, numbers, diagrams, or graphs," she said after the interns were in groups of ten. "Some are followed by a mathematical symbol. In each LAN group, nine members are holding a part of a single mathematical problem, and one member is holding the answer. For this activity, you will take the role of either a switch or a router. Your first task is to figure out who is who. If you are holding part of the problem, you are one of the switches in your group. If you are holding the answer, you are the router in your group." The interns began to read their cards and glance at the card of the person next to them.

"The first group to arrange themselves in proper mathematical order earns ten points," Aliyah said, gesturing a hand toward the scoring chart on the large dry erase board. Immediately, the students began reading their cards and asking to see the group members' cards. "You have five minutes, starting…*now*." The noise level in the room immediately rose as the students mingled and shuffled around as they tried to figure out their mathematical problems.

"Mentors," Aliyah said into the microphone as her eyes scanned the walls where her colleagues and superiors stood, "you are permitted to help the interns, but only in understanding their cards. You *cannot* give them the answer or tell them which group member comes before or after them."

The mentors nodded gratefully and walked toward the groups with an air of purpose. Aliyah could tell that they were relieved that they would not be relegated to the usual role of wall flies as a fellow mentor headed an activity. The previous week she had assumed that useless role and was left wondering why mentors had to attend the group activity at all.

Aliyah turned off the portable microphone and set it on the table that held a large cardboard "WAN" sign, where she would instruct the "routers" to come after their LAN group solved the mathematical problem. As Aliyah rounded the room and observed the interns and mentors interacting with each other, she felt that everything was right in her life. Her love for math and science education filled her so much that at times she imagined that if she remained only a mother and an educator for the rest of her life, she would be content.

*Marriage is half your faith*, she had learned in her Islamic studies classes. But no matter how eloquently the concept was explained, she never quite fully grasped what the prophetic teaching meant. When Aliyah was first exposed to the concept years after becoming Muslim, she had thought it meant that she *had* to get married.

But Aliyah hadn't been particularly interested in marriage. It wasn't that she frowned upon the arrangement. But she had grown up believing that she would meet her soul mate one day and fall in love. And because she hadn't yet met "the one", she saw no reason to get married.

*Muslims don't fall in love before marriage.* It was something that Aliyah would hear over and over again in Islamic classes and lectures. But her heart had recoiled at the idea. *How can you marry someone you don't love?* she wondered. But the more imams and scholars repeated the words, the more convinced she became that her dislike for the statement was due to religious ignorance and weak faith.

"True believers marry for the sake of Allah, not for their *nafs*," the local imam had told her when she spoke to him about Matt's proposal. Deanna had pushed the marriage so much that Aliyah had begun to doubt her Islamic sincerity in refusing Matt. Her internal turmoil eventually inspired her to seek advice from the imam. "But why can't we marry for our *nafs*?" Aliyah had asked him. "My *nafs* has to live in the marriage. I don't see what's wrong with wanting something for myself." "If you truly believe in Allah and the Hereafter," the imam had told her, "a good Muslim brother is all you'd want in a marriage."

Aliyah gritted her teeth at the memory. It was only in the last few months that she was beginning to explore her own feelings and needs guilt-free. After mustering the courage to cut off Deanna as a friend, Aliyah found that there were many other attachments that needed abating, the first of which was her blind trust of anyone labeled an imam, scholar, or Islamic teacher. It angered her that she had been so naïve as to assume that the imam's marital advice reflected divine guidance more than it did human opinion.

Like so many other converts to Islam and inexperienced, gullible Muslims, Aliyah had made the erroneous assumption that a "knowledgeable person" was actually a knowledgeable person. The Islamic classes she had attended had left her feeling so helplessly ignorant and in need of scholarly guidance that the obvious had escaped her. Any "knowledgeable person" was knowledgeable in only a certain field, not in *every* field. Only God had full knowledge and understanding of every aspect of life; thus, only He had the right to speak with authority on what someone should or should not do. Yet even God himself remained silent on exactly whom a person should marry. He gave a few basic, general guidelines then left the rest to human choice, desire, and opinion. Why then had the imam made Aliyah feel guilty for wanting a marriage that pleased her *nafs*? And why had Aliyah assumed that pleasing her *nafs*—her human choice, desire, and opinion—was mutually exclusive to pleasing Allah?

Would Aliyah's life had turned out differently if she had trusted her intuition more than she had trusted the imam? What if she had realized twelve years ago that, while the imam had a lot of knowledge regarding Islamic concepts, his understanding of the practical application of that knowledge might be lacking?

"We're done! We're done!" some interns from LAN 2 shouted, interrupting Aliyah's thoughts.

Aliyah smiled as she walked to the front of the room and retrieved the microphone and turned it back on. "Congratulations LAN 2," she said, prompting some clapping and cheers from the group. "But before you get your ten points, we need to check your mathematical problem and solution."

"We're done too!" the groups LAN 3 and LAN 1 shouted one after the other.

"Mentors," Aliyah said, nodding toward her colleagues and superiors, "see if LAN 2 have correctly assigned themselves to the roles of switches and router and if their problem is in the correct order for the solution they are proposing. If so, instruct the router to come to the WAN table. If not, then check the problem and solution of LAN 3."

*"You must not know how it feels to be in love,"* Reem had said when, a few days prior, Aliyah mentioned her thoughts on remaining single for the rest of her life and investing her time and energy into her son and her students. *"If you knew how true love felt, you wouldn't think you'd be content without it."*

Maybe Reem is right, Aliyah thought to herself. But even so, Aliyah was unwilling to trust Reem's thoughts over her own. *She might be more knowledgeable than me about Islam*, Aliyah considered. *But she's not more knowledgeable than me about me.*

***

"I like that." Jacob pointed to the framed quote on the wall of Aliyah's office from where he stood in the open doorway late Friday afternoon. He had already packed up and was dropping by Aliyah's office before leaving for the day.

Aliyah halted gathering her belongings to glance at the wall from where she stood behind her desk. *We are anxious to improve our circumstances, but are unwilling to improve ourselves. We therefore remain bound.* She'd hung the quote next to her desk earlier that week.

She smiled. "It's supposed to say, 'Men are anxious to improve their circumstances, but are unwilling to improve themselves; they therefore remain bound,'" she said, a shadow of a smile on her face. "But I figured Dr. Warren would ask me to take it down on the grounds of sexism."

Jacob chuckled in agreement. "*Adapted from a quote by James Allen*," he read aloud. "That was smart."

"I liked the pronoun *we* better anyway," Aliyah said sincerely. "I'm trying to get to a place where I focus on myself, and I think sticking to *I* and *we* helps when I'm being critical."

"It's a far cry from 'Don't argue with a stupid person,' huh?" Jacob said jokingly.

"You remember that?" she said self-consciously, laughter in her voice.

"Yes, because I'm trying to get away from the negativity myself," he said. "I've spent too many years being reactive and critical. It's time to focus on being proactive and self-reflective."

Aliyah rolled her eyes in agreement as she leaned forward to shut down her computer. "You can say that again. Sometimes I feel like I was sleepwalking for the last twenty years. It's unbelievable how much power I gave other people over my life."

"For me, it isn't so much other people as it is guilt and obligation," Jacob said. "I swear, those two feelings have been in the driver seat of my life for too long."

Aliyah nodded thoughtfully, and Jacob noticed how she seemed to be sincerely reflecting on his words. "That's an interesting perspective," she said as she put her iPad into her handbag and removed her keys. "You know, that might be where I went wrong myself."

"It's where a lot of us went wrong."

Aliyah pulled the straps of her purse over her shoulder then picked up a bulging manila folder before walking around her desk, a finger looped through her key ring. Jacob stepped backwards into the hallway as Aliyah approached the door and pulled it closed.

"*SubhaanAllah*," Aliyah said as she locked the door, speaking as if realizing something for the first time. "I think that's what has been bothering me all this time about some of my Islamic studies teachers. They made me feel guilty instead of inspired, so I did things out of obligation instead of trying to please Allah."

"You have to be careful with that though," Jacob said cautiously as he and Aliyah walked toward the elevator. "Guilty obligation isn't mutually exclusive to pleasing Allah."

"That's not what I mean," Aliyah said. "It's one thing to feel obligated to change because you know you're doing wrong and feel guilty about it. But it's another thing to feel obligated to change because someone made you feel guilty about something that you didn't even think was wrong."

Jacob's eyebrows rose in understanding. "That's a big problem amongst Muslims," he said reflectively. "But there's so much we really don't know, so sometimes it's best to just trust someone more knowledgeable."

Aliyah rolled her eyes in annoyance. "Someone more knowledgeable in *what* though?" she said. "I swear, I'm so sick of hearing that. They act like studying Islam in a university gives them authority over people's lives. You can teach me the basics of Islam, but don't tell me your knowledge gives you the right to dictate my personal life."

"Whoa," Jacob said, lighthearted teasing in his tone. "That's why I said *sometimes*. Obviously, a scholar can't tell you how to live your life. They can only teach you about Islam, and even that comes with conditions and limitations."

"If only *they* understood that," Aliyah said, frustration in her voice. "Too many of us trust everything they say. Don't they have an obligation to say 'I don't know' when they don't know?"

Jacob was silent as he and Aliyah stood outside the elevator waiting for it to open. In the seconds that passed, some of their colleagues joined them, inspiring Jacob to remain silent longer than he intended. *She's hurting*, he said to himself. This topic was obviously a sensitive one for Aliyah, and Jacob wondered what had happened in her life that hurt her so deeply.

The elevator chimed, and the doors slowly slid open. Aliyah groaned when she saw that it was already full. "I'm taking the stairs," she said. "You all have a good evening."

"See you Monday," some of her colleagues called out in response.

Instinctively, Jacob turned and followed Aliyah toward the staircase. He hadn't asked her what he had intended when he stopped by her office.

"Can I ask you something?" Jacob said as he hurried in front of Aliyah and pulled open the heavy exit door.

Aliyah shrugged as she walked past him and started down the stairs. "Sure."

He stepped forward and let the door close behind him. "Would you object to me going on television to talk about what happened?"

Aliyah halted her movements and turned toward him, a skeptical expression on her face. "Television?"

"Yes," he said. "I think it's the only way to correct the rumors."

Aliyah drew in a deep breath and exhaled as she continued down the stairs, this time walking more slowly. "Is that even possible?"

"I don't know," he said honestly. "But I think it's worth a try."

"Isn't it a bit late?" she said. "I mean, why now?"

"Because it's the first time I was given the opportunity."

Aliyah grunted. "You actually read all those emails and inboxes from the media? I don't trust those people."

"I don't either," Jacob said. "But I did respond to ones who sounded sincere."

"*Sounded* sincere?" Aliyah said skeptically. "Based on what?"

"A hunch," he said, shrugging. "And *du'aa*, of course."

Aliyah was quiet, but Jacob could tell she was listening, albeit reluctantly.

"Responding to them wasn't as stressful as I thought it would be," he said. "After I came up with a short, standard response, I just sent the same reply to all of them. It's similar to the one I posted on my Facebook page."

"I didn't see it," Aliyah said, her voice devoid of interest.

"It wasn't much," Jacob admitted apologetically. "But I basically said that none of the rumors are true and slandering believers is a serious sin."

"I can see why the media didn't respond," Aliyah said sarcastically, an amused grin on her face. "Slandering believers is a serious sin?" She chuckled. "They probably don't even believe in God, let alone the concept of sin. You probably sounded more self-righteous than helpful."

Jacob chuckled in agreement. "That part was only on my Facebook page. In my reply to the media, I said engaging in libel isn't a good idea. I then asked if they'd be willing to do a full, unedited interview with me to explain what really happened." He shrugged. "I didn't expect anyone to respond. But I felt it was the least I could do."

Aliyah drew in a deep breath and exhaled as they continued to descend the stairs. "I think it's fine," she said, "as long as you don't mention me."

"I don't have to mention you by name," he said tentatively, "but I'd have to mention you. Otherwise there's no point in doing the interview."

"Then don't do the interview," Aliyah said with a shrug. "I don't want to relive that nightmare. What if they edit the interview and twist your words? What then?"

Jacob walked alongside Aliyah in silence until they reached the first floor. He stepped ahead of her and held open the door as she passed in front of him. "I thought about that," he said broodingly. "And that's definitely a possibility. But I figured that since so much time has passed, there's nothing really newsworthy in that angle. They used it before, so it no longer has shock value, and the story isn't important enough to insist on it."

"How can you be sure?" Aliyah said as they walked through the lobby toward the doors leading to the faculty and staff parking lot.

"I can't," Jacob said. "But even my mother says doing the interview is probably a good idea."

"Your mother?" Aliyah said, pulling her head back in confusion.

"I do PR for her company, so I asked her advice."

*Oh.* Larry had mentioned their company to Aliyah. "I don't know, Jacob," she said, exhaustion in her tone. "I don't feel comfortable with it. But if you think it's a good idea, do it. I just don't want any part of it."

Jacob opened the lobby exit door then fell in step next to Aliyah after she walked ahead of him. "They asked if it was possible to make it a joint interview."

"Then absolutely not," Aliyah said. "I'd never agree to let Deanna talk about me while I'm not there, especially on TV."

"Not with Deanna," Jacob said. "With you."

There was an extended silence as Aliyah looked toward the rows of cars, but her expression suggested that her thoughts were elsewhere.

"I know it's not ideal," Jacob said. "But depending on how it's set up, it could be a good way to clarify the truth. I already explained to them that it's best if they interviewed us separately instead of at the same time."

"But what would we say?" Aliyah said. "I don't feel comfortable talking about my personal life to the world. It's none of their business."

"But you deserve exoneration. They had no right to slander you like that."

Aliyah shrugged. "To be honest, I'm less bothered by the secular media than by the Muslims. The media's focus is to stir up anything to get attention. You'd think Muslims would be focused on their souls."

Jacob nodded sadly. "I feel the same way. But the more I live, the more I realize that Muslims are people like everyone else."

"That's no excuse."

"I agree. But it's the truth."

"Not completely," she said as they walked the length of the parking lot. "It took me a while to figure out why Muslims were so willing to tear me down. First I thought it was because they felt that if something was mentioned in the news, they had a right to talk about it without sin."

"That's possible," Jacob said reflectively.

Aliyah shook her head. "But it was deeper than that," she said. "About a week ago, I read through my Facebook page for the first time since everything happened, and the majority of the tags and discussions by Muslims weren't about whether or not I was guilty of sleeping with a married man. That was discussed, of course, but it wasn't the focus. The focus was whether or not I was trying to steal my best friend's husband."

Jacob drew his eyebrows together. "I thought they discussed that because they assumed the mistress story was true."

Aliyah shook her head. "I thought so too," she said. "Until I actually read the threads."

"What were they saying?"

"That I was trying to get you to marry me as a second wife." Aliyah coughed laughter. "Some of them even mentioned how I apparently forced polygamy down my first husband's throat until he divorced me."

"*What*?" Jacob felt himself getting upset. "What is wrong with us?"

"But that's not all," Aliyah said. "When they discussed the possibility of me committing adultery, the sentiment was, 'Unfortunately, that's what happens when we work in mixed environments. May Allah forgive us.' But when they discussed the possibility of me trying to be a second wife, the sentiment was, 'Unfortunately, many women are backstabbers. Keep them out of your life.'"

Jacob was overcome with frustration. "That's terrible."

"Isn't it?" Aliyah shook her head. "It's like, it's acceptable if you anger Allah. But it's unacceptable if you anger me."

Jacob didn't know what to say.

"So for the Muslims, it was never really about my guilt or innocence in committing a major sin," Aliyah said. "It was about whether or not I wanted to marry a married man. And to many of them, polygamy was more unforgivable."

Jacob sighed. "It's really sad that we've come to this."

Aliyah shook her head in agreement. "It was amazing to see how adamant they were about making me out to be this vindictive woman. And not because they thought I was trying to do something wrong. But because they knew I wasn't."

A half hour later, Jacob had a heavy heart as he pulled in front of the school campus where his sons were enrolled in an all-day educational summer camp. After speaking to Aliyah, he was no longer convinced that the television interview was a good idea.

*What's the point?* That had been Aliyah's question, and now it was his own. If the people who mattered most to them viewed plural marriage as more blameworthy than major sin, then what exactly would he gain by clarifying the truth? And what crime would he be exonerating himself from?

*It was never really about my guilt or innocence in committing a major sin. It was about whether or not I wanted to marry a married man.*

*SubhaanAllah,* Jacob thought. What was he supposed to do with that?

***

As her mobile rang and vibrated in her purse, Aliyah quickly pushed open the door to her apartment. She set down the bulging manila folder then fished for her phone. After withdrawing her cell, she held the phone in front of her and hesitated when she saw the name on the display. *Larry Bivens.*

A flood of emotions came over her in the five seconds that it took for the name to disappear and the missed call symbol to appear. She was indignant and angry, yet sad and hopeful. But by the time the phone chimed and the voicemail symbol appeared, she was only annoyed.

*Try empathy.*

Last week Aliyah had typed the words in fancy font and framed the printout before hanging it on the wall in her living room near the front door. It was one of many printouts she'd hung on the walls of her home in an effort to think more positively and focus on herself. This one had been inspired by her mother's oft-repeated advice to Aliyah and her siblings whenever they were upset.

Aliyah drew in a deep breath as she dialed the voicemail then put the phone to her ear to listen to Larry's message. *Try empathy*, she said to herself in an effort to calm her annoyance.

"*As-salaamu'alaikum*, Aliyah," Larry's voice said, apology in his tone. "I know it's been a while. But we need to talk. Give me a call when you can."

Aliyah disconnected the call. Nikki would be dropping off Ibrahim soon, so Aliyah needed to start preparing dinner. She wondered if she should call Larry back now or later. Or at all.

She glanced at the clock. It was time to pray. She would have to worry about Larry later.

After *Asr*, Aliyah sat on the carpet of the living room and recited *Ayat al-Kursy*, as was the prophetic custom after obligatory prayer.

Her heart felt heavy as she realized what had gone wrong in her marriage to Matthew. Both she and Matt had been trying too hard to do "the right thing." Matt had been Muslim only a year when they'd met, and Aliyah had been Muslim for eight, but their understanding of marriage was strikingly similar despite the seven years between their Islamic experiences. Both had believed that "marrying for the sake of Allah" was somehow mutually exclusive to marrying based on one's needs and desires. Matt had not sought Aliyah in marriage, and Aliyah had not sought Matt. They had been encouraged to become a couple simply because they were "two good Muslims." But in the process, they became victims of a mentality that stripped from converts to Islam the right to their own hearts and souls, and the right to their own opinions and choices. Neither Aliyah nor Matt had been in any hurry to get married (to anyone, let alone each other), but friends and community leaders convinced them that they "needed" to get married.

Matt had been told that he needed to get married to protect himself from falling into *zina*, and Aliyah had been told that she needed to get married because a "good brother" was willing to marry her. It wasn't until years after they were married that Aliyah learned that Matt's incentive in getting married went far beyond a desire to avoid falling into fornication. Marrying a "good sister" was also his way of detaching his heart from his ex-girlfriend. His Muslim friends, as well as the local imam, had convinced him that if he had a righteous wife by his side, all his pain and worries would disappear. And Aliyah's Muslim friends (particularly Deanna), as well as the local imam, had convinced her that it was her Islamic duty to accept the proposal of a Muslim man whose character and religious practice pleased her. Though Aliyah hadn't known Matt well enough to assess either, she allowed herself to be persuaded that marrying Matt was the right thing to do.

"You don't have to marry him, you know," Benjamin had said after Aliyah eagerly introduced him to Matt for the first time. But by then, Aliyah was so enamored with the idea of having someone to love and care for her that she'd imagined that marrying Matt was what she wanted for herself.

It wasn't until this very moment, as she sat on the floor of her living room after *Asr*, that she realized that, at the time, she had been merely longing for a replacement family. Growing up as the daughter of Alfred and Naomi Thomas, Aliyah had felt part of something phenomenal. Everywhere she went, she met people who admired her parents' work. Alfred and Naomi were known in their church and their local community for their non-profit programs and the scholarships and internships they'd founded to benefit minority youth.

"You guys are so lucky," people would say to Aliyah and her siblings. And Aliyah felt lucky. She'd smile in pride whenever her mother and father were featured in the local news or received yet another reward for their volunteerism or non-profit work. Alfred and Naomi were best known for the love and care they showed to underprivileged youth. They went as far as to spend one-on-one time with youth to assist them in self-sufficiency and academic achievement.

And Aliyah had naively assumed that this unconditional love, care, and concern had extended to her, too.

"But she was the love of my life," Matt had told Aliyah when she told him she didn't feel comfortable having Nikki around anymore, even if it was only to teach her about Islam. Aliyah was particularly upset that she had to learn from Nikki that Nikki was Matt's ex-girlfriend. "Am I supposed to just abandon her now that I'm Muslim? She has the right to learn about Islam, and isn't it better if you teach her instead of me?"

Though Aliyah was deeply offended by Matt's tactics, she was genuinely moved by his honesty. She could almost feel his hurt at losing the woman he loved after he accepted Islam. As he spoke, Aliyah had sensed that Matt was hoping that Nikki would become Muslim so they could be together again, and that was when Aliyah realized what she had been to Matt from the beginning. She was merely a beautiful stranger tasked with making him forget the one who'd had his heart all along.

At the sound of a knock at the door, Aliyah sighed and stood, mentally preparing herself to greet Nikki as she dropped off Ibrahim.

***

"Because it's stupid. That's why." Arms folded across her chest, Deanna stood on the balcony that overlooked her parents' backyard Friday evening. The balcony's dark wood stairs spiraled down to the grassy area enclosed by the fence that divided her parents' property from the neighbors. Deanna knew she was pushing her luck by speaking to her mother like that, especially about something close to her mother's heart, but she was growing tired of her parents' browbeating. Why did they keep saying she had to go to church? She had been staying with them for a few months, and she had avoided church by running last minute errands or going to sudden appointments. But she was a grown woman. She shouldn't have to make up flimsy excuses to avoid something she shouldn't have to do in the first place.

"Jesus is our Lord, so you need to—"

"Jesus is a *prophet* of our Lord," Deanna interjected indignantly, "and the only thing I need to do is worship the same God he worshipped. Like *you* should if you really believe in him like you claim."

"You need to watch your mouth," her mother warned.

"And you need to watch yours." There was a part of Deanna that knew she was crossing every Godly and moral boundary by speaking to her mother like this, but the fury inside her had built up so much that she felt as if she were going to explode. She simply could no longer keep her mouth shut and play the role of obedient, submissive child while her parents tried to control even her thoughts and beliefs.

Deanna had come to stay with her parents because she needed their support and help in getting Jacob to realize his mistake in wanting a divorce. But instead of offering support, or even compassion or concern, everything was about proving that their religious beliefs were superior. It seemed that nothing mattered to them except their ability to look down on everyone who saw the world differently from them.

Though her mother had occasionally shown *some* compassion and concern, it quickly disappeared whenever the topic of religion came up. And those conversations never ended well. Like her father, Deanna's mother would usually resort to hitting and slapping if she couldn't get Deanna to renounce her Muslim beliefs or go to church with them.

"You're the one uttering blasphemy," Deanna said.

Internally, she dared her mother to lay a hand on her. Though Deanna imagined it would probably earn her an abode in Hellfire, she was no longer going to let her mother hit her without hitting back. She was tired of being her parents' punching bag whenever things didn't go their way. Their physical attacks would be understandable if Deanna was doing something openly disrespectful or harmful to them, but her parents would *instigate* arguments about religion then start hitting and slapping Deanna if she didn't agree with them.

"I am your *mother*. You have *no* right to speak to me like that."

"And you have *no* right to speak about God like that," Deanna retorted.

"Our Lord died for us and gave his *blood*," her mother said, voice rising authoritatively. "And if you want to go to Heaven, you need to accept his sacrifice."

"If our Lord died," Deanna said with a sneer, "I don't see how *anyone* is going to Heaven."

Deanna braced herself for her mother's attack. She could feel her mother's rage building as she glared at Deanna, her eyes thin slits of anger. "Your problem is you have no faith. You want everything to make sense."

"I don't need everything to make sense," Deanna said. "But I at least need *God* to make sense, and it makes no sense to believe somebody murdered Him. And you're telling me that God accepting His own murder is His greatest act of love toward humanity? You've *got* to be kidding me. Do you actually believe that nonsense?"

"And you think following a religion of terrorists and women haters is any better?"

Deanna contorted her face. "Terrorists and women haters?"

"That's what your religion teaches," her mother said, disgust in her voice. "Look at what your people do in the name of religion."

"And look at what *your* people do in the name of religion."

"*My* people are upstanding, God-fearing Christians who walk with the Lord."

Deanna snorted. "And what does that mean exactly?"

"If you went to church, you would know what it means."

Deanna gritted her teeth as the image of Bailey sneering at her in the church basement flashed in her mind.

“This is why your life is so messed up,” her mother said. “You’re selfish and immature. You have no regard for anyone but yourself. Even God means nothing to you.”

Livid, Deanna wrinkled her nose at her mother. Her heart raced at the audacity of that statement. How dare her mother, of all people, say that to her. “The apple doesn’t fall far from the tree,” Deanna said flippantly.

“How *dare* you.” Her mother stepped toward her, a finger hovering so close to Deanna’s forehead that she could feel the heat of her mother’s hand.

“Will you hit me?” Deanna held her mother’s gaze challengingly. “Because it seems like the only thing I can depend on in this family. I came here because I thought you and Dad would help me save my marriage. I was stupid enough to think you cared about me. I was stupid enough to think you *ever* cared about me.”

A shadow of indignant horror passed over her mother’s face as she dropped her hand, her fingers curling and tightening into a fist as if preparing to strike Deanna.

“If I’m selfish and immature,” Deanna said as her voice trembled, “it’s because I have selfish and immature parents. How *dare* you say I’m a bad Christian. *You’re* the bad Christian. I don’t have to love people who hurt me. That’s why I don’t love *you*.” Vision blurring in anger, Deanna stabbed her finger in the air toward her mother. “I hate you, and I hate Dad. And I hate Bailey too. You’re *all* sinful and wicked,” Deanna shouted until her throat hurt, “and I’m better than all of you!”

***

Aliyah forced a smile as Nikki stepped into the foyer holding Ibrahim’s hand. A wide grin spread on Ibrahim’s face when he saw his mother. After closing the door, Aliyah kneeled down and held her son in a tight embrace.

“*As-salaamu’alaikum*, Mommy,” he said, his voice muffled against her neck. “I missed you.”

“*Wa’alaiku-mus-salaam*, cookie monster,” she said. “I missed you too.”

“Is it okay if I use your bathroom?” Nikki said.

Aliyah looked up and nodded as she released Ibrahim then stood. “Yes, it’s around the corner on your left.”

Ibrahim removed his shoes and bounded toward the kitchen. “Are you hungry?” Aliyah asked as she followed him.

“I want a popsicle.”

“You can have one after dinner.”

“Can I have one now?”

“Himy,” Aliyah said, her voice soft, “you can have a popsicle *after* you eat.”

“I can eat another one after dinner,” Ibrahim said, his tone suggesting that he had come up with the perfect solution.

Aliyah chuckled and shook her head. “I don’t think so. But let’s fix some—”

A roaring sounding interrupted Aliyah midsentence, and she immediately hurried toward the sound. “Is everything okay?” she called out as she approached the bathroom door where Nikki was still inside. There was another roar-like sound followed by gagging. Concerned, Aliyah knocked on the door with the back of her knuckles. "Nikki?"

Aliyah heard the toilet flush, and seconds later the bathroom door opened. Nikki stood looking pale, eyes bleary. "I'm not feeling well," Nikki muttered, a hand on her abdominal area.

"Is it the pregnancy?" Aliyah said.

Nikki nodded, distracted. "I just need to sit down for a bit. I feel dizzy."

"You can sit on the couch until you're ready to drive home."

Nikki dragged her feet as she walked toward the living room, and Aliyah followed cautiously behind her. "Do you need anything to drink or eat?" Aliyah asked.

Nikki collapsed into the couch. "Do you have white bread or potato chips?" she said, her voice weak.

"I think so," Aliyah said as she started toward the kitchen.

"Are you okay, Ummi?" Ibrahim asked in a small voice, his expression concerned as he looked at his stepmother.

"Yes, I'm just tired," Nikki said as she stared at the ceiling, her head lying on the back of the couch.

Aliyah returned with a half-full bag of chips closed with a clip and a loaf of white bread still in its store packaging. "Do you need anything with it?" Aliyah said as she set them on the floor table in front of the couch, her eyes following Ibrahim as he retreated to his room.

Nikki sat up slowly and shook her head as she reached for the bread and opened the package. "No, I'm fine."

A concerned expression on her face, Aliyah sat next to Nikki and watched in silence as Nikki nibbled on a piece of bread. "Are you sure you're going to be okay driving back home? You look like you're barely holding it together."

Cheeks bulging slightly as she chewed, Nikki grinned humorously at Aliyah. "Don't worry about me," she said, her voice slightly muffled by the food. "I can't be broken."

A confused smile formed at Aliyah's lips. "What?"

Nikki chewed and swallowed before reaching for the bag of chips and removing the clip. "It's something one of my fashion design instructors used to say in college," Nikki explained, the strength coming back to her voice. "She struggled with alcoholism, so we'd get really worried whenever she got stressed, which was usually right before a show." A reflective smile lingered on Nikki's face. "But she'd joke and say, 'Don't worry about me. Attractive women can't be broken.'"

Aliyah's eyebrows rose in understanding, a hesitant smile on her face. "Oh my God. That's sad."

"Isn't it?" Nikki shook her head reflectively as she ate a handful of chips in silence.

"She was my favorite professor though," Nikki said. "She was so open and honest about her flaws, I was almost jealous. I couldn't understand how a professional, accomplished woman felt comfortable telling her students she was a recovering alcoholic. And it wasn't like she waited until we got to know her. She told us the first day of class."

"I can't imagine telling my students anything like that," Aliyah said. "I was mortified when all that 'hot Muslim mistress' crap was in the media."

"I can't either," Nikki said. "But she didn't just come out and say she's an alcoholic. She was telling us what inspired her to go into fashion. And she told us that her mother had taught her that her entire worth was based on how she looked and what she wore."

Aliyah wrinkled her nose in disapproval. "How is that inspiring?"

"I think she was saying that fashion and looking good was all she knew about," Nikki said, "so it was what she decided to go into for herself."

Aliyah nodded in understanding, but she still found the story bothersome.

"Anyway," Nikki said, exhaustion in her tone, "she said her mother would always say, 'Attractive women can't be broken.' Meaning, if you're good-looking and accomplished, nobody cares about you. So if you're hurt or having a bad day, you better just suck it up because you won't be getting any sympathy."

"*SubhaanAllah,*" Aliyah said, a look of distaste on her face. "That's a terrible thing to say to your daughter."

Nikki shook her head. "But from what I understand, her mother wasn't trying to be cruel. She just wanted her to understand the reality of the world. So she was trying to toughen her up for when she wouldn't be around to take care of her anymore."

Aliyah's gaze grew distant. "That's still sad."

"Perhaps," Nikki said with a shrug. "But it's not too far from the truth."

"You think so?"

"Look at what happened to you."

"To me?" Aliyah said, her forehead creased.

"The only reason people felt comfortable tearing you down was because they felt you deserved it."

Aliyah stared at Nikki in confusion, unsure how to form the question in her mind.

"Whenever a woman is attractive *and* intelligent," Nikki said, "people are jealous. So they're eager to tear her down, especially if they see something in her that they don't see in themselves."

Aliyah was reminded of her experiences growing up. She wrinkled her nose. "But that's so high school."

"No," Nikki said. "That's so *life* school. Women hate women they can't find anything wrong with, and men resent women they can't have for themselves."

"You really believe that?" Aliyah said, a troubled expression on her face. "I thought that whole saga was about people thinking I was trying to be a second wife."

A smirk formed on Nikki's face as she shook her head. "Girl, you are so naïve."

Aliyah felt a twinge of offence at Nikki's words, but she didn't respond.

"Even if they thought you were trying to be a second wife," Nikki said, "it wasn't *about* that. Girl, these are Muslims we're talking about. They know their *deen*, so they know you can marry a married man. If you were obviously broken in some way, they wouldn't have reacted like that. Because of our pride and insecurity, we approve of polygamy only if we can pity the woman somehow. That's why Muslim sisters are always talking about helping widows and divorced women instead of about marrying the person who's right for you."

"But I *am* a divorced woman," Aliyah said.

"No you're not." Nikki shook her head, still smirking. "You're a woman who *happens* to be divorced. There's a difference."

Aliyah narrowed her eyes, a question on her face.

"Look," Nikki said as if leveling with Aliyah, "I haven't been Muslim long, so I don't know a lot about Islam. But I'm just keeping it real. People are people. Women can put on hijab and pray five times a day, but beneath it all, they're still women. And women can stomach the thought of another woman only if we can be sure we're number one at the end of the day. In the *dunya*, that's how so many of us stay with men who cheat."

Aliyah nodded thoughtfully. "I see what you mean."

"So if you throw Islam into the mix," Nikki said, "the only thing that changes is the context. And the way I see it, those sisters were pissed off at you because, in their minds, polygamy is only acceptable if they can guarantee the man will be unjust."

Aliyah laughed out loud. "You *can't* be serious. *Forced* to be unjust? Men being unjust is the reason it's *not* acceptable to us."

"I'm not saying it's a deliberate thought," Nikki said. "But that's what it boils down to. If you were really unattractive or crippled, or even a bit up there in years, then Jacob would be the hero. And you would be the poor Muslim woman in need of a husband."

"That's possible," Aliyah said, laughter in her voice.

"But don't you get it?" Nikki said, a grin on her face. "We have to pity you before we accept you."

"I can see that," Aliyah said. "But what does that have to do with the man being unjust?"

"*Every*thing," Nikki said, humor in her tone. "In the hero scenario, Jacob can only marry a woman we think he doesn't *want* to marry. That way, women can feel he's doing her a favor instead of actually loving and caring for her like he does his first wife."

Aliyah nodded as she began to understand Nikki's point. "That's true."

"But if he *does* marry a woman he's not attracted to, then it's almost guaranteed he'll be unjust. Because, obviously, he'll prefer the first wife over her. And that's *exactly* what we want." Nikki grinned and shook her head. "But when he chooses someone he *can* be just with because he's actually attracted to her, we cry foul."

"Oh my God," Aliyah said, laughter in her voice. "You're so right."

"The worst part though," Nikki said, "is how disrespectful our polygamy requirements are to the women we think of as broken. They have feelings and needs just like we do, and they have the right to feel valued and desired as a wife. But we'll only accept them as co-wives if our husband *and* the women themselves understand they're a charity case with no real wifely value."

"*SubhaanAllah,*" Aliyah said, shaking her head. "I never thought of it like that."

"That's why no one thinks of you as a divorced woman. You don't look broken," Nikki said. "Because the minute a widow or divorced woman doesn't *look* widowed or divorced, then we don't care if she *ever* gets remarried. We start talking about how in the past, they didn't have a welfare system set up to help them out, and that's why polygamy was necessary. But now we have programs to help them, so they can just go apply for government housing and food stamps." Nikki grunted, the shadow of a grin on her face. "As if the only reason people get married is to eat dinner and have a place to sleep."

"As pathetic as that is," Aliyah said, humor in her tone, "it *is* how we think. May Allah forgive us."

Nikki nodded as a smile lingered. For a few minutes, the only sound between them was Nikki crunching on potato chips as her thoughts appeared to grow distant. Aliyah wondered if she should ask Nikki to stay for dinner.

"I owe you an apology," Nikki said, leaning back on the couch after she closed the bag of chips and put it back on the table.

Aliyah furrowed her brows as she looked at Nikki. "For what?"

"I was jealous of you," Nikki said.

Aliyah averted her gaze, uncomfortable with the sudden honesty. She didn't want to talk about this right now.

"When we first met," Nikki said, "I knew I could never accept Matt being with someone like you."

Offense stabbed Aliyah. When she was married to Matt, she'd felt like the soulless "good Muslim" tasked with keeping Matt's body warm at night. Aliyah wondered if she could ever forgive the imam and her friends for making her feel that it was her Islamic duty to marry "a good Muslim brother" just because he happened to be available.

"I asked Matt to divorce you."

It took a moment for Aliyah to register Nikki's words. When she did, her eyes widened as she met Nikki's apologetic gaze. "*What*?"

"I told him I couldn't handle it."

Aliyah's heart pounded in anger, and she had trouble finding her voice.

"At the time," Nikki said regretfully, "you were just the woman who stole my man. I was furious at him for falling in love with someone else."

Aliyah grunted, finding bitter humor in the term *falling in love*. It made sense for Nikki to believe that Aliyah and Matt had actually fallen in love. Why else would they have gotten married?

"I was happy to be with him again," Nikki said. "But I just couldn't accept being a counterfeit wife."

Aliyah focused her gaze on the wall near the front door where the inspirational quote hung. *Try empathy.*

"At the time, I really believed that all is fair in love,'" Nikki said reflectively. "It's practically the golden rule of relationships in the *dunya*."

"But you were Muslim," Aliyah muttered, her voice clipped.

"I know," Nikki said. "But I didn't know what being a Muslim meant. I was just learning about Allah and how to pray."

Aliyah moved her head in the beginning of a nod, but she was only half listening. It was infuriating how the people closest to her seemed to constantly use and abuse her whenever it suited them. Her own family had tossed her out of their lives when her presence was no longer convenient. When she had been only the quiet, starry-eyed girl who admired everything about her family, she was loved and welcomed. But as soon as she carved for herself a single part of her life as her own—her heart and soul— she was treated as if she had unleashed upon them some horrible, unforgivable affront.

"But this past year," Nikki said, her voice contemplative, "I've been reading a lot and going to a lot of classes and learning Qur'an with Reem. It's made me rethink a lot of things. I think I'm just now beginning to understand what it means to put Allah first and love for your sister what you love for yourself."

"That's good." Aliyah's tone was flat and emotionless. It was all she could do to keep from throwing Nikki out of her home and asking her to never come back.

"I know this is a lot to digest," Nikki said. "But I wanted to say I'm really sorry. I hope you can forgive me."

Eyes still on the inspirational quote, Aliyah tried to calm the storm of fury in her chest. "I don't know if I can do that."

"I understand," Nikki said, her voice subdued.

"No, I don't think you do," Aliyah said, surprised that she was speaking her feelings aloud. "If you would've spoken to me six months ago, I probably would have rushed to forgive you. Or at least I probably would have rushed to *say* I forgive you. Because I was taught that's what good Muslims do." She clenched her jaw and shook her head. "But I'm tired of saying and doing things just because everyone says I should. That's how I ended up marrying Matt." She grunted. "Which was probably the biggest mistake of my life."

"You didn't want to marry him?" Nikki sounded shocked.

“No,” Aliyah said, unable to temper the gloating pride she felt at knowing Nikki would find this revelation offensive. “And I never loved him,” she added for emphasis.

Aliyah turned and met Nikki’s gaze, her expression stoic. “But if you were willing to wrong me *and* your soul to get him, and if he was willing to wrong me and his soul to have you, then I think you two deserve each other.”

Nikki’s mouth fell open in shock. It took several seconds for her to regain her composure. “How could you say something like that?”

“Because it’s what I believe.”

“But Allah is forgiving and merciful,” Nikki said. “That’s what *I* believe.”

“That’s what *all* Muslims believe,” Aliyah said, her heart beat quickening as she spoke freely. “So don’t think you’ve uncovered some esoteric mystery there. Humans are pretty open-minded to things that favor them. It’s when it’s time to think about *others* that things get a little confused,” she said. “As you yourself pointed out when you mentioned women preferring injustice so long as it’s in their favor.”

Nikki contorted her face and stood. “I should’ve never opened up to you.”

Aliyah shrugged as she too stood. “Maybe, maybe not. I can’t speak on that. But if you’re sincere in wanting my forgiveness, then you have to accept that I’m not going to be overjoyed to hear that you set out to destroy my marriage while I welcomed you into it.”

Nikki shook her head as she walked toward the front door, her face pinched in distaste.

“I apologize that I’m not more excited to hear your confession,” Aliyah said as she followed Nikki to the door. “But this fiasco with Deanna has made me determined to make some serious changes in my life.”

“I just expected *you* to be more understanding,” Nikki said as she slipped on her shoes. “I thought you were different from people like Juwayriah and Deanna.”

Aliyah laughed, but it was apparent that she was not happy. “So because I’m upset about what you did, I’m like *them*?”

“To me you are,” Nikki said haughtily. “Cruel and self-centered, just like them.”

“*That’s* what you think of me?” Aliyah couldn’t conceal her shock and offense.

“It’s how you’re acting.”

“You have a right to your opinion,” Aliyah said as Nikki yanked open the front door. “But know this. I *definitely* don’t forgive you if you’re saying I’m a bad person if I *don’t*. That’s just not how seeking forgiveness works.”

Nikki lifted her nose, sniffing in offense as she straightened the strap of her purse and stepped into the apartment hall.

“I have feelings too, Nikki,” Aliyah said as she stood in the doorway. “And all I’m saying is I need time to work through them. I *want* to forgive you because I think that’s best for all of us. But you have no right to say I don’t have a choice.”

Nikki threw up a hand as she walked down the hall, her back to Aliyah. "Do whatever you want. I'm through. I'm just sorry I thought you were a good person."

Aliyah groaned and shook her head as she stepped backwards into the foyer. "*As-salaamu'alaikum*, Nikki," she muttered as she closed the door.

***

"Nine-one-one. What's your emergency?"

Deanna's palm was moist in sweat as she pressed the cordless phone against her ear and stood near the sliding glass patio door adjacent to the balcony. Her heart thumped so forcefully that she felt it in her throat. "My mother," she said, breathless. "She's not moving. I think I..." Her voice caught as she realized the enormity of her predicament. "We were arguing. I didn't do it on purpose. But, I, she…" Deanna's legs folded beneath her, and she fell to the floor on bent knees. "Can you send somebody, please?" she moaned. "Can you please send somebody to help my mommy?"

"Ma'am," the dispatcher said firmly and calmly. "What happened? Is she alive?"

"I don't know. I don't know..."

"Ma'am, please, I need you to tell us where she is."

"She's at the bottom of the stairs. She, I think… I… She fell."

"What stairs? Where are the stairs?"

"In the backyard," Deanna said, breathless, tears stinging her eyes. "Can you please just send help!" she yelled, growing impatient and annoyed.

"Ma'am, we are sending help," the dispatch operator said. "We just need to confirm your mother's location. Is she at the address of the phone you're using?"

"Yes! Yes!" Deanna shouted frantically. "Don't you have the location in your computer?"

"We have seven eight four Fr—"

"Yes, that's us!" Deanna shouted irritably. "Now send someone. Now!" She pressed the end call button and threw the phone on the floor before rushing back outside to her mother.

## 15
## Peace of Mind

Aliyah woke early Saturday morning with a sense of peace in her heart. "*Alhamdu lillaahil-lathee ahyaana ba'da maa amaatanaa wa ilahin-nushoor,*" she muttered into the darkness of her room. *All praise is for Allah who has given us life after taking it from us, and unto Him is the resurrection.*

After reciting the supplication for waking, Aliyah lay beneath the softness of her comforter, her thoughts on her plans for the day. It was an hour before dawn, but she wasn't inclined to go back to sleep. She had to take Ibrahim to basketball later that morning, and while she waited for him to finish, she would be taking tennis lessons with Reem, Mashael, and Nora.

Aliyah sat up and folded the comforter away from her body as she turned until she was sitting on the edge of her bed.

*You are the author of your life story.* In the dim light that glowed outside her window, she could make out the wooden frame of the quote that she'd hung on her room wall. It was too dark to see the words, but she knew them by heart. Like many people, she'd often heard the saying throughout her life. And like many people, she'd thought she knew what it meant.

The meaning was deceptively obvious, and like so many basic truths in life, the depth and complexity were often lost in the simplicity. It was like the saying, "All I really need to know I learned in kindergarten." Aliyah had never read Robert Fulghum's book by that title, but she could imagine what it would say. Or at least what it would convey. It was what she was embracing for the first time, in her thirties. She'd been estranged by her family, suffered an emotionally abusive friendship, and had gotten a divorce. It had taken all of this before the fundamental reality of life sank in.

*You are alone on this journey of life, if for no other reason than no one can take your journey except you.*

Perhaps she should pen that realization in a journal, she considered. In one of the self-help books she'd read about broken friendships, the author suggested journaling to help with healing from toxic and abusive relationships. Maybe Aliyah should give it a try. She wasn't much of a writer though she'd occasionally enjoyed writing poetry and personal essays when she was in high school. She wondered if there was a voice tucked away inside her that needed only emotional safety to find release.

*A lot of things happened to me when I was a child. And I think it just got too much for me to keep holding inside...*

At the reminder of Reem's words, Aliyah felt a lump in her throat. It was as if the words were being spoken from her own heart.

For a moment Aliyah sat in puzzlement at her emotional reaction. It made no sense for her to feel connected to those words. Nothing traumatic had happened to her when she was a child. There was no dark family secret that lurked in the shadows of her past. The Thomases had always been the good family. They were the ones whom everyone at church and in the neighborhood wanted to emulate. They were the ones parents mentioned when scolding their children. "Do you see the Thomases acting like that, huh?"

*"I might be looking at the world from my vantage point,"* Reem had said, *"but whenever I see someone like Deanna, it reminds me of myself...I wasn't mean-spirited by nature; at least I don't think I was. I just felt so pressured to be this perfect Arab girl that I couldn't take it anymore. My family was constantly comparing Arabs to Americans to show how we were better. Yet no one spoke about all the bad things we did behind closed doors. It was almost like it was our Arab duty to have a double personality. All that mattered was that we upheld our family's honor and image. It didn't matter who we were on the inside, or if we were suffering in silence about anything. So in the Arab-Muslim community, I acted like a meek, perfect Muslim girl. But at school, I was crying out for attention. I think I wanted somebody to see through all my rebellion and say, 'I can tell something's wrong with you. How can I help?'"*

Aliyah stood and walked toward her bedroom door as sadness weighed on her. She had no idea why, but she was fighting back tears when she stepped into the hall and flicked on the light before heading to Ibrahim's room to check on him.

"You should be grateful you have a mother and father in the home," her parents would often say whenever Aliyah was upset about something. "Do you know how many people don't even *know* their parents?" The shame these words had inspired in Aliyah would make her forget her troubles. *Who am I to be upset about anything in my life?* she'd say to herself. *I have a safe home and food every day. I have a family who love and care for me. I can go to school. I don't have to worry about stray bullets or bombs falling on my head. None of us are addicted to drugs or alcohol. No one is in prison...* "You think you have problems?" her parents would say, berating her or her siblings for complaining about their petty troubles. "You have no idea what a problem is."

Aliyah carefully turned the handle to Ibrahim's door and slowly pushed it open until a rectangular glow of light spilled into his room and illuminated part of his face. The love and protectiveness she felt for him at that moment nearly choked her. She couldn't fathom what she'd do if something ever happened to him.

*Show him the love you never got.*

The determination came to her so strongly that it was overwhelming. Before closing the door, she whispered to Ibrahim the prophetic supplication for placing children under Allah's protection. As she walked back to her room, she was reminded of something Jacob had said.

*"Guilt and obligation. I swear, those two feelings have been in the driver seat of my life for too long."*

In her bathroom, Aliyah performed *wudhoo'* in preparation to pray *Qiyaam al-Layl*, the voluntary prayer before dawn. As she rubbed the water of ablution on her hands, face, and arms, she realized that she too had been driven by feelings of guilt and obligation. But it wasn't for the reasons that she'd thought. Though attending Islamic classes had definitely contributed to these feelings, her Islamic teachers were not responsible for making Aliyah believe that her individual needs and desires didn't matter. Her parents were.

Her relationship with her mother and father hadn't been built on love and compassion. It had been built on guilt and obligation. That was why it had been so easy for them to ostracize her when she became Muslim. Because Ally as a person with individual needs and desires never existed in the Thomas household. The only things that mattered were the good Thomas image and the Thomases' responsibility to save the world. Everything in Aliyah's upbringing had been about her family's obligation to some greater cause. Feeding the hungry. Helping disadvantaged youth. Being there for those without parents in the home.

*You should be grateful you have a mother and father in the home.* Even as a child, Aliyah felt the sting of those words. But she had been too young and inexperienced to fully understand and articulate why they hurt so much. But now she understood their underlying message.

*You don't matter.*

Face and arms glistening from *wudhoo'*, Aliyah left the bathroom and walked toward her closet, grieving the thought of any child—or adult—actually believing that their suffering didn't matter simply because someone else was suffering too.

As Aliyah pulled the prayer garment over her head, she recalled reading a story about how Prophet Muhammad had comforted a boy whose pet bird had died. He even helped the boy bury the bird and offered condolences. Something like that could have never happened in the Thomas home, she reflected.

*Who are you to be upset about anything in your life?* That was the question her parents would ask if she shed a single tear over her "petty troubles." Years ago, Aliyah would have interpreted this question as a reminder to be compassionate towards others and grateful for her blessings. But now she understood it as a form of haughtiness. The Thomases were superior to everyone else, so they had an obligation to help everyone else. And if their children displayed even the slightest sign of neediness, they were scolded into guilt and shame. Because the Thomases were not needy. The Thomases helped the needy.

Aliyah unfolded her prayer mat and laid it in the direction of the *qiblah*. Guilt and obligation. Yes, they had been in the driver's seat of her life too. Like Jacob had said, these feelings certainly had their place. But without an environment of love and compassion—in which no one's pain or suffering was trivialized—guilt and obligation were merely tools of control and means to deny someone their rights. Telling a child that she had no right to be upset over her troubles because others had it worse was like a doctor denying a patient treatment for a gunshot wound because in a hospital on the other side of the world, patients had lost limbs after a bomb blast. "Who are you to be upset about a silly hole in your limb," the doctor might ask, "while others don't even *have* all their limbs?" But generous people did not view themselves as above needing generosity themselves, and they didn't see themselves as having the right to dismiss the legitimacy of another person's pain.

"What hurts her hurts me." When Aliyah had first read these oft-repeated words uttered by Prophet Muhammad whenever he sensed even the slightest distress in his daughter Fatimah, Aliyah was overcome with emotion and awe at the Prophet's compassion. She couldn't fathom that level of love and concern existing in her childhood home. Aliyah's father had "greater causes" to tend to than comforting and pampering his daughter. Alfred Thomas, along with his wife, was too busy feeding the hungry, helping the disadvantaged, and being there for those without parents in the home. Meanwhile their own daughter went hungry, became disadvantaged, and learned to survive without her parents. Yes, Aliyah had food to eat, enjoyed an advantaged lifestyle, and saw her parents every day. But emotionally and psychologically, she was starved, disadvantaged, and parentless.

And because Aliyah had been taught that guilt and obligation always superseded love and compassion, she had lived in self-flagellating denial, even going as far as to marry a man she did not love because she had convinced herself that it would fulfill some "greater cause."

***

*Kerri Michaels is in a coma.*

Jacob sat on the carpet of the living room and turned his head to the right then the left, signaling the end of *Fajr* prayer. "*As-salaamu'alaikum wa rahmatullaah,*" his sons recited in unison, repeating after Jacob as they sat behind him next to each other. "*As-salaamu'alaikum wa rahmatullaah.*"

Jacob turned his body until he was facing his sons and then recited the *dhikr* after obligatory prayer, his sons reciting with him. But his mind kept wandering to his mother-in-law who was lying in the hospital right then—and to his soon-to-be former wife who was being held at the county jail, pending an investigation into attempted manslaughter.

Barry Michaels had called Jacob late last night in such an unintelligible rage that Jacob had difficulty making out what his father-in-law was saying. "You people are responsible for this, you know that?" Barry spat through the phone. "So no, I'm not going to pay a single penny for that girl's bail. When she was in the church, she didn't have any problems. Everything went downhill when she joined the Muslims. And now my wife has to pay! You better hope she pulls through this, boy. You better hope!"

Though it had perplexed Jacob at the time, after he finally comprehended what his father-in-law was telling him, he felt a trace of peace in his heart. Perhaps hearing the horrible news and listening to Barry blame him for something that had absolutely nothing to do with him helped clarify for Jacob that he had made the right decision by divorcing Deanna. Jacob could no longer bear the laborious responsibility of saving and healing Barry and Kerri Michael's daughter, at least not in the role as Deanna's husband. As her Muslim brother and the father of their children, Jacob would always be connected to Deanna. But he could no longer subject himself (and potentially his sons) to daily emotional, psychological, and physical harm. His responsibility first and foremost was to protect his own soul (and the souls of his children), and remaining married to Deanna was pulling him away from his responsibilities as a Muslim and a father. Yes, men were the maintainers and protectors of women, but men could fulfill that role only if they were in a spiritually healthy environment that allowed them to first maintain and protect themselves.

It wasn't until Jacob woke up that morning about a half hour before *Fajr* that the gravity of his predicament weighed on him. Before praying *Fajr*, Jacob stood in *Qiyaam al-Layl* and supplicated to Allah for Kerri's recovery and for Deanna's psychological and spiritual healing. And he also prayed that Allah would help him and his sons during this difficult time.

"Your uncle Larry is going to be taking you to basketball this morning," Jacob said to Younus and Thawab after they finished reciting the prophetic supplications after *Fajr*.

"When is Mommy coming home?" Thawab said, his expression pained.

Jacob started to respond, but Younus spoke before he could. "She's not coming home for a while, okay?" Younus spoke with compassion, his eyes conveying insight and understanding as he looked at his younger brother.

"Why not?" Thawab said.

"She's really sick and needs to stay with her mother and father for a long time."

Taken aback by the maturity of his nine-year-old, Jacob creased his forehead in confusion. "She'll be gone for a while," Jacob said tentatively. "We're not sure how long though, little man. So let's make some cards and pictures for her. What do you think?" Jacob's eyes met Younus's briefly, and in that fleeting glance, Jacob saw that Younus was aware of at least part of what was going on.

Thawab shrugged noncommittally. "Okay."

"You want something to eat?" Jacob offered.

He shrugged again. "Okay."

"I'll get you some cereal," Younus said as he got to his feet. "Come on," he said, gesturing to Thawab, who stood and followed his brother to the kitchen.

Jacob leaned against the doorway to the kitchen and watched as Younus poured Thawab a bowl of cereal and milk, a reflective smile on Jacob's face. "But go to sleep after you eat," Younus said. "You don't want to be tired when it's time to go to basketball."

"So what was that all about?" Jacob teased Younus good-naturedly after they both left the kitchen.

Younus folded his arms over his chest, his expression troubled as he looked down, as if trying to figure out the best way to respond. "Are you and Mommy divorced?"

Jacob drew in a deep breath and exhaled. This was a conversation he had hoped he would never have with his sons, at least not for some time. Deanna's *'iddah* would be ending in a couple of weeks, and Jacob had decided that during the Islamic waiting period for divorce, he would persuade Deanna to go with him to marriage counseling. However, all of Jacob's attempts to convince her to accept professional or religious intervention were to no avail. She consistently maintained that she and Jacob were fully capable of solving their marital problems on their own (though she was adamant that Jacob was the only one with a problem).

"Not yet," Jacob said, deciding that honesty was the best approach with Younus. "But we might be soon."

Younus nodded. "Can we live with you then?" he said after a thoughtful pause.

Jacob furrowed his brows. "You already live with me, Younus. There's no need to worry about that."

"I mean, if we have to choose."

"You don't have to choose."

"Isn't that what the lawyers make you do?"

"Lawyers?" Jacob said, pulling his back in confusion. "What lawyers?"

"Divorce lawyers."

Jacob's eyebrows rose in understanding. "There won't be any divorce lawyers *insha'Allah.*"

Younus nodded, but he didn't look convinced. "I saw Mommy on TV," he said after a few seconds had passed. "Why is she saying bad things about Aunty Aliyah?"

Jacob was overcome with concern. "What bad things?"

Younus's arms dropped to his sides as he turned and walked toward the computer in the den. Jacob followed, dreading learning what Deanna had done this time.

***

"I'm telling you folks," the host of Will's Truth Hour said as he looked into the camera toward his television audience, "this story has inspired me to change the title of my show from W-T-H to W-T-F." He shook his head in disbelief, a smirk on his face. There was chuckling from the set.

Will turned to the two guests present as the camera zoomed out. "Remember that 'crazy Muslim woman' story from months ago?" The guests nodded knowingly, grins on their faces. "Well, that crazy Muslim woman has just gotten crazier. We've just gotten word that she approached Cassie Studios, a photography company, asking the owner to take pictures of her and tell the media, and I quote," he glanced at his notes before looking up, "'I'm the hot wife, and *she's* the crazy mistress.'"

There was laughter from the set. "But that's not all," Will said, humor in his tone. "She specifically requested that the photographer *lie* to the media. As it turns out, that 'hot Muslim mistress' she assaulted, who we're told goes by the nickname Aliyah, wasn't her husband's mistress at all. She was her *best friend.*"

"Unbelievable," one of the guests muttered.

"But our crazy marriage guru, Dr. Deanna Janice Bivens," Will continued, "author of *You Can Have Him All To Yourself*, wanted everyone to *believe* that her best friend was the mistress so that Aliyah would look like a crazy woman."

"That definitely puts a new spin on the blame-the-victim attitude that's really prevalent today," the female guest said as her name and the title *Feminist Lobbyist* appeared across the bottom of the screen. "One thing I speak about in my workshops is that women are often the first to blame the victim. Women put an enormous amount of pressure on other women to live up to sexist standards."

"What I want to know," the male guest said as the title *Relationship Psychologist* appeared beneath his name, "is what provoked the original assault. I mean, if Aliyah was this so-called marriage guru's best friend, and not her husband's mistress, then what on earth was she assaulting the woman for?"

"That's where the story gets really interesting," Will said, grinning hungrily. "Sources tell us that Dr. Bivens's husband actually wanted to *marry* Aliyah when they were in college, and after ten years of marriage, Dr. Bivens was still filled with jealous rage."

The guests nodded in understanding. "That makes sense," the feminist lobbyist said. "It's the part of blame-the-victim mentality that forms the foundation of rape culture. If a man finds a woman attractive, it's the woman's fault. So if she is attacked by a jealous woman or raped by a frustrated man, the logic is that she provoked the crime by being attractive."

"Or in this case," the relationship psychologist said, "Dr. Bivens may have been insecure due to a bad marriage and shifted blame to the symptom instead of addressing the cause. In my practice, I tell my patients that it's impossible for someone other than the spouses to create a bad marriage, even if one or both of them are having an affair."

"Well," Will said, doubtful humor in his voice, "I don't know if this is rape culture or a bad marriage, but Cassie Studios has provided us with those 'hot' photos from Dr. Bivens's photo essay. Editors," he said with contrived seriousness as he looked into the camera, "get ready to display that parental warning because these babies are *hot*."

The screen faded to a picture of Deanna wearing a business suit, her hijab pushed back displaying half of her hair, her lips in a pout, shiny with red lipstick. There was a roar of laughter from the set as similar pictures were displayed.

When the camera returned to the discussion desk, the guests were still recovering from laughter. "*Crazy* hot," Will added, an amused grin on his face as they transitioned to a commercial break.

***

"I just don't think that's the right attitude though," Reem said as she and Aliyah stood on the sides of the tennis courts holding their rackets, waiting for a court to open Saturday morning. Mashael had called to say that she and Nora wouldn't be able to make it that day. "What people think *does* matter. You just can't let it run your life."

"But I can't change how people think," Aliyah said. "So all I'm saying is I'm no longer expecting anything from friends or imams, and definitely not men. How is that being negative?"

"But you *should* expect things from people. That's the purpose of a community."

"Ideally, I agree with you, Reem," Aliyah said. "But we're working from two very different realities. I'm an American convert with no Muslim family, so I don't really have a community. If I were married, it'd be a different story. Because only married couples are welcomed in our community."

"Aliyah, come on," Reem said. "I don't think our community is *that* bad. They might post offensive stuff online, but it's just a bunch of talk. It might be hurtful, but they're not saying they don't want you around."

"Reem," Aliyah said, a lighthearted grin on her face, "can you step out of teacher mode for just one second? This is not a *tafseer* class. I know what I'm talking about. For the past ten years, I practically lived in that masjid, so I'm not guessing. If you're not married, you're not welcomed. Yes, people *tolerate* you because they have to. But outside community gatherings like *Jumu'ah* and *Eid* prayer, they practically have official rules that divorced women can't participate."

Reem laughed. "I don't believe that."

Aliyah shrugged, a pleasant expression on her face. "Denial is a luxury that only the privileged can afford."

Through the wide slit of her black face veil, Reem's eyes narrowed in hurt and confusion as she looked at Aliyah. "What's that supposed to mean?"

"Reem," Aliyah said, a knowing smile on her face, "all I'm saying is, I live a reality that you can't understand."

"Don't forget I'm part of this community too."

"You're *active* in the community," Aliyah said. "But you're not part of it. There's a difference. You don't even bring your son or daughter around. I'm not saying you have to, but the fact that you don't means you have the privilege of another community. I don't have that privilege."

"Everyone has options."

"I didn't say I don't have options," Aliyah said. "This whole conversation started when I said I'm pursuing other options for myself instead of depending on other people. But I'm saying I don't have the privilege of another community."

"That's not true though," Reem said. "You have the privilege of any community you want to be part of."

A shadow of a smile lingered on Aliyah's face. "When the Arabs get together," she said, "do you invite Americans?"

Reem narrowed her eyes in confusion. "They're speaking in Arabic. Why would we invite Americans? You wouldn't even understand what we're saying."

"That's my point," Aliyah said. "The Arab community is an option *only* for you, not me. So if I took your advice about being proactive in participating even when I think I'm not welcomed, I wouldn't even understand the conversation."

"I meant in *this* community, not with the Arabs."

"But why are those two different things, Reem?" Aliyah said challengingly. "If we're supposed to be a united *ummah* like you said, then why are Arabs excluded from that?"

"We're not excluded," Reem said. "I'm just saying there's no point in inviting English speakers to Arab social events. It makes no sense."

"We invite Arabic speakers to American social events," Aliyah said. "What's the difference?"

"Everyone is speaking English at your events," Reem said. "But at our gatherings, we only speak Arabic."

"I hear people speaking different languages at our events," Aliyah said. "But even if we did speak only English, don't you all know English?"

"Most of us do, yes. But our events give us the opportunity to relax and bond with other Arabs without the culture or language barrier."

"And why can't Americans also bond with Arabs?"

"You can," Reem said, "when we come to your events."

"Look," Aliyah said, "I don't have a problem with Arabs having their own events sometimes, because I'm sure if I were in a foreign country, I'd want to bond with people like me too. But my point is that the Arabs are your real community. I don't have a real community. When most Americans convert to Islam, we have in our minds that all Muslims are our brothers and sisters, and we really expect other Muslims to see us that way."

"And we do," Reem said.

"But that's not true," Aliyah said. "You keep us at a distance and come around only to earn blessings for teaching Qur'an or Arabic and being kind to us."

Reem's eyes conveyed hurt. "I don't keep you at a distance."

"I don't mean you specifically," Aliyah said. "I'm talking about the culture of how Arabs and other immigrant Muslims deal with Americans."

"I don't see you as any different from my Arab friends."

Aliyah's eyebrows rose. "I think you do."

"Aliyah, I'm really hurt that you'd say that," Reem said. "I love you like my own sister."

There was a thoughtful pause. "Think about it like this," Aliyah said. "My son is twenty years old and your daughter is nineteen, and they want to get married. Is that okay?"

Reem's eyes narrowed in distaste. "No. She'll have to marry someone who shares her culture and language."

Aliyah grinned and shook her head. "See? That's what I mean. Then you *do* see me as different from your Arab friends. And there's no way I could ever *really* be your Muslim sister because I don't share your culture or language."

"Marriage has nothing to do with what I'm talking about," Reem said.

"But it has *everything* to do with what *I'm* talking about," Aliyah said. "A real Muslim community should fulfill all our needs, not just Qur'an, Arabic, and Islamic studies. The community should be where we meet new friends, establish bonds of Muslim sisterhood and brotherhood, and where our children can meet their future spouses. If that's not even a possibility for us, then it's not a community. It's a charity project where we're sent home at the end of the day."

"That's why it's important for you to be more active in your community," Reem said. "For us, our parents and family help us get married. Americans can do something similar with each other."

"And why do you assume that Arabs should marry Arabs and Americans should marry Americans?"

"It's what makes the most sense," Reem said. "I know in Islam it's allowed to marry outside your culture, but it's not encouraged. It can cause too many problems in your marriage and family."

"I never heard that it's not encouraged," Aliyah said, "but I agree it can be a challenge for everyone involved. But that's not my point. I mentioned marriage because family is the foundation of a community. And if we just assume that Arabs and Americans should have their own separate families, then there's no such thing as the Muslim community you keep talking about."

"I don't think it's fair to expect Arabs and other Muslims to welcome strangers into their families," Reem said.

"Strangers?" Aliyah said, humor in her tone.

"You know what I mean."

Aliyah shook her head. "I don't think I do. You mentioned Arabs and other Muslims as one group and strangers as another. Who are the strangers you're talking about?"

"Aliyah," Reem said, annoyance in her voice, "it's not an obligation for Muslims to intermarry with no care whatsoever for lineage and culture. There's nothing wrong with preserving your bloodline and traditions."

"Preserving your bloodline and traditions?" Aliyah said in disbelief. "I thought Muslims married based on personal preference and spiritual compatibility. So I don't see how lineage and culture should even be mentioned in the context of marriage."

"That's why it's not a good idea for Muslims to intermarry," Reem said. "Understanding the importance of bloodline and family tradition is common knowledge in Muslim cultures. When they begin to intermarry, these things are lost because others don't respect our traditions."

"And they pollute the bloodline," Aliyah added, sarcastic humor in her tone.

Reem sighed. "Let's not talk about this anymore. It's not something I think you can understand."

"That," Aliyah said, nodding emphatically, "I agree with completely. I view my Muslim brothers and sisters as a single group regardless of what country they're from. And from what I read, that's what the Sunnah tells us to do. So unless it's based on someone's personal preference and not a family or cultural rule, the idea of preserving bloodlines and cultures is not something I have the capacity to understand."

"I think they're finished," Reem said, emotion gone from her voice. She gestured toward a court where the man and woman were gathering their tennis balls in preparation to leave. "We should go before someone else comes."

Aliyah nodded and followed Reem to the court, but her mind was still on the troubling conversation they'd just had.

***

"*As-salaamu'alaikum*, stranger."

Aliyah had just finished playing tennis with Reem and was standing on the sidelines of the basketball court waiting for Ibrahim's group to the finish their last round of drills. She turned at the sound of a familiar voice.

"Why do you look so shocked?" Larry said teasingly, a playful grin on his face. "I still exist."

An amused grin formed at Aliyah's lips as she shook her head and turned her attention back to the court. "Wow."

"Can I at least get the salaams?"

"*Wa'alaiku-mus-salaam wa rahmatullaah*," she said with measured deliberation. "Stranger."

"Man," Larry said, laughter in his voice, "a brother can't catch a break these days."

"A brother?" Aliyah repeated, playful disbelief in her voice. "You're the one who went AWOL on me."

"M-I-A, maybe," Larry said in lighthearted in apology. "But not AWOL."

Aliyah shrugged, a shadow of a smile on her face. "Same difference. Either way, you have a lot of explaining to do."

"Okay," Larry said as if in confession. "I messed up. I hope you can forgive me."

Aliyah was immediately reminded of Nikki saying something similar. Her smile faded at the thought.

"What?" Larry said, confusion in his voice. "Did I say something wrong?"

"No." Aliyah shook her head. "It's just that I seem to be hearing that a lot lately."

"Hearing what?"

"*I messed up*," she repeated. "*I hope you can forgive me*."

There was a thoughtful pause. "I take it you're talking about that social media madness from a few months back," Larry said.

Aliyah coughed laughter. "No, I haven't received any apologies for that."

"You're serious?" Larry sounded genuinely surprised.

"Dead," Aliyah said.

Larry exhaled in a single breath. "Wow."

"You can say that again."

"*Nobody* apologized?"

"Well, one, if you count Jacob," Aliyah said with a shrug. "But he wasn't even responsible for what happened."

An awkward silence followed.

"Have you spoken to Deanna or anybody?"

Something in the way Larry asked the question made Aliyah's heart stop. "What happened?" she said, her eyes wide in panic as she looked at Larry. He was probably here for Younus and Thawab, she realized. "Is Jacob okay?"

Larry averted his gaze. "*Insha'Allah.*"

"What do you mean, '*Insha'Allah*'?" Aliyah didn't mean to sound as if she were scolding Larry, but saying *insha'Allah* wasn't telling her anything.

"I mean *insha'Allah,*" Larry said firmly, a trace of annoyance in his voice. "You know who he's married to."

"Larry," Aliyah said, her voice a demanding plea, "tell me what happened."

Larry shrugged. "I don't know really. But it looks like Deanna and her mother had a fight or something."

Aliyah drew her eyebrows together and shook her head in confusion. "So…" she said, unsure how to form the question in her mind.

"So Jacob's mother-in-law is lying unconscious in some hospital."

"*What*?"

"It doesn't look good, Aliyah," Larry said, his voice subdued. "Deanna is being held at the county jail. Her bail hearing is scheduled for next week."

Aliyah felt lightheaded all of a sudden. There had to be some misunderstanding. "I mean, she couldn't have…you know?"

Larry pursed his lips and shook his head as if to say he didn't know any more than he'd shared.

"But that's so…" Aliyah's face was contorted in confusion. "Are you sure there isn't some mistake?"

"I'm sure."

"But Deanna practically adored her fam—"

"*As-salaamu'alaikum*, Aunty."

At the sight of Younus and Thawab, Aliyah quickly closed her mouth and forced a smile. Before she replied to the boys' salaams, Ibrahim appeared at her side.

"*As-salaamu'aliakum*, Mommy!" Ibrahim said, breathless. "I made a lot of shots today. The coach said I'm *really* good."

"*Wa'alaiku-mus-salaam*, Younus, Thawab, and my cookie monster," Aliyah said playfully. "I bet he did," she said to Ibrahim. "Because you *are* really good, *mashaAllah*."

Aliyah placed her hand on Ibrahim's back as he hugged her, and her eyes met those of Younus, who was looking at her with an odd expression on his face. The look in his eyes made her uncomfortable, and she was tempted to ask what was bothering him. But she forced a smile instead, imagining that he probably knew about his mother. In response, Younus made a poor attempt at a pleasant expression, his lips forming a thin line before turning his attention to his uncle.

"Will Daddy be back soon?" Younus asked.

"I'm not sure when he'll be back," Larry said. "But why don't we go get some ice cream?"

"Ice cream!" Thawab said cheerfully. "I want some."

"Oooh," Ibrahim said. "Can we get ice cream too?"

Aliyah's eyebrows rose in apology, and she started to shake her head.

"Why don't you two join us?" Larry said before she could refuse. "It'll be my treat."

"Yes!" Ibrahim said.

"Larry, I don't know…" Exhaustion was in Aliyah's voice as she spoke. She wasn't in the mood to hang out with Larry. She was still trying to wrap her mind around what he'd just shared.

"Can Ibrahim come with us then?" Younus said, folding his arms over his chest. He still had that odd look in his eyes as he looked at Aliyah.

Aliyah opened her mouth to refuse, but Ibrahim interrupted her.

"Mommy, please," he said, his face twisted in a pout. "I *never* see Younus and Thawab anymore."

The truth of his words stung, and she felt horrible. It had been months since Ibrahim spent time with his friends. "Okay, but I need to—"

"Yes!" The boys sang out the word all together, making Aliyah laugh midsentence.

"—go home and take a shower first," she finished. "And so do you."

"I'll pick up you and Ibrahim in an hour then, *insha'Allah*," Larry said.

Still smiling, Aliyah nodded. "Okay, *insha'Allah*."

***

*She'll have to marry someone who shares her culture and language.*

Reem cringed at the memory. *How could I say something like that?* she scolded herself, her gloved hands gripping the steering wheel as she drove home. Though it was how she honestly felt about the idea of her daughter marrying an American, it was incredibly rude. She shouldn't have said that to Aliyah. Perhaps Reem herself was being defensive. She had been offended by what Aliyah was saying about Arabs.

But Reem couldn't deny that Aliyah was right. It was true that Reem was not fully invested in the non-Arab community, and she did come around only to teach Qur'an and *tafseer* and to earn blessings for being kind to Americans. But Reem genuinely liked Aliyah. So what did it matter whether or not Reem would want Aliyah's son to marry her daughter? Why did everything boil down to marriage?

Was that really the measuring stick of sisterhood and brotherhood in Islam? Certainly, love for the sake of Allah was not limited to who could marry whom.

*Denial is a luxury that only the privileged can afford.*

Reem was really hurt by Aliyah's comment about privilege. All wasn't well in Reem's life, and all certainly was not well in the Arab community. Yes, Reem and Sayed preferred that Hana and Muhammad socialize with only family and other Arabs, but that didn't mean they were privileged. It was definitely a blessing to be part of two different communities and to not have to worry about whom their daughter and son would marry, but life was so much more complicated than that.

As Reem exited the interstate toward home, she was filled with dread as her thoughts shifted to the dinner party that her family was hosting that night. Her father's eldest son was visiting from Saudi Arabia with his wife and children, and they would be staying for three weeks. Reem loathed the idea of seeing Fahad sitting in her mother's living room relaxing and eating as if his presence were the most natural thing in the world.

"Don't worry about it," Sayed had told her early that morning. "I'll make sure Hana and Muhammad aren't around him too much."

Her husband's words had eased some of her anxiety, but not all. What if Fahad's teenage sons had turned out like their father had been at their age?

***

"Exactly!" Aliyah said, laughing in agreement as she and Larry sat across from each other at a table in the mall. Their bodies were turned toward the play area where Ibrahim, Younus, and Thawab were maneuvering bumper cars and ramming into each other at every opportunity. They had finished eating their ice cream thirty minutes before. "If there's not even a *chance* of our children marrying each other," Aliyah said, "then that's not a real friendship."

She had shared with Larry the conversation she'd had with Reem, but she didn't tell him that it was Reem who'd made the comments. To avoid backbiting, Aliyah had said that she had run into an old Arab friend from the masjid.

"They certainly keep us at a distance," Larry said, a smirk on his face as he shook his head.

"I really like the sister," Aliyah said reflectively. "But her comments about intercultural marriage really annoyed me. I don't see how they don't see that at divisive to say their children can only marry someone from their country."

"Because they're racist," Larry said. "And you're supposed to feel grateful if they even spend time with you. The minute you see yourself as more than a charity case, they feel insulted."

Aliyah was silent, uncomfortable with the offensive terminology in connection to her Qur'an teacher. "I don't think I'd call them racist," she said. "Because they do have a point."

Larry looked at Aliyah, eyebrows raised. "You're serious?"

"I don't agree with it," Aliyah clarified. "But you can't deny that there *is* some value to having your children only marry into families you already know."

"And your Arab friend doesn't already know you and Ibrahim?" Larry said skeptically.

"That's a good point," Aliyah said, chuckling self-consciously. "I guess I don't think of myself as being someone she *really* knows, if you know what I mean."

Larry narrowed his eyes in curiosity. "So you think you have to be from the same culture to really know someone?"

"No," Aliyah said tentatively. "But if someone thinks that no one should be in their family except people from their culture, then that thinking prevents them from ever really getting to know me. Because there's always this barrier and air of superiority that clouds everything."

"You think your friend feels superior to you?"

"Yes," Aliyah said honestly, frowning briefly. "But it's not intentional, so I don't blame her for it. It just makes conversations hard because she's always trying to teach me something instead of just taking a moment to actually listen to what I'm saying. It's like she feels obligated to make me see the world differently, but she almost never considers that *she* can benefit from seeing the world differently too."

"Did something happen to make her treat you like that, or is she like that in general?"

Aliyah furrowed her brows as she considered the question. "I don't know. But we did become close around the time I was getting divorced, so maybe she felt sorry for me and wanted to help."

"That happens a lot to introspective people," Larry said. "Especially if you tend to keep to yourself. Other people hide their pain through being talkative, sociable, and outgoing. They're so good at masking pain that they even hide it from themselves. But it's hard for people like you to wear a mask when you're hurting. So people feel sorry for you and think they need to save you."

Aliyah wrinkled her nose. "Maybe that's what Deanna thought she was doing."

Larry nodded thoughtfully. "I think the jury is still out on Deanna. But my hunch is that she was jealous of you and resented you for it."

Aliyah coughed laughter. "Deanna was always saying *I* was jealous of *her*."

"She was just projecting," Larry said. "Narcissistic people have a hard time processing negative feelings unless they're about other people. So anytime they feel something negative in connection to another person, they think it's because of that other person instead of themselves."

Aliyah creased her forehead. "You think Deanna is narcissistic?"

A disbelieving grin formed on Larry's face. "It's obvious, isn't it? That woman has some serious issues." He huffed. "I count it as a blessing that my brother will probably be finally free of her."

Aliyah contorted her face. "Don't say that."

"Why not?" Larry said. "It's the truth."

“There’s nothing good about Deanna spending the rest of her life in prison,” Aliyah said, frowning in disapproval. “What if her mother dies, Larry? Would you count that as a blessing too?”

“Of course not,” Larry said. “It’s terrible what happened to Mrs. Michaels, and I really pray she pulls through. I’m just saying there’s a silver lining here, and that’s my brother finally being able to move on with his life.”

Aliyah gritted her teeth in annoyance, her gaze on the boys bumping their cars into each other.

“I swear,” Larry said, “when I picked up my nephews this morning, Jacob looked like he was finally starting to have some peace of mind.”

“Did *he* say that?” Aliyah asked challengingly. “Because I have a hard time thinking he’s at peace with his wife in jail and his mother-in-law on her deathbed.”

“Of course not,” Larry said. “I’m talking about how he looked, not what he said.”

“Maybe you were doing a bit of projecting yourself,” Aliyah said flippantly.

Larry laughed and nodded. “Maybe I was.” He shrugged nonchalantly. “But I’m not going to apologize for being happy for my brother. Before he married Deanna, Jacob was vibrant, charismatic, and inspirational. I used to look up to him. But after he married Deanna, it was like a part of him died and I’d only get glimpses of who he used to be. And this morning I saw a glimpse of the brother I remember.” A reflective grin lingered on Larry’s face. “Call me insensitive or cruel or whatever, but I’m happy there’s a chance I’ll have my brother back.”

## 16
## Crash Course

Aliyah stood in front of Dr. Warren's desk, glancing uncertainly at the stack of files her supervisor had just handed her. "Did he say when he'll be returning?"

Dr. Warren raised an eyebrow. "I was about to ask you the same thing."

Aliyah creased her forehead, caught off guard by her supervisor's accusatory tone. "Excuse me?"

"Professor Thomas," Dr. Warren said, a knowing smirk on her face as she met Aliyah's gaze, "it is obvious that you and Dr. Bivens have strong feelings for each other and that you know each other outside of work. But I commend you both for your professionalism. So I'm asking this because I value Dr. Bivens as a colleague and an old friend." She narrowed her eyes in an effort to appear concerned. "Will he be returning to us any time soon?"

Aliyah's face grew hot in offense. "Dr. Warren," Aliyah said, struggling to keep her voice cordial, "I think there's been a misunderstanding. Outside of work, I know Dr. Bivens only through my friendship with his wife. And due to the unfortunate events over the past few months, I haven't seen her in quite some time."

"But you've seen Dr. Bivens, I assume?"

"Yes," Aliyah said, "at work."

"So you're telling me you have absolutely *no* contact with Dr. Bivens outside the office," Dr. Warren said with skeptical sarcasm.

"That's exactly what I'm saying," Aliyah said, unsure where all of this was coming from. "The last time I saw him was a week ago. At work," she added for emphasis.

Dr. Warren leaned back in her chair, the shadow of a smirk on her face. "That's interesting," she said. "Because from what I understand, you attend the same mosque."

"We do," Aliyah said cautiously, her gaze meeting Dr. Warren's unblinking. "But I've never spoken to him at the mosque. Like most Muslims, I go there only for prayer and religious study."

Dr. Warren huffed. "Well, on the off chance that you *do* see him," she said, "please find out how long he plans to stay away."

"On the off chance that I see him," Aliyah said, struggling to keep the sarcasm out of her tone, "I'll ask him to give you a call." Aliyah forced a tightlipped smile. "How does that sound?"

Dr. Warren's lips twitched in discomfort, and Aliyah sensed that this wasn't quite how her supervisor had envisioned the conversation. Aliyah had no idea what Dr. Warren was getting at or why, but Aliyah wasn't about to play the role of the ditsy new employee trying to impress her superiors. Perhaps Aliyah's willingness to help other professors run errands and make copies during her lunch break had been construed as evidence of her gullibility.

Yes, this job mattered to Aliyah—a lot. But not more than her integrity. She would rather go homeless or live with her uncle than reduce herself to pandering for approval. She would continue to go over and beyond what was required of her in work-related activities, but she was unwilling to open up her private life to scrutiny.

"Then I think we'll need to give you a little help with overseeing One Plus One," Dr. Warren said, as if in rebuke.

"Thank you," Aliyah said sincerely, conscious that Dr. Warren had imagined that Aliyah would want to run the internship alone. "I appreciate any help I can get."

"I think it's best if *you* were the one helping someone else," Dr. Warren said, her tone still in rebuke.

Aliyah nodded. "I agree," she said. "I'm still new here, so if a more experienced professor is able to run the program in Dr. Bivens's absence, I'm more than willing to assist wherever I can."

Dr. Warren's face was pinched in distaste as she leaned forward and opened up a file folder on her desk before removing a pen from a ceramic cup. "Then I think Dr. Stanley should replace you in running the internship."

It was obvious that Dr. Warren was trying to make Aliyah regretful for being uncooperative, but Aliyah was unable to feel anything but indignant.

*What on earth is going on here?* Aliyah thought to herself. One second Aliyah was a favored professor, and the next Dr. Warren was acting like she saw Aliyah as some sort of threat. The supervisor couldn't possibly think that Aliyah could vie for anyone's position after working at the college for less than a year. That was not even enough time to hope for tenure. And Aliyah didn't even have a doctorate yet.

***

"It could be several things," Larry said later that afternoon as Aliyah gripped the steering wheel with one hand and reached under her hijab with the other to push her earpiece in more securely. "But whatever's going on, it's not good."

"Well, I figured *that* much," she said, rolling her eyes in agreement as she slowed to a stop in preparation to exit the faculty and staff parking lot. "I'm just really not in the mood for *fitnah* at work. So if there's something going on, I wish someone would just come out and say it. I hate all this passive-aggressive stuff. I don't even *want* to run Jacob's internship program. I already have enough on my plate."

"But they don't know that," Larry's voice said through the earpiece. "As far as they're concerned, you all want the same things. So it's probably never crossed their minds that this job doesn't mean that much to you. For them, it's probably the sum total of their existence."

"If you ever work for anyone other than yourself," Aliyah recited aloud, "put your heart into the job. But don't put the job in your heart."

"Nice," Larry said. "Where'd you hear that?"

"My mom," Aliyah said reflectively as she eased her car onto the main road. "She didn't believe in professional slavery."

Larry chuckled in agreement. "Sounds like we grew up in the same house."

"I think today was the first time I really understood her advice though," Aliyah said honestly. "I want to keep my job, but not *that* much."

"It was a trap," Larry said, returning to the topic of Aliyah's predicament. "Jacob is obviously already in communication with his supervisor about his leave of absence, so it was completely unnecessary for her to ask you about it."

"I know…" Aliyah thoughtfully. "I just wish I knew what was going on. It almost sounded like she was trying to pin something on me. I just don't know what."

"She's probably just annoyed that Jacob suggested that you head the internship in his absence."

"But what difference does it make? The internship will be over next month."

"That's why I don't do nine-to-fives," Larry said. "This stuff never makes sense. There's always some insecure person on a power trip."

Aliyah rolled her eyes as she veered onto the ramp leading to the interstate. "Most people work a nine-to-five because they have to, Larry. We don't consider it a personal preference to work under people with superiority complexes."

"Didn't you say you wanted to start your own business?" Larry asked. "Maybe this is your chance."

"My chance?" Aliyah said, coughing laughter. "I still have to pay my bills."

"Not if you marry me," Larry said teasingly.

Aliyah felt dread in the pit of her stomach. As much as she enjoyed talking to Larry, the idea of being his wife, she just couldn't wrap her mind around. She was still in the dark as to why he had been suddenly MIA during the time the rumors were being spread about her, and thus far, all of his responses to her inquiries had been evasive.

"Larry, please," Aliyah said, exhaustion in her tone, "let's not go there."

"Why not?" Larry said lightheartedly. "I'm good enough to call for advice but not good enough to marry?"

Aliyah contorted her face. "What does getting advice have to do with marriage? I used to ask the imam for advice all the time, but I'd never marry him."

"Maybe that's why you're still single," Larry said, sarcastic humor in his tone. "You think everyone is beneath you."

Aliyah's face was aflame in offense. "*What*?"

"It's true," Larry said, laughter in his voice. "You can't deny that you could benefit from seeing other people as equal to you instead of beneath you." He added, "The imam's a good brother, so why isn't he good enough for you?"

"I didn't say he's not good enough for me," Aliyah said. "I said I would never marry him."

"But why not?" Larry said. "He's obviously a person of good character and has knowledge of the *deen*."

"Because we have *nothing* in common," Aliyah said, her eyes narrowed on the stretch of interstate in front of her. "He's like sixty years old. And *married*," she added.

"That didn't stop you from considering Jacob," Larry said, chuckling. "Except for their age difference, Jacob and the imam are very similar."

"*Jacob*?"

"Don't act like it's never crossed your mind. It's obvious how you feel about him."

"Why does *every*body keep saying that?" Aliyah said, face contorted in offense. "He asked about *me*."

"That doesn't mean you're not interested."

"Larry, please." Aliyah rolled her eyes.

"Are you begging me to marry you?" Larry joked.

"No I'm not," Aliyah said, annoyed. "I'm begging you to leave the topic alone."

"Should I leave you alone too?"

"Yes, I think you should," she said.

"Then why did you call me?"

"I called for advice, Larry. That's hardly an invitation for marriage."

"Just so you know," Larry said, "men don't like teases. So if you're not interested in marrying a brother, don't call him for advice. If you can't help him with what he needs, don't expect him to help you with what you need."

Aliyah was still fuming when she pulled into a space in the parking strip in front of the halal market. She had ended the call minutes before and was saying the *isti'aadhah* to calm herself. "*A'oodhu billaahi minash-shaytaanirrajeem*," she uttered as she turned off the car. *I seek refuge in Allah from Satan the rejected enemy.* "*A'oodhu billaahi minash-shaytaanirrajeem*."

Aliyah removed the key from the ignition then pushed the driver side door open as she was reminded suddenly of something Nikki had said.

*Women hate women they can't find anything wrong with, and men resent women they can't have for themselves.*

"Why is Islamic obligation only important after a *man* decides who he wants to marry?" Aliyah had vented to Reem weeks ago. "I've never heard an imam tell a brother, 'Fear Allah. The sister wants to marry you, so stop following your *nafs* and marry the sister.' But we're told things like that *all* the time."

After locking her car, Aliyah walked to the glass door with a large *We're Open* sign in red letters. A bell jingled above her head as she pulled the handle and stepped inside. Instantly, the smell of poultry and packaged food tickled her nostrils, and she momentarily shifted her thoughts from Larry as she made a mental note of what she needed to buy. As she made her way to the meat counter, rows of sugary treats in shimmery cellophane wrapping caught her eye. For a fleeting moment, her healthy resolve was weakened as she contemplated buying a sweet snack.

*What is going on with you?* she reprimanded herself. She must be more stressed than she realized. For years, the idea of eating processed sugar and high fructose corn syrup repulsed her. Yes, she sometimes had cravings for junk food, but usually her emotional eating amounted to consuming a gyro or a burger from a restaurant or making a halal salami sandwich for herself at home. But even when her cravings were at their worst, she never resorted to eating snack cakes or candy bars. Her guilty pleasure was generally white bread, and even that was usually organic.

"*As-salaamu'alaikum*!" At the sound of the cheerful voice, Aliyah turned and found a woman smiling at her, the woman's hand extended in greeting.

An uncertain smile creased one side of Aliyah's mouth at the sight of the woman's kind face and African-style head wrap and baby hair peeking out beneath. "*Wa'alaiku-mus-salaam wa-rahmatullaah,*" Aliyah said as she shook the woman's hand, a question still on her face.

"I'm sorry," the woman said, laughter in her voice. "I'm Salima. I met you in Sister Reem's Qur'an class."

An apologetic smile lingered at Aliyah's lips as she squinted her eyes in an effort to recall Salima.

"It's okay," the woman said, chuckling and waving her hand dismissively. "It was about a year ago. You probably don't remember."

*Oh,* Aliyah realized. That was probably why she didn't recall meeting the sister. They must have met around the time Aliyah and Matt were getting a divorce. Aliyah barely remembered anything from that period except the suffocating anxiety upon realizing her life was about to fall apart. Salima probably met her right before she dropped out the class.

"Well, it's good to see you again," Aliyah said cordially.

"You don't come to the classes anymore," Salima said.

Aliyah shrugged, an awkward smile on her face. "I started working full time, you know?"

"I was kind of sad when you stopped coming." Salima smirked. "When I met you, I was like, thank God, there's at least *one* person I can relate to in this class." She shook her head. "Those sisters are *fierce*."

Aliyah chuckled in agreement. "Well, at least they're in the right place."

Salima nodded reflectively. "That's true. Everybody can benefit from Qur'an."

Salima squinted as if remembering something just then. "You were Deanna's best friend, right?"

Aliyah shook her head, surprised by the instinctive gesture. "Not really," she said. "But we were friends in college."

"They were talking about her on WTH the other day," Salima said, concern etched in her voice. "Is she okay?"

Aliyah's heart dropped, her thoughts going immediately to Younus and Thawab. *O Allah.* She hoped the media hadn't learned of Deanna's arrest. They would have a field day, and Younus and Thawab would suffer the brunt of it and be scarred for life.

"You're talking about all that 'crazy Muslim woman' stuff from months ago?" Aliyah spoke in as casual a manner as she could muster.

Salima shook her head. "No, this is recent. She has some photo essay called 'I'm the Hot Wife.'"

Aliyah felt as if she were going to be sick. Though Salima didn't say it outright, Aliyah could read in Salima's expression that the photo essay had implied something negative about Aliyah. "I didn't see it," Aliyah said, finding her voice just then.

"Oh..." Salima looked embarrassed. "I thought..."

"I don't watch TV much anymore," Aliyah said.

Salima nodded in understanding. "I'm sorry. I didn't mean to..."

Aliyah shook her head. "No, it's not your fault. If it's on TV, it's public knowledge. So there's no need to apologize." She shrugged, a slight smile on her face. "I was going to find out sooner or later, right?"

"Well, we're all making *du'aa* for you," Salima said. "This whole thing is really messed up."

Aliyah grunted agreement and rolled her eyes.

"But how are you doing?" Salima said, her eyes conveying genuine concern.

"I'm good, *alhamdulillah*," Aliyah said, surprised by how convincing she sounded to her own ears. "I'm just trying to focus on my son and my job."

"That's good," Salima said sincerely. "Keeping busy helps."

"I'm in the car," a man said, appearing at Salima's side, a plastic bag of groceries in his hand.

Salima turned and smiled at him. "Okay, boo," she said. "I'm right behind you *insha'Allah*."

"*As-salaamu'alaikum*, sister," the man said, placing his right hand on his chest as he nodded a greeting to Aliyah.

"*Wa'alaiku-mus-salaam*," Aliyah said as he turned to go.

"I don't want to keep your husband waiting," Aliyah said as the bell jingled and the door closed behind him. "But it was really nice meeting you."

Salima smirked and placed a hand on her hip playfully. "Well, I'm flattered."

Aliyah chuckled, a confused expression on her face. "What?"

"That's not my husband," Salima said, her head turning as she smiled toward the parking lot. "That's Jamil, my little brother."

"Oh, I'm sorry," Aliyah said good-naturedly. "I just assumed..."

Salima waved her hand dismissively. "Don't worry. We get that all the time, especially since we live together. But I'm not his type anyway," she said jokingly. "He has a weakness for women he thinks he can save."

"It must be nice to live with family," Aliyah said reflectively.

Salima drew her eyebrows together, a playful grin on her face. "Now that's the first time anyone has said *that* to me," she remarked. "Usually people say, 'Oh *mashaAllah*, you must be really patient.'"

"Why?" Aliyah said, a confused grin on her face. "I wish I could live with one of my brothers. I miss them."

"Then you obviously have a good relationship with them, *mashaAllah*," Salima said. "For most of us grown folks, our relationship with family is polite at best."

Aliyah nodded, a sad smile on her face as she wished she could describe her relationship with family as *polite*. She hadn't seen her two brothers and two sisters, or her parents, in more than ten years.

"But let me get out of here before Jamil starts complaining." Salima pulled her purse in front of her and opened it before rummaging inside. "Come join us some time," she said as she handed Aliyah a business card. "Some friends and I get together every Friday night. You should join us."

"Muslim Marriage Monologues," Aliyah read aloud. "That sounds interesting."

"It is," Salima said. "It's like an open-mic poetry session and support group for Muslims in relationship crises."

"Oh my God," Aliyah joked. "Am I *that* obvious?"

Salima laughed. "It's nothing like that," she said. "It's for anyone. Married, single, divorced, or…" A shadow of sadness passed over her face as she maintained her smile. "…widowed, like me."

The pleasant expression fell from Aliyah's face. "I'm sorry. I didn't know."

"How could you?" Salima said, waving her hand. "I'm not saying it for sympathy. I just want you to know this isn't some snobbish married-women-only club."

Aliyah rolled her eyes knowingly. "That happens to you too?"

"All the time," Salima said. "But I get it. When you're young and insecure, you think the biggest threat to your marriage is out there somewhere." She shrugged. "I used to think the same until one night I went to sleep as a married woman with three children and woke up as a single mother of one."

"*SubhaanAllah*," Aliyah said, shaking her head in sadness. "May Allah reunite you in *Jannah*."

"Ameen," Salima said, her eyes growing distant momentarily.

"Will we see you Friday *insha'Allah*?" Salima said as she closed her purse.

"I usually have my son then, so…" Aliyah said apologetically.

"How old is he?"

"Five."

"Bring him," Salima said. "My son is the same age. Maybe they can hang out."

"Then I'll definitely think about it," Aliyah said sincerely. "It sounds nice."

"My number's on the card," Salima said. "Give me a missed call, and I'll save your number."

"Okay," Aliyah said, nodding. "I will *insha'Allah.*"

***

Deanna dreamt that she was choking on her mother's heart. As Deanna gagged, groping for life, her mother was reaching out for help, her right hand over the left side of her chest, her left hand waving frantically as she fought to stay alive. Deanna desperately tried to catch a single breath amidst the choking as a voice inside her screamed, *"It wasn't me, Mommy! It was Janice."*

Deanna woke with a terrible ache in her neck from having fallen asleep sitting up against the wall of the holding cell, her head against the sanded bricks. Still recovering from the delirium of sleep, Deanna brought a hand to her throat and exhaled in relief that she was breathing normally. But she winced as words fell upon her like a crescendo of guillotine blades. She pinched her eyes shut as if that would block the cryptic sonnets from racing like frenzied whispers inside her head. Once upon a time, in another life, she would have considered this lyrical invasion a writer's inspiration. But she had no laptop or pen and paper, and she had no desire to write. In fact, she had no desire for anything at all.

Yet the words were stubbornly unrelenting…

He hit her
Because
Her face came too close
To his
Hand.
*Janice.*
Or maybe
His hand came too close
To her
Face.
*Janice.*
But it wasn't a strike of anger
Or rage.
It was a desperate groping
For refuge
From
His pain.
*Janice.*
His pain stared at him every day
Glaring
But he called it determination
Strength
And wit.
*Janice.*

And others called it
His calling
To guide the wicked
And the blind.
*Deanna Janice.*
But that pain.
Oh that pain.
He didn't ask to be a father.
She didn't ask to be a wife.
It was just a burst of desire
A burning fire
To do
What's right.
*Janice.*
A life kicked inside of her.
And she too kicked
Herself.
He wasn't the man
She dreamed of
When she
Sang
To herself.
*But you should be grateful,*
*Janice Michaels*
*Because they chose*
*Life.*
So she sang
At the altar.
And the little girl
Danced and kicked
To the song
Even though every note
Seemed
Wrong
But it was a lullaby
A sweet chorus
Those adult lies
So she danced and kicked
Oblivious
Beneath her mother's heart
But even then
Like now
She thought she heard

Her mother
Cry
*Why?*

***

"*As-salaamu'alaikum*, Reem," Aliyah spoke into the small mouthpiece connected to the wire of her mobile earphones. "I was thinking about our conversation the other day, and I just wanted to apologize for saying you were privileged." Aliyah drew in a deep breath, hoping Reem hadn't let the call go to voicemail after seeing Aliyah's name on the display. "I've been frustrated about a lot of things lately, and I shouldn't have taken in out on you. *Jazaakillaahukhairan* for taking time to teach me Qur'an. That's the best gift any friend can give, and I shouldn't have expected any more from you. I'm sorry. I hope you can forgive me."

Aliyah squeezed the button on the wire, disconnecting the call, and she sat for a moment as her car idled in the driveway of the home that she used to share with Matt. She wondered if now was a bad time to drop by and say salaams to Ibrahim.

*"No,"* Aliyah had said in reply to Nikki's question as to whether she had wanted to marry Matt. *"And I never loved him."* It was true that Aliyah hadn't wanted to marry Matt, but it wasn't entirely true that she had never loved him. You couldn't be married to someone for ten years and not develop at least some mutual affection. Maybe she and Matt had never "fallen in love," but there were parts of Matt that she had grown to love.

Aliyah turned off the car and drew in a deep breath before getting out and walking to the front door. She hoped Matt wasn't there. But even if he was, she had to get home soon anyway because she had halal meat in the trunk that needed refrigeration.

Aliyah hesitated only momentarily before lifting a forefinger and pushing the doorbell to the tri-level brick house that she used to call home. For the past year, Nikki had been the one to come to Aliyah's apartment to drop off Ibrahim, so this was the first time that Aliyah had returned to her home since the divorce. It felt odd standing on the opposite side of the door. It was like she had been relegated to outcast in her own life.

The door opened so quickly that Aliyah's shoulders jerked in surprise. Matt's expression was one of confusion, but only briefly. Matt was dressed in a business suit, and Aliyah knew immediately that he had been expecting the airport taxi. For a fleeting moment, she felt the urgency to make sure he had packed everything necessary for his trip.

"*As-salaamu'alaikum*," Aliyah said quickly, averting her gaze in embarrassment. "Nikki told me I could drop by to see Ibrahim… I didn't know you were home."

"*Wa'alaiku mus salaam wa rahmatullaahi wa barakaatuh,*" Matt said, surprising Aliyah with the genuine smile that spread on his lips. "Come in." He took a step back and opened the door wide. "Ibrahim is right here."

"Mommy!" Ibrahim called out as Aliyah stepped into the foyer.

Aliyah laughed and kneeled as Ibrahim wrapped his arms around her neck. After a few seconds, she started to release him, but he locked his arms more tightly. "Now's not a good time for me to carry you," she whispered.

"Mmmm," Ibrahim murmured in protest, nestling his head closer.

Aliyah felt torn between wanting to comfort her son and worrying that Matt was watching. When they were married, Matt had often expressed concern that Aliyah was spoiling their son.

"It's okay," she heard Matt's voice above her head. "You can hold him if you want. He misses you. It'll be good for him."

Aliyah didn't know whether to feel relieved or mortified. But she decided that Ibrahim's needs took precedence over the awkwardness of the moment. As she stood, Ibrahim wrapped his legs around her.

"Actually…" Matt said as if something was on his mind. He glanced behind him cautiously. "I wanted to—" The chime of Matt's cell phone interrupted him mid-sentence, and Aliyah immediately knew it was the courtesy alert message informing Matt that his taxi was outside. Matt reached into a pant pocket and pulled out his mobile, his gaze on the screen. He frowned. "I have to go," he said, apology in his tone. "But," he said, lowering his voice, "we need to talk whenever you get a free moment."

Aliyah drew her eyebrows together, one hand on the back of Ibrahim's head. "Is everything okay?"

"Yes, yes," Matt said, his voice still low as he adjusted the strap of his laptop bag over his shoulder then pulled out the handle to his carry-on luggage. "It's about Ibrahim."

"Will Mommy live with us again?" Ibrahim said, his voice rising in hopefulness as he spoke into Aliyah's neck.

"No, buddy," Matt said apologetically then leaned forward and brushed Ibrahim's forehead with a kiss. "But maybe Mommy can come over more if you want."

"Yes," Ibrahim said in excitement, his head still leaning on his mother.

"Can I give you a call some time?" Matt whispered as he started out the door.

"Sure," Aliyah said, probably too quickly. But it was all she could do to conceal her shock that Matt was asking to speak to her at all. She was under the impression that he and Nikki felt it was an Islamic requirement that Aliyah and Matt never communicate directly.

"You leaving now?" Aliyah heard a tired voice call from upstairs. She imagined that Nikki must have seen the airport taxi from the bedroom window.

"Yes," Matt called out. "The car's outside."

"Have a good trip," Nikki said.

Aliyah was unable to temper the offense she felt right then. Matt divorced her for *this* woman? What kind of wife doesn't come downstairs to see her husband off before a trip? Pregnant or not, this was inexcusable.

"Thanks," Matt called out. He looked as if he were about to say something else but decided against it. Aliyah figured that he was debating on whether or not to tell Nikki that she was there.

"*As-salaamu'alaikum*," Matt said to Aliyah, his voice low as he walked out the door.

"*Wa'alaiku mus salaam*," Aliyah said, her anger subsiding as she watched him go. She sensed that life was not easy for him, and at that moment she found herself feeling compassion for him.

"Is that you, Aliyah?" Nikki called out after the airport taxi had driven away.

Of course Nikki had seen her car when she looked out the window. "Yes," Aliyah called back.

"I'm not feeling well," Nikki said, "so just... Well, you know your way around."

Aliyah closed the front door and wondered if she should bring the meat inside and put it in Nikki's refrigerator.

*Can I give you a call some time?*

At the reminder of Matt's question, Aliyah's curiosity was piqued, so she decided she would stay only a few more minutes and give Matt a call herself when she got in the car.

***

"You don't have to apologize," Reem said when she called Aliyah back as Aliyah drove to Salima's gathering Friday evening. "I was offended," Reem admitted, "but you didn't say anything wrong. I *am* privileged. I have options that you don't have, and I shouldn't trivialize that."

"I could have chosen a better word," Aliyah said regretfully, conscious that Ibrahim was in the backseat. "I was angry, and I shouldn't have taken it out on you."

"No," Reem said. "You had every right to say what you did. I don't believe in micromanaging people's pain. I went through that with my family when I was in high school, and I vowed to never do it to anyone else. So if you feel I've done something wrong, then say it. No matter how upset I get, we'll get through it *insha'Allah*."

Aliyah was quiet as she recalled Reem alluding to a rebellious stage she had gone through when she was a teenager. *"A lot of things happened to me when I was a child,"* Reem had said. *"And I think it just got too much for me to keep holding inside."*

"Why do you believe it's okay to choose who your children will marry?" Aliyah said after careful thought. If she and Reem were going to have an honest friendship, Aliyah needed to believe that Reem saw her as a full human being who was no less than an Arab.

Aliyah heard Reem exhale as if in exhaustion. "I don't think it's something you can understand, Aliyah," Reem said apologetically, her words reminding Aliyah of their conversation on the tennis court. "I know Americans have this idealistic view of Islam, but it's not necessarily what Allah asks of us. We can marry for culture and lineage if we want to."

"But you weren't talking about for yourself," Aliyah pointed out. "You were saying that about your daughter, and she's only four years old. How do you know what she'll want fifteen years from now?"

"We don't always know what's best for us," Reem said. "*Allahu'alam*," she said, acknowledging that ultimately God knew best. "But I don't see how Hana would have any idea what she needs when she's nineteen, or even twenty-five. That's why she has parents. There's a reason Allah requires a *wali* for marriage."

"And Muhammad?" Aliyah asked, referring to Reem's son, Hana's twin brother.

"And Muhammad too," Reem said. "But of course he has more rights to disagree with us."

The word *us* stung, making Aliyah feel as if Reem's entire family and circle of Arab friends were united against her and other Americans. "What about the hadith telling fathers to accept the proposal of a man whose character and religion pleases them?" Aliyah said.

"It's not as simple as that," Reem said. "It's like what you said about marrying Matt. You needed someone you were compatible with. And Hana and Muhammad will need the same thing."

*But I was talking about the need to make the decision for myself,* Aliyah responded in her mind. *And you're talking about making that decision for your children.* Aliyah decided against speaking her thoughts aloud. She already knew that Reem would have a logical explanation implying that Aliyah didn't have the capacity to understand her point of view. But to Aliyah's ears, it sounded as if Reem were justifying cultural discrimination under the guise of "I know what's best for my children." Aliyah couldn't comprehend how Reem's position was any different from the Arabs in pre-Islamic times.

"Sayed told me about Deanna," Reem said, her voice subdued. "*Laa hawla wa laa quwwata illaa billaah.*" Sadness was in her tone as she acknowledged that nothing happens except by the permission of God. "I pray there's some misunderstanding. I don't think she would harm her mother intentionally."

*"Intentional" is relative*, Aliyah thought to herself. She didn't believe Deanna would set out to physically harm anyone, especially her own mother, but Aliyah could see Deanna lashing out in anger. However, it was difficult for Aliyah to fathom an argument with someone's parents escalating to the level of physical violence. The thought was inconceivable. "All we can do is make *du'aa*," she said reflectively.

“Will she be out on bail until the trial?” Reem said. “Sayed said they just have to pay ten thousand dollars.”

*Just?* Aliyah repeated in her mind. *That's a lot of money.* “I don't know,” Aliyah said, her thoughts immediately going to Larry, whom she'd been avoiding for the past four days. She wondered if it would be wrong to ask him for an update. Asking about Deanna couldn't be the same as asking for advice, could it?

But just as soon as the idea came to her, she disregarded it. *“If you can't help him with what he needs, don't expect him to help you with what you need.”* Offense stabbed Aliyah at the reminder. Though Larry had texted and called to apologize for what he'd said, she refused to speak to him. It had taken some time for Aliyah to pinpoint why Larry always managed to get under her skin no matter how much she enjoyed his company. But after spending the last few days nursing her hurt over his words, she realized that Larry carried himself with a sense of entitlement.

Larry was intelligent, attractive, and wealthy, but none of these things inclined Aliyah to consider marrying him. But he was so accustomed to being sought after that it must have baffled him that Aliyah was not flattered by his company. *“Most women I date practically throw themselves at me,”* he'd said to Aliyah once. *“I like it when women play hard to get.”*

But Aliyah wasn't playing. She really wasn't interested in Larry, or any man for that matter.

As Aliyah slowed the car in front of the house that her navigation system had directed her to, she glanced back at Ibrahim and saw that his eyes were slowly closing though he was trying to stay awake.

“I think it's getting a bit too much for Nikki,” Matt had said when Aliyah called him four days ago when he was on his way to the airport. “And I'm worried that she won't be able to manage the baby and Ibrahim after the pregnancy.”

Aliyah sighed in exhaustion as she put the car in park. Naturally, she agreed to take care of Ibrahim full time once Nikki's baby arrived. After all, she had always wanted to spend more time with her son. But Aliyah was unsure how she felt about this sudden change of plans. She had a full-time job now, so she wouldn't be able to pick up Ibrahim from school each day. And if he stayed at school until she got off work, what would he do for three whole hours after school? Should she enroll him in an extracurricular activity? But he was only five years old and would be in kindergarten. Was it right to keep someone that young stuck in school from morning to evening each day? And then there was the question of financial support. Currently, she didn't receive any because, technically speaking, Matt had full custody while she had only visitation rights. But the arrangement was not legally binding. It had been mutually agreed upon after the divorce. At the time, Aliyah hadn't known if she'd have a place of her own, let alone a place for her son.

Aliyah's phone chimed and vibrated in her handbag as she walked to the front door of the home. Still holding Ibrahim's hand, she withdrew the phone and looked at the screen.

*That's how it is, huh?* Larry had texted. *Now that Jacob's divorced, you don't have any use for me? smh*

Hand trembling slightly, Aliyah locked the screen and dropped the phone back in her purse. *Jacob's divorced?*

Distracted by the news, Aliyah lifted the knocker and tapped it against the small metal frame on the door. She glanced down at Ibrahim and flashed a quick close-lipped smile before she stared straight ahead, thoughts distant.

"Who are you?" a tenor female voice said moments after the door opened. Aliyah found herself standing opposite an imposing woman with closely cropped hair who folded her arms authoritatively, waiting for an explanation.

"I'm…um…" Aliyah found it difficult to gather her thoughts.

"You straight, female by birth, and Muslim?" the woman asked as she narrowed her eyes at Aliyah.

Aliyah drew her eyebrows together, worried she'd knocked on the wrong door. She squeezed Ibrahim's hand tighter and pulled him closer. "Is this the poetry night club for married people?" she said, realizing immediately that she had completely botched the description.

"No, it's not."

The woman started to close the door when Aliyah heard someone call out, "Wait, Carly, I think that's the sister I invited."

The door opened again, and Salima peeked around the woman, and Aliyah's shoulders dropped in relief. "*As-salaamu'alaikum*, Aliyah!" Salima said, stepping around the woman to hug Aliyah. "I'm glad you made it."

"So you know her, I guess?" the imposing woman said, an arched eyebrow rising doubtfully.

"Yes, I do," Salima said, playful defensiveness in her voice. "Now chill with all the security detail."

"Is she str—"

"*Carly*," Salima interjected, her voice more serious. "I invited her. She's cool."

"I hope you're right," the woman said, huffing in annoyance as she walked away.

"Excuse her," Salima said apologetically as she ushered Aliyah inside and closed the door. "Carletta is just being extra careful. We've had some bad experiences in the past."

"Bad experiences?" Aliyah's voice rose in concern as she glanced at her son. "What do you mean?"

Salima's gaze went to Ibrahim, and a wide smile spread on her face. "Is this your son?"

"Yes." Aliyah smiled, a bit taken aback by the sudden shift in subject. "His name is Ibrahim."

"Ibrahim!" Salima exclaimed in the exaggerated excitement that adults often reserved for conversations with children. Salima clasped her hands together gleefully. "Ibrahim, I'm Sister Salima. And I have a son named Haroon. He's five and named after a prophet, just like you."

Ibrahim smiled, glancing up at Aliyah uncertainly. "Okay."

"Would you like to play with him? He has some really nice cars and action figures."

Ibrahim broke into a grin, and he looked at Aliyah. "Okay," he said tentatively, waiting for his mother's approval.

"That sounds good," Aliyah said, nodding politely.

"Carly," Salima called out, glancing behind her, "can you take Aliyah's boy upstairs to where Haroon and the other children are?"

Aliyah felt a tinge of discomfort at the thought of the rude woman accompanying her son up the stairs. "*As-salaamu'alaikum,*" Carletta said in forced cordiality after she returned to the foyer. She offered a tightlipped smile to Aliyah and an extended hand to Ibrahim. "Welcome to my humble home."

Salima laughed and shook her head as Ibrahim took Carletta's hand as they headed toward the stairs. "Sorry about Carly," Salima said. "She's not exactly a people person."

"I see," Aliyah said, her eyes following Ibrahim as he ascended the stairs alongside Carletta, excitement in his eyes.

"She hosted the monologues in her home about a year ago, and she said she wasn't going to do it again," Salima said as Aliyah slipped off her shoes, immediately realizing that she hadn't told Ibrahim to remove his.

"Why?" Aliyah said as she followed Salima down a hall.

"Because she went through something similar to what happened to you."

Aliyah creased her forehead. "What do you mean?"

"Name-calling, slander." Salima shook her head. "It was ridiculous."

"But why?"

Salima shrugged. "Who knows? We're still trying to figure that out."

"But what happened?"

"She hosted an open-mic with the topic 'Relationship Woes Among Judgmental Muslims,' and she made it an open invitation to all the sisters in the community," Salima said. "She wanted to start an open dialogue about how Muslims can be more understanding of diverse family make-ups. Like single-parent homes, blended families with stepbrothers and stepsisters being raised together, half-brothers and sisters living together after a parent divorces and remarries, things like that." Salima frowned and shook her head. "But it didn't turn out too well."

Aliyah grunted in understanding. "I could have told her that. This community only accepts homes that look like *Leave It To Beaver* and *The Cosby Show*. One mother and one father for all the children," she said. "And one marriage per person, preferably thirty years and counting."

"Well..." Salima said tentatively, turning to face Aliyah before entering the main room. "It was more than that. Some LGBTQ Muslims caught wind of it and came to the event."

Aliyah's eyes widened as she brought a hand to her mouth.

Salima shook her head. "Of course, it was a disaster. They used the open-mic session for all these lesbian Muslim poems and how so-called traditional Muslims are extremist and homophobic because they consider same-sex relations a sin."

"*SubhaanAllah*," Aliyah said. "I never heard about this."

"That's good to know," Salima said, a half smile on her face. "Because, I swear, it felt like the whole world was against us at the time. Even some of our friends got online and said we shouldn't exclude them in our sessions, otherwise we're hypocrites since our group is about relationship problems."

Aliyah rolled her eyes. "Some Muslims never cease to twist the message of Islamic sisterhood and brotherhood for their own purposes."

"Plus-minus Islam," Salima said in agreement.

Aliyah met Salima's gaze in confusion, a half smile lingering on her face. "Plus-minus Islam?"

"It's when Muslims add or take away things in Islam to suit their own purposes."

Aliyah nodded, understanding.

"The people who were slandering us believe in adding things to the religion," Salima said, "and the people who were slandering you believe in taking away things in the religion."

Aliyah huffed, an amused expression on her face. "Plus-minus Islam, huh?"

"Add LGBTQ practices," Salima said, "and take away polygamy."

"Because we live in different times," Aliyah said, mocking the commonly held argument to defend these changes. "And new times require new rules."

"Exactly," Salima said, smirking and shaking her head. "But we're not trying to go to Hellfire up in here. We're just a group of sisters trying to help each other strive for Paradise. And we don't put a footnote where Allah puts a period."

Aliyah smiled, nodding. "*MashaAllah*," she said. "I like that. We don't put a footnote where Allah puts a period."

"Good," Salima said, a grin spreading on her face. "Because that's the title of the poem I wrote for tonight."

Salima turned and walked into the main room, gesturing for Aliyah to follow. "Come on," Salima said. "Let me introduce you to everyone."

***

Deanna played the scene over and over in her mind. But the details remained jumbled and foggy. In her mind's eye, she saw her mother coming close to her, palm raised, threatening an attack. *"No,"* Deanna's heart cried in frenzied anguish. *"I will not let her hit me again!"* Deanna lifted a hand to stop her mother and furiously gripped her mother's arm. That was when Deanna felt her own feet slip beneath her.

For a moment, Deanna thought she would fall. But she propelled herself forward and steadied her disoriented stance…

Then found that she was at the top of the stairs holding onto the bannister. Alone.

## 17
## Muslim Marriage Monologues

"I'm not sure what you think your test in life is," Salima said as she stood in front of the crowd of sisters reciting the poem she'd written for the Muslim Marriage Monologues gathering that Friday night, "if you don't have to follow any rules…

I'm not sure what you think faith is
If there's absolutely nothing you *have* to do.
Why even claim Islam at all
If you're not going to submit?
Why even call yourself Muslim
If you can just call it quits?
No, I'm not judging you.
Okay, well, maybe I am.
But you can't deny this is all confusing
If you're standing where I am
I thought Islam was a complete religion
Established for all time
I thought Islam was Allah's religion
A gift to all mankind.
I thought the whole point of submission
Was that it requires a lot of work
I thought the whole point of faith
Was that you never give up
What happened to humility?
What happened to 'We hear and we obey'?
Or is that only when Allah says something you like
And otherwise it's 'We hear and we disobey'?
So, nah, I ain't feeling you
With all this love who you want to sh*t
If you wanna roll like that,
On the real, I ain't feeling it
We all got skeletons and ghosts
Stuff that's better left alone
You ever heard of hiding your sins?
Seeking refuge from Shaytaan?
So don't think you got a test so big
It can change Allah's Word
He knew what He was going to give you
Before you were even on this earth
So don't play that feel-sorry-for-me card
It's really getting old

We all got sob stories, girl
Some are just better left un-told
So if you want Paradise
You're going to have to get serious
And you can't put a footnote
Where Allah puts a period."

The crowd of about twenty women erupted in applause. "Tell it!" some shouted.

Smiling, Aliyah brought her hands together, clapping along with the crowd as her gaze followed Salima leaving the front of the room and joining the other women.

"I'm not much of a poet…" a soft voice said, prompting Aliyah to turn her attention toward the source of the sound. A tall, thin woman stood hesitantly in front of the crowd and held three sheets of paper worn with creases. A face veil sat under her chin like a bib, as if she were uncomfortable completely unveiling in front of the all-female crowd. "…so I hope you don't mind if I just read from the paper."

"Go 'head, girl!" someone shouted. "We're listening!"

"Okay…" The woman smiled awkwardly as she fumbled with her papers. "This is um… I just wrote something, um…" She forced laughter, as if in apology for her nervousness. "I'm sorry... I'm not used to speaking in front of people…"

"We're right here with you, *ukhti*! No judgment. Just share your truth."

"…so…um…okay…" She drew in a deep breath then exhaled, her breathing jagged from nervousness. "This doesn't really have a title, but it's about how I lost my best friend because of polygyny."

Aliyah was immediately reminded of her broken friendship with Deanna.

The woman shut her eyes as if to mentally coax herself into gathering her composure. "I lost my best friend because of polygyny," the woman said, her eyes opening as she looked at the paper in her hands. "But not for the reasons you might think. She didn't try to marry my husband, and I didn't try to marry hers." The woman smiled and shook her head, as if lost in a memory momentarily. "Allow me to explain," she said.

"My best friend and I met in high school," she said. "And I was always the strong one." She laughed nervously and glanced at the crowd. "If that's not too hard to believe," she added jokingly. "Lori had it rough growing up and was a bit quiet and withdrawn. So I was always fending off bullies and telling people to leave her alone. I guess I saw myself as her protector. But even back then, she'd tell me to let it go. She said everything doesn't require a fight. She said some things can just be ignored."

Aliyah averted her gaze, recalling having similar thoughts whenever her mother or siblings would say she should speak up more.

"But I knew better," the woman said sarcastically, "like I did for everything. So when she started hanging out with Arabs and Pakistanis, I told her she should be careful because they were probably terrorists or part of some sleeper cell."

There was a ripple of awkward laughter in the crowd.

"And when she decided to become Muslim and talked about wearing hijab, I rushed to call her parents and tell them their daughter was hanging out with a dangerous crowd." The woman smiled sadly. "Needless to say, Lori never wanted to speak to me again. 'You never see me,' she kept saying. 'You never *listen.*' And of course, I was offended that she couldn't see how I was just trying to help."

The woman drew in a jagged breath and exhaled nervously. "So anyway, after high school, we lost touch and went our separate ways. But a few years later, I met this wonderful guy and fell in love. But there was only one problem. He was Muslim." She smiled hesitantly. "Yes, I became *that* girl. I fell in love with religion because I fell in love with a man. But that's not the point."

Her hands trembled slightly as she looked at the paper. "I became Muslim and married him, and we ended up living in the same community as my friend Lori, who I found out was married now and had a child. She was ecstatic when she found out I was Muslim, and we reconnected just like old times. But this time, she was the strong one. I was really proud of the changes I saw in her. She was active and well-known in the community, and she and her husband were doing all these amazing programs at the masjid."

*Where do sisters find good men like that?* Aliyah wondered. If she were to ever get remarried, that's how she imagined her relationship would be. She and her husband working together doing community work.

"About a year after I joined Lori's community, I started hearing rumors about a brother trying to marry women in secret behind his wife's back. I dismissed it as gossip until a sister I knew came to me for advice about her friend accepting the brother's proposal. I was shocked and horrified, and of course I told her to tell her friend not to do it. But what was most troublesome to me was that it was Lori's husband who was trying to get married."

There were a few huffs and grunts from the crowd.

"I didn't know what to do, and, well—" She shrugged nonchalantly. "Okay, I admit, I was pissed. I immediately went into protective friend mode, and it was just like old times, except the bully I needed to ward off was Lori's husband."

"These men," someone muttered in frustration.

"So I talked to whoever I could to help figure out a way to tell Lori and have someone confront her husband. I even talked to the imam because I felt it was his responsibility to keep sisters from being manipulated like this."

*Okay, I can see where this is going,* Aliyah thought in annoyance, reminded of Deanna just then. Where do people like this come from? she couldn't help thinking. Who raises them? Who teaches them Islam? Were they really that self-absorbed as to think they had the answer to everyone's problems? Or were they just some sort of reverse misogynists who hated men instead of women? Aliyah could think of a million different non-incriminating explanations for what Lori's husband *might* be doing, and this woman couldn't think of *one*? No wonder Lori had said, "You never see me. You never *listen*."

A sad smile formed on the woman's lips. "Long story short, Lori's husband's reputation was ruined, and the imam asked him not to come back to the masjid except to pray. Lori and her husband eventually moved away, but before that, I found out that before they got married, Lori had told her husband that she didn't have any problem with polygyny so long as he didn't tell her until after it happened. Turns out, for her, the hardest part of polygyny was the suspense of not knowing what would happen. She felt like being taken through the rollercoaster of *maybes* and *what ifs* was too much for her, so she preferred to deal with only *what is*." The woman forced laughter, but it was apparent that she was not happy. "So of course, I lost my friend. And to add insult to injury, last thing I knew, Lori's husband married the sister my other friend talked to me about, and she and Lori are apparently not only co-wives but good friends."

The crowd clapped, and some women stepped forward to give the woman a hug, and Aliyah sighed, turning and walking toward the stairs to check on Ibrahim. It was hard for Aliyah to sympathize because all she could think about was how the woman ruined Lori's life. And based on what? Suspicion? An assumption? The belief that all men are evil?

As she ascended the steps, Aliyah wondered how the crowd would have reacted if the roles were reversed. What if a friend of Lori's husband had heard that Lori was secretly talking to a man whom they assumed she wanted to divorce her husband for? And what if that friend spread rumors about Lori until her reputation was ruined and she wasn't allowed to come back to the masjid? But to hear the woman tell it, it was as if her savoir complex were the most natural thing in the world. Of course the man was doing evil, and of course *she* had to save her friend. No need to verify the rumors. No need to mind your own business. Just go into immediate "save the woman from her evil husband" mode.

*SubhaanAllah*, Aliyah thought. Even *if* the rumors were true, was the community's reaction worth all that? Stopping Lori's husband from coming to the masjid except to pray? Apparently, the anti-polygamy police had given themselves promotions and were regulating who could serve Allah now.

At the top of the stairs, Aliyah heard the noise of children playing and saw that it was coming from a door that was slightly ajar. She walked toward it and carefully pushed it open wider and peered through the opening. After a few seconds of surveying the young faces, she saw Ibrahim and Haroon crashing action figures into each other and making pelting noises. She smiled and watched them for a moment longer before going back downstairs.

Salima was eating from a plate of vegetables and standing in the hallway when Aliyah reached the main floor. "You didn't like that one very much, huh?" Salima said, leaning into Aliyah with her voice lowered.

Aliyah forced a smile. "I really liked your poem, *mashaAllah*."

"But not Tina's?" A knowing smile was on Salima's on her face as she lifted a celery stick to her mouth and bit into it.

"Tina's the one who did the polygyny story?" Aliyah asked.

"Yes," Salima said.

Aliyah's gaze was drawn to the crowd of sisters now milling around in the room and getting plates of food. She saw Tina chatting amongst them, her face veil still under her chin. *She seems like a nice sister*, Aliyah found herself thinking as she studied the woman from afar. *And so did Deanna*, a voice retorted in her head.

"The story was interesting..." Aliyah said tentatively. "It's just hard to stomach, that's all."

"Because of what happened to you?"

Aliyah shook her head. "Not only that. It was just hard to follow."

"Really?" Salima sounded genuinely surprised. "I thought she did a good job connecting her thoughts."

"I don't mean in the storytelling," Aliyah said. "I mean in the logic behind her actions. I just don't get the 'save the woman from her husband' thinking. If I'd heard something like that about my friend, I think I would've just left it alone."

"You wouldn't feel obligated to tell her?" Salima asked between bites of celery.

Aliyah creased her forehead in confusion. "What is there to tell? It's a rumor."

"But it wasn't a rumor," Salima said. "Tina's friend was friends with the sister Lori's husband wanted to marry."

Aliyah chuckled. "That sounds like a game of telephone to me. Too many people in the chain of transmission, and too many possible misinterpretations between each link."

Salima nodded thoughtfully as she ate another celery stick in silence for some time. "But you don't think you owe it to your friend to let her know what people are saying about her husband?" she said. "I think I'd feel obligated to tell her *something*."

Aliyah shrugged. "I can see feeling inclined to let her know," she said honestly. "But there are other ways to go about it than creating an uproar in the community when you don't even know what's going on."

"Like telling her directly without talking to anyone else?"

"I don't think I'd feel comfortable," Aliyah said thoughtfully. "I'd feel tempted to," she admitted. "But I don't think I'd go through with it unless I had a really compelling reason to. I'm just not a fan of participating in the rumor mill. Part of the reason backbiting and gossip are so rampant is that each person feels justified to share what they think they know. It has to stop somewhere. And in Tina's situation, even if the worst was true, it's not a sin for the brother to ask about another sister without telling his wife. It's not like he got married in secret or anything. He was just *asking* about someone. And anyway, why did Tina assume Lori didn't know?" Aliyah contorted her face in distaste. "Like I said, there are just too many links in this telephone game, and I don't want any part of it."

"But what if you found out your friend's husband *did* get married in secret?" Salima said. "Would you still feel comfortable leaving it alone?"

Aliyah smiled in discomfort and shook her head. "I don't know about that one," she said honestly. "Because marriage should be announced. So there's a moral dilemma involved if it's done secretly."

"But with Tina's friend, she preferred not to know until after the fact," Salima said. "So wouldn't it ultimately be her husband's decision when to tell her?"

Aliyah nodded thoughtfully. "I would assume so…" she said, her voice trailing for a moment. "So I guess it's better left alone. Allah doesn't ask us to reveal people's private choices to other people. Marriage *should* be announced publicly," she said tentatively, "but it's not invalid if it's not. So I think staying out of it is safest for my soul."

Salima narrowed her eyes in deep thought. "I think you're right," she said. "Sticking to what you know Allah asks of you is always the safest route." She smirked. "But it's not easy when it's your friend on the other side."

Aliyah laughed in agreement. "That's true. So I guess I don't know what I'd do unless I'm in the situation."

Salima nodded emphatically. "That's true for most things in life. *What if*'s are so different from *what is*."

***

Friday evening, Jacob sat next to Attorney Bryan Schmidt who sat across from Deanna at the dingy foldout table in a cramped, musty meeting room at the county jail. Deanna's bail had been denied earlier that day, and because the attorney had been unsuccessful in communicating with Deanna himself, he'd asked Jacob to accompany him to the meeting.

"She's not speaking much," Bryan had told Jacob on the phone. "But she signed over power of attorney to you. So she's apparently thinking things through and wants you to decide how to move forward."

"Whose idea was it to give me power of attorney?" Jacob had asked. When he'd contacted Bryan to represent Deanna, Jacob had specifically asked Bryan not to tell Deanna that it was he and not her father paying the legal fees. It probably wasn't the most foolproof plan in protecting Deanna from learning that her father was eagerly working with the prosecution in the case against her. But Jacob had hoped that Bryan would give Deanna the impression that her father was paying for her lawyer and that he was only cooperating with the prosecution because he had been subpoenaed as a witness.

"It was your wife's idea," Bryan said, apology in his tone. "She told me last time we met."

"I thought she wasn't talking," Jacob said, a bit uncomfortable with the term *wife* being used in reference to Deanna. Her *'iddah* period was scheduled to end this week though he probably would never know the exact date. Deanna had more pressing issues to worry about than keeping track of her menstrual cycle. Besides, up until the accident with her mother, Deanna had refused to acknowledge the legitimacy of the Islamic divorce sans a legal divorce.

"If we follow the laws of the land for marriage," she'd kept saying, "then we have to follow the laws of the land for divorce, too." It had been frustrating trying to convince her that even in the case of marriage, a legal marriage was only valid if it met the conditions of an Islamic marriage; thus, the Islamic definition always took precedence. Jacob eventually left the issue alone and focused on taking the steps necessary to file for a legal divorce. But his efforts had been disrupted by the accident.

"She wrote it down," the attorney clarified. "But she occasionally answers yes or no questions, so I'm not sure we can consider her a selective mute at this stage."

*Then what should we consider her?* Jacob thought as he sat at the folding table studying Deanna's set jaw and her refusal to look in Jacob's direction. She seemed to be focusing her attention on the wall behind Bryan's head.

"*As-salaamu'alaikum,*" Jacob said, trying to keep his voice as cordial as possible. It disturbed him to see his wife dressed in a pale blue uniform and no hijab. But he tried to shift his thoughts to the more pressing issue.

Deanna turned her head slightly, her eyes still not looking in Jacob's direction. But Jacob thought he detected the tiniest hint of calm on her face at the sound of his greeting. He wanted to ask how she was doing, but he decided against it. She wasn't talking much, and in any case, what he really wanted to know, she wouldn't tell him, at least not in the presence of a stranger.

"Dr. Bivens," the attorney said, prompting both Jacob and Deanna to look toward him. "I'm sorry. I mean Mrs. Bivens," Bryan said. "I've spoken to the prosecution attorney, and they're willing to negotiate a plea deal that would reduce your time served to five years."

"If she pleads guilty," Jacob said in disappointment.

"Yes," Bryan said apologetically, "if she pleads guilty. But it's our best option right now. If Mrs. Michaels's condition takes a turn for the worst, they may change the charge from aggravated assault to second-degree murder, and that could mean a life sentence."

Jacob shook his head in disbelief. "And if she's innocent?"

"Mr. Bivens," the attorney said in as diplomatic a tone as he could manage, "without Mrs. Bivens's testimony or at least some documented non-incriminating account of the events on that day, the possibility of her innocence is an existential philosophy question. Right now, the prosecution has at least five witnesses, three of them neighbors who overheard the altercation between Mrs. Bivens and Mrs. Michaels, so without a strong defense, pleading innocent to aggravated assault is worse than pleading guilty to second-degree murder."

"I find that difficult to believe," Jacob said for Deanna's benefit.

"I agree. It *is* difficult to believe," Bryan said. "But unfortunately, this is how the criminal justice system works. Even if Mrs. Bivens were able and willing to testify in her own defense, I wouldn't advise it. The nine-one-one call itself is enough evidence to put her away for at least twenty years. We could find some character witnesses, but they are most helpful in cases that weigh heavily on premeditation as opposed to a crime of passion or emotion."

"What about the insanity plea?" Jacob had planned to posit the question later on the phone because he didn't want to offend Deanna. But after he learned that she appointed him power of attorney, Jacob felt obligated to discuss his thoughts while she was present. Deanna turned her head away from him until Jacob could see the unkempt ponytail at the back of her head and a profile of her face. He took her reaction to mean that she didn't like the proposition. "Strategically speaking, I mean," he added.

The attorney was silent momentarily as he considered what Jacob had said. "It's possible…" he said doubtfully. "But the plea deal is Mrs. Bivens's best chance at having a normal life again. With the insanity plea, best-case scenario, she'll be locked away in a psychiatric facility instead of a prison. And I don't recommend that."

"Even with a plea deal?" Jacob said.

"Currently, the plea deal is for aggravated assault," Bryan said. "I can speak to the prosecutors about a temporary insanity plea if you want."

Jacob looked toward Deanna, but she was still looking away from him.

"Why don't I give you two a few minutes?" Bryan said, collecting his papers as he stood. "I'll be right outside the door if you need me. But I suggest taking the current plea deal. It's our best option. This isn't a case you want to argue in court."

After the door closed, the room fell deafly silent except for a subtle ringing in the pipes buried in the walls. Jacob felt a surge of frustration as Deanna stared off into the distance. How did it come to this? Jacob thought. How did *we* come to this?

Jacob drew in a deep breath and exhaled. "Deanna, I'm really sorry you're going through this right now…" He shook his head. "I know you gave me power of attorney, but the truth is, I really don't know what to advise because I don't know what happened."

Deanna rolled her eyes in annoyance until she met Jacob's gaze briefly, her face contorted in offense. She grunted and looked away, folding her arms firmly over her chest.

*O-kay,* Jacob thought to himself sarcastically. *I guess this means I should just* know *she's innocent*. Some things never change, he thought to himself in exhaustion.

"Do you want to plead not guilty and fight the charges?" He spoke in the calm, diplomatic tone he often used whenever he was trying to avoid an argument with Deanna.

Deanna's nose flared in agitation, and she shook her head and folded her arms more stubbornly, as if too disturbed to speak.

"Then I guess we should accept the plea deal…" Jacob let his voice trail in hopes that Deanna would give him some indication as to what she wanted to do.

"No, I—" Deanna said in a grunt, her voice clipped. Her expression revealed frustration that she couldn't put together an intelligible sentence.

Her voice was so raspy and abrupt that for a fleeting moment Jacob thought someone else was speaking. She sounded like she was choking on her words. It pained Jacob to see her eyes glistening as she shook her head in annoyance. He wasn't sure if she was losing patience with herself or with him.

"Why don't you write it down?" Jacob said, opening up his brief case as the idea came to him just then. He withdrew a legal pad and pen and set them on the table before pushing them toward her.

For a few seconds she just sat there staring ahead obstinately.

"I can't help you if I don't know what you want," Jacob said softly. "And I want to help, Deanna. But I need to know what you want me to do."

Deanna's chin trembled, and for a moment Jacob thought she would cry. But tears shined in her eyes, refusing to fall. Deanna jerked her body forward so quickly that the table shook. She furiously slapped her hand over the legal pad and pulled it closer then picked up the pen.

Internally, Jacob sighed in relief. This wasn't ideal, but it was progress. Other than telling Attorney Schmidt in writing that she was giving Jacob power of attorney, she hadn't said much of anything.

The pen whistled across the pad in angry strokes, and after a few seconds, Deanna slapped the pen down. Jacob had to stand up to pull the pad toward him.

*You better NOT marry Aliyah*, the sloppy handwriting said.

***

"Reem, here are the rules," Aliyah said Saturday morning as she walked alongside Reem toward the tennis courts after taking Ibrahim to the indoor basketball court. Aliyah had rehearsed in her head what she would say, but she was unsure how to put her thoughts into words.

*You have no people skills*, she heard Deanna's voice in her head. Though Aliyah hated to admit it, Deanna was probably right. Aliyah had spent most of Friday night stewing about what Larry had said about not calling a man unless she's prepared to give him what he wants, but when Aliyah woke up this morning for *Fajr*, she realized that she had absolutely no idea how people came up with their rules of interaction.

In Aliyah's mind, she'd done everything she could to respect the limits of Allah, but apparently that wasn't enough. There were extra Muslim social codes to keep in mind. *But what are they?* she'd racked her brain earlier that morning. "Your uncle should be present whenever you're talking to a non-*mahram* man," a sister had told her once. But my uncle *is* a non-*mahram* man, Aliyah had thought to herself in confusion. Benjamin was her uncle by marriage, not by blood. So was the Muslim social code that she should talk to two non-*mahram* men at the same time?

After nearly giving herself a headache trying to understand Muslim social code, the only conclusion Aliyah could come up with was the one she'd come up with for most everything else. If Aliyah gave credence to the pseudo-religiosity of people like Larry, she'd be homeless and panhandling right then—because working in a "mixed environment" would make her a "tease" to all her male colleagues. So all she could tell herself was, *Worry about pleasing Allah, and leave people alone. They don't even know what* they *believe half the time.*

"You stay out of my life," Aliyah said, "and I stay out of yours." As soon as she said it, she realized it had come out all wrong.

Reem's eyes widened through the slit of her black veil. "Why would you say something like that?"

"I'm not upset," Aliyah said quickly, hoping to lighten the blow. "I've just given this a lot of thought, and I think it's better for both of us in the long run."

"I thought we were friends," Reem said, her voice tight in offense.

"We are," Aliyah said. "Just not *close* friends, if you know what I mean."

"No, I *don't* know what you mean."

"Look, Reem, I've thought a lot about what you said about intercultural marriage, and I realized I should respect your views, even if I don't understand or agree."

"*Alhamdulillah,*" Reem muttered.

"But since I view true friendship as only for the sake of Allah, I—"

"Are you saying I think it's *not* for the sake of Allah?"

"—can't open myself up to being hurt again."

Reem shook her head as they stopped at an open tennis court. "Now you think I'm trying to *hurt* you?"

"This is about me, not you," Aliyah said as she shrugged the tennis racket case from her shoulder then unzipped it. "I'm trying to learn from my bad experiences."

"Now I'm a *bad experience*?" Reem said in disbelief.

"Are you even listening to me?" Aliyah said, frustration in her tone. "This isn't about you. I know you mean well, but that's not enough. People use the good intentions excuse to do horrible things. And I'm trying to get away from that."

"What horrible things am I doing?" Reem asked challengingly, folding her arms over her chest. Her tennis racket was still in its case, the strap over her shoulder.

"I didn't say you were doing horrible things," Aliyah said as she pulled her tennis racket from its case. "If you were, I would just cut you off."

"Then what are you trying to say?" Reem's tone was defensive.

"I'm saying I respect that you and I don't agree on what an Islamic marriage should look like, so I'll just leave it alone and try to focus on what we do agree on."

Reem averted her gaze as she removed the tennis case strap from her shoulder and unzipped it. "I wish I never told you that," she muttered in frustration.

"You didn't tell me that," Aliyah said. "I drew it out of you. It was never really a secret to me. I just thought I could ignore it and focus on our Qur'an classes. But the closer we got, the more it bugged me. I felt like I was opening my heart to you while you were closing yours off. And I didn't like that."

"I did open my heart to you."

"I know you *think* you did." Aliyah hoped her words weren't offensive, but she really wanted Reem to understand her point of view. "And that's why I still value you as a friend. But what you call opening your heart is really just opening your mind to a new experience so you can earn blessings."

"And that's a *bad* thing?"

"No, it's not," Aliyah said. "It's a good thing. But it just means that to you, I'll always be lacking in some way."

"What is *that* supposed to mean?" Reem yanked the tennis racket from its case and walked toward the edge of the court to set it down.

"Look, Reem," Aliyah said as she followed her friend, "just like there are things I'll never understand about your cultural views, there are things you'll never understand about my spiritual ones." Reem stopped at the edge of the court and set down her racket case, and Aliyah glanced at the sky tentatively before setting down hers. The clouds had darkened, and it looked like it was about to rain.

"I get the whole preference thing," Aliyah explained as they walked back to the court. "But what I don't understand is why your culture doesn't allow you to see Allah's plan as bigger than yours."

At the net, gripping her tennis racket, Reem turned to Aliyah and folded her arms over her chest, her gaze stubborn and off to the side as she waited for Aliyah to finish.

"Normally, I'd consider your perspective racist," Aliyah said honestly. "But I'm realizing that things aren't as simple as one hundred percent good or one hundred percent evil. You have your reasons for thinking only Arabs are compatible with your children, so I accept that even in this, Allah knows best. But that doesn't make me change my opinion of spirituality and friendship. It just makes me change my approach to my friendship with you."

A soft rumble of thunder filled the brief silence.

"Why are Americans so obsessed with marrying other people?" Reem said, annoyed. "There are plenty of Americans you all can marry."

Aliyah smirked. "Trust me, Reem, there are plenty of Americans who aren't the least bit interested in marrying Arabs. And I'm sure there are plenty of Arabs who are open to marrying Americans. So for me, this is about Islam, not an obsession." Aliyah huffed humorously. "And after talking to you, I think I'll stick to considering only American men for marriage."

"Oh, so it's okay for *you* to be racist."

Aliyah shrugged. "That's one way to look at it. But to me, it's about avoiding another Matt situation. I don't want someone to think he's doing me some kind of favor by marrying me. I'm not the most confident person in the world, but I definitely think I'm worth more than *that.* I shouldn't have to prove I'm worth marrying." She paused thoughtfully. "And I shouldn't have to prove I'm worth having as a friend."

Reem shook her head in apparent irritation, but she didn't say anything.

"You might not understand where I'm coming from," Aliyah said sincerely, "and I accept that. But what I do need you to understand is that if you can draw the line at who your children can marry, then I can draw the line at who can be a close friend."

***

After playing tennis with Reem, Aliyah was grateful that the rain had been only intermittent and light, so their lesson was not disrupted. But Aliyah was pensive as she walked to the indoor basketball court. She wondered if she had done the right thing by telling Reem how she really felt. Reem had told her to be completely open about her feelings, but the conversation had left Aliyah feeling discomfited. Why couldn't she shake the feeling that she had said the wrong thing?

*"Because they're racist,"* Larry had said. *"And you're supposed to feel grateful if they even spend time with you. The minute you see yourself as more than a charity case, they feel insulted."*

Was it possible that Reem felt insulted that Aliyah was not content with being kept at arm's length?

"*As-salaamu'alaikum.*"

Aliyah turned at the sound of a female voice and saw Mashael walking briskly to catch up. Aliyah held the door to the gym open until Mashael was at her side. "*Wa'alaiku mus salaam,*" Aliyah said, forcing a smile. Mashael and Nora had come late to the tennis courts and played separately from Reem and Aliyah.

"I'm sorry about my sister," Mashael said, breathless, as she and Aliyah stepped inside the gym, the door closing behind them. "She told me about your argument."

"That was fast," Aliyah said, lighthearted sarcasm in her tone.

Mashael chuckled. "It doesn't take long to share something like that," she said. "Anyway, she and I have been arguing about this for weeks. Reem's a sweetheart, *mashaAllah*, but she's really hardheaded sometimes."

Aliyah raised her eyebrows. "You've been arguing about this?"

"It's a point of contention between us, to be honest."

"So you don't agree with the whole you-can-only-marry-an-Arab rule?" Aliyah hoped her joking tone would be taken as friendly banter and not condescension.

"No, I despise it," Mashael said, her face pinched in distaste. "My boyfriend's American, and my family thinks I've lost my mind. Some of them are saying I'm not even Muslim anymore."

The word *boyfriend* made Aliyah wince, but she told herself that Mashael might not mean the term in the way it was commonly used. Perhaps this was another Muslim social code Aliyah didn't know anything about. Was it possible that the word *boyfriend* varied in meaning as much as the word *friend*? Could Mashael simply mean that she was talking to the American for marriage?

"Is he Muslim?" Aliyah asked, turning her eyes to the basketball court where she saw Ibrahim standing in line to shoot the basketball into the lowered rim.

"No," Mashael said. "He calls himself a recovering Christian."

"And you think that's okay?" Aliyah said, her tone thinly masking her disapproval.

"I'm not convinced it's wrong," Mashael said tentatively. "So much of the Qur'an is misinterpreted to favor men, I don't know what to believe anymore."

Thoughts stormed Aliyah's mind, but she decided to keep quiet. She didn't know Mashael well enough to try to correct her beliefs. Aliyah didn't fully understand what Mashael was trying to say anyway, so how could she correct her? The last thing Aliyah wanted to do was what had been done to her. Everyone deserved to speak for themselves and have their words and behavior interpreted in the best possible light, and no matter how uncomfortable Aliyah felt with Mashael's words, she wasn't about to take that right away.

But Aliyah couldn't help feeling wary of Mashael's mention of a male-favored interpretation of the Qur'an. It always made Aliyah uncomfortable to hear any reference to a male or female view of Allah's Words. In Aliyah's mind, there were only two categories of Qur'anic interpretations, valid and invalid. Gender had nothing to do with it.

"I need your advice on something," Mashael said suddenly, leaning toward Aliyah with her voice lowered.

"*My* advice?" Aliyah turned and met Mashael's gaze, forefinger pointing toward her own chest. Aliyah didn't mean to sound so shocked, but her response was instinctive. She couldn't fathom what topic would warrant Mashael imagining Aliyah could be her advisor.

"Yes, yours," Mashael said, humor in her tone. "You studied Islam right?"

"Yes…" Aliyah said hesitantly. She was uncomfortable with anyone thinking she had "studied Islam" though technically she had. But hadn't every Muslim? "But I'm not knowledgeable about anything," Aliyah added for transparency.

Mashael chuckled. "*MashaAllah*," she said. "Reem told me you were humble."

"Um…I'm not sure what Reem told you," Aliyah said, uncomfortable with the implication that she knew more than she did. "But I'm not being modest. I really don't know anything."

"How long have you been taking Islamic classes?" Mashael asked.

"For about ten years…" Aliyah said, realizing how ridiculous she must sound.

"And in all that time," Mashael said, laughter in her voice, "you learned *nothing*?"

"I wouldn't say I learned nothing," Aliyah said. "But I'm not a scholar or student of knowledge or anything."

"Don't worry," Mashael joked. "I don't need a fatwa, just another perspective."

"Well, that's all I can offer," Aliyah said in apologetic warning.

"Can I drop by some time?"

"To my *apartment*?" Aliyah was surprised at Mashael's preference to speak to her in person. Perhaps all the Arab versus American discussions had made her assume that anyone from Reem's family would stay far from her unless they wanted to teach her something.

"If you don't mind…"

"Sure, it's fine," Aliyah said noncommittally. "It's just…" She creased her forehead. "Is everything okay?"

Before Mashael could respond, Ibrahim ran up to Aliyah and greeted her with salaams and a hug.

"I'll call you, *insha'Allah*," Mashael whispered. "*As-salaamu'alaikum*," she said as she lifted her hand in a wave and walked away.

"Aunty!" Thawab said, appearing at Aliyah's side. Aliyah smiled at him and rubbed his head. Her eyes drifted to Younus, who hung a few feet back from his brother. The odd expression she'd seen on Younus's face a week ago was still there. But this time, she decided to ignore it.

"*As-salaamu'alaikum*, Younus," Aliyah said.

"*Wa'alaiku mus salaam*, Aunty," he said, a look of uncertainty in his eyes.

Aliyah glanced around at the men and women meeting their children and walking toward the exit. "Younus, where's your father?"

Younus wrinkled his brow and glanced around. "Uncle Larry is supposed to be here."

Aliyah was overcome with dread at the mention of Jacob's brother. *"Men don't like teases,"* Larry had said to her. *"If you're not interested in marrying a brother, don't call him for advice. If you can't help him with what he needs, don't expect him to help you with what you need."*

"Who brought you here?" Aliyah asked.

"Uncle Larry," Younus said.

"Did he say he was going somewhere?"

"He said wait for him right here."

Aliyah frowned and glanced at her watch. She had hoped to be heading home by now so she could catch up on her preparation for One Plus One and the summer class she was teaching.

"Well, well, well," a boisterous voice called from the other side of the gym. They all turned at the sound of the voice and saw that Larry had just entered. "Who would've guessed?" Larry called out, prompting the other men and women to look at him curiously as he approached.

Aliyah sighed and turned to the boys. "*As-salaamu'alaikum*, Younus and Thawab," she said as she took Ibrahim's hand. "*Insha'Allah*, we'll see you later."

"*Wa'alaiku mus salaam*, Aunty," Younus and Thawab replied in unison.

"You're leaving so soon?" Larry said jokingly, a playful grin on his face.

Aliyah kept her gaze straight ahead as she walked toward the exit, firmly gripping Ibrahim's hand. *Maybe Larry thinks women shouldn't even* look *at men they don't plan to marry*, Aliyah thought sarcastically. *I don't want to send the wrong message.*

"Now *that* is just rude," Larry called out, humor in his tone. "I can't even get the greetings?"

Aliyah pulled open the exit door and let it close behind her and her son. She exhaled in relief as she passed through the reception area of the athletic complex and headed toward the door leading to the parking lot. As she and Ibrahim walked to her car, she thought of her uncle Benjamin. He and her aunt Valerie had left last night for a weeklong vacation. Right then she wished she could have gone too. She could really use the break, but there was no way she could take off from work. With Jacob gone and her supervisor acting ornery, now wasn't a good time to take any sick days or leaves of absence.

Aliyah lifted her keychain, pressing the button to unlock the car. She released Ibrahim's hand and opened the door for him. "Aunty!" she heard a small voice call out as Ibrahim settled into his place in the backseat.

Aliyah turned and found Thawab running toward her. She forced a smile as Thawab stopped breathless in front of her, handing her a rectangular package about the size of a book. "Uncle Larry said give this to you."

"Thank you, Thawab," Aliyah said as she took the package from him and deftly tossed it in the backseat next to Ibrahim.

"You're welcome, Aunty," Thawab said, still catching his breath. He turned and stood next to Aliyah as Larry and Younus came into view.

Aliyah rolled her eyes in annoyance as Larry approached with a triumphant smirk on his face. "You left so fast I didn't get to give you your box," Larry said.

"Well, I have it now," Aliyah said, giving Larry a tightlipped smile. "So *as-salaamu'alaikum*, Larry." She turned, standing at the open door and watching as Ibrahim buckled his seat belt. She then stepped back and closed the door before opening her own.

"*Wa'alaiku mus salaam wa rahmatullaahi wa barakaatuh*," Larry said, enunciating every syllable for exaggerated emphasis. He reached into his pocket and withdrew his car keys.

"Here, little man," Larry said as he tossed the keys to Younus. "You can start the car for us."

"Thanks, uncle!" Younus said as he caught the ring of keys with both hands, his gaze on the keys as if they were a rare prize. "Come on, Thawab," Younus said, gesturing to his brother. Thawab followed his brother to Larry's car, which was parked diagonally across from Aliyah's.

"I tried to call you before I got back to the gym," Larry said, his voice lowered. "But your phone was off."

Aliyah started to respond but realized that she had rushed out the apartment that morning without charging her phone.

"It's hot," she said finally as she climbed into her seat and turned on the ignition, her door still open. She reached to her right to adjust the temperature for the air conditioner. "I don't want to keep Ibrahim waiting," she said apologetically, raising her voice slightly as she closed the door and the automatic window came down.

"*As-salaamu'alaikum*, Larry," she said through the open window, keeping her voice cordial so that Ibrahim wouldn't sense that anything was amiss.

"I'm sorry," Larry said, his voice low as a hesitant smile played at one side of his mouth. "Just give me a call when you open the package."

"*As-salaamu'alaikum*, Larry," she said again, her voice slightly louder this time. But she didn't wait for a reply as she pressed the button for the automatic window and let it seal shut in his face. She put the car in drive and eased forward out of the parking space. For a moment she considered connecting her phone to the car charger. But she decided against it when she realized that Larry would most likely try to call during the drive.

As she exited the parking lot, she sighed, wishing she could visit Benjamin right then. She wanted to vent to her uncle about Larry's aggravating behavior. But she decided to let it go, at least for now.

Aliyah's mind drifted to her family as she slowed her car behind a line of vehicles at a stoplight. About a week ago, Aliyah had spoken to her aunt Valerie about the possibility of coming along when she visited her sister (Aliyah's mother) next time. Valerie had said she thought it was a good idea and that Aliyah's parents would be happy to see her. But Aliyah wasn't so sure.

The light turned green, and Aliyah drove in silence as she wrestled with whether or not to accompany her aunt to her mother's house. Yes, Valerie had a good relationship with the family, but Valerie was Christian; and that made all the difference. Benjamin himself rarely visited Aliyah's family except for official family events like weddings and family reunions. Aliyah suspected that he was tolerated only because he was married to Valerie and was father to the favored niece and nephew of Aliyah's parents. Though it was questionable whether or not Benjamin's children were Christian, Aliyah's two cousins (as far as the Thomases could tell anyway) were at least *not* Muslim. And in the Thomas family, that's all that had come to matter.

Or perhaps Aliyah had it wrong. Maybe there was underlying tension with Benjamin's children that Aliyah knew nothing about. One was recently married and the other one was still in college, so Aliyah imagined they couldn't possibly come around much anyway. Was Aliyah just assuming they were still favored by her parents while her cousins were hardly children anymore?

"Mommy, don't forgot your box," Ibrahim said from the backseat after Aliyah parked in front of her apartment complex and turned off the car.

Internally, Aliyah groaned as she removed the keys from the ignition. "Thanks, cookie monster," she said, forcing a smile into the rearview mirror before opening her door and getting out.

For a moment Aliyah considered leaving the box right where it was. She found it deeply offensive that Larry thought that it was inappropriate for her to call him for advice but that it was perfectly fine for him to buy her a gift—after she made it clear that she was not interested in marriage. His sense of male entitlement was grating her nerves.

It seemed that people like Larry made up Islamic rules to suit their own purposes. Would her desire for advice have been "appropriate" if the title *imam* was inserted before Larry's name? Were "imams" the only men permitted to advise the opposite sex? And were they the only men whom Muslim women should expect to look out for their wellbeing?

Aliyah watched as Ibrahim unbuckled his seat-belt and climbed out the car. She wondered what type of man her son would become. How would he view women? How would he treat them? Would Ibrahim be one of the magic-wand Muslims, who slapped labels on things and—*voila!*—right and wrong disappeared, and even Islamic obligations morphed into something else entirely? Would he think like Larry, that a woman shouldn't call the person she felt was best able to answer her question, but the one whose magic label would protect her from slander and arousing suspicion?

Did Aliyah's actions—calling the one person she thought could offer sound advice about her work dilemma—justify her being called a "tease"? Aliyah strived hard to stay away from sin and took very seriously the obligation to guard her chastity. After accepting Islam, she'd never committed *zina*, and outside the accidental handshake, she'd never even touched a non-*mahram* man. So it cut deep that anyone would accuse of her moral indiscretion.

After a moment's hesitation, Aliyah reached into the backseat and retrieved the box, her face hot in offense and mortification that she had inadvertently made Larry think she was immodest.

In the apartment, Aliyah plugged in her mobile phone and walked to the kitchen to prepare lunch for Ibrahim, sadness and regret weighing on her. If it had been wrong to call Larry, she wondered, who should she have called? Was it really better to face a dilemma alone than to call someone of the opposite sex? Or was what she thought of as "magic-wand thinking" merely a reflection of proper Islamic guidelines? Was it true that only men with honorary religious labels could offer advice and assistance to non-*mahram* women?

After Ibrahim had finished eating and had lain down for a nap, Aliyah picked up the box from the front table and opened it. Inside was a small card and the framed Mark Twain quote that she and Larry had seen in a store months ago.

*Never argue with a stupid person. They will drag you down to their level and then beat you with experience.*

She set the framed quote on the front table and lifted the card. The handwritten note said: *Forgive me, Aliyah. I have lots of experience being the stupid person, but I don't want to drag you down with me. I want you to lift me up. And maybe we can lift each other up. Give me a chance. I don't think you'll regret it.*

His words touched a soft spot in her heart, and for a moment, she considered calling Larry to thank him. She could then tell him, as politely and as straightforward as possible, that she wasn't ready for a relationship right then. But she stopped herself. *If you don't want to marry him, then don't call him,* she told herself. *Not even to tell him you don't want to marry him.* In Aliyah's mind, it sounded like the stupidest logic. But she accepted that this was how things had to be. She didn't want to risk having her "thank you" and polite refusal construed as a request for wedding plans—or an invitation for an inappropriate relationship. And she definitely didn't want Larry thinking she was "playing hard to get."

"Does *every* interaction between men and women boil down to sex?" she'd vented to Matt years ago after they attended a lecture where the speaker said that it was inappropriate for a man to "let his wife" record the standard greeting on the home voicemail or answering machine. "Brothers, have some shame!" the lecturer had said. "Do you want men imagining your wife?"

"*SubhaanAllah*!" Aliyah had exclaimed to Matt in the car. "Who imagines having sex with someone just from hearing her say leave a message after the tone?"

But apparently, Aliyah was in the minority in her belief that it was possible for men and women to interact respectfully without the assumption of sin or the expectation of marriage.

*Unless it's a male colleague during work hours or my uncle Ben,* Aliyah told herself with resolve, *I'll never speak to another non-*mahram *man again,* insha'Allah. If an emergency happened and she couldn't reach her uncle, for the sake of her dignity and saving herself the headache, she was probably better off reaching out to a trusted non-Muslim coworker than a Muslim man. Which meant she'd probably opt for death over asking for help, she thought bitterly. Because no matter how aggravating and confusing Muslim men could be, she didn't trust non-Muslim men at all.

Aliyah gripped the small card with both hands and hesitated only briefly before ripping it in half. The two torn pieces in hand, Aliyah lifted the Mark Twain frame and walked into the kitchen. At the trashcan, she stepped on the lever to open the lid, and after she released Larry's gift, there was a soft thud as the frame hit the bottom, the torn pieces falling closely, though more slowly, behind.

Aliyah returned to the front room and unplugged her mobile from the wall charger. She looked at the screen as she walked down the hall toward her room. The voicemail icon was displayed in the corner, indicating that someone had left a message.

"You have three new messages," the automated voice said as she put the phone on speaker. "First message," the robotic voice said before giving the time of the call. "*As-salaamu'alaikum*, Aliyah, this is Mashael," the message said as Aliyah entered her bedroom and closed the door, still holding the phone. "Can you call me whenever you're free? I want to get together as soon as possible. Thanks!"

Aliyah pressed a button to delete the message as she made a mental note to call Mashael later that evening or Sunday some time. "Message deleted," the robotic voice said as Aliyah reached behind her head with her free hand and removed the scarf pin holding her *khimaar* in place. "Next message," the robotic voice said as she pulled the now loosened cloth from her head. "So it's like that?" Larry's voice said, prompting Aliyah to roll her eyes. "I was just trying to—"

"Message deleted," the robotic voice said after Aliyah jabbed a finger on the keypad. "Next message," the voice said. "*As-salaamu'alaikum*, Aliyah." Larry sounded more reserved and respectful this time, but Aliyah doubted she had the patience for all this back and forth. Her forefinger pressed the keypad just as she heard, "This is Jacob. I tried to c—"

"Message deleted," the robotic voice said, sending Aliyah's heart racing. *Jacob?* Aliyah thought in confusion. Disoriented, Aliyah jabbed the keypad again. "Message restored," the robotic voice said.

Aliyah exhaled in relief. She stared at the phone nervously before pressing the keypad to listen to the message. "*As-salaamu'alaikum*, Aliyah. This is Jacob. I tried calling your uncle Benjamin, but I couldn't reach him. And a brother told me he's out of town until next week. But this can't wait. So if you can, call me back when you get this message. Or I'll just try back later *insha'Allah*. Again, I'm sorry for calling you like this. But I need to talk to you about something. *As-salaamu'alaikum*."

"Message saved," the robotic voice said.

Aliyah felt apprehensive anticipation as she pressed the "end call" symbol, her mind swarming with theories of why Jacob had called. Maybe it was about work, she considered. Perhaps Dr. Warren had called Jacob about the concerns she had expressed to Aliyah.

*"I tried calling your uncle Benjamin..."* Jacob had said.

No, Aliyah concluded. It couldn't be related to her position at the college. Otherwise, why mention calling her only after he couldn't reach her uncle?

*Unless it's a male colleague during work hours or my uncle Ben,* Aliyah had decided only minutes before, *I'll never speak to another non-*mahram *man again.*

Should she make an exception for Jacob since he was technically a colleague? Or was she merely allowing herself to fall into the same mistake she had with Larry? And the last thing Aliyah wanted was to disrespect Deanna during her most difficult time.

But what if Jacob was calling because he really needed her help for something?

*Don't be silly*, Aliyah told herself, drawing on the painful lesson she'd just learned. *No man calls a non-*mahram *woman for anything unless it's a pretext for having a relationship with her.*

Perhaps Aliyah didn't think of giving advice and helping someone as acceptable only in the context of marriage (or only when the title *imam* came before a man's name), but since other Muslims thought of male-female interactions in this way, it was probably better to err on the side of caution lest she send Jacob the wrong message.

But then how would she ever know why he called?

# 18
## Soul Talk

"You're talking about Jacob *Bivens*," Salima said, "the math professor?"

"Yes," Aliyah said hesitantly, holding the cordless phone to her ear as she sat cross-legged on her bed Saturday evening. After listening to Jacob's voicemail message earlier that day, Aliyah remained indecisive about calling him back. If he was calling to ask about marriage, she didn't want to endure an awkward conversation. But what if he was calling about work? He had appointed her to head the internship in his absence, so shouldn't she call him back if he wanted to discuss that?

"*Ukhti*." Salima's voice was soft as she referred to Aliyah by the endearing term *my sister*. "If you're trying to decide on whether or not to marry him, then there are only three things to consider," Salima said. "Allah, the man, and you."

"But I don't know if he's calling about marriage…" Aliyah said tentatively. "It could be about something else. Like work."

"And does your uncle work at the college too?" Salima said doubtfully.

"No," Aliyah said. "But he and Jacob are friends, so Jacob might have wanted my uncle to tell me something about the internship program we're working on together."

"Why wouldn't he tell you directly?"

"Well…" Aliyah was uncomfortable revealing anything about what was happening with Deanna. Thus far, it appeared as though the media hadn't gotten ahold of the story, and Aliyah didn't want to be the one to reveal Jacob's family crisis. She sensed that she could trust Salima, but Aliyah's general rule was, *If it's someone else's business, it's not mine to tell.* "…he's on vacation," she said finally, "and I'm not sure when he'll be back."

"Then what's the dilemma?" Salima said. "Just call him back."

"The thing is…" Aliyah said, wondering the best way to explain her apprehension. "Remember all those rumors about me and Jacob?"

"Yes…"

"They weren't completely false."

"Okay…" Salima said, as if unsure where the conversation was heading.

"He wanted to marry me when we were in college, and Deanna tried to make him marry her instead." Aliyah hoped she wasn't confusing Salima. "And then about six months ago, he talked to my uncle about marrying me as a second wife, and Deanna blamed me for it."

"But Aliyah, what does that have to do with calling him back?" Salima said. "He's your colleague and department head. You're going to have to talk to him sometimes. So I don't see what the problem is."

"I just don't want him to think I'm a tease or anything."

"A *tease*?" Salima said, humored disbelief in her voice. "What in the world would make you think something like that?"

"Larry said if I call men I don't intend to marry, then I'm a tease."

"Larry, *Jacob's* brother?" Salima said, surprise in her voice.

"You know him?" Aliyah said.

"I wouldn't say I know him..." Salima said in an apparent effort to sound diplomatic. "But he plays basketball with Jamil sometimes."

"Do you think he's right?"

"That you're a tease if you call men you don't intend to marry?" Salima spoke as it was the most ridiculous thing she'd ever heard.

"Not in those words..." Aliyah said, self-conscious all of a sudden. "But that it's wrong?"

"If you have no reason to call," Salima said. "But if you have a reason to call, then there's nothing wrong with it."

There was a thoughtful pause. "Does Larry want to marry you or something?" Salima said, as if a thought had come to her just then.

"He asked," Aliyah said tentatively. "But I said no."

Salima chuckled. "Okay, now it makes sense."

"What makes sense?"

"Why you're so confused," Salima said. "You have no idea whether you're coming or going."

Aliyah was unsure whether she should feel relieved or offended.

"You've been through a lot," Salima said. "And this situation with Jacob and Deanna, and now Larry, is making everything muddled in your mind."

"Well, this hasn't been my best year..." Aliyah said, sad humor in her tone.

"That much is obvious," Salima said, but Aliyah sensed that she meant it kindly. "You just have to give yourself time to heal. It's not going to happen overnight."

Aliyah started to respond then realized she had no idea what to say. She hadn't expected the conversation to shift to her personal struggles.

"I don't mean to criticize you," Salima said, her tone soft and apologetic. "But it's clear you're walking on eggshells."

"I really act like that?" Aliyah had hoped to sound lighthearted, but she just sounded sad.

"When I first met you in Sister Reem's class," Salima said, "I knew you were one step from falling apart. And I only knew it because I had been in the same place too."

Aliyah felt a lump in her throat as she was overcome with sadness.

"I don't know what's causing all your pain," Salima said. "But I know you're going to have to stop bottling it up for everyone else's sake. One day, you're going to have to just let go and do *you*."

"What do you mean?" Aliyah said, surprised that she found her voice. Tears stung her eyes, but she didn't understand her emotional reaction.

"First of all," Salima said, "you're going to have to talk to somebody. Whatever's bothering you, you can't keep trying to figure it out alone."

Aliyah coughed laughter, immediately reminded of her phone call to Larry. "Talking to someone is how I got into this mess."

"Not to a man," Salima said. "And not about work," she added. "And not about the Islamic ruling on phone calls or other meaningless stuff. Those are just distractions that keep you from focusing on what's really wrong."

"How do you know all of this?" Aliyah said, embarrassed humor in her tone.

"Once you've been through hell and back," Salima said, "it's not hard to see the fire in other people's eyes."

***

After the phone call with Salima, Aliyah sat on her bed, gaze distant and arms folded, the cordless lying next to her. *When I first met you, I knew you were one step from falling apart...*

Aliyah was the youngest Thomas girl, and her memories of childhood were relatively carefree. Her parents loosely ascribed to the "tough love" philosophy of childrearing, but other than the "You should be grateful you even have parents" mantra, Aliyah's memories of being the middle child in the Thomas home were one of security and comfort. Alfred and Naomi encouraged their children to share their thoughts and frustrations and told them they could talk to them about anything. Perhaps that was why Aliyah had been so open about her growing interest in Islam while she was in college.

Her uncle Benjamin was already Muslim at the time, but Aliyah had been oblivious to any serious family tension after his conversion to Islam. She was aware that her parents, as well as other family, did not approve of him leaving the church, but Aliyah was too young and naïve to really grasp what that meant. Yes, her parents and cousins and aunts and uncles gossiped about him at family gatherings and on the phone, and she heard a lot about how even members of the church felt sorry for Valerie because she was married to Benjamin.

But none of this prepared Aliyah for what would happen to her. For one thing, her family and church members gossiped about *everything*. A person could be gossiping about someone then get up and go to the bathroom, and the people still sitting at the table would gossip about that person, then get back right to gossiping *with* her once she returned.

So how was Aliyah supposed to know that the gossip about Benjamin "ruining" Valerie's life by becoming Muslim was any weightier than the gossip about the preacher having an affair? If anything, in Aliyah's mind, the latter was worse. But to Aliyah's surprise, her family and others still went to church faithfully every Sunday, gave generously when the preacher asked, and greeted the preacher and his wife with wide smiles and friendly enthusiasm. So Aliyah had assumed her unpopular choice would be treated similarly. "No topic is off limits," her parents would say. "Anything that you want to talk about, we're here," they'd say. So naturally, Aliyah confided in them about her spiritual transition.

Then her parents refused to speak to her ever again.

The shrilling of the cordless phone interrupted her thoughts, and Aliyah's shoulders jerked at the sudden sound. For a fleeting moment, Aliyah thought it might be Jacob but realized it was her home phone ringing, not her mobile phone. She picked up the cordless and saw Reem's name and mobile number on the caller identification display.

"*As-salaamu'alaikum,*" Aliyah said after pressing the talk button and putting the phone to her ear. Her voice was cheerfully cordial.

"*Wa'alaiku mus salaam.*" Reem's subdued tone made Aliyah sense that something was wrong. "I'm not going to keep you long," Reem said.

"It's no problem," Aliyah said sincerely. "I'm not busy."

"Well, I am," Reem said curtly.

Aliyah's eyebrows rose in surprise, but she didn't say anything.

"From now on," Reem said, "I won't be giving you any private tennis lessons or Qur'an classes."

"Okay," Aliyah said, surprised that she didn't feel offended or upset. Deep down, she was actually relieved at the news. An awkward silence followed, and Aliyah sensed that Reem had expected a different response.

"So if you want to study Qur'an," Reem said, her voice full of emotion, "then you can come to the masjid classes like everyone else."

"Okay," Aliyah said. "But I appreciate you taking the time to teach me," she said sincerely. She didn't want Reem to think she had taken the classes for granted. Amidst all the stress and chaos in her life, learning Qur'an was one of the few things that brought her peace of mind.

However, Aliyah couldn't deny that Reem's insistence on being part of her personal life was putting a strain on their relationship. One minute Reem wanted to be the Qur'an teacher, then the next she wanted to enmesh herself in Aliyah's personal life. But Reem had never taken a moment to ask what Aliyah wanted or needed, or if she wanted to be friends with Reem at all. Reem just offered advice, asked personal questions, and made unilateral decisions on what Aliyah *needed* to know. But whenever Aliyah showed the slightest sign of having feelings and limitations of her own, Reem took offense. To Aliyah, it was a lose-lose situation. Reem would always view herself as the generous giver and Aliyah as the humble receiver, and if Aliyah stepped out of the ingratiating role that Reem had assigned her, Reem behaved as if she'd been wronged.

"I know you're really busy and you didn't have to teach me," Aliyah said, hoping to part on good terms. "So *jazaakillaahukhairan.*"

"Next time someone offers to make special arrangements for you," Reem said, her voice tight in offense, "you should be more respectful."

"Reem," Aliyah said, "I apologize if anything I've said or done has offended you. But I really don't understand your definition of respect. If I've ever disrespected you, I didn't mean to."

"*If*?" Reem said in exasperation. "For the past few weeks, all you've been is disrespectful. I would've never imagined you would treat a Qur'an teacher like that."

"How did I disrespect you during Qur'an class?" Aliyah said, careful to keep her tone level.

"I'm not talking about Qur'an class," Reem said. "I'm talking about how you treat *me*."

"And how do I treat you?" Aliyah said, exhaustion in her tone.

"Are you seriously going to act like you have *no* idea what I'm talking about?" Reem's voice said through the receiver.

"I'm not acting," Aliyah said. "I really don't recall mistreating you during our classes."

"I just said this isn't about Qur'an class."

"But you said you would've never imagined I would treat a Qur'an teacher like this," Aliyah pointed out.

"A Qur'an teacher deserves respect in *and* outside of class."

Aliyah felt herself growing annoyed, but she struggled to keep calm. It had been Reem's idea for them to have a relationship outside of class. How could she blame Aliyah for that? Casual relationships weren't bound by formal rules. "Reem, if you recall," Aliyah said, "you were the one who initiated the idea of us being friends. When you and I became friends, the rules of student and teacher no longer applied."

"In Islam, for certain people, there is *adab* that applies at *all* times," Reem said in a didactic tone, referring to the rules of proper Islamic etiquette.

"You mean like how we're supposed to treat our *elders*?" Aliyah said, sarcasm in her tone.

There was an extended silence, and Aliyah sensed that Reem had forgotten that Aliyah was a few years older than she was.

"That's different," Reem said defensively. "A Qur'an teacher has a status above everyone else."

"I don't doubt that," Aliyah said. "That's why I asked you if I ever mistreated you during class. And since I haven't, I'm confused as to why you feel I've disrespected you as a Qur'an teacher. You can't mix friendship with a teacher-student status. Otherwise, I can claim you disrespected *me*. I'm the elder, whether we're in class or not."

"I didn't *have* to change my schedule around to suit you," Reem said, ignoring Aliyah's point. "That was a huge sacrifice for me. So you have no right to criticize my family and call us racist cultural Muslims."

"What?" Aliyah said, humor in her tone. "When did I call your family racist cultural Muslims?"

"Maybe you never said it outright," Reem said. "But that's obviously what you meant when you said Sayed and I are wrong to require that our children marry Arabs."

"And what does your family marrying only Arabs have to do with your status as a Qur'an teacher?" Aliyah said defensively.

"You know what, Aliyah?" Reem said, frustration in her tone. "I'm not going to have this conversation with you. I think you're really arrogant and self-centered. And the only person who seems to matter to you is yourself. I used to feel bad for you, but now I see I made a big mistake. No wonder Deanna pretty much lost her mind around you. You send so many mixed messages." Reem huffed. "The reason you don't have any friends is because no one fits into your narrow, judgmental image of what a friend should be. So find another Qur'an teacher, and find another friend. I refuse to subject myself to your disrespect anymore."

The dial tone hissed in Aliyah's ear, and she slowly set the cordless phone next her on the bed, shell-shocked as she pressed the off button.

*"Let me clarify something, Aliyah,"* Reem had said when she'd convinced Aliyah to let her teach private Qur'an classes without pay. *"This is not something I do for everyone. As you know, my schedule is really busy. But you're one of my best students,* mashaAllah tabaarakAllah, *and I'd hate to lose you. So this is something I want to do for myself, honestly. I know you might not understand this right now, but, truthfully, it would be an honor if you allow me to teach you privately."*

Aliyah got choked up as she recalled the conversation. *O Allah, what is wrong with me?* Aliyah thought in dismay. Was she really partly to blame for Deanna's deteriorating condition? And had she really done something to deserve Reem talking to her like that? Aliyah had apologized to Reem Friday night, and Reem had said Aliyah should always feel free to express herself without apology. So what happened?

*"You don't have to apologize,"* Reem had said Friday night. "*I was offended, but you didn't say anything wrong... You had every right to say what you did. I don't believe in micromanaging people's pain. I went through that with my family when I was in high school, and I vowed to never do it to anyone else. So if you feel I've done something wrong, then say it. No matter how upset I get, we'll get through it* insha'Allah."

Tears welled in Aliyah's eyes as she sat dumbfounded, her gaze staring distantly toward the framed quote on the wall. *You are the author of your life story.*

What should I write? Aliyah asked herself, pensive in the realization she was getting it all wrong.

*O Allah!* her heart begged. *Help me write this story!*

***

"Yes you will," Sayed said, raising his voice as he glared at Reem and pointed to her mobile phone that now lay on their bed.

"No I'm not," Reem said as she stood in front of the mirror affixed to their dresser, yanking the brush through her hair as it got caught in tangles. She couldn't believe that, after everything that had happened, her husband had the audacity to insist that *she* was wrong.

"I'm telling you as your husband," Sayed said, speaking firmly and deliberately, "you are going to pick up that phone and apologize to Aliyah. Nothing she's said or done deserves that. I've told you over and over again, you need to stop taking out your anger with Fahad on the people you love. If you knew what it meant to be a Qur'an teacher, then you would understand that the Qur'an isn't just rules of recitation, beautiful sounds, and *tafseer*. It's life, Reem. It's *life*."

"This has nothing to do with Fahad," Reem said flippantly, her head jerking slightly as she continued to brush her hair.

"You might *think* this has nothing to do with your oldest brother," Sayed said. "But it has *everything* to do with him. Do you really think it's a coincidence that you called Aliyah right after we sat through a difficult dinner with Fahad and his family?"

"No I don't," Reem said. "Yes, I was tired of Fahad, but I'm tired of Aliyah too."

"Why? Because she has feelings like everyone else? She doesn't *have to* be your friend, Reem. It's not a religious obligation."

"But I teach her Qur'an, so she should respect me."

"But what does respect mean, Reem?" Sayed said. "Our desire for our children to marry Saudis isn't an Islamic rule, so she has every right to disagree with it. Take a moment and look at it from her point of view. One thing I learned from Cathy is—"

"Do *not* mention her name to me," Reem interjected, speaking over him. She was offended that he would bring up the woman he almost married before he acquiesced to his family's desire for him to marry her.

"—that, for converts to Islam, Muslim friends are not just part-time playmates. They're people they hope to build an *ummah* with. They have no Muslim family, so every friendship is one step closer to building a future for themselves and their children."

"Then they need to understand that the world doesn't revolve around their idea of a perfect *ummah*," Reem said. "Part of the reason they have so many problems is they think everyone should live like the *Sahaabah*."

"Is that a wrong assumption?" Sayed said challengingly. "We *should* behave like the Companions of the Prophet, *sallaallaahu 'alayhi wa sallam*."

Reem slammed the brush down on the dresser and turned to face him. "Am I such a terrible person that Aliyah has the right to talk to me like that?"

"And is she such a terrible person that you have the right to talk to her like that?" Sayed said. "*SubhaanAllah*, Reem. Take a step back. She didn't disrespect you. She just expressed the same thing you'd feel if your Saudi friends said our children could never marry theirs. You wouldn't want anything to do with them."

"I didn't have to help her," Reem said. "I was doing it for the sake of Allah."

"Really?" Sayed said, sarcasm in his tone. "If this was about Allah, then you wouldn't have quit based on hurt feelings. Qur'an teachers don't pick and choose who learns Allah's Book."

"She can find another teacher."

"I sincerely hope she does," Sayed said reflectively, shaking his head. "I really do. May Allah replace you with someone better."

"What is that supposed to mean?"

"It means you're not in an emotional place to be her teacher right now, let alone her friend. So until you take a long, honest look at yourself and learn what it means to teach Qur'an, I think this is your loss, not hers. Allah doesn't need us, remember that. We need Him. And when we use His Book for our own purposes, there is no blessing in that."

Reem's eyes glistened in hurt, and she folded her arms in a pout. "I can't believe you'd say something like that to me. Everything I teach is from authentic sources. I don't speak from myself when I talk about Allah."

"Teaching is not only in words, Reem," Sayed said. "How you treat people *is* talking about Allah, especially when you expect privileges *because* you teach about Allah."

"Respect isn't a privilege," Reem said, sniffing indignantly. "It's a right."

"If it's a right, then Aliyah deserves it too."

Reem contorted her face. "Americans have *no* respect for religious knowledge. That's what I'm talking about."

"*Astaghfirullah,*" Sayed said, his voice stern. "Then why is it that Allah chose so many of them to become Muslim?"

A stubborn silence followed as Reem refused to respond.

"Look at the Saudis you're so excited to have our children marry," Sayed said. "How many of *them* are studying Qur'an? How many are even praying?"

Reem still said nothing, but her husband's words softened her solve slightly.

"Don't get ahead of yourself, Reem," he cautioned. "We don't have a monopoly on this faith. I think Americans are wise to view religious knowledge with distrust. Don't forget, that's how many of them came to accept Islam in the first place. And if they're sincere, that distrust will lead them to the religious knowledge they *can* trust."

"What have I done to make Aliyah distrust me?" Reem said, voice tight in hurt.

Sayed was silent for some time as he looked affectionately at his wife. "Reem, this isn't about Aliyah," he said. "This is about you. You're hurting, and when you're hurting, one-on-one relationships are hard for you." He drew in a deep breath and exhaled. "You need to go to a therapist to help sort this out. You can't keep lashing out at people every time Fahad comes around."

Reem clenched her jaw and tears welled in her eyes. "Where am I supposed to find a therapist?" she said in a small voice. "You know what our family thinks about American shrinks."

There was an extended pause as Sayed met Reem's gaze doubtfully. "Are you willing to go?" he said.

"As long as no one finds out," Reem said, averting her gaze.

"Then I'll talk to Jacob, *insha'Allah*," Sayed said. "I'm sure he'll know someone with no connection to the Arab community."

***

Early Sunday morning Jacob stood near the window in his home office. He had had a difficult time sleeping the night before, but he wasn't inclined to go back to bed. He had spent the latter part of the night in prayer and self-reflection. After praying *Qiyaam al-Layl*, he had sat on his prayer mat and read Qur'an until it was time to pray *Fajr*. In the *qunoot* during *Witr* prayer, Jacob had stood with his hands raised in supplication, begging Allah to forgive him and his wife and to cover their faults from the public. He beseeched Allah to heal Deanna, to protect her from harm, and to guide her to make the decision that was best for her.

Though it was a difficult conclusion (and one that he'd come to only after careful reflection and *Istikhaarah*), Jacob had told Deanna's attorney that he would not bear the responsibility for deciding Deanna's fate. Either they get her a psychological evaluation to determine her mental lucidity or they get Deanna herself to inform them, verbally or in writing, what she wanted them to do about the plea deal. It was obvious that Deanna's mental state was deteriorating, but Jacob wasn't completely convinced that Deanna was incapable of making a reasonable decision. If Deanna had the presence of mind to lure him to the jail just so she could vent to him about Aliyah, then she had the ability to decide whether or not she should fight the charges or accept the plea.

Besides, it was a lose-lose situation for Jacob no matter what he did. If he made the decision for her and she suffered a terrible fate, then Deanna would blame him for the rest of her life—and he would blame *himself* for the rest of his life. And if he made the decision for her and she was exonerated of all charges, then she would feel entitled to demand more of him. And no matter what happened, Jacob was firm in his resolve that he would not remarry Deanna.

The past few months had been terribly lonely and confusing for Jacob as he struggled to take care of himself and their sons in her absence, but the time had been surprisingly tranquil for him spiritually. He was even developing a healthier relationship with Younus and Thawab while their mother was gone. Whenever Deanna had been around, Jacob felt tense and anxious while interacting with his sons. Deanna's constant criticism about his parental decisions and her incessant yelling at the boys even while he was enjoying a pleasant moment with them put Jacob on edge. Ironically, he didn't realize just how much he had been on edge until she was gone. It was as if he was finally exhaling after having held his breath for too long.

*Call Dr. Warren!* The dry-erase marker note on the whiteboard reminded Jacob that he hadn't called Aliyah back. *Crap*, he thought to himself in self-rebuke.

He needed to talk to her before Monday morning. He glanced at the clock. Was it too early to give her a call?

***

Aliyah was still sitting facing the *qiblah* on the carpet of her bedroom when the rays of early morning spilled through her window. She had slept for only a few hours Saturday night before deciding to get up and pray *Qiyaam al-Layl*. But when she had gone to the bathroom, she discovered that she was menstruating. Her heart fell in sadness when she realized she would be unable to offer *Salaah* for an entire week. Usually Aliyah viewed her period as a "week off" from obligatory prayer, but moments like these she wished she could connect to Allah through formal prayer. Reem's words had cut deep, and Aliyah really wanted the tranquility of formal prayer to help clear her mind and heart. But since she couldn't pray, she had sat in self-reflection in between reading Qur'an and crying to Allah in *du'aa.* Facing the direction for prayer, she had remained there until sunrise, and the spiritual exercise helped calm her heart and unclutter her mind.

*"You stay out of my life, and I stay out of yours."* Aliyah cringed at the memory of how poorly she had translated her feelings to Reem. Aliyah had fallen asleep in a fit of agony, regretting how she had spoken to her now former Qur'an teacher, and she hadn't improved much when she had woken up that morning before dawn. Regret had gnawed at her as she reflected on how she could have better handled the exchange with Reem.

*It's for the better*, Aliyah said to herself as the rays of sun lit her room and she thought of Reem's angry phone call. She had no idea why she felt so certain, but there was a sense of peace in her heart. Everything with Reem would sort itself out, she felt, though Aliyah had no idea how or when. *Allah is in charge of hearts*, she reminded herself. *He is in charge of everything.* If Allah had decreed that Reem's heart would turn away from her, then it must be for a good reason. Aliyah hadn't intended to insult Reem, and Aliyah was sure Reem hadn't intended to insult her. Perhaps they were both nursing their own private wounds and simply needed time to heal.

"O Allah," Aliyah said bowing her head and raising her hands in *du'aa*. "Give me better than I lost, and give Reem better than she lost. And forgive us both and remove from us any *ghill* in our hearts. For you are *Al-Ghafoor*, *Al-Wahhaab*. Ameen."

After the prayerful supplication, Aliyah glanced at the clock and saw that it was just after seven o'clock in the morning. She wondered if it was too early to call Mashael. In a couple of hours, Aliyah would need to prepare breakfast for Ibrahim and start getting dressed. She was scheduled to meet Salima for breakfast at ten o'clock. When they had spoken the night before, they planned to meet at the mall restaurant where Aliyah had often taken her son to play with Younus and Thawab. Salima and Aliyah hoped that Haroon and Ibrahim could enjoy themselves in the children's area while they talked. So Aliyah should probably call Mashael within the next hour in case the conversation took longer than expected.

A vibrating sound interrupted Aliyah's thoughts, and she turned and saw that someone was calling her mobile. Confused, Aliyah stood and walked over to the nightstand by her bed, wondering who would be calling at this time.

*Jacob Bivens,* the caller ID display glowed.

After only a slight hesitation, Aliyah pressed the button to accept the call and put the phone to her ear. "Hello?"

"*As-salaamu'alaikum wa rahmatullaah,*" Jacob said.

Aliyah's spirits lifted at the sound of the familiar voice. "*Wa'alaiku mus salaam wa rahmatullaahi wa barakaatuh.*"

"I'm sorry to call so early," he said. "But I didn't want to miss you."

"It's okay," Aliyah said. "I was awake."

There was an extended pause. "Aliyah," Jacob said, concern in his tone, "did Dr. Warren meet with you last week to replace you with Dr. Stanley as stand-in coordinator of the internship in my absence?"

Aliyah got the sudden feeling that she had done something terribly wrong. "Yes…" she said hesitantly.

"And you accepted?"

Aliyah cringed as she was overcome with apprehension and mortification. "Yes…"

Jacob exhaled, as if disturbed by the news. "Then you need to talk to Dr. Warren first thing Monday morning and revoke that acceptance."

"Why?" Aliyah said, her tone concerned.

"This might not make a lot of sense right now," Jacob said. "But, trust me, if Dr. Warren appointed Dr. Stanley to oversee the internship, then it wasn't to help you or One Plus One."

Aliyah slowly sat on the edge of her bed, dread knotting in her stomach. "What happened?"

"I can explain more later, *insha'Allah,*" Jacob said, apology in his voice. "But for now, I need you to tell Dr. Warren that based on Article Three of the Faculty-Initiated Program Code, you decline to accept Dr. Stanley as the stand-in coordinator in your place."

"Okay…" Aliyah said, unsure how to process what Jacob was saying. She hesitated briefly before asking, "But why did you call my uncle about this? Does he know something?"

Several seconds passed before Aliyah heard Jacob exhale. "With everything that's happening," Jacob said, "I didn't feel comfortable calling you myself."

"You mean because of all those 'crazy Muslim woman' rumors?"

"No," Jacob said, as if choosing his words carefully. "Because Dr. Stanley has a history, and since I'm no longer at the college, at least for the time being, I wanted to make sure someone else was looking out for you."

“I’m not understanding,” Aliyah said, drawing her eyebrows together. “What history?”

“Aliyah,” Jacob said, “there’s a lot I can’t say because my position bounds me to confidentiality. Even this phone call itself is walking a thin line. But as your Muslim brother, it’s my responsibility to ensure your protection and safety. So I’ll say this. Part of the reason I made it a point to stop by your office each day and walk you to the elevator and to your car was so that Dr. Stanley and our other colleagues would associate you with me and leave you alone.”

“Leave me alone?” Aliyah repeated in confusion. “Why?”

Jacob drew in a deep breath and exhaled. “Aliyah, if I could, I’d tell you everything. But as a member of the staff disciplinary committee, I can’t reveal the details of cases that have come before me. So as far as Dr. Warren and any of our colleagues are concerned, this conversation never happened. But as your Muslim brother, I’m telling you that Dr. Stanley, with the implicit support of Dr. Warren, has been trying for years to have me demoted from department head, and it looks like they’re taking advantage of you and my absence to do it.”

Aliyah felt anxiety tightening in her chest. After having told Dr. Warren she welcomed any help for the internship, Aliyah loathed the idea of going back and telling Dr. Warren that she was formally refusing Dr. Stanley replacing her as One Plus One’s stand-in coordinator. Aliyah had tried so hard to stay out of problems at work, but now it looked like she had unwittingly walked right into a slew of them.

“When you look at the faculty handbook that I mentioned earlier,” Jacob continued, “pay particular attention to the section about faculty-initiated programs and the steps required to have a staff member replace another as the appointed stand-in coordinator. This is the part I need you to reference when you speak to Dr. Warren Monday morning. Right now, this might all sound cryptic, but trust me, with Dr. Stanley involved, your professional reputation, and perhaps even your position, could be at stake. My hope is that this is only a grievance they have with me, but we can’t afford to take any chances.”

“Okay,” Aliyah said, her mind racing to recall where she had placed the handbook. “I appreciate you letting me know.”

“And if you can,” Jacob said, “between now and next week, find out what you can about Dr. Stanley. As I said, I’m bound by confidentiality, so I can’t say much. But his indiscretions are well known on campus, even amongst students. So if you hear any rumors about him, they’re probably true.”

“Can you give me an idea of what I’m dealing with?” Aliyah said, feeling overwhelmed and anxious.

“I can’t speak on that,” Jacob said. “But you need to be careful, personally and professionally. He can’t be trusted.”

*How could I have been so naïve?* Aliyah thought in self-rebuke. When Dr. Warren first spoke to her about Dr. Stanley, Aliyah should have told her supervisor that she needed time to think over any changes different from what Dr. Bivens had suggested. But Aliyah had been so keen on being accommodating that the possibility that Dr. Warren had intended anything except to make Aliyah feel intimidated had never crossed her mind. No wonder Dr. Warren had seemed to anticipate Aliyah's resistance.

"And of course, don't let anyone know I told you to ask about him," Jacob's voice said through the phone. "Anything you learn, keep to yourself for future reference. You're gathering this information for your own protection, not to share with anyone else."

"Okay," Aliyah said, doubtful. "But who should I talk to?"

"You're probably safest talking to someone who's no longer at the college," Jacob said, apology in his tone, "if that's possible."

"Does my uncle know anything about Dr. Stanley?" Aliyah asked, hopeful that she could rely heavily on Benjamin instead of other people.

"Yes…" Jacob said noncommittally. "Through rumors. But some of the sisters who've attended the college should know more."

"I'll get on that right away, *insha'Allah*," Aliyah said. "*JazaakAllaahukhairan* for telling me."

"*Wa iyyaki*," Jacob said. "I was hoping you would never have to deal with any of this directly. But *qaddarAllah*," he said with a sigh. "Allah does what He wills."

There was an extended silence.

"I'm really sorry about everything that's happening with Deanna," Aliyah said, her thoughts shifting to her former friend. "If there's anything I can do to help, just let me know."

"I might take you up on that," Jacob said, his tone exhausted and reflective. "But right now, we just need your prayers."

"Of course," Aliyah said. "I pray for your family every day."

"Thank you," Jacob said. "That means a lot."

"How is Mrs. Michaels, by the way?" Aliyah said. "Is there any improvement?"

Aliyah heard Jacob exhale, and she hoped she hadn't touched on too sensitive a subject. "Allah knows best, but the doctors say they see signs of improvement, but nothing significant."

"Do they think she might wake up?"

"They're not sure," Jacob said. "But I'm praying she does. For everyone's sake," he said, "even mine."

Aliyah was unsure if she had the right to ask, but her curiosity was piqued. "Why yours?"

"I never really got to talk to her about Islam," Jacob said, "at least not in depth. There was always so much going on that it never felt like the right time."

"Well, I pray you get the opportunity," Aliyah said, unsure what else to say. She had no idea if it was realistic to expect Mrs. Michaels to wake up from a coma, let alone to be lucid enough to have conversations about religion.

"I do too," Jacob said reflectively. "I really do…"

A thought came to Aliyah suddenly. "If I run into any problems with Dr. Warren or Dr. Stanley," she said hesitantly, "should I call you or my uncle?"

There was a brief pause as Jacob considered Aliyah's question. "Whatever you think is best," Jacob said finally. "You're welcome to call me anytime, but depending on the nature of the problem, you may feel more comfortable talking to your uncle. Either way, I plan to stay in touch with both of you though I'll be pretty busy for the next few weeks."

"That's fine," Aliyah said. "I understand."

"But I do apologize for all of this," Jacob said. "I never intended for you to be in the middle of any of it. But unfortunately, every workplace has its set of problems, and Dr. Stanley is one of ours. And Dr. Warren, though well-intentioned at times, too often lets her resentment of religion, and Muslim men in particular, cloud her judgment, so Dr. Stanley takes every opportunity to exploit that."

"May Allah protect us," Aliyah said, unsure what else she could say. It was all so overwhelming.

"Ameen. That's my prayer," Jacob said sincerely. "In the end, it is Allah who is our Protector. I have to keep reminding myself of that."

***

At 10:30 Sunday morning, Aliyah sat across from Salima at a restaurant booth as they watched the boys play together in the mall. The bumper car section wasn't yet open, but Ibrahim and Haroon were enjoying themselves on the jungle gym next to it. In between smiling and laughing at the boys, Aliyah and Salima ate from their plates of waffles and omelets and sipped from glasses of orange juice and apple juice.

"You seem happy."

"What?" Aliyah said, still grinning as she looked away from Ibrahim and met Salima's gaze before putting a forkful of waffle in her mouth.

"You look happy," Salima said again, a smile creasing the sides of her lips.

Glancing at her son, Aliyah smiled with her eyes as she chewed her food. "I love it when Ibrahim gets out," she said after a few seconds.

"Ibrahim was out with you Friday night," Salima said, a friendly smirk on her face, "but you didn't look happy."

"Really?" Aliyah's tone conveyed genuine surprise. "I probably was just tired. I had a long day at work."

Salima narrowed her eyes as she ate in silence for some time, her expression playfully accusing.

"What?" Aliyah said, laughter in her voice as she grew self-conscious under Salima's gaze.

"You sounded really upset last night," Salima said.

Aliyah creased her forehead in confusion. "I did?"

"When we *talked*," Salima said slowly, as if to jog Aliyah's memory.

"Oh yeah," Aliyah said as if it were a long time ago. She waved her fork dismissively before using it to cut a piece of omelet. "I got up early and made a lot of *du'aa*, so I feel better, *alhamdulillah*." She looked toward the boys and laughed before putting the piece of omelet in her mouth.

Salima pursed her lips suspiciously after Aliyah met her gaze again. "You called Jacob back, didn't you?"

It took a few seconds for Aliyah to register what Salima was talking about. "Jacob?" Aliyah said, eyebrows drawn together after she swallowed her food.

"Yes, *Jacob*," Salima said, widening her eyes playfully, as if to remind Aliyah that he exists. "Jacob Bivens," she said. "*Dr.* Jacob Bivens, the math professor you work with."

Aliyah averted her gaze. "I decided not to call him back."

"Then he called you back," Salima said matter-of-factly.

Aliyah lifted a shoulder in a shrug, a hesitant grin on her face. "This morning," she admitted. "But it wa—"

"Ha, I knew it!" Salima shook her head. She lifted her glass of apple juice, took a sip, and set it back down, smirking. "I swear, if you didn't have melanin in your skin, you would be blushing right now."

"Blushing?" Aliyah said, humored disbelief in her voice. "Because my department head called me?"

"No," Salima said. "Because the man you want to marry called you."

The smile fell from Aliyah's face as she met Salima's gaze in confusion. "The man I want to marry? He's my best friend's husband."

"Former husband," Salima corrected.

Aliyah frowned thoughtfully. "How did you find out?"

"Jamil told me."

"Jamil?"

"My brother," Salima said. "He was with me at the halal store."

"Oh yeah," Aliyah said, remembering just then. "He plays basketball with Larry, right?"

"Sometimes," Salima said noncommittally.

"So Larry told him?" Aliyah said, surprise in her tone.

"Or Jacob," Salima suggested.

Aliyah drew her eyebrows together in confusion. "Jamil knows Jacob?"

Salima chuckled. "Everybody knows Jacob."

Aliyah smiled, nodding in embarrassment. "That makes sense. He's pretty well known in the community."

"Plus, Jamil works at the law firm that's representing Deanna."

A shadow of concern passed over Aliyah's face. "Everybody knows about the charges now?"

Salima shook her head. "Not everybody. But Jamil and I do."

"Why didn't you say anything?"

Salima pulled her head back in surprise. "Why does it matter?"

*Oh.* Aliyah shrugged. "I guess it doesn't. I just thought…" Aliyah didn't know how to finish her sentence.

"That you were keeping your friend's secret?" Salima finished, a knowing smile on her face.

"Yeah, I guess so."

"Keep doing that," Salima said, her tone serious. "We're praying the media doesn't get ahold of this."

"I am." Aliyah sighed as she glanced at the boys. "I'd hate to think what would happen if Younus and Thawab found out."

Salima raised an eyebrow. "Found out what?"

"Everything," Aliyah said, sadness in her tone. "Can you imagine?"

"They probably know a lot more than we do," Salima said reflectively. "Children aren't as naïve as we think. Don't forget they live with their parents."

"But Larry said it happened at Deanna's parents' house."

"That's not what I mean," Salima said. "They might not know all the details. But I'm sure they know something's wrong."

Aliyah drew in a deep breath and exhaled. "May Allah protect them. I don't want to see them hurt."

"Ameen to the *du'aa*," Salima said, her tone pensive. "But I think it's a little too late to hope they won't get hurt. Let's just pray their pain doesn't cause any serious long-term damage."

Aliyah ate in silence for some time, her gaze between the boys and her food. "How well do you know their family?" Aliyah said, glancing up at Salima hesitantly.

"Whose family?"

"Larry and Jacob's."

Salima averted her gaze and shrugged. "Not more than you, I assume," she said. "Jamil knows them better than I do."

Aliyah nodded thoughtfully. She felt inclined to inquire more, but she wasn't sure what to ask.

"Why?" Salima asked curiously.

"I don't know," Aliyah said with a shrug. "It's just that I—"

"Salima?"

At the sound of a strange voice, Aliyah turned and found an attractive young woman standing next to the their table smiling widely at Salima and holding a shopping bag.

"Yasmeen?" Salima said in pleasant surprise. She stood and drew the woman into an embrace.

The woman rolled her eyes in embarrassment and waved her hand dismissively. "Why do you keep calling me that?" she said after they released each other.

"A mother can hope, right?" Salima said teasingly.

"You're too young to be my mother," the young woman said, grinning. "But trust me." She lowered her voice and narrowed her eyes playfully. "I wouldn't mind having you instead."

Salima and the woman laughed at the private joke, leaving Aliyah feeling awkward.

"I'm sorry." Salima gestured a hand toward Aliyah as she sat back down. "Yasmeen, this is Aliyah. Aliyah, this is Yasmeen."

The woman rolled her eyes as she leaned forward and shook Aliyah's hand. "My name is Jasmine," she said as she side-eyed Salima playfully. "But Salima and my boyfriend think Arabizing my name will convince me to convert."

"You're not Muslim?" Aliyah said, more for friendly conversation than sincere interest.

"Not yet," Salima said quickly, answering for Jasmine. "But we're working on it."

Aliyah nodded, a polite smile on her face, but something in the way Salima spoke made Aliyah sense that Salima was rushing the conversation for her benefit.

"But give me a call sometime, okay?" Salima said, smiling broadly at Jasmine.

"I will," Jasmine said apologetically. "It's just that I've been so busy." She rolled her eyes again. "You know, with Larry and my family and everything that's going on."

Aliyah stiffened, the polite smile remaining frozen on her face. In her peripheral vision, she saw Salima eyeing her in between maintaining eye contact with Jasmine, but Aliyah couldn't bring herself to look at Salima. Aliyah felt pulsating at her temples as the conversation faded into the background then slowly became audible again.

"But let me go," Jasmine said finally. "I just stopped by the mall to pick up a gift for Larry's mother. I'm supposed to be meeting them for Sunday brunch."

"Tell everyone I said hello," Salima said.

"I will," Jasmine said before turning to Aliyah and smiling. "It was nice to meet you."

"You too," Aliyah managed to utter before Jasmine disappeared into the mall corridors.

Aliyah focused her gaze on her food and ate in silence for some time.

"I wanted to tell you when we discussed him last night," Salima said apologetically. "But I figured it didn't matter since you turned him down. I'm sorry about that."

"It's not your responsibility," Aliyah said sincerely, surprised that she found her voice. "It's just shocking, that's all."

"Is it?" Salima said doubtfully. "Larry doesn't strike me as a one-woman man."

Aliyah chuckled as she stabbed mindlessly at the food left on her plate. "I can see that."

"But he seems like a nice brother, *mashaAllah*," Salima said.

Aliyah rolled her eyes good-naturedly. "Don't they all?"

Salima grunted agreement. "My husband used to say, 'Everybody *seems* nice, Salima. Come up with a better line.'" She laughed and shook her head as if enjoying a pleasant memory. "I guess I'm just a stickler for seeing the good in people."

"*MashaAllah*," Aliyah said reflectively. "I'm the same way. But I'm learning that *good* is complex and layered."

"That's so true," Salima said, nodding in agreement. "When we see everything as black and white, it causes a lot of problems."

"But how do you work through the gray?" Aliyah said thoughtfully, setting down her fork and meeting Salima's gaze. "When Deanna and I were friends, I ignored all the warning signs, you know? I kept telling myself that she means well or that this is just her personality or she's just trying to help. Sometimes I don't know the forest for the trees."

"That's everybody," Salima said. "The closer a situation is to you, the more difficult it is to see what's really going on. That's why we have friends and family to help us figure things out."

"Or no one," Aliyah said in dry humor as she gazed toward the jungle gym for some time.

"We all have someone," Salima said, "even if it doesn't feel like it at times."

Aliyah nodded. "That's true. We always have Allah."

"I meant people," Salima said. "No one can do it alone."

"You sound like Reem," Aliyah said, meeting Salima's gaze with a hesitant smile. "But everyone doesn't have family and friends to depend on. Except for my uncle Benjamin, I have Allah and myself. And I'm starting to realize it's for the better."

"You don't have family?" Salima said, her tone conveying surprise. "I thought you mentioned you wished you could live with your brothers."

"Yes," Aliyah said tentatively. "Emphasis on the word *wish*. It could never happen. They don't speak to me anymore."

"Why not?" Salima said, shocked disapproval in her tone.

"I became Muslim."

Salima and Aliyah remained silent as they watched the boys climb the jungle gym and hang upside down, their legs locked in place on the bars. Droves of men and women slowly drifted into the mall as the gates of several stores opened, and a few more children joined Ibrahim and Haroon.

"How long have you been Muslim?" Salima asked.

"About eighteen years."

"And your family is still upset?"

"To be honest," Aliyah said, "I don't know. They never really offered any explanation. Except that I was being selfish and ungrateful after everything they did for me."

"Your *brothers* said that?" Salima asked, surprised.

"No, my parents," Aliyah said. "But everyone just went along with it."

"Maybe they didn't have a choice," Salima offered. "Whenever grown children fall in line with their parents on things like that, it's usually because the parents made it clear they don't have a choice."

Aliyah nodded thoughtfully. "I can see my parents doing that. They were really good at making us feel bad if we showed even the slightest disapproval of anything they did. When I was younger, I thought we were being raised to be respectful to our elders. Now I know we were just being raised to be compliant with whatever they wanted."

"Or both," Salima said.

"Or both," Aliyah agreed, nodding. "I just don't think my parents know the difference."

"Most parents don't," Salima said. "Parents learn parenting at about the same pace that children learn life. We're all going at this alone."

"You really think so?" Aliyah said doubtfully. "I think we know a lot more than we admit. It's not *that* difficult to just take a moment and listen to someone, you know what I mean?"

"I agree," Salima said. "I'm just saying it's not easy if you don't have the right guidance. Don't forget that a lot of what you know is because of the natural clarity that faith gives you. Without Islam, people are lost."

Aliyah huffed humorously. "Many Muslims are lost, too."

"Like I said," Salima replied, "without *Islam*, people are lost."

Aliyah nodded, understanding. "And Islam is sincere belief and humble submission."

"Exactly," Salima said. "Allah makes it very simple to be Muslim and go to Paradise. But that doesn't mean every Muslim understands and embraces what Islam really means."

"That's a lifetime effort," Aliyah said. "I'm still trying to figure it out myself."

"Good," Salima said. "It's when you're confident that you understand Islam fully that you need to worry."

There was a brief pause as Salima lifted her glass of juice. "So what's going on with you and Jacob?" she said before sipping from the glass, her gaze on Aliyah.

Aliyah shrugged. "Nothing," she said. "He was calling about work."

"Work?" Salima raised her eyebrows doubtfully then set her glass down. "Are you sure?"

Aliyah smirked and shook her head. "What is up with everyone? Do I have a sign on my head that says, 'Ask me about Jacob'?"

"No," Salima said. "But Jacob has a sign on *his* head that says, 'I want to marry Aliyah.'"

"I don't think so," Aliyah said, shaking her head and grinning self-consciously. She lifted her glass of orange juice and peered inside thoughtfully before setting it back down. "Maybe about thirteen years ago, but everything's different now."

There was an extended silence. "Not everything," Salima said reflectively. "Hearts don't change so easily."

Aliyah's gaze became distant momentarily. "But circumstances do," she said.

A loud humming noise came from the play area, and Aliyah turned and found a man preparing the bumper car station. Suddenly, there was a lot of commotion as the children left the jungle gym and rushed to line up, Ibrahim and Haroon among them.

"When Jamil was struggling in his marriage," Salima said, her eyes on the children pushing and shoving to get to the bumper cars, "he said Jacob gave him a lot of good advice."

"*MashaAllah*," Aliyah remarked, lifting her glass of orange juice and peering inside again before setting it back down, her thoughts distant.

"And he said Jacob was always talking about the lesson he learned after he let a good sister get away." Salima met Aliyah's gaze with a reflective expression on her face. "I remember listening to Jamil and thinking, I wonder who that sister was." Salima shook her head and smiled at Aliyah. "Now I understand what all the fuss was about, *mashaAllah*."

Aliyah averted her gaze, uncomfortable with the attention.

"Trust me," Salima said, "I don't think time or circumstance could make that man forget about you."

"Well," Aliyah said with a sigh, "for now, I'm focusing on myself and my son. I'll leave the rest to Allah."

"That's always a good plan," Salima said tentatively. "But there are some things Allah leaves to us."

"How did everything work out for Jamil and his wife?" Aliyah said, intentionally changing the subject. She didn't want to talk about Jacob right then.

Salima smiled as if enjoying a private joke. "Well, it turned out he didn't have to worry about solving any of his marriage problems after all. His wife's sheikh did it on his behalf."

Aliyah creased her forehead in confusion. "What do you mean?"

"The sheikh told his wife that she couldn't be married to him anymore."

"*What*?" Aliyah felt herself getting upset. "Why would he say something like that?"

Salima shook her head, a reflective frown on her face. "I have no idea." She shrugged. "But apparently, Jamil wasn't committed enough."

Aliyah contorted her face in disapproval. "How would the sheikh know how committed Jamil was to his marriage?"

"Not to the marriage," Salima said, a sad smile creasing the sides of her lips. "To the sheikh."

Aliyah's heart fell in sadness, recalling how betrayed she'd felt after she trusted the imam's perspective on Matt more than she did her intuition. "Why do they do that?" she said, shaking her head, upset. "What happened to focusing on Allah?"

"*Ukhti*," Salima said, melancholy in her tone, "for some people, focusing on Allah and focusing on their sheikh are one and the same."

Aliyah shook her head, still upset. "I don't understand that thinking though. Isn't a sheikh supposed to teach people about Allah and *Istikhaarah* and *du'aa*? Certainly, the sheikh didn't believe it was obligatory for Jamil to follow *him*."

"I don't understand it either," Salima said. "But it's rare to find someone who admits they don't have all the answers. Everyone wants to think their group, *madhhab*, or sheikh has the answer to everything."

"Even who you should be married to," Aliyah muttered, disappointment in her tone.

"Even who you should be married to." Salima nodded, pursing her lips. "But the good news is, it was for the best. Jamil is doing much better now, *alhamdulillah*. And if I'm completely honest, I was happy to see her go. She was pulling Jamil away from Allah, and it was hard to watch."

"*SubhaanAllah*. I can't imagine," Aliyah said, sighing. "I really miss my classes, but I'm not willing to go back to being taught that critical thinking and religiousness are mutually exclusive. When I became Muslim, I decided to submit to Allah, not to human beings."

"The problem is," Salima said reflectively, "we learn about Allah from human beings. So it's not as simple as people versus Allah."

Aliyah nodded. "That's true."

"But Jamil and I have been blessed to find some pretty good teachers in the last couple of years, *mashaAllah*," Salima said.

"You mean Reem's *tafseer* classes?"

Salima creased her forehead then shook her head. "I only review my *hifdh* with Sister Reem."

An expectant grin spread on Aliyah's face. "You memorized the *whole* Qur'an?"

A smile creased one corner of Salima's mouth as she nodded. "Yes, *mashaAllah*."

"Are you serious?" Excited laughter was in Aliyah's tone.

Salima chuckled. "Yes, *mashaAllah*, but I don't like to broadcast it."

"Why not?" Aliyah said, eyes still wide in pleasant surprise. "*MashaAllah, barakAllahufeek*. That's one piece of news that deserves to be broadcasted *everywhere*."

"It's a heavy responsibility though," Salima said, a hesitant smile lingering. "I got my *ijaazah* about ten years ago, so I want to—"

"You have your *ijaazah* too?" Aliyah said, unable to contain her excitement.

Salima chuckled. "So I want to find a teacher to recite to before I start teaching again myself."

"I thought you recited with Reem," Aliyah said.

"That's for my *hifdh*," Salima clarified. "Reem doesn't have her *ijaazah* yet, so we just focus on my memorization. But I'm still trying to find someone with a formal certification in reciting and teaching *Hafs*."

"Can you help me? I mean, if that's okay," Aliyah added quickly. "I've been studying *Hafs* for a while, but I need a new teacher."

Salima creased her forehead in confusion. "A *new* teacher?"

Aliyah averted her gaze momentarily. "Long story. But Reem stepped down from the position."

A shadow of concern passed over Salima's face. "Is everything okay?"

"Everything's fine. For me," Aliyah added for emphasis. "But Reem wanted more than a teacher-student relationship, and well..." Aliyah was unsure how much she should share. "…I'm not comfortable discussing my private life with someone just because they think I need a friend."

Salima nodded knowingly, a pleasant expression on her face. "I know the feeling," she said. "People take one look at my head wrap and start offering to teach me the Arabic alphabet and *Al-Faatihah* and even the fundamentals of *Tawheed*."

Aliyah laughed, relieved. "So it's not just me?"

"Trust me, I've been there," Salima said. "Sometimes people ask if I know how to pray and if my husband was Muslim." She shook her head, grinning. "It *never* ends."

"That doesn't bother you?" Aliyah asked, curious.

"Sometimes," Salima said honestly. "But they mean well, so I try not to get offended. And there *are* people who need help with those things. It's just hurtful that the assumption is either ignorance or neediness when they meet me."

"Do you think it's a cultural thing?" Aliyah asked thoughtfully. "Because we're American?"

"Yes," Salima said. "The general assumption is that people from Western countries are ignorant of Islam, even if they're Muslim. So well-intentioned people from Muslim countries see us as an opportunity to earn blessings by teaching us about our religion."

"But what if we know more than they do?" Aliyah asked rhetorically. "What then?"

Salima chuckled. "Then *we* have the opportunity to earn blessings." She shook her head, smirking. "But, trust me, that doesn't always go well. I've had people never speak to me again after they hear me recite Qur'an."

Aliyah drew her eyebrows together. "But why?"

Salima shrugged. "They probably just don't know how to deal with me anymore. But to be honest, I've experienced that with Americans too. For most Muslims, if they can't place you into a simple category, they get confused and leave you alone." Salima smirked. "That is, if they don't just call you misguided and try to convert you to their group."

"What type of Muslim are you?" Aliyah said in agreement, mocking the question she was often asked.

Salima laughed. "Or who's your sheikh?"

"Thank God I'm not the only Muslim who just wants to be *Muslim*," Aliyah said, "without the prefix." She shook her head. "But it gets lonely sometimes."

"Then stay lonely," Salima said. "It's better than doing something you don't believe Allah asks of you."

"*SubhaanAllah*," Aliyah said, relief in her voice. "I'm so glad I talked to you. I was starting to feel bad for keeping to myself."

"Never apologize for your personal boundaries," Salima said. "Wherever you can find authentic knowledge about your faith, take advantage of it. But don't let people bully you into committing yourself to one group, teacher, or school of thought. If that's what works for them, cool. But some of us are just trying to hold on to our faith and go to Paradise. And we don't need a special club membership for that."

"You can say that again," Aliyah agreed.

***

Aliyah was home from the mall and Ibrahim had already fallen asleep after lunch when she realized she hadn't called Mashael. After the conversation with Jacob, Aliyah had completely forgotten. Though Aliyah was exhausted after spending most of the morning at the mall, she decided to call Mashael before lying down herself.

"I'm sorry I'm just getting back with you," Aliyah said after Mashael answered and they exchanged salaams. "But if you still want to come over, you can."

"Can I?" Mashael sounded eager and grateful.

"Yes…" Aliyah said tentatively, sensing Mashael was ready to jump in her car right then. "But later this afternoon is better."

"That's no problem," Mashael said quickly.

There was a brief silence. "Can you give me an idea what this is about?" Aliyah said.

"It's about marriage," Mashael said in a low whisper, apparently in an effort to keep her family from overhearing.

"Oh…" Aliyah said, uncomfortable. "But you know you can't…" Aliyah's thoughts trailed as she realized it wasn't wise to offer advice before hearing everything Mashael wanted to say. Even if listening to Mashael's story wouldn't change Aliyah's advice, it would certainly affect Mashael's receptiveness to it.

"Today's not good?" Mashael said, concern in her voice.

"No, no, no," Aliyah said quickly, realizing that Mashael had misunderstood her unfinished statement to be related to the time of the visit. "Today's fine. I just need to lie down for a couple of hours."

"Is five o'clock okay?" Mashael said, hopeful.

Aliyah smiled. "Yes, *insha'Allah*. Five o'clock is perfect. I'll text you my address now."

# 19
# Wake Up Call

"He's terrible," Mashael said, wrinkling her nose as she sat on the couch in Aliyah's living room a comfortable distance from Aliyah Sunday afternoon. "I'm surprised he still works there."

"What did he do?" Aliyah said, eyebrows drawn together curiously.

"You never heard about Dr. Stanley?" Mashael said, a disbelieving grin on her face.

Aliyah shrugged. "I tend to keep to myself. I hear things here and there, but I never really pay attention long enough to know who anyone's talking about."

"That's good *mashaAllah*," Mashael said reflectively, her eyes growing distant momentarily. "I wish more people were like that."

Aliyah was unsure how to respond, as she sensed Mashael was distracted by an unpleasant thought. "Dr. Stanley and I are supposed to be working on a project together at work," Aliyah said finally, making it a point to avoid mentioning Jacob. "So I just wanted to get an idea of what type of person he is."

"He's an excellent math professor," Mashael said tentatively, "but he flirts with a lot of students. When I was there, girls were whispering about how easy it was to get an A in his class, if you know what I mean."

Aliyah contorted her face. "Are you serious?"

"Unfortunately." Mashael frowned. "One year I heard there was a sexual harassment suit filed against him by another professor, but I think the charges were eventually dropped. One of my friends said the college decided to handle the problem internally."

"By the staff disciplinary committee," Aliyah said aloud to herself, recalling that Jacob mentioned being a member.

"I guess so," Mashael said. "But from what I hear, that didn't really stop him. It just made him more careful. Last thing I heard, he focuses on girls who are loners and don't have a lot of support."

"Did you ever take any of his classes?"

Mashael nodded. "Two. But I never had any problem with him except when he made offensive comments about religion."

"During math class?" Aliyah said, wrinkling her nose in disagreement.

"Yes, all the time," Mashael said, her tone suggesting disapproval. "But he always found a way to relate it to what we were studying, so you really couldn't say anything."

Aliyah was quiet momentarily. "Is that where you met the guy who wants to marry you?"

"In math class?"

"No, at the college?"

"Yes." A reflective smile lingered on Mashael's face. "We've been together about three years now."

Aliyah's stomach churned in dread. She hoped Mashael wasn't involved in a *haraam* relationship. "Do you need to pray *Asr*?" Aliyah said, feeling the sudden need for a spiritual mood before they talked.

"Is it in?" Mashael said, lifting her wrist and looking at her watch.

"It just came in," Aliyah said, feeling relief that, whatever was going on with this "boyfriend," Mashael hadn't abandoned *Salaah*. "But I'm not praying, so you can go ahead."

"Where can I do *wudhoo*'?" Mashael asked, standing and glancing toward the hall where Ibrahim was in his room.

"The bathroom's the first door on the left," Aliyah said, gesturing toward the hall.

Aliyah's apartment phone rang seconds after Mashael entered the bathroom. As she stood to answer, Aliyah recalled leaving her mobile phone in her bedroom. Aliyah looked at the caller ID and saw Matt's name and her former home number on the display.

"*As-salaamu'alaikum*," Aliyah said as she answered.

"*Wa'alaiku-mus-salaam*," Matt said before pausing briefly. "Aliyah…" He exhaled in apology. "Nikki and I just got home from the hospital, and the doctors put her on bed rest, so we need you to keep Ibrahim for a few days."

Aliyah felt anxiety tighten in her chest. She had planned to arrive to work early in the morning so she could review the faculty handbook then meet with Dr. Warren before Dr. Stanley arrived. Where would she find a babysitter before then? Ibrahim wasn't part of any weekday summer program, so she had no place to take him. "I'm sorry to hear about Nikki," Aliyah said. "But I can drop off Ibrahim so she doesn't have to drive. I don't think he'll be too much trouble. He's become quite independent, *mashaAllah*."

"The doctor suggested that Nikki keep her stress level down, too," Matt said. "So she won't be able to keep Ibrahim until she's better."

Aliyah tried to keep from getting upset. She had already been racking her brain on what to do after school started when she had Ibrahim full time; and she still hadn't come up with any feasible plan. How was she supposed to come up with a solution overnight? It was aggravating that Matt and Nikki expected her to adjust to their sudden needs while they seemed to be completely oblivious to hers. If they wanted to keep Ibrahim during the weekend when he was supposed to be with his mother, they assumed that Aliyah would go along with it. And now when they wanted Aliyah to keep Ibrahim during the week when he was supposed to be with his father and stepmother, they assumed Aliyah would go along with that too.

Aliyah understood that it would be difficult for Nikki to care for Ibrahim while she was unwell, but how was Aliyah's predicament any better than Matt's? If Aliyah was capable of finding a last minute babysitter while she was at work, why couldn't Matt do the same while he was at work? Then Matt could pick up Ibrahim at the end of the workday, as he was expecting Aliyah to do. Did Matt imagine that his schedule was more strained than Aliyah's?

For a fleeting moment, Aliyah considered getting in her car and taking Ibrahim to his father's house. But she dismissed the idea. When Aliyah was a stay-at-home-mother, she had taken care of Ibrahim on her good *and* bad days, even when she was too sick to get out of bed. Because that's what mothers do. Calling in sick was never an option. If she was unwell, she mothered from the bed, and Matt took over when he got home. Why couldn't Matt and Nikki do the same?

"So she'll be better in a few days?" Aliyah asked doubtfully.

Aliyah heard Matt exhale. "I don't know… We hope so." That means *no*, Aliyah thought to herself in annoyance. So this was really about her keeping Ibrahim from now on. Even if Aliyah miraculously found childcare in the next few hours, she had no idea where she would get the money to pay someone for the rest of summer.

"Maybe Nikki can keep Ibrahim just for tomorrow?" Aliyah suggested hesitantly, hoping that Matt could understand the difficult predicament they were putting Aliyah in. "Then she can find a babysitter before Tuesday."

"Like I said," Matt said, apology in his tone, "she's trying to keep her stress down. So that might be too much for her."

"Then maybe you can find a babysitter?" Aliyah said, careful to keep sarcasm out of her tone.

"I have to work," Matt said, as if that explained everything.

"Yes, of course." Aliyah resisted the urge to say, "I do, too." It just didn't feel right arguing about the obvious. If Matt and Nikki were unwilling to take care of Ibrahim themselves or find childcare while Nikki was unwell, then Matt's home probably wasn't the best place for Ibrahim. No matter how frustrating this all was, Ibrahim's emotional and psychological well-being took precedence over everything.

"Where's the *qiblah*?"

Aliyah was holding the cordless at her side after ending the call with Matt when she heard Mashael behind her. "It's this way," Aliyah said, turning and using the phone to gesture toward a corner of the living room.

"Do you have a prayer garment and a *sajjaadah*?" Mashael asked.

"Sorry." Aliyah forced a smile as she returned the cordless to its base. Instinctively, she wondered what Mashael did when she was not at a Muslim's home. It was something that Aliyah often wondered about women who didn't wear hijab. Did they keep a prayer garment or *khimaar* in their handbag? Or did they delay *Salaah* until they got home? "They're in my room," Aliyah said before disappearing down the hall and returning with the garment and prayer mat a minute later.

As Mashael laid out the *sajjaadah* to face Makkah and put on Aliyah's one-piece prayer garment, Aliyah hurried to her room to call Salima on her mobile.

"I'm in a bind, Salima," Aliyah said hurriedly after they exchanged salaams.

"What's going on?" Salima said, genuine concern in her tone.

"I need a babysitter or a summer day camp for Ibrahim for the next four weeks," Aliyah said. "And it has to be affordable."

There was an extended pause. "Most summer camps ended last week..." Salima said, as if thinking out loud. "But most childcare centers are open year round."

"I don't think I can afford a childcare center," Aliyah said, doubtful.

"Matt won't be paying for it?" Salima asked.

"Eventually, *insha'Allah*," Aliyah said, uncertainty in her tone. "At least that's my prayer. But I need something for tomorrow morning."

"*Tomorrow* morning?" Salima's voice rose in surprise.

"You don't think it's possible?" Aliyah asked in a small voice, her heart constricting in panic.

"I don't know, Aliyah," Salima said apologetically, her tone suggesting doubt. "Best case scenario, you'll find something for Tuesday, and that's only if you're really lucky. But I don't know of any place open on a Sunday evening, so you'd have to wait until tomorrow to even see if there are any openings."

"Where do you take Haroon?" Aliyah asked hopefully.

"We have an onsite children's center where I work."

"That's nice *mashaAllah*," Aliyah said, sad reflection in her tone.

"Can you take Ibrahim to work with you just for this week?" Salima said. "He could just stay in your office."

Aliyah's thoughts went immediately to the fiasco with Dr. Warren that was awaiting her first thing in the morning. There was no way Aliyah could risk bringing her son to work. Even without the Dr. Stanley issue, Aliyah was still rebuilding her professional reputation following the Deanna incident. *"I have spoken to you at length about my concerns about any family coming to our offices during work hours,"* Dr. Warren had said during the meeting with Jacob and Aliyah, *"and you assured me that it's all under control. I hope this remains the case?"*

"I know it's not ideal," Salima said. "But during the summer, a lot of schools are relaxed about staff bringing their children to work."

"Not where I work," Aliyah said regretfully.

"You don't know any sisters who do childcare?"

Anxiety knotted in Aliyah's stomach. "One..." she said hesitantly.

"Call her," Salima said. "She might be willing to take Ibrahim tomorrow morning."

"But that was a while ago..." Aliyah said, feeling humiliated at the thought of calling the sister for anything. "I'm not even sure she does it anymore."

"Just ask," Salima said. "Even if she doesn't, she might be willing to take Ibrahim, at least for tomorrow."

"We're not exactly friends though..." Aliyah said weakly. "I don't even think she likes me."

Aliyah heard Salima chuckle. "*Ukhti*," Salima said, "it's normal for sisters to watch each other's children, even if they're not friends otherwise."

"Not for me," Aliyah said, sadness in her tone. "Those privileges are usually only for married women."

Salima was quiet momentarily. "I forgot about that… But it can't hurt to ask, can it?"

Aliyah paused doubtfully. "Do you know Juwayriah bint Abdullah?"

"The one who's always posting about marriage on Facebook?" Salima asked, confusion and disapproval in her tone.

"Yes…" Aliyah said hesitantly. "That's the only sister I know who does childcare."

There was an extended pause. "You might not want to go there…" Salima said.

"I don't think she'll harm Ibrahim or anything," Aliyah said for clarity. "But I just don't feel comfortable, you know?"

"Look," Salima said as if an idea had come to her suddenly. "Let me make some calls, and if I can't come up with anything, I'll call Juwayriah myself. I don't think she'll say no to me."

Aliyah's stomach churned in apprehension. "But won't she think you're calling for Haroon?"

"No," Salima said matter-of-factly. "Because I'll tell her I'm calling for Ibrahim."

Aliyah was still unconvinced. "But call me first," she said reluctantly. "I may decide to take my chances with keeping Ibrahim in my office."

Mashael had finished praying and was sitting on the couch thumbing through a book when Aliyah returned to the living room with her mobile phone in hand. Aliyah's prayer garment and *sajjaadah* were folded neatly on the floor table in front of the couch.

Mashael looked up and smiled when Aliyah came in. "This is pretty good," Mashael said, holding up the book she was reading. *The Purification of the Soul*.

Aliyah smiled hesitantly, an embarrassed expression on her face. She had left the book in the living room a couple of days ago when she had been looking for another self-affirmation quote to hang on the wall.

"Where'd you get it?"

"Probably from the masjid *sooq*," Aliyah said, resisting the urge to take the book from Mashael as she sat a comfortable distance from her on the couch. Seeing someone she didn't know well holding a book she had been reading made Aliyah feel vulnerable and exposed. "But sometimes I order my books online."

"I usually don't like religious books." Mashael opened the book to a page and read from it briefly in silence, making Aliyah cringe. "But this one seems interesting."

"You just have to find the right ones," Aliyah said, an awkward smile creasing the corners of her mouth. "Personally, my favorites are *tafseer*. But anything by

Ibn al-Qayyim Al-Jawziyyah, I'll read. It's not always easy to find a good translation though."

"Maybe Reem has it in Arabic," Mashael said as she nodded approvingly and put the book back on the floor table. Internally, Aliyah exhaled in relief. She was tempted to take the book to her room right then.

Aliyah chuckled self-consciously. "Oh yeah, I forgot you can just read the Arabic, *mashaAllah*."

"*Tazkiyatun-nafs*?" Mashael said.

"Yes," Aliyah said, feeling relieved as she sensed that Mashael was genuinely interested in the book. "And you'll probably like *Patience and Gratitude*, too," she added. "*Sabr wa Shukr*."

Mashael smirked. "If I tell Reem about the Islamic books you suggested, she just might change her mind about Americans."

Aliyah smiled uncertainly. "What do you mean?"

"She says Americans trivialize religious scholarship." Mashael shook her head humorously.

An awkward smile lingered on Aliyah's face. Aliyah had no idea if Mashael's comment was related to her directly, but Aliyah wasn't inclined to defend herself. Years ago, she would have tried to explain that she valued religious scholarship greatly. But her repeated experiences in some of her Islamic classes dissuaded her.

*Respecting religious scholarship is how I came to accept Islam and avoid shirk,"* Aliyah had told a sister once. *"Where do you think I learned how to pray, fast, and recite Qur'an?"* Aliyah had asked. But because Aliyah asked questions during class, requested prophetic evidence for a sheikh's position, and was unwilling to commit herself to a single spiritual teacher or *madhhab*, her Islamic faith was constantly questioned.

It was only recently that Aliyah had come to accept that there was a major difference between how she understood her duty to Allah and how other Muslims understood theirs. So she decided that her time was better spent focusing on pleasing Allah rather than constantly trying to find the right words to express appreciation for something to which only a person's life could bear witness.

"Does Reem know you're here?" Aliyah asked, intentionally shifting the topic of conversation to why Mashael had come.

"Probably not," Mashael said with a shrug. "But it's not a secret. She knows I plan to talk to you about Sheldon."

"That's his name?"

"Yes.

Aliyah felt uncomfortable all of a sudden. "Mashael…" Aliyah's thoughts trailed as she searched for the right words for what she was trying to say. "I'm probably not the best person to talk to..."

"Like I said yesterday," Mashael said, slight annoyance in her tone. "I'm not expecting a fatwa or anything. I just need another perspective."

“But would your family be okay with you talking to me?” As much as Aliyah wanted to help, she was wary of getting involved in something like this. Aliyah, like other American Muslims she knew, had had negative experiences with offering relationship advice to immigrant Muslims. Most situations ended with her being branded a bad influence or being cut off from the immigrant family entirely. It never made any difference whether or not the scandal or dilemma existed long before her advice was sought. In the eyes of the “good Muslim family,” if an American was involved at any stage, the moral corruption was somehow his or her fault.

“Of course not,” Mashael said, contorting her face. “That’s why I can’t talk to them about anything. They’re already calling me a *kaafir* for having an American boyfriend. How are we supposed to have a conversation about marriage?”

Aliyah drew in a deep breath and exhaled. “Okay, Mashael…” she agreed tentatively, warning in her voice. “But I’m not a scholar, so I really don’t feel comfortable sp—”

“Aliyah, it’s fine,” Mashael said, frustration in her tone. “I just want to talk to a human being for once. Every time I even mention Sheldon’s name, my family gets angry and refuses to speak to me.”

“I’m sorry,” Aliyah said sincerely. “It’s just that I don’t want to make matters worse.” She coughed laughter, embarrassment in that sound. “You said yourself that they don’t trust Americans.”

“But isn’t that wrong?” Mashael met Aliyah’s gaze with her eyes narrowed angrily. “Aren’t we supposed to accept everybody as equal? What difference does it make if Sheldon is American or Saudi? It’s not like Allah segregates us based on nationality. He looks at our hearts.”

Aliyah was silent momentarily. “But Mashael… Sheldon isn’t Muslim.”

“And?” Mashael snorted. “He’s a good person. That’s all that should matter.”

“But you can’t marry a disbeliever,” Aliyah said hesitantly, hoping she wasn’t offending Mashael. “Maybe that’s what your family is trying to say.”

“He’s not a disbeliever,” Mashael said, folding her arms in a pout. “He’s a believing Christian. Doesn’t that make him from *Ahl al-Kitaab*?”

Aliyah was overcome with dread. When Mashael had first mentioned her “recovering Christian” boyfriend, Aliyah had feared the conversation would go in this direction. It was commonplace for some Muslims to label Jews and Christians as “believers” if they felt they were good people. In Aliyah’s experience, these Muslims were either unaware or dismissive of the Qur’anic verses and prophetic statements that differentiated between the earliest Muslims who followed the prophets Moses and Jesus and those who committed *shirk* and disbelieved in Prophet Muhammad.

Aliyah sighed. “Mashael…” she said, hoping her reply wouldn’t lead to a longwinded discussion on Islamic *aqeedah*, as conversations on correct fundamental beliefs never seemed to go well. Most Muslims Aliyah knew were quite dogmatic in their incorrect beliefs, especially if the beliefs stemmed from love or admiration for a non-Muslim or if they stemmed from the teachings of a revered spiritual teacher. "…even if he is considered one of the People of the Book, you aren't allowed to marry him."

"You're saying only men can marry People of the Book?"

"No," Aliyah said. "Allah is saying that."

"So you're saying Allah favors men?"

"Mashael," Aliyah said, exhaustion in her tone, "I'm not going to argue with you about Allah. As far as I'm concerned, marrying non-Muslims isn't a privilege. So I don't see it as favoring anyone, except maybe the children who get to be raised Muslim."

Arms still folded, Mashael was silent as she appeared to consider what Aliyah was saying.

"But how do you know it's only men who can marry Jews and Christians?" Mashael said finally, frustration in her tone. "A lot of verses in the Qur'an apply to everybody even when Allah uses the masculine."

"I don't have the authority to reinterpret the Qur'an," Aliyah said. "So all I can tell you is, as long as Sheldon isn't Muslim, you aren't allowed to marry him."

"But that's not fair," Mashael said. "Women should be able to marry whoever they want, just like men."

"No one can marry whoever they want, Mashael," Aliyah said. "Men can't marry atheists or Buddhists or Hindus, or even Jews and Christians who don't fulfill certain conditions."

Mashael's expression conveyed annoyed disapproval. "But why does religion have to dictate our lives like that? It's so frustrating."

"Mashael, religion is a choice just like marriage is a choice," Aliyah said. "So if you're frustrated with anything, it should be with the person who feels that neither you nor God is important enough to make any changes for."

Mashael bit her lower lip as her eyes became distant momentarily. "I never thought about it like that," she said honestly.

"If a man is asking you to give up your beliefs to marry him," Aliyah added, "then it's just you converting to his religion instead of the other way around. So in the end, the real question is, who is your Lord?"

Mashael nodded thoughtfully. "I just feel like love is most important, you know?"

"It is," Aliyah said. "But only love of Allah."

"But does it really matter if he loves Allah or not?" Mashael said after a thoughtful pause. "My parents are saying Sheldon will never be a real Muslim, even if he converts."

Aliyah furrowed her brows. "Why would they say something like that?"

"They said if he becomes Muslim, it'll only be to marry me, so our marriage won't be valid."

"We can't say what's in anyone's heart."

Mashael snorted. "Tell that to my parents. When I told *them* that, they said most Americans aren't real Muslims anyway."

Aliyah tried to conceal her offense. "But is Sheldon interested in Islam?"

"He's asking a lot of questions, but my family refuses to help." Mashael shrugged. "I know I can just find some American Muslims to teach him, but he really wants to get to know my family."

Aliyah drew in a deep breath and exhaled. Despite how disturbing all of this was, as the one offering advice, Aliyah had the obligation to look at the situation from all angles. At the end of the day, Mashael's family were humans like everyone else, so they couldn't be blamed too harshly if they didn't like Sheldon. Besides, Aliyah had no idea who Sheldon was. It was possible that Mashael's parents had very good reason to protect their daughter from him.

"Mashael," Aliyah said, her tone soft with empathy, "I know it's not right what they're doing, but if they think Sheldon has ulterior motives, they're not going to want him around, even if it's just to learn about Islam."

"Why is marriage an ulterior motive only when it's an American?" Mashael blurted, her face contorted. "My family doesn't refuse dinner invitations of Saudi families whose sons want to marry me."

"But Sheldon isn't Muslim," Aliyah said.

Mashael rolled her eyes. "Do you really think that makes any difference?" she asked, meeting Aliyah's gaze challengingly. "If he became Muslim tomorrow, do you think it'll change how they feel?"

"Maybe they're upset that things didn't start off right," Aliyah suggested noncommittally. "Having a boyfriend isn't allowed in Islam."

"I never said it was," Mashael said flippantly. "That's why we're trying to get married." She snorted. "And just so you know, he doesn't believe in sleeping with anyone before marriage either. Muslims aren't the only ones with morals."

Aliyah nodded thoughtfully. "*MashaAllah,*" she said. "But maybe you should see if—"

The chime and vibration of Aliyah's mobile phone interrupted her midsentence, and she quickly reached forward and picked up the phone, anticipating a message from Salima. "Sorry," Aliyah muttered to Mashael, smiling apologetically before looking at the display. "I'm trying to find a babysitter for Ibrahim before tomorrow."

"That's fine," Mashael muttered, but Aliyah sensed that Mashael wasn't happy with the interruption.

*Do you mind if it's a brother who takes care of Ibrahim?* Salima's text message said.

Aliyah typed a quick reply. *As long as he's trustworthy. Do you know him?*

*He's a friend of Jamil's.*

*How much does he charge?*

*He said he'll do it for free.*

Aliyah couldn't keep from grinning as her index finger swiftly tapped the keypad: *Are you serious?* But before she pressed send, the phone rang, and Salima's name appeared on the screen.

"Jamil says it's Larry," Salima said after Aliyah answered.

Aliyah's heart sank. "*Larry*?" she repeated, defeated.

"Before you say anything, it was Jamil who made the suggestion."

"But why Larry?"

"Because he's keeping Younus and Thawab during the day now," Salima said. "The summer program they were in ended last week, and Jacob can't keep them because he's helping with Deanna's case."

Aliyah didn't know what to say. Had her childcare choices really been reduced to Juwayriah or Larry? This was beyond humiliating. She wondered if she should just take her chances with bringing Ibrahim to work.

"He's really not a bad person," Salima said sincerely. "I know he may not be your number one marriage choice, but he's good with children, *mashaAllah*. I even left Haroon with him a few times."

Aliyah glanced uncertainly in the direction of Mashael, whose stiff expression thinly veiled her impatience to finish the conversation they'd started. "Let me think about it."

"If you decide to leave Ibrahim with him, Jamil can call Larry if you want," Salima said.

"No, it's okay," Aliyah said, as if exhaling the words. "I just need to give it some thought."

After ending the call, Aliyah bit her lower lip and stared off into the distance for some time, still holding the mobile phone.

"Is everything okay?"

At the sound of Mashael's voice, Aliyah forced a smile and reached forward to set the phone down. "It's fine," she said. "I just have to decide who should keep Ibrahim tomorrow."

"Your family doesn't live nearby?" Mashael asked.

"My family?" Aliyah said, drawing her eyebrows together as she met Mashael's gaze.

"Your parents," Mashael clarified.

"They're two hours away."

"That must be hard," Mashael said sympathetically.

A sad smile lingered on Aliyah's face. "It is," she said, unable to temper the melancholy she felt at the assumption that her parents would help with Ibrahim even if they lived closer.

***

Aliyah woke early Monday morning with a sense of dread in the pit of her stomach. What had she been thinking when she decided to bring Ibrahim to work with her? Even if she arrived early enough so that no one saw her and Ibrahim come in, was it fair to ask her five-year-old son to sit quietly in a closed office all day? And what would she do when it was time to leave, or when he had to go to the restroom? And what if a student, or Dr. Warren, stopped by her office? Aliyah sat up in bed and tossed the covers from her body before going to the bathroom.

As she washed her hands, she wondered if it was pride more than judiciousness that had motivated her decision to refuse Larry's offer. While Juwayriah had shown Aliyah open contempt such that leaving Ibrahim with her would be unwise, Larry had only been annoying. Nothing he'd said or done suggested that Ibrahim shouldn't be around him. And even if Aliyah had other options, it was probably best for Ibrahim to be in the company of Younus and Thawab as opposed to complete strangers. So had her decision really been about Ibrahim's best interests?

On her way back to her bedroom, Aliyah peered into Ibrahim's room and watched the rhythmic rise and fall of his blanket as he slept soundly. *He deserves the company of friends, not a cramped office,* she thought to herself. Was it too late to call Salima to say she changed her mind? she wondered. Feeling mortified and regretful that she had inadvertently put her needs before her son's, Aliyah dragged herself to her room and wondered what she would say to Salima—and Larry.

"Call me first thing in the morning if you change your mind," Salima had said last night. "I leave for work around seven o'clock."

Aliyah glanced at the clock on her nightstand. It was 5:33. She picked up her mobile phone and bit her lower lip indecisively as she sat on the edge of her bed. Aliyah wanted to leave for work in an hour, so if she was going to arrange childcare, she needed to do it now. She powered on her phone, and her heart pounded nervously as she waited for the main screen to load.

*Pray Istikhaarah first*, a voice said in her head.

Aliyah set her phone down and raised her hands in prayer. Because she was unable to offer formal prayer due to her menses, she recited the *Istikhaarah* supplication without first offering two units of voluntary prayer.

"*Allaahumma…*" Aliyah muttered, her head bowed. *O Allah, I seek Your counsel by Your knowledge and by Your power I seek strength and I ask You from Your immense favor, for verily You are able while I am not and verily You know while I do not and You are the Knower of the unseen. O Allah, if You know this affair of me leaving Ibrahim with Larry to be good for me in relation to my religion, my life, and end, then decree and facilitate it for me, and bless me with it, and if You know this affair to be ill for me towards my religion, my life, and end, then remove it from me and remove me from it, and decree for me what is good wherever it be and make me satisfied with such.*

Aliyah lowered her hands and immediately felt the indecisiveness leave her heart. *I should leave Ibrahim with Larry so he could be with Younus and Thawab every day*, she realized. Though a sense of shame at her predicament still lingered, it was not as strong as before.

Aliyah drew in deep breath and exhaled as she picked up her phone and scrolled to Salima's name before putting the phone to her ear. Her hopes were deflated when the call went immediately to voicemail. Salima was probably still sleeping. As Aliyah prepared to leave a message, she heard an automated voice say that the voicemail box was full. Defeated, Aliyah ended the call and mentally kicked herself for having told Salima that she couldn't accept Larry's offer. Now what would she do?

*Call Larry*, the idea came to her just then. The thought filled Aliyah with dread. Perhaps Jamil had mentioned the idea to Larry, but there hadn't been any confirmation. So how would Aliyah explain herself, especially calling so early?

*"Bismillah,"* she mumbled, mentioning Allah's name to mentally block out her doubts. She had prayed *Istikhaarah* about this, she reminded herself. Aliyah scrolled to Larry's name and pressed call before she had time to convince herself that it was a bad idea. She put the phone to her ear and listened to it ring three times before it went to voicemail. But Aliyah couldn't summon up the nerve to leave him a message. A sense of helplessness enveloped her as she ended the call.

*Should I just call Matt?* As Aliyah considered the question, her mobile rang, causing her to start. She looked at the phone, and her spirits lifted as she saw the name *Larry Bivens* on the display.

"*As-salaamu'alaikum*," Aliyah answered after the first ring, apology in her tone. "I'm sorry to call so early," she said as he replied to the salaams. "But I was just wondering if—"

"Jamil and Salima already told me," Larry said, slight exhaustion in his voice as he cut her off. "Do you need me to pick up Ibrahim or you're dropping him off?"

"Whatever is best for you…" she said hesitantly. "Where are you?"

"Right now, we're at the masjid," Larry said, no trace of characteristic smugness in his tone. "We just finished praying *Fajr*, so we can pick up Ibrahim on our way home if you like."

"We?" Aliyah repeated in confusion.

"Jacob and I," Larry clarified. "We're here with Younus and Thawab."

Aliyah felt self-conscious at the thought of Jacob stopping by her apartment. "Where will the boys be today? Maybe I can meet you there."

"Now we're heading to Jacob's *insha'Allah*," Larry said. "Then I'm taking the boys to a soccer field close to the house."

Aliyah was even more uncomfortable going to Jacob's home than she was with him coming to hers. But if Larry was going to be taking care of Ibrahim, then she would have to get over her apprehension. "I guess, for today you can pick up Ibrahim and then we can talk later about what to do for the rest of the summer."

"Okay," Larry said, "then we should be there in about thirty minutes, *insha'Allah*."

"Okay…" There was an awkward pause. "Larry?"

"Yes?"

"Thank you."

"It's no problem," his voice said sincerely through the phone. "This is the least I can do after all the trouble I've caused you," he said, lighthearted humor in his tone. "I'm sorry about that, by the way."

"You didn't cause me any trouble," Aliyah said. "It's just…"

"You don't have to explain," Larry said. "I haven't been the best Muslim brother to you. I realize that now."

There was a thoughtful pause. "But just so you know," Larry said with characteristic smugness, but Aliyah sensed he was trying to sound cordial, "Jasmine is not my girlfriend."

"You don't owe me an explanation," Aliyah said, not wanting to talk about Jasmine right then. It was still a sensitive subject for her, and she didn't want to ruin the glimmer of affability they'd maintained so far. "I was just—"

"No," Larry interjected, apology in his tone, "I do. Salima told me about your run-in at the mall, so I just thought you should know that it's Jasmine who still considers me her boyfriend. But when I became Muslim, I ended the relationship."

"Well, *mashaAllah*," Aliyah said cordially, unsure how to respond. "At least she's thinking about becoming Muslim now."

Aliyah heard Larry cough in laughter. "Is that what she said?" he asked doubtfully, sarcasm in his tone. "Because last I knew, my family had given her the assignment of luring me back to my so-called senses."

"Oh…" Aliyah didn't know what to say.

"As in back to Christianity," Larry clarified, reflective disappointment in his tone. "But like the hypocrites Allah talks about in the Qur'an, she's Yasmeen whenever she tries to reconnect with me, but when she's around my family, she's telling them that she's really on their side." He grunted. "So I shouldn't be surprised they're inviting her over every second they get and telling me we should get back together."

"I'm sorry to hear that," Aliyah said sincerely. "I thought…"

"Don't be," Larry said. "I explained everything to Salima last night when she told me about Ibrahim." Aliyah heard Larry laugh, but it was clear he was not happy. "And don't worry," he teased good-naturedly, "Salima already apologized for painting me as a womanizer. So I accept your apology too, for believing her."

Aliyah coughed laughter, embarrassment in that sound. "We didn't think you were a womanizer…"

"Just not a one-woman man?" Larry finished knowingly, humor in his tone. "Well, I can't speak about the future, but so far, that's all I've been. That's how I was raised, and that's how I intend to remain in marriage."

"I'm sorry," Aliyah said again, unsure what else to say.

"It's okay," Larry said sincerely. "I can see how I gave off that vibe. So I accept part of the blame. I'm still learning all the Muslim social codes, you know?"

Aliyah laughed in agreement, immediately reminded of her own confusion in that department. "I can definitely relate to that," she said. "I still haven't figured them out."

"That's encouraging," Larry said jokingly.

"I'm sorry," Aliyah said humorously. "You'll probably catch on faster than me. I've never been good at socializing, even before I became Muslim."

"Thanks for the vote of confidence," Larry said. "Because I was quite the socialite before Islam," he said in a playful brag.

Aliyah laughed. "I can see that," she said sincerely, humor in her tone.

There was an extended pause.

"But you don't have to worry about me bothering you anymore," Larry said, his tone reflective and subdued. "I think you deserve someone better than me."

Aliyah started to reply but realized she had no idea what to say. "*MashaAllah*," she muttered in embarrassment.

"And with my brother back on the market," Larry said in lighthearted humor, "I'd rather we clash on something other than a woman."

"*MashaAllah*," Aliyah said again, feeling self-conscious and flustered.

"So I'm just going to keep praying that Allah sends me a righteous Muslim wife." He coughed laughter. "Whoever she is," he added. "So if you have any good friends, let me know."

"I will," she said sincerely, surprised by how much she genuinely hoped Larry would find a good wife.

When Aliyah hung up the phone, she couldn't help feeling a bit ashamed of herself. *"O you who believe*," Aliyah recalled reading in an English translation of the Qur'an, *"if there comes to you a disobedient one with information, investigate [and verify it], lest you harm a people out of ignorance and become, over what you have done, regretful."* This *ayah* from *Surah al-Hujuraat* would probably forever remain a lesson for both Salima and Aliyah. While Salima should have known better than to believe Jasmine's version of the story, Aliyah shouldn't have so readily believed the secondhand information.

"*Alhamdulillah*," Aliyah mumbled to herself, grateful that Larry had a forgiving heart. She was also grateful that she didn't have to feel stressed around him anymore. But it would probably take her some time before she forgave herself for judging Larry so harshly.

***

Monday morning after Sayed left for work, Reem sat on the edge of her bed staring indecisively at her mobile phone that lay on the nightstand. Sayed had given Reem the name of the psychiatrist that Jacob had told him about, and Dr. Melanie Goldstein fit all three of Reem's conditions. She was female, spiritual, and not connected to the Arab community. That she also was not connected to the Muslim community (and was in fact over an hour's drive away) was an added bonus. Why then was Reem hesitant about setting up an appointment?

Perhaps, it was her Arab blood paralyzing her. She would probably always feel inclined to protect her family's honor and image, even at her own expense. *And what's so wrong with that?* she thought defensively. Wasn't it betrayal to reveal to a complete stranger what her half brother had done? Though he was a teenager at the time and she was a young child, he was probably just as ignorant and confused as Reem was. Could she really blame Fahad for harboring resentment toward Reem's mother after his father married her as a second wife? Reem couldn't imagine how it would feel to see her mother have a nervous breakdown. It was only natural that Fahad would take out his frustrations on his father's second family, especially the children that had come from the union.

Anyway, what if she was remembering everything incorrectly? She didn't want to slander her brother. Maybe he didn't mean to touch her inappropriately and say that he had a right to because she was his sister. Maybe he really thought what he was doing was okay. Just because he was much older didn't necessarily mean that he knew better.

Reem's stomach convulsed as the sudden memory of Fahad's hand on her four-year-old chest flashed in her mind. She frantically shifted her thoughts to the phone call she needed to make. She didn't want to remember where else he had touched her—or if he had touched her at all. What if this was all a bad dream that she had fabricated because she hated him so much?

"*Halwah, wallah,*" Reem heard Fahad's guttural voice in her ear. Panicked, she looked over her shoulder toward the bed she shared with Sayed. She trembled when she saw that no one was there. Tears stung her eyes as she exhaled a jagged breath. *No*, she wasn't making this up, she realized in helplessness and despair. She had been the filthy little girl who had made her own brother desire and loathe her at once.

But why could Reem remember things only in flashes? And why, of the little she recalled, were the memories so choppy? For years she had interacted with Fahad normally, without even the slightest recollection of what had occurred. So why was everything coming back now? And why was she losing patience with people who had nothing to do with what Fahad had done? Maybe Dr. Goldstein would be able to help Reem sort out what was happening to her.

For the first time since she'd started teaching Qur'an at the masjid, Reem had called the imam to cancel all her classes. When she'd hung up, she had shortness of breath, fearing she had thrown away the last thing that had mattered to her. But she really didn't feel capable of teaching Qur'an right then. She barely trusted herself to leave the house. What if she had an angry outburst at the store or bank? Dressed like she did, she would probably end up in jail. No one would imagine that the veiled girl was having a panic attack or a bad day. To the rest of the world, Muslims were one dimensional and existed only in the context of religion. Human suffering and struggle were problems that only other people faced. So Reem couldn't trust herself in their presence. Any erratic behavior would be interpreted as a threat to their safety as opposed to a threat to her own.

What if the psychiatrist herself was an Islamophobe? Reem thought in panic.

"Jacob said she's respectful of Muslims," Sayed had said.

Before her anxiety got the better of her, Reem snatched up her mobile phone and dialed Dr. Goldstein's office.

***

"And you expect me to believe that, completely on your own," Dr. Warren said, regarding Aliyah sternly from where she sat behind her large desk, "without any coalescing with Dr. Bivens, you had a sudden inspiration, a week late might I add, to refuse to work with Dr. Stanley on the internship?"

Aliyah's cheeks grew enflamed in embarrassment. Aliyah was flustered, as she was completely out of her element. She wasn't used to openly contesting authority. "I'm saying that based on Article thr—"

"Save it," Dr. Warren said, lifting a palm to stop Aliyah midsentence. "I decline your request." She waved her hand dismissively. "Now get out of my office."

Bewildered, Aliyah walked slowly down the hall back to her office. *What is going on?* she thought in exasperation. Aliyah closed the door to her office and collapsed into the chair behind her desk. Why was Dr. Warren so insistent on Aliyah working with Dr. Stanley? It made Aliyah wonder if Dr. Warren was planning something more unkindly than even Jacob had surmised.

After a moment's consideration, Aliyah scrolled to Jacob's name in her phone. "I'm sorry to interrupt you," Aliyah said after giving Jacob the salaams. "But I did what you suggested, and it didn't go well."

"What happened?" Jacob said, his voice rising in concern.

Aliyah told Jacob point-for-point about her brief meeting with their supervisor.

"I was afraid she might do that," Jacob said, exhausted frustration in his voice.

"This isn't good, Aliyah," he said regretfully after a few seconds. "I can't lie to you. I was hoping this was only about me, but it looks like they have some vendetta against you too."

"But why?" Aliyah said, exasperated. "Dr. Warren and I were getting along just fine."

Aliyah heard Jacob sigh. "Aliyah," he said, as if trying to find the best way to convey what was on his mind, "at the end of the day, Dr. Warren is a professional, and she's not going to do anything to jeopardize her position, at least not overtly. But her suggesting you to be chosen for the internship was not only because she thought you were a good professor. She never liked my internship idea in the first place."

"But…" Aliyah didn't know how to form the question in her mind.

"I know it doesn't make sense," Jacob said apologetically, "but when Dr. Warren sees professors who have a good rapport with students and whose students improve noticeably under their tutelage, she doesn't have any choice but to reward that somehow. And in your case, I assume she felt the best way to do that was to assign you to the program she values the least."

"But *mashaAllah*, the internship is going really well," Aliyah said, a question in her voice. "It was even featured in one of the math journals this summer."

"I know," Jacob said, sad reflection in his voice. "And Dr. Warren resents that, probably not as much as Dr. Stanley though."

"I don't understand why she wouldn't be proud," Aliyah said. "It's her department getting all the attention."

"That's why I think she's coming at it from a different angle now," Jacob said. "When I first presented the internship idea years ago, she approved it halfheartedly because she felt that our department should be focusing on our own students instead of wasting time with high school kids, as she put it. Then when things started going well, she tried to have it dismantled completely so she could replace it with a summer program for our math students."

"Why couldn't you just do both?"

Jacob laughed. "That's exactly what I said, but Dr. Warren was adamant that the school didn't have the budget for it." He added, "Until the dean reviewed her proposal and came up with the same conclusion that you and I did. He was so impressed with the internship that he petitioned for the school to increase the budget for our department."

Aliyah chuckled. "I bet that shut her up."

"Not completely," Jacob said, reflective humor in his tone. "It just made her take credit for everything I was doing."

"Why am I not surprised?" Aliyah said, rolling her eyes and shaking her head as she held the phone to her ear.

"But recently, I got the feeling she was reverting back to having it dismantled," Jacob said. "But after talking to you, I think I was wrong."

"What do you mean?" Aliyah asked, brows furrowed.

"I think she's trying to have me phased out," Jacob said.

"And *Dr. Stanley* put in your place?" Aliyah said, shocked disapproval in her voice. "I thought she was a feminist. Why would she want someone like him in charge?"

"I think it's less about Dr. Stanley being assigned to my position," Jacob said, "than me being removed from it. It's just that Dr. Stanley is the only one who's vindictive and determined enough to do her bidding. Most of the other professors are focused on other things."

"Well, at least the department isn't corrupted by envy like most workplaces," Aliyah said.

"I wouldn't say that..." Jacob said doubtfully. "It's just that most of the staff channel their envy into pushing their own programs."

"Well, at least that's productive."

"I agree."

There was an extended silence.

"But what do I do about Dr. Stanley?" Aliyah said, her voice etched in worry. "I don't feel comfortable around him."

Aliyah heard Jacob sigh into the phone. "Just keep your distance as much as you can," he said. "But after I meet with Dr. Warren, I'm going to talk to him myself."

"You're meeting with Dr. Warren?" Aliyah said, fearful that their supervisor would think that she and Jacob were in collusion with each other.

"We agreed to have a phone meeting every week while I'm out."

"Oh..." Aliyah exhaled in relief.

"Look," Jacob said, "I have to go. But I'll probably need your help with Deanna if she pleads not guilty."

"Okay..."

"I can tell you more about it later, *insha'Allah*."

"Okay," Aliyah said, feeling unsettled at the mention of Deanna, "no problem."

They were silent for several seconds.

"Aliyah?" Jacob said, his voice hesitant.

"Yes?"

"I know this is something I said I'd never bring up again, but..."

Aliyah's heart constricted in anxiety, hoping there wasn't another work catastrophe awaiting her.

"...would it be okay if I talk to your uncle again about marrying you?"

Aliyah's face grew warm in discomfort and embarrassed flattery. "Sure," she said, cringing as she realized she had spoken her thoughts aloud. "I mean, if you want to," she added quickly.

"I just don't want to offend you," Jacob said uncertainly. "I know we said—"

"It's not offensive," Aliyah said, surprised that her words reflected how she honestly felt. "It's just..."

"I know it's not a good time," Jacob said, apologizing. "But I keep thinking it'll never be a good time, you know what I mean?"

"I think so," Aliyah said, averting her gaze to the calendar on her desk.

"An old friend of mine used to say, 'Every time is a bad time,'" Jacob said, embarrassed laughter in his voice. "'But it's up to us to change that.'" There was a brief pause. "That is, if you want to," he said hesitantly.

"I'll definitely think about it, *insha'Allah*," Aliyah said, picking up a pen and fidgeting with it. She was taken aback by how excited she felt.

"There's no rush," Jacob said, inciting in Aliyah a flutter of impatient excitement. Why did she fear that "no rush" meant it probably would never happen?

And why did she care anyway? It wasn't like she liked Jacob all that much.

"But I did want to put that out there." Jacob laughed self-consciously. "Now I can sleep better at night."

Aliyah laughed in agreement. "I know what you mean."

"You do?" Jacob said, surprise and curiosity in his voice.

Aliyah's cheeks grew hot in mortification as she scribbled mindlessly on the desk calendar. "I mean, when you get something off your chest," she said.

"That's true…" Jacob said.

Aliyah sensed that Jacob wanted to say more but was unsure if he should.

"Well," Jacob said finally, "I'll talk to you soon *insha'Allah*."

"Okay," Aliyah said, unable to keep the disappointment out of her voice. She wasn't ready to end the call just yet.

"*As-salaamu'alaikum wa rahmatullaahi wa barakaatuh*," Jacob said.

"*Wa'alaiku mus salaam wa rahmatullaahi wa barakaatuh*," Aliyah replied, wondering when she would get to talk to Jacob again. But when she ended the call and set her mobile phone on her desk, her lips twitched as she had tried to withhold giggling in pleasure at what had just happened.

***

"Kerri Michaels is awake," Attorney Bryan Schmidt said to Jacob as they sat across from each other in a conference room at the law office.

"Since when?" Jacob said, taken aback.

"Saturday evening, apparently," Bryan said.

Jacob drew in a deep breath and exhaled. He had the uncanny feeling that his life was about to shift in an unexpected direction and there was nothing he could do about it. "Okay, so what does this mean for us?"

"The prosecution intends to use her as a witness in their case," Bryan said regretfully.

Jacob nodded thoughtfully, his stoic expression veiling the frantic anxiety he felt at the news. "So what should we do?"

"You should talk to her."

Jacob creased his forehead in confusion. "To Mrs. Michaels?" he said. "About what?"

"Nothing," Bryan said matter-of-factly. "Or anything." He shrugged. "It doesn't really matter. Just show your face, and see how she responds. We need to gauge whether or not she's going to cooperate with them."

"Has Deanna said how she plans to plead?"

Bryan frowned. "Not guilty."

Jacob's heart sank. "So she didn't accept the plea deal?"

Bryan shook his head. "Unfortunately."

Jacob drew in a deep breath and exhaled, shaking his head. "I don't know why I'm surprised."

"Do you think you can visit your mother-in-law soon?"

"I can try…" Jacob said doubtfully. "But I doubt Barry Michaels will let me near his wife."

Bryan frowned thoughtfully. "What if I come up with something to ensure that Barry won't be at the hospital when you come?"

Jacob was unsure how he felt about the idea. "Is that feasible?"

"Yes…" Bryan said, the hint of a mischievous smile on his face. "I'll just have to give it some thought."

"Nothing that will put us in a compromising position," Jacob insisted. The last thing he wanted was to support something that would make Deanna's already weak defense worse.

"Of course not," Bryan said. "I'm thinking more along the lines of a meeting that he'll need to attend."

Jacob nodded. "Okay," he said finally. "Just let me know what you come up with."

***

"So Jasmine was the one who told you her name was Yasmeen?" Aliyah said into the wire mouthpiece that snaked from her ears to the phone that lay on her desk. It was her lunch break, and a paper bag of food was on the desk calendar in front of her.

"Yes," Salima's voice said regretfully. "But apparently, Larry gave it to her, at least indirectly, because she called him one day and asked what her name would be if she became Muslim. So of course, at the time, he got his hopes up. But that was before he met you."

"Wow…" Aliyah shook her head. "She made it sound like you and Larry came up with that name on your own."

Salima huffed. "Go figure. But I didn't even think much about what she said. I just thought she was being playful. But she just wanted to make it look like Larry was pushing her to become Muslim."

"But she's pushing *him* to become Christian," Aliyah muttered in disappointment. She shook her head as she reached into her lunch bag and withdrew a tuna and spinach sandwich that was sealed in plastic wrap.

"With the help of his family, it seems," Salima said, sad reflection in her tone.

Aliyah was quiet momentarily as she unwrapped her sandwich. "Do you think she'll ever become Muslim?" Aliyah asked curiously.

"I don't know…" Salima sighed. "With someone like that, you never know what they're thinking. But I was hopeful because I met her before Larry became Muslim, and she seemed like a really nice person."

Aliyah coughed laughter. "Everybody *seems* nice, Salima," Aliyah said, playfully mocking what Salima's late husband used to say. "Come up with a better line."

Salima laughed in agreement. "I know, right?"

Aliyah smiled and shook her head knowingly before mumbling "*Bismillah*" and taking a bite of her sandwich.

"But I can see why Larry isn't optimistic," Salima's voice said through the earpiece. "She thinks she can woo him back by getting in good graces with his family."

Aliyah was silent momentarily as she swallowed her food. "But why make them think she can make him leave Islam?" She contorted her face. "That's so stupid."

"Apparently, she has no idea what Islam really means."

Aliyah considered what Salima had said as she took another bite of her sandwich and ate quietly for a few seconds. "Was Larry even at that Sunday brunch or whatever she was going to?"

Aliyah heard Salima grunt humorously. "No. Can you believe it? It's a family tradition they do after church, so Larry and Jacob weren't even there."

"*SubhaanAllah,*" Aliyah said, setting her half-eaten sandwich on the crumpled plastic wrap. "She had me fooled."

"You're not the only one," Salima said regretfully. "I just feel bad for believing her. *Astaghfirullah,*" she said in self-rebuke, seeking Allah's forgiveness. "I should've known better."

"We both should have," Aliyah said reflectively. "But it's an understandable mistake," she said. "How would you know she was being deceitful?"

Salima sighed. "But Larry is Muslim," she said. "I should have made excuses for him. That's his right."

"*Astaghfirullah,*" Aliyah said in agreement, realizing she should have done the same.

"I'm just so used to meeting Muslim men who are playing games," Salima said, sadness in her tone, "and Larry fit the description."

"I know…" Aliyah said, sighing as she plucked a lone piece of tuna from the top of her sandwich. "But that goes to show you, you shouldn't judge."

Salima huffed in agreement. "And I thought I learned *that* lesson years ago."

"Like you said," Aliyah remarked, "we're all going at this alone. Every day is a lesson in life."

"It's just funny, you know?" Salima said. "As soon as you think you've learned something, Allah shows you that you didn't even understand *that*."

Aliyah drew in a deep breath and sighed. "I know. It's so scary. I think about that every time I learn something new about Islam."

"Me too…" Salima brooded. "But honestly, sometimes I envy the Muslims who feel content with what they know. It makes me wonder if I'm doing something wrong."

"You can say that again." Aliyah smirked and shook her head reflectively. "But the more I read the Qur'an and study the life of the Prophet, *sallallaahu'alayhi wa sallam*, and his Companions, I know the one thing you *can't* feel content about is your faith."

"I don't mean my *emaan* itself," Salima said. "I mean what I'm learning about Islam. It seems like everybody has found this one group or this one teacher they're satisfied with. And I wonder if I'm missing something."

"Everybody's *qadr* is different though," Aliyah said, referring to predestination. "Maybe that one group or teacher will help them get to *Jannah.* That doesn't mean it'll do the same for you."

"You really think so?" Salima said doubtfully. "My fear is always, what if they're wrong? It's not like every group or sheikh is actually teaching true Islam. Some of them are calling to themselves, or even *shirk*, you know what I mean?"

"I meant the ones who aren't doing that," Aliyah said. "But I feel the same as you. I think it's dangerous to put that much trust in one group or person. Allah didn't ask us to do that. He told us to stay on the *Siraat ul-Mustaqeem*, and nobody other than the Prophet can claim to always adhere to that."

"That's what I'm trying to say," Salima said. "So why are they content with just one teacher? The Prophet, *sallallaahu'alayhi wa sallam*, said the scholars are the heirs of the prophets," she said. "Scholars, as in plural," she added for emphasis. "And that means they're scholars only if they're inheriting and sharing what the Prophet actually taught, not anything else."

"Exactly," Aliyah agreed. "And everybody makes mistakes, no matter how good their intentions are."

"And no matter how much good you learn from someone," Salima added, "you still have to stand in front of Allah alone. So how can you just blindly follow someone? Other than the Prophet, *sallallaahu'alayhi wa sallam*, I mean?"

"But the way I look at it," Aliyah said reflectively, "as long as they stay away from *shirk*, then Allah can forgive them."

"That's true..." Salima said noncommittally. "I just don't think getting forgiven is that simple."

"I don't either," Aliyah said. "We can't walk around in blinders and think we'll be excused just because we're not scholars." She shrugged. "But then again, maybe they don't see it as wearing blinders. Someone told me that I'm the one wearing blinders."

"I'm not surprised," Salima said. "That's what Jamil's ex-wife used to say. She'd be like, 'Why are you so arrogant to think you know more than a scholar?'"

Aliyah rolled her eyes knowingly. "I've heard *that* before. It's like they pretend that no other scholar exists except their sheikh." She groaned. "I swear, sometimes I want to ask them the same question. Don't they realize that agreeing with one scholar automatically means you disagree with another?"

"Except for issues of *ijmaa'*," Salima added, clarifying.

"And how many issues have absolutely *no* disagreement amongst all the Companions and earliest scholars?" Aliyah asked rhetorically. "But to be honest, I don't think about it much anymore. I have my own soul to worry about."

"Yeah, but..." There was an extended silence as Salima apparently tried to gather her thoughts. "...when Jamil was married, I saw how it can hurt other people. What if they had children together? When I study the Qur'an, I see a lot of *ayaat* talking about the effect we have on others. Some people even lead others to the Hellfire. I don't want to be guilty of that."

"May Allah protect us," Aliyah said as she glanced at the clock.

"Ameen."

"I better get going," Aliyah said. "The interns are probably waiting for me."

"Well, at least Larry was a good sport about our little blunder," Salima said good-naturedly, apparently in an effort to lighten the mood before the call ended. "So that's one less thing to worry about for the rest of the day."

"*MashaAllah,*" Aliyah said sincerely. "May Allah bless him."

"Aliyah?" Salima said after a brief pause. "Can I ask you something before you go?"

"Sure."

"Would you ever reconsider Larry's proposal?" Salima said. "I mean, assuming Jacob doesn't propose again."

Aliyah drew her eyebrows together in confusion. "For marriage?"

"Yes."

"No way," she said, smirking. "We're too different."

"So you're content being single for the rest of your life?" Salima said jokingly, but Aliyah sensed that something was on Salima's mind.

"We'll see," Aliyah said as a smile creased one corner of her mouth, recalling the brief conversation with Jacob earlier that day. "Just keep me in your prayers."

"Well, let me know if you decide to see marriage in your future," Salima said, humor in her tone. "I just might know some good brothers I can send your way."

"No thank you," Aliyah said, laughter in her voice. "But I'll keep you posted *insha'Allah.*"

## 20
## Time To Heal

"You're suffering from PTSD," Dr. Melanie Goldstein said to Reem early Tuesday morning, a week after Reem had called to make an appointment.

Reem's veil was flipped back revealing her face, and her gloves were folded neatly on top of her handbag that she'd set on the floor. But Reem was having difficulty relaxing, and she kept pulling at loose threads on her black abaya.

*What does she think about Palestine?* Even as she asked the question in her mind, Reem knew she was being irrational. Was it possible that living in a close-knit Arab Muslim community had given her an unhealthy distrust of others? She hated when Americans viewed Arab Muslims as one dimensional, so why was she doing the same by behaving anti-Semitic? Certainly, Jacob wouldn't refer Sayed to someone unsympathetic to Muslims.

But what if Jacob was unaware of Dr. Goldstein's views on Palestine?

*Stop it*, Reem mentally commanded herself. *This is ridiculous.* Her question was merely a frantic attempt to avoid accountability for emotional healing. If she could convince herself that the psychiatrist had anti-Muslim views, then Reem would have an excuse to cancel treatment.

"What's PTSD?" Reem asked, mentally shifting her focus to the session.

Though the earliest time slot for an appointment with the psychiatrist had been two months away when Reem initially called, the office assistant had informed Reem that if she could arrive to the office by seven o'clock in the morning, Dr. Goldstein would see her as early as the following week. When Reem had mentioned to Sayed her pleasant surprise that a busy psychiatrist would come to work an hour early just for her, Sayed admitted that he had asked Jacob to personally request that the doctor view Reem's case as urgent. The gesture had been so moving that Reem had gotten choked up thinking about how compassionate and generous her husband and Jacob were being. But she couldn't deny how terrified the gesture made her feel. If her husband felt the need to have special arrangements made for her, then she was probably in worse shape than she realized.

"Post traumatic stress disorder," Dr. Goldstein said. "It's actually quite common for people who have experienced or witnessed something traumatic."

Reem averted her gaze. She hadn't revealed to the psychiatrist what Fahad had done. She had only mentioned her constant anxiety and angry outbursts. "I haven't experienced anything traumatic," Reem said, a nervous, reluctant smile on her face. She didn't want to mislead the psychiatrist into thinking she had survived a war or anything like that. "I'm just really stressed, that's all."

"Life can be stressful," Dr. Goldstein said. "So it's okay to not be okay sometimes."

A lump developed in Reem's throat. She'd often heard the saying, *It's okay to not be okay*, but right then it touched a deep part of her. "I'm doing okay," Reem said, her voice rising awkwardly as she tried to sound positive. "God has blessed me with a lot, so I'm grateful."

"He's blessed all of us," Dr. Goldstein agreed, her voice soft and empathetic. "But true gratefulness isn't possible without self honesty."

Reem nodded, and she felt her cheeks go warm in embarrassment. "I'm honest with myself." She didn't mean to sound defensive, but she didn't want the doctor to think Muslims weren't honest people. "In our religion, it's a sin to lie."

A faint smile formed at Dr. Goldstein's lips. "In every religion, it's a sin to lie," she said. "But struggling with self honesty is not the same as lying."

"Not in Islam," Reem said. *Now isn't the time to give da'wah*, she told herself. *You can teach about Islam another time.* But how could she leave the appointment without defending her religion? She couldn't allow the psychiatrist to think Muslims were deceitful. "We have to tell the truth, even about ourselves," Reem said. "God tells us that in the Qur'an."

There was a thoughtful pause.

"Reem," Dr. Goldstein said, prompting Reem to make eye contact, "I know how it feels to be misunderstood and to have others make assumptions about you because of your faith. And I know how it feels to carry the burden of presenting a positive image of yourself and your people to the world." Her lips formed a thin line. "But know that's not a burden you have to carry in my office. Here, you are free to be Reem, the human being, without the Saudi or Muslim label."

Reem contorted her face in disapproval. This was exactly what she'd feared. In the name of therapy, being forced to give up the parts of herself that mattered most. "But that's who I am," she said defensively. "I'm a Saudi and Muslim, and I'll never give that up, not even in here."

Dr. Goldstein smiled knowingly. "And I'm not asking you to," she said. "What I'm saying is, you have to allow yourself to heal. And to heal, you have to connect with the part that makes you human. Yes, you are Saudi and Muslim, just like I'm American and Jewish. But when we cry or stress because we feel overwhelmed, it's not because we're Muslim or Jewish. It's because we're human beings. And every human being struggles with carrying the weight of life's burdens. This is what I mean when I say you are free to be Reem, the human being."

Reem averted her gaze and started pulling at the threads of her abaya again.

"Oftentimes when we come from religious families, our religious label becomes a handicap," Dr. Goldstein said. "I don't mean that religion itself is a handicap," she clarified. "Like you, my faith in God means the world to me, and I wouldn't give that up for anything. But sometimes we confuse personal religious spirituality with public religious perception. And this is where our religious label becomes a handicap."

"I don't see being publicly Muslim as a handicap," Reem muttered, yanking at a black thread that wouldn't come loose. "I'm proud to be openly Muslim."

"As you should be," Dr. Goldstein said. "But being openly Muslim is about personal religious spirituality, not public religious perception. Being openly

Muslim is a natural result of doing what you believe," she said. "But how you're perceived as a Muslim is rooted in how others understand and view your beliefs."

"I can't help what others think about me," Reem said, annoyance in her tone. "So how is that a handicap?"

"When what people think about your religion matters more than your personal needs," Dr. Goldstein said.

Reem folded her arms in a pout. "I don't care what people think," she said. "I do what I know is right."

"But what happens when you don't know what's right?" Dr. Goldstein asked, narrowing her eyes curiously.

Reem shrugged. "Then I pray about it."

"Give me an example of something you'd pray about," Dr. Goldstein said, her tone conveying keen interest.

Reem shrugged again. "I don't know," she said. "Maybe if I should marry someone or have another child."

"Did you pray about telling me what he did to you?" Dr. Goldstein asked.

Reem's eyes widened, and her jaw dropped. "I can't believe this," Reem blurted in frustration. "Sayed told you already? How dare him…"

"Who's Sayed?" Dr. Goldstein asked, genuine curiosity in her voice.

Reem shook her head and pinched her eyes closed, as if to will the confusion from her mind. "I mean, Jacob. Sayed must've told Jacob."

"Jacob didn't tell me anything," Dr. Goldstein said. "Except that when a woman named Reem Muhammad calls, to make room on my schedule."

Reem rolled her eyes irritably. "Then how did you know about Fahad?" She met the psychiatrist's gaze challengingly. "And don't tell me you're psychic. I don't believe in stuff like that."

Dr. Goldstein drew her eyebrows together in confusion. "Who's Fahad?"

Reem grunted. "You know exactly who he is," she said accusingly. "You just asked me if I prayed about telling you what he did to me."

Dr. Goldstein nodded as if in confession. "I did say that."

"Then who told you about him?" Reem said as she met Dr. Goldstein's gaze.

There was an extended pause, and Dr. Goldstein's gaze grew distant momentarily. Reem sensed that the doctor was trying to find the best way to respond. "You told me," Dr. Goldstein said finally, looking directly at Reem.

Reem opened her mouth to reply but realized she had no idea what to say. Had Reem herself mentioned her half brother without realizing it? Was her anxiety so bad that she was becoming forgetful? "I don't remember saying anything about him," Reem muttered defensively.

"You didn't have to," Dr. Goldstein said. "I could say it was a wild guess, but that wouldn't be completely honest."

"Then how did you know?" Tears stung Reem's eyes, and her face was aflame in indignant mortification.

"I *didn't* know," Dr. Goldstein said. "But based on your symptoms…" She gestured toward Reem. "…those I see, as well as those you've shared, I know whatever happened to you violated something very personal. And with female patients, especially those from very traditional cultures, it's usually something sexual." She pursed her lips thoughtfully. "And often by a close relative, or a friend of the family."

Arms still folded in a pout, Reem averted her gaze.

"In the nine years that I've had this private practice, I've had only two Saudi female patients," she said. "You being the second. And I know it takes tremendous courage to seek professional help and talk to a stranger about something like this."

"It's not like my family is going to kill me if they find out I'm here," Reem mumbled. She wiped the moisture from her eyes with the bottom of her palm. "They're not like that."

"When I said courageous," Dr. Goldstein replied, "I don't mean your physical life is at risk. I mean your sense of self, your cultural and religious pride, and your psychological and emotional safety."

Reem started to respond, but the words got caught in her throat. She lowered her head and wiped her eyes again, hoping to hide her tears from the psychiatrist.

"And I'm not going to lie to you," Dr. Goldstein said. "Talking to a therapist, or to anyone for that matter, *is* taking a risk. How do you know you can trust me? How do you know I won't judge you? How do you know I even care?"

Reem tucked her chin to hide her face. She tried to discreetly wipe away the tears again, but they filled her eyes and slipped down her cheeks before she could stop them. Her nostrils moistened, and she sniffled as she rubbed the flat of her hand under her nose.

Reem heard slight commotion before she felt something being placed on her lap. Instinctively, she held on to it to keep it from slipping. In her blurred vision, she saw that it was a box of tissues. Chin quivering, she was overcome with shame as she pulled a tissue from the box. Her head was still lowered when she wiped her nose.

"And the scary thing is," Dr. Goldstein said, "the answer to all of those questions is, you don't know. Even if I were to assure you that I am trustworthy, that I won't judge you, and that I care, you can't be sure that any of that is true." Her voice was soft and empathetic. "This is where you have a difficult decision to make, and it's one you have to make alone."

Reem wiped her eyes again. It was embarrassingly cliché to cry in front of a therapist.

"Before you come to a follow-up appointment," Dr. Goldstein said, "ask yourself two questions. Do I want to heal, and can Dr. Goldstein help me in this?"

Reem nodded hesitantly, indicating that she understood. But she didn't try to respond.

"And even I can't claim to know the answers to those questions," Dr. Goldstein said. "So this is something you should pray about." She paused thoughtfully. "But

I'll go ahead and ask my assistant, Fredrick, to book you for the next available appointment, which is about three months from now. That will give you enough time to decide what you want to do."

"What if I want to come before then?" Reem said weakly, avoiding Dr. Goldstein's eyes.

"Then I'll tell Fredrick to book you before then, even if it's an hour earlier than I usually open."

***

"No!" Aliyah said, laughter in her voice as she spoke into the wire mouthpiece as she drove from work Tuesday afternoon to pick up Ibrahim.

"I swear to God," Salima's voice said through the earpiece, humor in her tone. "I called you right after I hung up with Jasmine."

"Does Larry know?" Aliyah asked curiously, her tone serious.

"I don't know," Salima said, as if exhaling her words. "I was tempted to call and ask him, but I figured I'll wait till I got home from work. But I assume he's the first person she called."

"You're still at work?" Aliyah said.

"Unfortunately," Salima said, lighthearted sadness in her voice. "I'll probably be here for another hour."

"The onsite childcare center stays open late?" Aliyah said, her voice rising in admiration.

"Only until six o'clock," Salima said. "But I usually bring Haroon to my office if I stay later than that. Unless my brother gets off before me. Then he picks up Haroon."

"Well, *mashaAllah*," Aliyah said after a moment's pause, her voice reflective and subdued. "May Allah preserve her."

"Ameen," Salima said noncommittally. "It's just hard to believe, that's all."

"I know..." Aliyah agreed. "But only Allah knows what's in people's hearts," she said, obligatory deference in her tone. "So we have to assume the best."

"That's true..." Salima said. "The timing is just funny."

"Is there a wrong time to become Muslim?" Aliyah asked rhetorically.

"I know, right?" Salima said, laughter in her voice. "I'm just worried because Larry's parents have been trying to convince Jasmine to use her relationship with Larry to make him leave Islam."

"I know..." Aliyah sighed. "But once someone says the *shahaadah*, we have to assume they're Muslim," she said. "Unless their words or actions prove otherwise."

"That's true," Salima said, as if regretful. "I just can't help thinking about the *ayah* in *Ali'Imraan* where Allah says, *Waqaalat taa-ifatummin ahlil-kitaabi aaminoo billathee unzila 'alallatheena aamanoo wajhan-nahaari wakfuroo aakhirahu la'allahum yarji'oon*."

As Salima recited the Arabic, Aliyah silently prayed that Allah would bless her to know the Qur'an like that someday.

"The general meaning is," Salima said, "some of the People of the Book tell each other to believe in Islam at the beginning of the day, then disbelieve later so that it will encourage the Muslims to leave Islam."

"*SubhaanAllah.* I remember reading the *tafseer* of that," Aliyah said. "Isn't that when some of them would pray *Fajr* with the Muslims then disbelieve later that day, so some of the Muslims would think they realized some contradiction in Islam that made them apostate?"

"Exactly," Salima said. "Or just something generally wrong with Islam."

"Let's just assume that's not what Jasmine is doing," Aliyah said, her voice firm in reproach. "Calling a Muslim a disbeliever is a serious sin."

"It's not Jasmine I was thinking of," Salima said. "It's Larry's parents. Even if Jasmine is sincere, they'll probably try to convince her to use her affiliation with Islam to steer Larry back to Christianity."

"*Allahu'alam.*" Aliyah sighed as she propped an elbow on the driver's side window seal, gripping the steering wheel with her other hand. "But I think about stuff like that when I read all those stories online about people leaving Islam. I mean," she said rhetorically, "how many of them are just doing what Allah is talking about in the Qur'an?"

"*Allahu'alam,*" Salima said, acknowledging that Allah knows best. "But today, we have enough real Muslims leaving Islam that they don't have to rely on that method too much."

"You think so?" Aliyah said doubtfully. "I think they use that tactic today more than they did in the past."

"Maybe," Salima said noncommittally. "But the Qur'an also talks about people who believe then disbelieve, so both are possible."

"But how can someone leave Islam?" Aliyah said, contorting her face. "I mean, I understand getting weak and struggling to hold on to your *emaan*. But giving up entirely?" She shook her head. "That doesn't make any sense to me."

"How can *kufr* ever make sense?" Salima said. "The whole concept of throwing away your soul is inconceivable," she said. "But if you understand how it feels to struggle in your faith, it's not too hard to understand giving up entirely."

"I see what you're saying," Aliyah said thoughtfully. "It's just scary to think about."

"Yes it is," Salima said, sincere reflection in her tone. "But life has a funny way of making the most harmful things feel like the right thing to do. That's why most people never enter Paradise." She grunted then added, "*After* they knew full well that Islam is true."

"May Allah protect us," Aliyah said.

"When I was in undergrad, I took off my hijab," Salima said as if lost in thought. "At the time, I really felt I was doing the right thing."

Aliyah was quiet momentarily, unsure if she had a right to ask what was on her mind. "Had you memorized Qur'an at the time?"

"Oh yeah," Salima said, as if it were the most natural thing in the world. "I finished the Qur'an when I was nine years old."

"*MashaAllah*," Aliyah said, admiration in the tone.

"But I'm not sure that made much of a difference," Salima said. "I don't mean there's nothing special about being a *haafidhah*, because *mashaAllah*, obviously there is. But I'm saying memorizing the Qur'an doesn't automatically protect you from spiritual struggles."

There was an extended pause. "But why did you take off your hijab?" Aliyah said. "If you don't mind me asking."

Aliyah heard Salima sigh thoughtfully. "I don't know," Salima said. "I guess I just felt there was too much emphasis put on it, you know? It was like everywhere I went, all that seemed to matter was who wore hijab and who didn't. And even if you wore hijab, Muslims were always nitpicking about right hijab and wrong hijab. I got sick of it. Especially when imams did lectures on how decorative hijabs are a *fitnah* for men," she said. "And how if men are attracted to us, it defeats the purpose of hijab."

Aliyah rolled her eyes and shook her head. "I know what you mean," she said. "I don't listen to those lectures anymore. It makes me feel like the whole measuring stick of correct Islamic modesty is whether or not some random guy thinks I look good."

"I wish I had thought to stop going to those lectures," Salima said. "That makes a whole lot more sense than doubting that Allah sees me as a human being."

"*SubhaanAllah*," Aliyah said. "Did you really feel like that?"

"To say the least," Salima said, lighthearted sarcasm in her voice. "I actually started to think the whole purpose of hijab had nothing to do with me."

"I've felt like that sometimes," Aliyah said, shame in her tone. "But I made a lot of *du'aa* and asked Allah to purify my heart and make me understand His religion better. Now, if I hear a lecture about hijab that talks about men's struggles instead of Allah's instructions or women's souls, I just turn it off or leave," she said. "Staying and listening causes too much spiritual confusion."

"I wish I had thought of that back then," Salima said. "But when you're young, you're so trusting of people who seem to know more than you. So I just figured Allah only created us to serve men and make their lives easier, and it made me feel distant from Allah," she said. "It sounds funny now, but back then, I felt that taking off my hijab would draw me closer to Allah."

"Do you feel like it did?" Aliyah asked. "In retrospect, I mean?"

"No," Salima said. "But, *wallaahi*," she said, swearing by Allah, "at the time, I felt like it did. I felt freer. I felt better about myself. And I even felt like I loved and appreciated Allah more."

"Then why do you feel it didn't draw you closer to Allah?"

"Because being close to Allah isn't a feeling," Salima said. "It's something only Allah can measure. But if we *are* close to Allah," she said, "then we certainly wouldn't feel comfortable disobeying Him every day."

"But none of us obey Allah perfectly," Aliyah said. "Some people struggle with hijab but are stronger in other things."

"That's true," Salima said. "So I can't speak for other women who took off their hijab. Maybe their obedience to Allah increased in other areas," she said. "But for me, I convinced myself I was taking off hijab because Muslims put too much emphasis on outer appearances. But trust me." She coughed laughter. "Once I took off my hijab, I started paying *way* more attention to how I looked. I spent more time styling my hair. I wore more make up. I took more pictures of myself. I even started being more friendly with guys."

"But how did you pray?" Aliyah said, reminded of when Mashael had asked to borrow her prayer garment. "Did you keep a hijab or prayer garment with you?"

"In the beginning I did," Salima said, her tone reflective. "But of course, over time, I just started delaying my *Salaah* or skipping prayers altogether. Sometimes I'd go a whole day without praying at all."

"*SubhaanAllah*..." Aliyah said in dismay.

"But that's how *Shaytaan* gets you," Salima said, referring to Satan. "He makes you feel righteous about doing wrong. For me, I kept thinking to myself, *See, I'm not a bad Muslim. A lot of people who cover don't even pray all their prayers.*" She coughed laughter. "Notice how *none* of my justifications had anything to do with Allah. It was all about what other Muslims were doing. Or were *not* doing."

"But what made you put it back on?" Aliyah asked.

"It wasn't one thing in particular," Salima said honestly. "Things just kept gnawing at my conscience."

"Like what?"

"Like Ramadan, for one," Salima said. "That's when I would review my *hifdh* the most and recite the whole Qur'an from memory. And as soon as I would recite *isti'aadhah*, I'd feel horrible. But I would try to focus on the *tajweed* and *hifdh* and not think too much about the meaning, *astaghfirullah*," she said, invoking Allah's forgiveness. "But it was hard, and sometimes I'd just break down crying because I hated myself so much."

"Did you ever put it back on just during Ramadan?"

"No," Salima said. "Because I felt like, what's the point? I'm just going to take it off afterward anyway."

"So what was the last straw, the final thing that made you cover again?"

"Two things," Salima said. "Seeing how I started getting annoyed every time someone said something good about hijab, and meeting Muslims who believed hijab isn't obligatory."

"Whoa... *A'oodhubillaah*," Aliyah said, seeking refuge in Allah.

"I think that was when I realized that taking off hijab isn't as simple as not covering," Salima said. "When you do something wrong, it's human nature to rationalize, so it almost never stops at the sin itself," she said. "And when I started socializing with people who said covering your hair isn't mandatory, I got scared I'd commit *kufr*."

"But you'd still be Muslim," Aliyah said, confusion in her voice.

"Not if I started denying clear parts of the Qur'an," Salima said. "Maybe the other Muslims didn't know what Allah says about hijab in the Qur'an. But I knew. So I had no excuse to believe something like that."

"I see what you mean," Aliyah said thoughtfully.

"But I did start philosophizing about the exact meaning of hijab," Salima said, embarrassed humor in her tone. "But even as I tried to convince myself that hijab was just dressing modestly, I knew it wasn't about Allah. It was about making my life easier. So I had to walk away from that and get myself together."

"*MashaAllah*," Aliyah said. "Maybe that's how memorizing the Qur'an saved you."

"Maybe…" Salima said noncommittally.

Aliyah paused thoughtfully. "Can I ask you something?" she said hesitantly. "Why do you wear a head wrap instead of a *khimaar*?"

Salima forced laughter. "Oh, let's not go there…"

"Why not?" Aliyah said, embarrassed laughter in her voice.

"I have a no-comment policy on that one," Salima said, humor in her tone.

"Really?" Aliyah said good-naturedly. "Why?"

"Because it reminds me too much of what I went through before I took off my hijab," Salima said. "All the your-hijab-is-wrong nonsense."

"You don't think there's a wrong way to wear hijab?" Aliyah asked curiously.

"I didn't say that," Salima said. "I'm just saying I'm not interested in justifying myself to anyone. The way I see it, everyone should do what they believe Allah asked them to. I may or may not be wearing hijab properly. But I'm just Salima, not the Prophet, *sallallaahu'alayhi wa sallam*. So what difference does it make why I do what I do? I'm not your example."

"Ouch," Aliyah said playfully.

"I didn't mean you specifically," Salima said. "I just have a pet peeve about Muslims pretending to care why I dress like I do, when their question is really just an underhanded attempt to tell me I'm wrong."

Aliyah creased her forehead. "But why do you assume they think you're wrong? Maybe they're just curious about something they're unfamiliar with," she said.

"Maybe *you're* just curious," Salima said. "But trust me, most Muslims take one look at me and think they have to save me from the Hellfire."

Aliyah frowned thoughtfully. "But is that a bad thing?" she said. "I know it can be offensive, but aren't we supposed to try to save each other from Hellfire?"

Salima huffed. "Judging someone and sincerely caring about their soul are two different things."

Aliyah was quiet momentarily as she considered what Salima said. "But how would you know whether or not someone sincerely cares?" Aliyah said. "I don't mean any disrespect to you. But isn't that the very definition of judging to claim to know someone's intentions? If it's wrong to judge someone for how they dress, isn't it just as wrong to judge someone for trying to help?"

There was an extended silence. "You make a good point," Salima admitted. "I just wish we could find a new topic, you know? I'm tired of talking about our clothes."

"I know how you feel," Aliyah said. "But I try to remind myself that obeying Allah is a topic that we should never get tired of. Though I do think we need to be more balanced when discussing women's issues. Women have a spiritual existence outside the context of hijab."

"If only the Muslim world realized that," Salima said reflectively.

"If only…" Aliyah agreed.

"But girl, let me get back to what I'm supposed to be doing," Salima said. "Just make *du'aa* that Allah preserves our new sister in Islam and guides Larry to do what's best."

"I will, *insha'Allah.*"

"Then I'll see you Friday *insha'Allah,*" Salima said.

Aliyah was confused momentarily. "Friday?"

"Muslim Marriage Monologues," Salima said.

"Oh yeah…" Aliyah said, chuckling at her forgetfulness. "But my aunt and uncle just got back from their trip a couple of days ago, so if I don't have to visit them, I'll come *insha'Allah.*"

***

Reem was sitting hunched over on the floor of the living room of their home when Sayed came home from work. Hana and Muhammad were running back and forth, chasing each other, seemingly oblivious to their mother's despondent state. Sayed wondered what time Reem had returned home. She was still wearing the black shoulder abaya from early that morning, and her *khimaar* sat on her neck like a loosened winter scarf. For a moment, trepidation gripped him as he wondered if his wife was conscious. But when he offered the salaams and closed the front door, she started, turning her head toward him.

As their gazes met, she smiled weakly and lifted a hand in a halfhearted wave. "*Wa'alaiku mus salaam,*" she mumbled.

"You okay?" Sayed said, his voice etched in concern.

His question seemed to bring life back to her, and she got to her feet and walked toward him, a tired but pleasant expression on her face. She embraced him without responding, and Sayed held her close for several seconds.

"*As-salaamu'alaikum*, Baba!" Hana and Muhammad called out cheerfully before they zipped out of the living room again.

Sayed smiled and replied to his children as he loosened his embrace in preparation to change clothes and prepare for *Asr* prayer. But Reem tightened her grip. Confused, he embraced her again, his heart aching for the pain she felt right then. Maybe it had been a bad idea to hire a driver to take Reem to and from her appointment. Sayed should have been there as emotional support. But Reem had insisted that she didn't want him to adjust his work schedule while he had insisted that she not drive herself.

"Do you love me?" Reem's muffled voice said, speaking into Sayed's neck.

"Of course," Sayed said. "More than anything."

"How is your love for me?"

Sayed smiled, relieved that even in her melancholic state, his wife had not lost her sense of humor. Whenever Reem was feeling sentimental or playful, she would ask Sayed the question that the Prophet's wife Ayesha would ask the Messenger of Allah. "Like a knot," Sayed replied, his voice soft as he mimicked the answer that the Prophet would give.

"Okay," Reem muttered. "Just checking."

Sayed brushed the top of her head with a kiss, his lips cushioned by her mass of hair. "I love you *too* much," Sayed said, playfully mocking the way some of their Arab friends who weren't proficient in English used the word *too* in place of *very* or *so*.

Sayed heard Reem chuckle, her shoulders moving rhythmically as she laughed. A wave of compassion swept over Sayed from how much he cared for his wife, and he pulled her closer and kissed her head again. Seconds later Reem's chuckles turned to whimpers, and Sayed felt the moist tears on his neck as her body trembled with the sobs.

"It's okay, *habeebti*," he said, pulling his head back just enough to meet her gaze. "It's okay." He wiped away her tears with the flat of his fingers then kissed her moist cheeks. "Allah is with you," he said as he held her close again. "And I am with you."

***

Aliyah was overcome with dread as Jacob and Deanna's house came into view and she slowed her car to a stop in front of the mailbox. When she put the car in park, she felt a shortness of breath, and her chest constricted in anxiety.

*Ever since we met,* Aliyah heard Deanna's voice in her head, *that's all I've ever done: listen to you and help you. I helped you get a husband. I helped you get a job. I help pay your bills. I listen every time you stress over your stupid, childish problems. But when will you listen to* me*?*

Guilt and shame choked Aliyah as she recalled telling Jacob it was okay to talk to her uncle about marriage. Was she out of her mind? What was she thinking? She couldn't marry Jacob. Everything about it was all wrong.

*You and Bailey are not going to do this to me!*

In her mind's eye, Aliyah saw the angry, contorted face of Deanna as she lunged at her. Aliyah leaned back in her seat and shut her eyes, waiting for the painful squeezing in her chest to subside. To steady her breathing, she inhaled through her nose and exhaled slowly through her mouth. Gradually, the anxiety loosened in her chest.

A shrilling sound caused Aliyah to start, and her eyes shot open. Heart thudding forcefully, she realized the cell phone next to her was ringing. Instinctively, she picked up the phone and looked at the display.

*Larry Bivens*

"*As-salaamu'alikum*," Aliyah said, speaking into the wire mouthpiece as she set the phone back into the compartment next to the driver's seat after accepting the call. "I'm outside."

"*Wa'alaiku mus salaam*," Larry said. "I can see that..." Lighthearted teasing was in his tone. "I was just wondering if there was any particular reason you didn't call to say you were here."

"I'm sorry. I was just—"

"It's fine," Larry said good-naturedly. "I'll send Ibrahim out now."

"Larry?" Aliyah said quickly, hoping to catch him before he hung up.

"Yes?"

"Will I be picking up Ibrahim here from now on?"

There was an extended pause. "Why?" Larry said.

"No reason," Aliyah said, her voice awkward in its forced cordiality. "I was just trying to...um, plan my schedule."

"Most likely," Larry said. "I'm not always at the same place with the boys each day, so Jacob and I thought it'd be easier if I bring them here each afternoon and stay with them until he got home."

"That makes sense..."

"But I can make other arrangements if you need me to," Larry said. "I'm flexible."

"No it's okay," Aliyah said, feeling self-conscious for having even asked. "This is fine."

"Okay..." Larry said, doubt in his voice. "Then I'll send Ibrahim out now."

Aliyah ended the call and bit her lower lip as she stared distantly beyond the windshield. *Beggars can't be choosers,* she told herself. It wouldn't be fair to ask Larry to disrupt his nephews' routine just to save her the discomfort of coming to Deanna's house every day.

The front door to the house opened, and Aliyah turned to see Ibrahim running out, an excited grin on his face. As he approached the car, a grin spread on her own face.

"Mommy!" Ibrahim said, breathless as he opened the back car door and climbed into his seat. "Uncle Larry said I run fast!" He closed the door and buckled his seat belt.

“*Wa'alaiku-mus-salaam*, Himy,” Aliyah said, playfully teasing her son for not giving her the salaams.

“Oh, sorry, Mommy,” Ibrahim said, giggling. “*As-salaamu'alaikum*.”

“So you run fast, huh?” she said, glancing at him in the rearview mirror as she put the car in drive and eased forward.

“Yes,” Ibrahim said eagerly. “And I kick the ball high!”

“*MashaAllah*,” she said. “I bet you do. You have strong legs.”

“Uncle Larry says I can be the best soccer player ever!”

“I think Uncle Larry is right,” Aliyah said, glancing in the mirror again. Ibrahim exhaled a sudden breath before leaning his head on the back of the seat and looking out the window. She smiled to herself. He was tired, but he was still wired from the exciting day. She silently prayed that Allah would bless and preserve Larry for helping with her son.

Her phone rang, and instinctively she glanced to the compartment next to her. *Larry Bivens.* Concerned, she answered immediately by squeezing the button on the wire that was still snaked to one ear. “Is everything okay?”

“Yes, it's fine,” Larry said, apology in his tone. “I just forgot to mention that Jasmine called to say she took her *shahaadah*.”

“Oh, *mashaAllah*,” Aliyah said, hoping she sounded genuinely surprised. But she couldn't help wondering why Larry thought it was important for her to know the news.

“And she asked if you could teach her how to pray.”

It took a few seconds for Aliyah to register what Larry was saying. “*Me*?”

“Yes, you.”

“But…”

“She says you seem like a good Muslim, *mashaAllah*.”

“But why not Salima?” Aliyah said. “Jasmine and I don't even know each other.”

“I asked her the same thing.”

“And what did she say?”

“That you seemed knowledgeable about the religion and that she felt she could learn a lot from you.”

“But…” Aliyah didn't know what to say.

“I guess you must have made quite an impression at the mall,” Larry said, lighthearted teasing in his voice.

“But we barely spoke,” Aliyah said as if genuinely confused.

There was an extended silence. “I can't say for sure…” Larry said, his tone suggesting that he was uncertain if he should share the information. “…but my hunch is that she put two and two together.”

Aliyah creased her forehead. “About what?”

“Remember that family dinner you went to at my family's house months ago?”

Aliyah's heart sank. She had completely forgotten about that. *Oooooh,* Aliyah could still hear the voices of Larry's family in her head. *It looks like Larry finally got over Jasmine!* "Yes…" Aliyah said tentatively.

"My guess is that she's curious about the mystery girl my family thought had stolen my heart."

Aliyah's stomach churned. "Larry, I…" she said, apology in her tone. "I'm sorry, but I can't…"

"I know, I know," Larry said good-naturedly. "I'm just passing on the message."

"Thanks," Aliyah said.

"But before she mentioned you," he said, "she asked whether or not it was her Islamic right to have her Muslim sisters help her learn everything."

Aliyah felt weak with dread. "*SubhaanAllah,*" she muttered.

"Jasmine's done her homework," Larry said, humored admiration in his voice.

Aliyah was silent for some time. "Can't she just go to the new Muslim classes at the masjid?" she said weakly.

"I'll mention that to her, *insha'Allah,*" Larry said as if the idea hadn't occurred to him.

"But don't say I suggested it," Aliyah said quickly.

"Of course not," he said, laughter in his voice. "But don't be surprised if she calls you up herself in the next couple of days."

Aliyah groaned. "Please don't tell me you gave her my number."

"I wouldn't do that," Larry said. "But Jasmine is very resourceful, so I thought I should give you a heads-up."

Aliyah was suddenly overcome with guilt and shame. It was wrong to purposely avoid her new sister in Islam, especially if all she wanted was to learn how to pray. Perhaps the phone call with Salima had prejudiced Aliyah against Jasmine. "If she calls," Aliyah said, exhausted obligation in her voice, "then I'll do what I can, *insha'Allah.*"

"I assume you don't want me to tell her that?" Larry said, slight teasing in his voice.

"Please don't," Aliyah said sincerely. "I was just thinking out loud."

"Got it."

***

"Are you sure?" Benjamin's voice said through the receiver as Aliyah held the cordless phone to her ear that evening after Ibrahim had fallen asleep.

Aliyah sighed as she slowly sat on the edge of her bed, letting the mattress receive her weight. "Yes, I'm sure." But even as she said it, sadness enveloped her, and she wondered if she was doing the right thing.

"Well, I'm sorry to hear that," Benjamin said, sadness in his tone. "I think Jacob would be perfect for you, *bi'idhnillaah.*"

"You really think so?" Aliyah said in a small voice.

"Absolutely," Benjamin said. "Like I told you when I first mentioned him, had I known he was open to marrying a second wife, I would have suggested him years ago."

Aliyah bit her lower lip as she considered what her uncle was saying. "It just doesn't feel right…"

"For you?" Benjamin asked doubtfully. "Or for how others will think of you?"

*Married ladies!* Aliyah recalled Juwayriah bint Abdullah's Facebook status from months ago. *Hold on to your husbands. I ain't one to call a sister out, so… #NuffSaid #YouHaveBeenWarned*

"I don't know…" Aliyah said, crippled by self-doubt. "Maybe a bit of both?" What if she *was* the home wrecker that Juwayriah accused her of being?

"When he was married, you felt uncomfortable with polygamy," Benjamin said. "So what's the problem now?"

"What kind of person marries her best friend's husband?" Aliyah asked, her voice tight in emotion. "Doesn't that make me a bad friend?"

"I don't know," Benjamin said honestly. "That depends on your definition of a friend."

"No real friend would take advantage of someone during their most difficult time," Aliyah said. "I can't do this to Deanna. No matter what she's done, she doesn't deserve this."

"But Jacob and Deanna aren't even married anymore."

"Well, I'm sure Deanna doesn't see it like that," Aliyah said.

Benjamin was quiet momentarily. "I'm sure you're familiar with the story of Zaid bin Haritha and Zaynab bint Jahsh, may Allah be pleased with them?"

Aliyah drew in a deep breath and exhaled, dreading the conversation being turned into an Islamic lesson. "Yes…"

"What do we learn from their story?"

"That an adopted son shouldn't be treated like a biological son," she said, speaking in monotone to underscore her disinterest.

"And?"

"Uncle Ben," Aliyah said after a few seconds, exhaustion in her voice. "I know it's not *haraam* to marry Jacob, so that's not what concerns me."

"I never thought you were under the impression that it's forbidden to marry him," Benjamin said. "I'm mentioning the story to remind you that sometimes you have to make the unpopular choice for the greater good."

"How can selfishness *ever* be the greater good?"

"Selfishness is a character flaw," Benjamin said, "not a marriage choice."

"But selfishness *can* be a marriage choice."

"True…" he said tentatively. "But all marriage choices are selfish on some level."

"Not the marriages of the Prophet, *sallallaahu 'alayhi wa sallam*," Aliyah said. "And he's our example."

"Ally," Benjamin said, reverting to her legal name as he often did, "all I'm trying to tell you is, if you think protecting other people's feelings is a condition to your own happiness, then you'll probably be unhappy and single for the rest of your life. So you have to decide who your Lord is. If it's Allah, then know that He hasn't put these unnecessary conditions on you. But if it's people, you're destined for misery no matter what you choose."

"It's not *shirk* to protect other people's feelings," Aliyah said defensively.

"I'm not talking about the type of *shirk* that takes you outside the fold of Islam," Benjamin said. "I'm talking about doing things for the sake of people instead of Allah."

"They're not always two separate things," Aliyah said. "Look at the story of Ali and Fatimah, *radhiyAllahu'anhumaa*."

"And is that story the exception or the rule?" Benjamin asked challengingly. "Or better yet, is it the *only* story that exists in our religion with regards to marriage?" he said. "If you want to derive a principle from Islamic history, then it should be based on striving to please Allah, and being compassionate to others while striving for the greater good."

"Exactly," Aliyah said. "How am I being compassionate to Deanna by marrying her husband?"

"Her *former* husband," Benjamin corrected. "Either way, pleasing Allah must be your starting point," he said. "And pleasing Allah does not always equal pleasing people. And pleasing people is not the same as compassion. Remember that."

"I know," Aliyah muttered.

"Don't make the same mistake of cultural Muslims," Benjamin warned.

Aliyah creased her forehead. "What is that supposed to mean?"

"I met a Muslim brother who was worried he wouldn't be able to marry the woman he wanted because in his country, all the elder relatives of the woman *and* man had to approve the marriage." Benjamin huffed. "And when I told him that Allah doesn't stipulate those conditions, he said it's part of Islam to respect our elders."

Aliyah rolled her eyes. "That's stupid."

"And how many other 'stupid' cultural rules have you heard from Muslims?" Benjamin asked rhetorically. "You *must* marry from a certain tribe," he said as if enumerating. "The person *must* have a specific lineage. You can't marry a divorced woman. The woman must be younger than you."

Aliyah sighed, recalling the difficult conversation she'd had with Reem about whom Hana and Muhammad could marry. "I know," Aliyah said sincerely. "And I don't agree with any of that."

"I know you don't," Benjamin said, his voice soft with empathy. "And I don't either. But I mentioned cultural Muslims because if your main reason for refusing Jacob is because he used to be married to your best friend, then you're no different than them."

"That's not true," Aliyah said, unable to quell her offense. "Being sensitive to other people's feelings isn't the same as forbidding what Allah has permitted."

"Have you ever met a cultural Muslim who says outright that it's *haraam* to go against their traditions?" Benjamin asked doubtfully. "Chances are, most will at least acknowledge that their customs are not Islamic requirements. But does this knowledge affect their behavior?" he asked. "For many, it only emboldens them because they don't feel they're changing the religion. They're just doing what's best for their children or trying to avoid problems in the family or marriage, they say."

*"I know in Islam it's allowed to marry outside your culture,"* Aliyah recalled Reem saying, *"but it's not encouraged. It can cause too many problems in your marriage and family."*

"Years ago, thinking about the hypocrisy of cultural Muslims would make me angry," Benjamin said reflectively. "But today, I realize that we have our own hypocrisy as American Muslims. We all have a lot of work to do."

There was a thoughtful pause.

"But it's not the same," Aliyah said. "Americans are much more open-minded about following true Islam."

"Not really," Benjamin said doubtfully. "It's just that the things we're close-minded about are widely accepted because of Westernization," he said. "So no one's going to call us on it. And even if they did, we wouldn't listen. Our Western arrogance makes us feel that our cultural adjustments to the religion are based on wisdom. But for others, we claim it's based on ignorance."

Aliyah drew her eyebrows together. "I don't see American Muslims doing that," she said. "We try hard to follow the Sunnah no matter what our culture says."

"I'm not denying our sincere efforts," Benjamin said. "But what we have in common with cultural Muslims is that we have our own un-Islamic traditions, and in the name of wisdom or some greater good, we dismiss Allah's teachings when it suits us."

"Like what?" Aliyah said doubtfully.

"Well, our anti-polygamy attitude, for one."

Aliyah groaned. "But polygamy is breaking the law, Uncle Ben," she said. "So no one is dismissing Allah's instructions. It's obligatory to follow the laws of the land."

"To follow or to respect?" he said challengingly.

"What's the difference?" she said, contorting her face defensively.

"One is placing human law above Allah's, and the other is avoiding breaking the law," he said. "There's a difference."

"Well, not partaking in polygamy is avoiding breaking the law," Aliyah said monotone, as if reciting the obligatory way to phrase her statement.

"No. Not marrying *legally* is avoiding breaking the law," he said. "Legal marriage isn't obligatory in America. So why do Muslims do it?"

"Because it makes the most sense," Aliyah said matter-of-factly. "That way, you follow the laws of Islam *and* your country."

"Ally," Benjamin said, "anyone who is sincerely trying to follow the laws of Islam *and* their country would never get legally married," he said, "in monogamy or polygamy. But that we do, then use it as an excuse to prohibit polygamy is just further proof of how we dismiss Islam whenever it suits us."

Aliyah contorted her face, glancing sideways at the cordless phone. "How is it *haraam* to get legally married?"

"I didn't say it's not allowed to get legally married," Benjamin said. "I said anyone who is sincerely trying to follow the laws of Islam and their country wouldn't do it. But this is just my opinion, not an Islamic ruling."

"But why wouldn't they get legally married? In your opinion?" Aliyah added.

"Because the requirements of a legal marriage contradict those of an Islamic marriage," Benjamin said. "And any Muslim with basic knowledge of Islam knows it's not permissible to enter into a contract that has conditions that go against our faith," he said. "Especially if you have a legal alternative."

"But I don't see any contradictions," Aliyah said. "We might have different conditions on who can marry whom, but whether it's legal or Islamic, marriage is marriage."

"But what if you want a divorce?" Benjamin said. "I know dozens of Muslims who have been divorced according to Islam for years, but they still don't have a legal divorce. And they knew full well before they got married that their legal contract would contradict Islamic laws if the marriage didn't work out. But they still got a legal marriage," he said. "Why? Because it never really was about doing what was Islamically required. It was about doing the best they could given that this isn't an Islamic country. But when it comes to polygamy, we want to claim that other Muslims can't do the same," he said. "And some of us even go as far as to claim Islam forbids it because America forbids it."

Aliyah was silent as she considered what her uncle had said.

"So yes, we have our own cultural traditions that we use to replace Islam," Benjamin said. "But it's easy to look at other Muslims and point out their faults," he said. "While the real challenge is to look in the mirror and be honest about our own."

"I see what you mean..." Aliyah said thoughtfully.

"And let me ask you something," Benjamin said. "Did you pray *Istikhaarah* when you refused Jacob's initial interest in marrying you?"

Aliyah creased her forehead. "You mean when he was still married to Deanna?"

"Yes."

"No," Aliyah said.

"And why not?"

Aliyah didn't know how to respond.

"Because your dislike for polygamy was so ingrained in your American psyche," Benjamin said, answering his own question, "that the idea of consulting Allah Himself didn't even cross your mind. "

Aliyah started to defend herself when she was reminded of what she had said to Reem. *"I get the whole preference thing. But what I don't understand is why your culture doesn't allow you to see Allah's plan as bigger than yours."*

Perhaps American Muslims we're so different from cultural Muslims, she considered. If she was genuinely convinced that it wasn't wise to marry Jacob at that time, why hadn't she consulted Allah before responding to her uncle? Certainly, praying about it would have only confirmed what she already felt. As it would for Reem and her husband regarding whom their children should marry.

"Don't complicate your faith, Aliyah," Benjamin said. "If Allah hasn't forbidden something, there's a very good reason for that."

Aliyah bit her lower lip as she listened.

"And as for Jacob's current proposal," Benjamin said, "there's no law against marrying the ex-husband of your friend. In Islam or America," he added.

"But how do I know I'm making the right decision?" Aliyah said weakly. "I could just be convincing myself I'm trying to please Allah while I'm just following my desires."

"You've said yourself that your biggest regret in marrying Matt was that you didn't consider what *you* wanted and needed," he said. "And if there's anything in which following your desires can also mean pleasing Allah, it's in the *halaal* bond of marriage."

There was extended silence as Aliyah considered what her uncle had said.

"Ally," Benjamin said compassionately, "don't get me wrong. I know this isn't an easy decision. And I acknowledge that I could be wrong about Jacob being right for you. Perhaps it *is* best for you to leave it alone. And maybe for all the reasons that make you uncomfortable," he said. "*Allahu'alam*. But I don't want you to say no until you've done some honest self-reflection and made *du'aa* and *Istikhaarah*."

She sighed. "Okay."

"I've known you most of your life," Benjamin said, "and if there's one thing I worry about, it's your tendency to overthink things and worry about protecting everyone else." There was a thoughtful pause. "So do me a favor," he said. "Think about what I said. Then get advice, and make *Istikhaarah*. If you still feel the same by this weekend, then I'll tell Jacob you said no."

"Okay…"

"Then *insha'Allah*, I'll see you this weekend," Benjamin said.

"*Insha'Allah*," Aliyah said.

"*As-salaamu'alaikum*, Ally."

"*Wa'alaiku mus salaam wa rahmatullaah*, Uncle Ben."

## 21
## Speak To Me

Deanna dreamt that Jacob was in a lush green field walking toward her, a smile on his face. "Thank you, Deanna," he was saying. "If it wasn't for you, I wouldn't be the man I am today." She was overcome with tears as she said, "I'm sorry, Jacob. Forgive me for everything." But he didn't seem to hear her. He continued to walk toward her, a smile on his face, but with each step, the grassy field expanded and stretched, until he was far from her, out of reach... *I don't want to lose you*, her heart cried as she lost sight of him. *Then pray*, she heard a voice in her head. *Pray...*

The stiff pillow beneath her cheek was moist from tears when Deanna opened her eyes. She squinted in the darkness, and her chest constricted as her eyes adjusted to reveal that she was not in her comfortable bed at home. The stale stench of the jail cell burned her nostrils, and she became nauseated as she lay in a fetal position. She clenched her teeth as her stomach heaved, and she swallowed to thwart the bile rising to her throat.

*"I divorce you."* Anger flared in Deanna's chest as she recalled Jacob pronouncing the blasphemous words that sealed her fate. If it hadn't been for him, she wouldn't be in jail right then. And if it hadn't been for him, she would never have fought her mother. What had he been thinking enraging her like that? Why had he threatened to annihilate their relationship? Or was the divorce pronouncement his idea of a cruel joke?

Or maybe Aliyah had put him up to it.

The possibility was so enraging that Deanna sat up in bed, eyes narrowed indignantly. The more she thought about it, the more it made sense. It was just like Aliyah to pull a stunt like this. Perhaps Aliyah had even expected Deanna to fight with her mother and end up in jail.

Oh, if only it had been Aliyah and not her mother on the balcony stairs that day. Then Deanna wouldn't be so racked with guilt about her lying in a coma. It would serve Aliyah right to be rendered practically useless after all of her surreptitious plotting to steal Jacob.

*"This is why your life is so messed up. You're selfish and immature. You have no regard for anyone but yourself. Even God means nothing to you."*

Deanna winced at her mother's words. For a fleeting moment, she felt a pang of guilt, and she was overcome with shame at her spiteful thoughts. Was it true that even God meant nothing to her?

*"Our Lord died for us and gave his blood,"* Deanna's mother had said. *"And if you want to go to Heaven, you need to accept his sacrifice."*

Deanna recoiled at the thought of returning to the religion of her parents. Her mother's words had only been a ruse to guilt Deanna back into joining the church. Ever since Deanna had accepted Islam, her parents had made it their life's mission to get Deanna to recant her faith. Perhaps Deanna *did* belong in Hellfire, she considered bitterly. But she would be remiss to fall prey to the trappings of a man and woman who lived only in the peripheral of God's Word. So how dare they judge Deanna for merely being a reflection of themselves.

But what kind of parents refused to help their daughter take revenge on the husband who had scorned her? What kind of parents would argue about religion, of all things, while their daughter needed their support? Where was the love? Where was the compassion? All Deanna had wanted was her husband to apologize and mend their relationship. But now *she* was in jail. *I want Jacob back!* her heart screamed. *Aliyah* cannot *win!*

*Then pray*, a voice said in her head. *Pray...*

The words from the dream tempered the fury in Deanna's chest as she recalled Jacob smiling at her. *If it wasn't for you, I wouldn't be the man I am today.* Chin quivering as she was overcome with emotion, Deanna was reminded that Allah could help her get her husband back.

*The supplication of the one who has been wronged is answered, even if it comes from a disbeliever.* She recalled the words from an Islamic lecture she'd heard years ago, and they gave her peace of mind. She had been wronged, so her *du'aa* would be answered. Jacob belonged to *her*, she said to herself, emboldened by possessive pride. And *no one* could take what was rightly hers.

***

Thursday morning after Aliyah had finished the final session with the interns, she walked down the hall leading to her office. It had been two days since her uncle had suggested that she pray and get advice about marrying Jacob. Aliyah's first thought had been to talk to Salima, but Aliyah had withheld, reminded that Salima had already offered her perspective. *"If you're trying to decide on whether or not to marry him, then there are only three things to consider,"* Salima had said. *"Allah, the man, and you."*

But that was easier said than done, Aliyah thought to herself.

"I barely even speak to Professor Thomas."

Hearing someone mention her name distracted Aliyah from her thoughts, and she slowed her steps, curiosity piqued, wondering where the voice was coming from.

"Then be sure to keep it that way."

Aliyah recognized the second voice just as she saw that Jacob's office door was open.

"The last day of the internship is tomorrow," the person said, impatient annoyance in his voice, "so you have nothing to worry about."

"Dr. Stanley," Aliyah heard Jacob say, his voice rising in upset, "you know full well this has nothing to do with One Plus One."

"That's the only project that I work on with Professor Thomas," Dr. Stanley said.

"Then let me put it to you another way," Jacob said. "If I so much as *hear* that you've looked at her the wrong way, or that you've said *anything* to make her uncomfortable, you'll regret it."

"Is that a *threat*?" Dr. Stanley said, disbelieving humor in his tone.

"I don't issue threats," Jacob said, his voice even and composed.

"You know what?" Dr. Stanley said in apparent aggravation. "I don't have time for this. I have work to do."

"Good," Aliyah heard Jacob say just as Dr. Stanley stormed into the hall, grunting. Dr. Stanley halted his steps, a shocked expression on his face when he saw Aliyah. Aliyah's eyes widened as they met each other's gaze. Her heart raced as she realized that Dr. Stanley would think she was eavesdropping.

After a few seconds, Dr. Stanley huffed, shook his head, and walked past her, his face contorted in disapproval. Fearing Jacob would come out of his office soon, Aliyah hurried to her office and fumbled with the keys until she unlocked the door and pushed it open.

"Professor Thomas?"

Aliyah turned and saw Jacob standing behind her, a confused expression on his face.

"Were you outside my office the whole time?" There was a tinge of disappointment in his voice.

Aliyah opened her mouth to speak but had no idea what to say for how mortified she felt right then.

"Do you have a class right now?" Jacob asked, disappointment still in his voice.

"No…" Aliyah said.

"Then meet me in the first floor conference room in five minutes," Jacob said, turning and walking away.

After Jacob disappeared behind the exit door, Aliyah exhaled in a single breath and bowed her head in embarrassment. She hoped she hadn't angered Jacob. Sighing, Aliyah closed her office door and locked it. She started to walk toward the staircase then decided against it. She didn't want to chance running into Jacob. As she made her way toward the elevators, she mentally prepared herself for an interrogation. Having a last minute meeting with her department head couldn't be good.

In the elevator, Aliyah's thoughts shifted to the conversation she'd had with her uncle about marrying Jacob. She had taken Benjamin's advice and reflected on the underlying reasons for her objections. It was true that, as an American, she had an inherent cultural bias against marrying Jacob. Intuitively, Aliyah understood that this prejudice wasn't rooted in her religion, but she still found it difficult to extricate herself from it.

It was one thing to know that something was wrong, but it was another thing entirely to do what was right. It was similar to the dilemma she'd faced when she was Christian and had learned about Islam for the first time. But this time, it wasn't as simple as renouncing false religious doctrine and affirming what she knew God required of her. She wasn't choosing between worshipping a prophet of God and worshipping God Himself. She was choosing between saying yes or no to marriage. And she didn't *have* to marry Jacob.

But she wanted to.

And she hated herself for it.

The elevator doors opened, and Aliyah stepped onto the first floor. As she rounded the corner, she smiled and greeted the students and colleagues passing in the hall. Through the soundproof glass that ran the length of the conference room, Aliyah saw Jacob standing with his arms folded, a troubled expression on his face as he looked toward the whiteboard, eyes distant.

*MashaAllah*, Aliyah muttered instinctively, averting her gaze. It was the most irrational thing to notice right then, but Jacob really did look handsome in the three-piece business suit and tie, though his suit jacket was hanging on the back of the chair behind him. Her heart ached for how much she would regret not marrying him.

Jacob turned at the sound of the conference door opening, and Aliyah gave him a tightlipped smile before finding a seat a comfortable distance from him. The door slowly closed and sealed shut, and Aliyah felt trapped and exposed at once. Ironically, reflecting on her marriage dilemma had highlighted not only the depth of her American cultural prejudices, but also the depth of her feelings for Jacob.

For years, Aliyah had felt at ease in Jacob's presence and found him easy to talk to, even in passing. But it was only in the last couple of days that she realized that this had never been the case with other men, even ones she'd dated or befriended before becoming Muslim. With other men, there had always been a grating discomfort, an invisible barrier that separated her from them. So Aliyah had made peace with forever being "socially awkward." It was simply her lot in life, she had concluded, that she would be unable to express herself effectively or be properly understood. Her friends misunderstood her, her classmates misunderstood her, and even her own family misunderstood her. No matter how hard she tried, she always managed to confuse or offend someone.

"I didn't intend for you to hear that," Jacob said apologetically as Aliyah sat down. He was still standing in front of the room, but he was facing Aliyah, his gaze distant as he looked at something beyond her. "I had planned to be gone by the time the morning session ended. I apologize for that."

Aliyah exhaled in relief as she realized that Jacob wasn't upset with her. "I'm sorry that I overheard. I didn't mean to h—"

"It's okay," Jacob said, waving his hand dismissively. "There's nothing we can do about it now." He coughed laughter. "Of course, now Dr. Stanley will think I planned it like that. I told him you didn't even know I was coming."

Aliyah chuckled. "Sorry about that," she said good-naturedly.

Jacob laughed and shook his head in response. "Don't worry about it," he said. "I should've closed the door or met somewhere else."

*Assuming the best*, Aliyah thought to herself, ticking off something else she'd come to like about Jacob. Whatever blunder she or anyone else made, he tried to put the best face on it. But it wasn't like that with other Muslims she'd met. For them, if you didn't speak a certain way, dress a certain way, or view the popular personality in a certain way, you were whispered about, made fun of, and cast out of social graces. Till today, it remained a confusing and frustrating experience for Aliyah. But she'd never felt that confusion and frustration around Jacob.

Even before Aliyah started working at the college (when she'd interacted with Jacob when visiting Deanna or attending one of their marriage workshops), she felt a sense of calm and safety in his presence. He was always unassuming and nonjudgmental. When someone spoke, he listened humbly and attentively. It was as if he actually valued what they were saying and wanted to understand their point of view. But with most others, their listening was merely obligatory and intermittent. And if a statement could be interpreted negatively, it would be interpreted negatively.

*"Why would you say something like that?"* Deanna often scolded Aliyah. *"You have no people skills."* But do *people* have people skills? Aliyah often wondered in aggravation. If others truly had the people skills they prided themselves in, why was it so hard for them to understand Aliyah, a *person*?

*Learn how to COMMUNICATE*, Juwayriah had posted on Facebook some time ago. *If you're a grown a$$ man or woman and you STILL don't know how to speak properly, then SHUT UP.*

"Could this cost us our jobs?" Aliyah asked Jacob, concern in her voice.

Jacob drew his eyebrows together and shook his head. "No, *insha'Allah*," he said. "If there's anyone whose job is at stake, it's Dr. Stanley."

"He won't tell Dr. Warren we ambushed him or anything?" Aliyah hoped her question conveyed the lighthearted humor she intended.

"*Allahu'alam*," Jacob said, acknowledging that God knew best. "But the most you have to worry about is an uncomfortable professional relationship."

"So he's not trying to take your position anymore or get me fired?" Aliyah said.

"I don't know about that..." Jacob said doubtfully. "I'm just saying that him seeing you outside my office won't affect much one way or the other. But the important thing is that he's going to leave you alone from now on, *insha'Allah*," Jacob said. "I assume he hasn't been a nuisance or anything?"

Aliyah shook her head. "No, *alhamdulillah*."

"Good," Jacob said, smiling to himself. "Then he got the memo."

Aliyah drew her eyebrows together. "The memo?"

Jacob shook his head, the shadow of a smile still on his face. "Nothing."

"But should I be worried about anything?" Aliyah said hesitantly.

"Here?" Jacob said rhetorically, humor in his tone. "Always. But after my meeting this morning, you shouldn't have to worry about Dr. Stanley bothering you directly."

There was an awkward pause as Aliyah debated whether or not to speak her thoughts aloud. "When will you be coming back?" she asked finally.

Jacob lifted a shoulder in a shrug. "I took off indefinitely," he said. "But the way things are looking, I could be back as early as next month."

"So everything is settled with Deanna?"

"No," he said, frowning. "But it looks like they'll keep pushing the trial date, so there's no reason to stay on leave."

"When is the trial supposed to be?" Aliyah said.

"For now, next May."

"Next May?" Aliyah repeated in surprise. "Why so late?"

"Well, apparently, in cases like these," Jacob said, "having a trial set for ten months later is the norm. And that's best-case scenario, I'm told."

"Best-case scenario?" Aliyah said, her face contorted. "And Deanna is just supposed to sit in jail until the court date?"

"That's what it looks like," Jacob said, a shadow of sadness in his eyes.

"What happened to innocent till proven guilty?"

"Did it ever exist?" Jacob said, lighthearted sarcasm in his tone.

There was thoughtful silence.

"So what will you do?" Aliyah asked, genuine concern in her voice.

Jacob shrugged. "Pray. Keep busy. Focus on Younus and Thawab."

At the mention of the boys, Aliyah was overwhelmed with sadness. There was so much she wanted to ask but was unsure if she had a right to. "How are they doing?" she said quietly, picking up a pencil that was lying on the conference table. She toyed with the pencil before adding, "I mean, with everything going on?"

"*Alhamdulillah*," Jacob said honestly. "They're good boys, *mashaAllah*, so they're taking it well."

Aliyah glanced up at Jacob hesitantly. "Did you tell Deanna?"

Jacob furrowed his brows. "About what?"

Aliyah averted her gaze and tapped the eraser of the pencil on the table absentmindedly. "About what you asked my uncle."

She heard Jacob sigh, and he was silent for some time. "I want to," he said sincerely. "But she's not well, and truthfully, I don't know if she will be any time soon."

Aliyah nodded, only slightly surprised to hear about Deanna's condition. Over the years, there had been several moments when she'd sensed that something wasn't quite right about Deanna. But Aliyah had brushed her suspicions aside, feeling guilty for thinking negatively about her friend. Aliyah didn't know much about mental health issues, so she'd always felt that it wasn't her place to pass judgment.

"Will she be getting help?" Aliyah asked.

"I'm working on it," Jacob said. "But given the circumstances, it's not easy. Involving psychiatrists at this point will complicate her defense," he said. "But not involving them will complicate her mental illness."

"So it's confirmed?"

"Is what confirmed?"

"Her mental illness."

He shook his head, a sad expression on his face. "She's still undiagnosed at this point."

Aliyah nodded, empathizing with the stress that Jacob must be going through.

"But I did talk to Younus and Thawab," Jacob said. "Younus more than Thawab, of course."

"About Deanna?"

"About everything."

"*Everything*?" Aliyah couldn't keep the surprise out of her voice.

"Yes."

Aliyah didn't know what to say.

"I didn't mention you by name," Jacob clarified, "but I talked about the different possibilities for our future."

"You don't think it's too soon?" Aliyah said, worry in her voice as she looked at him. "I mean, with everything that happened with their mother?"

Jacob's gaze grew distant, and he shook his head. "No," he said thoughtfully. "I know this isn't anyone's idea of a perfect family. But this is what Allah has given us, and I've made my peace with it."

"But won't it be hard for Younus and Thawab to adjust?"

"I imagine so," Jacob said. "But this is just one of many tests they'll face in life. I'm not doing them any favors by pretending that life stops when trials happen."

Aliyah's thoughts grew distant as she doodled on the table then erased the penciling.

"But no one loves my sons more than I do," Jacob said, "so I'll be there for them every step of the way *insha'Allah*."

"But what if they don't like me?"

"Like you?" he said, surprise in his tone. "You're practically family."

Aliyah recalled the awkward looks that Younus had given her the last couple of times she had seen him. "Younus doesn't speak to me anymore." Aliyah felt stupid for sounding like a little kid, but she felt it was important for Jacob to know.

"What makes you say that?" Jacob said, concern in his voice.

"He used to be excited to see me," she said. "But when I saw him at the basketball court, he was giving me strange looks."

Jacob nodded as if understanding. "He saw some YouTube clips from Will's Truth Hour when they were talking about the 'crazy Muslim woman' and 'hot Muslim mistress' rumors."

Aliyah felt sick all of a sudden.

"So he had a lot of questions," Jacob said.

"Did you answer them?" Aliyah said, barely finding her voice.

"Yes," Jacob said. "Younus and I had a long talk, a few actually."

Aliyah nodded, unsure what to say.

"But I don't worry too much about Younus," Jacob said. "*Insha'Allah*, he'll be okay."

"How can you be so sure?" she said doubtfully. "That's a lot to digest."

"How can we be sure about anything?" he asked rhetorically. "But I'm prayerful, and that's what keeps me from worrying too much."

Aliyah felt ashamed of herself momentarily. She wished she had that level of faith. "But what if we're wrong?" she said weakly. "What if we're about to ruin their lives?"

Jacob drew his brows together, vague amusement on his face. "Ruin their lives?" he said, a question in his eyes as he looked at Aliyah.

"This might traumatize them," Aliyah said weakly. "One day I'm Aunty Aliyah and the next I'm their new mother."

"Deanna will always be their mother," Jacob said. "So I would never tell them you're replacing her."

"But won't it be confusing?"

"In the beginning, yes," he said thoughtfully. "But they'll adjust *insha'Allah*."

"I don't think it's that simple," Aliyah said, casting her eyes to the side.

"Nothing is that simple," Jacob said, "even if everything turned out the way the world says it should."

Aliyah's thoughts grew distant, and she began doodling on the conference table again.

"There's no such thing as the perfect family, Aliyah," Jacob said. "In this world, the most we can hope for is living a life that's pleasing to Allah."

"And how do you know what that is?" Aliyah asked.

"We don't," Jacob said. "That's what self-reflection, *naseehah*, and *Istikhaarah* are for."

Aliyah thought of how, still, after reflecting on what was best, getting advice from her uncle, and praying about everything, she remained indecisive.

"But I'm not naïve," Jacob said. "I know we have a long road ahead of us. But as a father, what's most important to me is that my sons understand their higher purpose in life. I don't want to trivialize their struggles," he said. "But I don't want to exaggerate them either."

"What if the community doesn't accept us?" Aliyah felt self-conscious for worrying about what people think, but she couldn't help voicing her thoughts aloud. "You saw what they did when they thought you wanted a second wife."

"We either be patient," he said, "or find a new community."

"You're willing to move?" Aliyah said, her voice rising in pleasant surprise.

"It's something I've been thinking about," he said honestly. "For the sake of my sons more than anything. But I'm still praying about it because there are a lot of good people here, *mashaAllah*."

"But do you think it'll be better anywhere else?" Aliyah said doubtfully. "From what I hear, Muslims are pretty judgmental no matter where you go."

"*People* are judgmental no matter where you go," Jacob said. "But there's definitely something to say for a new start. People are most accepting when they aren't given the opportunity to have an opinion."

"What do you mean?"

"Do you really think we'd be the first blended family in this community?" Jacob asked. "It's just that others came to the community already remarried," he said. "Or no one knew anything about their former wives or husbands. So they were accepted for who they are, no questions asked."

Aliyah nodded reflectively. "I never thought about it like that."

"When people know anything about you," Jacob said, "they feel they have a say in what you should do with your life. It's just human nature."

Aliyah rolled her eyes. "I don't think so. It's just minding other people's business."

"I agree," Jacob said. "But that's why Allah talks so much about avoiding suspicion, assuming the best, and guarding our tongues. Humans have a natural tendency to get involved in things that have nothing to do with them. I'm not saying it's right," he said. "But it *is* natural."

Aliyah grunted. "Everyone is an expert in everyone's life," she said in lighthearted sarcasm. "Except their own."

Jacob chuckled. "That's the unfortunate truth," he said. "But there's not much we can do about it. All we can do is focus on our own lives and souls. People are people, and I don't think they'll be changing any time soon."

"But it's wrong," Aliyah said, a tinge of aggravation in her voice. "We're not just *people*. We're Muslim."

"And Muslims are people, Aliyah," Jacob said. "I'm not saying it's fair to have to move my whole family to another city just to live in peace. But this is the world we live in. If your life choices make people uncomfortable, they feel justified in mistreating you," he said. "Even if you've done nothing wrong." He shrugged. "It's sad. But it's really more their problem than yours."

"It doesn't feel like that," Aliyah grumbled.

"Allah is the best teacher," Jacob said. "Remember that."

Aliyah was silent as she considered what Jacob had said.

"So don't worry too much about people," he said. "They have their lesson coming." There was a thoughtful pause before he added, "As we all do when we focus on things that are none of our business."

"*Astaghfirullah*," Aliyah muttered reflectively, invoking God's forgiveness.

"But if it weren't for my sons," Jacob said, "I wouldn't even consider moving. Living your life based on people's definition of right and wrong is exhausting," he said. "Allah is my Lord, and that's who I'm focused on, *bi'idhnillah*."

Aliyah sighed. "I wish I had your resolve."

Jacob nodded reflectively. "It took me a long time to get here," he said. "But it's natural to worry about what people think. I don't think we can help it." He paused thoughtfully. "But I suffered so much from trying to do what everybody thought I should, I just don't have the capacity anymore."

Aliyah rubbed the eraser of the pencil on the table, her thoughts distant.

"Now I see these tests as an opportunity for my family to draw closer to Allah," Jacob said. "So I don't put too much stock in the superficial ideals of the world. I'm going on with my life, with or without people's approval."

***

"Are you sure you want to do this?" Sayed asked, an uncertain expression on his face as he looked at his wife. He was dressed for work and holding up his mobile phone as he asked the question, and Reem was in front of their walk-in closet, nervously sliding clothes to the left and right as she looked for something comfortable to wear under her abaya.

"No," Reem said without turning around. "But you already called in sick at work, so we should go ahead and do it."

"Reem, I'm more than happy to just spend the day with you. With Hana and Muhammad at your mother's house, we can do whatever you want."

"I need to heal," Reem said, still looking toward the closet.

Sayed creased his forehead. "Dr. Goldstein suggested this?"

"No," Reem said. "But it's something I need to do."

There was an extended pause. "Why?" Sayed said.

Reem yanked a maxi dress from a hanger and turned to face her husband. "I don't know," she said, slight agitation in her voice. "It's just the first thing that came to mind, so that must mean something."

"I support you," Sayed said tentatively. "I just don't want you to do anything you'll regret."

Reem coughed laughter. "It's a little too late for that," she said. "Being born into this family has made me do a lot of things I regret."

"But if your parents find out—"

"Mashael agreed to keep our names out of it," Reem said. "I'm trying to heal, not ruin our lives."

"What next though?" Sayed said. "I mean, if he agrees to become Muslim?"

"We plan a wedding *insha'Allah*," Reem said matter-of-factly as she slipped out of her housedress and tossed it to the bed.

"You can't be serious," Sayed said, his eyebrows drawn together in concern. "Your father should be involved before it goes that far."

Reem grunted as she pulled the maxi dress over her head. "He's been involved the whole time," she said. "Just in making sure it *never* happens."

"But that's his right," Sayed said defensively. "I'd hate to wake up and find out Hana is married and I didn't know anything about it."

"Then wake up *now*," Reem said, smoothing the cloth of the maxi dress with her hands. "Stuff like this only happens when parents go to sleep on their children and ignore their needs."

"He's trying to protect her."

Reem met Sayed's gaze with her eyes narrowed. "He's trying to *protect* her?" Her tone conveyed disbelief. "He's not trying to protect her, Sayed. He's trying to protect *himself*. And our family image."

"But we don't know anything about Sheldon."

"And why's that?" Reem said, folding her arms challengingly. "Because he's so mysterious?"

"You know what I mean," Sayed grumbled.

"We're losing Mashael. Did you know that?" Reem said. "Just like my family was losing me when I was in high school." She huffed and shook her head. "Right now, she cares what we think. But one day that will change, Sayed. Everybody has a breaking point."

Sayed nodded thoughtfully. "I just don't want you stressed out any more than you already are." He sighed. "And the truth is, I'm worried about Mashael. I wish she would just listen to your parents. What if Sheldon turns out to be a bad person? Then what?"

Reem drew in a deep breath and exhaled in a single breath. "I don't know, Sayed," she said, impatience in her tone. "There are a lot of what ifs. But what we *do* know is, Mashael thinks he's a good person. The least we can do is be there for her. If he turns out to be a bad person, at least we'll be part of her life when she finds out. If we turn our backs now, then she has no one to turn to when she needs help."

"But you're being impulsive," Sayed said, his voice soft in rebuke. "And we agreed to avoid that," he reminded her. "This decision has long-term consequences, so we have to be ready for everything that comes along with it."

"I'm ready," Reem said, walking to the closet and removing an abaya from a hanger. "If I'm going to rebel for the sake of anything, it should be this. I don't want to lose my sister."

"But you're not in high school anymore," Sayed said. "You have a lot at stake."

"Like what?" Reem said, meeting Sayed's gaze challengingly as she laid the abaya over the bend in her arm. "My parents' good opinion of me? Because I think I lost that years ago."

"It's more complicated than that," Sayed said. "There's no way you can know how this will affect your family long-term."

Reem was silent as she put her arms into the sleeves of her abaya and lowered her chin as she buttoned the front. "Did I tell you I tried to kill myself when I was seventeen?"

Sayed's expression conveyed shock, concern, and confusion. He opened his mouth to say something, but closed it.

"Yes, I know," she said sarcastically. "It's not exactly what you expect to hear from a good Saudi girl, is it? But that's how far this family drove me."

Reem looked pointedly at her husband. “Do you know how it feels to think dying is better than living?” she said. “Even though you *know* you might end up in Hell?”

Sayed’s lips formed a thin line, but he didn’t say anything.

“So don’t tell me about risks and sacrifice and family,” Reem vented, eyes glistening in emotion. “I almost lost my *life*, Sayed,” she said, her voice becoming shaky. “*And* my soul. And you know what my parents did about it?”

Sayed didn’t respond.

“Nothing,” she said angrily. She turned and yanked a *khimaar* from a hanger before meeting his gaze again. “Because they had no idea. And you know why they were so oblivious?”

There was an extended silence.

“Because they didn’t even *try* to see me,” Reem said as her eyes filled with tears and her chin quivered. “I walked around like some stupid robot.” Her voice became high-pitched from emotion. “I smiled at everybody and pretended like everything was okay. Then one day I decided to just end it all, you know? Eff it. And you know who saved my life?”

Sayed didn’t know what to say.

“A group of friends who saw me down the pills at school,” she said. “They forced me to throw it all up. And when I came home later that day barely even walking straight, you know what my father said to me?” She huffed at the memory. “‘Be more careful about your appearance, Reem,’” she mocked in exaggerated falsetto, “‘because if you look like you don’t care, who will want to marry you?’”

Silence filled the space between them for some time.

“So yes, maybe this is impulsive,” Reem said, wiping her eyes with the palm of her hand. “And maybe it’s the stupidest thing I’ll ever do. But right now, my sister is alive, and she still believes her family cares about her,” she said. “And I don’t want her to ever find out she’s wrong.”

***

Aliyah’s cell phone rang just as she and Ibrahim walked into the apartment late that afternoon. After she closed the door and locked it, Aliyah looked at the display. It was a number she didn’t recognize. Aliyah’s thoughts went immediately to the conversation she’d had with Larry about Jasmine. For a fleeting moment, Aliyah considered letting the call go to voicemail, but she felt bad for trying to avoid her new Muslim sister. She pressed the green icon instead.

“Hello?” Aliyah said as she put the phone to her ear.

“Is this Aliyah?” a female voice said.

“Yes…”

“This is Yasmeen,” the woman said. “I met you at the mall the other day? You were with Salima.”

“Oh, Jasmine?” Aliyah smiled knowingly.

Aliyah heard Jasmine laugh good-naturedly. "Yes, that's me," her chipper voice said. "But I'm Muslim now."

"*MashaAllah*," Aliyah said, excitement in her voice, unsure what else to say.

"But I'm still trying to learn everything," Jasmine said.

"Of course," Aliyah said sincerely. "It takes time."

"I want to start with the basics, you know?"

"I understand," Aliyah said as she motioned Ibrahim to the kitchen and walked behind him. "You have to take everything step by step."

There was an extended pause, and Aliyah sensed Jasmine was trying to figure out the best way to ask for her assistance.

"Can you help me learn everything?" Jasmine said in a small voice. "I mean, whenever you have time?"

Aliyah drew in a deep breath and exhaled as she opened the refrigerator and gazed absently inside for some time. "I'm really busy these days…" she said as she pulled out a glass casserole dish sealed with a plastic top. "So I'm not sure how much help I'd be."

"Anything you can do is fine," Jasmine's voice said through the phone.

"The masjid has new Muslim classes," Aliyah said as she set the casserole dish on the counter. "Maybe you can go to those?"

"I kind of wanted one-on-one, you know?" Jasmine said hesitantly. "I'd feel strange sitting in class with a bunch of strangers."

"I see…"

"So do you think you can help?"

Aliyah kneeled down to remove a nonstick skillet from a lower cabinet. "Not much," she said honestly. "But I can see what I can do."

"I really appreciate it," Jasmine said eagerly.

"When do you want to start?" Aliyah said, overcome with dread as she realized she was agreeing to precisely what she didn't want to do.

"This weekend?"

Aliyah set the skillet on the stove and poured a tad of olive oil in it, mentally kicking herself for agreeing to help. "I'm busy most of this weekend, so I'm not sure if—"

"I don't need much time," Jasmine interjected.

"O-kay…" Aliyah was unsure what to say.

There was a thoughtful pause.

"How about this?" Aliyah said. "I can meet you this weekend *insha'Allah*, and then I can introduce you to some other sisters who might be able to help. How does that sound?"

"That's fine…" Jasmine said tentatively.

"Good, *alhamdulillah*," Aliyah said. "Which day is best for you? Saturday or Sunday?"

"Saturday," Jasmine said quickly.

Aliyah wondered if Jasmine still planned to eat Sunday brunch with Larry's family after they came from church. "How does ten o'clock sound?" Aliyah said.

"Ten o'clock is perfect," Jasmine said. There was a brief pause. "Can you text me your address?"

Aliyah drew her eyebrows together and glanced sideways at the phone. She hoped Jasmine wasn't expecting a personal invitation to her home. "I'll text you the address to the masjid," Aliyah said. "We can meet there for about thirty minutes *insha'Allah*. But I won't be able to stay much longer because I have somewhere else to go."

"The masjid?" Jasmine sounded disappointed.

"Unless you have somewhere else we can meet," Aliyah said, trying to sound amiable. "I'm open."

There was an extended silence. "I guess the masjid is fine..." Jasmine said finally.

"Good, then I'll see you Saturday at ten *insha'Allah*," Aliyah said.

After ending the call, Aliyah chatted with Ibrahim about his day as she stood at the stove, heating the leftovers. As she set Ibrahim's plate of food in front of him and started to prepare her own, her phone chimed and vibrated from where it lay on the counter next to the refrigerator. Still holding her plate, she walked over to the counter and glanced at the screen.

*Any closer to your decision about Jacob?* Benjamin's text message said.

Aliyah hesitated briefly before powering off the phone and joining Ibrahim at the table. She didn't want to think about Jacob right then.

***

Friday evening Aliyah slowed her car to a stop in front of Salima's house for the Muslim Marriage Monologues gathering. Aliyah was running late because both she and Ibrahim had fallen asleep that afternoon and slept longer than they intended.

*Any closer to your decision about Jacob?*

Aliyah thought about her uncle's text message as she put her car in park. She still hadn't responded. She was supposed to visit Benjamin and his wife Saturday afternoon, but she really didn't know what to tell him. Aliyah couldn't deny that there was a part of her that was ecstatic about the idea of marrying Jacob. Other than the social awkwardness they'd face if they remained in their Muslim community, Jacob seemed like the perfect match.

But Aliyah couldn't bring herself to believe that this theoretical perfection would translate well into reality. As much as she shared Jacob's and her uncle's beliefs about doing things for the sake of Allah instead of for people, Aliyah wasn't convinced that she was up for another round of bullying from Muslims. Not to mention the humiliation she'd face once Deanna found out.

“Will Younus and Thawab be here?” Ibrahim asked as he unbuckled his seat belt, his eyes glistening in excitement as Aliyah looked at him through the rearview mirror.

She forced a smile as she thought of Younus and Thawab being bona fide brothers to Ibrahim. Her son would probably bask at the idea. “I don’t think so, cookie monster,” Aliyah said affectionately, unbuckling her seat belt. “But I think Haroon will be, *insha’Allah.*”

“Yes!” Ibrahim said as he opened his door.

“Whoa…” Aliyah said, laughter in her voice. “Wait for me.”

“Sorry, Mommy,” Ibrahim said, his body halfway out the door as he waited for Aliyah. She opened the driver’s side door, and Ibrahim shot out the car and ran to the door before she could call him back to walk with her.

After joining him at the door, Aliyah grinned at Ibrahim and rubbed his head before ringing the doorbell. He smiled back at her with the excited innocence that only a child could have. The door opened less than a minute later, and after offering a hurried greeting, Salima ushered Aliyah and Ibrahim inside. Salima told Aliyah that they had just introduced the first sister; she then led Ibrahim to where the other children were.

“Speak to me,” Aliyah heard a voice proclaim from the living room seconds before she joined the crowd of women. “Tell me what’s *really* on your mind. On your heart.” The woman was someone Aliyah didn’t recognize, but Aliyah felt connected to her at once. “Because I refuse to believe that a simple wedding invitation could tear your life apart….

I know he’s not the man you thought he should be.
And I know he’s not the ‘prince charming’ you envisioned for me
Oh, and I know, I’m not the daughter I *used* to be
But we already knew that, didn’t we?
What was it? Six years ago, when I said I believe in God now?
And maybe a year after that when I said I believe in Heaven and Hell?
And then I became Muslim, but you already knew that too
So I’m trying to understand what my being happy will ruin for you
Is it that our children will have funny sounding names?
Or that having a bearded son-in-law fills you with shame?
But don’t worry. You don’t have to claim him. I accept him as all mine.
But I thought that’s what the invitation said. Did you look inside?
Or how about this? Maybe you can just call him your daughter’s weird friend
Because I’m no more excited to introduce *you* to him
It’s not easy to know your future in-laws are casting you out
Before you even had a chance to find something stupid to fight about
But I get it. My marriage is like my religion. It’s all wrong.
It challenges your superior notions of right and wrong
But I wonder. Can *you* even keep up with what you believe?

I mean, since there's no God up there, and hence no rules, no clarity?
But you don't need to answer that. There really is no point
Because with atheists, there's only one possibility. Disappoint.
You have no critical thinking, or compassion, or an open mind.
You don't even have your own human heart on your side
But that's okay. The ceremony is still at end of June
Come if you like. But staying home is fine too.
But either way, we'll be there. He and I.
Saying I do and all that, planning the rest of our lives.
But I don't even know why I'm saying this to you
It's not like you even opened the invitation I sent you
Or at least that's what my mind keeps telling me
Since you don't— and *won't*
Speak to me."

There was an explosion of applause, and Aliyah forced a smile as she brought her hands together and clapped along with the rest of the women. But there was a part of her that had left the room while listening to the woman's words. The poem had touched Aliyah in a way that she did not fully understand. As the other sisters gathered around the woman to ask questions and compliment the poem, Aliyah excused herself and found the closest bathroom.

She stepped inside and closed the bathroom door softly then locked it. She stood still holding the handle, taking a moment to gather her thoughts. She then opened her purse and rummaged for her phone. She pulled it out and unlocked it before opening the text message conversation between her and Benjamin. For several seconds she stared at his words. *Any closer to your decision about Jacob?*

She hesitated briefly before typing her reply. *I can't marry him.*

But before she pressed send, her legs grew weak and tears filled her eyes.

*Speak to me*, a voice said in her head, and she thought of her parents and siblings and how much she missed them. She thought of Matt and Nikki and how they were starting a family together. She thought of Deanna and how she would probably never know happiness again. She thought of Mrs. Michaels lying helpless in the hospital. She thought of Salima losing her husband and two of her children overnight. She thought of Younus seeing those horrible media clips about his mother. She thought of Thawab running up to her and saying "Aunty Aliyah!" before giving her a warm hug. She thought of Ibrahim shouting, "Yes!" whenever he got to spend time with his friends. She thought of Jacob taking his sons and moving to another city…

And she thought of how unbearable it would be to know she'd never see him again.

*Speak to me. Tell me what's* really *on your mind. On your heart.*

Her gaze was fixed on the unsent message on her mobile screen. *I can't marry him.* The thin cursor blinked back and forth after the last word like a heart beating in uncertainty. The right arrow icon that would solidify the message remained dutifully in place, as if waiting for her command.

"But I'm scared," she muttered aloud as tears slipped down her cheeks. "I'm scared."

*But if you walk away now,* a voice in her head said, *you don't even have your own human heart on your side.*

There was a knock at the door, and Aliyah started, her thoughts interrupted.

"One second," she called out as she quickly set her mobile and purse on the sink counter. She reached forward and turned a faucet knob before filling the palms of her hands with water then washed her face.

*But I get it. My marriage is like my religion. It's all wrong. It challenges your superior notions of right and wrong.*

*But I wonder... Can* you *even keep up with what you believe?*

Hands shaking, Aliyah dried her face with a paper towel and tossed it in the small trashcan. She then picked up her cellphone and hesitated only briefly before pressing the right arrow icon. The swooshing sound confirmed that the message had been sent. Heart racing at the realization of what she'd just done, she averted her eyes from her reflection in the mirror as she picked up her purse and dropped the phone inside. She then pulled the straps of her purse over her shoulder before opening the bathroom door and rejoining the women.

## 22
## Then Where Are You Going?

Aliyah dreamt that she was in *sujood*, her forehead resting on the soft grass of a lush green field as she prayed to Allah. She remained in prayerful prostration as the field expanded and stretched beneath her. "*Fabi-ayyi aalaa'e rabbikumaa tukadh-dhibaan*," a voice recited in a strong, beautiful voice. *Then which of the favors of your Lord will you deny?*

There was a sense of calm in Aliyah's heart when her eyes fluttered open in the comfort of her bedroom. As she recovered from the grogginess of sleep, she wondered if Jacob had already prayed *Qiyaam al-Layl.* Instinctively, she reached out to see if he was still lying next to her…

*What?*

Heart pounding, Aliyah sat up in bed and searched the darkness for signs of her familiar surroundings. It took several seconds before she was able to convince herself that she was fully awake and no longer under the inebriation of sleep. But even as her eyes adjusted and revealed that nothing was amiss, there was still the lingering feeling that she was married and had not spent the night alone.

*Any closer to your decision about Jacob?*

A feeling of sickness sat heavy in her stomach as she recalled her uncle's text message—and her response: *I can't marry him.* The brief text conversation with Benjamin seemed like something from the distant past, but it had been only the night before.

Aliyah leaned to the side and turned on the small desk lamp that sat on the nightstand next to her bed. Her mobile phone still lay where she had left it. She hesitated only briefly before picking up the phone and powering it on. She couldn't remember if she had replied to Benjamin's response: *Can't now or can't ever?*

*Can't now*, Aliyah read her reply after she unlocked the screen. But the cursor was still blinking after the last word, indicating that she hadn't sent it. Aliyah started to press the right arrow icon but withheld. *Pray first*, she said to herself. *Then tell your uncle everything that's on your mind.*

***

Jacob's mobile rang late Saturday morning as he was walking out the exit doors of the hospital after a brief visit to Deanna's mother. He withdrew the phone from his pocket and looked at the display. *Benjamin Nelson.* A sharp pain stabbed Jacob's chest. *Aliyah said no*, Jacob figured. A part of him didn't want to answer the phone. He and Benjamin had already spoken briefly after *Jumu'ah* on Friday, and Benjamin had said that Aliyah was having second thoughts. "But don't worry," Benjamin had told him. "I'm working on it. She'll probably come around, *insha'Allah*. She just needs time." But even as Jacob held on to the barest of hope, he knew that Aliyah didn't need time. She needed someone else, a man who could offer a peaceful, uncomplicated version of marriage life.

“*As-salaamu’alikum*,” Jacob said as he put the phone to his ear. He tried to sound upbeat, but he was so distracted by the melancholy he felt right then that he doubted he even sounded cordial.

“*Wa’alaiku-mus-salaam.*” Already, Jacob could hear the apology in Benjamin’s tone.

“Any updates?” Jacob said in lighthearted humor as he reached into his pocket with his free hand and withdrew the keys to his car.

Jacob heard Benjamin sigh. “I’m sorry, Jacob,” Benjamin said. “But she said she can’t…”

“*Alhamdulillaahi ‘alaa kulli haal*,” Jacob said. *All praise is for Allah in every circumstance*.

“At least not right now,” Benjamin added. “But she might change her mind. I can see if—”

“It’s okay,” Jacob said sincerely, interrupting Benjamin midsentence. As much as he wanted to marry Aliyah, he didn’t want Benjamin to belabor the issue. If there was anything Jacob had learned about women, it was that they disliked persistent men. There was nothing admirable about a man who was so self absorbed that he refused to accept no for an answer.

While some men prided themselves in “the chase” and contended that women liked to play hard to get, Jacob believed that any woman genuinely interested in commitment wouldn’t refuse a man just for the fun of it. “I like a challenge,” Larry would often say, but Jacob felt differently. “I *accept* a challenge,” Jacob would say. “If it comes naturally,” he’d add. “But I don’t necessarily prefer it. A relationship isn’t a game.”

“But she didn’t say no outright,” Benjamin said, “so I still think there’s a chance.”

Jacob creased his forehead as he pointed the keychain remote toward his car and pressed the button to unlock it. “What do you mean?”

“I’ll just send you the screenshots of our conversation,” Benjamin said. “Then you can let me know what you think.”

Jacob tried to temper the hope that he felt right then, but it was difficult. He wanted to remain levelheaded about everything in case Benjamin was being overly optimistic. “Okay, *insha’Allah*,” Jacob said, his nonchalant tone veiling his true feelings.

“Will you be able to make it today?” Benjamin said after a few seconds.

Jacob drew in a deep breath and exhaled as he opened the driver side door and climbed into his car. “I should be able to,” he said, shutting the door. “Is it still after *Dhuhr*?”

“Yes, *insha’Allah*,” Benjamin said.

“I might be running a little late,” Jacob said as he buckled his seat belt. “I’m just leaving the hospital now, and I have a few more errands to run. Then I have to pick up Younus and Thawab from Larry’s.”

“How is she?” Benjamin asked, his voice subdued in concern.

"Deanna's mother?" Jacob said.

"Yes," Benjamin said.

Jacob coughed laughter as he put his key into the ignition and started the car. "You know how they say near-death experiences draw people closer to God?" he asked rhetorically. "Well, I'm not convinced that's true."

"What happened?"

"Nothing significant," Jacob said tentatively. "Except she grew angry when I recited Qur'an."

"*SubhaanAllah*," Benjamin said in dismay.

"And she started mumbling all this stuff about the blood of Jesus."

"Allah guides…"

"Yes He does…" Jacob said as he opened the compartment next to his seat and took out the wire that connected to the auxiliary port. He set down his phone after connecting the wire so that he could hear Benjamin through the car speakers. "So I'm just going to keep praying for her."

"Pray for Valerie too," Benjamin said, his tone reflective.

Jacob immediately regretted his comments about Deanna's mother. He had forgotten that Benjamin's wife wasn't Muslim. "Is she open to Islam?" Jacob asked as he backed out of his parking space, glancing in the rearview mirror.

Jacob heard Benjamin sigh. "Yes and no," Benjamin said reflectively. "She's probably the most devout Christian in her family."

"Do you think that makes her more, or less open to Islam?" Jacob said as he drove out of the parking lot.

"In some ways, more. But because of her family," Benjamin said, "probably less."

Jacob frowned as he thought of his own family. "Family can make things complicated," Jacob said. "There was a time I felt my father was close to becoming Muslim, but I think my mother dissuaded him."

Jacob heard Benjamin chuckle. "Valerie tried to dissuade me too. It almost tore apart our marriage, but giving up Islam wasn't an option," Benjamin said. "At least not for me."

"Allah guides…" Jacob said, echoing Benjamin's words from earlier.

There was a thoughtful pause. "If things don't work out with Aliyah," Benjamin said, "will you look into other options?"

Jacob was overcome with melancholy at the thought. "What other options?" he said, lighthearted humor in his tone. "I don't think there are any more Aliyahs in the world."

Benjamin chuckled, but there was a tinge of sadness in that sound. "*MashaAllah*, I can't disagree with you on that one."

Jacob felt a lump develop in his throat, and he tried to distract himself by remembering that there was still a possibility, albeit small, that he could marry Aliyah one day. Whenever "one day" would be, only Allah knew. Jacob wished it were easier to extricate himself from the desire to marry Aliyah. He hadn't lived with her a single day in his life, and still he couldn't imagine life without her. It would be easier if the prospect of marrying other women appealed to him. But right then, a dozen beautiful women of high status, good character, and deep spirituality could offer themselves to him, and he'd say no to each and every one. Even if four of them would agree to be his wives all at once, he doubted that the prospect would appeal to him any more.

*This must be how love feels*, Jacob thought sadly.

He'd had his share of girlfriends before accepting Islam, and none of them stirred the part of him that Aliyah did. The closest he had come to what could be considered love was the relationship he'd had with Melanie in high school. As early as middle school, there was a part of him that knew what he wanted in a wife. He didn't always know how to fully articulate it, but he felt his wife would be "educated and intelligent, yet humble and reserved." And he'd spent most of his young adult life searching for that woman. But everyone he'd dated would have, at most, two of those qualities, and he'd started to wonder if such a woman even existed. When he became Muslim, his hopes were renewed, as he imagined that perhaps his past disappointments were due to the women not having Islam in their life.

It was thirteen years ago that, for the first time in his life, Jacob felt intensely connected to a woman he had never even spoken to. Ironically, it was the day he and his future wife had met; and Jacob had only reluctantly attended the MSA dinner that Deanna had invited him to. Yet till today, Jacob's fondest memory of that evening was of the woman in a green hijab. She had been leaning against the wall reading a book, oblivious to all the commotion and chatter around her. He remembered how her expression was one of thoughtful intrigue, as if the words on the page offered a perspective she hadn't considered before. *Educated and intelligent, and humble and reserved*, he'd thought to himself; and the realization seemed to spring more from his heart than his mind…

*Whatever misfortune happens to you, is because of what your [own] hands have wrought. But He pardons [and forgives] much.*

"*Astaghfirullah*," Jacob muttered in regret as he recalled the Qur'anic verse that most certainly explained his current fate. It was heart wrenching to realize that a moment of carnal pleasure—with a woman to whom he had no meaningful attraction—would render a lifetime of heavy consequences. Would that he could remove that filthy stain from his heart. Would that he could take back the moment and refuse Deanna's invitation. Would that he could go back and speak to the woman in the green hijab. Would that he could walk up to Aliyah today, right then, and make her his wife…

"What's that?" Benjamin's voice said from the car speakers, asking Jacob to repeat what he had said. Jacob started, having forgotten that he was still on a phone call with Benjamin.

"I'm sorry," Jacob said. "I got distracted."

"Well, I'll let you go," Benjamin said. "*Insha'Allah*, we'll talk more once you get here."

"Okay, brother."

"Don't forget to read the screenshots I'm sending you."

Jacob forced laughter. "I don't think there's a chance I'll forget that."

"Okay, then," Benjamin said, laughter in his voice. "*As-salaamu'alaikum wa-rahmatullaah.*"

"*Wa'alaiku-mus-salaam wa-rahmatullaahi wa-barakaatuh.*"

***

Aliyah arrived to the masjid at a quarter to ten Saturday morning. As she entered the *musallaa*, she told Ibrahim to pray two units of prayer before sitting down and waiting for her in the front section of the prayer area that was reserved for brothers. She watched as Ibrahim walked swiftly to a space near the *mimbar* and raised his small hands as if in surrender, signaling the start of prayer. Aliyah smiled to herself then silently recited a *du'aa* that Allah would bless her son and preserve him upon Islam. She then walked to the sisters' area and prayed two *rak'aat* herself. After praying, she sat down in the section where there was no partition so she could see Ibrahim while she waited for Jasmine.

There were about fifteen men and women scattered throughout the *musallaa* reading Qur'an and praying. It had been months since Aliyah had come to the masjid herself, and she was surprised at how peaceful she felt. She had imagined that she would never again feel comfortable in the masjid after the "hot Muslim mistress" rumors were spread about her. Oddly, since the moment she'd offered to meet Jasmine here, she had thought nothing about the rumors. But even now, as she remembered everything she'd gone through, she didn't feel anxious or ashamed. She felt only relaxed and at ease, as if she were returning home after a long absence.

A shadow of a smile lingered on Aliyah's face as she saw Ibrahim shake the hands of two older brothers who had been reading Qur'an. He then walked over to the small floor shelf and removed an English translation of the Qur'an before sitting down and reading himself. The scene touched a soft spot in Aliyah, and there was a twinge of sadness that she hadn't thought of her son when she'd made the decision to stay away from the masjid. Ibrahim wouldn't always be a little boy, she thought to herself. One day he would be a young man, and he'd need the company of Muslim brothers to help him hold on to his faith.

"Aliyah?"

Aliyah was removing the small Arabic-English Qur'an that she kept in her purse when she felt someone standing near her. She looked up to find Juwayriah looking down at her with an expression of confusion. An awkward smile formed on Aliyah's face. "*As-salaamu'alaikum*," Aliyah said as she set the Qur'an on her lap and reached up to shake Juwayriah's hand.

"*Wa'alaiku-mus-salaam wa-rahmatullaah,*" Juwayriah said, her handgrip loose and reluctant. "What are you doing here?"

The question sounded like a rebuke, and for a fleeting moment, Aliyah felt offended. But the feeling passed as quickly as it had come. Though the inquiry was ostensibly rude, Aliyah sensed that Juwayriah hadn't meant it that way. In that moment, Aliyah was reminded of her sister, Cassie, who was uncomfortable with open displays of kindness and affection. Perhaps Juwayriah too masked her vulnerability behind grimaces and harsh criticism. Perhaps she too felt the need to carry herself like she had it altogether, while she was fragile and insecure like everyone else.

Why hadn't Aliyah noticed that before? It was confounding how someone who once seemed so overpowering and threatening suddenly appeared so tenuously human.

"I'm waiting for someone," Aliyah said. She paused before adding, "You?"

"Girl, I'm here almost every day," Juwayriah said, waving her hand dismissively, a mixture of a smirk and a frown forming on her face. Aliyah sensed that Juwayriah was attempting to be friendly, as if to tell Aliyah she no longer harbored ill feelings.

"You know you don't have to be a stranger," Juwayriah added, lighthearted teasing in her tone. She kneeled until she was eyelevel with Aliyah so that her voice wouldn't carry throughout the *musallaa*. "Nikki told me you're still upset about all that Facebook drama." She rolled her eyes and waved a hand. "But girl, it ain't that deep."

Aliyah's lips formed a thin line in an effort to maintain a smile. While it was comforting to know that Juwayriah had a conscience, it was troubling that she wouldn't take full responsibility for her actions. It reminded Aliyah of high school, when attempts by bullies to make amends were merely alternate forms of castigation. "Why you gotta be like that?" they would rebuke those who avoided them. "Ain't nobody thinking about you like that."

Now, in the social media age, bullying took the form of blatant or passive aggression via online posts and tweets. On the rare occasions that bullies actually acknowledged wrongdoing, they made light of it by painting those they harmed as overly sensitive or paranoid. And like Juwayriah's "it ain't that deep," they favored condescending dismissiveness over contrite apology. *Why is it always the ones inflicting the harm that trivialize the extent of the wound?* Aliyah often wondered.

"Well..." Aliyah said to Juwayriah, "if it's on the record that the angels record for us, it *is* that deep." She offered Juwayriah a closed-lipped smile, purposefully shifting blame back to where it rightfully belonged. "At least to Allah," she added, surprised and pleased by the frankness with which she spoke.

Juwayriah coughed laughter. "Girl, I'm not getting into all that," she said, smirking. But Aliyah could tell Juwayriah was more embarrassed than amused. "I'm just saying we moved on, so you should too."

*Yes, of course,* Aliyah thought to herself in amusement. *Bullies also dictate how long* you *can hurt—while there were no time limits or conditions on their self-assigned prerogative to "call people out," even on things as petty as grammar and communication skills.*

"So no more Facebook posts?" Aliyah asked, raising her eyebrows as if in pleasant surprise.

Juwayriah twisted her lips to the side, lighthearted humor in that gesture. "I don't know about all that," she said, a hint of sass in her tone. "I still got my opinions. You know how it is."

Aliyah smiled knowingly. "And I still got my feelings," she said.

*Self-righteous,* the term came to Aliyah right then. That was probably the description that Juwayriah and her friends would adopt for her from now on. Aliyah's refusal to accept Nikki's botched apology, compounded with Aliyah mentioning to Juwayriah the Book of Deeds and her right to her feelings, would almost certainly earn her the label that had been effectively coined by people who wronged others. Reminders about their souls didn't inspire self-reflection or temper their dismissiveness of wrongdoing; the reminders merely incited their insistence on shifting blame to the ones they harmed.

"Girl, you a trip," Juwayriah said, friendly teasing in her tone. But Aliyah could tell it was Juwayriah's way of evading the issue.

"What's Deeja up to these days?" Juwayriah said, changing the subject. "I keep calling her, but her phone is off. I don't see her on Facebook anymore."

"I don't know..." Aliyah said, casting her eyes to the side. "I haven't heard from her either."

"Well, if you see her, tell her I'm trying to reach her," Juwayriah said.

"Okay," Aliyah said, opening up the small Qur'an on her lap and turning to the page in *Surah Al-Baqarah* where she had last read.

Juwayriah rolled her eyes playfully. "But let me get out of here," she said, standing. "I'm supposed to be helping with this new Muslim class."

"It's today?" Aliyah asked curiously, looking up from the Qur'an. The last time Aliyah had heard anything about the class was a year ago, and she had been hoping that the class was still Saturday mornings.

Juwayriah glanced at her watch. "It's supposed to start at eleven," she said.

"You might have a new student today," Aliyah said, grinning.

"Who?" Juwayriah said, creasing her forehead.

"It's a new sister named Jasmine," Aliyah said. "Or Yasmeen, as she calls herself now."

Juwayriah raised an eyebrow. "*Larry's* Jasmine?" It was odd hearing Juwayriah mention Larry's name, but then Aliyah recalled that Juwayriah had been at the restaurant when Aliyah herself met Larry for the first time.

Aliyah drew her eyebrows together, not wanting to reveal that she knew about Larry and Jasmine. "Larry's Jasmine?" she repeated as if in confusion.

Juwayriah waved her hand, a grin on her face as if enjoying a private joke. "Never mind," she said, turning and walking away. "*Insha'Allah*, I'll talk to you later," she said, glancing over her shoulder.

After Juwayriah left, Aliyah looked toward where Ibrahim was sitting and found that he was in an animated conversation with a few older brothers, who seemed to be enjoying the banter. Aliyah smiled to herself then picked up the Qur'an and started reading the Arabic and then the English.

*And of mankind is one whose speech about this world's life may dazzle you, and he calls God to witness about what is in his heart; yet he is the most contentious of enemies. When he turns his back, his aim everywhere is to spread mischief through the earth and destroy crops and cattle. But God loves not mischief. And when it is said to him, "Fear Allah," he is led by arrogance to [more] crime. Enough for him is Hell, and worst indeed is that place to rest.*

"O Allah, protect me and forgive me," Aliyah muttered a silent prayer as she reflected on how easy it was to respond to reminders about Allah and the Hereafter with arrogance.

*And of mankind is one who dedicates himself to seeking the pleasure of God, and God is full of kindness to [His] servants.*

"O Allah, make me amongst them," Aliyah prayed.

*O you who believe! Enter into Islam wholeheartedly, and—*

Aliyah's cell phone rang and vibrated, and she immediately set the Arabic-English Qur'an on her lap and reached for her purse, embarrassed that she'd forgotten to turn off the ringer before entering the *musallaa*. Aliyah rummaged for the phone and pulled it out before it could ring a third time. A number appeared on the display that she didn't recognize, and Aliyah assumed it was Jasmine's since she had not saved Jasmine's information in her contact list.

"Hello?" Aliyah whispered as she put the phone to her ear and ducked her head so that her voice wouldn't carry throughout the prayer area.

"Salaams! I'm here," a cheerful female voice said. "Where do I go?"

***

*I can't marry him*
*Can't now or can't ever?*
*Can't now*
*Why not?*
*Bc it's too much to deal w right now*
*When would be better?*
*Idk. Maybe 5 or 10 yrs*
*5 or 10yrs?!*
*Or 3 maybe*
*What would change your mind?*
*What do u mean?*
*If everything worked out how u wanted, how would it look?*

*Deanna is fine & the boys r happy*
*And if Deanna is never fine?*
[sad face emoticon]
*It's OK to think of yourself, Ally*
*I know but it's hard*
*Do u like Jacob?*
*Yes*
*Enough to marry him?*
*Yes but it could never work*
*Allah knows best*
*Yes He does and I think this is best*
*U sure?*
*Yes*
*OK*
*But I think J will make a woman really happy one day* [happy face emoticon]
*I wish that could be u*
*Me too*
*But?*
*LOL, Uncle B. But life happens. We already talked about this*
*OK Ally. I'll tell him isA*
*Thanx*
*Yw*

Jacob frowned thoughtfully at the mobile display from where he sat at the kitchen table in Larry's home. He set down the phone on the table next to him and continued eating the tuna sandwich in silence while he waited for Younus and Thawab to finish a video game they were playing.

"Visiting that woman ruined your day, huh?"

Tuna sandwich still in hand, Jacob turned and saw that Larry had entered the kitchen. A smirk was on Larry's face as he opened the refrigerator and removed an apple before joining Jacob at the table.

Jacob made a weak attempt at a smile as he set his sandwich on the glass plate in front of him. "No, I'm just thinking about Aliyah."

Larry exhaled in a single breath, as if to indicate that the topic was weighty. "Good luck with that, man." He shook his head then took a generous bit of his apple.

"I think I'm going to need more than luck," Jacob said in lighthearted humor. "She thinks marrying me will complicate her life."

Cheeks bulging as he chewed, Larry shrugged. "She's right," he said, his voice slightly muffled. He chewed and swallowed before adding, "But it's worth it, so I think she'll marry you eventually. Aliyah's a smart girl. She's not going to let you go."

Jacob coughed laughter. "She already did," he said. "Twice."

"You know how women are," Larry said, gesturing dismissively with the partially eaten apple in hand. "They keep saying no, hoping you'll convince them to say yes." He shook his head as if amused before taking another generous bite of his apple.

"I don't think so, man," Jacob said sincerely. "Or at least not a woman like Aliyah. If she says no, she means it."

Larry nodded as he chewed, his expression suggesting that he was genuinely considering what Jacob had said. "Maybe…" he said finally. "Aliyah isn't your average woman."

"No she's not," Jacob agreed reflectively.

"But you're not your average man either," Larry said. "So you both can come up with something that works for the both of you."

"*Insha'Allah*," Jacob added, but he didn't sound optimistic.

"*Insha'Allah*," Larry agreed.

There was an extended silence as Jacob finished his tuna sandwich and Larry his apple.

"So what's up with you and Jasmine?" Jacob wiped the palms of his hands together, removing breadcrumbs from his hands. "You're getting married, now that she's Muslim?"

Larry angled his shoulders so that he could see behind him, then holding the apple core, he lifted a hand as if preparing for a jump shot and released the core toward the open trashcan. Hand bent at the wrist for the follow-through, he watched as it landed in the bin with a soft thud. "Nope," Larry said matter-of-factly, turning back around to face Jacob.

Jacob's eyebrows rose in surprise, and a confused grin formed on his face. "You serious?"

"As a heart attack," Larry said.

"Why the change of heart?"

Larry pulled his head back in surprise. "Change of heart? Who said I *ever* wanted to marry her?"

Jacob lifted a shoulder in a shrug. "I don't know…" he said. "I guess I just assumed."

"You know what they say about assuming?" Larry asked in friendly banter, a humored grin creasing one side of his mouth.

Jacob laughed. "I think I do, bro."

"But seriously, man," Larry said after a few seconds, his voice subdued and reflective, "I don't trust her."

Jacob was silent for several seconds, as if lost in thought. "Because of what Mom and Dad asked her to do?" he said, a somber expression on his face.

"I don't know…" Larry contorted his face, as if finding difficulty expressing what was on his mind. "She's just too eager, you know?"

"In what respect?"

Larry grimaced. "To get married," he said. "But she was like that before I became Muslim, and it was annoying even then."

Jacob shrugged nonchalantly. "She loves you, man. What do you expect?"

An expression of distaste lingered on Larry's face. "It doesn't feel like love," he said.

"Really?" Jacob said, growing concerned at his brother's sentiments. "On her part, or yours?"

"Both, I guess," Larry said. "She's been talking to Mom about joining the business, and it makes me uncomfortable. I feel like she loves what I can offer her more than she loves me."

Jacob huffed as if he'd never considered the possibility.

"So I don't know, man," Larry said, slight frustration in his voice. "And now she's suddenly Muslim when she realizes I'm not willing to marry a non-Muslim or give up my religion?"

"Most people go through a mental tug-of-war before they accept Islam," Jacob said reflectively. "I know I did." He lifted a shoulder in a shrug. "So maybe she just finally gave in. Becoming Muslim isn't an easy decision."

"But she was trying to get me to denounce Islam, man," Larry said, his face pinched in distaste.

"Benjamin's wife did the same thing," Jacob said. "But they're still married."

Larry grunted. "Benjamin was married for years before he even thought about Islam."

Jacob nodded. "That's true."

"I was never convinced I should marry Jazzy in the first place," Larry said, his eyes distant and conveying disappointment as he shook his head. "She never really felt like 'the one,' if you know what I mean."

"I thought you really cared about her."

"I do…" Larry said. Several seconds passed in silence before the shadow of a smile formed on his face, suggesting he was about to make a wry joke. "But what's love got to do with it?"

Jacob chuckled. "Well, if you ask the world," he said, "*everything*."

Larry huffed and shook his head, the beginning of a grin on his face. "I don't believe that."

Jacob's lips formed a thin line, unsure how to respond. He was thinking of Aliyah.

"I just can't picture her as the mother of my children," Larry said, frowning doubtfully. "That can't be good."

"People change…" Jacob offered.

"Not really," Larry said. "We are who we are. The only thing you can change is whether or not you'll end up in Hellfire at the end of it."

Jacob drew his eyebrows together as if perplexed. "You don't think Islam changes people for the better?"

"It changes people for the better," Larry said tentatively. "So that's why I mentioned the whether you end up in Hellfire part," he said. "But it doesn't *change* people."

Jacob nodded thoughtfully. "So what is it about Jasmine that makes you doubtful?"

Larry pursed his lips as if carefully considering the question. "She's not always forthcoming."

"In what way?"

Larry huffed. "In *any* way."

Jacob didn't know what to say.

"You know how some people have this deep, spiritual conscience?" Larry asked reflectively. "Jazzy never had that." He drew in a deep breath and exhaled. "She's more opportunistic than anything. So if she's doing something, there's always a carefully thought out reason why." He shook his head as his eyes grew distant. "And man, *I* don't even know what the reason is half the time."

***

Jasmine looked different from how Aliyah remembered her at the mall. Her face was framed by an off-white *khimaar* that was carefully wrapped about her head and secured in place by a scarf pin, and she wore a knee-length button-up blouse (or maybe it was a dress?) that fell over a wide floral skirt.

"*MashaAllah*," Aliyah said, a smile forming on her face after she exchanged the salaams with Jasmine in the lobby of the masjid. "You look…"

"Muslim," Jasmine finished, a proud grin spreading on her face as she extended her arms, as if inviting Aliyah to admire her attire more closely.

Aliyah's previous misgivings about Jasmine faded as she realized how much care Jasmine had taken before coming to the masjid. Though Aliyah wouldn't think less of any Muslim woman based on her appearance, especially a new Muslim, Aliyah couldn't deny that it was admirable that Jasmine had taken the time to not only research proper hijab but to also learn how to wear it as well—and for her first trip to the masjid.

"So what do you think?" Jasmine said, glancing down at her outfit and pulling at the sides of her skirt so that it flared. She twisted her torso to the right and left before letting go of the skirt.

"I love it, *mashaAllah*," Aliyah said sincerely. "If I didn't know any better, I'd think you had been Muslim at least a year."

"Good," Jasmine said. "I don't like making a fool of myself, so I did my research."

"Where did you study everything?" Aliyah said as she walked toward the *musallaa*, Jasmine falling in step next to her.

Jasmine shrugged. "Books, blogs, YouTube," she said, "wherever I could."

"So do you need any help?" Aliyah said jokingly as she opened the door to the prayer area and gestured for Jasmine to enter before her.

Jasmine chuckled as she stepped inside. "I need *a lot* of help," she said, lowering her voice as she glanced over her shoulder at Aliyah.

Aliyah took off her shoes as the door to the *musallaa* closed behind her, and she immediately looked toward the men's section and spotted Ibrahim still talking to the brothers. She smiled inwardly, pleased that he was comfortable in the masjid. Jasmine took off her shoes too as Aliyah kneeled to pick up hers and place them on the shoe shelf.

"Do you know about *wudhoo'*?" Aliyah asked in a lowered voice after Jasmine too had placed her shoes on the shelf.

"Is that the ritual washing before you pray?" Jasmine asked.

"Yes," Aliyah said. "Do you know how to do it?"

"I've watched some YouTube clips about it," Jasmine said tentatively.

"Maybe we can start with that," Aliyah said.

"But I did the ritual bath before I came," Jasmine said. "Isn't that enough?"

"*Ghusl*?" Aliyah asked as she walked across the soft carpet.

Jasmine hesitated. "I guess..." she said. "I read I should do it before coming to the masjid."

Aliyah shrugged. "That's fine then," she said. "But it's not obligatory unless there's a reason."

"A reason?" Jasmine repeated, confused.

Aliyah sat down near the partition and motioned for Jasmine to do the same. She made sure to sit where she could see Ibrahim while Jasmine could be behind the partition if she wanted. "*Ghusl* is obligatory after you finish your menses and after having relations with your husband."

"Relations?" Jasmine looked perplexed as she sat next to the divider.

"Sex," Aliyah said, an uncomfortable smile on her face.

Amusement glistened in Jasmine's eyes. "That sounds like fun," she joked.

Aliyah cast her eyes to the side, the shadow of a smile still on her face. She found Jasmine's joking unsettling, but she didn't want to discourage the relaxed mood. "*MashaAllah*," Aliyah muttered.

"So Muslims don't have to remain celibate for life or anything like that?" Jasmine asked, humor in her tone.

Aliyah couldn't tell whether Jasmine was asking in earnest or jokingly. "No, *alhamdulillah*," Aliyah said, erring on the side of clarity and truthfulness.

"Whew," Jasmine said as if relieved, humor still in her voice. "Then it'll be just like old times when Larry and I get married, huh?"

Aliyah shifted uncomfortably and glanced toward where Ibrahim was sitting and saw that more brothers had entered and were reading Qur'an and praying. "Have you studied anything about *Tawheed*?" Aliyah said, intentionally changing the subject. She refused to entertain inappropriate joking in the prayer area, even if it was from a new Muslim.

"So I take it, talking about sex isn't allowed in a Muslim place of worship?" Jasmine said, a smirk on her face.

"Look, Jasmine," Aliyah said, exhaustion in her tone. "If we're going to—"

"*A'oodhu billaahi me-nash-shaytaanir-rajeem*," a youthful voice reverberated from the masjid speakers.

Instinctively, Aliyah looked to the front of the *musallaa* and saw a boy who appeared to be about ten years old standing at the *mimbar* reciting into the microphone. Everyone in the prayer area had grown quiet and was facing the front, their attention on the thin boy in the white *thawb* and skullcap.

"*Bismillaahir-rahmaanir-raheem*," the boy continued, enunciating every syllable in a measured tone. "*Edhash-shamsu kuwwerat…*"

Aliyah immediately recognized the beginning of *Surah Al-Takweer*, a chapter of the Qur'an she had memorized some time ago. She bowed her head humbly and listened to the beautiful, captivating recitation. As the boy finished, she glanced toward the entrance to the prayer area and saw Juwayriah standing at the door, smiling proudly, as if she had come only to hear the recitation before returning to her duties. Aliyah was confused momentarily when Juwayriah spread her arms wide. But a second later, Aliyah saw that the boy had walked toward Juwayriah and was met with an embrace. Juwayriah kissed the boy on the top of his *kufi* before releasing him and disappearing behind the door while the boy returned to the prayer area and sat down with the rest of the brothers.

"*JazaakAllaahukhairan* to our young brother, Bilal," a deep male voice said into the microphone.

"Are you okay?" Aliyah heard a soft voice say in a hushed tone. She turned and saw Jasmine looking at her with a concerned expression on her face.

Embarrassed that she had been unable to hide her feelings, Aliyah nodded quickly and averted her gaze, her face aflame in shock and shame. "I'm fine," she mumbled as she pulled her purse onto her lap and opened it absently. But she had no idea what she was looking for.

"He's one of our top *hifdh* school students," the male voice continued, "and he just finished the Qur'an last week."

"*Takbir!*" one of the men called out.

"*Allaahu'akbar!*" the crowd shouted in unison, exclaiming the greatness of God for the blessings He had bestowed on Bilal.

"I asked him to open up this *Ta'aleem* session for us," the man continued, "and I'm honored that he agreed."

Aliyah glanced up and saw that the man who was speaking was the masjid imam. *"But why can't we marry for our* nafs*?"* Aliyah had asked the imam so many years ago, when she had been indecisive about marrying Matt. *"My* nafs *has to live in the marriage. I don't see what's wrong with wanting something for myself,"* she had said to the imam. *"If you truly believe in Allah and the Hereafter,"* the imam had replied, *"a good Muslim brother is all you'd want in a marriage."*

Aliyah thought of Jacob and was overcome with sadness. *He was right*, she said to herself as she reflected on the marriage advice that the imam had given her.

It was just that she had been too disconnected from reality to understand that getting religious advice came with the implicit understanding that the weightiest responsibility rested on the shoulders of the one seeking it.

The imam hadn't been incorrect in asserting that ultimately marrying a good Muslim brother was what was most essential in a marriage. It was just that the definition of "good" was much more complex than Aliyah had initially assumed. In the context of marriage, the concept of *good* encompassed more than superficial—or even genuine—Islamic traits. It further included compatibility, mutual physical attraction, and the actual desire to spend your life with the other person. If any of those factors were missing, then the man (or woman) was not a "good Muslim" for marriage.

No, the imam was not completely blameless in the ambiguous advice he had given, Aliyah thought to herself. But ultimately, the person seeking the advice understood his or her situation best—and that person was the only one who had to live with the consequences of the decision.

Perhaps when Aliyah had mentioned to the imam marrying for her *nafs*, he had misunderstood her to mean marrying *only* for her desires. What if her mentioning marrying for her *nafs* had inspired in the imam a similar discomfort and concern that Jasmine's joking about sex had inspired in Aliyah? Naturally, he would want to point Aliyah in a more spiritually healthy direction.

"...and in this *Surah*," the imam continued, and Aliyah realized she had missed what he had just said, "Allah, *subhaana wa ta'aalaa*, is evoking for us a vivid image of the Day of Judgment, and He begins by mentioning when the sun *kuwwerat*. And this term indicates that the sun is effectively folded or wound up."

*Am I ready for this Day?* Aliyah wondered to herself.

"Then He goes on to mention how the stars will fall and lose their luster," the imam said, "and how the mountains will vanish like a mirage, and how the pregnant she-camels will be neglected, and how the wild beasts will be gathered together..."

As she listened to his words, Aliyah reflected on her life thus far. How much time and energy had she wasted stressing over the wrongs others had done to her? Or worrying about what others would think of her?

"...And Allah goes on to say, 'And when the scrolls of deeds [good and bad] are laid open. When the sky is torn away. When the Blazing Fire is kindled to fierce heat. And when the Garden is brought near, [then] shall each soul know what it has put forward...'"

Instinctively, Aliyah glanced in the direction of Juwayriah's son, Bilal, and she felt a pang of guilt in her heart. Whatever faults Juwayriah had—and they were many, no doubt, Aliyah thought grimly—she hadn't sacrificed her priorities or those of her children in the face of them. And in that respect, she was better than Aliyah, *mashaAllah*. Perhaps Juwayriah had as many (if not more) gripes with the community as Aliyah had, but she still came to the masjid and benefited from her fellow believers. She had enrolled her son in a Qur'anic memorization program, and she volunteered to help new Muslims.

*But what are* you *doing?* Aliyah asked herself in self-rebuke. *And how much Qur'an does your son know?*

How was it that Aliyah could go to work every day and work alongside people who disbelieved in Allah, alongside a supervisor who scoffed at religion and openly plotted against her and her Muslim brother, and alongside a colleague who was *known* for sexual harassment—all for the sake of a paycheck? Yet she avoided the House of Allah and her Muslim brothers and sisters—and for what? Yes, she had to pay her bills, but she also had to save her soul and the soul of her son from the Hellfire.

"...Verily, this [Qur'an] is the word of a most honorable Messenger," the imam continued translating the Qur'an, "endued with power, with rank before the Lord of the Throne, with authority there [and] faithful to his trust..."

*We put too much pressure on our imams and scholars*, Aliyah realized in regret. *No soul can bear the burden of another*, the Qur'an taught. Then why was it that Muslims expected so much from each other? She would stand in front of Allah alone on the Day of Judgment, so she should start taking that solemn reality more seriously.

"*Astaghfirullah*," Aliyah muttered in a low whisper, invoking Allah's forgiveness.

"*Fa'ayna tadh-haboon*," the imam recited in a slow, measured tone. "In other words," he said, "Allah is saying... 'Then where are you going?'"

***

Reem was quiet as she stared out the passenger side window from where she sat next to Sayed, who was listening to a Qur'an CD as he drove. The truth was, despite all of her ostensible firmness in supporting Mashael's decision to be with Sheldon, Reem was terrified that she was making a horrible mistake. What if Sheldon turned out to be a child molester or serial killer? Yes, he had seemed like a respectable young man when Sayed and Reem met him the other day, but that didn't mean much, did it? To all outside accounts, Reem's half brother Fahad was an upstanding Arab Muslim man.

"What's this gathering about anyway?" Reem said, turning her head to Sayed as she looked at him through the opening in her *niqaab*.

"Benjamin just wanted to have a barbeque before the end of summer," Sayed said.

"You sure it's okay that we invited Sheldon?" Reem said doubtfully. "You don't think Benjamin will mind?"

"He said I could bring a friend if I wanted," Sayed said.

"And they have accommodations for children?" Reem glanced to the backseat where Hana and Muhammad were sitting looking out their windows.

Sayed chuckled. "Accommodations?" he said.

"You know what I mean," Reem grumbled.

"Well, I'm sure children are welcome," Sayed said.

"Did you ask?"

"No, but with Americans, that's pretty much a given."

Reem frowned, unsure as she glanced at her children again.

"Most of them don't have live-in help or family that babysits for every occasion."

"I know that," Reem said, slight offense in her tone.

Sayed smiled as he looked at his wife. "You're welcome to sit with the children if that makes you feel any better."

Reem didn't respond and instead resumed looking out the window. She knew why Sayed felt the need to reassure her, and it was difficult to accept that she actually needed the reassurance. Dr. Goldstein had told Reem that it was natural to have trust issues after what she had gone through, so Reem reminded herself that her anxiety was natural. Reem had always told herself that the reason she allowed Hana and Muhammad to be cared for by only her mom was that she wanted them to preserve their Arabic dialect. But now Reem knew it was more than that. She didn't want her son and daughter to be exposed to anyone who could harm them. Reem doubted she would feel comfortable leaving her children with her own father, but since her father worked a lot and was rarely home (not to mention that he wasn't exactly fond of children), she was able to leave Hana and Muhammad with her mother without being weighed down by too much distress.

"Is Mashael coming too?" Sayed asked.

"She didn't say," Reem said, still looking out the window.

"Well, I'm sure Sheldon probably told her he's coming."

Reem cringed at the mention of Sheldon possibly speaking to Mashael without her family's knowledge, especially in front of Hana and Muhammad. But it wasn't like they hadn't heard their aunt mention Sheldon herself. Mashael wasn't one to hide her views.

Reem sighed. *Why couldn't Mashael have picked an Arab boy to fall in love with?* she wondered. Their parents would still be furious, but at least then, it would make a whole lot more sense than the confusing mess they were getting into now. Their parents were right. There really was no way to know if Sheldon's interest in Islam was sincere. And what if it wasn't?

"*Mumken…*" Reem said. *Possibly.*

"Hopefully, meeting some American Muslims will convince him to go ahead and accept Islam," Sayed said.

Reem groaned and rolled her eyes. She didn't like the idea of a religion becoming more appealing just because people who shared your nationality were part of it. "Hopefully, realizing Islam is true will convince him to go ahead and accept Islam," Reem retorted.

Reem felt her husband looking at her briefly, but she refused to meet his gaze. In her peripheral vision, she could tell he was grinning at her, and she didn't feel like amusing him right then. *I love you* too *much*, she heard his voice in her head. And despite her grumpy mood, she felt the tiniest hint of a smile find its way to her lips.

***

Aliyah left the masjid later than she had planned because she had stayed for the entire *Ta'aleem* session then introduced Jasmine to Juwayriah so that Jasmine could attend the new Muslim class from then on. Fortunately, Jasmine and Juwayriah seemed to like each other right away, so Aliyah imagined she wouldn't be asked to be Jasmine's personal teacher anymore. She doubted she would be a good teacher anyway. Mathematics and computer science were her forte in the teaching field, but she had absolutely no idea where and how to begin helping someone learn the basics of Islam.

But Aliyah was glad that she had agreed to meet Jasmine at the masjid. It had been a cathartic experience. Had she not met Jasmine that morning, Aliyah had no idea when she would have gone to the masjid. She still felt plaintive about "the Facebook drama," as Juwayriah called it, but the saga didn't bother her so much anymore. Aliyah had no idea if she was ready to forgive Juwayriah for the part she played in inciting gossip and slander about her, but Aliyah couldn't deny that, after today, there was a soft spot in her heart for Juwayriah. How could she not feel softened after hearing the beautiful recitation by Juwayriah's son, Bilal, *mashaAllah*? Aliyah thought to herself.

"We have a part-time and full-time *hifdh* program," the imam had told Aliyah when she had stopped by his office to ask about the Qur'anic memorization programs available for Ibrahim in the fall. "But the best option for a boy as young as your son is the full-time program," the imam said. "The part-time students are mostly adults, and though Ibrahim is welcome to join, there are more children his age in the full-time program."

"But what do they do about school?" Aliyah had asked.

"Officially, our full-time *hifdh* students are homeschoolers," the imam had said, apology in his tone. "But we do offer basic classes in mathematics, English, and science depending on their grade level. However, we tell our parents not to depend on these classes alone because they won't cover everything your child is required by law to learn."

As Aliyah slowed her car to a stop at a traffic light, she glanced toward the passenger seat, where a *hifdh* school pamphlet lay. Sadness weighed on her as she saw the photo of young children reading Qur'an in the *musallaa*. Though she was sure Matt would pay the tuition fee for the program, she knew it was unrealistic to imagine that she would have the time and energy to homeschool Ibrahim after she returned from work. Already, with her schedule, he would have to remain at the masjid for at least three hours before she could pick him up after work. Though it was a blessing that the masjid wasn't far from the college, she couldn't expect a five-year-old boy to be willing to study school subjects after waiting for her so long. And what would happen when she couldn't leave work at exactly five o'clock, which happened often?

*It could never work*, she thought in regret as the traffic light turned green. Unless she could quit her job, or work part-time at the most, enrolling Ibrahim in the full-time *hifdh* program just wasn't realistic. She had to pay bills so that they had a roof over their heads, so she should just forget about it.

"The brothers said I read the Qur'an really nice," Ibrahim said from the backseat, as if on cue.

Aliyah glanced at her son through the rearview mirror and smiled at him with her eyes. "*MashaAllah*, Himy," she said. "And maybe one day you'll know the whole Qur'an without even looking at it."

"Wow," Ibrahim said, beaming and grinning. "That would be cool."

Aliyah forced laughter, her heart warming at how her son found the idea appealing. "Yes, that would be cool, wouldn't it?"

As Aliyah turned her car onto the street of Benjamin's house, she heard the distant sounds of excited shouts and laughter, and she saw a line of cars parked in front of his house. She creased her forehead curiously, wondering whom Benjamin and Valerie had invited to the gathering. Aliyah had been under the impression that it would be relatively small and informal.

The sweet scent of barbeque tickled Aliyah's nostrils, causing her stomach to rumble in hunger as she and Ibrahim walked up the walkway leading to Benjamin's front door. But as she heard the bustling excitement coming from the backyard, she wondered if it was best to just walk around the house instead of knocking or ringing the doorbell. The front door opened just as she lifted her hand to knock.

"Aliyah and Ibrahim!" Valerie greeted them with a wide smile. "I saw you drive up."

Aliyah smiled in reply and embraced her aunt warmly, and Ibrahim did the same. "How was your trip?" Aliyah asked as she stepped inside.

"Wonderful," Valerie said, beaming. "I have to tell you all about it when we get a chance."

Aliyah glanced around the living room.

"Everyone is out back," Valerie said over her shoulder as she walked toward the kitchen. "I'll be out there myself after I finish preparing this chicken."

"Do you need any help?" Aliyah asked, following her aunt into the kitchen, Ibrahim closely behind her.

Valerie laughed. "Don't try to escape the excitement on my account," she said. "Ben has been asking about you for the past two hours."

It was then that Aliyah had recalled turning off her phone at the masjid after Jasmine had called. She hadn't wanted to risk any ringers or alerts sounding while she was in the *musallaa*.

"He was under the impression that you would be here earlier," Valerie said.

"I'm sorry about that," Aliyah said, a half smile on her face as she watched Ibrahim approach the open back door then push open the screen door and rush outside. She had agreed to come early and talk to Benjamin and Valerie before the guests arrived and to help prepare for the barbeque, but she had been so distracted by the imam's talk and wanting to enroll Ibrahim in Qur'an school that she had forgotten.

Valerie waved her hand dismissively and chuckled. "Don't apologize to me," she said as she removed a tray of marinated chicken from the refrigerator. "Talk to your uncle."

An embarrassed smile lingered on Aliyah's face as she walked toward the back door. "Okay…"

"I'll be out in a bit," Valerie said.

Aliyah stood looking out the screen door briefly and saw the edge of the pavement basketball court where it appeared like a group of brothers were in the middle of a game, but she couldn't see everyone from where she stood.

"*As-salaamu'alaikum,*" Aliyah heard someone call out as she stepped outside and let the screen door close behind her. She looked in the direction of the sound and saw Mashael approaching, waving a hand, a wide grin on her face. Dressed in a T-shirt and baggy jeans, Mashael looked happier than when Aliyah had last seen her.

Aliyah smiled in surprise. She hadn't expected to see Mashael here."*Wa'alaiku-mus-salaam,*" she replied once Mashael was in front of her.

"You missed it!" Mashael said, grabbing Aliyah's hand and pulling her toward where Reem and Salima were sitting on a blanket on the grass.

"Missed what?" Aliyah said, walking quickly to keep up with Mashael.

"*As-salaamu'alaikum,*" Salima and Reem said in unison, lifting their hands in greeting as Aliyah approached.

"*Wa'alaiku-mus-salaam,*" Aliyah replied before turning her attention back to Mashael.

"Sheldon said the *shahaadah*!" Mashael said as she sat down on the blanket and pulled on Aliyah's hand, urging her to join her.

Aliyah squealed as she sat across from Mashael. "*MashaAllah!*"

"Can you believe it?" Mashael's eyes glistened in happiness. "Now we can get married."

Aliyah's smile faded only slightly as she tried to maintain a pleasant expression for the sake of Mashael. Given Reem and Mashael's family, Aliyah doubted that it would be that easy, but she didn't want to dampen Mashael's spirits. Mashael's happiness was so consuming that Aliyah wanted to hold on to this moment, Mashael's face glowing and her eyes alight. There was plenty of time for reality to set in, Aliyah told herself. It didn't have to be now.

"When did he say the *shahaadah*?" Aliyah said, careful to keep the excitement in her voice.

"About an hour ago," Mashael said, her voice still giddy.

"An *hour* ago?" Aliyah repeated, her eyes widening in genuine surprise. "How did you find out?"

"Find out?" Mashael said, laughter in her voice. "I was right there when it happened."

"We all were," Salima chimed in, a smile of satisfaction on her face. "Except you of course," she teased Aliyah good-naturedly.

An excited grin still on her face, Aliyah shook her head. "But where?" She stole a glance at Reem, whose gaze was elsewhere, as if she wasn't particularly excited about joining in the discussion.

"Right over there," Mashael said, gesturing to a place behind Aliyah.

Instinctively, Aliyah glanced behind her and saw the barbecue grill about ten feet from her, where her uncle stood arranging the coals with a wood-handle spatula.

"At the basketball court," Mashael added.

Still smiling, Aliyah turned her body so that she could see the basketball court, and Aliyah immediately saw a man with blond hair and a beard with his hands high in the air as he moved from side to side trying to block a shot. But before she could ask Mashael if that was Sheldon, she saw that the man opposite him dribbling the ball was Larry, and feet from him was Jamil, who appeared to be signaling for a pass. Sayed was standing on the sidelines, appearing to be enjoying himself watching the game. And near the basket was Jacob. He was wearing a sleeveless basketball jersey and knee-length shorts.

Aliyah's breath caught at the sight of him. Cheeks aflame in desire and embarrassment, she looked away and absently noticed that Haroon, Ibrahim, Younus, and Thawab were running through the yard alongside Hana and Muhammad, playing a game that Aliyah couldn't quite process right then.

"Aliyah, is that you?"

Aliyah glanced toward the sound and saw that her uncle, grill spatula in hand, was gesturing for her to come to him. Still distracted by thoughts of Jacob, Aliyah got to her feet and was careful to avoid looking toward the basketball court as she walked up to her uncle.

"*As-salaamu'alaikum*," Aliyah greeted her uncle once she was close enough to feel the heat of charcoal on her face.

"*Wa'alaiku-mus-salaam wa-rahmatullaah*," Benjamin said as he set the spatula on a plate on the glass-topped patio table behind him. "Where were you?"

"At the masjid," Aliyah said, casting her eyes aside in embarrassment. "I'm sorry," she said. "I lost track of time."

Benjamin placed the round wire tray back on the grill then closed it. "What were you doing there?"

"I had to meet a sister this morning," she said, apology in her tone. "But then I ended up staying for *Ta'aleem*, and—"

"So you're going to the masjid again now?" Benjamin said, a pleasant expression on his face.

A hesitant smile formed on Aliyah's face as she met her uncle's gaze. "Yes, I think so..."

"*Alhamdulillah,*" Benjamin said, nodding and smiling. "I'm happy to hear that, especially for Ibrahim."

Aliyah glanced toward her son, who was calling out something to the rest of the children, and she felt happy for him right then.

"He was with you?" Benjamin said.

"Yes," Aliyah said, her eyes lingering on Ibrahim for a few more seconds. "That's what took me so long," she said. "I was trying to find out about their *hifdh* program."

Benjamin's eyes widened in pleasant surprise. "You're thinking of enrolling him?"

Aliyah's expression grew serious as she drew in a deep breath and exhaled. "I want to…"

"Then you should," Benjamin said. "This is the best time to memorize Qur'an, while he's young."

"But it's full-time," Aliyah said. "And I work."

Benjamin frowned thoughtfully as he looked briefly in the direction of Ibrahim and the other children. "They don't have a weekend program?"

"Yes…" Aliyah said tentatively. "But it's mostly adults, so I don't know if he'd feel comfortable."

Benjamin nodded as if in understanding. "I see…" he said. "But it's better than nothing."

"I know…" Aliyah said, exhaling the words. "But I really want him to be with children his age."

"Won't he be with children his age at school?"

Aliyah grimaced. "But it'll be public school."

Benjamin drew his eyebrows together in concern. "You're not putting Ibrahim in a private school?"

She shook her head. "I can't afford it."

"What about Matt?" Benjamin said, his words thinly masking his disapproval. "Won't he be paying?"

"I don't know…" Aliyah said. "We haven't spoken much about it. He didn't even offer to pay for Ibrahim's summer childcare."

"*Summer* childcare?" Benjamin creased his forehead in confusion. "I thought he was with Nicole during the week."

*Oh.* Aliyah hadn't told her uncle what had happened, she realized just then. "Nikki's having a difficult pregnancy," Aliyah said, "so she's on bed rest now."

Benjamin shook his head, as if having a difficult time understanding. "But you work full-time."

Aliyah coughed laughter. "I know… I was thinking the same thing," she said. "But Matt said it was too stressful for Nikki to have Ibrahim around."

"Too stressful?" Benjamin said, disapproval on his face. "That's her stepson."

Aliyah smiled knowingly and shook her head, but she wasn't in the mood to rehash the subject. "But *alhamdulillah*, Larry takes care of Ibrahim for free while I'm at work."

Benjamin raised his eyebrows suspiciously. "*Larry*?"

Aliyah laughed and waved her hand. "It's nothing like that, Uncle Ben," she said. "Trust me."

"You sure about that?" Benjamin said doubtfully, folding his arms over his chest. "Larry's a full-time businessman at his mother's company. I don't see how babysitting fits into that."

"He's already taking care of Younus and Thawab for Jacob," Aliyah said. "So it's not a big deal."

Benjamin's expression relaxed somewhat, but it remained doubtful.

"Here we go," a female voice called out, and Aliyah and Benjamin looked toward the house and saw Valerie coming outside carrying a baking tray of chicken.

Benjamin took the tray from his wife and set it on the patio table as Valerie went back inside.

"I don't like the idea of Ibrahim going to public school," Benjamin said as he opened up the grill and peered inside.

Aliyah sighed as her gaze followed her son for a few seconds. "I don't either…"

"You sure there's no way you can enroll him in private school?" Benjamin said as he arranged the chicken on the grill. "Or at least the full-time *hifdh* program you were looking at?"

Aliyah shrugged. "Even if Matt agreed to pay for everything, it's probably too late to apply for private school at this point. School starts in about four weeks, and those schools usually have waiting lists. Then I'd have to figure out a way to get him to and from school. But with public school, he can take the bus, and there are free after-school programs I can put him in so he's not just hanging around waiting for me until I finish work."

"What about the full-time Qur'an school?" Benjamin said. "Even if there's no after-school program, at least he's at the masjid amongst Muslims."

"But then I'd have to homeschool him," Aliyah said. "And I could never do that while working at the college." She huffed. "Not to mention helping him review his *hifdh* on top of that."

"What if you worked part-time?" Benjamin said, still arranging the chicken on the grill as he talked. "Then we could see how much you'd need to cover your bills after that."

Aliyah's eyes widened, and she shook her head. "I couldn't let you do that."

"It would be only until I had a talk with Matt," he said.

She pulled her head back in surprise. "You're going to talk to Matt?"

"Why not?" Benjamin shrugged. "Ibrahim is his son. He has to be willing to contribute significantly if he expects you to care for him full-time."

Benjamin was silent momentarily before glancing at Aliyah. "You know people go to court for things like this?"

Aliyah grimaced. "Not me…"

"Then you'll need someone to speak to him on your behalf."

She frowned and shook her head. "I don't feel right about it… Nikki will probably convince him I'm just trying to take advantage of him or something."

There was a thoughtful pause.

"Then maybe you should go ahead and marry Jacob," Benjamin said as if it were the most natural solution in the world, his gaze on the chicken he was arranging. "That way, you can be a stay-at-home mom and not worry about work at all."

It took several seconds for Aliyah to register what her uncle was saying.

"I know you said you wouldn't be ready for another three to five years," Benjamin said as he closed the grill. "But I'm sure Jacob would be willing to wait to live together until then."

Aliyah coughed laughter. "You can't be serious," she said, disbelief in her tone. "Nobody's going to get married and live separately that long."

Benjamin regarded Aliyah skeptically. "Would *you*?"

Aliyah pulled her head back in surprise and pointed to herself. "*Me?*"

"Yes, why not?" Benjamin said. "It was your idea."

Aliyah coughed laughter again. "I was talking about getting married period."

"But I thought the point was you didn't want to make any drastic changes to your life too soon?"

"That's true…" Aliyah said tentatively.

"This way, you can do that without the demands of a normal marriage."

A disbelieving smirk was on her face as she shook her head. "No man would agree to that."

"I think Jacob would," Benjamin offered sincerely.

"I don't think so," Aliyah said, still smirking. But even to her own ears, she didn't sound convinced that it was impossible. Instinctively, she glanced to where Jacob was dribbling the ball and running toward the basket, and in that moment, Aliyah remembered the feeling she'd had when she woke up that morning. Had that been some sort of sign from Allah?

"Well, he's not planning on marrying anyone else," Benjamin said. "So I think it's fair to say he's open."

"Who told you that?" Aliyah said, unable to temper the flattery and hope she felt swelling in her heart.

"He did," Benjamin said simply.

Aliyah looked toward the basketball court again, and her heart raced in excitement at the possibility of being married to Jacob while changing little of her life at the same time. "No he didn't…" she said, hope and doubt in her voice at the same time.

"I'm serious," Benjamin said. "We spoke about it this morning."

Aliyah didn't know what to say.

"He loves you, Aliyah."

Her cheeks grew warm at her uncle's words, and she looked away.

"And I think you love him too," Benjamin said, his voice soft in sincerity. "You're just having a difficult time admitting it to yourself."

Immediately, Aliyah thought of Deanna and felt a tinge of guilt. But oddly, the feeling was not as strong as before. *No soul can bear the burden of another*, a voice said in her head.

"If you have a difficult time thinking of yourself," Benjamin suggested, "then at least think of your son."

Aliyah bit her lower lip as her gaze rested on where Ibrahim was playing with the children.

*And when the scrolls of deeds [good and bad] are laid open. When the sky is torn away. When the Blazing Fire is kindled to fierce heat. And when the Garden is brought near, [then] shall each soul know what it has put forward...*

"What do you think?" Benjamin said.

Aliyah was silent as she reflected on whether or not any of her misgivings were based on what she truly believed Allah wanted for her and her son in this world, or in the Hereafter.

*Fa'ayna tadh-haboon?* Allah asked in the Qur'an. *Then where are you going?*

*If you're not following the path that Allah has laid out for you,* Aliyah asked herself, *then where are you going?*

"You sure he doesn't mind living separately for a few years?" Aliyah asked tentatively, glancing up hesitantly at her uncle. "I mean... That's not exactly what a—"

"I'll ask him now," Benjamin said, a smile of triumph on his face as he interrupted Aliyah midsentence. He turned his back and walked toward the basketball court before Aliyah could stop him.

Her face grew aflame in embarrassment as she saw her uncle waving to the brothers and calling out to Jacob. Instinctively, Aliyah rushed into the house, the screen door closing behind her.

"Is everything okay?" Valerie asked, a concerned expression on her face.

Aliyah had forgotten her aunt was in the kitchen right then. "He's asking Jacob to marry me," she mumbled, peering outside uncertainly.

"What?" Valerie said, laughter in her voice.

"Uncle Ben," Aliyah said nervously, folding her arms over her chest. "He's asking Jacob if he wants to marry me."

"I thought Jacob already wanted to marry you," Valerie said, confusion in her voice.

"Yes, but..." Aliyah's words trailed as she lost her train of thought.

There was an extended silence.

"Go wash your face," Valerie said, a maternal smile on her face as she looked at Aliyah warmly. "You look like you've seen a ghost."

Aliyah nodded absently and walked toward the bathroom.

***

"You serious?" Jacob said, his heart nearly leaping from his chest in excitement as he wiped the sweat from his head with the back of his hand, a disbelieving grin on his face. His first instinct was to make *sajdah al-shukr*, prostration in gratefulness to Allah. But he wanted to make sure this wasn't some sort of joke, though rationally, he knew that Benjamin wouldn't make light of something like this.

"Dead," Benjamin said, smiling. "At least for the next twenty minutes," he added, lighthearted humor in his tone. "But after that, I can't make any promises."

"So what are you thinking?" Jacob said, creasing his forehead in curiosity.

A mischievous grin formed on Benjamin's face as he held Jacob's gaze.

Jacob's eyes widened in disbelief as he translated the tacit message, but he couldn't keep from smiling. "You're serious?"

"Why not?" Benjamin said, a smile lingering on his face. "I'm here, so that takes care of her *wali*." He shrugged and gestured behind him. "And we have much more than two witnesses."

Jacob raised his eyebrows and shook his head. "If it's okay with Aliyah…"

"But just so you know," Benjamin said, humor in his tone, "you just agreed to let her be a stay-at-home mom before you can even live together."

"Whatever she wants," Jacob said eagerly, a disbelieving grin on his face.

"And for the *mahr*?" Benjamin asked, referring to the obligatory dowry that a man paid to a woman upon marriage.

"Whatever she wants," Jacob said again, shaking his head.

"You mean that?" Benjamin said, his voice serious.

"Absolutely."

"What if it's a million dollars?" Benjamin said, raising an eyebrow jokingly.

"Then it's hers," Jacob said.

"But do you *have* a million dollars?" Benjamin asked, laughter in his voice.

"No," Jacob said, coughing laughter. "But I'm willing to pay in installments."

"Seriously?"

"No joke," he said sincerely.

"Then let's have a wedding." Benjamin clamped Jacob's shoulder briefly before walking toward the house.

"Oh yeah," Benjamin said, gesturing toward the grill. "Keep an eye on the chicken in case I'm gone too long."

***

By the time Aliyah had washed her face and emerged from the bathroom, she was filled with nervous excitement. It was still difficult to believe what she had just agreed to.

"He's ready right now."

Aliyah looked up and saw her uncle standing in the living room as she entered.

"Who's ready?" Aliyah said, confused.

"Jacob," Benjamin said. "He's ready to marry you right now."

Aliyah's eyes widened. "Right *now*?" she said.

"It'll just be the *nikaah*," Benjamin said. "You can do a wedding party later. But we have all the witnesses, so that's taken care of."

"But…" Aliyah looked down at herself and frowned. "I'm not dressed for a *nikaah*."

Benjamin shrugged. "You look a whole lot better than Jacob," he offered. "And you smell better too," he added, prompting Aliyah to laugh.

"But we haven't discussed anything…" she said.

"He's willing to provide for you so you can stay home even when you're not living together," Benjamin recited as if from memory. "And he's willing to pay any *mahr*," he said. "But only up to a million dollars."

Aliyah laughed and shook her head. "Ha ha ha," she said, her tone flat, letting her uncle know that she knew he was joking. "A million dollars?"

"*Wallahi*," Benjamin said, swearing by Allah, the shadow of a smile on his face. "He said he's willing to pay in installments if that's what you want."

Aliyah couldn't keep from smiling. "What would I need with a million dollars?"

"How about we settle for a home in your name?" Benjamin said.

Aliyah started to refuse then thought the better of it. A home would be expensive, but it was definitely practical. "Okay…" she said tentatively. "But a simple home."

"Sounds good," Benjamin said, clasping his hands together then walking toward the door. When Aliyah didn't follow, he looked behind him. "You coming?" he said. "This *is* your wedding, you know."

***

After Salima had taken the children inside to watch a movie in the den then returned to be one of the witnesses, Jacob and Aliyah were married outside near the basketball court in Benjamin's yard. The *nikaah* was so brief and simple that Aliyah wondered for a moment if it had really happened. Her uncle had merely stood in the center of the yard as Valerie alternated between smiling at Aliyah and managing the grill, and he'd asked Jacob and then Aliyah if they agreed to be married. When they both said yes, Benjamin asked if they had agreed upon the dowry, and when they said yes, he said, "Then as the *wali* of my niece, I announce in front of Allah and the witnesses today, that Jacob Bivens and Aliyah Thomas are husband and wife."

Someone called out, "*Takbir!*" and everyone shouted "*Allahu'akbar!*" Or at least it sounded like everyone. Aliyah couldn't be sure. She was so distracted by her excited disbelief that she was only vaguely registering what was happening around her.

"Go take a walk or something," Benjamin whispered to them before joining his wife at the grill.

***

Aliyah was overcome with shyness as Jacob took her hand and walked her to the house. Her face grew warm as she felt the strength and firmness of his hand holding hers, and her heart pounded in excitement. He let go of her hand briefly as he held the screen door open for her as she stepped inside. He gripped her hand again as the door closed behind them, both of them conscious that the children were in the house. Eyes cast down, Aliyah followed Jacob through the living room and out the front door. At the end of the walkway, hand-in-hand, they walked down the street.

They walked for some time until they came upon a wooded park and sat on a bench next to each other. Aliyah was grinning, but she was still unable to look Jacob in the eye.

"Tell me the rules," she heard Jacob say as he continued to hold her hand. "I want you to be one hundred percent comfortable." Even the sound of his voice sent her heart racing, and she wondered if she would last even one year living separately from him.

She shrugged, still avoiding his gaze. "We'll take it one day at a time," she muttered, surprised that she found her voice.

"No problem," Jacob said. "I'll do whatever is most comfortable for you."

"Okay…" she said, a shy grin on her face as she looked at a patch of grass.

"But can you do me a favor?" Jacob said.

"Okay…"

"Can you look at me?"

Aliyah coughed laughter, but she still couldn't look at him. A second later she felt his hand softly gripping her chin as he turned her face toward his. Hesitantly, she met his gaze, and he held her face between his palms.

"You are so beautiful, *mashaAllah*," he said in soft voice, their gazes locked.

She cast her eyes down again, but he gently lifted her chin until she looked at him again.

"Can I kiss you?" he said.

Aliyah's heart raced in embarrassment, and she instinctively glanced around her, making sure no one was around.

"I don't mean right now," Jacob said. "But whenever."

Aliyah smiled and nodded. "Now is fine too," she said, avoiding his eyes briefly.

A second later, she was wondering how she could have ever given up this beautiful moment for anything.

# 23
# A New Life

Aliyah held the door to the *musallaa* open as she watched Ibrahim pull off his shoes and place them on the designated shelf before walking swiftly to join the group of boys sitting on the carpet of the prayer area. Each boy held a Qur'an in his lap and recited quietly, the collective sound a melodious buzzing filling the masjid. A few boys rocked rhythmically back and forth in time with their murmured recitation. A smile lingered on Aliyah's face as she stepped back and let the door to the prayer area close as she turned and walked toward the masjid exit.

"*As-salaamu'alikum,*" a female voice called out as she stepped outside that late August afternoon. Aliyah looked up and found Juwayriah approaching the main entrance, flanked by her son Bilal and two other children.

"*Wa'alaiku-mus-salaam,*" Aliyah replied, lifting a hand in greeting.

"Bilal," Juwayriah said, her voice firm as she regarded her son, "take your brother and sister inside, and I'll be there in a second *insha'Allah.*"

Aliyah halted her steps, sensing that Juwayriah wanted to talk to her about something.

"How's Nikki?" Juwayriah said after the children disappeared behind the door. Her forehead was creased in concern as she met Aliyah's gaze.

"Nikki?" Aliyah shook her head in confusion. "What do you mean?"

"She had her baby a couple of days ago."

"She did?" Aliyah furrowed her brows. "I thought she wasn't due yet."

"She wasn't," Juwayriah said with a frown. "She and the baby are still in the hospital."

"I had no idea…"

"It's okay." Juwayriah waved her hand dismissively and shrugged. "I was just wondering if you'd heard anything. I haven't had time to stop by the hospital to check on her. But last I heard, they seem to be doing okay."

In her car, Aliyah considered texting Matt to ask about Nikki then stopped herself, thinking she should probably mention the issue to Jacob first. At the reminder that she was married, a smile toyed at her lips. It was still hard to believe. And now Ibrahim had a brother…or sister.

As Aliyah guided the car out of the masjid parking lot and headed to work, she wondered what she would do about her job as a college professor. Aliyah wanted to be a stay-at-home mother, especially now that Ibrahim was technically homeschooled, but she wasn't sure that it was wise to resign right away. Her tendency to overthink everything was probably making her paranoid, but she couldn't bring herself to relax in the knowledge that Jacob would take care of all her needs. It wasn't that she didn't trust Jacob. In only the few weeks they'd been married thus far, he had given her enough money to pay her rent for the entire year. But there was always that crippling *What if?* gnawing at the back of her mind.

*What if something happens? What if Jacob gets fired? What if he loses all his money? What if Deanna gets out of jail and wreaks havoc in our lives?*

*What if Jacob divorces me?*

Aliyah knew the last question was the most irrational of all. But it was only in the last few days that she was able to fully admit to herself that she was still getting over the shock from what had happened with Matt. Before the divorce, Aliyah had believed that Muslim men genuinely cared about Muslim women, or at least that the good ones did. Even after everything that happened between them, Aliyah didn't think of Matt as a "bad Muslim," so she couldn't make sense of why he'd treated her like he did. What kind of man divorces his wife just because his other wife asked him to? Or maybe Matt never wanted to be married to Aliyah in the first place.

*Jacob is not Matt.*

At the reminder, the anxiety loosened in her chest.

"You don't have to resign if you don't want to," Jacob had told her a couple of days ago. "I arranged your schedule so that you have only morning and early afternoon classes."

Jacob's words had given her a sense of calm and relief. "Thank you," she'd muttered through the phone, nearly exhaling the words. "I just don't know if I'm ready yet…"

"We can hire a private tutor for Ibrahim," he'd told her, his voice reassuring. "If you want," he'd added quickly, and Aliyah sensed he was hoping he hadn't offended her by the offer. He hadn't. She'd understood exactly what he meant. If she was going to be working fulltime, she might not have the energy to teach Ibrahim every subject.

Jacob's car was already in the faculty parking lot when Aliyah arrived to the college that Monday morning. It was the first day of classes, as it was for most schools and colleges in the area. Despite her decision to keep her job for the time being, Aliyah couldn't deny that she felt a marked sense of detachment from the college as she guided her car into a space near Jacob's. For each of the previous academic terms (spring, fall, and summer), Aliyah had come to work with a sense of anxiousness and uncertainty. She had been worried about her schedule, who the students would be, and if she'd impress her supervisor, colleagues, and students. But today, Aliyah was worried about none of these things. Even as she walked toward the college entrance, her mind was on Ibrahim's homeschooling curriculum and talking to Jacob after work. Right then, the only work-related concern she had was keeping her public relationship with Jacob professional.

"Good morning, Professor Thomas," Dr. Warren said as they passed in the hall after Aliyah swiped her badge to sign-in.

"Good morning, Dr. Warren," Aliyah replied, surprised by how genuinely carefree she felt upon greeting her supervisor. There was definitely something to say for psychological freedom, Aliyah thought to herself. She no longer felt bound to this job, and that was a good sign. Marrying Jacob had given her the internal emancipation she had sought for almost two years. Perhaps this was why marriage was half the religion. When you were paired with the right person, marriage provided the unfettering from worldly captivity and offered the spiritual and psychological freedom to focus on what was most important in life.

Aliyah unlocked her office, and as she pushed the door open, she was struck with a feeling of reminiscence. It was as if she had already moved on and was reflecting on all she'd learned from her experience as a professor. She set down her purse and powered on her computer, wondering what this feeling meant. Would she go ahead and resign after all? In the back of her mind, there was the reminder of what she would be giving up: a steady, dependable income of her own; more job experience on her résumé; and tuition reimbursement for her doctorate studies.

At the thought of giving up the opportunity for a PhD, Aliyah settled into her desk chair and bit her lower lip. She wasn't so sure that was a good idea. Perhaps she should stay at the college if only for this reason. Of course, she could obtain a doctorate even if she were not a professor there. But how would she pay for it? The likelihood of earning a full scholarship for her doctorate studies was slim, and she wasn't inclined to ask Jacob's assistance. Though she was sure he'd be more than willing to pay for her studies, she wondered if this was something she really wanted to use their own money for. She would rather use the money toward starting her own business, whenever that would be.

"Professor Thomas?"

Aliyah looked up and found Jacob standing in her doorway, the slightest hint of a smile on his face.

"Yes, Dr. Bivens?" she said, a grin twitching at her lips.

"I'm just doing my rounds to see if the professors in my department need anything."

Aliyah nodded and glanced around her office. "I think I'm good."

"You have any questions about your schedule or office hours?" Jacob asked.

She shook her head, a pleasant expression still on her face. "No, everything is pretty straightforward."

"I'll be meeting with everyone individually in the next four weeks, *insha'Allah*," he said. "So when you're free, drop by my office to let me know what date and time works best for you."

Seconds after Jacob walked away, Aliyah's phone chimed and vibrated, indicating a message. She withdrew the phone from her purse and unlocked the screen.

A grin spread on Aliyah's face at Jacob's message, and she quickly typed a reply. *Back at you <3*

Her heart fluttered in anticipation at the thought of talking to him after work. They had both agreed that their communication should be mostly through the phone until they could live together. The attraction they had for each other was too strong to meet in person on a regular basis. Already Aliyah had told Jacob they could live together after one year instead of three, and every day she wondered if she was underestimating her will power.

***

*Naomi is coming to visit this weekend.*

Aliyah's phone vibrated and the message appeared on her screen just as she slipped off her shoes in the foyer of her apartment. Mobile in hand and suspended in front of her, Aliyah's smile faded as she read her aunt Valerie's message. Aliyah had been laughing at something Jacob was saying as she closed the door and locked it, the earpiece still snaked to her ear as it had been during her drive home. Aliyah only vaguely processed the sound of pattering feet as Ibrahim rushed ahead of her to the kitchen.

"Aliyah?" Jacob's voice said.

"Uh… I'm here," she stuttered, trying to gather her thoughts. One hand was still on the bolt lock as the other held her phone.

"Is everything okay?" Jacob said, concern in his tone.

"Yeah, it's just…" Anxiety tightening in her chest, Aliyah felt the need to sit down.

"Aliyah?" Jacob's voice rose in heightening worry. "What happened?"

*Seriously?* she heard Cassie's condescending voice in her head.

"It's my mother…" Aliyah managed to say as she dragged herself to the couch and slowly let it receive her weight.

"Is she okay?"

"Yeah, yeah," Aliyah said quickly, her voice rising in an effort to allay his fears. "My aunt just texted me saying she's coming this weekend."

"*This* weekend?" Jacob said, echoing the surprise and confusion Aliyah felt right then.

Aliyah coughed in agreement. "I know."

"Did your mother ask you to come?"

"I'm not sure…"

There was an extended pause.

"You don't have to go if you don't want to," Jacob said, his voice soft in empathy.

"But it's my mother," Aliyah said, exhausted obligation in her tone. "I haven't seen her in over ten years. It would be wrong not to go."

There was another pause.

"Then I'll go with you," Jacob offered.

"No," Aliyah said quickly. "I mean," she said, apology in her tone, "I'm not ready for her to know about us. You know… with all that happened."

Jacob was quiet momentarily. “I understand,” he said sincerely.

“What if I come separately?” he suggested after a thoughtful pause. “As Benjamin’s friend?”

“That could work…” Aliyah said, anxiety easing in her chest at the idea of having some support. Of course, Benjamin would likely be there either way, but too often Aliyah felt that he didn’t understand the depths of the emotional difficulty she was going through with the family. Like Valerie, he seemed to think everything was as simple as Aliyah showing up uninvited at her parents’ house.

“I could bring Larry too,” Jacob said. “That way, it’ll be more difficult for her to associate me with you.”

Aliyah nodded, feeling better about the idea. “Okay, *insha’Allah.*”

“Did you talk to Ibrahim yet?” Jacob said after a moment’s pause.

At the shift in subject, the sides of Aliyah’s lips turned up in a smile. “I told him yesterday.”

“Really?” Jacob’s voice rose in pleasant surprise. “What did he say?”

“He just had one question,” Aliyah said, laughter in her voice.

“What’s that?”

“So Younus and Thawab will be my *brothers*?” She spoke in an excited whisper, imitating Ibrahim’s voice.

Jacob laughed out loud.

“Then he said one word,” Aliyah said, smiling.

“*Yes!*” Jacob said, mimicking Ibrahim.

Aliyah laughed and nodded. “Exactly.”

As if on cue, Ibrahim appeared in the kitchen doorway and looked at his mother, an uncertain expression on his face. “Can I have...” he began, his voice hesitant.

“*One* cookie,” Aliyah said, regarding him in compassionate sternness.

“Yes!” he said, disappearing into the kitchen and inspiring laughter in his mother.

“That’s the cookie monster, huh?” Jacob said playfully.

“Yes, that’s him.” Aliyah sighed pleasantly.

“What about you?” she said after a moment of silence. “Did you talk to Younus and Thawab?”

“Yes…” Jacob said tentatively.

Aliyah’s heart sank, and her smile faded. “They’re upset, aren’t they?”

“Not upset,” he said diplomatically. “Just…”

“Confused?” Aliyah spoke as if in self-rebuke.

“Aliyah,” Jacob said, coughing laughter, “it’s not you. Stop being so hard on yourself. They’re fine.”

“Fine is a euphemism,” Aliyah said, a tinge of accusation in her tone. “It’s almost always a placeholder for something worse.”

"Well, I don't mean it euphemistically," Jacob said. "They really are fine, *alhamdulillah*." The sincerity in Jacob's voice calmed Aliyah somewhat, but she couldn't help thinking Jacob was trying to spare her feelings.

"And I'm not saying that just to make you feel better," his voice said through the earpiece. "I really mean it. This isn't something I'd sugarcoat for you. It's too serious."

Aliyah exhaled in relief, having not realized she had tensed up so much. "So what did they say?" she asked, unsure if she really wanted to know.

"Thawab didn't say much of anything, to be honest," Jacob said. "So I guess you could say he took it well, at least ostensibly."

"And Younus?" Aliyah felt herself tensing up again. In her mind's eye, she saw Younus staring at her, that awkward expression still on his face.

"He asked if we did the *nikaah* at Brother Benjamin's barbecue while they were watching a movie."

Aliyah's heart dropped, and her face became aflame in mortification as she brought a hand to her mouth in shock. She slowly reclined so that her back was supported by the softness of the couch "*SubhaanAllah*," she muttered barely above a whisper.

Jacob forced laughter. "You can say that again," he said. "Talk about coming out of left field." He laughed again. "But it's all good, *alhamdulillah*."

"You told him we did?" Aliyah said, finding her voice.

"Yes," Jacob said matter-of-factly. "At that point, I didn't see any point in telling him anything different."

"*SubhaanAllah*," Aliyah said again, still registering the news.

"In a way, it made everything else easier," Jacob offered.

Aliyah contorted her face. "How?" she said challengingly. "Now he probably thinks all those rumors were true."

"I don't think so," Jacob said confidently. "That's reaching."

"But think about," she said. "If he—"

"He doesn't think the rumors are true, Aliyah," he said.

Something in the way Jacob spoke gave Aliyah pause. "How can you be so sure?"

"After he asked about the *nikaah*, I sat him down and told him everything," Jacob said. "I mean, from the very beginning," he added. "When I first saw you at the MSA dinner, how I met Deanna, why I didn't marry you then, how I asked about marrying you as a second wife, why I never—"

"Isn't that a bit much?" Aliyah said doubtfully. "He's only eight years old."

"Nine," Jacob corrected.

"But still…"

"Nine going on thirty-five," Jacob said, slight humor in his tone.

"Jacob, I don't know about this…" Aliyah said, feeling overwhelmed all of a sudden. "I don't think I can ever look him in the eye again."

"Why not?" Jacob said. "You didn't do anything wrong."

"But that's beside the point," Aliyah said. "Especially if Younus feels we did something wrong."

"I don't think he feels that way," Jacob said honestly.

Aliyah sighed and shook her head. "I hope you're right..."

There was a thoughtful pause.

"Aliyah…" Jacob said, as if trying to find the best way to explain what was on his mind. "Younus has always been very precocious," he said, "emotionally and intellectually. But his deep awareness has always been more about facts than ethics. So, really, you don't have anything to worry about."

Aliyah creased her forehead. "What do you mean?"

"I'm saying, if there's something more going on than he's being told, Younus will have an inkling about it," Jacob said, "and he won't rest till he knows everything there is to know. If there are any holes, he'll mentally fill them in with educated guesses and assumptions, and even then, that's only after he's done his own thorough research. But he won't accept ambiguity, fragmented truth, or dishonesty. His mind rests when he has the facts. But the facts themselves don't bother him as much as feeling as if he doesn't have all the facts. If that makes sense," Jacob said.

Aliyah nodded thoughtfully. "I see what you mean. I guess it's just hard to believe none of this will bother him."

"I didn't say none of it will bother him," Jacob said. "Younus has feelings, just like any other child. But as a general rule, he accepts that facts can't be changed. You just learn to live with them," Jacob explained. "When I say the ethics don't concern him, I mean it's not in his nature to insist that something be changed to fit what he feels should be done."

"But I'd hate to make him feel that his opinion doesn't matter."

"That's my job, Aliyah. I don't want you stressing over that," Jacob said. "Besides, I *want* him to believe his opinion doesn't matter. In the end, he is still a child, and I'm his father."

Aliyah wrinkled her nose. "I don't agree with that mindset though. Children aren't our property to do with what we want."

Jacob forced laughter. "I agree. And that's exactly why they need to understand where their opinions end and their boundaries begin. My marriage affects my children, so I'll definitely consider them in making that decision. But my marriage is not their marriage, and they need to understand that," Jacob said. "What kind of father teaches his children that they have the final word in his personal life? In my opinion, that's not showing empathy and compassion. That's emotional abuse."

"Emotional abuse?" Aliyah said, an expression of distaste on her face.

"Yes," Jacob said, his voice firm. "One aspect of emotional abuse is making a person believe they are responsible for your happiness or misery. Then you hold them accountable for it based on *their* opinions, choices, and behavior," he explained. "In the case of having a child decide whom I can marry, I'm not only emotionally abusing them, I'm teaching them that it's okay to emotionally abuse others."

Aliyah shook her head in genuine confusion, the wire to the earpiece moving with the head. "I don't see the connection," she said, doubt in her voice as she glanced at the phone she held on her lap, as if looking at Jacob himself.

"Or maybe emotional manipulation is a better term," Jacob offered. "But whatever the proper terminology, either way, that's an unfair burden to put on a child. Or yourself," he added.

"But how is it even manipulation?" Aliyah challenged. "If anything, it teaches children you really care what they think."

Jacob laughed good-naturedly. "No it doesn't. It teaches them that they have to parent you *and* themselves. From my perspective, that's wronging them. I'm a grown man, and I'd hate for my parents to put that burden on me. How much more a child? It sounds nice on paper, but, Aliyah, even you didn't ask Ibrahim's permission before you married me. And it would've been insane if you did."

Aliyah didn't know what to say.

"I guess the best way to see what I'm saying is to imagine your child says no," Jacob said. "Then when they grow up and understand the seriousness of the situation better, they begin to blame themselves if you're still single and unhappy. There aren't enough psychiatrist visits to fix that kind of guilt," he said. "Because it shouldn't have been there in the first place."

"I see what you mean," Aliyah said thoughtfully. "I guess what I was trying to say is, I just want Younus and Thawab to know that I care about their feelings, and I'm not just trying to throw myself into their lives."

"That's something only time and meaningful interaction can teach them," Jacob said. "It could never be conveyed in words, and definitely not in putting the burden of our personal decisions on them."

"That's why I'm uncomfortable with Younus knowing so much," Aliyah said. "I feel it's putting our personal burdens on him."

"Don't misunderstand me," Jacob said. "I didn't reveal anything that would incriminate you, me, or Deanna in his eyes. I didn't even tell him about his mother's lies and manipulation to get me to marry her."

"You didn't?" Aliyah's voice rose in pleasant surprise.

"Of course not," Jacob said. "I just told him that I didn't marry you because I was told you were engaged to someone else at the time. I didn't even say it was Deanna who told me."

"*Alhamdulillah*," Aliyah said, exhaling in relief.

"But because of all the online gossip," Jacob said, sad reflection in his tone, "it's possible he'll come across the information on his own."

"I hope not," Aliyah said sincerely.

"But the good news is that he'll likely chalk it up to media sensationalism," Jacob said. "Younus is well aware that the media mixes truth and lies just to draw an audience."

"That's good, *mashaAllah.*"

There was a thoughtful pause.

"But he *is* becoming a handful," Jacob said, laughter in his voice. "I'm considering pulling him out of school."

"Are you serious?" Aliyah said.

"I'm thinking about it," Jacob said honestly. "But we can talk more about it later because I want to know what you think."

"Did something happen?" Aliyah said, concern in her voice.

"No, it's just that his math and reading skills are on a ninth grade level, so he's really agitated and frustrated a lot at school."

"But it's only the first day."

"It's been going on for the last couple of years."

"Oh..."

"But we'll talk later *insha'Allah,*" Jacob said. "If you decide to homeschool Ibrahim full-time, I may ask you to homeschool Younus too. He won't need much one-on-one attention though, just guided independent study."

"What about Thawab?"

"For now, the Muslim school seems like the best option for him," Jacob said. "But we'll see *insha'Allah.*"

"Okay."

***

Friday night, after ringing the doorbell, Aliyah stood outside the door to Salima's home to attend Muslim Marriage Monologues for the first time since her marriage to Jacob. When the door opened, and Aliyah stepped past the threshold, the noise level rose as the ululations often used by Arabs to express extreme excitement reverberated throughout the house. An uncertain smile spread on Aliyah's face as she saw a group of about a dozen women beaming at her, most of them with one hand shading their mouths as their tongues moved in ululation. Salima grinned as she shut the door and locked it, and Aliyah met Salima's gaze with a puzzled and concerned expression on her face. Aliyah had hoped that the community hadn't yet heard about the marriage.

"Sorry," Salima whispered. "I didn't tell anyone. But word spread fast, and the sisters insisted on doing something for you."

"It's okay," Aliyah whispered back, waving her hand dismissively. "I don't mind." Oddly, Aliyah found that this was her true sentiment.

"I canceled the Monologues though," Salima said, her voice still low. "I didn't want anyone to come who hadn't heard about the *nikaah* yet."

"Thank you," Aliyah said honestly.

"Where's Ibrahim?" Salima said, forehead creased curiously.

"With Younus and Thawab," Aliyah said.

A knowing smile formed on one side of Salima's mouth. "You mean with Jacob."

Aliyah laughed as she followed Salima into the living room as the ululating died down. Immediately, the rhythmic pounding of a drum started, and sisters began to dance. Aliyah did a double take when she saw Reem and Mashael amongst them. Aliyah almost didn't recognize Reem because her hair was uncovered. When their gazes met, Reem grinned and ululated for a few seconds then moved her hips to the drumming, keeping her smiling eyes on Aliyah, and Mashael followed suit. Aliyah laughed before approaching them, exchanging salaams, and pulling them into a brief embrace.

"You look so good, *mashaAllah*," Salima said, appearing at Aliyah's side.

Aliyah glanced down at herself and frowned good-naturedly. "I'm not even dressed up."

Salima waved her hand dismissively. "Nobody is," she said. "But I wasn't talking about your outfit. I was talking about you." She grinned. "You're glowing.

"Really?" Aliyah averted her gaze momentarily. "I don't feel like I'm glowing."

"Are you happy?" Salima asked, still smiling.

At the thought of Jacob actually being her husband, Aliyah was overcome with so much joy that she couldn't find the words for it. It was still difficult to believe that it was really happening. "Yes," she said, unable to keep from grinning herself.

"Come on," Salima said, grabbing Aliyah's hand and pulling her where the sisters were moving to the rhythm of the drum. "Let's dance."

Aliyah felt a tinge of apprehension as Salima danced in front of her, holding one of Aliyah's hands at the same time. It had been a long time since Aliyah danced in front of people. Usually, her dancing was confined to the privacy of her home when she was exercising alone. Even when Reem had accompanied her during workout routines, Aliyah had merely followed the DVD program. It was difficult to fight the anxiety she'd battled for years in relaxed social settings. She always felt safer in structured environments or when she knew exactly what she was expected to do or say.

"Jamil asked me the oddest question the other day," Salima said later that evening when most of the sisters had gone home. She sat next to Aliyah, who was at the dining room table finishing the last bit of baklava, mentally preparing to leave herself. It had taken every bit of willpower to have stayed as long as she did. Aliyah had been looking forward to spending time with Jacob though neither he nor she had made any definite plans. Since their children now knew of their marriage, it would no longer be inappropriate for them to visit each other at home, though of course they still planned to interact primarily on the phone until they were ready to live together.

"What's that?" Aliyah said without looking up as she lifted the half-eaten diamond shaped baklava to her mouth. She discreetly glanced at her wristwatch as she chewed and lifted a cloth napkin to wipe the flaky crust from the tips of her fingers.

"He asked what I thought of Larry." The laughter in Salima's voice made Aliyah sense that Jamil's inquiry had made Salima both uncomfortable and confused.

Aliyah creased her forehead and met Salima's gaze, a question in her eyes as a smirk formed at her lips. "You mean…?"

"Girl, I know." Salima grinned in disbelief, breaking eye contact with Aliyah to smooth out the wrinkles on the tablecloth with the flat of her palms. "I was like, 'Boy, are you crazy? I'm old enough to be his mother.'"

The brief silence that followed was filled with the chatter of the remaining few sisters who were in the living room engrossed in a conversation of their own. In that moment, Aliyah knew that Salima was gauging Aliyah's approval more than she was asking her advice.

"His mother?" Aliyah said, still smirking, eyebrows raised.

"Well his older sister, at least," Salima said in playful defensiveness. "I have gray coming in."

"I do too," Aliyah said matter-of-factly. She shrugged. "But what difference does it make? Apparently, Larry doesn't care."

"How could he?" Salima coughed laughter. "He's never seen my hair."

"I don't think he cares," Aliyah said sincerely. "What he sees in you isn't superficial."

Salima's gaze became distant, and she frowned thoughtfully as she ran her palms over the tablecloth again though it was already flattened and free of wrinkles. "I wanted to be with Mikaeel in *Jannah*," she said, barely above a whisper.

Aliyah immediately knew that Mikaeel had been Salima's husband. At the mention of him, Aliyah didn't know what to say. Before that moment, he'd only been a concept, a symbol of Salima's pain. But hearing his name made it feel as if he had left the room only hours before.

Aliyah was silent, unsure what to say. There was nothing she could think of that could make it better for Salima, but she felt she should at least try. "Maybe you still can be with him in Paradise," Aliyah offered.

Salima sighed. "I've considered that," she said tentatively. "Over the years, I mean. And at first, it really mattered to me, you know, that I could be with Mikaeel, even if I married again." She shrugged dejectedly. "But what scares me now is, I'm not sure I care so much anymore."

***

"I'm sorry I'm running late," Aliyah said as she drove to Jacob's home to pick up Ibrahim after leaving Salima's.

"It's no problem," Jacob's voice said through the earpiece. "Just use the key. I'm in my office doing some work. The boys are in the playroom."

A tinge of guilt pinched Aliyah as she was reminded of the house key that Jacob had given her a couple of weeks ago. "For emergencies," he'd explained. She felt uncomfortable accepting a key to Jacob's home when she hadn't given him one to hers. "Ibrahim has my extra key," she'd told Jacob apologetically. "So if you ever need it…" Her voice had trailed awkwardly. Jacob had chuckled. "It's okay," he'd told her. "I just wanted you to have mine in case you ever need it for anything."

As Aliyah turned her car into the driveway of Jacob's home, a sense of sadness weighed on her as she thought of Deanna. It was a distant feeling, resignation mingled with grief. But there was no lingering shame for arriving at the home as Jacob's wife. She didn't even have the anxiety she'd had when she came to the house to pick up Ibrahim from Larry. Aliyah still felt bad for what had happened in her friendship with Deanna, but not for marrying Jacob.

These new feelings surprised Aliyah, but pleasantly. A faint, hesitant smile formed at her lips, a small but not insignificant reflection of the pride she felt in herself for her emotional growth. For perhaps the first time in her life, Aliyah was living out what was best for her, regardless of what others thought, and she didn't feel guilty about it.

A twinge of gloating pride surged at the thought of Deanna one day finding out that Aliyah was married to Jacob. For years, Deanna had plotted in tireless cruelty to ensure that her best friend would be denied the opportunity to marry a good man or have a good reputation. But Allah had turned everything around—in a way that only He could do.

But the feeling of gloating pride passed just as quickly as it had come and was replaced with heart-wrenching fear. If Deanna was capable of sinking to such spiritual lows, then anyone was—even Aliyah herself. Deanna was no more or less a flawed human being than anyone else. So what was it that had catapulted Deanna into emotional and spiritual self-destruction?

The depths of *hasad* that must have been eating at Deanna day in and day out, Aliyah couldn't fathom. But, as it was with all sins of wrongdoing, the destructive envy that Deanna had allowed to overtake her had ultimately not harmed Aliyah at all. Deanna harmed only herself—and with her own hands.

*Whoever uses his heart as a weapon destroys himself first,* Aliyah had read somewhere. And how true it was.

The car idled in the driveway of Jacob's home as Aliyah took a moment to gather her composure in the face of these terrifying thoughts. Was she really that different from Deanna if she allowed herself to feel triumphant at the thought of Deanna learning about her marriage to Jacob? Aliyah wanted so badly to never give in to negativity and pride, but it was difficult. She wanted so badly to be forgiving of any wrongs she suffered, but was that realistic? Or praiseworthy even? Did she really have to "turn the other cheek" whenever someone transgressed against her? Did she really have to smile and always be patient through every wrongdoing she suffered?

Aliyah sighed. *Probably not*, she concluded in resignation of the complexity of life. But with Deanna, Aliyah was at least determined to try, if for no other reason than Deanna would always be Younus and Thawab's mother.

But still, Aliyah thought as she turned off the ignition, the reminder of Deanna's cruelty hurt—viscerally. That someone whom Aliyah had considered her best friend would betray her on that level, and consistently, she doubted she would ever understand. There would probably always be moments that Aliyah would grow angry with Deanna. *And that's okay*, Aliyah told herself. Some things were just naturally enraging no matter how much time had passed and no matter how much you strived to forgive.

Recently, Aliyah found herself engaging in mental confrontations with Deanna more and more. *How dare you*, she'd say to Deanna in her head. *How* dare *you.*

The old Aliyah would have berated herself for these thoughts, but Aliyah was learning to allow herself the emotional release. Of course, she still believed in the Islamic injunction to make excuses for her Muslim sister, but she now understood that there was a vast difference between negative thoughts based on pure suspicion and negative thoughts based on confirmed truth. The former necessitated not only a litany of excuses, but also withholding oneself from a negative reaction. Because, ultimately, in the case of suspicion, you didn't even know what had really happened in the first place. *Allah does not like the public mention of evil*, the Qur'an said, *except by one who has been wronged.* How much more, then, was Aliyah's right to what she expressed privately, with only her hurting heart as a witness?

Aliyah reached next to her and pressed the button to unlock her seat belt, overcome with paralyzing sadness at the realization that there was no way to escape the emotional pain incited by Deanna's calculated and sustained betrayal.

*Revenge is almost never good*, Aliyah had penned in the journal she had recently started keeping. *But payback is nice. Mainly because it comes with no effort on your part, just God doing His work. And you can sit back and smile, saying, "That felt good." Allah is indeed the Best Teacher.*

At the reminder, Aliyah's spirits lifted slightly, and a reassuring smile creased one side of her mouth. Everything is going to be okay, *insha'Allah*, she told herself. Because it made no sense to believe anything else.

***

"*As-salaamu'alaikum*," Aliyah called out as she cautiously stepped into the foyer of Jacob's home, softly closing the door behind her. The house was quiet as she dropped her keys back into her purse and turned the bolt lock.

*"Wa'alaiku-mus-salaam,"* a voice responded as she slipped off her shoes.

Aliyah turned to find Younus standing about ten feet from her. Cradled in both his hands was a large glass bowl of freshly rinsed grapes. The red and green clusters glistened under the dim living room light, dangling over the sides of the bowl. Apparently, he had come to the kitchen for a snack when he'd heard her let herself in.

"My dad's upstairs in his office," Younus said, nodding his head toward the stairs. His voice was flat and matter-of-fact, betraying no emotion. Aliyah didn't know whether or not this was a good sign. "I can let him know you're here."

"That's okay," Aliyah said, perhaps too quickly. "I can go up and find him."

Younus pursed his lips and nodded, and Aliyah wondered if her response had come off as cavalier.

"Are you going to live here now?"

The question was so unexpected that Aliyah pulled her head back in surprise. "No, of course not," she said, an edge of defensive humor in her tone.

"Why not?" Younus asked, the same emotionless expression on his face. Aliyah wished she could tell what he was thinking. She didn't know if he was interrogating her or showing genuine curiosity given their new circumstances.

"This isn't my house," she said simply, hoping the answer sufficed. She offered Younus a close-lipped smile and started walking toward the stairs.

"But you're our stepmother now."

Internally, Aliyah cringed at the term *stepmother* as she halted her steps and met Younus's gaze. "That, I am," she said, maintaining a cordial expression.

"Then why did you say this isn't your house?" Younus squinted his eyes, his expression conveying genuine confusion. Aliyah thought she detected a tinge of hurt in his inquiry, and she felt bad for not knowing the right thing to say.

"I don't know," Aliyah said after an awkward silence, exhaling the words. It was at that moment that she remembered Jacob saying that Younus is more interested in full disclosure than in passing judgment.

She lifted a shoulder in a shrug as an embarrassed grin creased one side of her mouth. "I guess I'm still getting used to this stepmother thing."

Younus nodded, the shadow of a smile forming at his own lips. "Yeah," he said. "Me too."

Upstairs, Aliyah tapped the back of her knuckles on Jacob's office door. Though she rarely had come upstairs whenever she'd visited Deanna, the times that she did, Deanna had pointed out Jacob's office so that Aliyah would not accidentally enter it. It felt odd actually standing outside his home office—as his wife. The irony made her chuckle.

"Come in," Aliyah heard Jacob call out. "It's open."

Aliyah turned the handle and pushed open the door. When she stepped inside and closed the door behind her, a smile spread on Jacob's face as he got to his feet. Within seconds, he was in front of her and pulling her into an embrace. Her breath caught as she felt the firmness of his chest and the strength of his arms around her. She inhaled the sweet scent of musk as she nuzzled against him and locked her arms around his torso.

"I miss you," his deep voice rumbled above her head, weakening Aliyah's resolve.

"I miss you too," Aliyah whispered, surprised that her voice was steady given the thumping in her chest. She could stay like this forever, she thought to herself, slowly closing her eyes to drink in the moment. Right then she wished she hadn't made the condition that they wait so long before they lived together. Though she'd never stated it outright, she knew that the implication of the wait time also included delaying consummation of the marriage. She wondered if there was a way to implicitly revoke that implication.

Jacob pulled his head back then lowered his face to Aliyah's until their lips met. He kissed her softly, and Aliyah felt as if her head were spinning for how weak she felt right then. She had no idea if it was the combination of all the tormenting back and forth before their marriage and the now extended wait time before they could be together, but the emotional connection that she felt with Jacob right then was overpowering. She doubted she had the resolve to even go home that night.

When Jacob pulled away from her and walked back to his desk, Aliyah needed a moment to gather herself. *Breathe in, breath out*, she mentally coached herself. It took several seconds before her breathing was steady enough to allow her to speak.

"What are you working on?" Aliyah said casually as Jacob settled into his office chair and pulled it close to his desk. But she detected a slight quiver in her speech, as if her voice needed a moment more to recover. She walked over to where Jacob sat and stood at an angle opposite him so she couldn't see the monitor.

"Take a look," Jacob said, gesturing a hand in front of him. He leaned back as Aliyah stepped next to his chair and looked at the screen.

"Is this some sort of grant proposal for the college?" she asked skimming the document.

Jacob grunted laughter. "The college? I think I've given them enough of my creative ideas," he said. "This is something I'm working on for myself."

"Really?" Aliyah leaned into the screen and read more closely.

"You're applying for a grant?" she asked about a minute later, standing up straight and looking at Jacob.

"I hope to eventually," Jacob said, exhaling his words. "But this paperwork is for my non-profit status." He paused as he looked at the screen.

"What do you think?" he asked, his tone suggesting he wanted Aliyah's honest input.

Aliyah frowned thoughtfully and glanced at the document on the monitor. "I don't know much about non-profits," she said apologetically, reminded of the non-profit foundations her parents had founded. But she had been too young to know about the required formalities. "So I don't think I can be much help."

"I meant the idea," Jacob said, "not the proposal format."

"Oh..." Aliyah raised her eyebrows and looked at the monitor again. "Is it to help needy children?"

Jacob nodded thoughtfully. "That's one way to look at it," he said. "But more like needy adults."

"That's really good *mashaAllah*," Aliyah said. "If it works out, I mean."

"It's focused on emotional trauma though," he said self-consciously, his gaze fixed on the screen. "So I'm not really sure how to put it in words for the proposal." He looked at Aliyah, uncertainty in his eyes. "Maybe if I had a name for it?"

"Emotional trauma?" Aliyah furrowed her brows. "What do you mean?"

An extended silence followed, and Aliyah wondered if she'd asked the wrong question. Jacob's gaze grew distant as he seemed lost in a disturbing memory.

"What inspired you to start the project?" Aliyah asked curiously, hoping to shift his thoughts. "If you don't mind me asking."

Jacob frowned thoughtfully. "It's fine," he said. But Aliyah thought she detected a self-conscious hesitation in his voice. "It's just hard to explain because I'm not sure exactly..."

Aliyah glanced around the room, and when she spotted a chair, she walked over to it and dragged it to Jacob's desk. She locked her gaze with Jacob's as she sat down facing him at an angle. She leaned forward, her expression letting him know she was listening.

Jacob shrugged as he averted his gaze. "But I guess the short answer is you."

Aliyah drew her eyebrows together in confusion. "Me?"

Jacob coughed laughter in an apparent effort to offset the vulnerability he'd exposed. "You made me realize there's more to hope for in this life than just something better after death."

## 24
## Troubled Waters

Benjamin opened the door to his home early Saturday afternoon, and Aliyah heaved a sigh of relief when she stepped inside and saw both Jacob and Larry sitting on the couch in the living room. She had seen Jacob's car in the driveway and had begun to feel anxious about her husband being Benjamin's only male company. She didn't want her mother to suspect anything about her and Jacob's relationship. Naomi was visiting her sister Valerie, so whomever Benjamin entertained wouldn't be Naomi's concern. But Aliyah wanted to be careful. She had no idea what her mother was up to, showing up suddenly after more than ten years of refusing to even answer any phone calls or respond to a postcard.

Aliyah released Ibrahim's hand as she kneeled to take off her shoes, and her son followed suit. After aligning the two pairs of shoes on the rack, she stood and creased her forehead in confusion when she saw a strange man sitting on the couch to the right of Jacob, Larry on the left. Her aunt Valerie sat across from them on the loveseat, but Aliyah didn't see her mother anywhere.

Aliyah's eyes scanned the living room then met her uncle's with a question on her face. He discreetly nodded his head in the direction of the hall, and Aliyah understood that her mother had stepped out briefly, perhaps to the bathroom.

Aliyah's heart hammered nervously at the realization that her mother was nearby. Aliyah had no idea what to do with herself. She didn't see any place to sit except on the leather recliner, but she assumed her mother had been sitting there. She stepped into the living room, a tentative smile on her face, Ibrahim clinging uncertainly at her side.

"I'm Joseph."

Aliyah started, her shoulders jerking. The strange man seemed to have leapt from the couch and appeared before her suddenly, offering her a wide smile. It took several seconds for her to register his outstretched hand as he leaned forward in a stance of eager cordiality.

"Joseph Daniels," he said. "Cassie's husband."

The words *Cassie* and *husband* didn't seem to belong together, though Benjamin had told Aliyah years ago that Cassie was married. At the time, Aliyah had imagined Cassie's husband to be a feral-type creature with an evil countenance and only slightly human features, much like Cassie herself existed in Aliyah's mind. Growing up, Aliyah had often been told that she and Cassie resembled each other, and in her infantile naiveté, Aliyah had actually taken it as compliment. It was hard to believe that Cassie, with her sassy attitude and downright cruelty even so many years ago, had been beautiful to Aliyah once upon a time.

But who was this man with a kind face and easy smile, standing before her as if he was honored to merely be in her presence? If he had not introduced himself as such, Aliyah would have doubted that he had any connection to her sister Cassie. Based on Joseph's amiability and charisma alone, Aliyah wanted to offer him a wide smile and eagerly accept his peace offering in the form of a handshake. Everything about him said *family*, real family. He gave off the type of warm, genuine vibe that made it almost painful to *not* greet him with an all-out hug.

Instinctively, Aliyah glanced uncertainly at Jacob, whose expression was one of polite amusement. But Aliyah could see in his eyes reluctant disapproval of Joseph's gesture. If it were Jacob's home, he would most likely have intervened to politely discourage Joseph from shaking her hand. But Jacob was supposed to be merely a friend of Benjamin's, ostensibly with no significant connection to Aliyah. Though his intervention could be interpreted as merely friendly, for Aliyah's sake, Jacob was opting not to take the risk.

"Nice to meet you again, Joseph," Benjamin called out from behind them, stepping between Joseph and Aliyah in one motion, causing Aliyah to stumble back slightly. In a brotherly greeting, Benjamin slapped hands with Joseph then shook his hand firmly before guiding him back to his seat on the couch. Joseph's grin grew lopsided in confusion as he moved awkwardly backwards, his eyes narrowed humorously as if expecting an immediate explanation for Benjamin's apparent joke.

"As you know," Benjamin said good-naturedly, the expectant grin still on Joseph's face as his body reconnected with the couch, "this is my niece, Ally. But we call her Aliyah. That's her Muslim name." He offered Joseph a polite smile. "Muslim women don't shake hands with men."

Joseph's face fell in embarrassment as he leaned back into the couch. "Oh, I'm sorry. I didn't mean to—"

"It's okay," Aliyah cut in affably, flipping her hand dismissively to lighten the blow. "It happens all the time."

"Cassie never told me," he said, an embarrassed smile twitching at one side of his mouth. "So I didn't—"

"Cassie never told you *what*?"

The voice was thunderous in its authoritative tone, the familiar sound immediately inciting fear that twisted into a knot at the pit of Aliyah's stomach. Even before Naomi came into view, Aliyah felt her mother's towering presence. It was like Aliyah was a child all over again and in trouble for something she had no idea she'd done but was going to pay for mightily nonetheless.

Aliyah stiffened as her gaze met her mother's. But the fear loosened at the sight of Naomi's thin frame and level height. Naomi's expression was stern, but her aging brown face was weathered with the taut pride that was the signature of one who hid spiritual and emotional weakness behind formidable strength. In that moment, Aliyah's fear dissolved into sorrow that was so pained that it permeated every limb to physical weakness, and Aliyah felt too weak to stand. *I don't want my mother in Hellfire!* Childlike panic suffocated Aliyah and constricted her chest.

"Come here, baby," Naomi uttered in a tone that teetered between rebuke and compassion. A thin smile fought its way to her closed lips, but it was apparent that even this slight expression taxed Naomi to the point of emotional strain.

Aliyah offered an equally hesitant smile, but because she was holding back emotion more than she was fabricating it. Aliyah embraced her mother, slowly shutting her eyes as she inhaled the sweet scent of her mother's perfume, relaxing in that gesture. The aroma made Aliyah forget her agony of moments before and incited in her the assurance that she had a family and that she was loved. She had forgotten how it felt to belong to something bigger than herself, a collection of spirits bonded by the cozy shelter once offered by one woman's womb.

But Naomi's arms felt like steel bars locked around Aliyah's torso. Naomi's body was a steel rod in Aliyah's grip, erected in a show of obligatory affection that a mother long absent could not withhold from her child. It was in that fleeting moment that Aliyah sensed a cold barrier drop between them, a silent but resounding thud confirming that the battle lines were being drawn and that her mother was there to win.

Naomi released Aliyah too quickly, and Aliyah felt as if her mother had pushed her aside after the few-second timeframe of the obligatory display had expired. Naomi's eyes immediately went to Ibrahim, and something in the way she looked at him incited in Aliyah a panicked protectiveness. The feeling was so powerful that she had to actually keep herself from snatching her son out of his grandmother's reach.

"Is this my grandbaby?" Naomi placed her hands on her hips, baring her teeth to Ibrahim in what apparently was intended as a disarming smile.

"Yes," Aliyah said as she looked, smiling, at her son. Her tone was soft despite the growing protectiveness she felt in her mother's presence. "His name is Ibrahim. It's Arabic for Abraham."

Naomi grunted, her thin fingers moving in dismissiveness as if swatting away a gnat. "I know that, baby." The disarming smile returned to Naomi's face as she kneeled in front of Ibrahim. "Your mother doesn't know your grandma can read," she said to Ibrahim. "I've seen all those beautiful pictures of you in my email." She pinched Ibrahim's cheek, causing him to draw back and stand at his mother's side, finding Aliyah's hand with his own. "It would've been nice if your mother took the time to come visit her mother," she said, still smiling wide. "That's what a good *Christian* daughter would do."

Annoyance surged in Aliyah's chest, and she struggled to maintain a respectful countenance. She gently pulled her son closer and leaned his head against her hip with the flat of her palm.

"But you wouldn't know anything about that, would you, Abraham? Have you ever read the Bible, dear? Or is your mother making you read that awful Koran?"

"Naomi, that's enough." Valerie was on her feet, clipping her sister's shoulder and firmly guiding her toward the recliner. "Ally hasn't even had a moment to sit down."

Naomi whipped her head toward her sister, the sneer on her face unambiguous in the message she intended to send. But she stiffly and begrudgingly allowed Valerie to lead her back to her seat.

"This is *my* house," Valerie said, her soft tone becoming firm and authoritative as she looked her sister in the eye, unblinking.

Naomi's body met the leather chair in one sudden, angry bending at the knees. Though Aliyah felt anxious for what was about to unfold, she couldn't contain the pride and gratefulness she felt at seeing Valerie shush Naomi, the older sister and the family's heavy-handed matron who was known to keep everyone else in check.

"And you will *not* defame the name of Christ in *this* house," Valerie said, hovering near where Naomi sat, her eyebrows rising as if daring Naomi to counter her. "If you want to make this about Christianity, then the least you can do is *pretend* to know the loving message that our Lord taught."

The room grew silent. No one had expected this reaction from Valerie, and both Naomi's and Benjamin's expression testified to that.

This was a turning point for the two sisters, Aliyah knew it just as certainly as if they had spoken it aloud. She couldn't help feeling a tinge of guilt for being at least partly responsible for this rift.

"I'm going outside to shoot around for a bit," Larry announced, pushing himself to his feet and heading toward the kitchen without waiting for a reply. In all the commotion, Aliyah had forgotten he was there.

"You have a basketball court around here?" Joseph asked, his tone high-pitched in an effort to show genuine interest in another topic. But it seemed all wrong, the talk of sports amidst what was unfolding.

The sound of the backdoor shutting resonated in the room.

"Out back," Jacob said, his calm tone as contrived as Joseph's question. He pushed himself to a standing position then gestured to Joseph affably. "Come on, man. I'll show you."

"Joseph will be staying *right* where he is."

Joseph was half standing himself when Naomi gave her ultimatum, her voice rising in its obdurate command. He slowly sat back down, undisguised disappointment on his face as he appeared to grumble something under his breath.

It was awkward and disturbing to see a grown man react to Naomi that way. Aliyah wondered what sort of power her mother had over Cassie's husband to evoke that kind of deference from him.

"You're the one who insisted on taking this trip," Naomi said, "so you're going to sit right through it."

It was at that moment that Aliyah recalled the conversation in which Benjamin first told her about Cassie's marriage. *"She married a project manager from one of your parents' youth organizations."* Naomi was Joseph's boss—and his mother-in-law. Aliyah couldn't imagine a more deadly combination, particularly when the woman was Naomi Thomas.

"The other children are in the den," Benjamin said, his voice barely above a whisper as he appeared at Aliyah's side and laid a hand on Ibrahim's head. Aliyah nodded without looking at her uncle, and he guided her son out of the room. In her peripheral vision, she saw Benjamin motion to Jacob, who nodded in understanding then sat back down.

"I didn't expect to—"

"Don't tell me what you didn't expect," Naomi said, cutting Joseph off midsentence as she sat on the edge of the leather recliner as if preparing to get up any moment. "You wanted to learn more about this side of your family." She grimaced as if something distasteful was in her mouth. "And here we are." She gestured toward everyone in the room. "Now, *learn*."

"Naomi..." Valerie's voice was a mixture of a warning and a peace offering. "Why don't we just enjoy ourselves and catch up with everyone? It's not every day that we get to see each other."

"Catch up?" Naomi hissed, her eyes narrowed into slits. "When I learned my baby left the church and joined the Moslems, that was all the catching up I needed to do."

Because she didn't know what else to do, Aliyah sidled to the couch and sat on the edge of a cushion, perched as far from Jacob as was possible. Her legs were turned away from him, the side of her thigh touching the base of the couch's arm. Anxiety squeezing her chest painfully, Aliyah sat still, hoping that by remaining quiet and unmoving her mother would forget she was there.

***

"What was that all about, man?" Jacob was looking at Joseph when he asked the question, his forehead creased in genuine curiosity, annoyance etched in his voice.

Heavy-footed and fuming, Naomi had made her grand exit only minutes before, Valerie begrudgingly in tow, and the sound of the slamming front door still seemed to reverberate throughout the house.

Aliyah sat quiet, still perched on the edge of the couch, stiff as a statue, her gaze fixed distantly on something beyond her loosely folded hands on her lap. It was painful for Jacob to even look at her in that state. It took every bit of resolve to keep him from pulling his wife into an embrace, kissing her forehead and cheeks and telling her everything would be okay.

Joseph coughed laughter, an embarrassed grin creasing one side of his mouth. "I don't know, man," he said. "I wish I knew."

"Valerie mentioned you called a few days ago, wanting to talk to me," Benjamin said from where he stood in the middle of the living room, arms folded. He was looking at Joseph, an intense but kind expression on his face. "Did that have anything to do with what happened today?"

Joseph shook his head as a grim expression shadowed his face. "I *guess* so," he said sarcastically, his tone conveying frustration. But it was clear that his annoyance was directed at his mother-in-law. "Cassie probably told her about it."

"Joseph," Benjamin said sternly, as if insisting that Joseph level with him, "what's going on?"

There was thoughtful silence as Joseph seemed to come to terms with his need to be straightforward with Benjamin. "I've been reading about Islam," he said finally, an edge of defensiveness in his tone. "And Cassie's threatening to leave me if I convert."

The room grew quiet.

"And I guess Dr. Thomas told her she'll take care of it," he added, referring to Naomi.

***

As they walked toward the tennis courts, Mashael was smiling so wide that it was contagious. "What?" Reem said, laughter in her voice, a question on her face as she narrowed her eyes through the slit of her veil and adjusted the strap of the tennis case on her shoulder.

Mashael lifted her left hand in front of her face then wiggled her fingers, the glint of a diamond blinking in the sunlight. Reem's eyes widened, and her mouth fell open behind the soft black fabric on her face.

"Let me see," Reem demanded good-naturedly as she reached up and yanked Mashael's hand toward her. Mashael giggled as Reem halted her steps to get a closer look. "*MashaAllah,*" Reem said, her voice barely above a whisper as she dropped Mashael's hand and averted her gaze.

"So you're officially engaged now, huh?" Reem said as she resumed walking toward the courts, her eyes straight ahead as Mashael fell in step next to her. Reem hoped she sounded excited for her younger sister, but it was hard to quell the jealousy that enflamed her heart right then. *Why does Mashael get the happy ending?* Reem thought pensively.

Yes, Reem was happy for her sister and had of course known this moment would come. She'd even had a hand in making it happen. But Reem couldn't deny that it felt so unfair. What had Mashael done to deserve escaping the trial of sexual abuse at the hands of their own brother and thus avoiding subsequent emotional trauma? What had Reem done to deserve suffering it?

"Yes." Mashael beamed in a full-teeth smile. "Isn't it crazy?" she bubbled. "I didn't expect him to buy me a ring until after the wedding."

*She doesn't even cover properly,* Reem thought bitterly. *Why does she get Sheldon?*

Reem stopped herself, reminded of what Dr. Goldstein had told her during the follow-up appointment. "You're going to have to be patient with yourself. The price of self-honesty after trauma is persistent pain and frustration. Sometimes it'll be directed at yourself, but sometimes it'll be directed at others, often toward those you love. When you feel this happening, just stop and tell yourself to be patient with yourself. Lashing out at others usually means there's a part of you crying out for healing. Find out what part that is, and tend to it. But take your time. The discovery won't happen overnight."

"When's the wedding?" Reem heard herself say, pleasantly surprised to hear genuine excitement in her voice.

Mashael's silence prompted Reem to repeat the question. "When's the wedding, *habeebti*?" Reem teased, hoping her playful tone would let Mashael know that she only wished her the best.

Mashael's face crumpled, and she looked as if she were about to cry. She turned her face away from Reem as they reached the only vacant court. She quietly walked over to the edge and stopped to unzip the soft case. As she withdrew her tennis racket, she kept her back to Reem.

Concerned, Reem quickened her pace until she stood next to her sister. She grabbed Mashael's bare arm just below the fabric of the short-sleeved polo shirt. "What's going on?" Reem said, her eyes narrowed and voice lowered so that no one could overhear. "Are you okay?"

Mashael clenched her jaw as she jerked her shoulder to release herself from Reem's grip. "I'm not talking to you about the wedding," Mashael said, cold defensiveness in her tone as she folded her arms, the tennis racket raised with the handle against her chest. "So don't ask me about it again." She was still avoiding Reem's gaze.

Behind her veil, Reem's face contorted. "*What*?"

Mashael met Reem's gaze, unblinking in defiance. "I said don't ask me about the wedding again," she said, making no effort to lower her voice. "I'm not going to talk about it with you. Ever."

Reem pulled her head back in shock and offense. "What is your *problem*?" she hissed, indignant. "How do expect anyone to support your decision, or even come to the wedding, if you act like this?"

Mashael grunted and rolled her eyes, a knowing smile on her face as she shook her head. "See? This is why I don't want to talk to you about the wedding. Everything is always about *you*, and how you can make someone's life miserable if they do something you don't like."

"You're the one flaunting your engagement ring. How am I wrong to ask about it? You're practically throwing your wedding in my face."

Mashael's eyes widened, a look of amused disbelief on her face. "Seriously? You're even going to turn my *happiness* into a slight against you? *Yaa salaam!* You are so self-centered."

"Then why did you show it to me if you didn't want me to talk about it?" Reem shot back.

"Because it's on my *finger*," Mashael said. "And the least I can do is tell you what it means, even if it's already obvious. But that doesn't mean I want to do wedding plans together."

"I never asked to be a part of your wedding!" Reem said, her tone laced in offense. "I don't even know if we'll *come*."

Mashael glared at Reem, hurt in her eyes, but she didn't say anything. Instead, she slowly turned around and started putting her racket back in its case. She yanked the zipper closed in angry jerks of her hand.

"*SubhaanAllah,*" Reem said in disappointment and rebuke as she followed her sister across the court. "So you're canceling *tennis* now? That's so immature."

"Really?" Mashael spun around to face Reem, causing Reem to nearly run into her. "Is it any more immature than ending your friendship with Aliyah? Or canceling Qur'an with her and everyone else just because they don't worship *you* properly?"

Mashael grimaced. "*Wallah,* sometimes I'm ashamed that you're my sister," she said. "It's not enough that you walk around *looking* like an extremist. You have to act like one too. And you have the nerve to say it's all for Islam. It's all for you, Reem, and only *you.*" She wrinkled her nose in disgust. "You dress like that and call yourself a Qur'an teacher just so you can feel better than everyone else. Because you know if you took off your hijab and stopped teaching Qur'an, you'll have nothing left you can say about yourself. Then it'll be obvious to everyone that so-called ignorant Muslims like me, Sheldon, and Aliyah are way better *people* than you."

***

As soon as Mashael saw Aliyah enter the apartment corridor, head down and feet nearly dragging while flanked by three energetic children, she knew it had been a bad idea to come. She had knocked on Aliyah's door a half hour ago, and when no one answered, she'd texted Aliyah to say she was at her apartment, hoping to drop by and chat.

*I'm on my way home now*, Aliyah had texted in response, *if you want to wait.*

A tired smile crept on Aliyah's face when her gaze met Mashael's. Mashael smiled apologetically in return and warded off the tinge of guilt she felt at the realization that Aliyah was being cordial for her sake.

"*As-salaamu'alaikum,*" Aliyah said, raising a hand in greeting. Her smile spread as she gestured to the boys. "Ibrahim wanted his brothers to come over."

"It's okay," Mashael said quickly, feeling bad for the apology she heard in Aliyah's tone. "I don't want to interrupt anything."

Aliyah forced laughter as if enjoying a private joke. "Don't worry about that," she said, waving her hand as she held her keys. "I welcome the interruption."

Mashael waited as Aliyah unlocked the door then pushed it open.

"Did you pray *Dhuhr*?" Aliyah asked, glancing over her shoulder as the boys zipped past them and pulled off their shoes.

"I can't pray," Mashael said, indirectly referring to her monthly cycle. Aliyah held the door as Mashael stepped past her and took off her shoes.

"Younus," Aliyah called out before the boys could disappear into Ibrahim's room. He turned and met her gaze, a question and slight irritation on his face. "Can you call the *adhaan* for us?" she said casually as she closed the door and bolted it.

Younus smirked in male pride and walked into the living room. Mashael smiled to herself as she watched Younus make the formal call to prayer. The sight made her eager to get married and have children of her own.

"Sorry to stop by unannounced like this," Mashael said after Aliyah and the boys finished praying and the boys had retreated to Ibrahim's room. Aliyah set a tray of snacks and drinks on the floor table before settling on the couch next to Mashael. Aliyah still had that look of exhaustion in her eyes, but her overall aura seemed more relaxed after praying. "But I didn't know who else to talk to."

A shadow of concern passed over Aliyah's face. "Is everything okay?"

"Sheldon and I are going to get married," Mashael blurted, "and I don't want my family there."

Aliyah's eyebrows rose, and her gaze became distant for some time. "Not even Reem?" she asked, still looking at nothing in particular. Mashael could hear the disappointment and concern in Aliyah's voice.

"Especially not Reem," Mashael said bitterly.

Aliyah shook her head in confusion as she met Mashael's gaze with her eyebrows drawn together. "Why not? I thought she was the only one who supported you and Sheldon."

Mashael felt a surge of irritation at the thought of Reem's hypocrisy. "She supported Sheldon becoming Muslim because she had to, but she doesn't support the marriage."

Aliyah look confused and disturbed. "Are you sure? Did she say that to you?"

"Yes," Mashael said irritably, recalling the numerous arguments they'd had before Sheldon became Muslim. "She wouldn't shut up about it." Mashael sighed and leaned back on the couch. "But she did say she'll be there for me, no matter what."

Aliyah's face brightened somewhat. "*MashaAllah*, that's really good."

"I guess so," Mashael muttered, unconvinced.

"Reem was probably just trying to be completely honest with you about how she feels," Aliyah offered. "It's normal to worry about someone you love. Remember, they don't know Sheldon like you do."

"And whose fault is that?" Mashael grumbled, folding her arms.

"Nobody's." Something in the soft way Aliyah spoke prompted Mashael to look at her. "Sometimes things just happen," Aliyah said with an almost imperceptible shrug, "and nobody wanted it to turn out like this."

"I just don't want the happiest day of my life ruined with their negativity and judgmental attitudes."

"I doubt Reem will be negative on your wedding day. She'll be happy for you *insha'Allah*."

Mashael wasn't so sure, but she kept her thoughts to herself. "We had an argument today," she said in a low voice, eyes averted. "And I told her never to ask me about the wedding again."

An extended silence followed, and Mashael sensed that the news made Aliyah sad.

"It's a blessing to have a family," Aliyah said, but she seemed to be talking more to herself than to Mashael. "Especially a Muslim family."

"I know," Mashael said with a sigh. "And I'm grateful for them. It's just..." Mashael tried to find the words for what she was feeling right then. "...I don't think of my family as real Muslims, you know?"

Aliyah drew her head back in surprise. "What do you mean?"

Mashael shrugged, unsure how to put her thoughts into words. "Islam is just something they use to guilt you into doing what they want. Especially my parents. They're always talking about the rights of the mother and father in Islam because they want to control everything I do, even my thoughts and feelings. But they don't really care about my soul." She grunted. "I doubt they even care about their own."

"That's a bit harsh, don't you think?" Aliyah interjected. "Don't they believe in Allah and pray?"

"Yes, but—"

"Then they care about their souls."

"But they don't even do everything they're supposed to. They're alw—"

"Do *you* do everything you're supposed to?" There was lighthearted amusement in Aliyah's tone as she regarded Mashael, a confused smile on her face.

The boldness of Aliyah's question stopped Mashael midsentence, and for a fleeting moment, Mashael was offended. But in that moment she became self-conscious of her uncovered hair and exposed arms and legs. Her very presence was an obvious answer to Aliyah's question, and she felt a flicker of shame for her appearance.

Mashael had always defended not wearing hijab by saying she was in America, not in Saudi Arabia. But right then she saw the hypocrisy in her own mindset and behavior. Why did she feel comfortable disregarding Allah's instructions about hijab but grew angry with her family for disregarding Allah's instructions about whom she could marry? No, the two crimes were not of equal magnitude, in Mashael's view, but they were crimes nonetheless. *Look not at the size of your sin,* a popular saying advised, *but at the magnitude of the One you're disobeying.*

"Nobody's perfect, Mashael," Aliyah said. "I'm not saying your family is right, or even that you have to invite them to your wedding. But if you don't want them there, make sure it's because you believe that's what is wisest given the circumstance, not because they're humans with faults just like you."

Mashael felt ashamed of herself all of a sudden, and guilt sat heavy in the pit of her stomach as she thought of how she'd spoken to Reem.

"But I don't want them there," Mashael said quietly, overcome with emotion at the honesty of her words. "I want it to be just me and Sheldon."

A thoughtful silence followed.

"What about your *wali* and witnesses?" Aliyah asked tentatively. Mashael sensed that Aliyah was trying to sound helpful instead of judgmental.

Mashael contorted her face. "So I really have to have my father and other people there?"

"You'll need someone qualified to represent you," Aliyah offered, "and at least two adult Muslim witnesses, from what I understand."

Mashael heaved a sigh of frustration as she folded her arms across her chest and collapsed against the couch, laying her head back, staring at the ceiling. "Then I'll probably never get married."

Sounds of stomping and playful shouting came from Ibrahim's room.

"You guys are so lucky, *mashaAllah*," Mashael said broodingly, still looking at the ceiling.

"Who?"

"Americans," Mashael said. "As soon as you turn eighteen, your families let you do whatever you want."

"That's not necessarily true." Aliyah's tone sounded sad and reflective.

"But it's the law," Mashael said, venting. "Arabs would never allow something like that."

"But don't you have American nationality?"

Mashael grunted. "Technically, yes."

"Then it's the law for you too," Aliyah said. "But that doesn't mean your family will let you do whatever you want."

Mashael turned her head to Aliyah from where it still lay on the back of the couch. "Would your parents stop you from marrying who you want?"

Aliyah's expression was difficult for Mashael to read. "No..." she said, almost cautiously. "But—"

"But what?" Mashael said, laughter in her voice. "What could be better than that? *Wallah*, I wish I could have your parents, at least until after the wedding."

Aliyah's expression became so disturbed that Mashael feared that she had angered Aliyah somehow. "Don't say that," Aliyah said finally, looking away. "Don't ever say that again." Her voice rose in firmness. "That is *not* something you want."

At that moment Mashael recalled Aliyah's tired expression when she'd seen her in the hall earlier. She wondered if Aliyah's stress was connected to her parents. "I only meant—"

"I know what you meant," Aliyah said, her voice still firm. "But still, don't ever say it again, especially if you're swearing by Allah. That's not a small thing, Mashael."

"Swearing by Allah?" Mashael asked, sitting up and staring at Aliyah in genuine confusion. "I didn't swear by Allah, I—"

"You said '*Wallah.*' That's swearing by Allah."

Mashael started to respond then realized that Aliyah was right. She had used the term for swearing by Allah. "But that's just a way of emphasizing a point," Mashael explained. "It's not meant to be taken that seriously."

Aliyah stared at Mashael with what appeared to be genuine fear in her eyes. "*A'oodhu-billaah,*" Aliyah exclaimed, seeking refuge in Allah. "How can taking an oath in Allah's name ever be a joke?"

"I didn't mean it's a joke," Mashael said, flustered. She didn't understand why Aliyah was making such a big deal out of a simple phrase. "I mean, it's just something Arabs say. It doesn't mean anything like you're thinking."

"To Allah or to you?"

Mashael's lips were already parted in preparation to respond, but Aliyah's question silenced her. She had no idea what to say to that. For a moment, trepidation gripped her as she wondered if her casual use of Allah's name was sinful.

"Anyway," Aliyah said with a sigh, apparently in an effort to lighten the mood, "my point is, be careful what you wish for. My parents are disbelievers, Mashael. There's nothing admirable in that."

Mashael was quiet. She hadn't thought about it from that perspective. She'd only meant that she wanted parents who wouldn't make getting married so difficult.

"I thought they were Christian," Mashael said more for conversation's sake than genuine interest.

"They are in name," Aliyah said sadly. "But they hate Islam so much that it doesn't even make sense."

Mashael wrinkled her nose. "Really? Why?"

Aliyah shrugged. "Who knows? Sometimes I feel they're more upset that I chose something without their permission or approval than that I chose to become Muslim. To them, children are property whose sole purpose in life is to do their bidding."

"*Wallah*?" Mashael said, eyes wide. "Sorry," she said, quickly shaking her head to correct herself. "Really?"

"Unfortunately, yes."

"*SubhaanAllah,*" Mashael said. "I thought the Amish were the only Americans who were like that with their children."

Aliyah coughed laughter. "The Amish?" she said. "I heard they were really kind and family oriented."

"Maybe some of them are," Mashael said. "But they excommunicated Sheldon after his *rumspringa*, and they won't even speak to him or see him anymore."

The confused expression on Aliyah's face told Mashael that she should explain. "*Rumspringa* is a time when Amish teenagers can act like regular Americans, but they have to fully recommit to the Amish lifestyle after that. But Sheldon didn't really want to. He wanted to go to college instead of working on the farm."

Aliyah creased her forehead. "Do they know he's Muslim now?"

Mashael shook her head. “He lives with some distant family now, but he hasn’t told them yet. It’s almost unheard of for an Amish to convert to Islam, so I don’t know how they’ll take it.”

“I thought he was excommunicated from his family.”

“From his Amish family,” Mashael clarified. “But the relatives he lives with are Mennonites, so they’re fine with him going to school and doing what he wants.”

“Except converting to Islam?” Aliyah said rhetorically, light humor in her tone.

Mashael coughed laughter. “We’re crossing our fingers on that one.”

“You mean you’re making *du’aa*?” Aliyah said playfully.

Mashael laughed self-consciously and nodded. “We hope to get our own place soon though,” she said. “So hopefully, it won’t matter.”

“Soon?” Aliyah said, creasing her forehead in confusion. “You already have a wedding date set?”

Mashael grew quiet. She hadn’t intended to reveal her plans to Aliyah. She knew Aliyah would never approve. “What’s the point in waiting?” Mashael said defensively.

Aliyah shook her head, a confused expression still on her face. “I’m not saying you should wait,” she said. “I was just asking because I thought your parents didn’t give their approval yet.”

“I’m not waiting for it,” Mashael said, defiance in her tone. “I heard that if my father doesn’t have an Islamic reason to stop me from getting married, he can’t.”

“That’s true…” Aliyah said tentatively. “But you don’t think it’s too soon to go that route? Sheldon wasn’t Muslim when they first met him. So they couldn’t approve of him marrying you.” She frowned, empathy in her eyes. “Why not give your father a chance to say yes now that Sheldon’s Muslim?”

Mashael was overwhelmed with exhaustion at the question. She had no idea how to explain to Aliyah that it didn’t matter how much or little time had passed, or whether or not Sheldon was Muslim now, her parents would never agree to the marriage. In her family, being American was synonymous with being a disbeliever, even if a person took his *shahaadah* and officially accepted Islam.

One of the few exceptions to this general rule was when the family could earn bragging rights for guiding the person to Islam. But even then, it was a trophy-like pride, not one that respected the new Muslim as fully human with rights equal to their Arab brothers and sisters. When it came to marriage, non-Arabs’ Islamic rights almost disappeared. Sometimes this cultural rule was bent for American females marrying Arab men, but it was almost never bent for American men marrying Arab females. It was a huge dishonor to have non-Arab lineage in the family of a respectable Saudi family, and in families like Mashael’s, family honor took precedence over religion.

“Sheldon’s parents are similar to mine,” Mashael said finally, though she imagined that Aliyah probably wouldn’t understand entirely where she was coming from. "So he understands why there's no point trying to convince my parents. We're just going to do a private ceremony then tell them later," she said. "If ever."

Aliyah nodded, and Mashael was surprised to see genuine empathy on Aliyah's face. "Sort of like what Jacob and I did?"

Mashael raised her eyebrows as she recalled the sudden *nikaah* at Jacob's house the day Sheldon accepted Islam. Reem had told her not to talk to anyone about it. "Yes, I guess so…" she said, smiling.

Mashael looked at Aliyah, a curious expression on her face. "You didn't tell your parents or family about Jacob?"

Aliyah shook her head, a close-lipped smile teasing her lips. "No, not yet."

"Is it because of all those rumors about you and Deanna?"

She paused before moving her head in the beginning of a nod. "Partly, yes. But like you mentioned about Sheldon's family, my parents pretty much excommunicated me after I became Muslim. So I'm not sure I want them involved in any part of my personal life."

Mashael grew quiet, immediately ashamed of her comment about wishing she had Aliyah's parents.

"I saw my mother today for the first time in more than ten years," Aliyah said in a low voice, her gaze looking at something beyond the floor table. She coughed laughter. "And it was the first time I was grateful to Allah that my family had cut me off and wanted nothing to do with me." A lopsided smile formed on her lips as she looked at Mashael. "And now I think I don't want anything to do with them either."

***

"You think I'm wrong for feeling this way?" Aliyah asked Jacob later that evening when he'd come to her apartment in preparation to take Younus and Thawab home. They were sitting at the kitchen table after having eaten, Jacob at the head and Aliyah at an angle to him.

"No," Jacob said honestly. "I think it's only natural after everything that's happened. I'd be more worried if you never felt angry with them. A person can only take so much. We're all human, in the end."

"But what about all the rights they have over me?" Aliyah said, a hesitant smile on her face. She was feeling guilty for what she'd said to Mashael earlier.

"You don't have to *want* to be around your family, Aliyah. You just have to keep ties with them."

Aliyah used her fork to toy with the cold food leftover on her plate. "But it feels wrong. I never felt like this before."

"After all you've gone through," Jacob said in lighthearted humor, "I imagine you're going to feel a lot of things you've never felt before."

Aliyah was quiet as she played with her fork. There was so much she wanted to say, but she didn't want Jacob to judge her harshly for it.

"I've been thinking a lot about Deanna these last couple of days," she said finally, deciding it was best not to keep her feelings bottled up any longer. She wanted to be able to relax and be herself around Jacob, and the only way to do that was by being fully honest with him.

"Really?" he said. Aliyah could feel him looking at her, but she couldn't meet his gaze. "In what way?"

She lifted a shoulder in a shrug. "It's sort of how I feel about my family now," she said. "Except with my family, I feel guilty for not wanting to see them again. But with Deanna, I feel guilty for not really caring what she thinks anymore." Aliyah drew in a deep breath and exhaled slowly, her heart beat quickening at the realization that she was actually speaking her thoughts aloud. "In a way, I almost want her to know about us. The more I think about everything she's done, the more I think she deserves this as payback."

There was an extended silence.

Nervous that she had disappointed Jacob with this confession, she hesitantly glanced at him. To her surprise, she found him grinning at her.

"What?" she said, laughter in her voice.

"I'm just happy to see you finally sticking up for yourself."

She chuckled and averted her gaze. "I don't know if I'd call it that…"

"I would," he said. "It's unhealthy to be as passive and forgiving as you've been all this time. Forgiving and overlooking is good, but only if you're being honest with yourself about how the betrayal makes you feel. But for you, it seems like you force yourself to deny that the betrayal ever happened at all."

As Jacob's words took meaning, Aliyah realized that he was right. She wasn't so much forgiving as she was willfully blind, and there was nothing praiseworthy in that. Only with sight could you be forgiving because only then would you see the harm and feel the pain of what you're forgiving.

"*Astaghfirullah*," Aliyah uttered, seeking God's forgiveness. "I never thought about it like that before. It makes me feel like a bad person now that I feel more upset than inclined to forgive."

"You're not a bad person for being upset because someone wronged you," Jacob said. "Forgiving them is an option, not an obligation."

"But isn't forgiveness best?"

"Yes," Jacob said matter-of-factly. "But only if it's really forgiveness. And forgiveness isn't of the tongue. It's of the heart. So before you can forgive, you need to consult your heart to see if it's ready."

Aliyah nodded thoughtfully.

A question came to her, but she was unsure if she had the right to ask it. "Do you forgive Deanna?" she said after a moment's hesitation.

Jacob seemed to be contemplating the question. "Yes…" he said tentatively. "As long as I don't have to be her husband," he said. "And as long as she doesn't harm my sons or my wife."

Hearing herself referred to as "my wife" in the same context as Deanna made Aliyah feel awkward—and proud.

"I guess I just feel like I don't know who I am anymore," Aliyah said. "My emotions are all over the place." She shook her head. "Even today, as I watched my mother try so hard to keep Cassie's husband from becoming Muslim, I felt like I hated her, *astaghfirullah*."

Jacob lifted a shoulder in a shrug. "Was there anything to love in what she did?"

"But I don't mean just her behavior," Aliyah said. "I felt like I hated *her*." Her expression conveyed distaste. "But what kind of person feels like that about her own mother?"

"A person who's suffered abuse one time too many times and can do nothing about it except lash out in her heart."

"But isn't that sinful?" Aliyah said, feeling choked up all of a sudden. "Doesn't Allah punish people who disrespect their parents?"

"You didn't disrespect her," Jacob said. "You felt dislike for her. There's a difference."

"But how do you honor and respect someone you dislike?"

"The same way you honor and respect all those teachers and bosses and supervisors who turn your stomach at the very sight of them," he said simply. "The same way we honor and respect court judges by referring to them as 'Your Honor,' regardless of how we feel inside." He shrugged. "What goes on in your heart is between you and Allah."

"But that's what I'm afraid of," Aliyah said. "What if Allah is displeased with me? Doesn't this make me a hypocrite?"

Jacob nodded, understanding. "I think I know how you feel," he said. "I went through something similar with my mother, and of course Deanna year after year."

"How did you come to terms with it?" Aliyah asked, looking intently at Jacob.

"I made *du'aa*," he said. "And I asked Allah to purify my heart."

Aliyah pursed her lips, her eyes growing thoughtful. "I need to do that…"

"We all do," Jacob said, "no matter what we think is going on in our hearts."

Aliyah grunted. "I just hate feeling like this. I'm not used to it. I've always been really positive and loving and optimistic with my family and friends."

"But have they been positive, loving, and optimistic with you?"

Aliyah frowned thoughtfully. "No, but…"

"Then you can understand why you're feeling different now. You've probably never experienced what it feels like to have a real friend," he said. "Or a real family even."

A feeling of sadness overcame Aliyah as the truth of his words settled upon her. He was right. She had no real friends or family.

Aliyah was fighting the urge to cry when she felt Jacob take her hands in his. She hesitantly met his gaze with a sad smile. He lifted her hands and kissed the top of both, one after the other.

“But I pray that Allah will give you both in me,” he said.

## 25
## Her Release

*"You are my relief,"* Jacob had told Aliyah, *"and my release."*

*"What do you mean?"* Aliyah had asked him, unable to contain her flattery.

*"You are my relief because Allah sent you after the difficulty,"* he said. *"And you are my release because I can finally breathe and be myself around you."*

These were the thoughts swimming in Aliyah's mind as she drove to Nikki's house Sunday afternoon. A reflective smile was frozen on her face as her eyes were on the road in front of her. *"Then you are my relief and release, too,"* she'd replied.

Aliyah glanced in the rearview mirror and saw Ibrahim mumbling rhythmically to himself as he looked out the window. Headphones were on his ears, and he held an iPod in his hand. Aliyah smiled at the sight. He was practicing his Qur'anic memorization in preparation for Monday. Yes, Jacob was definitely her relief after the difficulty, *mashaAllah.* Now she could focus on being a mother without feeling forced to work fulltime due to her financial situation.

And now her son was a big brother.

When Aliyah had told Jacob about Nikki's baby, he'd told her she should go visit and take Ibrahim to see his little sister (Nikki confirmed in a text message that the baby was a girl and that she was having some sisters over Sunday afternoon and that Aliyah was welcome to come).

Aliyah slowed the car in front of Matt and Nikki's home, and she was pleasantly surprised that not the least bit of emotions were stirred at the sight of her old house. In that moment, she was actually happy for Matt and Nikki. If they could please Allah by the union, people who loved each other belonged together, Aliyah thought to herself.

*I forgive you, Nikki,* Aliyah's thoughts resonated from the heart, *and I forgive Matt, too.* As she put the car in park and turned off the ignition, she whispered a silent prayer for them both. She asked Allah to bless their marriage; have mercy on them; forgive them for their past, present, and future sins; and admit them to the highest level of Paradise. At the heartfelt supplication, Aliyah felt moisture in her eyes as she imagined the angels making the same prayer for her and Jacob.

***

"Aliyah!" someone called out after Aliyah removed her shoes and placed them on the rack. She looked up to find Jasmine coming toward her with her arms outstretched.

"*As-salaamu'alaikum,*" Aliyah said as Jasmine drew her into an embrace as soon as she stepped into the living room.

"*Wa'alaiku-mus-salaam*, stranger!" Jasmine teased. She leaned into Aliyah until her face was right next to her ear. "Is it true what I heard?" she whispered. "You and Jacob got secretly married?"

The question took Aliyah off guard, and she didn't know what to say. She felt wary divulging anything to Jasmine. Aliyah tried to think of a way to neither confirm nor deny the rumor, but Jasmine spoke before she could.

"It's okay," Jasmine said, standing up straight again. She flashed Aliyah a wide smile as she squeezed her arm affectionately. "I'll take your silence as a yes." She winked. "That's not a question you hesitate on if the answer is a no."

Aliyah didn't know whether to feel concerned or offended.

"Congratulations though," Jasmine said, a playful grin on her face. "Now at least I know you won't be trying to steal *my* man."

The comment stung, and Aliyah's face grew hot in offense. Jasmine's emphasis on the personal pronoun *my* was clearly a passive aggressive insinuation that Aliyah had stolen Deanna's man.

A thousand retorts stormed her mind, but Aliyah held her tongue. Ibrahim was right behind her, within earshot, and she didn't want to ruin this day for him.

"*As-salaamu'alaikum,*" Aliyah called out to the women scattered throughout the living room. Some were sitting on the couches, others on the floor, and a few standing and chatting. On a small couch was Nikki cradling a baby in her arms.

"*Wa'alaiku-mus-salaam,*" a chorus of voices sang out.

"*Wa'alaiku-mus-salaam,*" Nikki said after them, a tired smile on her face. She gestured with her head. "Come and see your goddaughter."

It wasn't until after she grasped Ibrahim's hand and led him to where Nikki sat with the baby that Nikki's words finally registered. "Goddaughter?" Aliyah repeated in disbelief, laughter in her voice.

"Yes, why not?" Nikki said, meeting Aliyah's gaze without a hint of humor or sarcasm in her tone. She lifted the baby and turned her to Aliyah. "It makes the most sense, doesn't it? With her being Ibrahim's little sister. You can be a second mother to Bushra like I'm a second mother to Ibrahim."

Taken aback by Nikki's kindness, Aliyah didn't know what to say. "You named her Bushra?" she asked as she kneeled slightly to take the baby in her arms.

"Yes. Matt says it means good news or glad tidings."

Aliyah nodded as Bushra reached out a tiny dimpled hand in a stretch and a yawn before relaxing again. "It's a beautiful name *mashaAllah,*" Aliyah said sincerely. "May Allah give all of you much *bushra* through her."

"*Ameen,*" the women in the room murmured.

"*Ameen,*" Nikki added, a reflective expression passing over her face.

"Ibrahim, this is your sister Bushra," Aliyah said, lowering herself so that her son could see the baby.

A shy smile played at Ibrahim's lips. "Really?"

"Yes. Your Daddy and Ummi just had a baby girl," Aliyah explained. "So you're a big brother now."

His smile widened. "I know," he said, trying to play down the big moment.

Aliyah and Nikki laughed. "You want to hold her?" Nikki offered.

Ibrahim looked uncertain then finally nodded.

“Then sit down first,” Aliyah said, and Ibrahim obeyed, his eyes eager as he settled on the floor. Aliyah kneeled and carefully handed the baby to him, and arranged his hands so that he held his sister securely.

Ibrahim looked nervous at first, but after a few seconds, he found a comfortable grip. A grin spread on his face, and he glanced up at his mother to see if she saw how well he was holding his sister. Aliyah smiled and nodded at him, then he went back to staring at his sister, unable to keep from grinning proudly the whole time.

“How does Ibrahim like the *hifdh* school so far?” Juwayriah asked from where she sat on the couch. “When Bilal first started, he had a hard time.”

“It seems okay so far,” Aliyah said as she settled on the floor next to Ibrahim. She glanced at her son. “How is Qur’an school?”

“It’s fine,” he said, his eyes still on Bushra.

Aliyah and Juwayriah chuckled.

“How long does it take for someone to memorize if they’re starting from the beginning?” Aliyah asked after a few seconds.

Juwayriah shrugged. “It depends on the child,” she said. “If they have a really good memory, they could finish in a year.”

“Wow, *mashaAllah*,” Aliyah said, eyes widening. “I don’t know about that…”

“But it’s not recommended,” Juwayriah said. “The teachers say it’s better for them to take their time to make sure their *tilaawah* is right. Usually when they rush the memorization, there are a lot of mistakes in the *tajweed*.”

Aliyah nodded. “That makes sense.”

The doorbell rang, and Aliyah was pleasantly surprised to see Salima walk in after one of the sisters opened the door.

“*As-salaamu’alaikum*,” Salima greeted everyone with a smile and a wave.

“Haroon!” Ibrahim called out over the chorus of salaams.

Aliyah immediately reached toward him and took Bushra. As soon as the baby was in Aliyah’s arms, Ibrahim shot to his friend’s side before Haroon even finished taking off his shoes.

Aliyah carefully got to her feet then handed Bushra back to Nikki. In that moment, she saw a grimace pass over Jasmine’s face as Salima walked into the living room to shake everyone’s hand. Instinctively, Aliyah did a double take. But by then, Jasmine was all wide smiles and eagerly greeting Salima. Aliyah was overcome with dread as she imagined that Jasmine probably had heard of Larry’s interest in Salima, though she couldn’t imagine how.

*“But Jasmine is very resourceful,”* Larry had told Aliyah when Jasmine was ostensibly looking for someone to teach her about Islam, *“so I thought I should give you a heads-up.”*

“How about Ummi, like Ibrahim calls you?” Aliyah said as she sat back down on the floor near Nikki, speaking low enough so that only the sisters right next to them could hear. “I don’t want to call myself *godmother*.”

Nikki nodded, considering it. “That’s fine.”

"*Alhamdulillaah.*"

A grin formed at Nikki's lips. "So I take that as a yes?"

Aliyah drew her eyebrows together in confusion, then realized a second later what Nikki was referring to. "Yes, of course," Aliyah said sincerely. "I'd be honored, especially since she's Ibrahim's sister."

"Good," Nikki said, exhaling but still smiling. "Matt kept warning me you might say no."

Aliyah chuckled.

"You know, because…" An awkward expression lingered on Nikki's face, and Aliyah sensed that Nikki expected her to understand the unfinished thought.

Aliyah nodded. "I understand," she said, even though she didn't. There were a host of reasons that could make them think she'd refuse the offer, but she couldn't imagine the one Nikki was referring to. But Aliyah decided that it wasn't important to discuss right then. There were too many people around.

"I need to talk to you," Salima whispered, leaning over and clipping Aliyah on the shoulder. "After we leave here, *insha'Allah*," she added before standing upright and cooing at the baby.

***

"Can you come to Muslim Marriage Monologues this Friday?" Salima asked an hour later as she and Aliyah walked to their cars, Haroon and Ibrahim behind them throwing each other friendly punches.

Aliyah frowned apologetically. "I'm not sure," she said. "Between squeezing in time for me and Jacob, homeschooling Ibrahim, and trying to figure out what to do about this job at the college, I can hardly think straight."

Salima nodded. "I know what you mean," she said sincerely. "That's how I felt after I went back to work after Mikaeel died."

"Well, I'm sure it's nothing like that," Aliyah said, coughing in embarrassed laughter.

"Stress is stress, girl," Salima said, waving her hand dismissively. "May Allah make it easy for you."

"Maybe I can try next Friday, *insha'Allah*?" Aliyah said.

"That's fine," Salima said tentatively. "It's just that I wanted you to meet Mikaeel's sister. She's coming to stay with me for a few days *insha'Allah.* And Friday's probably the only day we'll be still long enough for her to meet anyone." The shadow of a smile played at her lips. "And she asked to meet you."

Aliyah's eyes widened slightly. "Really?" she said, smiling.

"I told her a lot about you."

"*MashaAllah*," Aliyah said, unsure what to say to this. "I didn't know he had a sister."

Salima halted her steps near the cars parked along the curb then opened her handbag and withdrew her car keys. "We're not exactly friends though," she said with a wry smile. "But we make it work. She's Haroon's only Muslim family on his father's side."

"They converted?" Aliyah asked, glancing down as she rummaged for her own keys.

Salima shook her head. "She and Mikaeel grew up Muslim. His parents accepted Islam together and raised Mikaeel and Kalimah as Muslims. But his parents passed away."

Aliyah felt a stab of pity for Kalimah. She felt strangely connected to Mikaeel's sister at that moment, perhaps because Aliyah herself was the only Muslim in her immediate family.

"I'll come *insha'Allah*," Aliyah said with a shrug, smiling. "I can make time."

Salima's face seemed to brighten. "You sure?"

A grin creased one side of Aliyah's mouth. "Why not? I don't know if I'll ever get this opportunity again."

"She'll be happy to meet you."

"And I'm sure I'll be happy to meet her," Aliyah said.

"But I have to warn you," Salima said, slight humor in her tone, "she's pretty feisty."

"That's fine," Aliyah said, waving her hand dismissively. "I can do feisty."

A reflective smile lingered on Salima's lips as she looked toward where the boys were playing. "Kalimah and I didn't always get along though."

Aliyah looked toward the boys too, frowning thoughtfully. She sensed this was a sensitive topic for Salima. "Why's that?"

"I don't know..." Salima exhaled broodingly. "I used to think it was because she had such a strong personality." A look of distaste passed over her face. "We argued a lot too, so I figured that might be it," she said.

Aliyah thought of her relationship with Cassie and how even before she became Muslim, they never really got along.

"But now I realize it was because I felt she was a bad influence on my husband."

Aliyah drew her eyebrows together and turned to look at Salima. "Really? Why?"

Salima narrowed her eyes thoughtfully. "Kalimah and her husband have been married for about ten years now," she said. "But I never agreed with the marriage, and I wasn't quiet about it." She heaved a sigh that came out ragged, as if she was steadying a wave of emotions. "So she and Mikaeel didn't see each other that much."

Aliyah watched Haroon and Ibrahim run through the front yard as they waited for their mothers to finish talking. "Why didn't you agree with the marriage?"

Salima grunted. "Pride. Stupidity. Self-righteousness," she said. "If you want the truth."

Aliyah was silent, her gaze still on the boys.

"But honestly..." Salima's lips formed a thin line momentarily. "...I felt if Mikaeel spent a lot time with Kalimah and his brother-in-law, then he'd want to marry a second wife too."

Aliyah met Salima's eyes, a question on her face, but Salima was still looking toward the front yard. "Kalimah's husband was already married when she married him?" Aliyah asked, surprised curiosity in her tone.

Salima nodded then looked at Aliyah. "Remember when we first met and I invited you to Muslim Marriage Monologues and I told you it was for Muslims in relationship crises?"

"Yes," Aliyah said, nodding. "We were at the halal market."

"And I told you why everyone's welcome?" Salima said.

Aliyah nodded, remembering. *"When you're young and insecure, you think the biggest threat to your marriage is out there somewhere,"* Salima had said. *"I used to think the same until one night I went to sleep as a married woman with three children and woke up as a single mother of one."*

"That was when you told me you were a widow," Aliyah said.

"Well, it wasn't just losing a husband that inspired my new perspective," Salima said. "It was watching how Mikaeel's sister suffered his loss, too."

Aliyah was silent, unsure what to say.

"I know it sounds crazy," Salima said. "But that was the first time I actually saw Kalimah as human being just like me. Before that, she was just his annoying home-wrecking sister."

"*SubhaanAllah*," Aliyah said. "That's really how you thought of her?"

Salima moved her head in a nod, an entanglement of emotions apparent in that small gesture. "And every time she and her husband wanted to visit, I pitched a fit." Salima's eyes glistened in sadness. "Because of me," Salima said, her voice breaking and her face crumpling slightly, "she didn't get to spend a lot of time with her brother before he died."

Aliyah looked away, unable to withstand the agonizing regret in Salima's eyes.

Salima wiped her eyes with the tips of her fingers, her keys dangling and jingling with the motion. "But anyway," she said, her voice rising in an effort to sound positive, "*alhamdulillah*, we're on better terms now."

"*Alhamdulillah*," Aliyah said, agreeing, hoping to say anything to make it better for Salima.

"But it'll be nice if you can come Friday," Salima said, her voice and expression returning to a semblance of pleasantness. "Kalimah will probably share something she wrote a few years ago," she said. "It's about her experience with how Muslims mistreat sisters who marry into polygyny."

"Ouch," Aliyah said, humor in her tone. "I'm not sure I want to hear that one."

"Me either, if I'm honest," Salima said, smirking, laughter in her voice. "But I already heard it before, so I think I'll be all right hearing it a second time," she said. "I was the one who suggested she perform it at Muslim Marriage

Monologues," she added with a shrug, her expression going reflective again. "It's the least I can do."

Aliyah nodded. "That makes sense."

"But girl," Salima said, lifting a hand and waving Haroon over, "let me get this boy home so he can do his homework and I can get everything ready before work tomorrow."

"I'll see you Friday night *insha'Allah*," Aliyah said.

"I'm going to call you," Salima said, embarrassed laughter in her voice. "I got to talking about all this Kalimah stuff, I didn't even get to ask you what I wanted."

Aliyah creased her forehead. "That isn't what you wanted to talk about?"

Salima smirked. "Girl, no. I could've texted to ask you about Friday," she said, waving her hand dismissively. "I wanted to ask your advice about Larry."

"Oh okay," Aliyah said, feeling awkward as she recalled Jasmine's strange behavior earlier. She wondered if it would be appropriate to mention her suspicions about Jasmine knowing about Larry's interest.

"Haroon!" Salima called out, slight irritation in her voice as she waved him over again. "Let's go!"

Aliyah turned and gestured to Ibrahim, but he was already trailing behind Haroon.

"I just need someone else to bounce all this off of," Salima said, humored self-consciousness in her tone, a hesitant smile on her face. "Sometimes I feel like I'm losing my mind even taking this boy seriously."

Aliyah started to say, "I understand." But she stopped herself, fearing that the acknowledgement would carry an unintended connotation based on her past with Larry.

"No problem," Aliyah said finally. "Give me a call. I'm free all day. Jacob has a lot of work to do for the college, so I doubt we'll even get a phone call in today."

"All right then, *ukhti*," Salima said, drawing Aliyah into a brief perfunctory hug. "*As-salaamu'alaikum*."

"*Wa'alaiku-mus-salaam wa-rahmatullaahi wa barakaatuh*," Aliyah replied.

***

"You can't be serious," Larry said, a disbelieving smirk on his face as he turned his body to look at Jamil, who sat next to him at the dining room table in Jacob's home Wednesday evening. Jacob sat at the head while Aliyah sat at an angle next to him, across from the men and next to Salima.

It was Aliyah's idea to have the dinner that night. After she and Salima had talked on the phone Sunday, Aliyah suggested that Salima take Larry up on his suggestion to at least get to know him better before saying no. Salima and Larry had then discussed "*halaal* dating" options, and the only one Salima felt comfortable with was "*halaal* socializing" wherein Aliyah and Jacob, as well as her brother Jamil, would get together whenever possible.

Since Mikaeel's sister would be visiting Salima for a few days through the weekend, Aliyah had suggested that Salima and Larry's first "*halaal* date" be a casual dinner that week before Kalimah arrived. When Aliyah mentioned the dinner idea to Jacob, he was more than happy to offer his home. It was heartwarming to see how much he cared for his brother, and Aliyah was left wondering how it would feel to have blood family who loved her and valued her happiness in that way.

"You mean to tell me that you would be one hundred percent happy," Larry said in a humored tone, eyebrows raised skeptically, "if you married a woman and she wanted to prioritize her career over her family?"

Jamil coughed in self-conscious laughter. "I didn't say I'd be *happy* about it," he said. "I'm just saying I wouldn't have a problem with it."

"Bull," Larry proclaimed, shaking his head and shifting his position back toward the table. He reached forward and lifted the pitcher of water and poured some into his almost-empty glass then set the pitcher back down in soft thud. He took a few gulps of water before turning his head and narrowing his eyes skeptically at Jamil. "If these two young ladies weren't either already taken or family to you, I'd think you were trying to impress them."

Salima's expression suggested that she was humored by the remark, and Aliyah sensed that Salima was genuinely attracted to Larry.

"Maybe he's just saying it's not worth the fight," Salima offered, apparently in obligatory sibling compassion.

Larry looked directly at Salima then, the smirk still on his face. Salima averted her eyes, an embarrassed smile playing at her lips. "Okay, then," Larry said, his tone suggesting he was going to ask Salima a probing follow-up question, but Aliyah noticed how his voice became gentler when he addressed Salima. "Do *you* think it's completely rational for a man to be okay with his children being in the care of strangers when he makes enough money for his wife to stay home?"

Salima nodded. "Yes, I do," she said frankly. Her pleasant, self-conscious expression remained, but there was no shyness in her voice.

Larry threw his back against his chair in exaggerated disbelief. But the soft expression on his face when he looked at Salima made Aliyah smile at the obvious affection there. "No," he said to Salima in playful devastation. "You're killing me."

Salima raised a finger, a smile toying at her lips as she prepared a clarification. "You asked if it would be completely *rational*," she said. "And I think it would be, especially if he knows this is something his wife really wants and that fighting about it might break up their marriage." She smirked as she looked directly at Larry for the first time. "But if you'd asked if the situation would be *ideal*," she said, "I would've given a different answer."

"Lord have mercy," Larry said, shaking his head before turning his attention back to Jamil. "I thought you were the only lawyer here tonight. What mind games are you teaching your sister?"

Everyone chuckled or grinned at Larry's comment.

"It's not a mind game," Jamil said, offering his sister a grateful smile as he glanced in her direction. "It's the truth. You do what's right for the situation, not just what would make you happy as a man."

Larry shook his head, as if he wasn't having any of it. "Nah, man, I'm not into all this political correctness, feminist ish. Men's feelings and needs should be respected too, and I'm not feeling my wife putting our children in daycare just because she watched too many Hilary Clinton speeches and has Beyoncé's song 'Who Rules the World?' on repeat."

Jamil grinned. "I think it's called 'Run the World,' man."

"Seriously?" Larry asked, his eyes narrowed at Jamil as if this piece of information genuinely surprised him enough to halt his argument.

Jamil nodded. "I'm pretty sure."

"Damn," Larry said. "That's even worse. The question is less rogue than the command. That chick is sending women subliminal messages to wreck their homes."

Everyone laughed.

"I'm serious," Larry insisted. "You don't think I'm right?" He was looking at Jacob now.

Jacob threw up his hands, a close-lipped smile on his face, as if to say he's not in it. "I don't know, bro. I'm just a student here."

"Come on, Jacob, you know these songs are teaching men and women to disrespect each other."

Jacob nodded. "That's true. I just don't know if Beyoncé is intentionally sending that message."

"I agree with Larry," Salima said sincerely. "Whether it's intentional or not, Beyoncé and other singers are corrupting a lot of people, and when people try to live out what they hear in these songs, it wreaks havoc in their homes."

"Exactly," Larry said, slapping the flat of his hand on the table, causing some of the dishes to rattle.

Jacob shook his head. "I think we're being overly simplistic here," he said. "I don't disagree that most of these songs are problematic. But to say that they wreck homes is a bit extreme. It takes a lot more than a rebellious song to dismantle a family. If that happens, then the problem started somewhere else. I think it's possible to listen to these songs and not be negatively affected."

Aliyah raised her eyebrows at that one. It wasn't that she disagreed with her husband. It was just that she'd never considered the perspective before. But she didn't speak her thoughts aloud. She didn't feel it was respectful to Salima to actively participate in any discussions that took place in the context of Salima and Larry getting to know each other. Everyone else there had the right to chime in. Jamil was Salima's brother, Jacob was Larry's brother, and of course Larry and Salima themselves were expected to interact. That was the whole point of these gatherings. But Aliyah was there only because Salima didn't want to be the only woman, and because she wanted Aliyah's honest opinion on what she thought of Larry as a person. However, given Aliyah's past with Larry, Aliyah felt it wisest to offer no more than Salima had requested: her presence.

"Bro, are you serious?" Larry said in humored disbelief. "Everything you watch or listen to affects you either negatively or positively. And I don't see how Beyoncé songs can be the latter."

Jacob shrugged. "Actions are by intention, man." A vibrating noise followed by a chime sounded in the middle of his comment. "Everybody isn't listening to music so they can learn about life," he said as he patted his pockets and glanced around the room, apparently in search of his mobile phone.

"It's on the floor table in the living room," Aliyah said in a low voice, leaning toward Jacob and nodding her head in the direction of where his phone lay.

He twisted his body until he was looking behind him, then nodded. "Thanks," he muttered as he got up and walked over to it.

"Subliminal messages are called subliminal for a reason, bro," Larry said, raising his voice so that Jacob could hear him from the living room, where he stopped at the floor table to pick up his phone. "They exist in a realm beyond our conscious. So intentions are irrelevant."

Jacob shook his head as he glanced at the screen of his phone and ran his forefinger over it to unlock it. "No," he said, looking up at Larry as he walked back over to the table. "*Lack* of intentions is irrelevant for subliminal messaging. That's what they depend on, passive, mindless listening. But subliminal messages aren't as powerful in the face of conscious intentions, especially if I'm aware of the possibility that the message could be harmful to me in some way." With the hand he was using to hold the phone, he gestured toward Larry as he sat down. "That's something these conspiracy theorists don't talk about. You have more power over your mind than anyone else does, no matter how grand the plan is to corrupt it."

"But you're still affected," Larry said, "even if you intend *not* to be."

"That's why I said the messages aren't *as* powerful," Jacob said. "I didn't say they have no effect whatsoever. But with conscious intentions, you can actually get something beneficial out of an otherwise corrupt message."

"I hope you're joking," Larry said, a playful sneer on his face.

"I'm with Larry on that one," Jamil said, laughter in his voice. "You're going to have to explain how you can benefit from a bad message."

Salima leaned forward, eyebrows raised as she looked at Jacob, as if she too was awaiting an explanation. But she didn't demand it verbally.

"First of all," Jacob said with a knowing smile as he looked at his mobile screen and scrolled down with his forefinger, apparently reading the text message that had just come in. There was an unnatural extended pause as his smile faded and a shadow of concern passed over his face as he stared at his phone. When he lifted his gaze, he looked directly at Jamil, whose expression suggested that he had some idea what this text could be about. There was a troubled question in Jamil's eyes, and Jacob's frown as he put the phone in his pocket seemed to give Jamil affirmation of what he feared. Jamil nibbled at his lower lip, and Jacob seemed distracted by sudden aggravation.

"Is everything okay, bro?" Larry said, genuine concern in his voice. Aliyah and Salima looked at Jacob, their expressions mirroring Larry's question and concern.

"Yeah, yeah, yeah," Jacob said too quickly, waving his hand. "Just some work stuff at the last minute." But Aliyah sensed that he was just saying that so that he didn't ruin his brother's first official meeting with the woman he wanted to marry.

"What were you saying?" Jacob said, looking at Larry, keen interest in his eyes.

"I wasn't saying anything, man," Larry said, brotherly teasing in his tone. "You said, 'First of all,' then left it at that." He coughed laughter. "Like your point was so profound you didn't even have to finish it."

Jacob laughed, and Aliyah could hear gratefulness in that sound, as if he knew his brother was being a good sport about Jacob wanting to pretend the unpleasant interruption hadn't occurred.

"But I'd be grateful if you could explain how we can earn good deeds by listening to bad songs," Larry said.

"My pleasure," Jacob said, as if Larry's last statement was all he needed to put the conversation back on track. "I don't think I put it quite like that," Jacob said. "But what I meant was that it's not impossible to listen to a song with the specific intentions of getting something beneficial from it."

"For example?" Larry challenged.

Aliyah noticed that Jamil was consciously making an effort to appear interested in the conversation, but it was obvious that the silent exchange between him and Jacob about the text message had truncated his interest in the topic.

"Okay," Jacob said, as if accepting the challenge. "Take any love song, for example."

"Ohhh," Jamil said playfully, "I want to see where this is going."

"But seriously," Jacob said, his voice rising in an effort to make his point. "Let's be honest," he said. "Most of the time they're singing about *zina*, or at least wanting to commit the sin."

"I can't argue with that one," Larry said, nodding in agreement.

"But let's say I'm listening to it and consciously thinking about my wife."

"And if you're not married?" Larry countered with a smirk.

"Then my future wife."

Salima and Larry glanced at each other and smiled. Aliyah smiled herself upon seeing the obvious attraction between them.

"If that's what I'm thinking of when I listen to the song," Jacob argued, "then I'm getting some benefit from it that perhaps the singer himself didn't even intend."

"Okay…" Larry said tentatively, nodding, as if he hadn't thought of that.

"They have their intentions, and I have mine," Jacob said with a shrug. "That's what I tell myself whenever I watch or listen to something that I know wasn't crafted with me and my religion in mind."

"But what about the subliminal messages though?" Salima asked, her tone suggesting genuine curiosity more than disagreement. "Aren't you still affected?"

"Perhaps," Jacob conceded. "But if you pray five times a day every day, and at their proper times. And with sincerity and concentration," he added for emphasis. "I don't see how the effect could be that strong. Especially if you also read Qur'an, make *du'aa*, and do the morning and evening *adhkaar* that the Prophet, *sallallaahu'alayhi wa sallam*, taught." Jacob shrugged. "Call me a fool, but I think the effect of Allah's Words and messages are more powerful on your psyche than anyone else's."

***

"Is something wrong?" Aliyah asked a couple of hours later as she helped Jacob clear the dining room table and clean up the kitchen. Their sons were in the playroom, but Aliyah had told Ibrahim to start getting ready to go home so he could review his *hifdh* and homeschool work before bedtime.

"What do you mean?" Jacob said as he carried a plate to the kitchen, Aliyah following with a glass in each hand.

Aliyah hesitated, unsure how much she had the right to ask. She didn't want to appear nosy or obnoxious. But Jacob's entire aura had changed after he received the text message during dinner, and he still didn't seem himself.

"That text message from earlier," Aliyah said finally, keeping her gaze on the glasses as she set them on the counter then loaded them into the dishwasher. "It seems to have really bothered you."

Jacob was silent as he used a fork to scrape the food remains from the plate into the trashcan.

"It was from Deanna's lawyer," he said finally, frowning as he carried the plate to the sink and rinsed it. It was then that Aliyah recalled Salima telling her that Jamil worked at the law firm that was representing Deanna.

When Jacob met Aliyah's shocked, concerned gaze, she knew what he would say before he said it. "The charges were dropped against her," he said. "She's being released."

## 26
## A Job Well Done

Aliyah sat in her college office Thursday afternoon, nibbling at her lower lip thoughtfully. She had finished all her classes for the day and was considering going home early to prepare Ibrahim's homeschooling materials that she was using to supplement the minimal subject study that he was receiving at the Qur'an school. When Jacob had arranged her class schedule so that she would have most of the afternoon free, he'd told her that she was free to use her office hours to work on homeschooling preparation so long as she'd finished all her college duties. He told her she was also welcome to step out and check on Ibrahim at the masjid if she didn't have a meeting or an appointment with a student, but he cautioned her to be careful about going home early every day lest Dr. Warren use it as yet another strike against her. But right then, Aliyah didn't care. She was too distracted to think about work. She hadn't finished all her college duties for the day, but she wasn't making any progress just sitting in her office. So what was the point?

*She's being released.*

A sick feeling came over Aliyah at the thought of seeing Deanna again. A part of Aliyah, the angry part, felt that Deanna deserved to remain in jail, if for no other reason than the crime of being a horrible human being. But the angry thought passed just as soon as it had come, and Aliyah was left with feeling horrible herself. She hated these sudden waves of anger. It was difficult reconciling this sporadic rage with the calm, peaceful, non-confrontational personality that had defined her since childhood.

*"But everyone has a limit,"* Reem had told her once, when she was warning Aliyah about how she'd be treated if she married Jacob, "*and I think you're reaching yours."* Jacob himself had told Aliyah something similar, though for a different reason.

Aliyah wondered why she hadn't seen the warning signs herself. *"I'm just happy to see you finally sticking up for yourself,"* Jacob had said. But was that really what was happening? Or was she changing into a different person entirely?

"Deanna is at her parents' house now," Jacob had told Aliyah that morning on the phone as they both drove to work. Aliyah actually had a surge of jealous protectiveness over her husband when he'd said that. She almost dared Deanna to come near Jacob and try anything. But a second later, she was worried about former best friend. Deanna staying at her parents' house just didn't seem like the best idea. But what other option did Deanna have? She certainly couldn't stay with Jacob.

"I changed all the locks," Jacob had told Aliyah when she asked if he thought Deanna might try to come back to her old home. Aliyah had immediately thought of the key he had given her. "Before I gave you a key," he'd added, as if reading her mind.

"But what if she pretends she lost her key and gets a locksmith to make another one?" Aliyah had asked, concerned. "Especially since it's still technically her home?"

"Actually," Jacob's voice had said through the earpiece, "it's technically *my* home."

Aliyah had creased her forehead, her eyes on the road. "It's not hers too?"

"No," he said, "at least not on paper. It's only in my name."

"Really?" For reasons she didn't fully understand, Aliyah laughed, finding this bit of information humorous.

"What?" Jacob's voice said, confused humor detectable in his tone.

"I don't know," Aliyah said honestly, laughter in her voice. "I guess it's just something I never expected. A man doesn't put his own wife's name on the house they share?" She continued cackling and actually felt tears of laughter springing to her eyes. She wiped them away with one hand, her other still gripping the steering wheel. "Man, I'm scared of you," she said jokingly.

"It's not what you think," he said. "It's something Deanna actually insisted on after we got married."

"*Deanna*?" Aliyah said, taken aback. For some reason, this information sapped the last bit of hilarity from the scenario.

"When we got married..." he began, his tone suggesting self-conscious humor, "she had this notion that she was going to strike it rich from all her books and marriage workshops and business ideas, so she made sure we had separate bank accounts and that whatever was of any value was in only one person's name."

"Oh…"

"I honestly have no idea how much money she has to her name."

"So you don't have a shared bank account?" Aliyah said, genuinely surprised.

"One," he said. "But it's a savings account that we planned to put in Younus's and Thawab's names when they're old enough."

"Hmph," Aliyah said, nodding, finding the whole scenario interesting. She wondered what it would mean for her and Jacob's marriage.

"But I was the breadwinner, obviously," Jacob said. "She never had to pay any bills or buy any necessities," he said. "For us or the boys."

"*MashaAllah*," Aliyah said, unsure what else she could say.

"But we didn't put anything in writing about it," Jacob said, sounding slightly disappointed. "It was just something she thought was best for both of us." He grunted. "At least that's what she said."

Aliyah was silent, unsure what to think about all of this.

"But as far as the home is concerned," Jacob said, "it worked out for the best."

"*Alhamdulillah*," Aliyah muttered.

"I'm assuming her lawyer will give her good advice," Jacob said. "If that's the case, then I doubt she'll try anything like getting a key copy to my home."

"Her lawyer?" Aliyah asked, eyebrows furrowed. "I thought he was just representing her in her mother's assault case."

"Well, he is…" Jacob said. "At least that's the only representation that I agreed to pay for. But now that—"

"*You* paid for her lawyer?" Aliyah interjected, surprised.

There was a pause, as if Jacob was taken aback by the question. "Yes...why?"

"*MashaAllah, barakAllahufeek*," Aliyah said sincerely. "You have a big heart."

"*Alhamdulillah*," he said, downplaying his generosity. "I just didn't want her to know her father wasn't exactly on her side throughout all this."

"She thinks her father's paying for the lawyer?"

"I think so," Jacob said.

"When's the last time you talked to her?" Aliyah said.

"That's a hard one…" he said as if exhaling his words. "Because I'm not sure you can say we've talked at all since she's been arrested."

"Really? But I thought—"

"She became practically mute after what happened," Jacob explained. "So we don't really get to talk."

Presently, Aliyah got up from her office chair and leaned forward to power off her computer. She wondered, perhaps irrationally, if she there was any way she could check on Deanna to see how she was doing. Learning about her having suddenly become mute was deeply troubling, and that news alone made Aliyah feel bad for her. No, Aliyah wasn't ready to forgive Deanna for all of her backstabbing and betrayals over the years, and she didn't feel the least bit guilty for being married to Jacob right then. But she couldn't deny that she still cared about Deanna as her Muslim sister.

Whatever transformation was happening with Aliyah now that she was no longer suppressing her negative emotions and denying her right to her own feelings, she was pleasantly surprised that she was no longer plagued by the irrational notion that human beings were the personal property of the person they married—even when they were no longer married to the person. Allah certainly didn't put that humiliating burden on His servants. Why then did they put it on themselves?

*Plus-minus Islam*, she heard Salima's voice in her head. *It's when Muslims add or take away things in Islam to suit their own purposes.*

Though Salima had been talking about LGBTQ beliefs and anti-polygyny sentiments, Aliyah saw how the same plus-minus mentality applied to the "friend codes" she'd held herself after Jacob divorced Deanna and wanted to marry her. Aliyah could understand being compassionate and respectful to your friend, but being compassionate and respectful was not the same as denying yourself the blessings that Allah had made lawful to you, seeking to please someone else.

*O Prophet! Why do you ban [for yourself] that which Allah has made lawful to you, seeking to please your wives?* Allah asked in the Qur'an. Aliyah had read in the *tafseer* that this *ayah* was revealed in response to an incident when Prophet

Muhammad had vowed to never eat a certain type of honey because he believed it changed the smell of his breath and thus displeased his wives.

And right then, Aliyah's heart asked the same question of herself, as well as her Muslim brothers and sisters, regarding whom Allah made lawful for them in marriage—seeking to please their friends and cultures.

So no, Aliyah thought to herself, she wasn't obligated to deny herself the joys of a lawful marriage to the man whom Allah had shown was right for her, especially in seeking to please the person who'd done everything in her power to strip that opportunity from her. *If there's any compassion and respect that I owe Deanna,* Aliyah said to herself in firm resolve, *it's in not openly gloating about having married Jacob in the end, after all.*

***

"This is something I wrote a few years ago," Kalimah said as she stood in front of the women Friday night at Muslim Marriage Monologues in Salima's home.

Aliyah couldn't help thinking that Kalimah didn't seem the least bit feisty. If anything, she seemed calm-spirited and gentle. She could almost feel the emotional pain Kalimah had battled after both losing her brother and withstanding emotional abuse from Muslims for doing nothing other than marrying for the sake of Allah.

"And it's really personal to me," Kalimah said. "When I first wrote it, it was an angry entry in my diary after dealing with some really hurtful treatment from my brothers and sisters in Islam." A reflective frown formed on her face, as if the memory alone still pained her.

But Aliyah wondered if the pain was merely a memory for Kalimah. Perhaps the hurtful treatment was an ongoing experience for her.

"I'd just come back from a Muslim conference," Kalimah explained. "Something I'd paid good money for," she added, her tone suggesting strong emotion for the first time. "And one of the brothers, a well-known and respected Muslim figure, was doing a marriage lecture during the main session." She paused and shook her head, as if she still couldn't believe what had happened. "And he did this really long tirade, blasting men who married another wife before they, quote, *deserved to*," she said, a slight sneer in her voice.

Kalimah drew in a deep breath and exhaled in preparation to recite the poem. "It's called, 'I Am Not a Good Job Sticker'...

I am not a "good job" sticker in his life's notebook,
A trophy or award plaque on his wall,
Or a badge of honor pinned to his chest,
Telling the world that he was a good boy and "Job well done!"
How dare you objectify me to a soulless object presented only when he's done enough to prove he's deserving of me.
I suppose you imagine you are speaking *for* me when you say all those fancy things to discourage a man from taking another wife...

*Until* he's proven himself.
*Until* he's rich enough.
*Until* he's acceptable enough.
*Until* he's accomplished enough.
*Until* he's good enough.
Oh, how I will meet you on the Day of Judgment and plead my case to my Lord, telling Him of how you robbed me of my humanity in this world.
How you said the only woman with a soul is the one covered in the only part of the polygyny verse that happens to *not* exist: "One is best for you, if you only knew."
If you only knew what is best for you, you'd shut your mouth.
If you only knew your Lord, you'd focus on what was best for *you*—and that is a job never done.
So no, I am not a "good job" sticker in his notebook, a trophy or award on his desk,
Or a sign he's deserved me as a badge of honor on his chest.
I am not your topic of interest used to win a petty debate.
I am not your topic of apology used to say that not *all* Muslims live this way.
Oh, sometimes I pity you—if only that would matter at all.
But it doesn't.
Because I am a soulless object plastered to your debate wall.
I am the one who isn't best for him, if he only knew.
I am the sticker who shouldn't be—except for the non-existent few.
I am the badge of *dis*-honor pinned to his chest.
I am the objectified nothingness because he chose what isn't best.
So it doesn't matter what I feel, what I think, or what I see.
Because I am not even *human* to you…
Even as I pray, cry, and make *du'aa* to Allah—just like you.
But for now, I find peace in the words of Prophet Ya'qoob from the Qur'an…"

The Arabic recitation was so powerful and unexpected that the hush that had fallen over the room during the poem became even more hushed still. Every woman in the room bowed her head in humble reflection upon hearing the beauty of Allah's Words.

"He said," Kalimah finished with the English meaning of what she'd just recited, "*'Nay, but you have contrived a story [good enough] for you. So patience is most fitting for me…'*"

***

"I don't think I have any judgment left in me," Aliyah said jokingly. The women sat in Salima's living room discussing Kalimah's poem, the only one that had been performed that night. "After everything I've experienced this past year,"

Aliyah said, "I've learned to keep my mouth shut and ask only one question when I hear about somebody else's life."

"What's that?" Kalimah asked from where she sat on the floor amongst the other women.

"What is *Allah's* view on this?" Aliyah replied. "And if I can't be one hundred percent sure that the answer is that He's displeased, then I don't see how I have a right to express my own displeasure."

At that, the women grew quiet, and a few said, "Hmph" in deep reflection.

"*Astaghfirullah*," Kalimah said sincerely. "May Allah help us love what He loves and hate what He hates."

"*Ameen*," the women muttered in agreement.

"I don't have a problem with polygyny…" one of the women piped in, her tone rising with the last word, suggesting that the infamous *but* would follow. Her voice sounded awkwardly loud in the room and broke the reflective atmosphere. "I'm just waiting to hear a *good* story of it." Her half smile only thinly veiled the smug expression on her face. "So far, I haven't."

She shrugged, an unapologetic sneer in that gesture alone. "*MashaAllah*, if your marriage is good…" she said to Kalimah, as if she were really saying, *No offense, but…* She huffed, a smirk creasing the side of her lips. "…but yours would be the first."

A tense silence fell over the room, and Aliyah watched as Kalimah's calm expression became tight in offense. "My marriage is not a good or bad *story*," Kalimah said, her voice rising authoritatively, firm in conviction as it matched the challenge the woman had thrown at her. Her unapologetic tone was Aliyah's first glimpse into the feistiness that Salima had warned her about. "It's my *life*," Kalimah said, contorting her face as she regarded the woman with distaste. "How *dare* you demand to know the good or bad details of somebody's life before you even *attempt* to trust that your Lord knows better than you."

A suffocating quiet permeated the tense atmosphere. The woman who'd expressed her opinion shifted uncomfortably, an embarrassed but defiant look on her face. She looked as if she was about to say something flippant in response.

Aliyah glanced uncertainly at Salima, hoping the hostess would intervene to quell the growing tension. But Aliyah pulled her head back in surprise when she saw the close-lipped smile on Salima's face. Salima was leaning forward, her chin resting on a loose fist, as if enjoying the emotional scene.

"If you need to hear, quote," Kalimah said, lifting her hands and making a downward movement with two fingers on each hand, indicating quotations marks, "*good stories* about polygyny before you accept its goodness in people's lives, then that's *your* problem, not mine." She lifted her upper lip in an undisguised sneer as she regarded the woman. "Why aren't *Allah's* Words sufficient for you?"

The woman threw up her hands, her face twisted in annoyance and defensiveness. "It ain't that deep," she said, rolling her eyes. "I was just expressing my opinion."

"*No*," Kalimah said, her voice rising in insistence, driving home her point. "You were just being *arrogant*." She met the woman's gaze, unblinking. "It's none of your damn business whether my marriage, or anyone else's for that matter, would count as a *good* story according to your self-righteous, contrived standards."

The woman's nose flared as she glared at Kalimah. Her lividness was almost palpable, as if it were all she could do to keep from physically striking Kalimah.

"Do you go around asking sisters in monogamy whether or not their marriage is *good*?" Kalimah challenged, eyes narrowed.

Aliyah cringed, feeling obligated to step in to diffuse the situation. "I think she was just trying to say th—"

"I don't care what she *thinks* she was trying to say," Kalimah said, raising the flat of her palm to Aliyah, halting her midsentence. "But what she *is* saying isn't too different from a *kaafir*."

There was the sound of several women sucking in their breath at once. Even the woman whom Kalimah was talking to appeared too shocked to speak. Her mouth fell open, her eyes narrowing in irate disbelief.

"You're like someone who recognizes the truth of Islam," Kalimah said, unperturbed by the stunned silence, "yet rejects it because she's heard only, quote—" She moved her fingers in the quotation mark gesture again. "—*bad stories* of Muslims."

Aliyah exhaled, having not realized she was holding her breath. She was relieved that Kalimah wasn't calling the woman a disbeliever. The relieved expressions on other women's faces suggested that they had been thinking similarly.

But the impenetrable tension remained.

"Islam is not your personal storybook to like or dislike," Kalimah said, her voice suggesting finality with the issue. "It's a way of life." She shrugged smugly. "Live it, or don't live it. There is still goodness in it, no matter how many, or few, so-called *good stories* you hear about it during your life."

***

Deanna stood in the kitchen of her parents' home Monday afternoon still wearing the soft fluorescent pink bathrobe she'd put on that morning after taking a shower. The cloth belt was tied securely at her waist, the hem of the robe stopping just above her shins. Her back was leaning against the counter next to the refrigerator, one arm crossed over her chest, the other hand holding the stack of papers from the package that had arrived only two days after she was released from jail.

Deanna had read through the contents twice each day since the package arrived. It was the first thing she did in the morning after waking up and the last thing she did at night before going to bed. It was as if with each new reading, she expected to uncover some hidden evidence that none of it was real. But today, she'd already read through the paperwork three times because she needed to decide what to do. The thirty days she had to respond were waning with each day.

For the divorce petition to have arrived that quickly, Jacob must have been meeting with a lawyer while she was awaiting trial—when she was trusting him to represent her best interests. The mere thought of him plotting revenge after she'd gone as far as to assign power of attorney over to him was enraging. His behavior reeked of the most vicious betrayal.

*Is he out of his mind?* she thought angrily to herself, slamming the stack of papers on the counter behind her. As if filing for a divorce was not enough of an affront, he was seeking ten percent of all of her business assets and book proceeds, as well as significant ownership in her marriage business. Apparently, he felt that he had carried the greater financial burden of funding both her consultation business and book promotion—and that he was an integral part of their success.

Yes, Jacob had been very generous with his money during their marriage, and she had often sought (and occasionally insisted on) his participation in many of her relationship workshops and book projects. But she had assumed that he had agreed from the goodness of his heart, not so that he could lay claim to what was rightly hers. She didn't owe him a single cent for mere marital kindness. Her money was hers and hers alone, and she would not allow him to touch a single penny of it.

*Fine*, she thought in aggravation, *if he wants full custody of our sons, he can have it.* But she wasn't parting with any of her money, and she was not sharing ownership in her business. If she was going to be left high and dry, abandoned and alone to fend for herself as a single woman, she wasn't about to be held down by kids. She wasn't going to let him get off scot-free, starting life with a clean slate, while all she received were child support checks to compensate for twenty-four hour childcare—and having not even the *hope* of another man looking her way. Because she was some *other* man's "baby mama."

No, she wasn't going down that road, not now, not ever. She certainly didn't want a divorce, but if Jacob wanted to pretend that he actually did, she was going to call his bluff. Then she'd make him regret that he'd even thought about letting her go.

There was the sound of movement coming from her father's office, and she immediately snatched up the stack of papers and left the kitchen. She hurried up the carpeted steps and walked down the hall to her room, where she locked the door behind her. At her dresser, she yanked open a drawer and lifted a stack of neatly folded clothes and placed the papers beneath it before shutting the drawer again.

As Deanna walked over to her bed, she caught a reflection of herself, and she halted her steps to study herself in the full-length mirror. She turned her torso from left to right, in awe at how attractive she was. As she admired her reflection and thought about how Jacob would be miserable without her, an idea came to her. Grinning, she slid her fingers into her entangled mess of hair, then turned her face from side to side to see which angle was more flattering. Her eyes traced her reflection from head to toe, and her heart raced as the idea took on a life of its own in her mind.

With the divorce filing, Jacob lost any right to an opinion about her life. Her days of playing the "good Muslim wife" were over, and she refused to assume that degrading role again. When he came crawling back to her in the end, as she knew he would, their relationship would be on her terms, not his.

But first she had some work to do.

The mischievous grin spread on her face as she studied her reflection. She still had her figure, and now that she no longer felt any obligation to "guard her body from men's eyes" out of respect for Jacob, she was going to do what she had set out to after Aliyah's media ruse: use her sex appeal to get Jacob's attention. Her efforts had flopped last time mostly because she had been so busy trying to balance Muslim modesty with sensuality, and it just didn't work. This time she would definitely be the "hot Muslim." And with Jacob filing for a divorce, the new photos would likely have a much more powerful effect. Not only because she had a more foolproof strategy this time, but because his male jealousy—and desire—would almost definitely kick in.

But first she needed to devise a way to keep Jacob out of her pocket during the divorce—without paying a single cent in lawyers' fees. She wasn't even going to waste her time telling her parents about the divorce papers. Of course, they'd find a way to blame her or come up with some stupid plan about getting custody of the kids. But Deanna had a better plan. Her father wasn't speaking to her anyway, and her mother was always holed up in her room most of the day, recovering from that stupid fall that Deanna had taken the blame for.

If only Deanna could reconnect with at least one male friend who either was a lawyer himself or knew someone who was, then her plan would be complete. Then, she could kill two birds with one stone: pro-bono legal representation and arm candy to make Jacob fly into a jealous rage.

Then after he came crawling back, she could sit back and gloat, telling herself, "Job well done."

Her smile faded as she was reminded of her struggles with her voice. She lifted her chin and studied the smooth skin of her neck in the mirror. Using the tips of her fingers, she massaged her throat, wondering when her speech would return to normal. Though her voice itself had returned, it was raspy and she hated the sound of it. And several days out of the week, she felt as if she had a sore throat.

"Hi, I'm Deanna," she spoke aloud to her reflection. She grimaced. She sounded like a lifelong smoker.

How would she be able to resume workshops and interviews sounding like this? And how could she find a man who would be willing to even pretend to like her if she couldn't even hold a decent conversation?

Sadness and frustration overwhelmed her. It wasn't supposed to be like this. She wasn't supposed to be living in her parents' house struggling to utter an intelligible sentence.

What had she ever done to deserve this? Why was Jacob punishing her like this?

And how was she supposed to punish him in return if she couldn't even speak properly? What handsome male lawyer would offer free legal services to someone in her condition? She probably couldn't even call some of her old male friends from college. They probably wouldn't even believe it was she, with her voice like it was.

*Asher.*

The thought came to her so suddenly that it halted all her others. The mere thought of reconnecting with her older brother made her physically sick. The last time she'd seem him was in passing at a family reunion several years ago, and she never made any effort to keep in touch. And neither did he.

But her parents often mentioned that he had a successful real estate company that specialized in business property. Deanna couldn't imagine him not knowing at least three male lawyers offhand who'd been clients of his.

But would he help her? was the question.

*He owes me*, Deanna thought in indignant aggravation, reminded of how he had remained a friend of Bailey's for years. Finding her a male lawyer friend was the least he could do.

*But* would *he?*

Deanna grunted. There was only one way to find out.

## 27
## People of Unknown Value

"Where is she?"

Aliyah had barely gotten the door to her apartment open Wednesday evening in response to the knocking before she heard the demanding question. Reem didn't even offer the salaams as she stood with her arms folded defiantly, her eyes glaring at Aliyah as if she'd stolen something.

"*As-salaamu'alikum,*" Aliyah said, her eyes narrowed in concern as she waved Reem inside. "Is everything okay?"

Reem stepped into the foyer, but she didn't go any further. "You tell me," Reem said, still wearing her veil even after Aliyah had reached behind her and closed the door.

Aliyah shut her eyes and shook her head in a quick motion, as if to clear her head. "Can you tell me who we're talking about here?"

"So you're going to act like you don't know?"

"Know *what*, Reem?" Aliyah said, growing annoyed. "Can you please stop speaking in code?"

Reem yanked her *niqaab* up to reveal her face, throwing the black fabric behind her head like a cape. She kicked off her shoes and walked heavy-footed to Aliyah's couch, where she sat stiffly on it, arms still folded. When Aliyah went to sit down next to her, she saw that Reem had tears in her eyes.

"She's gone, Aliyah," Reem whimpered, her voice awkwardly high-pitched as her chin quivered. "She didn't come home last night, and her phone is off."

Aliyah's heart fell in the realization that Reem was talking about her younger sister Mashael. *"But I don't want them there,"* Mashael had told Aliyah when she'd come over and talked about her fight with Reem about the wedding. *"I want it to be just me and Sheldon."* Aliyah had never thought Mashael would actually run off and elope. It just wasn't a scenario that she associated with Reem's family.

"And the police won't treat it as a missing persons case because she's an adult," Reem said. "So they're not helping at *all*." She exhaled a ragged breath. "What if something bad happened to her?"

"Did your family try to reach Sheldon?" Aliyah asked.

Reem nodded, her face still contorted in pain. "But his phone is off too."

Reem looked at Aliyah, eyes pooled with tears. "What if he kidnapped her and did something to her? What if—"

"Mashael told me that she and Sheldon wanted to get married without any family there," Aliyah interjected, feeling obligated to at least share what she knew. "But I didn't think she meant they'd run off together."

Reem stared at Aliyah in disbelief, her crumpled expression conveying hurt. "What else could it mean?" she asked accusingly in rebuke, as if the little Aliyah knew made her fully culpable in the crime. "You should've called me as soon as she told you that."

"I forgot about it to be honest," Aliyah said, slight defensiveness in her voice. She wasn't about to take the blame for this.

"You *forgot* about it?" Reem said, incredulous, eyes widened in disbelief. Aliyah sensed Reem needed a tangible target for her pain. "How could you forget something like that?"

"Because Mashael just wanted advice," Aliyah said, still defensiveness, "and there's nothing alarming about that."

"When people want advice, Aliyah," Reem said, her voice didactic, "it's usually because their whole predicament is alarming. Seeking advice is always a warning sign for something bad."

Aliyah pulled her head back in surprise. "A *warning* sign?" she repeated in humored disbelief. "No, Reem," she corrected, intentionally making her didactic tone mirror Reem's. "When people want advice, it's usually because they want advice. End of story."

"Not for an Arab," Reem said.

Feeling exhausted all of a sudden, Aliyah exhaled impatiently in a single huff. "We're not going to do this right now," she said, rolling her eyes. "I was in the middle of working with my son on a homeschool assignment when you came." She slapped her hands on her thighs and stood. "And I'd like to continue that undisturbed if you don't mind," she said, walking toward the front door.

In the foyer, Aliyah pulled the front door open and held it so that Reem would know she had to leave. "If I hear anything else from Mashael, I'll let you know *insha'Allah*," she said. "But for now, my hunch is that she's married and trying to live her life in peace. I imagine that she'll be reaching out to you soon to let you know that she's okay." She added, "As I honestly believe she is."

"And if she's not?" Reem said challengingly as she pulled her *niqaab* back over her face and walked over to the front door. Her voice still carried the accusatory tone from earlier, as if this was all Aliyah's fault.

"Then all we can do is pray to Allah for her safe return," Aliyah said sincerely, a tinge compassion in her exhausted tone. "And if something terrible *has* happened, it's nobody's fault, Reem. Remember that."

***

Later that night after Ibrahim had gone to bed, Aliyah sat on the prayer mat on the floor of her bedroom, feeling emotionally and mentally exhausted. She'd just finished praying two units of voluntary prayer and was reflecting on her brief encounter with Reem, which had left her a bit annoyed though Reem had apologized before she left and asked Aliyah to forgive her for her outburst.

"I'm just so worried about her," Reem had said, her voice full of emotion.

Aliyah imagined that Reem must be going through a lot of emotional pain herself to have repeated angry outbursts like the one she had earlier—and like the one she'd had months ago when she canceled their Qur'an class. In many ways, Reem reminded Aliyah of Deanna. Both seemed to allow their personal battles to disrupt their relationships with friends and family. But of course, Deanna's disruption had a much more sinister component.

*Could I end up like that?* Aliyah wondered in pensive self-reflection. She herself was battling a lot of emotional pain and was finding her patience waning in her dealings with other people. Perhaps her pain had already begun to disrupt her relationships with others and she just didn't realize it.

Her phone vibrated from where it lay on the nightstand next to her bed, interrupting her thoughts. Sighing, she pushed herself to a standing position and pulled the one-piece floral prayer garment over her head. She balled up the cloth and tossed it on her desk chair as she walked over to the nightstand and picked up the phone. She slid her forefinger across the screen to unlock it then tapped in the passcode so she could read Jacob's full text.

*You still awake?*

A smile creased the corners of her mouth and she quickly tapped her finger on the keyboard in reply.

*Yes. Why?* ☺

*I just miss you, that's all*

*<3*

*Can I call you? Or is it too late?*

Aliyah started to type, *It's never too late for you*, then erased it, fearing it was too forward at the moment. *You can call*, she typed finally. *I'm up*.

"This year is going by *really* slowly," Jacob said, as if exhaling the words when Aliyah answered her mobile phone on the first ring. Aliyah could hear the smile in his voice.

In the loose, faded blue knee-length cotton tee that she favored at bedtime and with her hair frizzy and in need of grooming, Aliyah didn't particularly feel like a heartbreaker. But as she pulled back the heavy comforter and climbed into bed, the phone held against her ear with her free hand, she felt like the most beautiful woman in the world, if for no other reason than Jacob's deep voice made her feel that way.

"How long do we have left?" he said, his voice heavy in impatient longing.

Aliyah giggled flirtatiously. It was the first he'd mentioned of the difficulty he was having with the extended wait, and she was relieved to know that she wasn't the only one. There had been fleeting moments, albeit irrational, that she'd begun to fear that Jacob wasn't as attracted to her as she'd initially thought.

"About ten months, I think," she said, a smile in her voice as she pulled the phone from her ear and tapped the speakerphone icon. He groaned in playful annoyance, the guttural sound coming out as a deep bass, the speaker giving the utterance an almost music-like quality. Heart racing, Aliyah wondered why she hadn't thought to propose the option of birth control instead of this extended, torturous waiting.

"Seriously?" Jacob sounded genuinely surprised, lighthearted disappointment in his voice. "*That* long?"

That was when Aliyah remembered that this extended celibacy was what she herself had wanted, and in fact insisted on. Up until the *nikaah* itself, she hadn't even allowed herself to believe that she wanted to be married. How then could she have known that her three- to five-year "preferred" wait time was as preposterous as her initial preference not to marry Jacob at all?

"You giving up so soon?" she asked teasingly. But what she really wanted to say was, *"I feel like giving up too."* But how could she admit that the now extensively reduced one-year time frame was unbearable too? She wanted to maintain at least a shred of female dignity, but how could she do that if she were the first to give in?

"No…" Jacob said in a thoughtful sigh, as if resigning himself to patience. "I waited this long to be with you, I can wait another ten months." He huffed, humor in that sound. "But I'm telling you, it's not easy."

"Really?" Aliyah teased. "You seem to be doing fine."

He coughed laughter. "I'm trying to be strong for you. I just don't want to mess this up."

His honesty was refreshing and moving. With that confession alone, she felt connected to him more strongly than before. Aliyah hesitated before saying, "I don't think you could mess this up, no matter what happens." She bit her lower lip nervously, wondering if he caught the hint.

There was a thoughtful pause. "Even if my ex-wife came back acting like a raving maniac?" There was self-conscious humor in his tone.

Hopes deflated with mention of Deanna, Aliyah sighed in disappointment. But she knew Jacob wasn't trying to be a killjoy. His reason for mentioning his ex-wife was likely the same reason for his weathering the storm of the extended wait. Aliyah had made a big deal about both. She'd practically told Jacob that Deanna's contentment with their marriage was a prerequisite to her own. So naturally, Jacob would want to gauge Aliyah's feelings about Deanna storming back into his life.

But still, it was annoying to hear any mention of her. Right then, Aliyah couldn't care less whether or not Deanna tried to come back into Jacob's life, calmly or raving. Aliyah wasn't going anywhere *insha'Allah*, regardless of what tricks Deanna thought she had up her sleeve.

"*Insha'Allah*, we'll cross that bridge once its laid," Aliyah said, her calm resolve veiling her irritation with the topic.

"It's already been laid," Jacob said, slight humor in his tone. "We just didn't get to it yet. But I think we're fast approaching."

"Why? Because she's been released?" Aliyah's tone suggested genuine curiosity, but she really wished they could talk about something else.

"Not only that…" The extended pause suggested that Jacob was trying to find the best way to put his thoughts into words. "She was served the divorce papers after she got home from jail."

*Oh.*

In her mind's eye, Aliyah saw Deanna's face twisted in indignant disgust as she used her thumb and forefinger to leaf through the papers as if they were contaminated.

*"The way to keep a man from marrying someone else is you keep the subject of divorce and polygamy out of your marriage,"* Deanna had told Aliyah when Aliyah was still naïve enough to view her as both friendly and wise. "*Jacob would never marry another woman because I don't give him any reason to...I take care of myself. I give him sex every night. I pamper him...*"

The memory was almost heartbreakingly sad right then, and Aliyah found herself feeling sorry for Deanna. How many other women—and men—suffered from this "God complex"? How many married couples genuinely believed that their ostensibly healthy, lasting, committed relationships were due to their hands alone? Yet how many of these same people were so fixated on bragging about their "long, happy marriage" that they were tragically blind to the daily emotional suffering of their husband or wife—at their own hands?

*O Allah!* Aliyah silently prayed, moving her lips and bowing her head in humility as trepidation gripped her. *Protect me from self-deception!*

***

"So you decided to keep your job at the college?"

It was a Saturday morning in early October, and Salima sat in the restaurant booth across from Aliyah where they'd often met before, and today Aliyah had accepted Salima's request to get together for breakfast. Ibrahim and Haroon were in the play area enjoying themselves, having eaten at home before they came.

Aliyah smiled self-consciously as she pulled a grape from the bundle on her plate and slipped it into her mouth. After chewing and swallowing, she nodded. "It's crazy, isn't it? All that time I wanted to be a stay-at-home mom again, and now that I have the opportunity, I throw it away."

"I wouldn't call it throwing it away," Salima said. "Ibrahim is homeschooled," she said. "But he's not technically *home*."

"That's true..." Aliyah said, feeling better about it when Salima put it that way.

"And sometimes the biggest stress of working fulltime is knowing you *have* to go in," Salima said, "no matter what."

There was a shadow of sadness on Salima's face that made Aliyah's heart hurt. She sincerely hoped that Salima would remarry one day and have the same psychological freedom that Aliyah had right then.

Aliyah nodded. "I think that's what was happening with me. I felt like I didn't have a choice." She coughed laughter. "And having my husband as my superior certainly helps."

Salima laughed in agreement. "Especially when you know he's in your corner."

Aliyah watched the boys race up the side of the jungle gym then dangle upside down, their knees locked in place, keeping them steady as they swayed their bodies back and forth.

"And Ibrahim's a fast learner, *mashaAllah*," Aliyah said, smiling toward him as she spoke. "And he's really independent. I think I would've quit if he was struggling academically. I couldn't live with myself if I kept my job when he needed all of my energy when he got home."

Salima smiled knowingly at Aliyah. "And you like your job," she said.

Aliyah nodded, chuckling. "Yes, I do." She shrugged. "I don't like my supervisor and some of my colleagues, but I love my students. And I love teaching."

"Then that's all that matters."

Aliyah ate a few more grapes as she and Salima watched the boys for a few minutes. "I reapplied to my old PhD program," Aliyah said.

"Really?" Salima's voice rose in excitement as her eyes met Aliyah's. "That's really good *mashaAllah*."

"I figured, why not? Now that I'm a fulltime employee, the college will pay for it."

"When will you know if they accepted you?"

"In a few weeks, *insha'Allah*," Aliyah said. "My old advisor said it's just formality at this point since I was already accepted before."

"*MashaAllah*," Salima said, shaking her head in admiration. "Maybe one day…" she said, referring to herself.

Aliyah creased her forehead as she looked at Salima. "What's going on with you and Larry? Did you get together again after that dinner at Jacob's?"

The barely restrained grin that formed on Salima's face told Aliyah everything she needed to know.

"We've talked…" Salima said tentatively.

"Okay," Aliyah said, nodding and smiling. "You don't have to say anymore. Just tell me when the wedding date is."

Salima laughed.

"But I swear," Aliyah said, humor in her tone, "after that dinner, I feared you'd run the other way."

"Why?" Salima seemed genuinely surprised.

"All that talk about women and careers and subliminal messages."

"Oh that." Salima laughed and flipped her hand. "That's actually what made me take him more seriously."

"Really?" Aliyah said good-naturedly, eyebrows raised.

"It's refreshing to meet a man who's just *honest*," Salima said. "So many try to think up the right things to say to women, and it's so annoying. Almost every man would agree with everything Larry said, but they won't admit it. It's like they're constantly looking over their shoulder to check if their opinions about women and family fit the status quo or some political feminist agenda."

Aliyah nodded. "He's definitely honest, *mashaAllah*."

"But we'll see where it goes, *insha'Allah*." That initial grin returned to Salima's face.

"How's Kalimah doing?" Aliyah asked, remembering Mikaeel's sister just then. "Did she enjoy her visit?"

"She did actually…" Salima said, the smile on her face suggesting that she was enjoying a private joke.

Aliyah ate in silence for several seconds, mulling over whether or not she had a right to speak her thoughts aloud. "Why didn't you stop her?" she said finally, genuine curiosity in her tone. "When she was arguing with that sister?"

"*Stop* her?" Salima spoke as if it were the most farfetched concept in the world. "Why would I?"

Aliyah shrugged, unsure if she had the right words for what was on her heart. "It just felt like it was a bit much, you know? That sister probably went home really shaken and hurt."

"I agree," Salima said, lifted a shoulder in a dismissive shrug. "And if she did, that was her own doing, not Kalimah's."

Aliyah drew her eyebrows together, a curious smile on her face. "You don't think Kalimah's reaction was a bit over the top?"

"No. I don't," Salima said, but Aliyah could tell Salima's defensiveness was directed at the topic, not at Aliyah herself. "Kalimah had every right to say what she did, and *how* she did." There wasn't even a hint of ambivalence or doubt in Salima's tone. "I wish more sisters in polygyny had her guts."

"You don't think it was rude and disrespectful?"

Salima contorted her face slightly. "Not as rude and disrespectful as the question itself," she said. "If you're a stranger openly making assumptions about someone's marriage, you deserve any tongue lashing that comes your way. And I certainly am not going to intervene in your defense."

Aliyah nodded, having not considered it from that perspective. "But maybe the sister felt comfortable expressing her opinion because of the relaxed atmosphere of Muslim Marriage Monologues?"

Salima huffed, a smirk on her face. "No," she corrected. "The sister felt comfortable expressing her opinion because it was against polygyny." She huffed again. "Like I felt comfortable expressing mine to keep my husband from spending time with his own sister and brother-in-law."

At that, Aliyah grew quiet, reminded of the deep emotional scars that Salima was suffering after losing her husband and realizing the wrongs she'd done to his sister.

"If anything," Salima said, "Kalimah was being nice. If you compare her strong reaction to the bull she has to put up with from Muslims every day, it's no comparison. We're definitely ruder and more disrespectful, hands down," she said. "It's just that our point of view is more widely accepted, so we don't have to take responsibility for our cruelty."

Aliyah was immediately reminded of her uncle Benjamin talking about the hypocrisy of American Muslim culture.

"It's like telling African-Americans to stop getting so upset about racism," Salima said. "That's an easy suggestion when you don't have to suffer from it every day." There was an expression of distaste on her face. "Or when you don't have to worry about being handcuffed, thrown into the back of a police car, and spending the rest of your life in prison," she said. "Or getting your brains blown out just for *looking* suspicious."

Aliyah was quiet as she considered the analogy.

"Just like all the discussions surrounding race in this country are watered down so as to not offend the very ones who put the system of racism in place," Salima said, "all our discussions surrounding marriage in the Muslim community are designed to sustain a system of mistreatment and marginalization of brothers and sisters in polygyny." She grimaced. "And we want to pretend like we're doing this for some greater good." She huffed. "When it comes to our beliefs about marriage, it's a shame that homosexuals have more honesty and self-respect than we do."

Aliyah didn't know what to say to that.

"So, no." Salima shook her head, her expression conveying conviction. "I'm not worried about that sister's feelings. Call me insensitive, but if I were going to feel bad for anyone, it would be Kalimah," she said. "At worst, that other sister went home feeling offended. But Kalimah probably went home feeling unwelcome amongst the Muslims. And that's far, far worse."

Aliyah nodded. "I see what you mean," she said sincerely.

"The sister should be grateful to Kalimah," Salima said. "Sometimes the only way we learn is to be confronted head-on about our wrongdoing, especially when it's about our faith."

There was a thoughtful pause.

In a lower, more reflective tone, Salima added, "I wish someone had done that for me." She drew in a deep breath and exhaled, the sound coming out ragged in emotion. "But because my privileged mindset went pretty much unchallenged amongst Muslims, to say the least," she said with a thoughtful frown, "I wronged myself, my husband, *and* his family, and I have no idea if Allah will forgive me."

***

```
I know several lawyers. But they're usually licensed
by state, so I don't know how much they can help you.
```

Aggravated, Deanna closed the email window, and pushed away from her desk. She had humiliated herself by reaching out to her brother only for him to shut her out. She hadn't told Asher why she needed the lawyer, but she'd expected a little more enthusiasm than his two measly lines in reply.

*Now what?* she thought in annoyance.

Melancholic heaviness weighed on her as she sat feet from her desk, the email window a horizontal icon at the lower border of her monitor. Deanna tried to ward off the depressed feeling. She didn't want to reduce herself to sulking over a man who didn't appreciate her.

*You better NOT marry Aliyah.*

Deanna winced at the memory. Those were the only words she'd said to Jacob when she saw him last. That she'd put them in writing instead of speaking them aloud made the scenario all the more incriminating.

*I don't want to lose you,* Deanna's heart had cried as she lost sight of Jacob in her dream. *Then pray*, a voice told her. *Pray...*

"Child, you need to stop fighting yourself." The elder inmate at the jail had shouted the words as she passed Deanna one day, when Deanna was in one of her customary funky moods. Before that moment, Deanna and the woman had never exchanged a single word. The advice had shaken Deanna, and no matter how hard she tried to deny it, she knew that woman's passing comment was a sign that she should turn to Allah for help.

*Then pray...*

There had been a few other Muslim women at the jail, but Deanna had kept her distance. Sometimes she'd see them pray together, lined up next to each other in their pale inmate uniforms. Some days the sight was annoying because it reminded her of the self-righteous sisters she'd known from the masjid, women who were no better than anyone else but felt the need to flaunt their religiosity in everyone's faces. But there had been other days that the sight incited guilt in Deanna regarding her own spiritual neglect. Whatever troubles these women had in their lives that had landed them in jail, at least they had not abandoned *Salaah.*

One day while in jail, Deanna had found herself in front of the row of sinks, feeling awkward as she rubbed water over her skin. She couldn't even recall the last time that she'd performed *wudhoo'*, and a part of her had wanted to give up right then. But as the cold water ran between the recesses of her fingers, a calming, humbling feeling struck her. When she rubbed the water over her face, there were tears forming in her eyes.

Minutes later, she'd lined up next to the other Muslim inmates, and as soon as she raised her hands as if in surrender to signal the start of prayer, she had a jolting epiphany. *Whatever misfortune happens to you, is because of what your [own] hands have wrought...* They were the same words she'd read from the Qur'an after Jacob had divorced her. At the time, she'd promptly shut the Qur'an and didn't want to read anymore. She knew it wasn't merely coincidence that it had come to mind as soon as she'd begun praying at the jail that day.

Turning her head to the right and then to the left, signaling the end of prayer, guilt had sat like a nasty pit in her stomach. She loathed herself something unimaginable right then. *You're a hypocrite and a fraud,* her mind had jabbed in self-rebuke. And she sat feeling like an imposter amongst the prayerful Muslims. *You can't blame Aliyah just because Jacob wanted to marry her*, came the begrudging thought thereafter. *She was never plotting to marry him, and you know it.*

Deanna had clenched her teeth, irritated at the haranguing thoughts. When she got up and left the women, she had no intention of joining them again. This pitiful self-loathing was why she'd stopped praying in the first place. All praying did was make her feel like a horrible person, like she was bound for Hellfire no matter what she did. And this was the effect of prayer when she was actually concentrating. Otherwise, it felt like a meaningless burdensome ritual that God had forced upon her, and she really didn't understand why He insisted on it so much. Neither the deriding guilt nor the empty ritualism inspired her to continue *Salaah* with any regularity. Why pray when the best she could hope for was feeling drastically worse than she had before she prayed?

But even as the mere thought of prayer continued to annoy Deanna, she was never able to shake the effect of that single prayer that day. *Stop blaming Aliyah. She's not a backstabber. You are.* The bitter realization that only she was to blame for what had happened in her marriage continued to haunt her up until her release. *Whatever misfortune happens to you, is because of what your [own] hands have wrought…*

But Deanna despised Aliyah nonetheless. Perhaps she always had, though Deanna couldn't say with any truthfulness that this was due to any fault of Aliyah's. Aliyah had never been a bad friend. Aliyah had never lied or betrayed her. In fact, Aliyah was sickeningly loyal, someone you could always count on, in that stereotypical "bestie" way. Deanna despised Aliyah because Aliyah was a weak, pathetic person who was a poor excuse of a woman, a poor excuse of a human being in fact. She never stood up for herself and was an easy target for anyone who wished to take advantage of her. She saw the good in *everybody*, in a blind, stupid, naïve way.

But what Deanna resented most about Aliyah was that women like her were the archetype of the "perfect wife." Perhaps it was a life rule of sorts that all good men would fall for the helpless, dimwitted religious-type at least once. It was like a childhood fantasy of theirs or something.

"Oh, child," the elder inmate had uttered sympathetically after Deanna had confided in her with angry, indignant outbursts that taxed her raspy, aching voice. "No man wants a needy, desperate woman. So make sure you don't become one. And if your friend is as pathetic as she sounds, he'll be over her real quick. Sometimes you just got to let a man taste his fantasy. Then he'll come back to you on his knees."

Aliyah had *no* right to give the media those pictures of herself, Deanna thought bitterly, standing up and pacing her bedroom, clinging on to any excuse to remain angry at Aliyah. *Yes*, her mind retorted, *but she would never plot to steal your husband.*

Deanna nodded at the revelation, halting her pacing and sitting firmly on the edge of her bed. It was true. Betrayal wasn't in Aliyah's makeup. Deanna had been merely projecting when she'd assumed that Aliyah was savvy enough to hook someone else's man. Even Aliyah's marriage to Matt had been Deanna's handiwork. And as useless as that man was, to anyone, Aliyah hadn't even been able to keep *him*. How then could she win someone like *Deanna's* husband? Jacob had only been interested in Aliyah because she represented that stereotypical "righteous" brainless damsel that all men thought they wanted. Deanna just needed to convince him that she was the only real woman he'd ever know.

"Apologize to him and your friend," the elder inmate had suggested. "Especially if you don't have any proof she was betraying you. Men like women who show regret and humility, especially for things that mean a lot to them."

Deanna grunted at the memory. But she didn't dismiss the advice, however difficult it was to swallow. Though she hated to admit it, Aliyah *did* deserve an apology. She just wondered if she'd ever have the wherewithal to give it to her. But she couldn't think about that right now. She needed to focus on getting a lawyer.

*Attorney Bryan Schmidt*, the idea came to Deanna just then. He was the lawyer her father had hired for her representation in the assault case. Of course, he wouldn't be able to double as arm candy to make Jacob jealous, but Deanna was running out of time—and options. She had less than ten days to respond to the divorce filing, and the last thing she wanted was the divorce decision to automatically default in Jacob's favor.

But Bryan was all business, so it was highly unlikely that he would offer any free legal advice, and asking her father to pay the fees was out of the question. She had money of her own, but until her voice situation was settled, she didn't want to touch any of it because she had no idea when she'd be able to earn money again.

But if she already knew exactly what she wanted before she consulted him, then all she'd need him to do was type it up formally and submit it to the court. That way she could save herself an astronomical legal bill.

***

*Racism makes sense.* The timing of the epiphany was odd, and completely out of context. But later, even the timing and context would make sense to Aliyah. She was standing in front of a small lecture hall conducting an algebra lesson when the realization came to her. She had just finished explaining how any lettered variable that was part of a mathematical equation containing other definite values had a single definite value itself.

"What this means is, the term *unknown value* is actually quite narcissistic," she'd joked, setting off a ripple of uncertain laughter amongst the students. "Because if all of the other values are known, then it's impossible that this single one can be truly *un*known. It's only unknown to the extent that a person lacks the knowledge or willpower to work out the single answer that everything else is obviously pointing to. A truly unknown value exists only outside the sphere of other definite mathematical values," she explained. "In other words, in the realm of definite realities, the answer to the unknown is literally right in front of you if you have both the knowledge and willpower to see it."

There was the whistling of pen strokes across student notebooks, and Aliyah pondered the completely obvious reality of *why* racism made sense: *Believing that someone deserves the harm that consistently comes to them is much easier (not to mention much more convenient) than admitting your part in inflicting that consistent harm.* After the self-serving belief is firmly in place, the rest is left to confirmation bias—that tendency to view any new information that supports your belief as proof that your belief was right in the first place, while completely ignoring or discarding any new information that contradicts or disproves your belief.

In this self-serving contradictory mindset, Aliyah reflected, Divine truth was the necessary arbiter in human justice. Without evidence from God Himself that all humans were created equal—and exceeded each other only in sincere faith and good character—there would be many who would live and die genuinely believing they themselves were inherently superior (or inferior) to others.

But amongst even professed believers in God, racism had permeated the hearts so much that even God's Words did little to deter the self-contradictory disease. Because the person did not want it deterred. For reasons perhaps unknown to the racists themselves, racism was subconsciously viewed as *necessary* to their existence. Their fragile egos and faulty self-serving biases gave them a sense of purpose on earth, as if they were here only to "civilize" everyone else.

When Salima had made the analogy between the systematic mistreatment of racial minorities in America and the systematic mistreatment of marriage minorities—namely men and women in polygyny—in Muslim communities, Aliyah had thought the parallel was hyperbole, a gross exaggeration. But now she understood that, until that moment of her epiphany during her algebra lesson, the reality of the bigotry that people like Kalimah regularly faced was merely a variable of "unknown value" in Aliyah's world.

It had been much more convenient for Aliyah, a person of marital privilege, to believe that "disadvantaged" people in polygyny deserved their bad reputation and social ostracizing. That way, she didn't have to admit that her negative view was merely a small but necessary tool in the same sinister beliefs that perpetuated the system of racism in America—and was fueled by both confirmation bias and discarding God's Words.

***

"I don't think I would've thought to put it like that," Salima said later, when Aliyah shared her epiphany. "But *mashaAllah*, you're right." Laughter was detectable in Salima's voice through the earpiece as Aliyah drove the short distance from work to the masjid to pick up Ibrahim.

"It's kind of scary though, isn't it?" Aliyah said, gripping the steering wheel, the earpiece snaking from her ear to her mobile phone in the compartment next to the driver's seat. "How we only get upset when *we're* being wronged, but we have no problem seeing others wronged in a similar way. Then we blame them for the suffering that was at least partly our fault."

"It *is* scary," Salima agreed. "Especially when I remember how I used to vent to Mikaeel, saying that any problems that women like Kalimah face are ones they created themselves, so I have no sympathy for them whatsoever."

"*SubhaanAllah*," Aliyah said in lighthearted humor. "You were a completely different person back then, huh?"

There was a thoughtful pause. "Not completely, no," Salima said. "Just a bit more self-centered and insecure."

"A bit *more*?" Aliyah said jokingly. "You consider yourself self-centered and insecure?"

"Don't you?" Salima spoke as if it were the most natural assumption in the world.

"No…" Aliyah said, as if waiting for the punch line of the joke.

"Well, you should," Salima said matter-of-factly.

Aliyah laughed out loud. "Are you serious?"

"Dead," Salima said. "Everybody's self-centered and insecure about *something*. It's just a matter of staying away from the selfishness and insecurity that doesn't benefit you."

"And when is either of those beneficial?" Aliyah said.

"When you're trying to save your soul or get married."

Aliyah started to ask what Salima meant then stopped herself. *"All marriage choices are selfish on some level,"* Benjamin had said during their conversation about American culture.

"You better be selfish when it comes to saving your soul," Salima said, "no matter whose feelings get hurt."

When Aliyah thought of how her family was hurt after she became Muslim, she realized that she was living proof of believing that she had to put herself first sometimes.

"And like I told you when you were stressing over Jacob," Salima said. "When you're deciding about marriage, then all you need to consider are Allah, the man, and you."

Aliyah slowed her car behind a long line of cars at a stoplight down the street from the masjid. "But what about insecurity?" she said. "How is that good?"

"You should never be too sure of yourself," Salima said. "That's why we have *naseehah* and *Istikhaarah*." She grunted. "And trust me, I didn't seek advice or ask Allah's guidance before I treated Kalimah like I did. That's why I say I was a bit more self-centered and insecure than I am now," she said. "And for all the wrong reasons."

"But it's a difficult subject," Aliyah said. "I don't think I would've ever married Jacob while he was married to Deanna."

"And I think you're right for that," Salima said. "I'm not pro-polygamy. But today, I'm a bit wiser when it comes to staying out of matters that don't concern me. Now I just know polygamy isn't something I want for myself."

Aliyah immediately thought of the hadith, *Part of a person's good Islam is that he stays out of matters that don't concern him.*

"But," Salima added, "not wanting it for myself is a far cry from screaming, 'What women in her right mind would marry an already married man, especially in a country where it's not allowed? You reap what you sow!'" Salima grunted. "*Astaghfirullah*," she said in self-reproach. "I used to say that all the time.'"

Aliyah was quiet momentarily. "I guess knowing someone in polygyny kind of brings a human face to it though," she said in thoughtful reflection, wondering how she would feel about plural marriage if she had someone like Kalimah as a friend. "So that helps."

Aliyah heard Salima cough laughter. "Not necessarily," Salima said. "For most of us, it just gives us a tangible target for our vitriol. And believe me, we're *searching* for their faults so we can announce to everyone why *nobody* should do it."

"*SubhaanAllah*," Aliyah said. "In a way, I think I'm guilty of that. I know it's allowed, but I still can't wrap my mind around it."

"Like you said, racism makes sense," Salima replied. "We can tell a lot about what's *really* in our hearts based on what we defend and what we condemn." Salima added, "And what we work to fix and what we work to tear down."

Aliyah nodded thoughtfully as the light turned green, and she lifted her foot off the break pedal and eased the car forward. The masjid came into view, and her thoughts immediately shifted to Ibrahim.

"Marriages have always been fraught with problems," she heard Salima's voice through the earpiece. "But Muslim communities are constantly working to *fix* problems in monogamous marriages," Salima said.

"That's true," Aliyah uttered non-committedly.

"We have lectures, counseling, and of course community support," Salima said. "But with plural marriages, we do everything we can to tear them down." She huffed. "And we guilt men and women into never doing it. We use legal arguments, we pass around bad stories as cautionary tales, and in some communities," she said, her voice rising in disapproval, "imams refuse to even perform the ceremonies."

Aliyah put on her right signal before turning into the parking lot. "But that's to protect women from being taken advantage of," she said.

Salima coughed laughter. "No, it's to protect the imams and masjids from legal and social backlash if they're ever accused of supporting bigamy in this country," she said. "But it sounds better to say they're doing it for women's protection."

Aliyah wasn't sure she agreed with that, but she didn't speak her thoughts aloud.

"So yeah," Salima said. "Racism definitely makes sense."

“That’s a difficult position to be in though,” Aliyah said, maneuvering the steering wheel as she guided her car into a parking space in front of the masjid. “In America, you *do* have to worry about legal and social backlash. No community wants a reputation for supporting people who are doing wrong.”

“Well, I’ll tell you what Kalimah said when I argued the same thing.”

“What’s that?”

“Then why not start programs to support people who are doing it right?” Salima responded.

Aliyah didn’t know what to say to that.

“And counsel the people who are doing it wrong,” Salima added. “Just like we do with monogamy.”

The shadow of a smile formed on Aliyah’s face. “Well, she has a point there.”

“Kalimah was saying, that way, we can build more positive polygyny marriages that Muslims can look to as an example,” Salima explained.

Aliyah opened her mouth to respond then stopped when she heard the sound of the *adhaan* through the earpiece. “Salima?” Aliyah said, flustered momentarily. “Are you at work?”

“No,” Salima said. “I left early to come to the masjid. The imam asked to meet me *insha’Allah*.”

A knowing smile formed on Aliyah’s face. “Is it about you and Larry?” Aliyah teased.

Aliyah heard Salima laugh. “No…” Salima said. “They asked Reem if—” She stopped midsentence at the sound of someone else talking, the *adhaan* still reverberating in the background.

“I have to go,” Salima said quickly then gave salaams before disconnecting the call.

When Aliyah entered the masjid and opened the door to the prayer area and quietly stepped inside, Ibrahim was still sitting in the *musallaa* in front of the Qur’an teacher, who was giving him instruction though most of the other children had gone home. Several men and women were standing, bowing, or prostrating in *Sunnah* prayers, scattered about the *musallaa* in their respective sections.

Aliyah slipped off her shoes and kneeled to place them on the rack. When she stood again and walked toward a place in the back of the *musallaa* where there weren’t many women, she was overcome with a feeling of gratefulness for being Muslim. Perhaps it was the spiritual tranquility of the masjid at the moment or seeing her son studying Qur’an, but her heart swelled with a happiness that was difficult to contain. And the smile on her face was only close-lipped and restrained because she didn’t want to draw too much attention to herself.

Amidst all the pain and confusion in the last year, Aliyah had forgotten that being guided to Islam was a gift from Allah. That He’d given His gift to her while so many others were misguided was something for which she could never be properly thankful. It hurt that she’d lost her birth family in the process, but after the jarring encounter with her mother, she was beginning to realize that not being in direct contact with them was not necessarily a bad thing.

After praying the congregational prayer, Aliyah walked over to Ibrahim and greeted him, and he enthusiastically told her how his day had gone. Apparently, he was advancing well in his Qur'anic studies.

In the lobby of the masjid, Aliyah heard someone call her name. She turned to see a familiar face framed by the floral cloth of a hijab. It took a second for her to realize who it was.

"Salima?" she said, a confused but pleased grin spreading on her face.

"Does it suit me?" Salima said when they were face-to-face.

"Anything would suit you *mashaAllah*," Aliyah said sincerely, unsure how much she should compliment Salima's *khimaar* since she knew the head-wrap was what Salima favored. "But you look really good in hijab."

Salima raised an eyebrow. "In hijab?" she said good-naturedly.

"I mean *this* hijab," Aliyah said quickly, embarrassed laughter in her voice.

Salima flipped her hand dismissively, a hesitant smirk on her face. "It's okay," she said. "I get it. Everyone's proud of me for dressing like they do."

Aliyah couldn't tell if Salima was being sarcastic, so she just maintained a friendly expression.

"But I think I can get used to it," Salima said, nodding thoughtfully. "I don't look half bad."

"What made you wear it today?" Aliyah said, feeling that was safe to ask.

Salima lifted a shoulder in a shrug. "I thought it was the respectful thing to do," she said honestly. "Reem told the board about me when they asked for a replacement Qur'an teacher, and I wanted to look fully Muslim when I met with them."

Aliyah's eyebrows rose in surprise. "*MashaAllah.* You're going to start teaching Qur'an here?"

"That's what it looks like…"

"What days will you be teaching?"

"We haven't worked out all the details," Salima said. "But for now they want me at least once a week, either in the evenings or on weekends."

"So you might teach more than that?" Aliyah said, a smile in her voice.

Salima coughed laughter. "When they found out I have an *ijaazah*, they wanted me here every day," she said. "They said it's hard to find a qualified female Qur'an instructor who can teach on that level."

"That's really good, *mashaAllah*," Aliyah said sincerely.

She drew her eyebrows together after a moment's pause. "But you work fulltime…"

"Exactly," Salima agreed with a knowing smirk. "So now I have to decide what to do."

"You're willing to quit your job?" Aliyah asked, unrestrained surprise in her voice. She hoped she didn't sound like she disagreed.

Salima shrugged, uncertainty in her expression. "I'm willing to do a lot of things these days," she said, humor in her tone. "Thanks to you and Larry."

Aliyah pulled her head back in surprise, a confused smile creasing the sides of her mouth. "Me and Larry?"

"I keep hearing your voice in my head," Salima said. "So I'm trying not to be one of those anti-hijab activists that we were talking about."

Aliyah shook her head in genuine confusion. "Anti-hijab activists?"

"You know..." Salima said. "Judging people because I feel they're judging me."

The confused expression remained on Aliyah's face a moment longer before she recalled the conversation that Salima was most likely talking about. *"Judging someone and sincerely caring about their soul are two different things,"* Salima had said in defense of her reasons for not getting into conversations with people about why she wore the head-wrap instead of the *khimaar*. *"But how would you know whether or not someone sincerely cares?"* Aliyah had said. *"I don't mean any disrespect to you. But isn't that the very definition of judging to claim to know someone's intentions? If it's wrong to judge someone for how they dress, isn't it just as wrong to judge someone for trying to help?"*

Aliyah nodded, chuckling. "I don't think I mentioned anything about anti-hijab activism though."

"I know," Salima said, a smile in her voice. "Those are my words." She shrugged. "But the same difference."

"If you say so..." Aliyah said good-naturedly.

"Well, if I'm fighting for the right to *not* wear hijab while insisting that anyone advising me to obey Allah is judgmental, then I'm an anti-hijab activist."

Aliyah maintained a polite expression, unsure what to say to that. "And Larry?" she said. "What does he have to do with any of this hijab talk?"

The way Salima's face softened at Aliyah's mention of Larry made Aliyah see just how much Salima really liked him. Salima averted her gaze momentarily. "We were talking the other day," she said, "and he asked if there was any religious significance to the different way I wear my hijab."

Aliyah nodded, but she didn't understand fully where Salima was coming from. Why hadn't she just explained to Larry what she had to Aliyah months ago? Larry would probably understand.

Salima coughed laughter. "I think that was the first time I was tongue-tied about the subject," she said, embarrassment in her tone. "In my head, I'd always rationalized the way I dress, saying 'At least I'm covered.' But when he asked that question, expecting me to have this deep, Islamic answer, I felt so stupid. I had no idea what to say to him."

Aliyah nodded again, this time understanding Salima's reasoning.

"And all I kept thinking about was *ayah* thirty-one in *An-Noor* where Allah instructs women to take their *khimaar* and draw it over their bosom area," Salima said, embarrassed humor still in her tone. "And I couldn't think of one good reason that I did the exact opposite with my headscarf."

"Is Haroon here?" Ibrahim's small voice said from next to Aliyah as he looked at Salima. Aliyah had almost forgotten that her son was standing there.

"No, sweetie," Salima said softly to him, switching subjects seamlessly. "He's with Uncle Larry."

"Ooooh," Ibrahim said, his voice full of excitement as he turned to look at Aliyah. "Can I go with Uncle Larry too?"

Aliyah smiled down at him and rubbed his head. "Not today," Aliyah said.

***

Salima fought the twinge of envy that stabbed her as she witnessed the mutual compassion between mother and son. It wasn't that she resented the connection that Aliyah had with Ibrahim, but it reminded her of how Mikaeel had been with his children. There wasn't a day that went by except that a piece of Salima grieved for what both she and Haroon had lost when Mikaeel and their eldest son and only daughter died in a car accident one night.

"Let me go and speak to the imam again real quick," Salima said, polite apology in her voice. "I forgot to ask him something."

"Okay. *Insha'Allah*, we'll talk later," Aliyah said. "Let me know how it goes." She offered Salima a smile. "It'll be nice to have you here. I might re-enroll in Qur'an myself if you're the teacher."

Salima shook her head and squeezed Aliyah's arm affectionately. "Don't say that, *ukhti*. You should enroll in Qur'an because it's offered, not because I'm the teacher."

Aliyah brought a hand to her mouth, a humored expression on her face. "I'm sorry. I didn't mean…"

"It's okay," Salima said, releasing Aliyah's arm. "Reem will be missed, and I doubt I'll be able to do her precedent justice, *mashaAllah, barakAllaahufeehaa*."

Aliyah nodded in humble acknowledgement. "She was a good teacher, *mashaAllah*."

"She's the one who suggested to the imam that I take her place," Salima said, feeling obligated to give credit where credit was due.

"*MashaAllah*," Aliyah said. "You mentioned that."

There was a brief silence before Aliyah offered Salima the salaams and turned to go, lifting her hand in a wave as she gripped Ibrahim's hand with her other.

"Aliyah?" Salima said. When Aliyah glanced back, Salima leaned into her, clipping her on the shoulder, and whispered so that Ibrahim wouldn't hear, "Don't be too hard on Reem, okay? She's not a bad person. She's just going through a lot. You two should keep in touch."

Ignoring the puzzled expression on Aliyah's face, Salima returned Aliyah's salaams then walked away.

***

*"I'd rather be single than share my husband!"*

Salima winced at the memory, dropping her head momentarily to gather her composure before walking into the imam's office. It was probably the most irrational thought in the world, but that single utterance in a moment of anger was what had come rushing back to her after she'd learned the news of her husband's death.

*"Don't say that,"* Kalimah had said so many years ago following Salima's outburst. Kalimah's voice was low in warning though she had been as hotheaded as Salima only moments before. "*Say,* 'Astaghfirullah,'" she said, her voice teetering between sternness and trepidation.

"*So it's a* sin *to prefer the Sunnah of monogamy now?"* Salima had retorted, indignant.

*"No,"* Kalimah had said. *"You just shouldn't utter* du'aa *in vain."*

*"First of all, it's not a* du'aa,*"* Salima had said. *"And it's not in vain. It's what I truly feel."*

*"Just be careful what you wish for..."*

*"It's not a wish. It's a fact."*

Feet from her, a smile spread on the imam's face at the sight of Salima at his door. "*As-salaamu'alaikum*, sister," he said, waving her inside. "Come on in."

"*Wa'alaiku mus salaam*," she muttered in reply, thoughts still distracted as she walked into the office.

Was she overdoing it? Salima wondered, doubt gripping her. Her atonement for that careless statement? Had she become so fearful of Allah's punishment that she was going to the opposite extreme? Were her strong views in support of Kalimah and other women who chose polygyny making her callous and insensitive to those who held other views?

She hoped not.

*Astaghfirullah,* she mouthed inaudibly, heeding Kalimah's advice from so long ago, as she did so many times a day since her life was turned upside down.

## 28
## The Marriage Story

"You can contest it, of course," Attorney Bryan Schmidt told Deanna as she sat across from him at his office Thursday morning, less than seven days from the thirty-day deadline to respond to Jacob's divorce petition. "But if saving money is your goal, the best route is reaching a mutual agreement about the terms of divorce as opposed to contesting it altogether," he said. "And the best route for that is to avoid court completely."

Deanna grimaced and leaned back in her chair. "So if he wants a divorce, he just gets it?" Her voice was still a bit raspy, but she was getting used to the sound of it though she doubted she'd ever find it palatable.

"Not necessarily," Bryan said. "A judge can refuse to grant a divorce, but divorces are usually refused without prejudice. So a person can keep seeking a divorce until he or she fulfills the requirements of the court."

"I'll take that as a yes," Deanna muttered in aggravation. "So what am I paying *you* for?"

Bryan frowned thoughtfully. "That's a question only you can answer," he said. "My retainer is twenty-five hundred dollars, and I charge five hundred dollars an hour after that. I occasionally grant discounts for potentially lucrative cases, but—"

"Potentially lucrative cases?" Deanna sneered.

"—I make exceptions to even that every now and then."

"So basically you just make money off of everyone else's problems and misery?" Deanna said.

The hint of a smile appeared at the corners of Bryan's mouth. "That's definitely one way to look at it," Bryan said. "So I suppose you and I have something in common."

Deanna contorted her face. "What's that supposed to mean?"

"You're a marriage counselor, right?"

Refusing the bait, she remained quiet, face still contorted as she looked at him.

"Without other people's problems or misery, neither you nor I could make a living, could we?"

She grunted. "Just tell me what I need to do to get this over with as fast as possible." She added for emphasis, "Without going broke."

The smile continued to play at Bryan's lips, and Deanna sensed he was enjoying a private joke. "Like I said, that's mostly your decision. With the exception of this meeting that I offered free of cost because of your recent representation in the aggravated assault case, every meeting, phone call, or work done for your divorce will be billed at the price I mentioned."

"Okay, fine," Deanna said. "Just tell me what I need to do."

"As I said, that's your decision. I can only help you with the most legally sensible approach to what you want."

"Can you stop speaking in riddles?" she said, feeling herself growing annoyed. "I don't know *what* to do. I don't even *want* a divorce, for God's sake."

"Well, the fastest and cheapest route is to just sign the paper and agree to all his terms."

"That's ridiculous," Deanna said. "I'm not giving him a penny."

Bryan leaned forward and typed something into his MacBook. "What about custody of your sons?"

Deanna felt the fire of rage building inside her. "I refuse to live as a single mother. So if he wants a divorce, then he loses his right to free childcare."

"Well, that wouldn't be free. He'd have to pay child support."

She huffed. "No," she said, her voice tight in fury. "He can have custody, but I get visitation rights, and I don't pay a single cent to him for *any*thing."

"So you aren't willing to pay child support?"

"Of course not," she said, glaring at Bryan as if he'd lost his mind. "He's the one who wants the divorce, so he should be paying *me*."

"Okay..." The tapping on his keyboard filled the silence between them momentarily. "But I have to warn you, if you demand any money from him, it'll most likely be contested, which means the divorce could end up being a back-and-forth case, which can get really expensive."

"You asked what I wanted," Deanna said, aggravated, "so I'm telling you. But I'm not willing to pay a lot of money for this."

"Then I suggest making demands he's most likely to fulfill."

Deanna glanced at her watch, wondering if this free hour was almost up. She still had just under twenty minutes.

"Like what?"

"Give him everything he asked for—"

"Absolutely *not*."

"—except you pay nothing to him, and he pays nothing to you. Any accounts or assets that are in both of your names are split fifty-fifty, and neither of you seeks alimony. He gets custody of your sons, and you get weekend visitation rights." Bryan was typing as he talked, glancing from his MacBook to Deanna then from Deanna to his MacBook. "How does that sound?"

Deanna was quiet momentarily. "I don't like it," she muttered, clenching her teeth momentarily. Bryan glanced at the clock as a shadow of impatience crossed his face, and Deanna could tell he felt she was wasting his time. "But if he agrees to it, I guess that's fine." She shook her head firmly. "As long as I'm not paying *anything* except lawyer fees."

***

Saturday morning Jacob was sitting in his home office, engrossed in making the final notations on his non-profit application when he heard the sound of pounding on his front door. He immediately wheeled his office chair back to the window behind him and peered outside. When he saw a FedEx truck idling in front of his house, he hurried downstairs before the driver could leave an attempted delivery notification.

After signing on the electronic panel, Jacob closed the door and locked it with one hand and examined the package with the other. He creased his forehead as he saw the familiar name Attorney Bryan Schmidt and Associates on the return address label.

He tore along the perforated strip in the cardboard and tossed the envelope on the front table as he pulled out the stack of papers. It was disappointing seeing Bryan Schmidt's name and law office logo above his and Deanna's names, but Jacob had expected as much. Who else would Deanna have found to represent her?

Jacob had to read through the papers twice before he allowed himself to exhale in relief. A triumphant smile played at his lips as he returned the papers to the FedEx package then walked into the living room, where he fell on his knees and rested his head on the ground in the *sajdah* for gratefulness.

He had felt a bit guilty for insisting on such overreaching terms in the divorce petition. He was not the least bit interested in taking a percentage of Deanna's money or owning any of her business. In fact, he would have voluntarily forfeited any joint ownership in her business if he'd had it, without taking a single cent. He wanted nothing but freedom from the emotionally tortuous marriage while maintaining full custody of his sons. He was even willing to pay Deanna alimony for the rest of his life if that was the price tag attached to being free of her. "She can have anything she wants," he'd told his lawyer, "as long as it's not me."

But his lawyer had advised him that this wasn't a sentiment that Jacob should put in writing. "Coming off as greedy and demanding is less risky than coming off as overly generous and desperate," the lawyer had said. "So let's reserve your diplomacy as a last resort. If she's as narcissistic as you say she is, then it'll never occur to her that you're not the least bit interested in her money, business, or book proceeds. So she'll fight tooth and nail to keep you out of her pocket, even if it means giving you uncontested custody of the children."

Jacob hadn't been so sure about Deanna's narcissism equaling her willingness to relinquish custody of Younus and Thawab. He'd assumed most narcissists used their children as both pawns in getting what they wanted and tools of punishment if their spouse no longer wanted to be married to them.

"That's only when their pride and ego are more valuable to them than their pockets," the lawyer had explained. "So unless she's in it for the fight itself, or as a personal vendetta against you, or she really does love her children more than she loves herself, she'll want to minimize her lawyer fees and come to a quick agreement to protect her assets."

Jacob had no idea where Deanna's ultimate values lay, but he knew that having custody of his children meant more to him than any wealth or assets. So that was one fight he was willing to take to the last penny in his pocket, or even debt, if it came to that.

***

Deanna's eyes shot open as she sat up in bed suddenly Saturday morning, feeling as if she'd been punched in the stomach. The aching had her bent over and clutching her abdomen as she let out a blood-curdling scream of anguish. The sound seemed to come from something feral and incorrigible. Even as her neck ached and the beastly sound burned her throat, she couldn't stop the screaming. It was elongated and repetitive, dropping off in a horrible sobbing moan followed by a quick, audible inhalation of breath before picking up again full force.

It wasn't until she heard the insistent pounding, then her father's demanding voice and the rattling of her locked door that she tried to remember where she was. In those first moments, she had no cognizance of being in any definite location. She'd only known that she was utterly and terribly alone, that heart-wrenching reality delivering a blow that was palpable in the gut. But even as she recognized her father's angry voice, she felt as if she were in her prison cell but on the bed that she and Jacob had shared. Except Jacob was not there, and she knew with a certainty that pulsated in her veins that this was a tragedy that her own hands had brought forth. And she feared that God Himself was looking down on her with a sense of smug satisfaction for giving her exactly what she deserved.

"Deanna, baby!" It was her mother's voice now.

But even as the reality of her surroundings slowly quieted the confusion of her mind, she couldn't stop the screaming.

The door banged open, slamming against the wall in a crash, the brass handle dangling off its screws. Then there was the sudden rushing of footfalls, and a moment later she was being rocked and squeezed so tightly that Deanna could barely catch her breath between screams.

"It's okay," her mother consoled. "It was just a bad dream." It was then that Deanna realized that her mother had left her own bed to come to her side. Though Kerri Michaels had regained full control of her limbs, she had been directed to remain on bed rest, only getting up when necessary.

"What's all this fuss about?" Barry demanded, a thick fold of annoyance between his brows.

Deanna's screams had died down, but she was sobbing inconsolably. Unable to stand the look of contempt on her father's face, she laid her head on her mother's chest and tried to catch her breath between sobs.

"Why don't you go on to bed, Barry?" Deanna heard her mother say, an edge of irritation in her tone.

It wasn't long before Deanna heard the retreating sound of his heavy footsteps and the clanking of her door against the frame. But she could tell by the sound of it that the door would need to be repaired before it could close properly.

"Now tell Mommy what's bothering you," Kerri said, gently moving Deanna back so she could look her in the eye.

The compassionate way her mother asked the question sent Deanna into a fit of sobs again.

"It's okay," Kerri said, patting Deanna's shoulders gently and squeezing her again. "Tell me when you're ready."

"I want—" Deanna's high-pitched voice came out as a pitiful whine that was interrupted by the sudden need to inhale. "I want—" she tried again. But she sounded more pitiful than before, as if she were a child just learning to speak.

"What do you want, baby?" Kerri said, gently pushing Deanna back until they made eye contact again.

"I want…" Deanna spoke slowly, giving herself time to suck in her breath then exhale slowly. "…to be..." *Inhale, exhale.* "…a better person."

***

"So that's it?" Aliyah asked, a confused but pleased expression on her face. "If she signs it, the marriage is dissolved?"

"That's what it looks like."

It was Saturday afternoon, and Aliyah and Jacob sat on a quilt in the backyard of his home as Younus, Thawab, and Ibrahim played a war game that Aliyah couldn't quite figure out. Freshly fallen leaves scattered the grass around them and cushioned the ground beneath them. The air was cool but comfortable with an occasional chilly breeze. Jacob wore a thin black leather jacket and Aliyah a dark green button-up sweater over her shoulder *abaya* and matching *khimaar*.

Aliyah didn't know how she felt about the news. In a way, it made her sad because it reminded her of when she'd gotten a divorce from Matt. That sinking feeling of suffocating loneliness was something she'd never forget. Any time she heard of someone getting a divorce, she felt herself getting a little choked up.

"May Allah make it easy for her," Aliyah muttered just above a whisper, swallowing the lump in her throat.

She felt Jacob looking at her, an odd expression on his face.

"What?" she said, self-conscious laughter in her voice as she met his gaze.

"Did you just make *du'aa* for Deanna?" There was a smirk on his face, as if he were about to make fun of her.

She averted her gaze and shrugged, the shadow of an embarrassed smile forming on one side of her mouth. "Yes, why not? Divorce is horrible. I don't wish it on anyone."

"It doesn't feel horrible to me," Jacob said. "I'm actually pretty excited, to be honest," he said. "And I certainly wish it on me and Deanna."

"I didn't mean it like that," Aliyah said quietly, unsure how to put her thoughts into words. "I just remember how it felt, that's all."

Jacob nodded thoughtfully, squinting his eyes toward the boys. He was quiet for so long that Aliyah feared that she had offended him.

“I make *du’aa* for her too,” Jacob said finally, his gaze still looking out over his yard. “It’s good to know I’m not the only one.” He turned his head and smiled at Aliyah. “But I still want the divorce.”

“I do too,” she said, smiling because she didn’t know what else to do. It all felt so awkward, and exhilarating. It was difficult to believe that in just a week’s time, they might be able to actually start building their lives together without the constraints of social discretion. Yet her former best friend would be suffering through their happiness. And though there was the empathy for what Deanna would be going through, there was the freeing heartfelt conviction that Deanna’s suffering was not hers to bear.

“Will you come live with me once the divorce is final?” Jacob said, his thumb rubbing the back of Aliyah’s hand that was on the quilt next to him.

Her instinct was to pull her hand away out of fear that someone would see them, but his touch was so comforting that she kept her hand right where it was. His touch was a soft, cool warmness that matched the autumn scene around them, but it incited a firestorm inside her. Her heart raced wildly, and she found herself catching her breath though she did everything she could to mask her weakening resolve.

“Maybe…” It was the only thing she trusted herself to intelligibly utter right then. Anything else would betray the dizzying desire she was trying to quell.

The flat of Jacob’s palm moved to the back of her hand as he continued the massage. Aliyah closed her eyes and let herself enjoy the moment, a smile lingering on her face, her face lifted slightly toward the sky.

“Come with me,” Jacob’s deep voice said in her ear. A moment later, he was on his feet, tugging at her hand.

“But…” Aliyah said as she opened her eyes and stumbled to her feet, unable to keep from giggling in self-conscious excitement. As she trailed only slightly behind him as he gripped her hand and walked toward the house, she felt like a schoolgirl about to cut class for the first time. But she trusted her experienced guide, and her heart pounded with such fierce anticipation that she imagined there wasn’t anything he could ask from her right then that she wouldn’t give.

“Don’t worry,” Jacob said, a smile in his voice as he guided her through the house and up the stairs and down the hall. But there was no need for the warning. Aliyah was not worried, even as he stopped in front of his room to gaze at Aliyah a moment more, a mischievous grin on his face. Though her heart would not steady to a normal rhythm and she couldn’t hold his gaze for long, she’d never felt safer and more at ease in her adult life.

When Jacob reached behind her to push open his office door instead of the door across the hall, Aliyah knew he just wanted to spend some time alone together, away from the children. And this made her resolve even weaker, knowing that he was doing everything to respect her wishes.

After pulling her inside, he closed the door and locked it. “Relax,” he told her as he held her face in his hands. “I’ll never do anything you’re not ready for.” Then he slipped his arms around the waist of her sweater, and he held her tighter than he ever had before, and she relaxed in his possessive embrace. He kissed her softly at first, then expressed the same fire of passion that Aliyah was battling right then. It was only a matter of seconds before the flame erupted in her, and she eagerly returned his affections.

Aliyah felt his hand trace the fabric of her *khimaar*, and a second later, she heard his deep voice in her ear. "Why don't you trust me?"

"Wh-at?" Because she was having trouble catching her breath, the question came out in two syllables.

He pulled his head back until they were looking into each other's eyes, then he smoothed down the cloth of her headscarf again. "Why don't you trust me?" he said again. "You always wear hijab and *jilbaab* around me."

Aliyah averted her gaze, and her cheeks grew warm in embarrassment. It was something she'd hoped they wouldn't have to talk about. But for some time, she sensed his confusion, and perhaps even offense, at her remaining fully covered in his presence. Initially, she'd told herself it was because their children didn't yet know of their marriage. But now she knew it was something else, and she had a pretty good idea what was inspiring the discomfort.

"I'm sorry," she murmured, flustered and ashamed, eyes still averted. A minute passed in silence between them, and Aliyah could feel him looking at her. But she couldn't bring herself to look him in the eye.

"Is it something I did to make you uncomfortable?" she heard him ask, concern and apology etched in his voice.

Aliyah took a step back from him as she shook her head. "No, nothing like that."

She felt him reluctantly let go of her, his arms dropping to his sides as she turned away from him and walked toward his office desk.

"Then what is it, sweetness?"

Aliyah's heart softened at the term of endearment. He'd never used a nickname for her before. She pulled out his office chair and lowered herself into it, offering him a polite but distant smile as she looked at him. "It's not a big deal," she said, but she didn't even sound convincing to herself. "It's nothing you did."

"Is this something you want to wait for too?" he asked, genuine curiosity in his tone. "Because I don't mind. I just want to make sure it's not something I've done."

"It's not that," she said. "It's just..." She searched her mind for the right way to explain the truth without incriminated herself. Self-conscious, she coughed laughter. "...I don't know. It's just..." She drew in a deep breath and exhaled. "...two things, I guess."

"What two things?" Jacob said, walking over to her and standing directly in front of her so that she had to look up at him.

"Well... Matt..." As soon as she uttered his name, she felt self-conscious all over again.

"What did he do?" Jacob's voice rose, the instinctive male protectiveness surfacing.

"Nothing," Aliyah said quickly. "He just didn't like my hair, so…"

Jacob contorted his face as if that was the most ridiculous thing he'd ever heard.

"…I guess I'm just a little self-conscious about it, that's all."

"Well, you don't have to feel like that around me," Jacob assured her.

"I know," Aliyah said, laughter in her voice, averting her eyes again. "But it wasn't just Matt…"

"What do you mean?" The male protectiveness was in his voice again, as if preparing to come to her defense in response to anyone who'd dared to hurt her.

"It was Deanna too," she said finally, unable to look at him. "She said I didn't know how to take care of myself." There was embarrassed laughter in her tone. "And that part of the reason that Matt wanted Nikki was because her hair looked better than mine."

"*What?*"

"And that since she had good hair, she never had to worry about problems like that with you in her marriage."

Jacob huffed. Aliyah hesitantly looked at him and saw that his face was twisted in upset.

"She actually said that your *hair* had made Matt want another wife?"

Aliyah chuckled self-consciously. Now that it was spoken aloud, it did sound ridiculous. "Yes…" But as ridiculous as it sounded, Aliyah couldn't shake the feeling of insecurity that the memory incited. "And that she'd never have that problem with you."

There was an extended silence as Jacob seemed to gather his thoughts. "Sweetness…" Jacob said softly as he lowered himself until he was kneeling in front of Aliyah so that she had to look down at him. Using both hands, he gently squeezed her legs above the knee, and this relaxed Aliyah somewhat. Even over the fabric of her abaya, his hands felt warm. "...listen to me."

Aliyah held his gaze to let him know he had her attention, but it was difficult not to look away.

"The love that Allah has put in my heart for you is something that is beyond my control," he said.

Aliyah lowered her eyes momentarily before meeting his gaze again.

"It's something I prayed to Allah to help me fight," Jacob said, "and it's something I tried to fight myself for years. So even if I wanted to, I don't have the power to remove from my heart what I feel for you."

He offered her a gentle smile. "When I saw you at that MSA dinner," he said, "it wasn't your hair or body that drew me to you. Because I couldn't see either," he explained. "It was your spirit and character."

Aliyah's cheeks grew warm, and she averted her gaze again.

"But *maa-shaa-Allaah,*" he said, gripping her hands and squeezing them affectionately as he elongated each syllable, his voice rising in emphasis with each sound. "There isn't a woman I met before or after Islam who is more physically beautiful to me than you."

He shook his head, shutting his eyes momentarily then opening them to underscore the earnestness of his words. "And you could be *bald,*" he said, "or suffering from some incurable scalp disease, and it wouldn't make me see you as any less beautiful than you are to me right now."

Aliyah felt tears welling in her eyes, moved by his words, but she willed herself not to cry.

"*Wallaahi,*" he said, swearing by Allah, "I have been tested in so many ways in my life, and I haven't always lived like I was supposed to. And on account of my sins alone, I would've never dreamed I could even *look* in the direction of a woman like you." He lifted her hands and kissed each of them, his lips resting on them for several seconds before he lifted his head and met her gaze again.

"So *please,*" Jacob said, his eyes conveying every bit of emotion Aliyah sensed from his words, "let me love *all* of you. Because there isn't a part of you that I don't fall on my knees every day and thank Allah for."

Nodding, Aliyah lifted a hand and quickly wiped her eyes before the tears could fall.

"And if the blindness of Matt and the superficiality of Deanna were the two things keeping you from relaxing in my company," Jacob said, "just know that you don't have to worry about either with me. By Allah, I see you in a way Matt never could," he said. "And your beauty is far beyond superficial to me."

Aliyah felt herself getting choked up again, but a grin formed on her face as she and Jacob held each other's gazes. When the tears slipped from her eyes, it was Jacob who reached up and wiped them away, his fingers gentle against her cheeks. He then lifted himself up from where he was kneeling and kissed the parts of her face where the tears had fallen.

A second later, they were kissing each other again, and Aliyah didn't squirm or protest when his hands reached beneath her *khimaar* until his fingers played with the kinky tangles of her puffy ponytail. The scarf pin loosened from where it held the fabric in place, and she relaxed as she felt the cloth slip from her head and fall to the floor. Jacob continued kissing her and running his hands over her natural hair until he tugged at the elastic-cloth ponytail holder, her thick hair releasing itself into an afro at the back of her head.

"I love your hair," he murmured then continued kissing her. He pushed his fingers into the kinky curly mass and let them get stuck in the tangles. "So beautiful," he said. "So so beautiful."

His words and gentleness made her feel as beautiful as his utterances made her sound, and she felt as if even her heart was smiling at the intense connection between them.

"That was only…" Aliyah said, catching her breath between words, as he moved to kiss her forehead and hair. "…the first reason."

It took a few seconds before he processed what she was saying. "What do you mean?" he said, slightly breathless himself.

"Matt and Deanna were only the first reason I never took off my hijab in front of you."

He immediately pulled back from Aliyah, apology and regret in that sudden motion. "I'm sorry," he said quickly, glancing around for her *khimaar*.

Chuckling, Aliyah reached out and grabbed his hand and tugged him back toward her. "It's okay," she said, then quickly kissed him on the lips to reassure him. "I just thought you should know."

The pain of apology in his eyes almost made Aliyah regret that she had mentioned that there had been a second reason. But she felt it was important for him to know.

"It's okay really," Aliyah said, laughter in her voice. "I'm happy this happened."

Jacob looked uncertain, as if he wanted to believe her but wanted to make sure she wasn't just saying something for his sake.

"*Wallaahi*," Aliyah said, her tone lower and gentle because she really wanted him to know she was speaking from her heart. "This moment couldn't have been better."

"But there's a second reason…" Jacob said, as if fearing that hearing it would make him feel bad for what he'd done.

Aliyah nodded. "Yes, but it's not a big deal."

"What is it?"

An embarrassed smile toyed at her lips as she averted her gaze. There really was no easy way to put this. She heaved a sigh to gather the strength to say what she needed to before looking him in the eye again. "I feared that taking off my hijab and abaya when we're together would make it that much harder to wait a full year."

***

"So Aliyah, huh?"

Salima heard Larry groan at her question, lighthearted dread in the sound. But she could tell he was genuinely uncomfortable with the question. It was late Saturday afternoon, and she held the cordless phone between her shoulder and ear as she stood in front of the sink in her kitchen, rinsing the dishes then placing them in the dishwasher.

"We're going *there*?" Larry said in a pained voice, humor in his tone.

"Yes, we are," Salima said, laughter in her voice. But she was not joking in the least. If they were going to get serious, then he had to be completely honest with her about what had happened between him and Aliyah, and about whether or not his heart was still attached to her.

"I'm telling you…" Larry said as if expressing a complete thought, his voice a warning. He gave a light whistle, as if to underscore the fact that this topic was not a good idea.

"What?" Salima said, exaggerated defensiveness in her humored tone. "Were you *that* attached that you can't even handle her *name* being mentioned?"

"No, it's nothing like that," Larry said. "It's just I know how you women are."

"What's that supposed to mean?"

"It is what it is," he said, smugness in his tone. "You know how y'all do."

Salima felt a twinge of offense, but she fought it. "No. I don't," she insisted, her voice rising to underscore her point. She tried to sound as if she were joking, but she sounded confrontational.

"Here we go," Larry said knowingly, exhaustion in his voice. But he managed to sound as if he was humored by the exchange.

"What do you mean, 'Here we go'?" Salima said defensively. "You're the one who made a snarky remark about women."

"I was just stating the facts,"

"Such as…"

"Such as you don't need a man to tell you how women are," Larry said. "That's either a trap or a fight."

"Well, with me it's neither," Salima said. "I really want to know what you think of us."

"It's not about what I think of you," Larry said. "It's what I've experienced."

Salima rolled her eyes to the ceiling as she picked up a mixing bowl and held it under a thin stream of water. "Then tell me what you've experienced," she said. "It sounds like this Aliyah situation has touched a chord."

"Now see, that's what I'm talking about." Larry spoke as if he felt he'd been wronged. She heard him cough laughter. "If you're going to make this about Aliyah, then it's a lose-lose situation."

"Why?" Salima taunted. "Because you still have feelings for her?"

"Aww man, seriously?" Larry said, laughter in his words. "You taking it there?"

"Just answer the question."

"Why? So you can crucify me for being a man?"

"So you're admitting it?" Though Salima was making light of the possibility, a surge of disappointment weighed on her, and she wished she didn't care so much about what he felt for any woman.

"I didn't admit anything," Larry said, humored defensiveness in his voice. "I just know any conversation about another woman never ends well."

"Why's that?" Salima said, her voice more serious.

"Because you women like to believe that if a man loves you, it's impossible for him to have feelings for anyone else."

Salima's heart softened at his casual mention of the word *love.* It was flattering that he would discuss it in connection with her, even if indirectly. "I don't even believe that's true for women," she countered. "So I definitely don't expect it from a man."

The extended silence on the other end of the phone told Salima that Larry hadn't expected that response.

"You serious?" Larry said, humored disbelief in his tone.

"Yes, why not?" Salima said. "We're all human."

Larry huffed, conveying in that small sound how impressed he was with her perspective. "That's different," he remarked reflectively.

"What's different?" Salima said, a smile in her voice.

"Women being honest."

Salima laughed out loud, unable to suppress how hilarious she'd found his statement. On one level, she felt that she should be offended, but Larry's frankness was so honest that it was both refreshing and comical.

"What?" she heard Larry ask. Hearing the laughter and genuine confusion in his voice only made her laugh harder.

"I'm sorry," she said finally, trying to pull herself together. "It's just funny how blunt you are."

"Oh," Larry said, coughing laughter, uncertainty in that sound. "That's new," he remarked. "Most women are offended by my bluntness."

"Well, I can't fault them for that," Salima said, smiling and shaking her head as she leaned over to place the mixing bowl upside down on the bottom rack of the dishwasher. "You certainly have a way with words."

He was silent momentarily. "I'm going to take that as a compliment," Larry said finally.

Salima shrugged, still smiling. "Well, it certainly wasn't meant as an insult. It was just an observation."

There was a thoughtful pause. "You don't have anything to worry about with me," Larry said. "I hope you know that."

Salima drew her eyebrows together in confusion. "What do you mean?"

"With Aliyah or Jasmine or anyone," he said. "The only reason I didn't approach you sooner is because you were way out of my league."

Salima's cheeks grew warm, and the smile returned to her face. "Out of your league? How?"

Larry huffed, as if the answer was obvious. "Are you kidding me? You're like this…" He paused, searching for the word. "…spiritual icon," he said finally, making Salima overcome with self-conscious flattery.

"*MashaAllah,*" she muttered humbly.

"*MashaAllah,*" he repeated, but more heartfelt, as if he were more certain of her amazingness than she was.

"So you didn't think I was some washed-up old widow?"

She heard Larry laugh, and the sound was so heartwarming that she felt herself laughing too. "Have you looked in the mirror, girl?" Larry said, the last word coming out as a groan of admiration. "There's nothing old about you."

"Except my age…" she said tentatively.

"Age ain't nothin' but a number," he said.

She smiled wide.

"But *Salima* is not a number," he said with a huff, a litany of flirtatious implications in the way his voice rose with her name.

"Then what is she?" Salima said, humor in her tone.

"She's—" He huffed again, and there was a pause that was a beat too long. "Let's not go there," he said, his voice serious, as if in self-rebuke. "I want to save some things for later."

Salima's eyes widened as she brought a hand to her mouth. "I didn't mean…" she stuttered, her face going warm.

"I know, I know," Larry said sincerely, his voice subdued. "But as you know, subtlety is not my strength. And the last thing I want to do is disrespect a Muslim queen like you."

"*MashaAllah*," Salima said, as if thanking him.

"I'm just keeping it real," Larry said honestly.

"Well, I appreciate the respect," she said, her voice low and reflective. "Truly."

"Well, I appreciate the honor of you letting me speak to you." He spoke as if he knew she'd never agree to marry him. "Someone as regal as you deserves nothing but respect."

She was quiet momentarily, uncomfortable with the way his words seemed to lower himself while raising her up. "And someone as honorable as you deserves no less respect," she countered.

Larry coughed in self-conscious laughter. "I don't think so."

"I'm serious." The tone of Salima's voice mirrored the honesty of her words. "You *are* honorable, *mashaAllah*."

"I still have a lot to work on," he said, as if still beating himself up over the misunderstanding between him and Aliyah and Salima.

"We all have a lot to work on, Larry," Salima said, her voice soft but firm in its insistence. "The fact that you realize that about yourself is in itself honorable. And that's a lot more than I can say about most brothers in this community." She grunted. "Or sisters."

The extended silence made Salima's heart drop in sadness. She feared that her thoughtless remarks to Aliyah many months ago had left him with deep insecurities regarding his spiritual worth.

"Just make *du'aa* Allah blesses me with a righteous wife." Though his words came out confident, Salima sensed that they were laced in melancholic self-rebuke.

"So you're giving up on me already?" Salima teased, hoping to lighten the mood.

"Nah," he said, drawing out his response as if he were still lost in thought. "I just want to see you with the right person."

"And why can't that be you?" Normally, Salima wouldn't be as forward as this, but she didn't want Larry to hang up thinking she thought she was better than he was. Larry wasn't giving himself enough credit, and she wanted him to know it.

"Come on, Salima…" he said, as if egging her to admit that she already knew the punch line of a joke that had been left unfinished.

"I believe in Allah, Larry," she said firmly after a thoughtful silence. "Do you?"

He didn't respond immediately. "Yes," he said finally. The single utterance was so humble and sincere that it sounded as if he were testifying to his *shahaadah* again.

"Do you believe that He is *Al-'Aleem*, *Al-Hakeem*?" she said. "The All Knowing, the All Wise?"

"Yes."

"Do you believe in *al-qadr*, His divine decree, the good and the bad?"

"Yes."

"Do you believe in *al-Lawhil-Mahfoodh*, the Preserved Tablet above the heavens in which Allah inscribed everything that will happen until the Day of Judgment."

"Yes," he said, his voice low, as if in humble submission to the glory of his Creator. "I do."

"Then can you tell me, with certainty, that as we speak," Salima said, her voice a gentle challenge, "the All-Knowing, the All-Wise has decreed that you and I should never get married, and that someone else is written for us in that inscription above the heavens?"

Larry was silent for a few seconds, and Salima could sense that he was moved to self-reflection. "No, I can't," he said quietly, subdued emotion in that sound.

"Then let's find out what is written for us."

***

Aliyah and Jacob talked for hours, taking a break only to call their sons inside to shower, pray *Asr*, and eat. After Jacob led everyone in prayer and everyone had eaten, Younus, Thawab, and Ibrahim retreated to the playroom while Aliyah and Jacob returned to Jacob's home office to continue talking.

After Jacob closed the door and locked it, Aliyah removed the *khimaar* and abaya she'd worn for prayer, revealing a white low-neck long-sleeved fitted T-shirt and wide-legged jeans. It wasn't the outfit that she would've chosen that morning had she known that Jacob would see her uncovered for the first time. Nevertheless, she felt comfortable and relaxed in his presence, even as she wished that her hair had been plaited or twisted in an attractive style before he'd removed her *khimaar*. But she figured that it was better this way. If he could appreciate her casual, homey look, then she wouldn't feel pressured to keep up a stellar appearance. And he'd be more enamored with her beauty when she took the time to dress up for him.

"But I'm grateful for my marriage to Deanna," Jacob said, lowering himself onto one of the large floor pillows that lined a wall. He motioned for Aliyah to join him, and after hanging her *khimaar* and abaya on the back of his office chair, she sat down on a pillow next to him.

"*Alhamdulillah*," Aliyah said. "I think that's the best way to look at it."

He put his arm around Aliyah and pulled her to him. It was as if it were the most natural gesture in the world. She laid her head on his shoulder, and he forked through her hair with his fingers, even as they kept getting caught in the tangles.

"It's the only way to look at it," she heard him say above her head. "It taught me so much."

"*MashaAllah*," she muttered, enjoying the relaxing comfort of his hands stroking her head.

"I think Deanna was a blessing and a punishment for me."

Aliyah pursed her lips thoughtfully. "At the same time, you think?" she asked.

"Yes," Jacob said reflectively. "But I didn't realize the punishment part until a year ago."

Aliyah drew her eyebrows together, intrigued. "So before that," she said, "you thought of your marriage as a blessing?"

He huffed, humor in that sound. "Can you believe it?"

She didn't know what to say to that. "I don't really know what your relationship was like," she said tentatively, unsure if uttering *yes* or *no* was an appropriate response. She didn't want to taint the sincerity of his reflections by saying anything negative about Deanna. For this sensitive subject, Aliyah wanted to offer a compassionate listening ear, and no more.

"Well, it was rough to put it lightly," he said. "I was miserable almost every day since we got married."

Forehead creased, Aliyah moved her head so she could look Jacob in the eye. "*Every* day?"

"We had our moments," he said tentatively, exhausted regret in his voice.

The irony of the statement was not lost on Aliyah. Both his confession and subdued tone was like that of one confessing to the occasional argument or fight in a relationship rooted in mutual love and compassion. But he was speaking of the occasional moments of happiness in a relationship filled with agony and regret. The realization was so weighty in its sadness that she just quietly laid her head back on his shoulder. Her thoughts grew distant as she relaxed under the massage of his fingers through her hair.

"But they were few and far between," he said with a sigh.

"Then why did you view it as a blessing for so long?" Aliyah said, finding her voice.

"Because that's what living in guilt and obligation does to you," he said. "You don't allow yourself to interpret anything in your life except through the lens of a blessing. And if you feel even slightly frustrated or angry, you fight it and tell yourself you're just being ungrateful to Allah."

"*SubhaanAllah*," Aliyah said, realizing she'd done the same for many years. "But isn't that a *good* thing?" she asked rhetorically, reflecting on her own soul. "Is there ever a time that that could be bad?"

"Looking at everything through the lens of a blessing?" he asked aloud to answer his own question. "No, that can never be bad. But attributing every feeling of frustration and anger to some deficiency in your relationship with Allah? Yes, that can be very, very bad."

Aliyah nodded thoughtfully, moved by his insight.

"Pleasing Allah isn't about ignoring problems that are literally right in front of your face," he said. "It's about handling them in a way that respects the boundaries of Allah and the rights of others at the same time."

Aliyah was silent for some time as she reflected on what he had said. "But why are we so blind to that?" she asked. "Why are we so addicted to our own misery?"

"Because it's hard to tell the difference between patience through natural hardships and suffering through self-imposed misery."

Aliyah nodded. "That's true…"

"And also because so many of us trust the institution of marriage more than we trust Allah."

Aliyah leaned her head back and narrowed her eyes at him, a confused smirk on her face. "What?"

He returned her smirk with a disbelieving smile. "Isn't it obvious?"

Aliyah just looked at him, shaking her head slightly. "No…"

"You and Matt," he said. "Deanna and I."

She blinked, holding his gaze, waiting for a less cryptic explanation.

"Why did we hold on so long when it was obvious early on that we should let go?" he asked rhetorically.

"Oh…" Aliyah shrugged, laying her head back on his shoulder. "I thought I was doing it for the sake of Allah."

He forced laughter. "Exactly," he said. "And even more than that, we believed in the 'till death do us part' marriage vow that we heard at every wedding growing up. But it never occurred to us to reflect on why it's not part of the Islamic ceremony."

"But Allah hates divorce," Aliyah said.

"Allah hates sin and disobedience," Jacob corrected. "And divorce is neither when Allah is the One who made it obvious that it's the better option for you."

Aliyah didn't know what to say to that.

"What most Muslims won't tell you is that *not* getting a divorce can also be a sin."

Aliyah turned her head, the confused expression returning to her face as she looked at Jacob again, grinning in disbelief. "How?"

"See?" Jacob said, laughing out loud, as if her question itself proved his point.

"What?" Aliyah said, laughter and genuine confusion in her voice.

"Think about it," Jacob said. "What if you're in a marriage that's harming your soul?" He raised his eyebrows to underscore his point. "And you've tried everything in your human power to make the marriage work, but it's tearing at your *emaan*?"

Aliyah nodded, seeing his point, but she maintained eye contact, listening.

"Or you're in a relationship with someone who's abusive and you know it's harming you and your children? And there's nothing you can do to help the person because they refuse to believe they have a problem?"

Aliyah frowned, her lips forming a thin line. "But it's not easy for those women to leave," she said.

"I'm not talking about ease," Jacob said. "I'm talking about doing what's necessary given your situation."

"But maybe they still think they can make it work," Aliyah offered. "Nobody can say someone's sinning for staying in a bad relationship."

Jacob shook his head. "I'm not talking about what someone *else* says," he said. "I'm talking about what you know Allah has shown *you*."

He gestured a hand in dismissiveness, a look of distaste on his face. "You know how I feel about Muslims poking their noses into other people's marriages and offering their so-called *opinions*. You and I suffered from that insanity with all that 'hot Muslim mistress' crap."

Aliyah felt Jacob's body tense in anger at the memory.

"And *bi'idhnillaah*," Jacob said, raising his voice in emphasis, "unless clear sin is happening right in front of my eyes, I'll *never* be okay with even *having* an opinion on someone else's relationship." His voice was full of emotion and conviction. "Especially when I have *no* idea how Allah sees their choices."

*"I've learned to keep my mouth shut and ask only one question when I hear about somebody else's life,"* Aliyah herself had reflected to Kalimah. *"What is Allah's view on this?"* It was interesting to see the parallels between her and Jacob's thought processes.

"I'm talking about when you *know* you're no longer in let's-make-it-work mode," Jacob said. "But you stay because you're addicted to the marriage story you've heard since you were a child. And you'd rather be able to tell the world that you put your marriage first than be able to tell Allah that you put Him first."

## 29
## The Better Person

*Apologize to Aliyah.* Deanna's hands were shaking so badly that the script was scraggly and off the lines. Just writing the note itself was so emotionally taxing that she had to push back from her desk and gather herself for a moment before continuing. It was Sunday morning, and her parents had gone to church while Deanna stayed in her room sitting in front of her computer poring over internet articles about starting life as a new person.

*If you want to be a better person today than you were yesterday,* one article read, *then the first thing you need is new vocabulary.* After that line, it had been pretty much the same suggestion mentioned in every other article she read: *Start with "I'm sorry."*

The first time she'd read this advice was Saturday night in a self-help book her mother had given her. *YOU CAN BE A BETTER PERSON!* As soon as Deanna had seen the title—in all caps followed by an exclamation mark—her stomach churned. She had to resist throwing the book out right then. But her mother's face was so full of compassion and motherly concern when she'd given it to her that Deanna wouldn't be able to look her mother in the eye if she didn't at least read the first page. Whoever this hyperactive, nauseatingly optimistic author was, she'd apparently touched Kerri's life in a significant way. Otherwise, Kerri wouldn't have offered the woman's worn, dog-eared book to her daughter.

Deanna had made it through the acknowledgments and the introduction before going to bed Saturday night. But she'd reached her limit of patience when she turned to the first chapter and saw "SAY I'M SORRY!" printed in large font at the top. She'd promptly closed the book, wondering how this author could have a single trusted friend if she could write an entire book with titles in all caps—followed by actual exclamation marks—without anyone telling her it was a bad idea, and a very off-putting one at that. The effect of this literary *faux pas* was like being yelled at through a megaphone while you were standing right in the person's face.

Deanna would have to reconsider the pros and cons of this self-improvement journey. Besides, what was the point? She wasn't a bad person, and she'd sacrificed a lot carrying the responsibility of being Aliyah's only friend. And Aliyah wasn't an easy burden to bear.

At worst Deanna had occasionally said some things she shouldn't have, particularly when she'd first met Jacob and he'd expressed interest in Aliyah. But Deanna refused to beat herself up about setting Aliyah up with Matt so she couldn't marry Jacob. Like they said, *All is fair in love and war.* And that situation was arguably both. Aliyah really wasn't good enough for Jacob, and why should Jacob have to settle for less just because he had no idea what he'd be getting himself into?

But Sunday morning, Deanna had awakened from a fitful sleep full of aggravation and annoyance. She kicked the duvet from her body, her mind racing as she lay awake infuriated that she couldn't pinpoint why she was so disturbed. An image of Jacob, face and arms glistening from the water of *wudhoo'*, had flashed in her mind, and she'd become even more enraged. *How dare you divorce me!* Deanna thought angrily. *Do you think you're* better *than me?*

But seconds later Deanna was doubled over in bed, writhing in pain as she clutched her stomach. She felt the scream in her throat but clamped her teeth shut so forcefully that her jaws hurt. The noise escaped in growling moans of high-pitched whines that her clenched teeth only slightly suppressed. Not wanting a repeat of the day before, she let go of her stomach and grabbed a pillow and pressed her face against it, muffling the feral cries.

*Involuntary screaming.* It was the first thing she'd typed into the search engine when she sat in front of her computer after her parents had left for church. Before these two episodes, she'd had no idea that such a thing even existed in human experience. And it had only been out of annoyance at having absolutely no idea what was happening to her—and her refusal to talk to anyone else about it—that she'd keyed in the term at all.

It was both comforting and alarming to see the dozens of internet search results appear on the monitor in front of her. Deanna found herself getting choked up as she read about so many others suffering from the same uncontrollable shouts and feeling utterly helpless to do anything about it.

There wasn't a plethora of expert information on the topic, but what Deanna did find was in the field of psychiatry. Suppressed anxiety and unresolved trauma were the top reasons that mental health professionals postulated were at the source of the screams. The only physiological cause that Deanna had found any information about was body tension or physical ailments caused or worsened by stress having gone unaddressed for too long. Some patients' involuntary screaming first began during something as simple as a massage, in which they were forced to relax their bodies to release tension.

*So you're stressed.*

The answer was so simple that it was almost offensive. *What am I supposed to do with that?* she thought bitterly. For all the professional mumbo jumbo these so-called experts had scattered throughout their research articles, they weren't very helpful at giving any tangible solutions. *Tell me something I can* do *about it!* she wanted to shout.

*YOU CAN BE A BETTER PERSON!*

The book was lying on the desk near the monitor, and the mere sight of it at that moment was infuriating. This time, Deanna didn't feel obligated to pretend to appreciate the book. She stood, slapping the flat of her palm on it before picking it up and throwing it against the wall in an angry grunt. She was breathing heavily though the book had merely hit the wall and tumbled right back down to her desk.

But this time it wedged itself in the wires behind the central processing unit. And that was fine with her. There, it could remain out of sight, out of mind.

Deanna slammed her body back into her chair and with the force of her weight, yanked the chair toward the desk. She then reached forward and pulled the mouse over the mouse pad until the arrow on the screen rushed across the article on involuntary screaming that she still had open. She then closed each window, having had her fill of self-incrimination for the day.

*But you* can *be a better person.*

Her heart dropped at the thought, and the heaviness of grief sat in her stomach like acid. She felt sick at the thought of living as a spinster for the rest of her life. How could she face anyone as a divorced woman? How could she face herself? *Oh my God,* Deanna's thoughts raced frantically. *I'll be like Aliyah!* The thought was so repulsive that she felt weak. *Will my business collapse? Will I be invited to do interviews and workshops anymore?* No one in their right mind would take relationship advice from someone with a failed marriage.

*But it's not my fault!* Deanna's heart screamed. *I was the perfect wife. Jacob just—*

Jacob just *what*?

For one of the first times while fuming about all the wrongs she'd suffered in her marriage, she drew a blank.

*What did Jacob do?* The question was like a taunt, and Deanna felt herself growing annoyed with the self-reproaching voice in her head.

"Only people without a proper understanding of God and the sacred bond of marriage have serious problems in their lives and marriages," she'd said in an interview once. Deanna frowned at the memory. It seemed like a lifetime ago.

"But what about divorce?" the interviewer had asked. "Certainly, people of your faith experience this problem like everyone else."

"Yes, they do," Deanna had replied, her voice full of confidence and conviction. "But only the Muslims who are ignorant and take marriage lightly. If they were really following their faith and valuing their relationships, they wouldn't be in that situation."

The acid bubbled in her stomach, making her sick in mortification. *Then how do you explain* your *predicament, Dr. Deanna Janice Bivens?*

Deanna's nose flared in aggravation. *I'm not the one taking marriage lightly! Jacob is!*

Wanting the voices in her head to stop, Deanna stood and reached behind the CPU and withdrew the worn book that her mother had given her. She narrowed her eyes at it skeptically, wondering if there was something to this hyper-optimism after all.

*YOU CAN BE A BETTER PERSON!*

This time the words hit a soft space in her heart, and she felt tears stinging her eyes. *Somebody loves you, Deanna,* a voice said. *Somebody cares about you.* Then the author's perky voice: *And we're rooting for you to win!*

With her free hand, Deanna wiped away the tears before they could fall. Book still in hand, she sat down in front of her computer and searched *How to be a better person.*

Then Deanna read blog after blog and article after article saying essentially the same thing as the perky megaphone author: You need a new mindset, and it starts with taking responsibility for your actions.

Deanna groaned in begrudging acceptance of her predicament. Somehow she would have to learn to say, "I'm sorry." She wrinkled her nose as the first person who came to mind was Aliyah. The idea of apologizing to anyone, especially Aliyah of all people, was so repulsive that Deanna felt physically sick at the thought. There had to be a more sensible way to become a better person than kowtowing to pathetic people.

But still Deanna pushed herself to write the scraggly note at the top of her self-improvement "to do" list: *Apologize to Aliyah.* Deanna then slammed the pen down and pushed away from the desk.

*Aliyah should be apologizing to* me, Deanna thought angrily.

*For what?*

The voice came from her own mind, so it made no sense for Deanna to get offended. But she did. *What kind of question is that?* she thought in disdain. *What do you mean, "For what?"*

But even in her indignant state, she couldn't think of a single thing that Aliyah should definitely apologize to her for (key word being *definitely*).

*If you think you deserve an apology too,* one online author had written, *take a step back and honestly ask yourself, "Is there another plausible explanation for what I'm upset about? Am I projecting my own anger, bad thoughts, and insecurity on my friend or partner? Did they do something that was definitely wrong?"*

But Deanna wasn't quite ready to let go of her anger and resentment. Aliyah wasn't some faultless angel. She should be apologizing too, even if for no more than being a constant irritation in Deanna's life.

*On the first page of your self-improvement journal, write: "I'm sorry, [Insert his or her name here] for [Here, write everything in detail that you are sorry for]."* At that, Deanna had closed the browser and decided it was time to prepare herself some breakfast.

When she came back upstairs an hour later, her stomach full and having thumbed page by page through the latest issue of every magazine that had arrived in the mail in the last couple of days, she begrudgingly returned to her self-improvement tasks.

Deanna mentally wrestled with herself, searching for any way she could skip the apology and jump straight into self-improvement. But either guilt or the article she was reading would remind her that there was no self-improvement without self honesty, and that there was no self honesty without acknowledgement of wrongdoing. So whether she liked it or not, the first painful step was contrition.

After an excruciating back and forth, Deanna had begrudgingly decided to do the apology—but on her own terms. She wasn't about to write some soppy, longwinded "I'm sorry" friend's love letter. If Aliyah was going to get an apology in writing during Deanna's self-improvement, it would be in the form of a "to do" list. That was all Deanna was willing to offer Aliyah right then.

Exactly what Deanna was sorry for, she'd figure out later.

Having had enough of stressing over her life, Deanna stood and walked over to her closet to find something to wear. If she was going to have any hope of becoming a better person—and getting Jacob back—she would have to reach Jacob where it mattered most. And the best place to start was with his parents. She hoped they still had their Sunday brunches after church because she planned to join them today.

***

*Can I ride with you to N's aqeeqah? My car's in the shop till tomorrow and Jamil can't take me.*

Aliyah was sitting next to Ibrahim in his room early Sunday afternoon, helping him with his reading and math when she unlocked her phone and stared at Salima's cryptic text. Nearly a full minute passed before she realized that Salima was most likely talking about the *'aqeeqah* for Nikki's baby. But that didn't make any sense because Aliyah was the godmother ("Ummi") and she'd heard nothing about the event.

*Nikki's aqeeqah???* Aliyah texted back.

*Yes.*

*Today?!*

*Yes. Did you get FB invite?*

Oh. Facebook. That would explain why she didn't know. *Haven't been on in a while,* Aliyah replied.

*Masjid @ 3*

Aliyah sighed. She and Ibrahim had made a lot of headway today, and she didn't want to interrupt that by leaving in the middle of their homeschooling work. He still had Qur'an homework to complete before tomorrow. But how would it look if she didn't show up or at least bring Ibrahim to his own sister's *'aqeeqah*?

*Ok. ETA 2:30,* Aliyah texted, already standing in preparation to get dressed and pick up Salima and Haroon.

***

The massive home of Mr. and Mrs. Bivens was surrounded by a tall iron fence that framed the peripheral of their expansive 10-acre land. Neatly trimmed evergreens stretched the length of their property and lined the winding driveway that led to the gated entrance. Two stone statues of growling lions sat on either side of the gate, the call box wedged into the side of the left one.

Deanna slowed her car to a stop as the driver's side window slid down. She reached out the window and punched in the code that she had memorized years ago. The automatic gate squeaked as the right and left sides opened wide as if welcoming an honored guest. A twinge of anguish stabbed her as she realized that this was no longer her family, and she wondered how long it would be before they changed the key code so she could no longer come unannounced.

It's the small things, she'd always heard, that you miss most when a relationship falls apart. And that moment was the first that she understood what that meant. Jacob had been the first and only real relationship in her life. *Listen to your body, and listen to your heart,* her therapist had advised when she was in high school trying to heal from the trauma of Bailey's rape. Though it was on prom night that she'd followed that advice for the first time, it wasn't until she'd met Jacob that her soul was awakened too.

"I don't see any reason why Muslims can't have the best of both worlds," Jacob had said during his speech at the MSA career day event that Deanna attended when she'd seen him speak for the first time. She didn't often attend MSA events because her doctorate degree work took up most of her time. But when she'd overheard, more than once, some of the female students speak in admiration of a "Professor Jacob Bivens" who was a convert to Islam, Deanna's curiosity was piqued, so she made it a point to attend the next event in which he was slotted to be a speaker. "We pray for Allah to give us the best in this world and the best in the Hereafter," he'd said during that speech. "So why should we settle for less than the best in anything that we do?" Those were the words that had stayed with Deanna. *So why should we settle for less than the best?*

After the speech was over, swarms of students had walked up to him and eagerly introduced themselves and told him how much they'd enjoyed his talk. Though Deanna had been no less eager to introduce herself and meet the charismatic adjunct professor, she hung back, watching from a distance. When she saw how Jacob merely shook their hands or nodded politely before going on to greet the next person, Deanna knew this was not the right time or place to show herself. She needed his undivided attention. She needed him to focus on her and her alone. She needed him to remember her. She needed him to *want* her. *Why should I settle for less?* she asked herself.

On the days that followed, she'd registered as an official member of the MSA and signed up for the email list so she would get alerts whenever they were having events. She also looked up the university's roster for adjunct professors and learned which classes Jacob was teaching. Then she made it a point to go to each one before it ended if she didn't have a class herself. But she wouldn't enter the classroom or lecture hall itself. She would wait outside until the crowds of students spilled out the door and watch where Jacob went after class each day. That was how she'd learned where he liked to study and eat, and when.

His favorite spot was a relatively unpopular food court on a part of campus that was far from the residential halls, student center, and buildings where most of the classes were held. The only significant part of campus that was near his favored food court was an old library that few students frequented unless they couldn't find what they were looking for in the large, renovated library in the middle of campus. The food court itself was located in the small welcome center near the campus's main entrance, a center most students and faculty never entered, as it was mainly for prospective students and their parents who wanted general information about the school or for visitors or students who lived off campus and needed directions to a specific building or event.

It was the perfect place, Deanna had thought when she first saw him enter the building. She watched from afar as he left his books and notebooks on an empty table and went to order himself some food. But it would be a month before Deanna actually walked up to him and introduced herself. She had been waiting for the right pretext to strike up a conversation, and merely saying her name and talking about herself was not enough. She needed a reason for them to see each other again and spend time together. When she received the MSA email announcement about the dinner, she knew it was the perfect opportunity. She could simply ask if he was going and find a way to convince him to go if he hadn't planned to attend. That way they could get to know each other at the dinner.

*"Who was that sister with the book?"*

Deanna grimaced as she slammed the driver's side door closed and pointed the keychain remote toward her car. She pressed the button to lock the vehicle before walking up the paved pathway leading to Jacob's parents' front door.

The memory of that single question still stung as she remembered the unmistakable contrived casualness in his voice as he pretended that neither the inquiry nor the answer meant anything to him. Deanna had known exactly whom he was talking about when he asked the question, and she'd felt a fire of offense at both his audacity and Aliyah's. How dare him ask *her* about another woman when she was the one who'd invited him that night. And how dare Aliyah draw attention to herself by leaning against a wall and reading a book. Deanna had begun to wonder if Aliyah had planned the whole thing until she recalled that she hadn't told anyone that Jacob was coming.

*"What sister?"* Deanna had asked him, mustering all her strength to keep from giving him a piece of her mind and schooling him on how rude it was to talk about another woman in her presence.

*"You were talking to her when you were getting our plates,"* he'd said. *"She had on a green hijab."*

Presently, Deanna's nose flared. A man remembering the color of anything a woman wore was always a bad sign, at least when it wasn't Deanna he was noticing. So Deanna had known exactly what it meant when Jacob mentioned the color of Aliyah's hijab. He was attracted to Aliyah and wanted to get to know *her* instead of Deanna. Deanna hadn't taken Jacob to be a man of poor tastes. But a man was a man, and thus susceptible to foolishness every now and then. But why should he have to settle for less than the best when Deanna was right there? Jacob deserved someone like Deanna, and Deanna was going to do everything in her power to make sure he understood the flimsy, broken package he would be getting with someone like Aliyah.

*Apologize to Aliyah.*

At the memory of the scraggly note atop her "to do" list, Deanna felt nauseated. What had she been thinking when she wrote that? Was she out of her mind? Was she really to be blamed for simply fulfilling her Islamic responsibility of warning a person before they chose a bad match for marriage?

No, there was no way she was going to allow herself to feel bad for anything she'd said about Aliyah or to Aliyah. That girl was so horribly needy and pathetic that Aliyah should be thanking Deanna for even being her friend. The task was so painstaking and time consuming.

*Right now*, Deanna thought as she lifted her forefinger and pressed the doorbell, *I'm focusing on making amends with Jacob and Jacob alone.*

***

"I'm working on him," Jasmine said, smirking as she cut a slice from her waffle and lifted it to her mouth.

"But you said you told Larry you converted to Islam," Mr. Bivens said, leaning back in his chair from where he sat at the head of the dining room table of his home. His wife sat at an angle to his right, Jasmine to his left. Only three of the other five chairs were filled—by his wife's sister, Sadie, and her husband who sat across from each other, and by the reverend, a close friend of the family, who sat at the other end, opposite Mr. Bivens.

"I did," Jasmine said after she chewed and swallowed.

"Then how are you still working on him?" Mr. Bivens said doubtfully.

Jasmine grew uncomfortable under his cautious gaze.

"If Larry thinks you've joined his religion," Mr. Bivens continued, "I don't see how that will help him come back to the church."

The ringing of the doorbell sounded throughout the house, but they ignored it and continued eating, as the maid usually answered the door. Jasmine figured it was probably someone from the Bivens's family or close friends, as it was not uncommon for someone to stop by and visit after church even if they had been unable to attend the entire Sunday brunch.

"I figured it doesn't make much of a difference to them what I am," Jasmine said, choosing her words carefully. "A Christian and a Muslim are pretty much the same religion according to them. So I think of it as an interfaith experiment."

The reverend coughed laughter. "A Christian and a Muslim are pretty much the same religion?" he repeated. "How's that?"

Jasmine smiled, pleased that she had the reverend's attention. Because it was the church Larry and his family attended, she had been baptized in the reverend's church shortly after her and Larry's relationship grew serious. "They say Muslim means anyone who submits to God."

The reverend nodded but waved his hand as if dismissing her comment. "I know what they say the word *Muslim* means," he said. "I'm asking how you can believe they're the same religion?"

"*I* don't believe they're the same religion," Jasmine said, gesturing a forefinger toward herself, emphasizing the personal pronoun. "But Muslims say they're the original Christians." She forced laugher. "And the original Jews."

The reverend and the other guests at the table coughed laughter and huffed their disapproval, offense in that sound.

"Do you wear that…" Mr. Bivens interjected, making a circular motion around his head, apparently unable to remember the word.

"Hijab?" Jasmine finished for him, her voice rising in eagerness to respond. "Yes, sometimes," she said. But she wasn't wearing it today. "It makes them feel more comfortable if you look like them."

"So you're still Christian then?" the reverend said, his eyebrows drawn together.

"Of course," Jasmine said. "I just think it's—"

"Deanna," Mr. Bivens said, his voice rising as he stood suddenly, his legs banging the table in front of him, causing his plate with half-eaten food to rattle slightly. A wide, awkward smile spread on his face as he stretched out his right arm in an exaggerated gesture of welcome.

Jasmine felt her blood go cold. The Bivens Sunday brunch after church was the last place she would expect to see another Muslim. Chest constricted in apprehension, Jasmine slowly turned in her seat and followed Mr. Bivens's line of vision. For a fleeting moment, Jasmine felt relieved that it wasn't Deanna after all. But the woman responded to Mr. Bivens's greeting with a polite smile and nod, her eyes cutting at Jasmine in disapproval. That was when Jasmine recognized Deanna's familiar features, though something about Deanna seemed off.

It wasn't until Deanna had sat down at the table near the reverend that Jasmine realized why she didn't recognize Deanna right away. Deanna wasn't wearing her hijab. The realization gave her some relief, as she wondered momentarily whether or not she and Deanna were in the same predicament. But then she remembered that Deanna wasn't in *any* predicament. Deanna had already married into the Bivens family and had been welcomed for more than ten years.

Why then wasn't Deanna wearing her hijab?

"To what special occasion do we owe the pleasure of this visit?" Mrs. Bivens chimed, a pleasant but demanding expression on her face.

"I'm not here to interrupt anything," Deanna said, and Jasmine noticed that Deanna sounded as if she had just gotten her voice back after a bout of laryngitis. Deanna flicked her eyes at Jasmine suspiciously, and Jasmine looked away and clumsily picked up her fork, deciding to focus her attention on finishing the food on her plate.

"Here." Still standing, Mr. Bivens reached forward and moved his fingers in a gesture to tell Deanna to pass him the unused plate in front of her. "Let's get you something to eat."

Looking a bit uncomfortable, Deanna lifted the glass plate and handed it to him and let him put some food on it before passing it to his wife, who eagerly added some other food items from her seat as her husband sat down and pulled his chair back in place in front of the table. Their nervous movement told Jasmine that she was not the only one who hadn't expected Deanna's visit today.

"Thank you," Deanna murmured as she accepted the plate full of food from Mrs. Bivens and set it down on the place in front of her.

"Are you rejoining the church too?" The reverend addition of the word *too* prompted Jasmine to look up nervously to gauge Deanna's reaction to the question.

Deanna contorted her face and stared at the reverend as if he'd lost his mind. "No," she said so sternly that Jasmine flinched. But Jasmine envied Deanna's boldness right then. Once Jasmine was in the family herself, she could speak freely too. "I'm just here to apologize," she said, her raspy voice rising with such confidence that one would think that Deanna herself was the one who invited everyone there that day.

An awkward silence followed as everyone discreetly glanced at each other in confusion. "For what, dear?" Larry's aunt said.

"For anything I might have done to offend you while Jacob and I were married," Deanna said.

An uncomfortable quiet fell over the table, and Jasmine narrowed her eyes at Deanna, unsure if she'd heard her correctly. "You and Jacob aren't married anymore?" Jasmine blurted before she could stop herself.

Mrs. Bivens eyed Jasmine in disapproval, but Jasmine sensed that Larry's mother wasn't as upset as she felt obligated to be. From the expression on Mrs. Bivens's face, Jasmine surmised that this was news to her too, and no one else at the table looked as if they knew any more than Mrs. Bivens did.

"I received the divorce papers a couple of days after the charges were dropped, and I—" Deanna clamped her mouth shut as if suddenly realizing something, and her eyes darted around the table from person to person in trepidation. Jasmine sensed that Deanna had erroneously assumed that Jacob had given everyone his version of events, so she'd felt obligated to give hers.

"Charges?" Mr. Bivens said, his voice rising in concern. "What charges?"

"I meant…" Deanna said quickly, her voice trailing, making it painfully obvious that she was backpedaling in a frantic attempt to make up for her mistaken assumption. "…the children."

"After the *children* were dropped?" Sadie said, her voice conveying the incredulity that Jasmine, and perhaps everyone else present, felt right then.

"They've been staying with Jacob," Deanna said, offering a disarming smile that was less convincing than the verbal blunder.

"So you mean a couple of days after they were dropped off?" Sadie said as if coaching a child in what would best make her tale believable.

"Yes," Deanna said. "I've been staying at my parents because…" She smiled again. "…well, you know."

"No," Mr. Bivens said, his eyes conveying genuine confusion as he shook his head, "we don't know."

"So I guess Jacob didn't tell you about the divorce then?" Deanna said, a lopsided smile forming at her mouth then disappearing as a shadow of what looked like anger flashed on her face.

Deanna's behavior was so odd that Jasmine momentarily forgot that she should be concerned about what Deanna most likely overheard only minutes before.

"So divorced women don't wear the hijab cloth?"

It was Sadie's question, and for some reason, Deanna looked shocked by the inquiry. It was almost as if until that moment, Deanna didn't even realize she wasn't wearing it.

"I think I should get going," the reverend said, standing and pushing his chair back as he nodded politely at everyone. "My wife isn't feeling well today, so I need to go and check on her." Mr. Bivens and his family immediately stood and gave their polite farewells.

"I'm not here to talk about hijab," Deanna said after the reverend had left the room, slight irritation in her voice. "I just wanted to make sure you understood that I respect your family very much." Her voice was monotone, as if she were reading from a paper or reciting the words of a memorized speech. "I'm working on being a better person, and if there's anything I can do to be a valued member of the family, please let me know." Then Deanna smiled at everyone, baring her teeth in an eagerness that made Jasmine cringe and look way.

Jasmine couldn't watch this. Whatever Deanna had intended by today's visit, she certainly wasn't achieving it. If she hadn't known that Deanna was Muslim, Jasmine would've wondered if Deanna was sober right then.

"Well, we thank you for coming," Mr. Bivens said, the cordiality in his voice lessening the awkwardness of the moment but highlighting the awkwardness of Deanna's presence.

Deanna nodded and offered her father-in-law a polite close-lipped smile, lowering her gaze modestly as if to downplay her generosity of the moment. The effect was like a person of royalty bowing her head to her subjects after her kindness had moved her to bestow on them something they valued greatly. "It's no problem, really," Deanna muttered, the smile twitching at her lips as she flipped her hand at the wrist.

"So you and Jacob are getting divorced?" Mrs. Bivens asked, the directness of her question crumbling the fragile cordiality of the moment.

"*He* wants to," Deanna said, the accusation in her voice unintentionally adding tension to the moment. But she remained oblivious to the lack of judiciousness of her blaming tone in the presence of his family. She flashed another smile. "But I'm trying to be the better person."

***

Matt was standing outside in front of the masjid with Benjamin, Larry, Jacob, and Sayed when Aliyah pulled her car into the parking lot Sunday afternoon. Salima sat in the passenger seat next to Aliyah, and Haroon and Ibrahim sat in the back. It was odd seeing the men talking together as if they were old friends, but it was also heartwarming. It gave Aliyah the feeling of being part of a genuine community.

It was at that moment that Aliyah realized that the entire atmosphere of the Muslim community seemed calmer and less intimidating now that Deanna was no longer part of her life. Perhaps all of her previous anxiety was due mostly to Deanna being her constant companion. Even occasionally running into Juwayriah didn't inspire as much apprehension as it did before. Aliyah doubted that Juwayriah would ever be someone she considered a close friend, but Juwayriah was no longer someone she felt she had to avoid.

"So you're no longer on Facebook, huh?" Salima said as Aliyah navigated the parking lot in search of a good space.

Eyebrows drawn together, Aliyah glanced at Salima. "What makes you ask that?"

"You didn't know about the *'aqeeqah.*"

"Oh yeah," Aliyah said, as if that were a sufficient answer. But she really didn't know what else to say. At one point, during the "hot Muslim mistress" saga, she had made a conscious decision to stay offline, but now she had forgotten about it.

"It's really that stressful for you?"

Aliyah shook her head. "I don't even think about it, to be honest."

Salima coughed knowingly, laughter in that sound, as if she and Aliyah were sharing a private joke. "I say the same about checking my voicemail."

Aliyah turned the steering wheel as she maneuvered the car into an empty space not too far from the entrance. "Your voicemail?" she repeated, a question on her face.

"Most of the time my voicemail is full, so people have a hard time reaching me if I don't answer the phone," Salima said. "Unless they text me." She shrugged. "I guess I'm better at texts."

As Aliyah put the car in park, she recalled calling Salima when she needed last minute childcare for Ibrahim and getting the automated message that Salima's voicemail was full.

"I used to say it was because I keep forgetting to check the messages and delete the old ones. But now I realize it's because I'm afraid of what I'll hear if I check the messages," she said, "and because I'm afraid to delete the old ones."

"Why?"

"Because of what happened with Mikaeel," Salima said. But her voice sounded matter-of-fact, not sad. "I'm still afraid to hear voicemails because I don't know what they'll say, and I'm still afraid to delete old ones because I never know if I'll hear from that person again."

A thoughtful silence followed as Aliyah turned off the car and unlocked the doors. "I don't think it's anything like that for me," Aliyah said, but her voice sounded uncertain, even to her own ears. "I just…" Her voice trailed, as she was unsure what she was trying to say.

"I'm not saying it to criticize," Salima clarified as they opened their doors and got out the car, Haroon and Ibrahim following suit. "It makes sense, honestly," she said raising her voice over the roof of the car. "I'm starting to hate social media myself. I feel like for most of us, it does more harm than good."

Aliyah was silent as they closed their doors and she lifted the keychain to the car to lock it. When she and Salima were side by side, each holding her son's hand, she said, "I don't know if I'd say I hate social media. I just haven't had time to get on lately."

"Well, to *me*," Salima said, pointing to herself with her free hand, "it's like how the combination of credit cards and online stores creates impulse buying. Except now, it's the combination of internet and social media that creates impulse bickering," she said. "Half the stuff people post about, they don't even remember a week or a month later."

Aliyah forced laughter. "I think I can remember everything I've posted in the last *year*."

"That's because you don't post much," Salima said, lowering her voice slightly as they neared the masjid entrance. The group of brothers shouted salaams and they passed, and Aliyah and Salima gave salaams in reply, waving their hands and offering Jacob and Larry smiles.

"Maybe," Aliyah replied with a shrug.

Salima sighed. "I don't know, girl. I'm probably wrong, but I just figured you were avoiding Facebook because of all the stress of dealing with people online."

At the main doors, Haroon and Ibrahim let go of their mothers' hands and walked ahead into the masjid.

"So how's everything going with you and Larry?" Aliyah asked in a low voice after Haroon and Ibrahim were out of earshot.

Salima glanced over her shoulder as a grin formed at her mouth. "We'll see, *insha'Allah*," she said, the finality of her tone letting Aliyah know that Salima wouldn't be sharing any more than that. But Aliyah was pleased with the response, taking it to mean that things were going well between Salima and Larry. She smiled to herself as they walked passed the *musallaa* and followed the signs pointing to where the women's section would be for the *'aqeeqah.*

***

The noise level rose as Aliyah and Salima descended the stairs into the basement, and when they opened the doors to the large room where the women were gathered, they found many of the women dressed up as if it were a wedding party instead of an *'aqeeqah.* The sound of the *daff* pounded rhythmically from a stereo, and some of the women were dancing. Aliyah and Salima grinned at each other and exchanged questioning glances.

"You came!"

Aliyah looked up to find Nikki coming toward her, arms spread in the beginning of a hug. Aliyah was a bit taken aback by the warm welcome, and by Nikki's elaborate appearance. Nikki wore an off-white satin dress and a diamond studded gold necklace, and white teardrop earrings dangled from her ears.

"Of course I came," Aliyah said, laughter in her voice. "I'm the Ummi now,"

"I just didn't know if you'd feel comfortable," Nikki said, still smiling but averting her gaze momentarily. "You know…"

A confused expression lingered on Aliyah's face. Though she had no idea why Nikki would imagine she'd feel uncomfortable, especially after their godmother agreement, Aliyah decided to lighten the mood. "I wish I would've known to dress up!" she said jokingly. "I feel like a party pooper dressed like this."

Nikki frowned sympathetically. "Oh it's okay. A few other sisters didn't get the event change notification either."

"Event change?" Salima said, creasing her forehead as she looked at Nikki.

Nikki laughed self-consciously. "Oh, I guess you didn't either." She flipped her hand at the wrist. "It's okay. A couple of weeks ago, Matt and I decided to make it a *waleemah* and *'aqeeqah* together." She wasn't looking at Salima or Aliyah when she said this. "You know… because we never got to do our wedding party."

*Oh.* Aliyah maintained the cheerful expression, but she had no idea what to say to that.

"*MashaAllah*!" Salima exclaimed, pulling Nikki into an effusive hug, saving Aliyah from the mortification of saying anything congratulatory. "*Mabrook*!" she said, wishing blessings upon Matt and Nikki as she held Nikki in an extended embrace.

By the time Salima released Nikki, a few other sisters had come up to greet Nikki and congratulate her, so Aliyah was spared any further conversation.

"You okay?" Salima whispered, leaning into Aliyah after the women had whisked Nikki away.

Aliyah nodded. "Yes, *alhamdulillah*," she said. "I'm fine." And she was. After the shock of the moment had passed, she actually felt herself feeling happy for Nikki.

"Good." Salima slapped Aliyah on the shoulder playfully. "Because your man is upstairs, and it's all good."

Aliyah smiled and nodded. "It certainly is," she said, thinking of the intimate moment she'd shared with Jacob. The memory itself made her cheeks go warm, and the familiar anticipation made her heart quicken as she looked forward to the time when she and Jacob could live fully as husband and wife.

"Now let's get something to eat," Salima said, tugging on Aliyah's hand.

As they stood in the line for food, Aliyah took a moment to look around the room. It was heartwarming to see all the Muslims present to support Nikki and Matt. Aliyah wondered how her life would have turned out differently if she had been surrounded by real friends instead of only Deanna after she became Muslim. She wondered if her marriage itself would have felt different if she had other friends.

Aliyah felt something flat and stiff being placed in her hand, and she looked down to see that Salima had passed a paper plate to her. The aroma of food tickled Aliyah's nostrils, and her stomach grumbled as the array of food came into view. Stainless steel food warmers were aligned on a row of tables, and Aliyah scanned the options to decide what she would eat.

When she was in front of the warmers, she served herself some natural rice, grilled chicken and baked kale then followed Salima to a table that had a few empty seats. They had just settled down and started to eat when Aliyah glanced up then did a double take when she saw Jasmine enter the room, face framed by a gold-trimmed black *khimaar*. Aliyah instinctively looked at Salima, who had a pleasant expression on her face as she enjoyed her food and chatted with the sister who sat in the other chair next to her. Hoping Jasmine would not see them, Aliyah turned her body slightly and continued eating, pretending to be engrossed in Salima's conversation.

"Oh. My. God."

Aliyah cringed when she heard Salima say these words, eyes fixed on the door where Jasmine had just entered. From the sound of Salima's voice, Aliyah knew Jasmine must have done something more shocking than merely arriving. But Aliyah willed herself not to look in Jasmine's direction. After witnessing Jasmine's disapproving look at Salima when they'd visited Nikki's house to see the baby, Aliyah feared that Jasmine knew about Salima and Larry and would cause trouble.

"Don't worry," Salima said in a low whisper, leaning into Aliyah and gripping her leg under the table in an apparent effort to be discreet. "I'll take care of this."

Creasing her forehead, Aliyah opened her mouth to ask Salima what she'd meant. But when her eyes followed Salima's line of vision, her heart dropped. Walking next to Jasmine was Deanna. Aliyah clamped her mouth shut and felt her palms moisten in perspiration. Deanna's face was tight in an expression of contempt as her eyes swept the room as if she had somewhere else she'd rather be. She was dressed in a long fitting black dress and a long-sleeved short jacket. Her hair was styled loosely around her shoulders, and there was no evidence of a hijab anywhere.

"Just relax and stay calm," Salima whispered as Jasmine and Deanna drew closer to their table. This time, Aliyah listened, drawing in a deep breath and exhaling slowly to calm herself.

"Well, well, well," Jasmine said in an exaggerated tone of pleasant surprise, loud enough for anyone standing nearby to hear. Her voice was rivaled only by the sound of the *daff* thumping from the speakers and distant laughter and chatter from parts of the room far from them. "*MashaAllah*," she said, her expression conveying that she was proud of herself for some reason. "I guess this is the table for husband stealers?"

A hushed silence fell over the room like a rippling wave until there were no sounds except the hushed whispers of women eagerly enlightening oblivious guests about the background of what was unfolding and the rhythmic beating of the *daff* like a quickened heartbeat of tense anticipation.

"May we join you?" Jasmine said mockingly, a sneer on her face as she glanced sideways at Deanna in an obvious effort to impress Deanna. But Deanna didn't seem to be paying attention to what Jasmine was saying, a look of annoyance and boredom on her face as she continued to glance around the room. Aliyah wondered if Deanna had even seen her sitting there. She hoped by some miracle or divine intervention that Deanna hadn't.

"These seats are actually taken," Salima said, apology in her tone as she offered Jasmine a polite but contrived smile.

"You're saving them for Larry and *Jacob*?" Jasmine said, her voice rising at the last word. Mention of Jacob seemed to jar something in Deanna, and she snapped her head in the direction of Salima and Aliyah and gave them once-over.

Deanna opened her mouth to say something, but the screeching of a microphone interrupted her as the music was suddenly turned off. Everyone's head turned to the back of the room where there was a small platform with a microphone.

"*A'oodhu billaahi me-nash-shaytaanirrajeem*," a soft, beautiful melodic voice reverberated through the microphone and filled the room, silencing everyone at once. "*Bismillaahir-rahmaanir-raheem*," the voice recited, elongating the syllable beautifully, and Aliyah found herself searching for the source of the sound. A second later she found Reem standing before the microphone, her eyes shut as she concentrated on the meaning of the words. She wore a long bronze Arab-style wide dress with gold embroidering on the front and sleeves, her hair in a single braid, gold earrings dangling from her ears. Before that moment, Aliyah hadn't even realized Reem was there. "*Yaa-ayyuhalladheena aamanoo laa tuqaddemuoo bayna yadillaahi wa rasoolih, wattaqullaah*," Reem recited the opening verses of *Al-Hujuraat* from the Qur'an. "*InnAllaaha samee'un 'aleem...*"

Reem continued reciting the *soorah* in a slow measured tone, taking her time and allowing the tranquil power of Allah's Words to settle over the room. Women who were standing discreetly shuffled across the room to find a seat, and those who were serving themselves food slowly moved along in the line, their eyes on Reem as they listened to the beautiful recitation.

Jasmine and Deanna stayed where they were, the only ones still standing except for the women serving themselves food. But Jasmine and Deanna were quiet as they looked toward Reem.

"*...InnAllaah ya'lamu ghaybas-samaati wal-'arDh,*" Reem recited. "*Wallaahu baseerum be-maa ta'maloon.*" Even as Reem came to the closing of the *soorah*, the room remained quiet.

"I chose this *soorah*, this chapter of the Qur'an, to recite today," Reem said, her voice shaking slightly, and Aliyah wondered if Reem had been scheduled as part of the program or if this was an impromptu speech to halt the trouble that had been unfolding, "because it explains so beautifully the blessings and the warnings Allah gives us as a community. And as we know, the family forms the foundation of the community," she said. " And today, Matthew and Nicole are celebrating not only the birth of their daughter Bushra but their marriage as well."

There was a slight rustling noise from where Jasmine and Deanna stood, and Aliyah glanced in their direction and found them walking toward the food.

"Allah also tells us in this *soorah* that we are a single brotherhood and sisterhood, joined by our *emaan*, our faith in Him," Reem continued. "And it is through holding together this bond and having *taqwaa* that we attain His mercy. And one of the most beautiful ways of bringing together hearts and fearing Allah is through the bond of marriage and having children."

Reem's eyes seemed to follow Jasmine and Deanna momentarily before turning her attention back to the crowd. "In this *soorah*, Allah makes reference to this bond when He says that He created mankind from male and female," Reem said. "He then goes on to tell us that He made us into nations and tribes so that we will come to know each other. And amongst these diverse groups, the ones who are the best are those with the most *taqwaa*. In other words, they are those who are the most conscious of their meeting with Allah and work daily to protect themselves from Allah's punishment. And what better path to *taqwaa* than through marriage, starting a family, and joining the hearts of Muslim brothers and sisters like we're doing today?"

After Reem's speech, the reflective, tranquil atmosphere that had settled over the room lingered, even as the wedding nasheeds and the dancing resumed, and the social chatter picked up.

***

*Thank you*, Nikki mouthed to Reem as Reem walked away from the microphone after her impromptu speech. Reem smiled and mouthed, *You're welcome.* But she didn't return to where she had been dancing amongst the other women. She was too shaken up from what had just happened to resume her carefree, festive attitude from a half hour before, though she was pleased that others were able to. Seeing Jasmine, Deanna by her side, confront Aliyah and Salima so nastily, and at Nikki's *waleemah*, had stirred something in Reem that was a mixture of rage, shame, and compassion.

It was enraging to see the cruelty that people were capable of, and to their own Muslim sisters. And for what? The scene itself incited in Reem shame for Jasmine's and Deanna's sakes. If only they could see themselves, Reem had thought in empathetic mortification. If only they could see what others saw. If only they could see the evil of their actions.

But still, she was overcome with compassion for Deanna, and Aliyah. It couldn't be easy to let go of someone you love and watch them start their life over with someone else. Reem wasn't sure how much Deanna knew about Aliyah and Jacob, but that Deanna had even known that Jacob wanted to marry Aliyah while still being married to her was enough agony. How could a woman's heart handle that level of pain? Reem couldn't imagine facing that level of emotional turmoil with Sayed. She loved him too much to even entertain the thought. She couldn't even handle him mentioning the name of the woman he was interested in marrying before her. Reem herself tried not to even mention her in her thoughts.

But didn't everyone have the right to love, no matter who loved the person before them? And given that Allah was in charge of hearts—and had made both divorce and polygyny permissible—how much could you really blame a man and woman for remarrying after divorce, or a man for marrying another woman while he was still married to someone else?

There was a burst of laughter from the food table, and Reem looked in the direction of the sound and saw Jasmine, Deanna, and Juwayriah laughing together about something as they held their half full plates. Immediately, Reem stiffened in apprehensive preparation for a repeat of the scene she had interrupted with her speech only moments before. *Yaa salaam*, she thought to herself in dread. *I hope they're not going to confront Aliyah again. Do they have* any *shame?*

That was the part of American culture that Reem could never understand. That unabashed cruelty. That complete disregard for the feelings of others. That unapologetic trampling upon social etiquette.

Everybody had things that had hurt them in life, Reem reflected indignantly. Everyone had things that angered them. Everyone had *feelings*. Why was it that so many Americans felt that the world had to stop to soothe theirs?

*O Allah, I'm trying*, her heart cried as she reflected on her painful attempts to overcome the disdain she felt toward Americans. But it was a difficult process. After her friendship with Aliyah went downhill and Sayed appealed to her to think of her views on intercultural marriage from Aliyah's perspective, Reem had engaged in a lot of self-reflection. And she'd come to realize that she definitely harbored more than a harmless dose of pride in her view of Arab culture *vis-à-vis* American culture. But how was she to overcome it? In her mind, her concerns were valid, and the incident today with Jasmine and Deanna was a prime example.

There seemed to be no line with Americans, no boundaries, nothing they respected as sacred and inviolable. You could mention their own mother or father, and at least one of them would say something dismissive, if not outright disrespectful. You could mention a renowned scholar, and they'd speak of him as if he were a politician who had to win their vote. You could mention something from the Qur'an or Sunnah itself, and they'd dissect it as if were a topic open to debate.

No matter how hard Reem tried, she just couldn't view that culture as offering more good than harm. Yes, Arabs had their problems, but in her view, Americans were worse. Maybe that was why she could barely stomach the thought of having one in her family.

*And you're surprised you haven't heard from Mashael?* the self-reproaching voice asked in her head. Reem's heart fell in sadness at the reminder of her sister's sudden disappearance. "*Astaghfirullah,*" she muttered, realizing that Sayed was right. She had a lot to work on within herself.

Perhaps to prove to herself that she was at least making an effort, Reem approached the table where Salima and Aliyah were sitting with another sister.

"*As-salaamu'alaikum,*" Reem said, offering the women a wide smile as she rounded the table and shook their hands.

"*Wa'alaiku-mus-salaam wa-rahmatullaah,*" each of them replied as they gripped her hand.

*O mankind! We have created you from a male and female, and made you into nations and tribes, that you may know one another...* The Qur'anic verses she'd recited during her speech settled over her heart as she sat next to Aliyah.

"How are you?" Aliyah asked, a warm smile on her face.

"*Alhamdulillah,*" Reem said, nodding her head humbly. "How are *you*?" She emphasized the last word teasingly to subtly indicate that she was talking about the new marriage.

"I'm good, *alhamdulillah,*" Aliyah said, an affectionate grin forming on her face. "Allah is Merciful," she said sincerely. "I'm really glad how everything's turned out."

Reem smiled, struck by how Aliyah didn't seem the least bit shaken by the disrespectful scene that had just occurred. Yet when Reem was upset with Aliyah, she hadn't even been able to handle the *possibility* that Aliyah was disrespecting her, and that had been in private. How does Aliyah do it? she wondered. Where does she get her strength from?

*Verily, the most honorable of you in the sight of Allah is [the one who is] the most righteous...*

No, Reem certainly didn't know the heart of any believer, but she couldn't help admiring the forgiving nature that seemed to come naturally to Aliyah.

***

"*Jail*?" Juwayriah repeated, disbelieving humor in her tone as she stood in front of the line of stainless steel food warmers, holding a half-full plate of food.

Deanna hadn't intended to mention her brief stint behind bars. But after Juwayriah had asked Deanna how she was doing and mentioned that she hadn't heard from her in a while, Deanna had mentioned that she was still adjusting to life after being released. It wasn't until after she had said it and saw Juwayriah's expression that it occurred to her that Jacob probably hadn't told anyone what she was going through.

The thought of Jacob being that ashamed of his own wife was unnerving and humiliating. Maybe his crippling shame was what sealed his final decision to send the divorce papers. He didn't want to have anything to do her, lest she stain his pristine image and reputation. The thought was infuriating. She had half a mind to go upstairs and find him so she could give him a piece of her mind. But she resisted. *"Don't do anything that will make your case more complicated,"* Attorney Schmidt had told her. *"If you want to talk to him, let's arrange a meeting with your attorneys present."* And the last thing Deanna wanted was to give Jacob an excuse to take more from her than he already was trying to do.

"Yeah, girl," Deanna said, smirking. "My mother fell down the steps in our backyard, and they tried to say I pushed her."

"*SubhaanAllah*," Juwayriah said, shaking her head, a sad expression shadowing her face. "That's terrible." She narrowed her eyes curiously. "Your mother told them that?"

"No," Deanna said. "She couldn't tell them anything because she was in a coma."

"A *coma*?"

Deanna rolled her eyes and flipped her hand at the wrist. "Yeah, but she's better now. She's almost fully recovered."

"Well, I'm glad she's better," Juwayriah said sincerely.

She gestured a hand toward Deanna. "That's what you meant when you said you almost lost your voice due to stress?"

"Yes," Deanna said. She twisted her lips to the side. "I've been going *through* it."

"But as soon as she gets out," Jasmine said, her tone a bitter complaint, apparently in an effort to empathize with Deanna, "Jacob slaps her with divorce papers."

Deanna clenched her teeth. It was all she could do to resist glaring at Jasmine as if she'd lost her mind. Deanna did *not* want anyone to know about that. She was planning to give Jacob what he wanted then woo him back after he realized what he was missing. She didn't mind Jacob's family knowing, but she didn't want anyone at the masjid to know. It was humiliating enough that they knew he had been interested in marrying Aliyah as a second wife. The memory of that alone was enough to make her want to strangle him. But like the elder woman had told her in jail, sometimes you just had to let a man have his fantasy. And what man didn't pine after another woman every now and then, especially the stereotypical "damsel in distress"?

Juwayriah brought her free hand to her mouth as she looked at Deanna, her eyes widening in shock and sympathy. "No…"

Deanna grunted laughter, concealing her true feelings. "Girl, I ain't worried about him. He just didn't want somebody with a criminal record."

"But I thought the charges were dropped," Juwayriah said, placing her hand on her hip in disapproval, her other hand still holding the plate.

"You know men," Deanna said, rolling her eyes. "They don't know the difference."

"But it hasn't gone through yet?" Juwayriah said, as if that would make everything better.

"No..." Deanna said, slightly annoyed at Juwayriah's optimism.

"And he hasn't pronounced divorce?"

Deanna contorted her face in offense. "*Pronounced* divorce?"

"For the Islamic divorce," Juwayriah clarified.

"What difference does it make?" Deanna retorted, recalling the morning after she'd locked Jacob out the house and he emerged from the master bathroom, face and arms wet with water of *wudhoo'*. *"Then I divorce you,"* he'd said after she refused to agree to marriage counseling.

"It determines whether or not you're in *'iddah*," Juwayriah said, her voice soft in an apparent attempt to let Deanna know that she only meant well.

"What's that?" Jasmine said, her upper lip upturned in disapproval.

"*'Iddah* is the three-month waiting period after a woman is divorced," Juwayriah said matter-of-factly, as if it were a simple fact recited from some Islamic text and not an indication of what Deanna had suffered.

"So a man just says the word," Jasmine said, undisguised contempt in her tone, "and just like that, you're *divorced*?"

Juwayriah looked as if she was offended by Jasmine's question. She blinked repeatedly as she met Jasmine's disapproving gaze challengingly. "You have a problem with that?"

Jasmine shrugged. "It just sounds stupid that's all," she said. "If men can do that, then what rights do women have?"

"Women can get a divorce too," Juwayriah said defensively. "And all they do is give back their dowry and wait *one* month."

Jasmine huffed indignantly, as if unimpressed.

"What difference does it make to you?" Deanna shot back, having had enough of Jasmine for one day. "You're not even Muslim."

The look of horror on Juwayriah's face made Deanna wonder momentarily what catastrophe had just happened. "Don't say that," Juwayriah said sharply, scolding Deanna as if she were her mother. "If you call a Muslim a *kaafir*, it comes back on you."

Deanna twisted her face in offense. "Call her a *kaafir*?" She jabbed her thumb in the direction of Jasmine. "*She's* the one who said she's not Muslim."

"*What*?" Jasmine spoke with a horror that mirrored Juwayriah's expression.

"Don't sit up here and like you don't know what I'm talking about," Deanna said, glaring at Jasmine. "You told my in-laws you were just pretending to be Muslim to impress Larry."

Juwayriah's face contorted in disgust as she looked at Deanna. "Deeja, you shouldn't—"

"I. Did. Not." The firmness in Jasmine's voice was so forceful that Deanna momentarily doubted her memory. "If you had joined the conversation instead of *eavesdropping*," Jasmine said, fury lacing her words, "you would've heard me say that I *am* Muslim. What you *think* you heard was me telling them that Muslims and Christians have a lot in common, so sometimes people consider them the same religion."

"But you s—"

"Don't tell me what *I* said," Jasmine interjected, her forefinger stabbing at the air in front of Deanna. "I know what *I* said. Maybe all that stress is messing up your memory, and not just your voice?" she taunted.

"Deeja, seriously," Juwayriah said, her voice teetering between a plea and a warning, "you shouldn't say things like that. You must've heard her wrong."

"She *definitely* heard me wrong," Jasmine said, her icy glare still on Deanna.

The look in Jasmine's eyes made Deanna flustered and defensive. She didn't trust her memory anymore, but she didn't feel Jasmine had any right to talk to her like that.

"You need to worry about your own life instead of obsessing over mine," Jasmine said viciously. "Your man is the one dumping you so he can secretly marry his mistress."

Deanna hadn't known that she had raised her hand at Jasmine until she felt Juwayriah's firm grip on her arm. "Let's just—"

"*Allaahu-akbar! Allaahu-akbar!*" the *adhaan* reverberated throughout the building, proclaiming God's greatness and announcing that it was time for *Asr* prayer. A second later, the music stopped and the voices quieted. "*Allaahu-akbar! Allaahu-akbar!*"

A sense of calm settled over Deanna, and embarrassed, she lowered her hand, Juwayriah still gripping her arm cautiously. For some reason, Deanna felt choked up all of a sudden, sadness suffocating her.

*"Ash-hadu-an laa ilaahi illaAllaah..." I bear witness that nothing has the right to be worshipped except Allah*, the muezzin proclaimed.

*I want to be a better person.* The feeling was so heartfelt and overwhelming that Deanna had to fight the urge to call Jacob right then and beg him to take her back.

*Apologize to Aliyah*, another thought urged. Even in her melancholic regretful state, Deanna felt her stomach churn in repulsion as she recalled the scraggly note she'd written to herself.

*I don't care about Aliyah*, she mentally retorted. *I just want my husband back.*

As the muezzin continued the call to prayer, Deanna recalled the dream she had had urging her to pray. *Then pray...*

But Deanna hadn't prayed since she'd stood in line next to the Muslim women at the jail. She hated the horrible discomfited state that prayer often left her in. She wanted to become a better person, not worse.

*Then pray...*

Deanna watched with a detached sense of envy as the women walked in different directions in search of their abayas and hijabs. Some women stood near their seats, buttoning up their over-garments, others arranging the fabric of their *khimaar* around their heads.

"Can you pray?" Juwayriah asked Deanna and Jasmine after the *adhaan* was finished.

"Yes," Jasmine said, a tinge of offense still lingering in her voice.

Deanna merely shrugged in response, refusing to look at Juwayriah. In the world of people like Juwayriah, there was no such thing as a Muslim who didn't pray, Deanna thought bitterly.

"Then let's go join the *jamaa'ah,*" Juwayriah said, referring to the congregational prayer about to be held upstairs in the *musallaa.*

Jasmine immediately followed Juwayriah toward the door, but Deanna hung back.

"I don't have anything to wear," Deanna muttered.

She didn't think they'd heard, but Juwayriah immediately halted her steps and said, "Hold on," causing Jasmine to halt her steps too.

Deanna didn't even bother looking when Juwayriah returned to where many of the women were still sitting. She already knew Juwayriah was asking to borrow the abaya and *khimaar* of someone who couldn't pray due to menses, and Deanna didn't feel like withstanding the women's judgmental looks when they tried to figure out who'd come to the masjid without hijab.

"Here," Juwayriah said, pushing a thick bundle of charcoal colored cloth with blue trim into Deanna's hands.

Deanna stared at it for a moment as if still undecided. She stiffened when Juwayriah reached up and ran her palms over Deanna's hair, pulling it back into a ponytail. The friendly gesture made Deanna uncomfortable, but she didn't resist. Instead, she laid the *khimaar* on a nearby table then slipped her arms into the capacious abaya before buttoning it up in the front. When Juwayriah finished with Deanna's hair, Deanna reached for the *khimaar* then walked out the room with Juwayriah and a group of other women heading upstairs for prayer.

## 30
## The Badge of Honor

"What's this we hear about you and Deanna getting a divorce?"

It was his father's question, but Jacob didn't respond right away. This was not the way Jacob had planned to spend Monday evening after work. He had wanted to stop by Aliyah's for a few minutes. But even before he decided to go to his parents' house (as he told them he might when they'd called the day before, upset), he decided against the impromptu visit to his wife.

Though Jacob was trying hard to be patient for Aliyah's sake, it was getting increasingly difficult to spend time with Aliyah while respecting the temporary celibacy they had agreed on. He knew that Aliyah was becoming as impatient as he was, but he valued their relationship too much to take advantage of her weakening resolve. And reducing their face-to-face visits would make it easier for them both. He sensed that Aliyah was ready to compromise, but he refused to allow himself the luxury of entertaining any changes to their plan until the legal divorce from Deanna was final. He wished there was some way to expedite the process and free himself from Deanna sooner, but he had no choice but to be patient. He had made the recklessly stupid decision to marry Deanna twelve years ago, and he had to accept the consequences of that decision.

"Is it true?" His father's voice rose.

There was a time that his father's demanding tone would have stirred something inside of Jacob. Regret, guilt, obligation, and perhaps even shame. But today it stirred nothing but slight irritation. And it wasn't because he was upset with his father, but because he wanted to be somewhere else.

Years ago, Jacob would have been tongue-tied at being confronted with the topic of divorce, especially from his parents. But now, in his late thirties, Jacob saw through even his parents' façade of unity and strength. Marriage was a badge of honor for them, Malcolm and Ruth, as it was for the entire Bivens family; and Malcolm didn't want his eldest son to tatter that badge.

"Yes." Jacob replied in a matter-of-fact tone, devoid of any emotion.

"Marriage is not something to be taken lightly, son."

Jacob heard the offense and accusation in his father's voice, and Jacob couldn't tell what was more offensive to his father, the divorce or the fact that Jacob didn't consult him first. But because it wasn't a question, Jacob remained quiet, a loose fist beneath his chin as he leaned an elbow on the arm of the small couch that was situated at an angle to where his parents sat on the larger, wider sofa. He did not feel even the slightest inclination to respond. But in his mind, he marveled at how parents could remain so stuck in time as to imagine that their son, a grown man, was still a child. Did they really imagine that he had taken marriage lightly simply because they were unable to personally validate his struggles?

"Your father and I are just concerned about you," Ruth interjected, her tone soft, but Jacob detected the offense in her tone too. She was hoping her gentle approach would convince him to open up and confide in them. "Please help us understand what happened."

"I filed for a divorce," Jacob said, "and I hope by this time next week, it's final."

Ruth drew in a deep breath and exhaled audibly, a clear sign that she was losing patience with her son. "Jacob, this is not a game," she said, her voice tight in offense. "Marriage isn't something you throw away when you get tired. It's for life."

"Not necessarily," Jacob said.

"In *God's* eyes," Malcolm said authoritatively, "marriage is for life." It was obvious that the mention of God was supposed to make Jacob feel guilty.

"I don't believe marriage is a divine prison sentence," Jacob said, careful to keep his tone level. "Marriage is a divine mercy, not a punishment."

"Marriage is what *you* make it," Ruth said, her tone conveying the offense she'd felt at Jacob's statement. "If it feels like a punishment, it's because you didn't put in the work to experience the mercy."

Jacob shook his head. "I don't agree with that. There are people in abusive relationships, and it's not their fault."

"Don't change the subject," Malcolm said. "We're not talking about abusive relationships. We're talking about *your* relationship."

"You and Deanna are a beautiful couple," Ruth said as if chiding him.

"And that means we should stay together?" Jacob said, looking at his mother with a hurt expression on his face.

"Look, son," Malcolm interjected, lifting his hand as if to request a truce. "All we want to do is understand what happened so we can help."

"There's nothing you can do," Jacob said, his voice apologetic. "I've already made my decision. You don't have to blame yourselves."

"But this is unacceptable," Ruth blurted. "No Bivens has ever gotten a divorce."

*So there it is*, Jacob thought bitterly, *the real reason they're so hurt*. He was almost relieved that it was out in the open. Now they could talk more honestly. "I hope to change that," Jacob said, careful that there was no trace of sarcasm in his voice.

But his mother sucked in her breath as if he'd slapped her. "*What*?" Ruth said, indignant, and Malcolm patted his wife's leg to calm her. "How could you say something like that?"

"Because it's true," Jacob said, speaking more confidently. "It's not an *honor* that none of us are divorced. It's a burden. I suspect there are others in a similar situation who don't realize getting out is an option."

"And what about the children?" his mother said, voice rising in an accusatory tone.

"What about them?" Jacob said, careful not to sound as defensive as he felt. He hated when people behaved as if they cared more about his sons than he did.

"What will happen to them, Jacob?" Ruth spoke as if he knew exactly what she was talking about. "They can't just be tossed back and forth with no real home."

"They have two parents, and that's not going to change," Jacob said.

"Have you read the statistics on children of divorce?" she challenged. "They're significantly more likely to get a divorce themselves."

"Yes, I have," Jacob said. "And I have no problem with that."

"How could you have *no* problem with being the cause of your children being more likely to break up their family?" she said in exasperation.

"Because I'll never understand how in the name of happily-ever-after," Jacob said, voice rising in conviction, "a family breakup could be worse than the emotional and psychological breakdown of another human being."

The room grew quiet, and the weight of Jacob's words hung in the room. He had no idea if his parents' silence was due to the profundity of his statement or the depth of their shock and disagreement.

"Yes, maybe my decision *will* make divorce a more likely option for Younus and Thawab when they're older," Jacob added confidently. "But I'm happy to be an example to them so they'll know when enough is enough."

The look on his parents' faces was difficult to read, but Jacob went on. "And that's much more preferable," he said, "than raising children who confuse being driven to mental illness with being patient in marriage."

The silence in the room remained so long that Jacob was almost certain he'd offended his parents.

"No one wants what's best for my sons more than I do," Jacob said sincerely, his voice low out of respect for his parents' heightened sensitivities. "That's why I didn't leave Deanna sooner."

A troubled expression lingered on his parents' faces, but he could tell they weren't inclined to respond.

Jacob shook his head, eyes narrowed thoughtfully. "I know you want to understand what happened. But that's not something I'm ready to share with you or anyone right now," he said. "Yes, we're getting a divorce, and it's for a good reason." He paused before adding, "But our privacy and dignity are more important than your understanding and agreement."

***

Aliyah heard her mobile phone ringing just after she'd finished working with Ibrahim on his homeschool assignments. She walked out of his room and hurried down the hall to her own and quickly glanced at the caller ID before accepting the call and putting the phone to her ear.

A grin spread on her face as she said, "*As-salaamu'alaikum.*"

"*Wa'alaiku-mus-salaam wa-rahmatullaahi wa barakaatuh,*" Jacob replied, happiness evident in his voice.

"Why the good mood?" Aliyah said, giggling as she closed her room door then walked over to her bed and sat on the edge.

"Because I get to hear your voice after an aggravating meeting with my parents," his deep voice said through the phone.

Aliyah smirked. "Well, I'm glad there's an upside to this."

A second later she frowned and her tone became more serious. "But is everything okay with you and your parents?"

She heard Jacob let out a laugh. "No," he said, humor in that sound, "but that's nothing new. They just want to save me from the horrible fate of divorce."

"Oh, that," Aliyah said, smiling and rolling her eyes to the ceiling. "At least they're not trying to save you from the horrible fate of Islam," she said in grim humor.

"That'll probably be our *next* meeting," Jacob said.

"Really?" Aliyah said as if genuinely surprised. "I thought they'd given up trying to get you to change your religion."

"Maybe they have…" Jacob said thoughtfully. "But I think it's more of a temporary truce."

"So how'd they find out about the divorce?" Aliyah asked.

"Apparently, Deanna paid them a surprise visit yesterday," he said, exhaustion in his tone.

Aliyah frowned empathetically. "Oh no…"

"And she told them *I'm* the one who wants the divorce, but she's trying to be the better person and reconcile."

Aliyah rolled her eyes, unable to temper the aggravation she felt right then. "She's still talking about reconciliation?"

"*Still*?" Jacob repeated, laughter in his voice. "She never wanted reconciliation," he said. "She just wanted me sentenced to being her husband for life. Every time I suggested marriage counseling, she refused."

"You told them that?" Aliyah asked curiously.

"No," Jacob said with a sigh. "I didn't tell them much of anything. But they kept pushing for details."

"That's understandable," Aliyah said sincerely. "They have no idea what happened."

"And they don't need to," Jacob said, irritation in his voice, but Aliyah could tell it wasn't directed at her. "I told them our privacy and dignity are more important than their understanding and agreement."

Aliyah nodded thoughtfully, reflecting on what Jacob had said. "I like that, *mashaAllah*," she said. "I need to pen that in my journal or hang it on my wall."

"Well, I'm glad somebody agrees," Jacob said.

"Agrees?" Aliyah repeated, laughter in her voice. "Why would I disagree?" she said. "I wish I would've thought to say that to every nosey person who kept asking why Matt and I got a divorce." She rolled her eyes. "It's like people feel your divorce isn't valid unless you tell them every single private detail of what happened, *and* they agree with you," she said. "It's like they have some 'invalid until proven valid' rule they operate off of." She shook her head. "I swear, I can't tell you how many times people lectured me about the importance of marriage, as if Matt and I tossed a coin for the decision."

"Exactly," Jacob said, relief in his tone. "That's how I feel with my mother and father."

Aliyah was quiet momentarily. "But it's different with parents," she said. "They usually do really care about what happened."

"Not necessarily," Jacob said. "Sometimes they're more offended than concerned. They just don't want anyone to ruin their family name."

Aliyah thought of how proud her parents were to have been married for so long. "That's true," she said. "Having a long lasting marriage is definitely a bragging point in the Thomas home." She paused thoughtfully. "That's probably why my mother is so up in arms about Cassie and her husband."

There was extended silence.

"Have you heard any more from them?" Jacob asked.

"No," Aliyah said with a sigh. "But I don't expect to. Cassie and I aren't really close, and I doubt my mother will ever speak to me again." She grunted. "Like she didn't for ten years."

"I meant from Benjamin and Valerie?"

Aliyah frowned. "No," she said. "But they don't talk a lot about other people's lives unless there's a reason."

"Well, I gave Joseph my phone number in case he had any questions about Islam or anything."

"That's good *mashaAllah*," Aliyah said, but she didn't feel optimistic. Her mother had a way of making sure she got her way, by any means necessary. And with Joseph being a project manager in one of her organizations, there was no end to the manipulation she'd likely subject her son-in-law to.

"I hope he calls," Jacob said sincerely. "If not me, then Benjamin at least."

Aliyah bit her lower lip. "Just make *du'aa*," she said finally. "Between Cassie and my mother, he'd have to be pretty committed to still be interested in becoming Muslim."

"Is there any other way to be when it comes to your soul?" Jacob asked rhetorically. "I mean, God doesn't disappear just because people don't want you to submit to Him."

"They probably think they already are submitting to Him," Aliyah offered. "That's how *Shaytaan* works," she said. "He makes you believe you're on the right path when you're not."

"That's true," Jacob conceded. "Satan is certainly good at his job."

"Yes he is," Aliyah agreed reflectively.

"It's just difficult to comprehend how someone wouldn't become Muslim after they heard about Islam," Jacob said. "It's one thing if you've rationalized yourself out of ever learning about it in the first place, like many people do. But after you *know?*" He let out a low whistle. "That's not something I want to face Allah with on the Day of Judgment."

"They're the same thing though," Aliyah said. "All ignorance isn't excusable in front of Allah. Rationalizing yourself out of learning about Islam is pretty much the same as knowing it's true and rejecting it."

"You think so?" Jacob asked, his voice skeptical.

"Yes, absolutely," Aliyah said. "That's like skipping class then asking the teacher to excuse you for not knowing about an upcoming exam. But excusable ignorance is not knowing there's a class to attend in the first place."

"Hmm…" Jacob said, as if considering the perspective for the first time.

"There are even hadiths about people answering the last question in the grave by saying that they just said about Prophet Muhammad, *sallallaahu'alayhi wa sallam*, what they heard everybody else saying."

"That's true," Jacob said, as if recalling a hadith just then. "*SubhaanAllah*."

"So ignorance isn't always an excuse," she said.

Jacob was quiet for some time, and Aliyah sensed that he was reflecting on what she'd said. "That makes me feel a bit better about the divorce," Jacob said finally.

Aliyah drew her eyebrows together in confusion. "About the *divorce*?"

"Sometimes I feel bad," Jacob said, "because I know Deanna never really *knew* me, you know?"

Aliyah didn't know, but she was listening.

"It's like I was her caretaker more than her husband." His tone suggested that he was lost in self-reflection, speaking more for his own benefit than Aliyah's. "I tried to let her get to know me," he said. "But she always shut me down. She never wanted to talk about anything that made her upset." He huffed. "Unless it was about someone making *her* upset. I felt like there was this wall constantly between us, and every time I tried to climb over it, she punished me."

"*SubhaanAllah…*"

"I know all of it isn't her fault."

The tinge of sadness in Jacob's tone made Aliyah curious about all he'd gone through. But she didn't pry. She understood that some of the more intimate pain of marriage remained sacred even after the bond of marriage was broken. *What's between husband and wife stays between husband and wife,* her parents would often say. And after her divorce with Matt, Aliyah mentally added, *Even if they're no longer husband and wife.*

"But she's not the first person to go through severe trials," Jacob said, the self-reflective tone still in his voice. "And she won't be the last. And no matter what we go through, we can't punish other people for it," he said. "And we can't always say we didn't know, thinking that gives us a pass. In a marriage, it's your responsibility to get to know the person you're married to, especially if they're doing all they can to introduce themselves to you."

Aliyah frowned thoughtfully. "I think some people are just incompatible."

Jacob let out a sigh. "Yes, that's true," he said tentatively. "But more people are just *impossible*. There's a difference."

***

"*Marriage* counseling?" Jacob repeated incredulously. It was Tuesday morning as he shut the door to his college office to increase privacy, speaking into the Bluetooth earpiece of his phone.

"Her lawyer says she'll agree to everything if you agree to go to couple's counseling."

"*Before* she signs for the divorce?"

"They didn't specify," Jacob's attorney said. "So I suggest agreeing to it, but only after the divorce, perhaps for co-parenting purposes."

Jacob gritted his teeth. This was a bad sign. Deanna was stalling, and he knew what this meant. She was testing the waters to see if they still had a chance. But the Islamic divorce had already gone through, and to Jacob, this legal paperwork was just the final aggravating red tape to free him completely.

He drew in a deep breath and exhaled to calm himself. Then he walked over to his desk and picked up the phone and tapped the icon for the *du'aa* app. He opened up the *Istikhaarah* prayer tab and read from it, quickly moving his lips to recite the supplication. He hated rushing through this prayer, especially without praying two units of voluntary prayer first, but he was on a tight schedule today, and this was the only time he had a moment free to speak to his lawyer.

"Fine," he said as if it took the last bit of patience from him. "But specify that it's *after* the divorce, for co-parenting purposes." He sighed. "Then please let's set up a time for us to sign and counter sign the final divorce papers."

"You got it."

***

"I don't want to sign it," Deanna said, folding her arms defiantly as she stood looking out the window of the office of Attorney Schmidt's office Tuesday afternoon, her back to him. She heard her attorney sigh in impatience, but she ignored him. "I don't want a divorce. How can we stop him from divorcing me?"

She turned to face Bryan then, her eyes filling with tears, but she refused to give into weakness. "Make him stay married to me."

"I can't do that," Bryan said. "All I can offer is the best divorce deal possible. But I have to be honest with you and say, your case doesn't look good on paper. He put tens of thousands of dollars into your business. He personally endorsed and promoted your books. He participated in your marriage workshops and television interviews. Then there are the cases of assault—"

"That was dropped," Deanna said irritably.

"No," the attorney correct. "That was with your mother only. You have two restraining orders on public record, and one from—"

"But not from Jacob," Deanna said.

"—Jacob's place of work," the attorney finished, his voice firm. "No, it's not as strong as from Jacob himself, but it doesn't look good in court. Jacob changed the keys to his office, and during that time, you weren't living at the house. And if he also changed the locks during the time you were gone, then that's enough evidence to at least *argue* that you were a physical threat to him and the children."

"*What*?"

"You also worked on your business fulltime," Bryan continued, boredom in his voice. "And according to the uncontested divorce documents, you were less present with the children than Jacob was because of your numerous interviews, workshops, and traveling for speaking engagements."

Deanna huffed, lifting her nose in annoyance.

"And Jacob also mentioned in the documents that at least one of your sons personally requested *not* to live with you when he found out that there was a chance for divorce."

Deanna clenched her jaw, but she didn't respond.

"I'm fully willing to argue for a better deal," her attorney offered. "But if saving money is still a concern of yours, then I feel obligated to let you know you don't have a strong case here. Even some of the videos of your interviews suggest that you have an uncontrollable temper that you're barely keeping at bay. And I can't say I disagree with your husband regarding the possibility of you suffering from an undiagnosed personality disorder."

"I. Am. Not. *Crazy*," Deanna said through gritted teeth.

"I didn't say you were," Bryan said. "I'm just telling you how all this will look to a judge. It's definitely possible to argue your case to delay the divorce, but—"

"I didn't say delay it," Deanna interjected in annoyance. "I said cancel it."

"—I don't advise it," he said. "If your husband is agreeing to leave all of your assets untouched, I think that's a pretty good deal, considering his financial contributions to both the family and your business projects," he said. "But we can push for alimony if you think—"

"I don't want his money," Deanna said, putting up a hand to stop Bryan mid-sentence. "I want *Jacob.*"

***

Deanna felt the screaming in her throat before she even reached the exit of the office building. She clamped down her teeth and breathed heavily, hurrying her steps to the glass exit doors and pushing a door open before anyone could ask what was wrong. The cold October air slapped her face, and she opened her mouth wide to breathe in the fresh air, her breaths audible and deliberate, as if she were suffering an asthma attack. Miraculously, that seemed to stifle the screams, and she broke into a slow jog to her car, continuing the deep breaths with her mouth wide open.

She pointed the keychain remote to her car then yanked open the door and let her body collapse into the front seat, still breathing audibly. But as soon as she shut the car door, a shrilling scream escaped her throat. She fumbled with her keys before putting the correct one into the ignition and starting the car. Engine idling, she quickly stabbed at the controls to the radio and held down the button for the volume until the fuzzy music was almost as loud as her screams.

Deanna had no idea how long she sat in that parking space screaming like a maniac, desperately sucking in her breath after each one. But tears were streaming down her face like rivers by the time she glanced behind her and put the car in reverse. As she backed out of the space, her heart was pounding erratically, her screaming now repetitive moans.

*Just give him the f—ing divorce,* an angry voice said in her head. *Then make him regret it.*

***

"But we don't have to wait for the legal divorce if you don't want to," Aliyah said, her soft hands squeezing his as she looked up at him Tuesday evening from where she stood in front of him in the foyer of her apartment.

Jacob looked away from her. He couldn't stand the innocent kindness he saw in her eyes. It was probably a bad idea for him to have come. Though Larry said it was no problem for him to hang out with Younus and Thawab at Jacob's house, Jacob knew that being in Aliyah's presence was too difficult for him. But he needed her comfort right then, and hearing her voice on the phone was not enough.

"But I *do* want to wait," Jacob said, aggravated with himself. "I want everything to be right for you. You don't deserve to be dragged into this. This is my life, and you didn't choose it."

Aliyah shook her head then placed her hands on the short hair of his cheeks. "This is *our* life," she said, holding Jacob's gaze. "And I *did* choose it."

"That's all the more reason to make sure everything is perfect for you," Jacob said. "I just wish there was some way we could just—" He huffed and pursed his lips, too upset to even finish his thought.

"*SubhaanAllah,*" he said seconds later, a trace of aggravation still in his voice. "This really makes me appreciate the wisdom of Allah.

"I know…" Aliyah said sympathetically, her soft hands still on the hair of his closely-cropped beard.

"Divorce shouldn't be a *fight.*" Jacob grunted. "I did everything I could to just be *free* of her. What else does she want?"

"Deanna isn't a rational person," Aliyah said. "You can never know what's going through her mind, so it's not worth trying to figure it out."

***

*Apologize to Aliyah.* Standing and hovering over the desk in her room, Deanna angrily picked up a pen and scribbled out Aliyah's name then ripped the page from the notebook, crumpled the paper in her fist then threw it across the room.

"I'm not apologizing to anyone!" Deanna yelled. She then let the chair receive her weight and folded her arms defiantly.

*YOU CAN BE A BETTER PERSON!*

Annoyed, she reached for the book and turned it over, slamming the face of it on her desk so she wouldn't have to read the cover.

*Then pray...*

At the reminder that she hadn't offered a single obligatory prayer that day, Deanna's shoulders slumped in exhaustion. What was the point? It wasn't like Allah was going to give Jacob back to her if she suddenly became a good Muslim.

*I want to be a better person.* It was more an aching longing from somewhere deep in her heart than an annoying voice in her head. Deanna felt a whimper crawl in her throat as she realized that she genuinely did want to be better. She just didn't know where to begin. She had no idea what was even wrong with her. Exhausted from the mere thought of making so many changes, she stood and dragged herself to the bathroom for *wudhoo'*.

***

Jacob's legs folded beneath him after he tore the contents from the FedEx package Saturday morning and saw Deanna's signature on the revised divorce papers. He had already signed the revision himself, so her signature made the divorce final.

Initially his lawyer had thought that he and Deanna would have to meet in person for the signature and counter signature because Deanna kept going back and forth. And Jacob had been prepared to do that if that was the price of his freedom. But Tuesday he had begun to lose hope after his lawyer had told him that Deanna wanted to make marriage counseling a condition for the divorce. He hadn't gotten a full night's sleep since then, and he was fighting a migraine each day at work due to stress. But despite the despair threatening to tear him apart, he prayed to Allah each night in *Qiyaam al-Layl*, begging Allah to forgive him and to free him from Deanna.

Hunched over on his knees, Jacob held onto the side of the couch with one hand as he tried to catch his breath, still grasping the stack of divorce papers with his other hand. Tears stung his eyes, and he immediately let go of the papers and fell into *sujood*, his head resting on the carpeted floor in gratefulness to Allah. His shoulders shook, and his voice came out as a moaning whine as he muttered prayers to Allah.

When he sat up and leaned his back against the bottom of the couch, his face was still moist with tears and his breaths were still audible. But he felt a smile of relief forming on his face. Elated that Allah had answered his prayers, Jacob made the firm intention to give money in charity. As the reality of what had just happened settled over him, he felt life come back to his limbs, and he pushed himself to a standing position so he could call Aliyah.

"*Alhamdulillah*!" Aliyah exclaimed as soon as he told her.

"I know," Jacob said, unable to keep from grinning. "It's still hard to believe."

"This is really good news, *mashaAllah*," Aliyah said, and he could hear the smile in her voice.

"I know…" he said again because he didn't know what else to say.

"I have good news too," Aliyah said, excitement in her voice.

"What?" Jacob said, smiling curiously.

"I restart my PhD program in January *insha'Allah*."

"So they sent you the acceptance letter?"

"Yes."

"May Allah bless it for you." He chuckled. "So I guess this means you're keeping your job at the college, huh?"

"Definitely *insha'Allah*," she said, excitement in her voice. "At least until I have my doctorate degree in hand."

"I'm just happy you're not so stressed about it anymore."

"I am too," Aliyah said sincerely. "I guess this made me realize how much I actually like my job," she said. "I don't think I could just give up on my students like that."

An extended silence followed, as neither knew what to say.

"Soooo," Aliyah said, slight teasing in her voice as she stretched out the word, "what now?"

Jacob creased his forehead, a curious smile on his face. "What do you mean, what now?"

"You know…" Aliyah said, shyness in her tone. "With us."

Jacob smiled wide. "Well, the ball's in your court on that one," he said. "I'm still willing to wait your required year."

He heard Aliyah sigh thoughtfully. "I don't know if I want to anymore," she said sincerely. "I realize now that I was just afraid of the unknown, you know?"

"I understand," Jacob said. "But give it some thought, okay?"

Aliyah coughed laughter. "I think I've given it enough thought," she said, conviction in her tone. "I think we've waited long enough. Any longer and I think I'll just get frustrated."

"As long as you're sure…" Jacob said uncertainly.

"I'm sure."

"Then let's take a vacation somewhere."

Aliyah sighed empathetically. "You don't have to go through all of that, Jacob, really. To me, it's enough of a vacation to know that we're free from Deanna."

"I know," he said tentatively, "but I've given this a lot of thought myself, and I don't want you to be burdened with living in Deanna's old house. I want us to start anew."

"You plan to sell the house?" Aliyah asked, surprise in her tone.

"Yes, *insha'Allah*," Jacob said. "I'm already looking at some other properties."

"Well, my lease isn't up until February," Aliyah said, "so I'm fine living at my apartment until then."

"Then we can plan a honeymoon in the meantime," he said.

The sound of Aliyah giggling made him smile.

"Don't worry," he said. "I'll pick something simple. I know you don't want anything extravagant."

"Thank you," she said, gratefulness in her voice.

"And of course Larry is fine watching the boys for us."

"You already asked him?" Aliyah sounded surprised.

"Not for this specifically, but he told me he's willing to if we ever want to get away for the weekend or something."

"*MashaAllah*, may Allah bless him."

"Ameen," Jacob said sincerely. "I'm really blessed to call him family."

Aliyah didn't immediately respond, and Jacob sensed that Aliyah was thinking about her own family. "I wish I knew how that felt…" Aliyah said, her voice sad and reflective. "I feel like an orphan."

Jacob grew sad for Aliyah. "I'll do what I can to make you happy, *bi'idhnillah*," he said and meaning it. "I can't imagine how it feels to be going through that."

"Allah tests everyone in different ways," she said, her voice a sigh. "But *alhamdulillah*." She sounded slightly more cheerful. "I *do* have you."

"And I you, *alhamdulillah*," Jacob said with a smile, his heart filling with so much happiness that he wished he could hug her through the phone.

## 31
## A Beautiful Name

"That's a huge blessing, you know," Larry said, "growing up Muslim."

"Yes, *alhamdulillah*, it is," Salima said noncommittally. "But I think anyone's path to Islam is a huge blessing, *mashaAllah*."

"Isn't there a hadith about the person who grows up Muslim being under Allah's Shade on the Day of Judgment?"

Salima smiled into the cordless phone from where she sat curled up on the couch of her living room early Saturday morning in mid-November. Jamil and Haroon were still sleeping after having gone back to bed after *Fajr*, but Salima had stayed awake after prayer, anticipating Larry's call. The after-*Fajr* early morning phone call had become their weekend routine after Larry had texted Salima one Sunday morning after he'd prayed *Fajr* in the masjid, asking if she was awake. And she had been, though she had awakened only to make sure that Jamil and Haroon were up for prayer since she hadn't been able to pray that week. She hadn't even realized she'd left her phone on the night before until she heard the chiming alert indicating an incoming text message after returning to her room.

"Yes, there is actually," Salima said. "But the hadith isn't only about a person who grows up worshipping Allah. It's about seven categories of people who'll be under Allah's Shade." She grinned. "And one of them is a man whose heart is attached to the masjid."

Salima could almost see the smile of recognition on Larry's face. "Oh yeah," he said, "I remember that now."

"And who knows?" she said. "That could be you."

Larry chuckled self-consciously. "I don't know about that…"

"And there's another hadith," Salima said, "about the double reward of the Christian who believed in Jesus, peace be upon, then accepts Islam."

"Really?" Larry sounded genuinely surprised.

"Oh, you'd be surprised the endless rewards that exist for believers from every background," Salima said teasingly. "There are even rewards for simply moving your tongue."

"Moving your tongue?" There was laughter in Larry's voice.

"In *dhikr*," she said. "Like saying *subhaanAllaahi wa bihamdi wa subhaanAllaahil-'atheem*. The Prophet, *sallallaahu'alayhi wa sallam*, said these words are light on the tongue but heavy on the Scale."

"What does it mean?"

"A loose translation is, 'Highly glorified is Allah and praise to Him, and Highly glorified is Allah, the All-Mighty.'"

"And reciting Qur'an too, right?"

"Absolutely," Salima said, laughter in her voice. "That's at the top of the list. Every letter that you recite earns you ten blessings each."

"*MashaAllah*," Larry said, admiration in his voice. "Then you must get millions of blessings, knowing the whole Qur'an and teaching it."

A reflective smile lingered on Salima's face, but she felt sad all of a sudden. She was thinking about Mikaeel and their two children, and how shocked and terrified she felt the moment she found out about the accident. She thought about Kalimah and what she must be going through. She thought about her sins of the tongue and the limbs, in being a believer who had been so full of Allah's blessings that she thought she had the right to dictate how they were manifested in other people's lives.

"I hope so," Salima said quietly, her breath catching as tears filled her eyes.

There was an extended pause, and Salima sensed Larry's concern through the phone. "Are you okay?" he said.

Salima forced laughter. "I'm fine," she said, taking a ragged breath. "It's just—" She quickly wiped her eyes then took a moment to steady her breathing. "It's just I get a bit emotional sometimes," she said, finding her voice. "Sometimes everything just hits me all at once, you know?" She coughed laughter as fresh tears sprung to her eyes and she wiped them away. "We're so ungrateful, *astaghfirullah*."

"*Astaghfirullah*," Larry muttered.

"You know how they say, 'The more you have, the more you think you deserve; and the less you have, the less it takes to make you thankful'?"

"Yes."

"Well…" Salima huffed, humor in that sound. "It's true."

"That's a hard trap to *not* fall into," Larry said reflectively.

"But why?" Salima said, narrowing her eyes as if confounded. "I mean, you'd think…" She sighed and shook her head, letting her thoughts go unfinished.

"I know," Larry agreed. "That's one thing Aliyah taught me."

At the mention of her friend, Salima stiffened in annoyance. Larry had never given Salima a completely forthcoming explanation as to what had happened between him and Aliyah. More than anything, he'd been consistently dismissive of the topic, and that nagged Salima to no end. She hated that it bothered her so much, but she really wanted to know if his heart was attached to someone else, even if only marginally. "*Aliyah*?" she repeated, hoping she sounded as lighthearted as she intended.

She heard Larry laugh self-consciously. "I don't mean Aliyah the person," he said. "I mean Aliyah the experience."

"There's a difference?" Salima said in lighthearted sarcasm.

"For me there is," Larry said.

Salima drew her eyebrows together. "What do you mean?"

"I never got to know Aliyah the person," Larry said. "And frankly, I'm glad I didn't."

Salima winced at the harshness of his words. She wasn't so sure it was right to hear what he had to say about her friend, but she felt relief nonetheless. At least the question of Aliyah was a little less mysterious. "Ouch," she said, laughter in her voice, hoping Larry took the subtle hint to take it easy on Aliyah.

"I don't mean any disrespect to her," he said, as if realizing just then how his statement must have sounded. "I meant that I'm glad I didn't get to know her as a person because I don't think it would've been good for either of us."

"Why not?" Salima asked, genuinely curious.

"Because I realize now that the whole thing was just this huge, exciting challenge to me, and most of it had more to do with Jacob than me."

Salima drew her head back in surprise and glanced sideways at the phone. "*Jacob*?"

"I know it sounds stupid," Larry said, laughter in his voice. "But when I first met Aliyah at the restaurant, I was just flirting, you know, being a man. You see a good-looking woman and you just want to find out a bit more about her."

A tinge of jealousy pinched Salima. "*MashaAllah*," she said, more for herself than for any connection to his story.

"But it wasn't really that deep to me." He spoke as if he was lost in thought. "I mean, sure, I would've married her if it came to that. But not because I really wanted to," he said. "It would've been because it was the natural next step. It was more scientific than emotional. I'd read all these stories about the prophets and righteous people of the past, and I was on a spiritual high. I'd just broken up with Jazzy, and I was ready to experience what being with a real woman was like."

"A *real* woman?" Salima said, humor in her tone.

He coughed laughter. "You know…"

"No, I don't," she said in lighthearted firmness.

"A righteous woman," he said, "someone who submits to God and her husband."

"Can't forget the husband part," Salima joked.

"Of course not," Larry replied, mirroring her joking tone.

"So what does any of this have to do with Jacob?"

"Because he wanted to marry her too." Larry spoke as if that were the most logical explanation in the world.

"And…"

"And that made her more of a challenge," Larry said simply.

"I hope you're joking," Salima said, half-humored, half serious.

"Sadly, I'm not," Larry said, embarrassed humor in his voice.

"So that whole thing was just some stupid sibling rivalry, male ego trip?"

"I wouldn't put it like that…"

"Is there another way to put it?"

"It's like you said," he explained. "The more you have, the more you think you deserve."

"And exactly *what* did you have at that time," Salima said, "except a lot of nerve?"

She heard Larry laugh through the receiver. "My own money," he said, "good looks, a solid track record."

"A solid track record?" Salima said, chuckling. "You hadn't even been Muslim that long."

"I mean with women."

She rolled her eyes. "Okay," she said, "you were really full of yourself."

"I know," Larry said in agreement. "That's the whole point of me mentioning the Aliyah situation. It humbled me. She wasn't impressed by any of it."

Salima laughed out loud. "I can't say I blame her."

"Cut a brother some slack," Larry said, laughter in his voice. "I thought I was doing something good."

"By trying to marry the woman your brother wanted to marry?"

"It didn't start off like that."

"But it didn't deter you."

"Of course not. You have to understand," he said, reflective humor in his tone. "I grew up looking up to my brother. He always had things I could never have. So learning that he wanted to marry Aliyah made her more valuable to me."

Salima rolled her eyes and shook her head, a grin on her face. "I'm not sure I'm up for hearing all of this," she said jokingly.

"You're the one obsessed with knowing every detail of every thought I've ever had about any woman," he teased good-naturedly.

"Well, I'm officially healed from that obsession."

Larry laughed then said in a more serious tone, "But we weren't compatible anyway."

Salima sighed reflectively. "*Allahu'alam.*"

"Allah knows best," he agreed. "But I think He made His signs clear on this one."

"In what way?"

There was a thoughtful pause. "You know that Mark Twain quote?" he said. "Never argue with a stupid person?"

"Because they'll just drag you down then beat you with experience?" she finished.

"Yes, that one," he said.

"That's one of my favorite quotes," Salima said. "I wish I could find a bumper sticker of it. Then maybe I can stick it to my forehead or something."

"Your forehead?" Larry said, chuckling, momentarily distracted from his point.

"Yes, why not?" Salima joked. "That way, I'll never forget it," she said. "Or I can stick it to my office wall. Because that's where most of the stupid people are in my life."

"Well…" Larry said, returning to his point. "Aliyah thought quotes like that put pride in your heart," he said, coughing laughter. "So she didn't like it."

Salima contorted her face. "Put *pride* in your heart?"

"Yeah…" He laughed again. "Like it made you think you're better than other people."

Salima wrinkled her nose. "O-kay," she said, as if she had no idea what Larry was talking about.

"Exactly." He huffed. "I swear, that girl was so uptight, it was suffocating."

Salima grew quiet, uncomfortable with the seamless shift from reflecting on their blessings to speaking badly about their Muslim sister. "Let's not backbite her though."

"*Backbite* her?" Larry said in humored disbelief. "I'm just telling you what happened," he said defensively.

"I know, but…" Salima didn't know how to explain the reason for her sudden discomfort with the conversation.

"Sorry," Larry said sincerely, his voice subdued. "I shouldn't have called her uptight."

Salima was quiet as a thought came to her. "You know, Aliyah wasn't completely wrong about that," she said finally.

"About what?" Larry said.

"The quote. It *can* put pride in your heart if you're not careful."

"Oh no," Larry said humorously, in mock dread. "Not you too."

"Seriously though," Salima said good-naturedly. "She has a point."

"You're joking, I hope."

"I'm not saying I see it the way she does," Salima clarified. "But like the Prophet, *sallallaahu'alayhi wa sallam*, said, 'Actions are by intention.'" She shrugged. "Used in the wrong situation, quotes like that *can* make you look down on people and reject the truth, which is essentially the definition of *kibr*."

"*Kibr*?"

"Blameful pride."

Larry was silent for some time. "I guess I can see where you're coming from," he said honestly. "But if you think like that, then you'll stress over *every*thing."

"Well, like I said," Salima replied, "I don't see the quote negatively. But to each his own, you know? Everybody has to do what works for them."

"Live and let live, huh?" Larry said, humor in his tone.

"Exactly," Salima said with a shrug. "Unless they're doing something Allah doesn't like."

***

*Is the "hot Muslim mistress" now the secret wife? Some people really know how to halalify on the down-low! #MuslimScandal #HalalHomeWreckers*

JazzyQ and 48 others like this. 13 comments.

Nicole Nikki Willis: *Are ya'll seriously starting this sh*t again?* (3 likes)

JazzyQ: *Guilty conscience, **Nicole Nikki Willis**?* (24 likes)

Nicole Nikki Willis: *This is straight-up backbiting! 'A'oodhubillaah!* (2 likes)

Juwayriah bint Abdullah: *Did I mention any names in my status? I just asked a question. #iftheshoefits* (17 likes)

Nicole Nikki Willis: *You didn't have to say a name. It's obvious who you're talking about!* (3 likes)

JazzyQ: *Who would that be* ***Nicole Nikki Willis****? You?* (18 likes)

Juwayriah bint Abdullah: ***Nicole Nikki Willis*** *why do you care so much? Are you bi or something?* (12 likes)

JazzyQ: ^^^ *LMAO* (9 likes)

Nicole Nikki Willis: *She's your Muslim sister. Fear Allah.* (2 likes)

Juwayriah bint Abdullah: ***Nicole Nikki Willis*** *in Islam marriage is public. So we have a right to inquire about who's married to whom. And if a marriage is done on the DL, then we have a right to ask questions! Why all the secrecy? Makes me wonder if all those HMM rumors were true!* (19 likes)

Muslimah Amreekiyah: *How you get him is how you lose him! I have no sympathy for secret wives AKA halal home wreckers! So tired of the polygyny is halal argument!!* (22 likes)

Imrah Wahidah: ***Muslimah Amreekiyah*** *does that apply to first wives too? They got him thru halal marriage, so they lose him thru halal marriage (when he marries someone else)?* (7 likes)

Reem Muhammad: *Bismillah. fyi Jacob is divorced from Deanna.* ***Juwayriah bint Abdullah*** *if the wedding you're talking about took place (and only Allah knows), just keep in mind, you not being invited to a wedding doesn't make it secret. All Islamic marriages have witnesses. So there's no such thing as a "secret marriage." There are marriages you know about and those you don't. Learn the difference. Neither case implies adultery beforehand. Be careful what you "wonder" about in public. It'll be on your record on the Day of Judgment. No one is obligated to call every child of Adam after they get married. So if YOU want to know who's married to whom, pick up the phone and ask them. All this passive aggressive BS on FB is really childish. You're backbiting and you know it. You can lie to the people, but not to Allah.* ***Muslimah Amreekiyah*** *"polygyny is halal" isn't an argument. It's an Islamic fact. If you're tired of your religion, that's called spiritual crisis. Get help if you need it. And fyi: There's no such thing as "halal home wreckers" in Islam. Anything that's halal brings good. But hating what Allah loves can wreck your home and everything else in your life. And it seems like this whole discussion was started to wreck someone's home. Is that halal?*

Reem's hands were trembling in anger as she typed the last words then grunted as she pressed *enter*. She snapped her laptop shut and left it balanced on the comforter covering her legs as she folded her arms over her chest, her eyes narrowed in aggravation. She huffed and shook her head in disbelief at the cruelty of these women.

*What's their problem?* she wondered, fuming. Why were they so fixated on other people's lives?

"You still up?" Sayed's voice was groggy and muffled against the pillow where he lay facing Reem, the comforter pulled over his shoulders.

"I couldn't sleep," Reem said softly, her calm voice concealing her annoyance with the Facebook discussion.

"What happened?" Sayed said knowingly, a lazy smile forming on his lips as he squinted his eyes at Reem, his head still against the pillow.

"Nothing," Reem muttered, shaking her head, arms still folded in agitation.

Sayed slowly sat up next to her then put an arm around her shoulder. "What happened?" he said again, this time more sincerely.

"It's this stupid—" Reem gestured a hand toward her laptop then huffed before folding her arms again, too upset to explain further.

"Some social media madness again?"

"Pretty much."

"Anything you want my perspective on?"

She lifted the laptop and handed it to him then resumed her pout, shaking her head in disbelief. When he opened the laptop and silently read the contents on the screen, she grew self-conscious, wondering if she'd handled the situation correctly. Perhaps she had been too impulsive in her response, something she'd told Sayed she was trying to avoid. But it was so infuriating seeing the way Juwayriah and her friends were talking so badly about Aliyah.

"*SubhaanAllah*," Sayed muttered, shaking his head at the screen. "Is this why women get social media accounts? To multiply their sins?"

Reem bit her lower lip and glanced at her husband hesitantly, wondering if he'd read what she typed.

"Well, at least you have a few people who seem to fear Allah," Sayed commented with a sigh, lifting the open laptop and handing it back to Reem. "But I don't think it's anything you need to get involved in."

Reem creased her forehead as she set the laptop back on her legs, looking at Sayed. "You didn't see what I said?"

"*You* were part of that discussion?" His eyebrows were gathered in disapproval as he regarded Reem.

"Yes, I thought you…" Her voice trailed as Sayed reached over and took the laptop back and quickly skimmed the screen, scrolling down in search of her name. Seconds later, he frowned, apparently as he re-read what she'd wrote. "Just keep in mind," he read aloud, causing Reem to cringe and shut her eyes, "you not being invited to a wedding doesn't make it secret... And it seems like this whole discussion was started to wreck someone's home."

At the sound of laughter, Reem's eyes shot open as she looked at Sayed in disbelief, a hurt expression on her face.

"This short essay is yours?" he said, gesturing his hand toward the long comment, a grin on his face.

Reem opened her mouth to respond but didn't know what to say.

"It's fine, *habeebti*," he said, leaning over to brush her cheek with a kiss. "It's the third most sensible comment on the thread."

"The *third*?" Reem repeated, unsure if he was mocking her.

"*Tab'an*," he said. *Of course.* "In situations like these, the best advice is shortest and most meaningful."

"It wasn't that long," Reem said, but she detected the uncertainty in her own voice as she leaned over and read her comment again.

"'She's your Muslim sister. Fear Allah' was by far the best comment on that thread, *mashaAllah*," he said. "The Prophet, *sallallaahu'alayhi wa sallam*, was known for giving very brief, meaningful pieces of advice. 'Love for your brother what you love for yourself,'" Sayed enumerated. "'*Laa tagh'dhab.* Don't get angry.'"

"Then what was the second best comment?" Reem said, eyes still on the screen, feeling embarrassed as she compared her comment to the others.

Sayed put his forefinger beneath the comment by the person named Imrah Wahidah, then read aloud, "'Does that apply to first wives too? They got him thru halal marriage, so they lose him thru halal marriage?'"

Reem wrinkled her nose in disagreement. "Why?" she said. "It's sarcastic."

Sayed shrugged. "Maybe. But it's also a simple, thought-provoking rhetorical question," he said. "And it takes their faulty logic and throws it right back at them. You'll find these sorts of rhetorical, thought-provoking questions all throughout the Qur'an and Sunnah, especially in response to people doing or believing things that are wrong."

Reem sighed. "I see what you mean," she said. "Maybe I should delete my comment then…"

Sayed furrowed his brows. "Why? There's nothing wrong with it."

"But you said it's a short essay."

He chuckled. "But it's a *good* short essay, *mashaAllah*. It'll just come off as a bit whiny and self-righteous," he said with a shrug. "And no one will probably read the whole thing. But deleting it won't do any good either."

"No one will read it?" Reem said, her tone conveying hurt. She had put a lot of thought into what she'd said, even if she had been upset.

"Except the people who don't need to because they already fear Allah," he said. "Other people generally have short attention spans," he said. "And it's even shorter when it's something they disagree with. So no, the Facebook *fitnah*-mongers won't give it more than a quick skim, then miss the whole point. But they'll read enough to decide they don't like you," he said with a chuckle. "*That*, you can depend on."

Reem frowned, folding her arms over her chest again. "Then what's the point of *amr bil ma'roof wa nahi 'anil munkar*?"

Sayed nodded, as if realizing something just then. "*Astaghfirullah*," he said, seeking Allah's forgiveness. "I shouldn't have said *no one* will read it. *Allahu'alam.* A few probably will. And besides getting blessings for doing what you're supposed to, that's the point of commanding the good and forbidding the evil. The reminder benefits the believer."

"But why do they keep doing that?"

"Who?" Sayed said, looking at Reem quizzically.

"These sisters." She gestured toward the laptop screen. "You'd think they had enough after all those lies they spread about Aliyah and Jacob the first time."

"Some people like *fitnah*," Sayed said simply.

Reem contorted her face. "But why? It makes no sense."

"It makes sense," Sayed disagreed. "Think about it," he said. "When you're not doing what you're supposed to, is what makes you happy connected to what Allah loves? Or something that you personally have strong feelings about?"

Reem immediately thought about her struggle to view Americans as equal to Arabs.

"We all fall into this sin sometimes," Sayed said.

"Yes, *sometimes*," Reem emphasized. "But every single day, all day? That's stupid."

"I can't answer that," Sayed said thoughtfully. "Because it *is* stupid. You're not gaining anything, in this world or the Hereafter, by living like this."

Reem huffed in annoyance. "I swear, sometimes I wish that sister would change her name."

"What sister?"

"Juwayriah bint Abdullah."

Sayed glanced at the screen again but didn't say anything.

"How can she take the name of one of the mothers of believers," Reem fumed, "then say she's the daughter of the servant of Allah, and act like that?"

A thoughtful silence followed. "I don't think she *took* the name. Her parents probably gave it to her," Sayed said reflectively. "And it's a beautiful name, *mashaAllah.* So she shouldn't change it."

"She should if she's acting like that!"

Sayed shook his head. "No, she shouldn't," he said. "She should change her *behavior* if she's acting like that. But she should keep the name. It could be a reminder to her one day."

"But—"

"Should *you* change your family name from Muhammad whenever you sin?" Sayed asked gently. "No one is perfect."

At that, Reem grew quiet, but she was still upset.

"Remember when you and Mashael were discussing hijab and you said if a woman can't cover properly or act like a Muslim in public, it's better she doesn't cover at all?"

Reem frowned at the memory, but she nodded.

"Like I said then," Sayed continued, "we should never wish someone harms their soul just because we're embarrassed by them. Islam is not a PR campaign to impress non-Muslims. And it's a very dangerous mindset to wish bad upon your Muslim brothers and sisters just so you can make Islam look better to disbelievers."

***

"Did you find anybody for Jamil yet?"

"Yet?" Salima repeated, smiling into the cordless phone that she held with one hand as she now stood in the kitchen, glancing around for what she could eat for breakfast.

"Isn't he single?" Larry said.

"Yes…" Salima said, a question in her tone. "For now. Why do you ask?"

"A brother is looking for someone for his daughter."

Salima chuckled and shook her head. "And I assume he asked you because he wanted *you* for her."

She heard Larry laugh self-consciously. "Well…"

"And you told him…?"

"I told him I was already talking to someone for marriage."

"And who would that be?" she said teasingly.

Larry chuckled. "Come on, Salima. Don't give a brother a hard time."

"So you're thinking about marriage now?"

"That's all I've ever been thinking about."

Salima grinned as she reached for a box of cereal from atop the refrigerator then set it on the counter. "I mean, is it more than just *thinking* this time?"

"I'm praying on it," he said in a serious tone. "But I think I'm ready." There was a thoughtful pause. "If you are."

Salima opened a cabinet and removed a glass bowl. "Then I have some praying to do myself," she said, a smile in her voice.

"Let me know what you think," Larry said. "Because the ball's pretty much in your court."

"Let me talk to Jamil and my parents and get back with you."

"I'm willing to meet them," Larry said. "Your parents, I mean. If you want me to."

"Of course, I do," Salima said. "But they prefer to be informed only after I'm sure what I want."

"I heard that Muslim parents micromanage their children's marriages," Larry said, light humor in his tone.

Salima grunted, mirroring his humor. "Not mine," she said. "I'm too grown for that." She added, "And they're too secure."

"So it's not like a rule or something that the parents have to agree?" There was genuine curiosity in his tone.

"It's definitely preferred," Salima said tentatively. "But previously married women have more autonomy."

Larry chuckled self-consciously. "So us getting married doesn't hinge on what they say?"

Salima grinned. "No," she said. "But I value what they think."

"I can live with that," Larry said.

"So let me see what they say and get back to you."

"Okay," he said. "Sounds fair."

"But who's this mystery woman you think is good for Jamil?" she said, returning to the original subject.

"Oh, I don't know her," Larry clarified. "I just know she's eighteen, in her first year of college, and never been married before."

Salima felt a twinge of jealousy. "Sounds like a good catch."

"Nah," Larry said. "Not for me."

"Why not?" Salima asked curiously, opening a drawer to get a spoon.

"Too young," Larry said.

"She and you have about the same age difference as you and I," Salima pointed out.

"It's not the age difference," he said. "It's her *age*."

"Some eighteen-year-olds are pretty mature."

"In theory maybe, but not in reality."

Salima creased her forehead as she opened the refrigerator and removed a half-gallon of milk. "What do you mean?"

"I'm not saying an eighteen-year-old isn't mature enough for marriage," he clarified. "I'm just saying an eighteen-year-old isn't mature enough for *me*."

Salima raised her eyebrows as she poured her cereal and milk then returned the milk to the refrigerator. "And why not for *you*?"

"I'm almost thirty years old," he said. "What would we have in common?"

"What do you and I have in common?" Salima asked rhetorically.

"That's different," he said.

"Why?"

"You and I have been in previous relationships," he said. "This girl's probably never dated a man in her life, and she's most likely a virgin."

"And that's a problem?"

"For me it is."

"Why?"

"Because I'm not a virgin," he said simply. "Aren't virgins supposed to marry virgins?"

"You mean in Islam?"

"Isn't that a rule in the Qur'an or something?"

"No," Salima said. "Chaste people can only marry chaste people," she said. "What's forbidden is for someone living a life of fornication or adultery to marry someone who's living properly."

"What if you sinned before becoming Muslim?"

"Then you've repented *insha'Allah*, and so long as you're no longer living like that, then you're considered chaste."

"Oh," Larry said, as if this was the first he'd heard of this.

"You know, Jamil is divorced..."

"Really?" Larry's voice rose in surprise.

"You didn't know that?"

There was extended silence. "Oh yeah…" Larry said, as if remembering just then. "I forgot about that. Probably because he doesn't have any children."

Salima sat down at the kitchen table with her bowl of cereal and mumbled "*Bismillaah*" before bringing a spoonful of cereal to her mouth. A thought came to her after she'd eaten a few bites. "Do you want to reconsider our situation now that you know you have more options?"

There was a long pause, and Salima sensed Larry's confusion. "What do you mean?"

"Now that you know it's not *haraam* for you to marry a virgin."

Larry laughed out loud. "No thank you."

Salima chuckled, a question in that sound. "Why do you say that?"

"Not interested," Larry said. "Like I said, I don't think they're mature enough for me."

"Why not?"

"They're clingy, needy, and possessive, for starters," he said.

"Ouch," Salima said before eating more cereal in silence.

"I don't mean it offensively," he said. "It's just that I'm ready to start a family, and I want my wife to have some life experience to pass on to our children. I don't want to have to raise my children *and* my wife."

"You really think it would be like that?"

"For me, yes."

Salima was overcome with sadness all of a sudden, but she finished her cereal before voicing what was on her mind. "What if I can't have any more children?" she asked quietly.

"You mean because of your age?" Larry said.

Salima frowned. "Yes."

"We'll cross that bridge when we get there, *insha'Allah*."

"But what if it's the bridge we're at right now?" she asked. "What will you do?"

There was a thoughtful pause. "I don't know," he said honestly.

Salima lifted the spoon and played with it mindlessly. "Would you want to marry another wife?"

Larry was silent for several seconds. "I don't know." Her heart fell at his words. "But I don't think so," he added.

Salima set the spoon down, her eyebrows drawn together, perplexed. "You mean you're willing to never have children of your own?"

"I don't think it matters what I'm willing to do," Larry said. "It only matters what's written for me. Even if you can't have children, marrying another woman doesn't guarantee anything," he said. "If Allah has written I'll have children, then I will. If He's written I won't, then I won't. So what's the point of chasing the unknown?"

"But you're okay with not even *trying*?"

Larry chuckled. "You're speaking as if you believe we don't have a chance. Of course I want to try. But marriage is about more than having children. It's about what we can offer each other in this world. Even if we're never able to offer it to anyone else."

A reflective smile played at Salima's lips. "That's true. The husband and wife are helpmates to each other," she said, "helping each other worship Allah and go to Paradise."

"And that's what I'm looking for," Larry said. "If Allah wants to bless us with children too, then I'm more than happy to enjoy that blessing."

They were both lost in thought for some time.

"You can go ahead and tell Jamil about that sister," Salima said finally, hoping to drop the subject of polygyny. It inspired too much discomfort. After repenting for how she'd treated Kalimah, Salima often wondered if Allah would humble her further by decreeing that she live as a co-wife herself.

"You don't want to tell him?"

"No," she said.

"Why not?"

"Because he's back in touch with his ex-wife." She lowered her voice in case Jamil was awake.

"Back in touch?" Larry repeated, confused. "In what way?"

"That's what I don't know," Salima said. "But he might be considering remarrying her."

"Really?" Larry sounded disappointed.

"You sound like me," Salima said in dry humor.

"I don't know anything about his marriage," Larry clarified. "But it made me think of Jazzy."

"Jasmine?"

"Yes, I'm sorry," he said quickly. "I'm so used to calling her Jazzy."

Salima laughed. "It's okay," she said. "I don't mind."

"You don't?" Larry sounded genuinely surprised.

"Why would I mind?" she said. "If you call someone by their nickname long enough, you tend to forget their real name."

"Well, I'm glad you understand," Larry said, sounding relieved.

"I don't know everything that happened with you and Jasmine," Salima said after a thoughtful pause, "but Jamil's situation is kind of complicated."

"Then do you think it's a good idea to mention someone else?"

"*I* think so," Salima said, emphasizing herself. "If only to let him know he has options. But I can't be the one to do it because it might sound disrespectful."

"But if he's thinking of remarrying the woman…"

"I think that's exactly what he's thinking," Salima said. "But I can't be sure she's thinking the same."

"Are you serious?" Larry sounded concerned.

Salima sighed then stood and left the kitchen, deciding this was a conversation that was better had in the privacy of her room. "Hold on a minute," she said then ascended the steps to her room. She closed the door and locked it before sitting on her bed.

"Let me put it like this," Salima said. "I don't like the sister. But it's not my place to say that."

"Why not?"

"Because my role is to be the supportive big sister."

"And you can't tell him the truth?"

Salima drew in a deep breath and exhaled, thinking of the difficult relationship she'd had with Kalimah when Mikaeel was alive. "I wish I could, but my opinions have gotten me into trouble in the past, and I don't want to make the same mistake. If I had something concrete to tell him, I would." She sighed. "But the main problem I had with her, she says she's no longer involved in."

Larry chuckled knowingly. "Sounds like Jasmine after I became Muslim," he said. "Now she's suddenly Muslim."

Salima frowned thoughtfully. "That's the thing though. You don't know what's in someone's heart. I don't feel good about his ex-wife, but what is a feeling?"

"Trust your gut," Larry remarked. "That's what I say."

"But I'm not the one interested in marrying her," Salima said. "So my gut is irrelevant, don't you think?"

Larry was quiet momentarily. "I wouldn't say it's irrelevant…"

"Your gut told you not to marry Jasmine," Salima said. "But Jamil's gut is telling him *to* marry this sister."

"He told you that?" Larry sounded doubtful.

"No, but…"

"Because what you want and what you know deep down are two different things," he said.

"But not everyone knows the difference."

"I think we do," Larry said. "We just don't want to believe we do."

Salima drew in a deep breath and exhaled. "I'll have to think long and hard before I say anything to him though."

"Why?"

She sighed. "Because, like I said, I don't have a good track record with my opinions. And I have to figure out if this is really my gut saying something's wrong, or if it's just *me* saying something's wrong."

There was a thoughtful pause before Larry asked, "What are your objections?"

Salima folded her legs in front of her, trying to decide how much she should share. "Her practice of Islam mainly."

"She doesn't pray?"

"She prays," she said tentatively. "And wears hijab," she added.

"Then what's the problem?"

Salima pursed her lips, deciding the best way to put her thoughts into words. "She's what some would call a Muslim groupie."

"A *groupie*?" Larry said, and Salima could hear in his voice how appalled he was.

Salima chuckled. "Not that type of groupie," she clarified.

"Is there another type?"

"I mean, she feels she has to attach herself to people before she can attach herself to Allah."

There was a thoughtful pause. "What do you mean?"

"You know how in Christianity, people worship Jesus to draw closer to God?"

"Yes."

"It's sort of like that," Salima said. "Some Muslims feel they need something tangible to turn to before they can worship Allah."

"But isn't that *shirk*?" Larry sounded confused.

"Yes, if it's done in the literal sense," Salima said. "But with this sister, her sect believes you have to commit to a particular sheikh and spiritual path before you can be a real Muslim."

There was an extended silence, and Salima sensed Larry's confusion. "So…" he said, as if having a difficult time formulating his question. "…how is that different from Islam? I mean, isn't Prophet Muhammad, peace be upon him, our sheikh, and his Sunnah our spiritual path?"

"Yes."

"Then…"

"It's hard to explain," Salima said, "because each group is different. But in this sister's group, they believe their sheikh has reached such a high spiritual state that's he's incapable of sin, and that if you draw closer to him, you draw closer to Allah."

Salima heard Larry laugh out loud. "You serious?"

"Dead," she said, no humor in her tone.

"But how does that work?" he said, sounding genuinely confounded. "Do they have their own *shahaadah* and everything?"

"Pretty much," Salima said. "Though they don't call it that. Some of them call it *bai'ah*, but some of them don't call it anything. They just commit themselves to following their saint, then they—"

"Their *saint*?" Larry interjected, humored disbelief in his tone.

"—pretty much treat him like he's Allah or the Prophet, *sallallahu'alayhi wa sallam*."

"Is this Muslim Catholicism or something?" he said incredulously.

"To me it is," she said. "But to them it's just venerating the *awliyaa'* of Allah."

"The what?"

"*Awliyaa'*," Salima said. "They're the believers who are closest and most beloved to Allah. It's a term from the Qur'an and Sunnah talking about the prophets and messengers and the believers whom Allah has singled out due to their high level of *emaan* and commitment to Him."

"Oh I think I read something about that," Larry said. "These are the people of *ihsaan*, right?"

"Yes," she said. "But this group translates *awliyaa'* as saints. But either way, Muslims aren't permitted to claim this station for anyone other than the prophets and messengers and anyone specifically mentioned in the Qur'an and Sunnah." She huffed. "And you certainly can't claim it for yourself."

"People *claim* to be saints?" Larry asked in disbelief.

"Yes, unfortunately."

"I thought you meant some Muslims treat their sheikhs like the Christians treat prophet Jesus, peace be upon him," Larry said, "but the sheikhs didn't ask them to."

"That happens too," Salima said. "But the group Jamil's ex-wife is part of, the sheikh *himself* says he's a saint. And he says people are obligated to follow him." She grunted then added, "And that you can't follow any other sheikh along with him."

She heard Larry suck in his breath. "Wow, that's some crazy stuff," he said, and Salima could almost see him shaking his head, a disbelieving smirk on his face. "That sounds like how I was taught to think about Allah. I can't worship any other god along with Him."

Salima coughed laughter, agreeing.

"Jacob told me about the different sects of Muslims," Larry said. "But I didn't know it was like that. Makes me wonder if these people ever really learned about Islam."

She shook her head, a reflective smile lingering on her face. "Trust me," she said. "Many of them have. They just don't see anything wrong with adding their own spice to it."

There was a thoughtful pause. "Is Jamil into that kind of stuff too?"

Salima drew in a deep breath and exhaled. "No, *mashaAllah*," she said. "He's just really into this sister."

"Fatal attraction, huh?" Larry said in dry humor.

"*Allahu'alam*," Salima said, acknowledging that Allah knew best. "I could be wrong about this whole thing."

"But what they're doing sounds really messed up."

"I don't mean about the beliefs," she said. "I mean about the sister. She says she's no longer part of that group."

Larry was silent momentarily. "And you believe her?"

"No," Salima said. "But I don't have any proof."

"What makes you doubt her?"

"Because that's still her social circle," Salima said. "And one thing I know about these sects is, unless they see you as a potential convert, they're not welcoming to outsiders," she said. "Any whiff of you having doubt about their sheikh or their group, you're ostracized and shut out of everything, even dinner invitations."

"So you think she's lying?"

Salima frowned thoughtfully. "No…" She was unsure how to put her thoughts into words. "I just don't think she realizes what she's gotten herself into."

Larry was quiet for some time. "That sounds like a cult." His voice was etched in concern.

"Sometimes it is," Salima said.

"Sometimes?" Larry repeated, humor in his tone.

"Because every group that has mistakes isn't a cult."

"And you don't think this one is?"

Salima was silent momentarily. "I don't know," she said honestly. "But even if it were, I don't think the sister will realize it until it's too late."

"What do you mean?"

"Because usually people don't realize what's happening until their life is turned upside down and they have no one to turn to," she said. "Because all their connections are through their group. And if you reach out to someone you think is a friend, they'll only help you if you fully commit to everything you're trying to get away from."

Larry was silent for some time. "Can I ask you something?"

By the tone of his voice, Salima knew Larry's question was completely unrelated to Jamil and his ex-wife. "Sure," Salima said.

"And this is just hypothetical," he said, as if in lighthearted warning.

Salima immediately grew concerned. "Okay…" she said, caution in her voice.

"What if one day I did want to marry another wife?" Larry said, and Salima immediately felt weak at his words. "Would you support me?"

Rage flashed through Salima, and she tried to calm herself. *"We didn't think you were a womanizer…"* she recalled saying to Larry. *"Just not a one-woman man?"* Larry had replied. *"Well, I can't speak about the future,"* he'd said, answering his own question, *"but so far, that's all I've been. That's how I was raised, and that's how I intend to remain in marriage."*

"Support you?" Salima repeated, hoping the curious tone she was trying to maintain masked the horror she felt right then.

"Yes." Larry spoke as if supporting her husband's efforts to sleep with another woman was the most natural reflection of wifely righteousness.

"I thought you were a one-woman man," she said teasingly, hoping she sounded as lighthearted as she intended.

"I am," Larry said. "I was just wondering how you'd react if that changed." He chuckled. "You're not going to go Deanna on me, I hope."

Salima gritted her teeth. "Don't talk about Deanna like that."

Larry laughed. "Okay fine," he said non-committedly. "But would you fight me about it?"

"I wouldn't be happy," Salima said, deciding that was a safe response.

"I wouldn't be either," Larry said.

Salima creased her forehead, as if waiting for the punch line. "Why wouldn't *you* be happy?" This time, she made no effort to mask her sarcasm.

Larry chuckled. "You women really think men have no hearts, huh?"

"The jury is still out," Salima said, a smirk on her face.

"Now, that's cold," Larry said in lighthearted humor.

"Well, I'm not the one bringing up polygamy before we're even married."

Larry laughed out loud. "Are you joking?" he said. "You asked me if I'd want to marry another woman if you can't have children. I wasn't even thinking about polygamy before you brought it up."

*Oh.* Salima's face was aflame in embarrassment. *"Would you want to marry another wife?"* she'd asked him only minutes before. "Well, I didn't mean it like that," she muttered defensively.

"Like what?" Larry said, unmasked amusement in his voice.

"I was speaking hypothetically."

"So was I."

*"And this is just hypothetical,"* Salima recalled Larry's words just then. Mortified, she didn't know what to say.

"You know this is why women get a bad rep, don't you?" Larry said, humor still in his tone. "You guys start stuff then pin it on us." He chuckled. "I swear, before I became Muslim, I laughed out loud when I read that verse in the Qur'an about having two women witnesses."

*And if there are not two men [available], then a man and two women, such as you agree for witnesses, so that if one of them errs, the other can remind her...* Salima recalled the part of the *ayah* in *Al-Baqarah* that Larry was referring to.

"I was like, this Book is the real deal," Larry said. "It talks about things we all know are true but people try to deny in the name of feminism and what not."

Salima didn't know whether to feel proud or offended. "Women have good qualities, too," she said.

"Of course," Larry said. "Being emotional and forgetful aren't bad qualities. It is what it is."

"Men can be emotional and forgetful," she said defensively.

Larry chuckled. "Are we really going to do this? This politically correct back-and-forth? You memorized the whole Qur'an, so you know better than I do that men and women are different."

*And the male is not like the female...*

"Why do you all do that though?" Larry asked, genuine curiosity in his tone. "Try to prove women are equal or better than men? There's nothing wrong with having human fault. Men have their faults too."

Salima grew irritated all of a sudden. "Maybe because we've been oppressed too long."

"Fair enough," Larry said. "But then shouldn't your focus be on fighting oppression instead of denying who you are? How does denying your female traits help you?"

"We're not all dimwits," she said bitterly.

Larry sighed. "Look, Salima," he said, his voice soft in empathy and exhaustion. "I don't mean to offend you. I think we both know I'm not saying women are stupid. It's just hard to have a serious conversation with women sometimes because you all get offended over stuff that has nothing to do with anything."

Salima huffed and rolled her eyes.

"All I'm asking is the same question you asked me. You asked what I'd do if things didn't turn out like we expect with you having children, and I'm asking you how you'd feel if things didn't turn out like we expect with me being married to only you."

Salima understood his point, but it was hard to let go of her hurt. "I'm sorry," she muttered after a few seconds. "It's just a really difficult subject for me."

"I can understand that," Larry said. "But it really is just a question. I don't have any plans on marrying another wife."

Salima drew in a deep breath and exhaled, her eyes growing distant. "I used to be dead-set against polygamy," she said. "But now the whole concept just terrifies me."

"What do you fear most?"

"My *emaan*," she said. "And my *ikhlaas*."

"Your faith and sincerity?" Larry asked.

"Yes."

"Why?"

"I fear for my faith because I don't want to question Allah," she said. "And I fear for my *ikhlaas* because I'm scared I won't even care what's best for me. I just don't want it in my life."

# 32
# We're SAFE Now

*I hate myself.*

The words wriggled their way through the recesses of her mind, then her heart. They now sat heavy and idle in the pit of her stomach, a nasty internal bruising. It was as if someone had sucker punched her in a fit of rage, leaving a painful loathing that had been there long before the fight.

Aggravated, Deanna yanked the covers over her head and switched positions, now laying on her other side.

*"I guess this is the table for husband stealers?"*

Jasmine's question hung in the darkness of the bedroom, haranguing, as if addressing Deanna herself. It incensed the loathsome bruising in her stomach and crawled like stealthy fingers around her neck until her throat closed. Tears stung her eyes, and she gasped for air.

*Nobody wants you. Nobody loves you. Nobody cares.*

Deanna clamped her teeth down and bolted upright, letting the comforter fall to her waist as she silenced the scream before it found her voice. Her lips wrestled to stay closed as a horrible moaning escaped with each breath.

Deanna hated the night, and slumber itself provided little refuge. If asleep, she was haunted by nightmares of an enigmatic world that she was certain reflected the reality of her depraved life. If awake, she was haunted by the inescapable nightmares of her reality itself. And the day was merely the brief and foggy, though welcomed, reprieve offered the hopeless insomniac.

*I want to be a better person.*

These words settled upon her just as the moaning of her thwarted screams subsided. Though once heartfelt, the declaration was now but a ridiculous mantra that did not belong to people like her.

*You cannot be better because you have no good in you to begin with.*

Deanna grunted in angry annoyance. "So what?" she called out, her voice loud in the stillness in the room. "So what if I'm not a good person! Who is? Aliyah? I don't think so!"

*But what about Jacob?*

At the reminder of the divorce, a mournful whine escaped her throat as the clutches of loneliness clamped around her. Tears spilled from her eyes before she could stop them, and she covered her face with her hands as her shoulders shook. This time, she made no effort to quiet the wailing screams into the night.

And this time, she heard no stirrings of her mother or father coming to her aid.

***

"I love you."

Jacob uttered these words as he held Aliyah close to him, his voice fading as he drifted to sleep. His snore was a soft wheezing in the darkness of the hotel suite, a rhythmic aphrodisiac that made Aliyah snuggle even closer to him.

"I love you too," she whispered even though she had no idea if he was conscious enough to hear her. But a faint smile played at her lips as she lay with her head against his bare chest, the flat of her palm massaging the coiled hair there. She felt herself becoming exhausted, but she wanted to lie awake a moment more, imbibing the electrifying pleasure that still weakened her even an hour later.

"This was well worth the wait," Jacob had teased her earlier, and she'd laughed out loud.

"Muslim women aren't stiffs, you know," she'd teased in return. "Just because we cover and lower our gazes doesn't mean we don't know how to enjoy ourselves *and* please a man."

Jacob had coughed laughter. "Well, I'm certainly not complaining."

The smile on her face spread into a grin before she closed her eyes and drifted to sleep herself.

***

*Perspective.* The epiphany came to Deanna as her eyes blinked open under the strain of grogginess, the light of day hesitantly filling her room through the closed curtains, an indication that she had drifted to sleep after all. *I need perspective.*

The mere thought of reaching out to someone during this difficult time made her stomach knot in anxiety and dread. She hadn't even been online since her arrest and subsequent release except to email Asher and read his reply. There were literally hundreds of unread messages in her account, but she couldn't bring herself to open a single one. She'd already deleted the Facebook app from her phone, and if it hadn't been for her email alerts about bills and her occasional communication with her lawyer, she would have deleted the email app as well. Even without having read a single message or post online, she'd already become angry imagining what others would be saying about her.

*Talk to Asher.*

Deanna hated her brother with paralyzing resentment, but she really had no idea whom she could turn to right then, at least not without being billed by the hour. Her mother and father lived with her under the same roof, and one would think that the parent-child bond would inspire more than begrudging tolerance of her presence. But to them, the provision of a home and food each night was much more than they owed her, no matter what she was going through. They knew nothing of the divorce, at least not officially, and Deanna doubted they cared either way. Asher himself might not even care, but his indifference remained a theory because her brother was not someone she had ever taken time to get to know.

Asher was Barry and Kerri's firstborn, the pregnancy that had inspired their marriage. But Deanna often felt that she was the unwanted child, the pregnancy that neither of them expected or wanted, the pregnancy that forced them to spend money they could have used for more important and valuable things. In Deanna's darkest dreams, she was their firstborn, the child they resented because she forced them to commit to each other in marriage when they had plans for a better life. Their resentment of her was almost palpable while Asher enjoyed a distant respect of which she could only imagine.

But Asher was her brother, and perhaps there was within him a trace of the familial connection of blood ties that went beyond mere begrudging obligation and tapped into the veins of emotional bonds.

***

Asher's house reeked of beer and cigarettes, and Deanna breathed through her mouth. She was unable to temper the annoyance she felt at him for not even taking time to clean up though she had called before making the five-hour drive early that afternoon. But now it was evening, and she was tired and hungry, and the sight of books and newspapers sloppily stacked all over the living room floor and unwashed clothes thrown about and piled carelessly on the couch made her want to turn around and head right back home.

"You want a drink?" Asher said from where he stood opposite his sister in the foyer. He wore a dingy wife beater shirt and faded blue jeans that sagged below the waistline, revealing a hint of blue and red striped boxers. The beginnings of a beard framed his face in unkempt graying coils and offered Deanna only a semblance of the countenance she associated with her older brother. He held her gaze as he walked over to the couch and shoved a pile of clothes to the side then gestured for Deanna to come in and sit down.

She hesitated only momentarily before entering the living room and walking around to the couch, not bothering to remove her shoes. A musty smell stung her nostrils as she let the sofa receive the weight of her body.

Deanna did want something drink, but she felt leery about consuming anything from his house, even water. "Sure," she heard herself say. Her stomach lurched as he disappeared into the kitchen, and she swallowed hard to keep from throwing up right then.

There was clanking and banging coming from the kitchen, and Deanna glanced about her in repulsion, her lips pinched closed in distaste. She did a double take as she saw on the small circular table next to her a single framed picture. It was of two men standing outside in front of what looked like Asher's house, laughing together about something. Deanna immediately recognized Asher as the man clipping the shoulder of the other, as if to keep from laughing more. The other man's eyes were shut, his mouth wide open and teeth bared mid-laugh. There was something eerily familiar about him that made Deanna's insides convulse. She quickly turned away, shifting her entire body away from the frame.

"Here we go," Asher said, appearing suddenly and slamming a clear glass mug and a can of beer on the circular table next to her. He reached under his arm to retrieve his own can of beer as he settled on the single-cushion loveseat at an angle opposite the couch.

There was a soft hissing sound as Asher opened his beer before leaning his head back and taking a gulp. He wiped his mouth with the back of his hand then leaned forward, can still in hand, and asked, "What did you want to talk about?"

"I'm divorced," Deanna said, shifting stiffly on the couch, unable to get comfortable next to the pile of musty clothes. She'd thought she would have a more eloquent introduction to her problems, but she didn't want to stay longer than she had to.

Asher chuckled, a half grin forming on his face. "Join the club."

Deanna pulled her head back in surprise. "You were married?"

"Yep," Asher said, folding in his lips as his eyes lost focus momentarily. "And I despise the institution."

"Did you have any children?"

"Three," he said with a grunt, a shadow of anger passing over his face. "And I despise that institution even more than marriage."

Deanna felt disgusted with her brother right then, but she kept her judgment to herself.

"That wench lives like a damn princess while I can barely afford satellite TV," he said bitterly. "On *my* dime. But apparently, that's not enough. She had me put in jail."

At the mention of jail, Deanna's interest was piqued. "You were in jail?"

"Mom and Dad didn't tell you?" Asher spoke in distracted anger, as if venting to himself. "Twice."

A suffocating silence followed, and Deanna averted her gaze, remembering her own experience in jail. "What did you do?"

"What did I *do*?" Asher said, his voice rising in irritation, his eyes meeting hers in an icy glare. "Why do you assume I did anything?" Deanna opened her mouth to respond, but he continued before she could, "I didn't pay *enough* child support, apparently." He grunted and shook his head before leaning his head back and taking another gulp of beer. "But the whole damn system is extortion, if you ask me."

"Do you see them often?" Deanna asked, missing Younus and Thawab just then. "Your children, I mean?"

"I used to," Asher muttered. "But even that was a fight with her. So I just said f— it." Deanna winced at his profanity. "She put all these crazy ideas in their head about me anyway, so what's the point?" he said. "I'm a deadbeat whether I show up or not. But she sure cashes those checks every month." He huffed then took another generous sip from the can. "And she doesn't even bother to have a job."

Deanna's eyes traveled cautiously to the unopened beer can next to her. "Do you have bottled water?"

"What?" Asher contorted his face as he looked at her.

"I'm Muslim," she said. "I don't drink."

Asher rolled his eyes in annoyance. "Oh yeah, I forgot about that." But his voice was more compassionate than his expression.

He shook his head. "I drink tap water," he said. "Feel free to fill your glass as much as you like."

Deanna couldn't tell whether or not he was being sarcastic, but she smiled nonetheless. She knew right then that she would be reserving a hotel that night if she was too tired to drive home.

"Don't the Moslem women wear some type of headdress?" Asher said, making a circular motion around his head.

"Yes," Deanna said, stiffening in offense. She hated when her entire identity as a Muslim woman was summed up in that piece of cloth. "But I don't."

"Hmph," he said, a slight grin on his face as he regarded her with an expression that was difficult for Deanna to read. "Was your husband abusing you or something?"

Deanna twisted her face in disgust. "Of course not," she said. "I would *never* let a man lay a hand on me."

"So I guess you were abusing him then, huh?"

Deanna's eyes widened in offense. "*A'oodhubillaah*," she exclaimed before she realized that Asher would have no idea what the Arabic utterance meant.

"Aw hell nah," he said, that grin still on his face. "I don't want any of that Moslem voodoo in my house."

"Why would you even ask me something like that?" Deanna fumed, ignoring his insult on her religion.

"Ask you what?" Asher said, his expression becoming angry and defensive all of sudden.

"If I abused my husband."

"Oh, girl, get over yourself." Asher flipped a hand at her, as if shooing her out of his sight, and in that moment, he reminded her of their father. "You're a smart girl," Asher said, a frown on his face. "You went to college and all that, so you know about the cycle of abuse." He huffed. "But without child support bills, you probably have enough money to pay some stupid shrink to fix all your problems."

Deanna looked at Asher as if he'd lost his mind. "The cycle of *abuse*?"

"Don't tell me you're almost pushing forty and you still haven't figured out what the hell is wrong with you?"

Deanna just stared at him, unable to soften the indignant expression on her face.

"That's why you're here, right?" he said. "To find out how I cope and all that?"

"We-were-not-abused," she said through gritted teeth, insulted that he would even suggest something like that. "We're *Michaels.*"

The explosion of laughter was so sudden that Deanna started. Still holding his beer in one hand, Asher slapped his free hand repeatedly against the arm of the loveseat, his legs moving up and down as if running in place, his body rocking back and forth in amusement.

Deanna's face was aflame in mortification at having incited this delirium, but her expression remained set in obstinate offense.

"Thanks, sis." Asher drew in deep breaths as if trying to gather his composure. He placed his free hand on his chest and shook his head, a smile still on his face. "I'm glad you came. I haven't had a good laugh since I destroyed my marriage."

Deanna's nose flared. "What's so funny about what I said?"

Asher raised an eyebrow as he regarded his sister, a smirk creasing one side of his mouth. "You're not joking, are you?" he asked rhetorically, a trace of sympathy in his voice. "You really think we had some stupendously great upbringing, don't you? The up-and-coming Michaels, right? The sign to the world that underprivileged minorities can fulfill the American dream," he sang out before erupting in laughter again.

Seconds later he sighed, shaking his head. "Damn, girl. And I thought you were the smart one."

"No family is perfect," Deanna said defensively, but she detected a falter in her voice.

"Is that the story you tell yourself?" There was a sneer on his face, but a moment later his expression became reflective. "I used to tell myself the same," he said, a distant sadness in his eyes, a slight smile lingering at his lips. "But I can live with the truth now. We have one f—ed up family."

He gestured a hand toward Deanna. "You get raped in the basement of our church. Bailey gets a pat on the back," he said, as if enumerating the Michaels's litany of faults. "Dad blames you. I beat my wife." He shrugged. "I blame her."

A shudder went through Deanna at the casual mention of what had happened to her. She was never sure that Asher even knew about it though she'd always suspected he had. He had been twenty-three and living on his own when she'd written the letter to her parents before running away from home. But he had stopped calling her Janice around that time, so perhaps their mother or father had told him. It was touching to learn that all this time Asher had believed Deanna, even without having spoken to her about it directly.

"You see that picture there?" Asher pointed to the frame that sat next to the glass mug and beer. "That's me with the only friend I still have."

Deanna's eyes cautiously slide in the direction of the frame.

"You know who that is next to me?" There was humor in Asher's voice. "Bailey."

Deanna shuddered and turned away from the frame. She felt lightheaded all of a sudden and gripped the arm of the couch to steady herself.

"He's a disgusting misogynist." Asher leaned his head back and took another gulp from the can.  A smirk was on his face as he swallowed and looked thoughtfully at the picture. "But I like him."

Deanna's stomach lurched, and she felt the bile rising to her throat. But she clamped her teeth shut and swallowed hard, refusing to let Asher's words unnerve her.

"You know why?"

Asher's question hung in the air like the stench of the room, but Deanna didn't respond. She refused to even look at her brother right then.

Asher grunted, humor in that sound. "Because he knows he's full of crap." He spoke as if that were the most admirable trait in the world. "And that's more than I can say for anyone else I know." He huffed. "Including our self-righteous parents."

***

The sound of the shower woke Aliyah, and she felt the emptiness of the space in the bed next to her as her palm lay on the tussled sheet instead of the warmth of Jacob's chest. A smile formed on her lips as she recalled the night before, and she immediately uttered the supplication for waking, translating the Arabic words in her mind. *All praise is for Allah who gave us life after having taken it from us, and unto Him is the resurrection.*

She instinctively glanced at the clock and saw that it was time for *Fajr*, the dawn prayer. She sat up and pulled the heavy duvet around her as she glanced around the bed for her gown. When she saw it lying in a small heap on the carpeted floor, she reached down then said "*Bismillaah*" as she shook it before pulling it over her head. She heard the shower water stop just as she sat down on the edge of the bed and picked up the breakfast menu from the nightstand to see what time breakfast was served.

"*As-salaamu'alaikum*," Jacob said, a smile spreading on his face as he emerged from the bathroom, a hotel-issue towel secured firmly around his waist. He walked over to the side of the bed where Aliyah was thumbing through the breakfast menu and brushed her forehead with a kiss. She smiled up at him and returned the salaams, returning the menu to the nightstand as she stood in preparation to shower herself.

"How'd you sleep?" Jacob asked as he walked over to the other side of the bed and picked up his clothes then shook them as Aliyah had done minutes before.

"Good *alhamdulillah*," she said and meaning it, a smile in her voice as she walked toward the bathroom. She looked over her shoulder, watching him as he pulled his shirt over his head.

"You?" she asked, halting her steps at the open bathroom door.

"Slept better than I have in years," he said sincerely, winking at her.

She chuckled and shook her head as she stepped into the bathroom and closed the door.

***

*You went to college and all that, so you know about the cycle of abuse.* Deanna gripped the steering wheel so firmly that her hands hurt. Her tired eyes were narrowed and fixed on the silver darkness of dawn beyond the windshield. The words were Asher's, but the voice in her head was her own, as if they'd sprung from her own thoughts. *Don't tell me you're almost pushing forty and you still haven't figured out what the hell is wrong with you.*

Abuse.

The word carried with it so much weight, so many accusations. It was a word that Deanna associated with helpless women, women she was burdened with saving because they were too weak to save themselves. Abuse existed only in the context of someone else's life, not Deanna's.

She was a Michaels, so it was impossible that she had been abused. Other than her aunt, there was no one in her family who'd subjected themselves to such a lowly existence. Yes, Bailey had raped her, and that could count as abuse. But she had been only eight years old then, and she'd never let it happen again. She *refused* to let it happen again. Unlike Deanna, abused women suffered from learned helplessness and feigned weakness when they were really just addicted to their victim status.

No, Deanna would not claim victimhood for herself. She was above being a victim. Victims were people like Aliyah and her cohorts, people who could barely hold themselves together, let alone their lives and marriages. That's why they needed Deanna's expertise, to help them stand up straight and learn the basics of keeping a man.

*But you're divorced too.*

The words slammed down upon her like the heavy blade of a guillotine.

She was repulsed at the thought of being categorized as a divorcée. She was not a divorcée. She was a marriage guru who prevented the category from even existing in the first place.

"You know what I suggest?" Asher had said when she'd told him of her insomnia and nightmares, and the involuntary screaming and internal tug-of-war with herself. "Apologize to every person who's ever crossed your path." His words were slightly slurred, as he was on his third beer by then, having consumed Deanna's a half-hour before. "Start with your ex-husband and friends, then your children and colleagues, and don't stop until you feel completely humiliated and exposed." He laughed then took another swig of beer before gesturing the can toward her. "I wish I'd thought to do that before I f—ed up my life and everyone else's."

***

After her shower, Aliyah put on an abaya and *khimaar* before lining up at an angle behind Jacob in preparation for prayer.

"You want to pray your *Sunnah*?" he asked, turning to look at her from where he stood facing the *qiblah*. "I prayed mine while you were in the bathroom."

"Sure," Aliyah said, probably too quickly. Though she often prayed the two voluntary units before *Fajr*, she hadn't planned to pray them right then. But after her husband's reminder, she immediately raised her hands and offered the extra prayer, her heart lifting at the blessing of having such a good man in her life.

***

*There it is again*, Deanna had thought bitterly when Asher made the suggestion. *That apology*. Why was it that so many people believed that self-improvement was connected to appeasing someone else? Why couldn't she just become a better person without humiliating herself? Why should she have to apologize to anyone? They were no better than she.

"You did *what*?" The look on Asher's face had been a mixture of horror and disgust, and Deanna immediately regretted telling him of how she'd convinced Jacob to marry her instead of Aliyah.

"She didn't deserve him," she'd muttered defensively. "She had no idea how to keep a man."

Asher just looked at her then, his disgusted expression unchanged except now there was a trace of pity. "And I thought I was a bad husband."

"I did *not* abuse anybody." Deanna was indignant, insulted that he would imply that her crime was greater than his.

He laughed out loud but left the subject alone. "We should get together some time," he'd said minutes later. "The three of us."

"I'm not speaking to Jacob anymore," she'd said stiffly.

"Girl, I'm not talking about your ex-husband," he said, a sneer in his voice. "I'm talking about me, you, and Bailey."

Deanna glared at Asher, but she couldn't tell whether he was speaking in earnest or jest. "I-refuse-to-have-anything-to-do-with-that-monster," she said, speaking through gritted teeth.

Asher cackled and shook his head, setting his empty beer can at his feet. "That's a shame," he said, a smirk on his face, "because you two have so much in common."

"I have *nothing* in common with him," Deanna said, her voice trembling in fury.

"But you do," Asher insisted, his eyes traveling to the framed picture as he spoke. "You both steal things from other people then insist that the victim deserved the crime."

Deanna opened her mouth to respond but found she'd momentarily lost her voice.

"Except Bailey is better than you," Asher said, his eyes reddened and unfocused from insobriety. But his voice was surprisingly steady and clear. "He doesn't pretend to be good."

***

*"Let me tell you how I snagged Jacob."*

These were the words that came to mind as Jacob sat on the carpeted floor of the hotel room, a thin travel prayer mat in front of him. Aliyah sat diagonally behind him with her own travel prayer mat in front of her. "*SubhaanAllah,*

*SubhaanAllah, SubhaanAllah...*" he said, glorifying God while enumerating with his fingers, and he heard the muttered whispering of Aliyah doing the same.

Sitting there after *Fajr* prayer, Jacob was overcome with gratefulness for the blessings that Allah had given him through Aliyah. Even as he'd suffered daily in his marriage to Deanna, there were times that Jacob had allowed himself to imagine what it would be like to have a righteous wife. The concept of having as a life partner a woman who loved and respected him as the leader of the household was something he'd begun to associate with generations past. Yet still, he hadn't been able to quell his desire for a woman with at least a semblance of those qualities. But he'd imagined that it was his ungratefulness for what Allah had given him in Deanna that made this desire constant even as he was already married with children. "If you want a righteous wife," the imam had said at *Jumu'ah* one day, "then ask yourself this: Am I a righteous husband?"

The imam's question had given Jacob pause. Jacob had come to the Friday prayer that day mentally exhausted from yet another argument with Deanna, even as he had been at work all morning. On her best days, Deanna would make Jacob feel belittled and emasculated. Jacob knew she wasn't always doing it on purpose, but that didn't make the situation any better. There was constantly an air of entitlement and superiority with her, as if she viewed it as Jacob's sole responsibility in marriage to fulfill her every desire, even if left unspoken.

On that particular Friday, Deanna had woken up in one of her nastier moods, when it felt as if her primary purpose was the argument itself. Even after an hour of back and forth, Jacob had no idea what on earth she was upset about. Every word that she uttered was so vicious that it was as if her only goal was to inflict as much pain as possible. Jacob had left the house angry and frustrated, wondering how much more of her cruelty he could take. *Isn't a wife supposed to respect her husband?* he'd fumed.

However, listening to the imam's words, Jacob asked himself, *But am I a righteous husband?* Could he honestly say that he himself was righteous and thus deserving of a righteous woman? Upon careful reflection, Jacob knew with certainty that the answer to that question was a resounding no. He hadn't even been sure that he knew what righteous meant. Yes, he lowered his gaze, avoided unnecessary interactions with women, never committed adultery, and prayed the five daily prayers on time every day. But did that make a person righteous, he'd wondered? *Ascribe not purity to yourselves*, the Qur'an commanded. Then no, there was no way he could say with any truthfulness that he deserved a righteous wife.

The buzzing and vibration of his phone interrupted his thoughts, and he glanced toward the hotel dresser where he'd placed his mobile. He started to stand to get the phone, but Aliyah stood and reached for it before he could. Without looking at the mobile display, she quietly handed him the phone then sat back down on the floor and resumed her *adhkaar*.

Surprised at this gesture, Jacob stared at Aliyah, a question on his face as he wondered if she was upset with him for something. But her eyes were looking at something beyond her prayer mat as she quietly recited *Ayat al-Kursy*, which was a prophetic custom after each obligatory prayer.

*What are you thinking?* he asked himself once the confusing moment had passed. The phone continued to buzz and vibrate in his hand, but he didn't look at the screen, distracted by the fact that Aliyah's simple gesture had surprised and worried him at all. It took several seconds for Jacob to realize that the reason for his surprise and concern was that Deanna would hand him his phone only if she was annoyed by the interruption or if she was insisting that he take a call that was about a workshop or interview she wanted him to do for her.

*SubhaanAllah,* Jacob thought to himself. *Is that really how I lived?* The realization made him shudder. How had he lasted more than a decade in that relationship, where the simplest display of kindness was either withheld or done for ulterior motives? And how had he lived with all of that pent-up anxiety? Every day that he was married to Deanna was like walking on eggshells. If a day was going well, he viewed it with suspicion, as if waiting to learn something he'd done wrong. He'd lived in apprehensive expectation of her next verbal or physical attack.

*0-4-1-9.* Jacob used his forefinger to type in the numeric passcode to his phone.

*1 missed call. Larry Bivens*

As Jacob pressed the phone icon next to Larry's name and placed the phone to his ear, he remembered why he'd chosen the 0419 numeric passcode so many years ago. *And live with them honorably*, Allah commanded men in the Qur'an with regards to their wives. *If you dislike them, it may be that you dislike a thing and Allah brings through it a great deal of good.* This verse was from the chapter entitled *Al-Nisaa*, The Women; and it was *soorah* 4, *ayah* 19, hence Jacob's chosen passcode. It was his daily reminder to look to the good in Deanna and be grateful for her as a wife.

"*As-salaamu'alikum*," Jacob said as soon as he heard the phone stop ringing. "Are the children okay?" Aliyah's recitation stopped suddenly, and Jacob sensed her heightened concern.

"The children are fine, man," Larry said. "But we have another problem."

"What's going on?" Jacob said, his voice etched in concern. Aliyah moved closer to Jacob, intense worry lines between her eyebrows.

Phone still against his ear, Jacob turned to Aliyah and offered her a reassuring smile. "The children are fine," he whispered. Her face immediately relaxed, and she stood and walked over to the bed and sat down and picked up the food menu again.

"It's Deanna," Larry said.

"What about her?" Jacob said, his concern heightening.

"She's here at your house."

"*What?*"

“I didn’t let her in, of course,” Larry said. “But she’s ringing the doorbell like a maniac, pounding on the front door, and blowing up the house phone. It sounds like she’s trying to use her key to get in.”

At that moment, Jacob remembered preparing for the weekend trip by programming all of Deanna’s calls to go directly to voicemail. He drew in a deep breath and exhaled.

“Thanks man,” Jacob said, exhaustion in his voice. “Tell her I’m not there.”

“I did.”

Jacob groaned.

“She doesn’t believe me.” Larry chuckled. “For all I know, she thinks I *am* you.”

“Okay,” Jacob said, sighing. “I’ll call her myself. But as a last resort, if she doesn’t leave, call the police.”

***

“I am better than the wicked and sinful. I am walking with the Lord.” Deanna recited this mantra to herself as tears streamed down her face and she alternated between pressing the doorbell, pounding on the front door, and wiggling the door handle because her keys were not working. She needed to talk to Jacob immediately. She had made a mistake in agreeing to the divorce. She needed to tell him she was willing to do marriage counseling like he’d suggested before the divorce.

The mere thought of having as her only family her emotionally distant parents and her misguided brother was terrifying. Deanna had left her brother’s house late the night before and came directly to her and Jacob’s home. How she had lasted so many hours on that filthy couch was beyond her. It was as if her brother’s home was inhabited by *shayateen*, demons lurking in the corner of every room. Listening to him speak in admiration of Bailey felt as if Asher himself had transformed into a *shaytaan*, and it terrified Deanna that this was actually her own flesh and blood, her only family.

*I need Jacob back.* The epiphany came to her minutes before she came upon the exit leading to her parents’ home. But she’d been overcome with anxiety so intense that her chest hurt at the mere thought of spending another second in that house. *I need Jacob back!* her heart and mind screamed in a cacophony of frantic desperation.

“I’ll do anything you want,” she’d sworn aloud as she passed her parents’ exit and headed toward Jacob’s instead. “I don’t care what it is. I just need you back.”

“Jacob, just give me a minute,” she spoke into the front door while pounding the flat of her palm against it. “We need to talk. It’s really important.”

The familiar ring tone on her phone wafted into her consciousness as if coming from a distance. She recognized it immediately as the special ring she’d assigned to Jacob. At the sound, she scrambled for her purse and opened it then quickly withdrew her phone.

"Hello?" she said, breathing heavily, making no effort to conceal her anxious excitement to speak to him.

***

The mere sound of Deanna's voice incited annoyance in Jacob, but he tried to remain calm. She was probably having a nervous breakdown, but he found it extremely difficult to muster up even the slightest sympathy for her state. For years he'd pleaded with her to get professional help, but she would scoff at him and hurl insults, as if he was the one with the problem.

"*As-salaamu'alaikum*, Deanna," Jacob said, speaking as calmly as his frustration would allow. He stood with his back to Aliyah, who now sat cross-legged on the hotel bed, a concerned expression on her face as she listened intently to his side of the conversation. Before calling Deanna, he'd briefed Aliyah on what Larry had told him.

"Can you let me in?" Deanna said, her breathing sounding as if she'd just run a marathon. "I have something important to tell you."

Jacob drew in a deep breath and exhaled. "I'm not home right now, Deanna. Larry is there watching the children for me. I won't be back until tomorrow, *insha'Allah*."

"But I heard you—"

"That was Larry, Deanna," Jacob said, enunciating every word carefully, as if speaking to a child. "My brother."

"But I thought—"

"What time is good for us to meet on Sunday?" Jacob interjected, wanting to end this call as quickly as possible. It aggravated him that she had chosen this weekend of all times to create a disturbance.

There was an extended pause, and all Jacob could hear was her breathing. "You'll see me?" She sounded surprised and ecstatic.

It was odd witnessing this level of vulnerability from Deanna. She sounded as if she were doing a horrible impersonation of his ex-wife. Her desperation when there was no other option was so cliché that it was almost sad. It reminded Jacob of the predicament of people who would beg God to return them to the world so that they could live righteously, but even if Allah did return them to the world, they would go right back to living a life of arrogant disobedience.

"We have to choose a counselor for co-parenting, remember?" Jacob said.

Her silence suggested that she had completely forgotten about the single aspect of the divorce agreement that she herself had insisted on. "And we can talk about other things too," she said quickly.

"What time?" Jacob said, doing his best not to sound annoyed.

"Any time."

"Then I'll call you tomorrow *insha'Allah*."

"We made a mistake, Jacob," she said. "We should do marriage counseling instead."

Jacob's nose flared as he felt himself losing patience. "We'll talk tomorrow *insha'Allah*," he said again, his voice rising slightly.

"Did you hear me? We made a mistake."

"I heard you," he said with a sigh. "Let's talk about it tomorrow."

"I'll wait for you here."

"*No*." Jacob himself flinched at the sternness of his tone. He silently recited *isti'aadhah*, seeking refuge in Allah, then tried again. "No," he said more gently. "If you don't leave right now, my brother will call the police." Jacob hated threatening Deanna, but he was running out of options. Besides, she didn't seem to be in her right mind, and he imagined that nothing else would register.

"But this is *my* house." With those words, it was as if she were Deanna again. Jacob could hear the signature pompous arrogance in her voice.

"No," Jacob said firmly, making no effort to sound diplomatic. "It's *my* house. And if you don't leave now, you'll be back in jail, and then, we won't be able to talk tomorrow."

Jacob heard Deanna grunt in aggravation, but he sensed that the threat of not being able to meet with him was more troublesome than the threat of going back to jail.

"Fine," she said. "But I never liked your brother. You should find someone else to watch our children."

"I'll call you tomorrow, *insha'Allah*," he said again, but he detected the stillness on the other line, indicating that she'd already hung up on him. Dropping his hand to his side, still holding his phone, he exhaled in relief. If he had been forced to hang up on her, he had no idea if she'd leave Larry and the children alone. So it was a good thing that the call had ended by her initiation. It gave Deanna the sense of control she needed in nearly every interaction.

"I've been thinking a lot about my mother and sister…" Aliyah said as Jacob walked over to the hotel dresser and set his phone next to the large television screen. "And it made me realize that—"

"We're going to have to meet Deanna together tomorrow," Jacob said. He turned to face Aliyah as he folded his arms and met her gaze with a serious expression on his face. He hated to cut off his wife mid-thought, but he didn't want to delay sharing what had been on his mind. Deanna's erratic behavior only confirmed what he'd already thought. It was time to tell her about him and Aliyah. "I can ask Larry to come too," he said tentatively. "But we need to meet with her sooner rather than later."

Aliyah's lips formed a thin line, her expression contemplative and troubled.

"I know it's not ideal," Jacob said apologetically. "But I don't know what other choice we have."

Aliyah looked pained as she regarded him, a question on her face. "But is she mentally stable?"

Jacob grunted, a trace of humor in that sound. "Has she *ever* been mentally stable?" he asked rhetorically.

"What if she goes crazy?"

"I think she's already past that point," he said. "She passed that a long time ago."

Aliyah shook her head, doubtful. "I don't know, Jacob…"

"If you feel uncomfortable," he suggested, "I can speak to her alone. With Larry," he added, clarifying. "But my hunch is that she needs to see you in person to really process what I'm saying. Otherwise, she'll probably be in denial."

"Deanna can get violent…"

The fear that Jacob saw in Aliyah's eyes gave him pause. He had become so accustomed to Deanna's physical attacks that he'd forgotten that they could cause bodily injury. He was definitely physically stronger than Deanna, but the scar on his forehead from a girlfriend's violent attack before he'd become Muslim was proof enough that his size alone wouldn't protect him from physical harm. Moreover, he'd sustained his share of bruises and broken skin during fits of rage by Deanna herself. Deanna's volatile nature had become so much a part of his marital life that he'd forgotten that there were actually men and women who lived out their lives free from fear in their own homes.

"I'm sorry," Jacob said quietly. "I forgot about that."

"I can still come with you," Aliyah said tentatively. "It just needs to be in a public place." She added hesitantly, "You know, with security around."

Jacob nodded thoughtfully. "The masjid?"

Aliyah creased her forehead doubtfully. "Maybe the mall?" she said. "I'm not sure the masjid is the best place for this. There will be too many people she knows there, and it'll probably make her more defensive."

"That's true…"

"Plus some of the main gossipers and Facebook *fitnah*-starters hang out at the masjid on the weekend."

Jacob nodded thoughtfully.

"The mall has some quiet areas," Aliyah said. "We could even make a reservation at a restaurant."

Jacob's eyebrows rose as a smirk formed at his lips. "The irony…" he said, reflective humor in his tone. "You know the Day of Judgment is near when the mall is a better option than the masjid."

Aliyah chuckled, as if just then realizing the irony herself. "I know…"

"The *shayateen* love the marketplaces."

She shook her head, a reflective smile lingering on her face. "We live in strange times…"

They were silent for some time.

"What if we asked your uncle if we could meet at his house?" Jacob said. "I know it's not public and doesn't have security, but I think her seeing Brother Benjamin will have the same effect. He's pretty well-respected in the community," Jacob said. "And if anything happens, we can always call the police."

Aliyah sighed, and she became lost in thought momentarily. "Sometimes I feel sorry for her, you know?" She shook her head. "I know she never really talked about it much, but I never got the feeling she had a really supportive family." She shook her head again. "And now this? She's probably losing her mind."

Jacob huffed, thinking of how Deanna's father was working against her after the accident with her mother. "Her not having a supportive family is an understatement," he said. "She's practically an orphan."

"I know you know a lot more about her situation," Aliyah said. "But I always felt like she had this wall up around me, as if she needed me to think she was stronger than she really was."

"Sounds about right," Jacob said. "She kept the same wall up around me."

"Really?" Aliyah sounded genuinely surprised.

"Of course," Jacob said. "A person like Deanna doesn't let anyone in. The only reason I know a bit more than anyone else is because I lived with her. There's only so much you can hide from someone you sleep beside every night."

Aliyah coughed in agreement. "That's so true…"

"It really is a sad situation she has with her family," Jacob said reflectively. "But it's hard to feel sorry for someone who brings so much misery to your life."

"I know what you mean," Aliyah said quietly.

"You know, they have all these categories of mental illness," Jacob said, "and I would spend hours online researching how to help someone like Deanna, and how to…" He paused, unsure how to put his thoughts into words. "I guess I just thought if I loved her enough, she would get better."

"I didn't even realize she had a mental illness."

Jacob shrugged. "*She* doesn't even realize she has a mental illness." He sighed and shook his head. "Like they say," he said. "You can't help someone who doesn't want to be helped."

There was a thoughtful pause. "Do you think some mental illness is self-inflicted?" Aliyah asked.

Jacob raised his eyebrows thoughtfully. "Self-inflicted?"

"Like they brought it on themselves?"

He drew in a deep breath and exhaled. "I suppose it's possible…"

"I'm asking because it seems like arrogant people are all a bit touched in the head, if you know what I mean."

Jacob laughed out loud.

"I'm serious," Aliyah said, laughter in her own voice. "Think about it. How mentally healthy can you be to openly disobey God?"

"But Deanna is Muslim…" Jacob said, feeling obligated to say something positive.

"I don't mean Deanna *per se*," Aliyah clarified. "I mean anyone who is living in a way they know is wrong, but they insist on doing it anyway."

Jacob frowned thoughtfully. "I don't know…" he said. "Wouldn't that apply to all of us?"

Aliyah shook her head. "I don't mean people who keep sinning because they fall into human weakness. I mean people who insist that the entire definition of sin or right and wrong should be changed just because they disagree with it."

Jacob was quiet as he considered Aliyah's point. He had never thought about mental illness from a spiritual perspective.

"I know some people are mentally ill because of things out of their control," Aliyah said. "But I think there *are* people who make themselves mentally ill."

Jacob nodded thoughtfully. "You might have a point there," he said. "Especially considering that jinn are usually involved in enticing us to sin in the first place."

"The disbelieving jinn," Aliyah clarified.

"And how sane can you be to listen to someone who you *know* wants you in Hellfire?" Jacob asked rhetorically.

Aliyah bit her lower lip and seemed lost in thought for some time. "I think my mother is mentally ill," she said finally.

Jacob furrowed his brows. "Your *mother*?"

"You saw her," Aliyah said, gesturing a hand toward him. "Does she seem like she's in her right mind?"

Jacob recalled the disturbing scene that Naomi had made at Benjamin's house. "Maybe you're thinking of mental sickness and spiritual sickness as the same thing?"

"No," Aliyah said. "Because not all mentally ill people are spiritually sick. But I think all spiritually sick people are mentally ill."

"But aren't we all spiritually sick on some level?"

"Yes," Aliyah said, "which means we all have a touch of mental illness to the extent that we voluntarily give ourselves to those sicknesses."

Jacob was silent momentarily. "But what about people who are possessed by jinn?" he said. "They didn't voluntarily give themselves to that sickness."

"Like I said," Aliyah replied, "this wouldn't apply to every person with mental illness, but I think it applies to people like my mother."

Jacob pursed his lips thoughtfully. "I don't know…" he said. "I think you make a good point, but I think mental illness is much more complicated than that." He shook his head. "And I don't think your mother is mentally ill." He shrugged. "But then again, I'm not sure if there's anyone who can claim to be one hundred percent mentally healthy."

"I read a book one time," Aliyah said reflectively, "and it said we're all on the verge of mental illness to a certain extent."

"I hope that's not true."

Aliyah shrugged. "Maybe it's not. But it was written by a famous psychiatrist, and though that doesn't mean he's right, I do think he's on to something."

There was an extended pause, as it seemed that there was nothing left for either of them to say.

"You think we can meet at your uncle's house tomorrow?" Jacob said, returning to the subject of speaking to Deanna.

Aliyah was silent as she considered the suggestion. "I guess that could work…" she said. "As long as Uncle Benjamin is fine with it."

Jacob creased his forehead as he looked at Aliyah, a thought having come to him suddenly. "What were you saying about your mother and sister earlier?" he said. "When I cut you off?"

"Oh yeah," Aliyah said. "I was saying that dealing with them made me realize that the non-profit you're trying to do is really important, *mashaAllah*."

Jacob felt so uncomfortable with the vote of confidence that he had to fight the urge to change the subject. He wasn't used to having his ideas praised or supported.

"So many people are dealing with emotional trauma," Aliyah said, "and they have no idea what to do about it." She huffed. "We have so many resources to help people who insist on being victims. But what's out there to help people who are suffering but are just trying to *live*? Not everyone wants to blame others for their problems and then pay a therapist to tell them they have a right to."

Jacob nodded. "I just can't figure out how to start it though," he said. "I can't even come up with a name."

"That's what I was starting to say earlier," Aliyah said. "I thought of name that might work."

A smile spread on Jacob's face. "You did?" It was heartwarming to learn that she'd taken time to work on his idea when he didn't even ask her to. This was definitely a new experience for him in marriage.

"But I'm not sure if it's what you're looking for…" Aliyah averted her gaze, and Jacob sensed that she was becoming suddenly self-conscious about her suggestion.

"What is it?" he said, optimism in his voice. "So far, I've come up with nothing." He added, "At least nothing worth using."

"Safe."

It took a moment for Jacob to register what Aliyah was saying. "Safe?"

She frowned self-consciously. "You don't like it, do you?"

"Oh, was that the name you came up with?" Jacob said.

Aliyah laughed, embarrassment in that sound. "It's stupid, isn't it?" But Jacob could tell she was hoping he disagreed.

"No…" Jacob said tentatively, hoping he sounded grateful and diplomatic. "It's just… I mean, will people understand what we do? I want the name of the organization to speak for itself, if you know what I mean."

Aliyah nodded. "Sorry," she said.

"No, no, it's fine," Jacob said, reassuring her. "I'm still racking my brain about this myself."

"I just thought it was a good acronym…" she said, her voice trailing. She coughed laughter. "But it does sounds silly, huh?"

"Safe is an acronym?" he said, his curiosity piqued just then.

"It's okay," Aliyah said, waving her hand dismissively. "We don't have to use it."

"But what does it stand for?"

"Surviving Abuse and Family Estrangement."

Jacob's spirits lifted immediately. "*You* came up with that?"

An embarrassed grin creased one side of her mouth. "Yes, but I know it could be better. So we can think up something else."

"No, no, no," Jacob said, a smile in his voice. "I like it."

Aliyah's expression showed childlike excitement. "You do?"

"SAFE." He nodded, as if getting used to the name. "I like it," he said sincerely.

"It doesn't sound stupid?" Aliyah wrinkled her nose, humored doubt in her expression.

"Absolutely not," Jacob said. "I just didn't know it was acronym at first."

Aliyah laughed out loud. "Oh yeah, that could be a problem."

"But it could definitely work for what I'm trying to do."

There was a thoughtful pause. "And you don't mind the family estrangement part?" Aliyah said doubtfully. "I know you were mainly focusing on abuse, but I think emotional trauma goes beyond that. That's why I mentioned my mother and sister," she explained. "I could use an organization like this myself. It's not easy being estranged from your family."

"I definitely don't mind," he replied. "Like I said, I'm still vetting out everything myself, and I think the addition of family estrangement allows us to reach more people in our work."

Aliyah nodded. "I like how your proposal was speaking of helping people overcome their abusive tendencies instead of only helping people who've been abused."

"The funny thing is," Jacob said reflectively, "they're actually the same people. It's just that it's more in style, so to speak, to say you were abused instead of admitting you have abusive tendencies yourself." He shook his head. "My father used to always say, 'Hurt people hurt people, son. And show me *one* person in this world who hasn't been hurt at least once in their life.'"

"Wow, *mashaAllah*," Aliyah said. "He sounds like a wise man."

Jacob shrugged. "Or just a man with a bit of wisdom," he said. "Anyone who's lived and learned has wisdom to impart."

"But some people are wiser than others," Aliyah said.

Jacob nodded thoughtfully. "True. But it's hard for me to think of anyone as wise who's heard of Islam then turned away from it while knowing it's true." He shrugged. "So like I said, to me, he's just a man with a *bit* of wisdom. I could respect him more if he at least accepted his purpose of life."

"I know what you mean..." Aliyah said, and Jacob sensed that she was thinking of her own family.

“But we’re SAFE now,” Jacob said in lighthearted humor. “So *insha’Allah*, we can help people with a bit of wisdom get a bit more help in life.”

## 33
## The Marriage Announcement

Early Sunday afternoon Salima pulled her car into the driveway of her parents' home. She was unable to keep from grinning from the excitement she felt. Losing her husband and eldest children in a car accident years ago had left her numb with shock and grief. But the suffering was nothing like she had read about in books or had seen in movies. While the tragedy certainly inspired deeper appreciation for the time they had together, the death of a loved one didn't erase from your mind and heart all the troubles you'd faced while they were alive. It didn't even erase the anger and frustration you felt toward them.

But the truth was, Salima realized, grief wasn't something that could be explained or shown to you. There were no words you could read or film you could watch that could make you understand. Fate knocked your legs right from under you just when you stood firmly on the ground. It punched the wind from your lungs just when you were breathing freely, full of life. But grief wasn't all tears and anguish, she reflected. It was also delirious laughter, immeasurable silence, and feeling nothing at all.

The one thing the books and movies did get right, Salima thought, was the difficulty of starting again. But it wasn't because your heart was so attached to the one you'd lost that it was unimaginable to move on. It was because every limb and vein in your body was paralyzed in fear. It felt like a single step in the wrong direction could cause someone else to tumble from your life. And at times, your suffering even felt like divine punishment, payback for every sin you committed and every careless word you'd spoken.

It felt like what you deserved.

But more than anything, Salima reflected, sudden tragedy was the violent removal of the veil of pretense. And though that was the most painful part, it was also the most blessed. Because it forced you—if you had even the slightest remnants of faith and common sense—to look at the life of this world from the vantage point of your purpose of creation, instead of from the vantage point of fulfilling your desires.

"I'm glad I met you," Larry had said to Salima once. "No matter what happens, I think it's a blessing that we crossed paths." A smile twitched at her lips as she put the car in park. She was almost embarrassed for how giddy she felt, but she couldn't help it.

Salima liked Larry more than she had been able to fully admit. His frankness and confidence might be interpreted as rudeness and false machismo to some, but Salima liked these qualities. She admired a man who wasn't ashamed to be a man. In this age of increasingly effeminate and emasculated men, it was refreshing to connect with someone with obvious masculine qualities. That he was not afraid to disagree with her and call her on her own contradictions only made her admire and desire him more. His straightforwardness could be offensive at times, but it was comforting to know she would be marrying a man who wasn't afraid to lead.

Mikaeel had been an absolute sweetheart, but it wasn't until Salima got to know Larry better that she realized that Mikaeel, though sincere in his role as husband, had too often bowed under pressure. That he had allowed Salima to create a rift between him and his sister was evidence enough that he could have done a better job at being the man of the house.

"You shouldn't blame yourself for that," Larry had said after Salima told him about her refusal to have Kalimah and her husband around. "I'm sure your husband was a good man, may Allah have mercy him and give him *Jannah*, but if the only reason he didn't see his sister often was because you made a fuss about her being a second wife, then that's on him, not you." Taken aback by the new perspective, Salima had listened, intrigued that there was a kinder explanation for her wrongdoing.

"Women are women," Larry had said. The comment stung, but Salima remained quiet as she tried to hear him out. "They're irrational and emotional when it comes to things they don't want to deal with. That's why it's a man's job to head the household."

He clarified, "I'm not saying you were right for what you did." He huffed, proud humor in that sound. "Because I sure as hell wouldn't have let any wife of *mine* act like that. You would've been put in your place real quick," he said with conviction. "There's no way I would've cut ties with my sister, especially when my sister was doing something good."

"I wouldn't call marrying another woman's husband *good*," Salima had muttered, feeling defensive. "Maybe it wasn't *haraam*," she said. "But it definitely wasn't good."

Salima heard Larry laugh out loud through the phone. "Girl, you can try that female sob story on someone else," he said. "Marriage is a good thing. And you're smart enough to know that doesn't only apply to yours."

"But we should love for our sister what we love for ourselves," she said, offended. "I know I shouldn't have treated Kalimah like that, but that doesn't mean she wasn't being a bit selfish when she married that sister's husband."

"You mean when she married her *own* husband," he corrected.

"But he was already married," Salima said, voice tight.

Larry huffed, humor in his tone. "And why shouldn't that sister love for Kalimah what she loved for herself?" he asked rhetorically. "I just find it funny that you all use that statement to argue what someone should do for *you*, when the whole point of the hadith is to tell us what we should be doing for someone else."

Salima didn't know what to say to that.

"Look," Larry said, apology in his tone, "I get that this whole polygamy thing is hard for women. But I just don't understand why you all have such a hard time telling the truth."

"What's that supposed to mean?" Salima said, indignant.

"You're just jealous and insecure," he said. "There's nothing wrong with that."

"Are you being sarcastic?" she said, her voice teetering between disbelief and outrage.

"Sarcastic?" Larry spoke as if it were the most ridiculous suggestion in the world.

"I don't see how jealousy and insecurity are positive traits," Salima said, an edge of haughtiness in her tone.

"I didn't say they were positive traits," Larry said. "I said there's nothing wrong with them. They're *human* traits."

"But you said they only apply to women."

"I *did*?" There was amusement in his tone. "That's where you're wrong. I mentioned them in the *context* of women. I didn't say they applied to women exclusively."

"But you said—"

"Every unflattering observation of women isn't a sexist insult," he interjected. "But since we're on the subject, yes, I think men are jealous and insecure too. And if you ask me, they're *more* jealous and insecure than women," he argued. "The fact that Allah gave you all the ability to share your husband without killing each other is a miracle, if you ask me. That kind of arrangement would never work the other way around." He huffed, humor in that sound. "Trust me. Most men I know can't even handle the idea of their *former* wife or girlfriend being with another man."

"Women have a hard time with that too."

Larry laughed again. "So now you *want* the negative traits to apply to you? I swear, I've never been able to figure out why all the feminist movements and anti-sexism campaigns even claim to be about supporting women, when almost all of them seem to have as their underlying theme hatred of anything female."

"That's not true," Salima said, hurt in her voice.

"Yes it is," Larry said. "Look at what just happened with us. I mention the real reason women have a problem with polygamy, and you get all upset and defensive. But when I mention those same traits as connected to men, you want equal representation." He coughed laughter. "Women have a serious inferiority complex if you ask me. And it's rooted in self-hate."

Larry's words had infuriated Salima, but she could think of no intelligent response.

"Nothing is good enough," he continued amidst her silence, "unless you can be sure it's good enough for men too." He grunted. "And everything negative about you, you deny unless you can apply it to men too. And when we leave you alone and describe only the negative traits of men, you want *those* too."

In her parents' driveway, Salima turned off the ignition. She pulled down the visor and checked her appearance in the mirror. She was wearing her favored African-style head wrap today. If this were any other visit, her parents would likely be proud to see Salima in the traditional Muslim hijab she'd begun wearing occasionally. But because she was coming to talk to them about remarrying, the *khimaar* that was often associated with Arab and South Asian Muslims would probably rouse their concern. She had already told them that Larry was an American convert, but seeing what appeared to be a drastic and sudden change in her appearance could lead them to believe that Larry was spiritually abusive.

"*As-salaamu'alaikum*, baby!" A broad smile spread on her mother's face as Salima stepped into the foyer of her parents' home. The sweet aroma of food and baked dessert tickled Salima's nostrils and made her realize how hungry she was after the three-hour drive.

Before Salima could respond, her mother drew her into a warm hug, and Salima returned the salaams as she embraced her mother, her voice slightly muffled. She noticed that her mother had put on weight since they'd last seen each other, but it suited her. It often worried Salima whenever her mother would get excited about the latest diet or weight-loss regiment touted as revolutionary on television. Her mother had recently developed heart problems, and Salima was worried that the diets would only make the problems worse.

"*As-salaamu'alaikum*, sweetheart." Salima heard her father's voice just as her mother released her, keeping an arm around Salima as if she feared her daughter wouldn't stay long.

"*Wa'alaiku-mus-salaam*, Abi," Salima replied, offering her father a hug too, her mother's hand still on her shoulder.

"You hungry, baby?" her mother asked, immediately guiding Salima to the dining room.

"I'm starving," Salima said with a grin, her eyes eagerly surveying the array of food laid out on the table. "But I want to pray first."

"Is it time yet?" her mother asked, looking toward Salima's father.

"We still have a half-hour before *Dhuhr* is in," he said. "So we have time to eat and catch up."

"Oh, when was the last time you were here?" her mother said as they settled into their seats at the dining room table.

"A year ago, I think?" Salima asked, a half-smile on her face.

"You know that's too long a time for us to go without seeing you," her mother scorned good-naturedly. "We worry about you."

"I'm so swamped with work and taking care of Haroon that I barely have time to think straight," Salima said, taking a seat across from her mother as her father sat at the head.

"I keep telling Jamil he makes enough to take care of the both of you," her father said, shaking his head in disapproval as he situated himself in his chair. "A man's job is to take care of a woman, especially if she's a widow. And since you don't want to move in with us, Jamil needs to step up and be a man."

An uncomfortable smile formed on Salima's face. "Jamil does a good job *mashaAllah*," she said. "But he has his own life to worry about."

Her father huffed. "We all do. That doesn't change the fact that we're men and we still need to take care of our women."

"I don't want to be a burden on him though," Salima said, forcing a smile. "When he remarries, what will I do?"

Hushed silence fell over the table.

"Remarries?" her father said, a concerned expression on his face. "He didn't mention anything to us about a new young woman."

"I meant hypothetically," Salima said quickly. She didn't want Jamil to think she had traveled to their parents' house to talk about him. They were less fond of his ex-wife than she was, and the last thing she wanted was to cause a ruckus over something that might not even happen. They were of the opinion that it was not permissible to marry sectarian Muslims, and they would certainly make a fuss if he tried to remarry her. They didn't even agree with the initial marriage, and that was before her religious views were fully known.

"Is he back in touch with Muslimah?" her mother asked as she held out a hand for Salima to hand over her plate.

"Uh…" Salima averted her gaze as she lifted the plate in front of her and placed it in her mother's grip. "I'm not sure."

"I hope you advised him against remarrying her," her father said.

"We haven't really talked about it," Salima said, hoping to change the subject to why she'd come. "I've been trying to figure out my own situation."

An awkward silence permeated the room, and the only sound that could be heard was the clanking of serving spoons as Salima's mother prepared her plate. Salima noticed her parents exchanging glances, as if there was something they knew but was not saying.

"I never liked hypocrites," her father said. "You and Jamil know that." He spoke as if he were scolding Salima, but he kept his voice level. "Wearing one face in front of the people and another behind closed doors."

"I'm not sure I think Muslimah is a hypocrite…" Salima said, choosing her words carefully. "She's just confused."

"Is that right?" her father said, a slight smile on his face, inciting discomfort in Salima.

The plate now full, her mother reached across the table to hand it to Salima. When Salima accepted it, her mother went on to prepare another plate.

"Your sister tells us Muslimah is always involving herself in some mess or another," her mother said, meeting Salima's gaze, a concerned expression on her face. "Aren't you two in communication?"

"Muslimah and I?"

"You and your sister."

Salima lifted her shoulder in a shrug. "We talk sometimes…"

"She says you and Muslimah are friends."

Salima pulled her head back in surprise. "Friends?"

"I think she was talking about Facebook, honey," her father said gently, looking at Salima's mother.

"Oh," Salima said. "She's on my friends list, but I don't follow her." The expression on her parents' faces told Salima that they had no idea what she was talking about. "I mean, we don't really keep in touch or anything."

"But you're friends online?" Her mother's tone suggested that she was genuinely perplexed.

"And Yasmeen?" her father said, his gaze toward the food his wife had just placed in front of him. He glanced at Salima as he picked up his fork and muttered *bismillaah*. "Are you in touch with her? Apparently, she's a friend of Jamil's."

Because the name had no logical context to her family, Salima had no idea whom her father was talking about. "Yasmeen?" she said, drawing her eyebrows together as she picked up her fork in preparation to eat. She pronounced Allah's name before slicing the salmon with the side of her fork and lifting it to her mouth.

"She says most people know her by her non-Muslim name," Salima's mother interjected. "Jasmine."

Salima suddenly lost her appetite. She had no idea why, but she knew in her gut that no good could come from Jasmine's name being mentioned at her parents' table.

***

At the apartment building, Jacob carried Aliyah's compact luggage bag upstairs then waited in the living room as Aliyah changed clothes in preparation for their meeting with Deanna. Larry had initially agreed to join them, but he'd called to cancel when he found out that Salima was out of town for the day. Before then, Larry had told Jacob that he was sure that Salima would be happy to keep Ibrahim, Younus, and Thawab while he joined them during the meeting. But after learning of Salima's trip, Larry had said that Jamil would probably be willing to watch the boys since he was already watching Haroon, but neither Jacob nor Larry felt completely comfortable with that arrangement.

Both Jacob and Aliyah had prayed *Istikhaarah* about the meeting with Deanna today, but Jacob was beginning to wonder if the signs were pointing to not having the meeting instead of going ahead with it. Benjamin had agreed to allow them to meet at his house, but he didn't sound enthusiastic about it, though Jacob doubted that enthusiasm was even possible given the circumstances. But even Larry had sounded apprehensive when Jacob told him about the meeting.

"You sure you want to do that, man?" Larry had asked. "I'm sure," Jacob had said. But now he wondered if that were true.

***

Salima took another bite of food so she could avoid looking her parents' in the eye. "Yes, I know Jasmine," she said as casually as she could manage.

Her parents' exchanged glances again.

"Are you aware that she was Larry's girlfriend before they accepted Islam together?" her mother asked.

Blinking in confusion, Salima set down her fork and shook her head. "She was Larry's girlfriend, but they didn't accept Islam together. Larry accepted Islam first."

"But they both converted to Islam, right?" Her mother's voice conveyed confusion as to why Salima was being so technical.

"Yes, but—"

"How well do you know this boy?" her father interjected, his fork suspended in the air as he regarded Salima with eyes narrowed in concern.

Salima cringed. Her father referring to Larry as a "this boy" wasn't a good sign. Anyone he respected he referred to as "the brother" or "young man."

"I…" she stammered, unsure how to answer the question. "…um, pretty well."

"How did you meet?"

Salima became flustered. "At the masjid, I think," she said. "Or maybe it was through Jamil."

"*Jamil* introduced this boy to you?" Her mother's voice conveyed shock and disapproval.

Salima shook her head. "Not for marriage," she said. "They're friends."

"Jamil is *friends* with this boy?" Her father contorted his face in confusion.

Her parents exchanged a look again, and Salima was at a loss for words. She felt like she was being ambushed, but she had no idea where the attack was coming from and why. "What's going on?" Salima said finally, concern in her tone as she looked back and forth between her parents.

Her father nodded in her mother's direction before resuming eating.

"Are you aware that this young man is facing a potential lawsuit?" her mother asked.

It took a moment for Salima to register what her mother was saying. "A lawsuit?"

"Jasmine came by here a couple of weeks ago," her mother continued. "And she said—"

"*What*?"

"—that she's in the process of seeking damages for some things that happened while they were dating."

Salima felt herself growing upset. "She came *here*?"

"Jamil suggested that she come."

Salima's stomach knotted in shock and dread. "*Jamil*?"

"Apparently, he's representing her in the case against—"

"Representing her…?"

"—this young man."

"But that doesn't make any sense," Salima said, her thoughts racing. "He didn't mention anything to me about it."

"You mean Larry or Jamil?" her mother asked.

“Either of them,” Salima said, her face aflame in furious mortification.

“Well, Jamil couldn’t mention it because of attorney-client privilege,” her mother said. “And it sounds like the case is still in the elementary stages, so I’m not sure if Larry has even been served yet.”

Salima coughed laughter, a disbelieving expression on her face. “Please tell me you don’t believe this girl.”

Her mother frowned and exchanged that look with Salima’s father again. “She has no reason to lie,” her mother said finally.

“I doubt that,” Salima said, a sneer in her voice.

They were silent for some time, and Salima sensed her parents’ growing concern. “*SubhaanAllah*,” Salima said, shaking her head. “I knew she had issues, but this is way over the top.”

“Salima, sweetheart,” her father said, “it’s not a good idea to start off by blaming the victim.”

“The *victim*?” Salima recoiled. “We don’t even know who the victim is.”

“Fake victims are very rare,” her mother said, as if trying to reason with Salima. “You know that.”

“Trust me,” Salima said bitterly, “Jasmine is definitely *rare*.” She huffed. “And not in the praiseworthy sense.”

“So you think she’s lying?” Her mother sounded disappointed.

“Don’t you?” Salima said, hurt in her eyes as she met her mother’s gaze.

“But you don’t even know what the charges are,” her mother said, her voice a plea. “So how can you say she’s lying?

“I mean,” Salima said, contorting her face, “what kind of person drives three hours to a stranger’s house to say horrible things about a man she’s trying to marry?”

A pregnant silence followed.

“Excuse me?” her father said, setting down his fork. “Are you saying that you’re trying to marry a man who’s engaged to *someone else*?”

“No, no, no.” Salima shook her head and gestured a hand in the air, as if to ward off a misunderstanding. “Larry broke up with Jasmine after he became Muslim, but Jasmine is trying everything to get him back.”

“But she’s Muslim now,” her mother said.

“But he doesn’t like her anymore,” Salima said. “He wants to marry me.” As soon as she said it, her face was aflame in embarrassment as she realized how she must sound to her parents. Even in the best-case scenario, with Larry innocent of whatever Jasmine was accusing him of, this whole situation sounded insane.

Her parents ate in silence for some time, and because Salima didn’t know what else to do, she ate too, though she was too shaken up to concentrate on food.

“You’re still grieving Mikaeel, baby.” Her mother’s voice was soft in motherly affection. “I know it’s been four years now, but suffering doesn’t have a timeframe. You don’t have to rush into anything. You have Haroon to think about.”

Salima felt herself getting choked up, and she swallowed the lump in her throat, her gaze on the food she was toying with.

"I'm sure this… Larry seems like a good brother," her mother said. "But I don't think he's good enough for you, baby. You need someone like you, a brother who was raised Muslim, who's memorized Qur'an, and whose heart is attached to Islam. Perhaps, he'll mature one day and turn out to be a good Muslim," she said gently. "But right now, it's obvious he still has one foot in the *dunya*."

Salima felt that she should say something in Larry's defense, but she couldn't think of anything to counter her mother. Though she felt her mother's view was a bit overly idealistic, she couldn't deny that her mother did have a point.

Her mother sighed. "Most of these young converts have no idea what it means to be Muslim," she said. "They come to this religion full of zeal. They read the books of the past and want to recreate it in the present, and they search for a good woman so they can marry their troubles away." She frowned, a sad and compassionate expression on her face. "But life doesn't work like that."

Salima felt overcome with sadness all of a sudden. At that moment, she felt so distant from Larry that she felt like a complete idiot for even considering him. Her mother was right. What was she thinking? Salima couldn't marry someone who'd barely been Muslim two years. She would probably have to treat him like a grown son instead of a husband.

"Maybe this young woman *is* lying," her mother offered. "Allah knows best. But even if she is, you have to ask yourself what kind of man attracts this type of woman in the first place. Certainly not a righteous one," she said firmly. "If we're living right, the people closest to us will reflect that. And this Larry person sounds like one immature, zealous, confused young man."

***

Aliyah felt the onset of chest pains before she even left her apartment, but she ignored them. From years of suffering anxiety in stressful situations, she had grown familiar with the uncomfortable tightening of her chest and the occasional difficulty breathing. Even at Nikki's *aqeeqah*-turned-*waleemah,* because of the large crowd, Aliyah had felt the constriction in her chest. Upon seeing Deanna there, the uncomfortable sensation had been exacerbated. But Aliyah had been able to push herself through, her interactions and mannerisms betraying nothing of what she felt, as she'd done so many times in life.

But today was different. There was no escalation from discomfort to pain. The chest constriction started out as pain.

*"I think you're jealous of me,"* Aliyah heard Deanna's voice in her head. *"No woman in her right mind lets her husband marry another wife."* It was as if Deanna were sneering at her, eager to let Aliyah know how pathetic she was. *"The only reason I'm asking your advice is because you represent my ideal client."* As if reliving the humiliation all over again, the pain sliced through her chest. *"You're divorced. You're depressed. You're broke. You have no marriage prospects. And*

*you have no idea how to fix your relationship problems on your own. So my workshop idea is to help people like you."*

Before Aliyah was even halfway to her uncle's house, she was steadying her breaths to prevent a full-fledged anxiety attack. She was grateful that she and Jacob were in separate cars because she didn't want to incite his concern. For someone unaccustomed to her social anxiety, her symptoms could be mistaken as a medical emergency, and Aliyah didn't want to create a scene. She'd already mentioned to Jacob her increasingly frequent anxiety attacks, but so far he'd never witnessed one. And Aliyah wanted to keep it that way. The last thing she wanted was to make Jacob feel that Deanna had been correct in saying that Aliyah was burdensome and needy.

Aliyah's body was trembling by the time she pulled in front of her uncle's house. In addition to the sharp pain in her chest, she was now battling a migraine. She put the car in park then took a few moments to breathe in and out. She recited a *du'aa* asking Allah to help her get through this meeting.

Aliyah had been so distracted by her anxiousness that she didn't notice Deanna's car in the driveway until she was almost to the front door. Her heart nearly stopped, and Jacob glanced over his shoulder at her, a puzzled and disturbed look on his face. They had come an hour early for the expressed purpose of avoiding Deanna seeing them come in together.

Unsure what to do, Aliyah slowed her steps, and Jacob made a motion with his head to indicate he'll go on inside. Aliyah nodded and hung back until Jacob was let in the house and the door closed behind him. Outside alone, Aliyah felt her chest pains increasing. Not wanting to seem idle in case someone looked out the window, Aliyah reached in her handbag and withdrew her phone. She punched in the code and scrolled down to Salima's name.

***

The chiming and vibrating of her phone startled Salima. She instinctively reached behind her and pulled her purse onto her lap from where it hung on the dining room chair as she sat with her parents. She'd already looked at the caller ID and accepted the call before she registered why her parents were giving her disapproving looks. It was extremely rude and out of character for Salima to interrupt a family meal to accept a personal call. But even as she realized her error, she pushed her chair back then whispered to her parents, "Sorry, I have to take this."

She greeted Aliyah with the salaams as she walked quickly up the stairs and closed herself in the hall bathroom.

"*Alhamdulillah,*" Aliyah said as she breathed a sigh of relief, apparently too distracted to realize she hadn't returned Salima's greeting. "I know you're not in town, so I was afraid you wouldn't answer."

"It's okay," Salima said, speaking in a low voice though her parents were most likely still downstairs and out of earshot. "I have a few minutes."

"Deanna's here."

"What?" Salima drew her eyebrows together. "At your uncle's house?"

"Yes," Aliyah said, sounding panicked. "What do I do?"

Salima shook her head in confusion. "But wasn't she *supposed* to be there?"

"Yes, but not *now*," Aliyah whined. "We came early to avoid bumping into her."

"Oh…"

"This just…" Salima heard Aliyah take several breaths after the utterance. "I don't know what to…" More breathing. "Can you…"

"*QaddarAllaahu maashaa'a fa'al*," Salima said, careful to speak as gently as possible in response to Aliyah's anxiety. "This was already written for you, *ukhti*. So Allah has a better plan."

Salima paused as a thought came to her suddenly. "Are you inside or outside?"

"Out-side," Aliyah said with a jagged breath.

"And where is Jacob?"

"He…went in-side."

"Then go to your car and sit down for a moment okay?"

"O-kay…"

"Recite *isti'aadhah* and the *du'aa* for when you're facing a difficult situation," Salima said. "You know it, right?"

"Ye-es."

"Start saying it now."

She heard Aliyah muttering the supplications over and over again, and she silently supplicated to Allah herself for Aliyah.

"There's nothing Deanna can say or do that Allah hasn't already written for you," Salima said when she heard the car door slam and Aliyah's voice steady with her prayerful utterances.

"*Jazaakillaahukhairan*," Aliyah said, her breathing returning to normal. "You're right." She drew in a deep breath and exhaled. "I just need a few minutes to gather myself."

"No problem," Salima said. "And I'll stay right here with you until you feel better, *insha'Allah*."

"I'm sorry," Aliyah said, embarrassed humor in her tone. "I hope I'm not keeping you from your parents. I know they have more rights."

"They'll be fine, *insha'Allah*," Salima said, and it was then that she registered how relieved she was to hear a familiar voice. In just the few minutes she'd been on the phone with Aliyah, she was already feeling guilty for her negative view of Larry. In the presence of her parents, the new perspective had felt like wisdom, but now it felt like betrayal. Yet still, even then, Salima wasn't able to convince herself that her parents were entirely wrong in the advice they'd given her about Larry.

"Then I won't hold you long," Aliyah said apologetically. "But can you recite Qur'an really quick? I think that'll help calm me down more."

A grin formed on Salima's face. "You can recite yourself, you know," she teased.

Aliyah laughed self-consciously. "I know. I just..."

"It's okay," Salima interjected good-naturedly. "I need to hear another reciter myself sometimes, especially when I'm stressed."

"I like your recitation, *mashaAllah.*"

"*MashaAllah,*" Salima muttered humbly, stepping out of the bathroom so she was standing in the hall. "Any specific requests?"

"The last part of *Sooratul-Hashr,*" Aliyah said, gratefulness in her voice. "Starting from *'yaa ayyuhalladheena aamanoo.'*"

Salima smiled to herself at this touching moment, one friend comforting the other with the highest source of comfort, the Words of the Creator. "*A'oodhu billaahi minash-shaytaanir-rajeem...*" she began, raising her voice confidently as she was taught to do during her studies, then recited what meant:

*O you who believe, fear God (Allah). And let every soul look to what it has put forth for tomorrow—and fear Allah. Indeed, Allah is Acquainted with what you do. And be not like those who forgot Allah, so He made them forget themselves. Those are the defiantly disobedient.*

*Not equal are the companions of the Fire and the companions of Paradise. The companions of Paradise—they are the attainers [of success].*

*If We had sent down this Qur'an upon a mountain, you would have seen it humbled and coming apart from fear of Allah. And these examples We present to the people that perhaps they will give thought.*

*He is Allah, other than whom none has the right to be worshipped, Knower of the unseen and the seen. He is the Most Gracious, the Most Merciful. He is Allah—there is no god but He—the Sovereign, the Pure, the Perfection, the Bestower of Faith, the Overseer, the Exalted in Might, the Compeller, the Superior. Exalted is Allah above whatever they associate with Him. He is Allah, the Creator, the Inventor, the Fashioner; to Him belong the most beautiful names. Whatever is in the heavens and earth is glorifying Him. And He is the Exalted in Might, the Wise.*

***

Aliyah breathed a sigh of relief when her uncle opened the front door and she found Deanna in *rukoo'*, bowing in prayer, facing a corner of the room.

*You didn't start yet?* Aliyah mouthed to Jacob, who was sitting on the couch and had turned when she came in. Jacob shook his head and gestured to Deanna, indicating she had been praying since he'd come inside. A smile creased the corners of Aliyah's mouth. If she hadn't feared that Deanna might see her in the corner of her eye and misinterpret the action, Aliyah would have made *sajdah al-shukr*, the prostration for gratefulness, right then. Whatever would happen at this meeting, starting it with prayer was definitely a good sign.

***

"What was that about?" Salima's father said, lighthearted teasing in his voice as she returned to her seat at the table. Salima could tell that hearing her recite Qur'an during the phone call was the most unexpected surprise, but she detected fatherly pride in his voice. Her mother's expression conveyed equal pride, her eyes compassionate and pleased as she watched Salima settle back into her seat. Salima sensed that they had been upset about her abruptly leaving the table but that hearing her recitation erased from their hearts any offense.

"That was Larry's sister-in-law," Salima said. She thought nothing of it when she said it because it was merely a matter of fact. But a moment later, she realized how significant the information was in light of the conversation they'd just had. "She was nervous about a meeting she had to attend and wanted to hear Qur'an to calm her."

Eyebrows rising in surprise, they exchanged glances that seemed to say, *Well, who would've guessed?*

"His whole family is fond of Qur'an actually," she added.

A few seconds passed in silence.

"But…" her mother said, eyes narrowed. "…I thought he converted."

"He did," she said. "But his older brother has been Muslim for about fifteen years now, I think. And Larry spent a lot of that time learning Islam from him. And his brother is married to one of my best friends, who I was just talking to now."

They nodded thoughtfully. "And you say Larry is fond of Qur'an too?" her father asked.

"Definitely," Salima said. "That's what we have in common. But his focus is more so on the meaning as opposed to only memorization."

"Well, memorization *is* important…" her father said.

"That's why he started memorizing," she said. "He's taking classes at the masjid, and if he has any questions, he asks me. Sometimes I listen to his recitation, and I correct him." She smiled to herself at the thought, her heart feeling renewed appreciation and admiration for him.

"Well…" her father said, as if feeling obligated to balance out their views from earlier, "that's not something common amongst the more zealous converts."

Her mother nodded. "That's true… The extreme ones don't spend a lot of time studying Quran."

Salima's spirits lifted in hopes that they were changing their mind about Larry. But then she saw her mother frown.

"But I still don't think he's good enough for you," her mother said.

"I agree," her father said, as if he'd given this a lot of thought. "It's good that he's studying Qur'an, but it'll take years before he's qualified to marry someone like you."

***

Deanna heard Aliyah's voice responding to Benjamin's salaams, and she stiffened in annoyance as she sat for the last part of prayer. But she willed herself to concentrate on her Creator, wanting to stay focused on why she'd come, and what had inspired her prayers.

That morning, Deanna had prayed *Salaah* for only the second time since the congregational prayer in jail, and she was surprised by the calming effect it had. Yes, there were moments that she was racked with so much guilt that she was tempted to abandon prayer right then, but then tranquility settled over her and made her throat close and her eyes fill. It was then that she realized that she missed this, the feeling that she had a higher purpose in life. She missed feeling the certainty that there was a God and that He would take care of her, as long as she took care of herself. It was why she'd become Muslim in the first place.

Visiting her brother Asher had left her feeling filthy, alone, and abandoned. Returning to the emotionally cold atmosphere of her parents' home only made her loneliness more suffocating and pronounced.

*I can't live like this anymore*, she'd said to herself. She was anguished and disgusted at that tiny voice telling her that Asher was just a godless version of herself—or at least someone she was on the fast road to becoming. And she feared that his summation of the Michaels was more accurate than the fairytale version she'd created of her family in her head.

*All people are naturally self-centered and think of themselves as fundamentally good*, the self-help book had said. *They readily recognize evil in the world around them, but almost never as readily recognize it within their own worlds or within themselves. Even those of us who are honest about our evil usually do so from a point of self-compassion, contextual justification, or stubborn self-defense. It is almost unheard of for someone to stand up and angrily condemn themselves. That's why self-honesty about one's evil is usually discussed in the context of a confession or a contrite apology, but almost never condemnation. This self-centered view extends to our families and loved ones as well. No evil committed by our own hands or by those we love feels as horrific as that committed by others or by other people's friends and family. For most of us, true evil is and will always be somewhere "out there."*

Deanna was reluctant to turn her head to the right and utter the *tasleem* to end the prayer. The reason that she was praying at all, even though *Dhuhr* had not yet come in, was because she didn't want to be left to her own devices in starting over with Jacob. She'd come over an hour early so that she could spend it in prayer. Benjamin and Valerie had seemed a bit surprised to see her before the scheduled meeting, but they were gracious in welcoming her and pointing her in the direction of the *qiblah* so she could pray as many units of *Duhaa* that she desired.

But now Jacob had arrived (she heard him give Benjamin salaams earlier) and Aliyah too, though Deanna wasn't completely sure why her former best friend would choose today of all days to visit her uncle. *Whatever*, Deanna thought to herself, turning her head to the right then the left, ending the prayer. *Be the bigger person*, she said to herself. *You are walking with the Lord.*

***

Jacob felt a twinge of pity as he watched Deanna complete her voluntary prayer then walk over to where he was sitting and give him salaams. Her burnt red *khimaar* sat loosely on her head, making his stomach convulse at the reminder of the day they'd first met.

She offered him a wide smile and sat down a few feet from him on the couch, a pungent scent of perfume wafting in his direction with that motion. It was the same scent she'd worn the night she'd invited him to her apartment under the guise of a double date. He instinctively glanced around for Aliyah, but he did not see her. He heard the hushed banter of women coming from the kitchen and realized that she was visiting with Valerie. Benjamin sat across from Jacob and Deanna, offering Jacob a subtle but reassuring smile.

"*Bismillaahir-rahmaanir-raheem*," Benjamin said, his firm authoritative voice relieving Jacob of the pressure of starting the meeting himself. "Because you haven't yet agreed on a co-parenting counselor," Benjamin said, "I'm going to be your mediator today in hopes of you both coming to an agreement on how to work together for the sake of your children."

Deanna started to say something, but Benjamin raised a hand to stop her. "I know each of you have other matters you want to discuss," he continued. "And since those things will most likely affect your approaches to co-parenting, I'll let you share those before we move on to making arrangements for caring for your children."

Benjamin nodded and gestured toward Deanna. "We can start with you, Sister Deanna," he said.

When Deanna lifted her head haughtily and looked directly at Jacob, Jacob knew the meeting wasn't going to go as smoothly as he'd hoped.

"You married Aliyah, didn't you?" Bitterness was in her tone, her eyes narrowed in accusation.

Jacob instinctively glanced at Benjamin, unsure how to handle this sudden, unexpected slap in the face. Benjamin's expression revealed neither approval nor disapproval, and Jacob took that as a sign that he was permitted to speak.

"Yes," he said more firmly than he intended, detecting an edge of defense in his tone. The hushed silence in the kitchen let Jacob know that Aliyah and her aunt were hanging on to every word. "After our divorce, I asked her to marry me."

"After our *real* divorce?" Deanna's upper lip was upturned in a sneer. "Because that was fast."

"Yes, after our *real* divorce," Jacob said, "the one recognized by Allah."

Deanna tossed up her hands as if disgusted and losing patience. "You were wrong for that," she said. "But I want you to know that I forgive you. This doesn't have to ruin anything between us."

Aliyah appeared in the doorway, arms folded defensively. Valerie was next to her, caution on her face. Jacob glanced briefly in their direction before returning his attention to his ex-wife.

Deanna shifted herself until she was looking at Aliyah. "And I forgive you too," she said. "I knew you always wanted to be me, so I can't blame you for trying when you had the chance." She grunted. "I suppose your best friend being locked away was the perfect opportunity to steal my man?"

"I am not your personal property, Deanna," Jacob said, speaking firmly, his voice rising in upset. "I can marry whomever I want, whenever I want," he said. "I belong to no one except Allah."

She flipped a hand at Jacob. "Like I said, I forgive you. You're a man, so you can't help yourself. And Aliyah…" Deanna contorted her face as she regarded her. "…she can't help herself either because she's never had a real man in her life." Deanna shrugged smugly and looked at Jacob. "So I'll share you with her if that's what you really want."

Jacob shook his head, as if finding it difficult to comprehend the depths of Deanna's narcissism. "I'm not interested in remarrying you, Deanna. I'm married to Aliyah now, and that's not going to change *insha'Allah.*"

"Jasmine told me you went behind my back." Deanna was looking at Aliyah now. "But I didn't want to believe it," she said. "Because that girl's a liar and a hypocrite. So I thought she was slandering you just to impress me." Deanna shook her head, frowning in distaste. "But I see I overestimated you. I thought you were the good Muslim, the one who really feared Allah." She huffed. "But you're just like the rest of us. Selfish, pathetic, and greedy."

Jacob could see signs of offense on Aliyah's face, and she looked as if she was going to respond and take the bait. "Do you have a point?" Jacob said to Deanna. "You said you wanted to talk, so let's talk."

"Why *her*, Jacob?" Deanna's eyes glistened, but she kept her face stern. "Couldn't you have chosen someone more…" She gestured her hand flippantly and wrinkled her nose. "*…worthy*?"

"Worthy of what?" Jacob said, puzzled disapproval on his face.

"Worthy of sacrificing our marriage over."

He narrowed his eyes in disbelief. "Do you really believe that Aliyah is the reason I divorced you?"

"Isn't she?" Deanna said, stubbornness in her voice though her face crumpled from hurt.

"No she is not."

"Then why did you marry her?" Her chin quivered and tears shined in her eyes, but her firmness in tone suggested that she wasn't registering her deteriorating state.

Jacob glanced at Aliyah, who was shaking her head and looking down, apparently in effort to maintain her composure. "Because I wanted to," he said, not a trace of regret or apology in his voice. "And because I knew she would make me happy, *bi'idhnilllah.*" At that, Aliyah glanced up, a surprised expression on her face as she looked at him.

"But what about *us*?" Deanna said, her words laced in fury.

"Was there *ever* an us?" Jacob countered.

"Of course there was." The tears pooled in her eyes and rounded her cheeks. But she seemed so detached from her pain right then that it was as if the tears were coming from someone else.

"No," Jacob said firmly. "There was only you and your husband project." He clenched his jaw as he momentarily relived what he had gone through. "A project you started long before we met."

"Who told you?" Deanna said, her eyes wide with shock.

Jacob pulled his head back in confusion. "Told me what?"

"I only looked up your schedule and followed you so I could know where to find you," she said defensively. "What's so wrong with that?"

"*Followed* me?"

"I knew you wouldn't notice me unless I could meet you alone," she continued as if not hearing him. "And so I followed you to the welcome center so we could talk."

It took several seconds for Jacob to register Deanna's words, and their meaning. "You *followed* me there?"

"Only for a few weeks."

"A few *weeks*?"

Deanna contorted her face and glowered at him, fresh tears pooling in her eyes. "But I don't appreciate you calling it a husband project."

Jacob shook his head, too overwhelmed by what she was saying to respond immediately. "I was talking about the way you think about men in general," he said finally. "Not about how you approached *me*."

Deanna was still glowering at him, her expression unchanged, so he wasn't sure if she'd registered what he said.

"You treat people like they're all pawns in some master plot you've crafted for them," Jacob said, feeling pent-up anger rise to the surface as he was able to express himself freely. "You don't think about anyone but yourself, unless they can benefit you in someway." He shook his head, nose wrinkled in disappointment.

"So yes, I was your husband project," he said. "I was just a soulless man put on earth for you to toy with. You slander your own best friend. You rush to pair her up with a man you wouldn't even marry yourself. And heck," he said with a huff, "for all I know you even faked a pregnancy to convince me to marry you."

He shook his head again. "But I blame myself," he said. "Because I was young, stupid, and full of myself. I should have never let myself go that far. But in you, Allah gave me exactly what I deserved. He gave me the female version of myself. Our marriage was my penance as far as I'm concerned. And, *bi'idhnillaah*, I'll *never* go back to that nightmare," he said, earnestness in his tone. "Even if Allah took Aliyah from me and I had to live alone for the rest of my life."

***

Jacob's words unsteadied Deanna until the ground seemed to open up beneath her. It was as if she were falling with nothing to hold on to. Her hand fumbled behind her in search of the arm of the couch, and when she found it, she dug her fingernails into it for fear she would collapse.

*We live in a world dominated by science and corporeal reality,* the self-help author had said. *Anything that cannot be measured, simulated in a lab, or confirmed by the five traditionally recognized senses is cast into the worlds of superstition, imagination, and myth. Science is not looked at as a microcosm of a wider world. It is looked at as the wider world itself. Consequently, the spirit world, like that of religion, is largely ignored and shoved under one (if not all) of the three aforementioned categories. Thus, discussing concepts like contrition and atonement become extremely difficult because the concept of morality itself cannot be proven, and therefore, can only exist (allegedly) as part of one's imagination or "mythological" beliefs. But the truth is that the human is made up of both body and spirit. This is undeniable, even if you reject the notions of God and religion. Somewhere deep inside us, we have a barometer of right and wrong, and if we do wrong, we feel horribly and often pay for it for the rest of our lives.*

"I'm sorry," Deanna said, resentment in her tone, the words leaving a bitter taste in her mouth. "I'm sorry for ruining your life, Jacob," she said, shivering in anger. "And I'm sorry I ever met you, Aliyah. I think we would've both been better off if I was never part of your life.

***

Salima arrived home Sunday evening with a heavy heart that left her restless in frustration and self-doubt. A part of her was grieving, but she wasn't fully cognizant of what she'd lost. Feeling suffocated in her parents' presence, she'd left their house a couple of hours before she'd planned, having fought off a tinge of guilt for making up an excuse to leave. During the three-hour drive home, the urge to call Larry was almost painful, but she withheld, fearing it was unfair to him.

*"I'm sure this Larry seems like a good brother,"* she heard her mother's voice in her head. *"But I don't think he's good enough for you, baby. You need someone like you..."*

Salima had considered calling Aliyah to ask her perspective, but she reminded herself that Aliyah couldn't relate. Aliyah didn't have parents who displayed affection or emotional concern for her well being, so the concept of having parents deeply concerned about whom she chose to marry would probably be quizzical at best. Then there was the possibility that the perspective of Salima's parents could be considered offensive. Aliyah probably wouldn't understand why Salima's family put so much emphasis on marrying a man who was raised Muslim.

As Salima recited the supplication for entering the home and closed the door, she heard the patter of footsteps hurrying down the stairs. A smile spread on her face as Haroon greeted her with salaams and a hug. Jamil appeared at the top of the stairs a moment later. The sight of him incited a bit of annoyance at the reminder of Jasmine visiting their parents, but she held her tongue and smiled up at him.

"*As-salaamu'alaikum,*" she said.

"*Wa'alaiku-mus-salaam wa-rahmatullaah,*" Jamil replied, offering her a warm smile. "How was it?"

She shrugged, glancing down at Haroon as she pulled him closer to her. "I'm still trying to process everything."

"That bad, huh?" he said teasingly.

There were silent for several seconds. "Did Haroon eat dinner yet?" Salima said finally.

"Yes," Jamil said. "We just finished eating right before you came."

"Did you brush your teeth?" Salima asked, looking down at her son.

Haroon shook his head. "Uncle Jamil is letting me watch a movie."

Salima drew her eyebrows together in concern, but a smile lingered on her face. "On a school night?"

"I told him if he finished his homework and helped me clean up we could watch *The Boy and the King*."

Relieved that it was at least a beneficial film, she nodded. "Okay, but brush your teeth first and go to bed right after it's over."

"Okay," Haroon said as he hurried back up the stairs.

"Thanks for watching Haroon," Salima said after she heard a room door close.

Jamil came down the stairs, a hesitant smile on his face. "So I guess they told you about Jasmine's visit?"

Salima glowered at her brother, his casual question infuriating her. "Why would you invite her to our *parents'* home, of all places?"

"I didn't invite her there," he said, walking past Salima to the living room. "I wanted to talk to you about it, but I couldn't."

Salima followed him into the living room then grunted and rolled her eyes as she sat down on the couch, arms folded. "Attorney-client privilege?"

"It might not mean much to you," Jamil said, a tinge of annoyance in his voice as he sat a comfortable distance from her. "But violating that could cost me my job *and* license."

"You know they think I'm a fool for even considering Larry," Salima said, accusation in her tone. She shook her head in disbelief, but she detected a hint of self-doubt flickering inside her. She looked at Jamil. "Do you agree with them?"

Jamil folded his lips as if the subject was an uncomfortable one.

Salima's face grew hot in offense. "But he's your *friend*."

Jamil regarded Salima as if seeing her for the first time. "And that's supposed to mean I'm excited for him to marry my sister? Yes, I like Larry. But that doesn't mean I like him for you."

She shook her head and rolled her eyes to the ceiling. "You sound like Mom and Dad."

"So what if I do?" Jamil said defensively. "We're worried about you."

His use of the word *we* struck a soft place in her heart, making her momentarily forget what she was about to say.

"They kept asking me what I knew about the brother who wants to marry you, and if there's anything at all that could make him bad for you," he said, exhaustion in his tone. "I didn't want to lie."

"So you send Jasmine to do it for you."

Jamil shook his head, an expression of frustrated amusement on his face. "I knew you'd say that about her."

"Why? Because I'm judgmental, or because you know she's a liar?"

"And if she's not?" Jamil said, looking Salima directly in the eye.

"Then that's for me to worry about."

"Yet you worry about me and Muslimah all the time."

At the mention of his ex-wife, Salima didn't know what to say.

"This is what families do, Salima," Jamil said. "We worry about each other. I just don't think you can be too careful."

Salima was lost in thought for some time. "Be honest with me, Jamil. What exactly is Jasmine accusing him of?"

"Mom and Dad didn't tell you?"

"Do they *know*?" Salima said, doubt in her tone. "They were so vague that I got the impression that Jasmine only said enough to incite their suspicions and disapproval."

Jamil's lips formed a thin line. "I don't know what they know because I didn't ask what she told them."

"But what do *you* know?"

Jamil drew in a deep breath and exhaled. "Salima, you know I can't tell you that."

"But you can send Larry's ex-girlfriend to our parents' house?" she said in exhausted disappointment.

"Her talking to them about what she experienced is different from me divulging what a client told me."

Salima felt herself growing upset. "You're my brother and a Muslim before you're a lawyer, Jamil. So if there's something I need to know about the man I want to marry, I think you're obligated to tell me, attorney-client privilege be damned."

Jamil exhaled in a single breath and appeared to be considering what Salima had said. But he remained silent, not looking at her.

"In the name of *Allah*," Salima said, irritation in her voice, "I ask you to tell me anything I need to know."

Jamil remained silent for a full minute before he sighed. "Look…it might be nothing."

"An entire lawsuit based on nothing?" Salima huffed. "I highly doubt that."

He folded in his lips and shook his head, as if the conversation was painful for him. "She's not going to file a lawsuit," he said finally. "She was just meeting with me to see if she had a strong case if she decided to."

Salima squinted her eyes in aggravation. "But a strong case about *what*, Jamil?"

Jamil was silent for several seconds before he responded. "Suffering emotional distress and financial loss due to a broken engagement."

Salima's eyes widened in disbelief, and she coughed laughter. "Are you kidding me? So she's trying to sue him because he's going on with his life?"

Jamil looked irritated. "It's not that simple, Salima."

"And you thought that warranted a meeting with our *parents*?"

"She invested a lot of time and money into that relationship."

"And I invested a lot of time and money into my marriage," she said. "But Allah took my husband's soul. So should I sue *God*?"

"This isn't a joke, Salima."

"That's what it sounds like to me."

"Her emotional distress isn't just about a broken engagement."

"Then what is it about?" she said sarcastically. "Losing out on cashing into the Bivens family business?"

"She says he was verbally abusive."

Salima laughed out loud. "Before or after she found out he was interested in me?"

Jamil shook his head, clearly annoyed. "This is why I didn't want to talk to you about this."

"I don't blame *you*," Salima clarified, but offense was still in her tone. "It just sounds like the classic revenge lawsuit."

"And if it's not?"

"Oh, it *is*."

"But it's not even a lawsuit yet."

"And I doubt it ever *will* be," she said flippantly. "She only hired you for legal advice because you're my brother, and she was banking on your guilty conscience making you warn me and our parents against the marriage."

"Have you ever taken a moment to *listen* to Larry?" Jamil said, hurt and offense in his eyes as he looked at Salima. "He talks like he has this chip on his shoulder, and like women don't deserve crap. That might make for a good debate over dinner, but imagine living every day with a man who thinks your troubles are laughable at best."

Salima shook her head in disagreement. "He's just honest about how he feels."

"Is that what they're calling misogyny nowadays?" Jamil said saracastically.

"*Misogyny*?" Salima recoiled. "Larry doesn't *hate* women."

Jamil raised his eyebrows doubtfully. "You sure about that?"

Salima opened her mouth to respond, but Jamil spoke before she could.

“As a friend, I found his frankness humorous, though it was annoying as hell sometimes,” Jamil said. “But when Jasmine came to me for legal advice, I saw it from a different perspective.”

Salima didn’t know what to say, but she had a difficult time letting go of her offense.

“Maybe she did come to me for revenge,” Jamil said with a shrug. “I don’t know. Maybe she even wanted you and I to have this conversation. And maybe she does want to keep him from marrying you so she can have him to herself. But that doesn’t mean she’s lying.”

## 34
## Atonement

It was a Friday afternoon in mid-December and Aliyah was clearing her desk in preparation for winter break when she heard a light knock on her office door. She looked up and saw one of her algebra students peering in the open doorway, a hesitant expression on her face, a loose fist poised mid-knock.

"Professor Thomas?"

"Hello, Robin," Aliyah said, offering the student a weary smile. "I thought all the students had gone home already."

Robin smiled self-consciously. "I commute."

"Well, I've already packed away my grade book..." Aliyah said apologetically, glancing around the office as she placed her hands on her hips. "But your reports should arrive to your home by next week."

Robin shook her head. "I'm not here to ask about my grade."

"Oh?"

Robin glanced cautiously over her shoulder into the hallway before looking at Aliyah again. "Can I come in?"

Aliyah felt a wave of exhaustion. She was one of the last professors still on campus and was planning to head home soon. Jacob had signed out before leaving for the Friday prayers and had just texted to say he had picked up Ibrahim after *Jumu'ah* and they would meet her at the apartment. But her expression remained cordial as she gestured for Robin to take a seat opposite her desk.

"Thank you," Robin muttered, walking in quickly and sitting down, her petite frame almost swallowed up by the chair. She was one of Aliyah's quiet students, rarely raising her hand and only speaking when she absolutely had to. She had a nervous habit of biting her thumbnail throughout class while she took notes with the other hand. Robin said nothing as Aliyah continued placing her belongings in a cardboard box atop her desk then opened a desk drawer.

"Is everything okay?" Aliyah said, glancing up as she leaned forward to thumb through the file folders.

Robin offered a reassuring smile that did little to veil the nervousness hidden beneath. "I'm good," she said, her voice awkwardly high-pitched as she used her thumb and forefinger to push back the hair that had fallen over her eyes.

"How can I help you?" Aliyah said, regarding Robin skeptically.

Robin chewed on a thumbnail nervously before speaking. "I've been thinking about that lesson you gave on narcissism and unknown values."

A puzzled expression lingered on Aliyah's face. Several seconds passed before she recalled the lesson. *"The term* unknown value *is actually quite narcissistic,"* Aliyah had said. *"Because if all of the other values are known, then it's impossible that this single one can be truly* un*known. It's only unknown to the extent that a person lacks the knowledge or willpower to work out the single answer that everything else is obviously pointing to."*

A smile of recognition passed over Aliyah's face. "I was joking," she said.

"I know," Robin said, pushing her hair away from her face again. "But I can't get it out of my head." A crooked smile formed on her face. "In the realm of definite realities, the answer to the unknown is literally right in front of you," she said, reciting Aliyah's words from class, "if you have both the knowledge and willpower to see it."

Aliyah shook her head, impressed. "You have a good memory."

"I wrote it down."

"I guess I should've told you that wouldn't be on the exam," she said in lighthearted humor.

Robin chuckled and nodded. "Yes, I guess so…"

An awkward silence followed, and the only sound that could be heard was Aliyah opening a drawer and shuffling through papers.

"I'm an atheist," Robin said with nervous laughter.

Aliyah raised her eyebrows quizzically, feeling on guard all of a sudden, unsure where the conversation was heading. She immediately thought of Dr. Warren and wondered if this student intended to voice a complaint against Aliyah. But Aliyah had made it a point to never mention God or religion during her lessons, even in passing or jest the way other professors did. Though things had calmed down considerably after the incident with Deanna, the atmosphere between her and Dr. Warren remained tense, and Aliyah sensed that her supervisor was waiting for the moment to officially pin something on her.

"I'm a *math* professor," Aliyah said, her tone firm as a cordial expression remained on her face.

"I know, I know," Robin said quickly, apology in her tone as she pinched her eyes shut and shook her head, as if willing the wrong words from her mind. "I just wanted you to know that what you said made me rethink a lot of things. So I wanted to thank you."

Unsure Robin's meaning, Aliyah nodded hesitantly, but she decided against inquiring further. "You're welcome…"

"That was the first time I realized it's not mathematically possible for God to be unknown." She smiled nervously. "Or non-existent."

It was then that Aliyah registered what Robin was saying. *In the realm of definite realities, the answer to the unknown is literally right in front of you if you have both the knowledge and willpower to see it.*

"Because if all of the universe is known," Robin recited, a hesitant smile thinly veiling the spiritual discomfort this realization had uncovered, "then it's impossible that the existence of the Creator can be truly unknown. He's only unknown to the extent that a person lacks the knowledge or willpower to work out the obvious truth that everything else is pointing to."

Aliyah forced laughter as she heard her words rephrased in that manner. "Just so you know," she said, humor in her tone, "I wasn't talking about God or religion when I said that."

"I know, I know," Robin said with a grin, waving her hand dismissively. "And I wasn't thinking about God or religion when you said it either," she said. "At least not at first."

"Well, I'm glad it helped clarify some things for you." Aliyah lifted the box from her desk, pulled out her chair, and kneeled to put the box on the floor under the desk.

"My dad is Jewish, and my mom is Methodist," Robin shared, her voice sounding more relaxed.

As Aliyah stood, she heard Robin chuckle self-consciously.

"So I think I'm just more confused now," Robin said.

"I'm sure you'll figure everything out," Aliyah said, cautious not to say anything that could be construed as proselytizing. Though she was fairly certain that Robin had no intention of accusing her of actively trying to convert her to Islam, Aliyah was aware of how even the most innocent comment could be misunderstood or interpreted as intimidating.

There was an extended pause. "You converted to Moslem, right?"

Aliyah paused thoughtfully as she walked around her desk and reached up to remove her coat from a hook secured into the wood of a wall cabinet. "Yes…"

"What were you before?"

Aliyah's lips formed a thin line as she slipped her arms into her coat, weighing the wisdom of responding. "Christian," she said finally, glancing down as she pushed each button through its hole.

Robin stood and walked out the door and waited in the hall as Aliyah lifted her handbag from the desk and pulled the straps over her shoulder.

"I was wondering…" Robin said hesitantly as Aliyah walked toward the door and turned off the lights. "…do you know of anything I can read to learn about the Moslem religion?"

Aliyah was silent as she pulled the door closed and locked it. The hall was quiet, and it seemed that everyone else had gone home. But she headed toward the stairs, not wanting to chance Robin continuing her line of questions in front of Aliyah's colleagues in the elevator.

"What sort of thing do you have in mind?" Aliyah said as Robin fell in step next to her.

"Anything," Robin said eagerly. "I mean, anything about the Moslem God and how you guys believe in Him."

"Do you like to read?" Aliyah said. "Or are you looking for a small pamphlet or website with quick FAQs?"

"That's fine," Robin said quickly. Clearly, she hadn't expected the conversation to progress this far.

"But do you *prefer* a book?" Aliyah said as she opened the heavy exit door leading to the staircase. "You know, something lengthy you can read over the holidays?"

"Um…it doesn't matter," Robin said, and Aliyah couldn't tell if this was Robin's way of politely declining. "But a few books would be nice. I plan to read what I can during the break."

Aliyah was quiet as their footfalls fell heavy on the steps. "Do you have your phone with you?" she asked. "Or an iPad?"

"Yes," Robin said, quickly opening up her purse and rummaging inside with one hand.

"Then I'll use your Notes app to input the names of some books and websites you might find helpful." College policy strictly forbade interactions between professors and students outside of school, and Aliyah sensed that Robin felt a bit disappointed that Aliyah wasn't making an exception so that they could exchange numbers. But Robin tapped in the passcode and handed her phone to Aliyah.

Aliyah slowed her steps as she typed in the information then handed the phone back to Robin as they stepped through the exit door leading to the first floor.

Aliyah's phone chimed and vibrated just as Robin thanked her and waved goodbye in the main lobby of the math and science building. Aliyah swiped her badge at the console near the security desk before reaching in her purse and looking at her phone.

*Running late,* Jacob's text said. *Just picked up Younus and Thawab. Stuck in traffic.*

***

It was nasty outside, Aliyah noticed with a frown, the cold air stinging her face as she pushed open the exit door. A thin layer of freshly fallen snow covered the walkway and the mostly vacant faculty and staff parking lot. In the main street that ran along the front of the college, cars crawled cautiously forward in the foggy late afternoon, headlights glowing bleakly ahead of them and crimson break lights turning on and off intermittently.

Aliyah tucked her chin toward her chest to protect her face from the cold, and she pushed her hands into the deep pockets of her coat. Her gaze was on the round toe of her low-heel patent leather boots, where snowflakes fell then melted from the warmth of her body heat as she tried to remember when her last menstrual cycle had been. She couldn't remember whether it was before or after the weekend trip she and Jacob had taken. She was on birth control, so either way, it wasn't necessarily a cause for alarm.

Aliyah's birth control regiment included placebo pills that allowed her body to menstruate according to a 28-day cycle, but it sometimes took a couple of days before she saw the initial spotting. But this week, she hadn't seen any spotting, and she was five days beyond her normal start date. The prescription she was on currently was different from the one she had used when she was married to Matt, so Aliyah couldn't be sure whether or not the extended delay was due to the hormonal difference in the pills. When giving her the prescription, her obstetrician-gynecologist had told her not to be alarmed by any variation or abnormalities in her cycle.

Yet Aliyah had been feeling different for the last couple of weeks, and she couldn't shake the fear that sat in the pit of her stomach, telling her that she was pregnant. There was no nausea or significant mood changes, and she wasn't having unusual food cravings. But there was this heavy, dreary feeling that permeated her every morning, making her want to stay in bed. It wasn't melancholy or dread, but something else. It was like a gnawing sense that the comfortable world she had just settled into was shifting beneath her feet and she didn't have the capacity to comprehend the change or the wherewithal to face it. So she would lie still reciting *adhkaar* in soft whispers until the feeling passed.

In front of her car, Aliyah halted her steps and pulled her handbag in front of her then removed her keys. She thought of Deanna as she pointed the remote toward her car and unlocked it before opening the door and climbing inside. Early that morning before *Fajr*, Aliyah had awakened from a dream in which she'd seen herself lying asleep next to Jacob only to wake and go to the bathroom and find Deanna in there brushing her teeth. In the dream, Aliyah had felt familiar irritation, as if she wasn't surprised to find Deanna there. She had been tempted to complain to Jacob but decided against it, knowing he'd just tell her to leave Deanna alone, as she didn't have a bathroom of her own.

The air in the car was stiff with cold as she inserted the key into the ignition and turned on the engine. She leaned forward to adjust the heat settings and to activate the window defroster, reflecting on the odd sensation that continued to linger even then, following the dream. It was as if she and Deanna had recently spoken and spent time together and that there was no lurking animosity between them. There was no joy or sadness, just the acceptance of the sober reality of life.

"She says she's sorry," Jacob had told Aliyah a few days after the tense meeting at Benjamin's house, his tone devoid of emotion as he recited this news with a detached sense of obligation in passing on a message.

Aliyah's first instinct had been to ask why Deanna couldn't simply tell Aliyah herself, until she remembered she had never taken the block off of Deanna's contact information in her phone and email. But that morning, after praying *Fajr*, Aliyah had cleared the block, accepting that she and Deanna would have to be in contact since Aliyah was now the stepmother to Deanna's children.

The vents blew out cold air as the car lazily heated itself, and Aliyah glanced toward the main street, overwhelmed with a sense of dread for the journey home. Sighing, she reached for her handbag and withdrew her phone then connected it to the auxiliary port, knowing she would need something to distract her during the drive. As she scrolled through audio options, her phone chimed and vibrated, the chiming magnified through the car speakers.

*Streets are really bad,* Jacob texted. *Be careful. Interstate is at a standstill, and the snow keeps coming. I'm near Jamil's exit, so I'll wait out rush hour there.*

*Is he home?* Aliyah texted back.

*Yes, alhamdulillah.*

Aliyah wondered if she should head to Salima's herself. Then maybe she and Salima could go to Carletta's together later that night for Muslim Marriage Monologues if the weather had improved and the streets had been cleared. But Aliyah dismissed the idea, however tempting it was. Her apartment was closer to the college than Salima's house, so if she went anywhere besides home, it should probably be the masjid, which was down the street. But the idea of sitting in the masjid alone filled Aliyah with even more dread than the extended drive home. So she decided to take the long way home, avoiding the interstate altogether.

***

"No, I'm home," Salima said, smiling into the mobile phone from where she sat cross-legged on the bed in her room, a *mus-haf* in her lap. "Haroon's school dismissed the students at noon, so I left work early to pick him up."

"Our school let out early too," Carletta said, "but hardly no students were there anyway."

There was a thoughtful pause. "How do you like your new job?" Salima asked. "I know you don't prefer teaching public school."

The extended silence on the other line made Salima realize that something heavy was on Carletta's mind. She heard Carletta draw in a deep breath and exhale before responding.

"It's going fine..." Carletta said tentatively. "But I don't think I'll be able to participate in Muslim Marriage Monologues anymore," she said apologetically.

"Teaching fulltime is a bit overwhelming, huh?" Salima said, humored admiration in her tone. "I don't know how you teachers do it. I substituted a few times, and it was the worst job experience of my life."

"I'll have to cancel tonight." Carletta spoke as if she hadn't heard anything Salima said. Her tone was firm in resolve, making Salima wonder if she'd offended her friend somehow.

"Because of the weather?" Salima asked, confusion in her voice.

There was a thoughtful pause, and Salima sensed that Carletta was trying to find the best way to explain. "I had a meeting with the principal today."

Salima drew her eyebrows together, unsure how the statement was related to the Friday night gatherings about marriage.

"Remember all that fuss the LGBTQ community made about my 'Relationship Woes Among Judgmental Muslims' topic at Muslim Marriage Monologues?"

"Yes..."

"I have no idea how," Carletta said, irritation in her voice, "but somehow my new job heard about it and they asked me outright if I was homophobic."

"*What*?"

"I know," Carletta said, clearly perturbed.

"What did you say?"

She grunted. "I wanted to tell them, not homophobic, *Hell*-ophobic."

Salima burst out laughing. "I have to use that one," she said as she recovered from laughter.

"But of course I had to act all prim and proper and dutifully appalled," Carletta said.

"But how did they even find out?" Salima said.

"Who knows?" Carletta said. "This is the internet age, so anything posted on Twitter, Facebook, or some random blog is accessible to anyone with some free time on their hands."

"So you think they just randomly googled your name?"

"That, or someone told them something about me." She huffed. "Probably both."

Salima shook her head in disbelief. "This is crazy…"

"You're telling me," Carletta said in agreement.

"But is it even legal?" Salima said. "To hold someone accountable for what's posted online about them? Isn't that hearsay?"

"Does it matter?" Carletta said. "Today, most people view it as their patriotic duty to mistreat religious people. We don't have any rights as far as they're concerned."

"I remember reading about a teacher who lost her job because of something she posted on Instagram," Salima said.

"*A* teacher?" Carletta said. "There are dozens, if not hundreds, of others losing their jobs because of stupid stuff like this."

There was a thoughtful pause. "Are you going to fight it?" Salima said.

"Fight what?" Carletta said. "They didn't take any action against me. It was just a meeting. I'm still employed." She grunted before adding, "For now."

"Do they know you're Muslim?" Salima said. Carletta didn't wear hijab and would often mention that she didn't feel someone's religious affiliation should be officially revealed for a job.

"They do now." There was a tinge of frustration in her tone.

"*SubhaanAllah*."

"You can say that again."

A thought came to Salima, and she hesitated briefly before putting it into words. "Did you tell them…" she said, intentionally leaving her thoughts unfinished. "…you know?"

Carletta sighed. "I thought about it," she said. "But then I figured it's not fair to me or my husband. Why should I have to tell them my private business just to prove I'm not a bigot?"

"You think your husband would mind if you told them?"

There was a brief pause. "I don't know," Carletta said reflectively. "But when we talked about it before marriage, it was something we decided to keep between ourselves. It was never an explicit agreement or anything though."

"I understand," Salima said sincerely.

“Plus I don’t want it to get out,” Carletta said. “Especially amongst the LGBTQ Muslims. They’d try to either recruit me or vilify me.”

“You think so?” Salima said doubtfully.

“They don’t like success stories,” Carletta said. “They want everyone to believe that sexuality is an underlying orientation that’s impossible to control. So they’ll try to convince me I’m just denying who I, quote, *really* am. Or they’ll say I’m lying.” She huffed. “Or that it’s oppressive to ask other people to do what I’m doing.”

Salima was silent momentarily. “I know it’s not my call,” she said. “But sometimes I wish you would share your story. I think it can help others.”

“I don’t know…” Carletta said, uncertainty in her tone. “I just hate the whole concept of, quote, coming out.”

“*A’oodhubillah*,” Salima said, seeking refuge in God. “I didn’t mean *that*.”

“But how else could I do it?” Carletta asked rhetorically. “If I don’t, then they’ll just think I’m one more person who says people can be fixed.” She grunted. “Call me old-fashioned, but I prefer the closet.”

“I hear you…”

“Anyway, you can only help someone who wants help,” Carletta said. “Plus, I don’t want sisters giving me the side-eye. I’m just not into making people uncomfortable. Like you said in your poem, there are just some things that are better left untold.”

“But what if you shared your story anonymously?”

Carletta chuckled. “I’ve thought of that too. But still, I don’t see the point. Either you want to do what you’re supposed to, or you don’t. I don’t see how hearing my story will change the state of someone’s heart.”

“But it can’t be easy for the people struggling alone,” Salima said. “And maybe hearing someone else’s story can encourage them.”

“Is life *supposed* to be easy?” Carletta said. “I still have my private battles, but they’re nothing like they used to be.”

Salima closed the Qur’an that was on her lap and set in on the nightstand then shifted her position on the bed. “What helped you the most?”

Carletta was silent as she considered Salima’s question. “I know this will sound crazy,” she said, slight humor in her tone. “But my parents.”

“Really?” Salima said, surprised. “I thought you never told them.”

“I don’t mean directly,” Carletta said. “I mean with how they raised me in the church. They would always say that sex was something sacred that was more about pleasing God than pleasing yourself.”

“But it’s supposed to be pleasurable to you too.”

“I agree,” Carletta said. “But the point is, worldly pleasure alone is not really pleasure. There has to be an underlying spiritual and emotional component to it.”

“Can’t you just tell people that?” Salima said. “Maybe they’ll see it differently.”

"You're assuming people *want* to see it differently," Carletta said. "Most people want what they want, end of story. I'm not saying they don't go through a lot of hardships. Because I know they do. I've been there," she said. "I'm just saying they see their struggle against sin as some gift they're begrudgingly bestowing on God. And when it gets hard, they resent the struggle, and sometimes God Himself. So it's easier to just change the script than to change yourself."

"*SubhaanAllah*," Salima said. "That sounds like every sin we don't want to give up."

"It is," Carletta said matter-of-factly. "People who identify as LGBTQ don't have a monopoly on personal struggle. But most of them want you to believe they do."

Salima was silent as she considered Carletta's words.

"They hype up this whole victim status thing," Carletta said, "because their whole campaign hinges on appealing to people's emotions instead of appealing to our sense of right and wrong." She paused then added, "They want everyone to believe our struggle is *so* different from everyone else's that right and wrong shouldn't even apply to us." She huffed. "And if you treat them the way they *say* they want to be treated, they label you a homophobe."

Salima creased her forehead in confusion. "What do you mean?"

"They say we're like everyone else, right?" Carletta said.

"Yes."

"Well, the rest of the human race accepts that being disagreed with is a part of life."

"That's true..."

"My parents think I'm going to Hell for eternity because I don't believe Jesus is my Lord and Savior," Carletta said. "And guess what? I don't care. Because I don't believe that about myself. And I certainly don't believe that their Christian beliefs make them Islamophobes."

Salima frowned thoughtfully. "But aren't there *any* LGBTQ religious groups established to help people *overcome* their desires?" She shook her head. "It's just hard to believe that religious people, especially Muslims, wouldn't want a safe space to obey God instead of change the religion. At least if you really want to go to Paradise in the end."

There was a thoughtful pause. "I suppose there must be," Carletta said reflectively. "But I don't know of any. Though some groups seem to be more focused on rooting out bullying and shaming than arguing about religious issues," she offered.

"That's true," Salima muttered.

"But there are definitely a whole lot of people like me," Carletta said. "People just quietly living their lives and trying to do what they're supposed to without making a big fuss about our private struggles."

"*MashaAllah*," Salima said sincerely.

“We’re the majority, in my opinion,” Carletta said. “Most of us are wary of groups because they tend to have pretty blatant political or anti-religious agendas. And for those of us who came to religion for spiritual salvation, and not only for a sense of belonging,” she said, “that’s just not a bandwagon we’re willing to join.”

“I always wondered about that…” Salima said. “I mean, how common can it be for religious people to want to challenge God?”

Carletta sighed thoughtfully. “That’s the thing though. A lot of these groups are changing the terminology of religion altogether,” she said. “Whenever these topics come up, you’ll hear a lot about, quote, hetero-normativity, as if believing in the way Allah created us is really about being influenced by some underhanded bigoted agenda, instead of living how you’re supposed to.”

“That’s scary…”

“You can say that again,” Carletta said with a huff. “But the way I see it, any group that includes the letter *T* in their acronym can’t possibly be about fighting temptation and overcoming sinful desires. I don’t care how religious they claim to be.”

It took a moment for Salima to register Carletta’s meaning. “But what about people who became Muslim after they went through surgery and hormonal treatment?”

“But their gender is still whatever is was at birth. They just need to repent and accept that.”

Salima was silent for some time as she considered what Carletta was saying. “But bullying and shaming is a real problem for some of them, I hear. I’m sure that makes healing more difficult.”

“I realize that,” Carletta said sincerely. “But that’s another topic completely. When the principal met with me today, she wasn’t concerned that I was going to beat up anyone or make fun of my students. All she wanted to know was whether or not I had any, quote, prejudicial beliefs against the gay and lesbian lifestyle.”

“What did you tell her?”

“I told her no.”

Salima chuckled. “That was smart.”

Carletta coughed laughter. “And it happens to be true. Having a religious belief that something is sinful is not a prejudice.”

“Good point, *mashaAllah*,” Salima said with a smirk.

“But then she mentioned Muslim Marriage Monologues and asked if I was part of that, quote, homophobic group.”

“*What*?”

“No joke,” Carletta said. “Those were her exact words.”

“O Allah…”

“So I said I had no idea what she was talking about.”

Salima felt a tinge of offense, but she understood why Carletta felt compelled to respond like that. “Did she say anything else about it?”

“Muslim Marriage Monologues, you mean?”

"Yes."

"Not really," Carletta said. "But I did explain to her that I had gone to and hosted many informal marriage events and discussions, so it's possible that the misunderstanding could have come from that. I told her that anti-gay sentiments are quite common in religious communities, and it was impossible for me to control what other people thought or said."

Salima chuckled. "You should've become a lawyer."

"In another life, perhaps," Carletta said jokingly. "But for now, I'm just trying to pay my bills."

The doorbell rang, and a second later, Salima heard Jamil's heavy footsteps in the hall then a knock at her door.

"Let me go," Salima said with a sigh. "It looks like we have company."

"Salima?" Jamil called through the closed door. "That's Jacob with the boys. He's going to hang out here until the streets are clear."

Salima groaned and rolled her eyes. She wished Jamil would have told her earlier. Then she could've fixed herself something to eat while she was on the phone. "Okay!" she called out, holding the mobile phone away from her head then putting it back to her ear.

"So you'll text everyone?" Carletta said.

"That's no problem," Salima said. "Most people probably wouldn't have come anyway because of the snow."

"I'm sorry about this," Carletta said, sadness in her tone. "That was the highlight of my week."

"Don't worry about it, Carly, really," Salima said. "We live in the age of social terrorism," she said in wry humor. "So it's better to be safe than sorry, especially when your job is at stake."

"But I really hate all this policing people's thoughts and beliefs." Carletta groaned. "It's unconstitutional, if you ask me."

"But that's the thing," Salima said jokingly. "No one's asking you. Because you don't matter."

"I know, right?" Carletta chuckled in agreement. "Apparently, constitutional rights only apply to the non-religious."

"The *anti*-religious," Salima corrected.

"You have a point there," Carletta said, laughter in her voice.

***

Aliyah halted her steps in the hallway of her apartment when she saw the homeless person hunched over against the wall near her door. She glanced around her, uncertain what to do. For a moment, she considered calling Jacob but decided against it because she didn't want to alarm him. Besides, there was nothing he could do while he was stuck on the other side of town, and it wasn't like the person was threatening her or anything. From where she stood, it looked like the person was sleeping.

Taking cautious steps forward, Aliyah held her keys in her fist to keep from making noise as she approached. At her door, she turned her hand up and pinched the edge of the house key in preparation to slide it into the lock.

"What took you so long?"

Aliyah yelped and jumped backwards, dropping her keys, her heart thumping fiercely. When the woman reached for the keys, Aliyah scrambled forward and snatched them up.

"What's your *problem*?" the woman said. It was then that the contorted face with the winter hat pulled down to the forehead and the stern voice became familiar. "Why does everything have to be so dramatic with you?" Deanna rolled her eyes as she came to her feet, a small brown paper bag in her hand.

It took several seconds for Aliyah to catch her breath and calm her racing heart. "What are you doing here?" she finally managed to say.

"What are you *not* doing here?" Deanna said flippantly. "It's rude to make people wait for you."

For a fleeting moment, Aliyah wished she still had the restraining order against Deanna, but it had expired a long time ago.

Deanna grunted. "Open the door," she said. "I'm cold."

Aliyah gritted her teeth to stay calm as she inserted the key into the lock then mouthed the *du'aa* for entering the home. "I have to pray," Aliyah said as she set her purse on the front table then shrugged off her coat.

"Then I'll pray with you," Deanna muttered, aggravation still in her voice as she closed the door after stepping inside.

Aliyah quietly hung her coat on the rack in the foyer before kneeling to pull off her boots. *Leave her alone. She doesn't have a home of her own.* The words came to Aliyah as if from the dream she'd had the night before, and they tempered, at least for the moment, the annoyance she felt at being thrust into Deanna's presence.

"Where are you manners, girl?"

Aliyah was walking toward the hall bathroom in preparation to make *wudhoo'* when she heard Deanna grumble these words. She cringed, bracing herself for the insult that she knew was coming.

"Aren't you going to ask if I need anything?" Deanna said. "I'm your guest, for goodness sake."

Pursing her lips in irritation, Aliyah slowly turned around. "Forgive me for not being prepared to receive you," she said, making no effort to conceal the sarcasm in her tone. "But I have to use the bathroom, if that's okay with you."

"I have to use the bathroom too," Deanna said, offense in her tone. She walked past Aliyah into the hall then abruptly turned around.

"Here," Deanna said, extending the crumpled brown paper bag toward Aliyah. "I bought this for us," Deanna said as Aliyah reluctantly accepted the offering without looking at it. "But it's probably cold now." Deanna was already in the bathroom with the door shut before Aliyah had opportunity to respond.

Sighing, Aliyah dragged herself to the couch and collapsed into it. This was not the way she had planned to spend her Friday evening. As if on cue, her phone buzzed and chimed from her purse next to her, and she already knew before looking at it that Jacob was texting to tell her he was being delayed further.

*No Muslim Marriage Monologues tonight,* Salima's text said. *Stay safe everyone!*

***

"So how's that brother of mine treating you?" Jacob said as he and Jamil settled on the couch after praying *Maghrib* and the boys had gone upstairs to Haroon's room. Salima was setting a tray of tea on the floor table in front of the couch when he saw her offer a reluctant smile.

"He's treating me well, *mashaAllah*," she said.

Jacob detected the obligatory cordiality in her tone, and he wondered if everything was okay between Salima and Larry.

"Our parents are doing their share of meddling," Jamil said in lighthearted humor as he reached forward and filled a ceramic cup with hot water then dropped a teabag in it before setting it on a saucer in front of Jacob, "now that marriage is part of the discussion."

"Marriage?" Jacob said, raising his eyebrows in pleasant surprise as he put sugar in his tea. "So things are getting pretty serious, huh?"

"Actually," Salima said as she settled on the chair at an angle to them, " it's Jasmine who's doing the meddling."

Jacob sensed a marked change in Jamil's mood, but Jacob kept his gaze on the tea he was stirring. The tension in the room was almost palpable, and Jacob felt reluctant to even lift his hand to sip his tea.

"She drove three hours to my parents house just to tell them that she's in the process of filing a lawsuit against Larry," Salima said, bitter satisfaction in her voice, as if her words were punishing Jamil somehow.

"*What*?" Now it was Jacob's mood that had changed as he looked at Salima in disbelief.

"Apparently," Salima said, sarcasm in her tone, "your brother is a women-hating abuser who's caused Jasmine irreparable emotional damage during their relationship."

"Excuse me?" Jacob said, unable to hide his offense. He sat back and folded his arms over his chest, momentarily forgetting about the tea.

"What do you think, Jacob?" Salima said sweetly, the sarcasm in her tone unmasked. "Is Larry a sexist monster that I need to be protected from?"

"Do my *parents* know about this?" Jacob said, his voice etched in concern. But as soon as he said it, he realized the irrationality of the question. How would Salima know if his parents knew? She probably hadn't even met them herself.

"I'm not even sure Larry knows about it," Salima said, the bitterness still in her voice. "I didn't mention it to him yet. You know, since I might have to tell him that his friend Jamil is representing his ex-girlfriend in the case against him."

***

*The most dreaded apologies are usually the most essential ones.*

In the bathroom as she completed her *wudhoo*, Deanna drew in a deep breath and exhaled as she recalled the words of the self-help book. She mentally scolded herself for starting off on the wrong foot with Aliyah. No matter how annoying Aliyah was, Deanna had to push through this. She doubted she could ever forgive Aliyah for marrying Jacob behind her back, but even that, Deanna couldn't fully blame Aliyah for.

*I don't care what your religious beliefs are*, the book had said. *But somewhere in everyone's life there is proof for karma in some form. Call it what you want. But when you do wrong to someone, it's coming back to you. And in the most unexpected, painful way. But the good news is you can reverse that cycle. Make it right with the person you've wronged. Not because they're such a great person. But because you want to be a better one.*

***

Frowning thoughtfully, Aliyah peered into the brown paper bag and saw two semi-wrapped gyros. *"She says she's sorry."* Jacob's words came to Aliyah just as the flame of fury rose in her chest and she heard the water in the bathroom being turned off. Was it possible that Deanna really was sorry? The question was one that Aliyah hadn't seriously considered. Everything with Deanna had always felt so much like some underhanded plot to prove her superiority that it was difficult to trust any signs of positivity from her. The concepts of *Deanna* and *sincere regret* just didn't seem to belong in the same context.

*"You brought gyros?"* Aliyah had said in childlike excitement so long ago, before the call from her uncle forever changed the course of both of their lives.

*"Yes, against my better judgment,"* Deanna had said. *"You know that bread has too many carbs."*

*"I love you, Deeja!"* Aliyah had sang out.

*"Yeah, yeah, whatever..."*

"You can go in the bathroom now." Aliyah started at the sound of Deanna's voice, and she turned to see Deanna standing near the couch, gaze averted, her expression still reflecting a shadow of annoyance.

"Thank you," Aliyah muttered then set the paper bag on the floor table before quietly walking to the bathroom herself.

***

*Try empathy.*

Deanna did a double take from where she sat on the couch waiting for Aliyah to finish making *wudhoo'*. The wall hanging near Aliyah's front door had probably been there for a while, but Deanna had never noticed it before. At least she didn't recall having noticed it before.

*"Don't tell me you're almost pushing forty and you still haven't figured out what the hell is wrong with you?"*

Asher's words incited annoyance in Deanna, and she looked away from the quote. Hearing water running in the bathroom and realizing that she was about to stand next to Aliyah in prayer filled Deanna with so much irritation that she had to resist the urge to leave right then. Though Deanna had begun praying again, she wasn't consistent, and there were times that she resented the ritualistic obligation that continuously disrupted her day.

*What's the point?* she often asked herself. It wasn't like prayer had given her anything she wanted. In fact, she'd just lost the one thing that had meant the most to her. And for what? So some soft-spoken, brainless bimbo could run away with everything she'd put her heart and energy into all these years? Deanna had *made* Jacob into the man he was today. It was infuriating that he could repay her hard work by bestowing it on someone so undeserving and beneath her.

*If you really want to be better, then shut up.* The blunt advice from the author of *YOU CAN BE A BETTER PERSON!* returned to her like a slap in the face. *I know it sounds harsh, and maybe it is. But one of the things that keeps you stuck where you are is saying the same things to yourself over and over again. If there's something you find consistently annoying, you have to ask yourself, is it really* that *annoying? Or are you just repeating to yourself the same negative triggering words each time you encounter it? I'm not saying there's nothing genuinely annoying in the world. Because let's face it. Life sucks. But you don't have to suck, too.*

Deanna heard the bathroom door open, and the muscles in her cheeks ached as she offered Aliyah a wide smile. "You ready to pray?" Deanna said, her voice cheerful and eager even as a scream crawled in her throat, as if begging her not to put herself through the spiritual torment right then. The last thing she wanted was to feel like a horrible person.

*You can't feel better until you feel worse!* the author had said.

Internally, Deanna groaned and resigned herself to her fate, swallowing hard and feeling a wave of relief as the scream quietly retreated and settled into a knot in her stomach.

***

"This is why I didn't want to talk to you about it," Jamil said with an edge of aggravation in his voice.

"Me talking about Jasmine going to our parents house doesn't violate attorney-client privilege," Salima said. The bitterness she heard in her voice made her realize she needed to calm down. Jacob was still there, sitting quietly, his uncomfortable expression suggesting that he hadn't planned to avoid the storm outside by walking headlong into a worse one inside.

*"I just need some time to think about this,"* Salima had told Larry the night she'd returned from her parents' house.

*"What happened there?"* he'd asked, his voice etched in hurt and concern.

*"They just mentioned some things I hadn't considered."*

*"Like what?"*

The sincerity she'd heard in his voice that night left Salima guilt-stricken even now. She had never given him a straight answer, and it tore her apart to know that he'd merely come to accept that she now realized what he'd known all along. *"You deserve someone better than me,"* he'd told her many times before. And she knew that was why he'd pulled back and left her alone. He hadn't even attempted a phone call or text since that night, and though a part of her felt offended, a greater part, her more rational side, knew that it was his way of respecting the wishes she had been too shy to speak aloud.

***

"What happened to all that 'women like to play hard to get' nonsense you're always talking?" Jacob had teased his brother a few days ago when Larry had stopped by to visit, saying he was thinking to leave Salima alone. At the time, Jacob had thought little of Larry's words, having assumed that Larry was just being Larry. But Jacob did recall that Larry's mood had been more somber than usual, even as he'd chuckled and reluctantly participated in light banter with Jacob.

"I guess I'm getting old," Larry had joked in response.

"Or tired of the chase maybe?" Jacob had teased.

"Something like that," Larry had muttered noncommittally, an awkward smirk on his face.

But right then, as Jacob witnessed the argument between Salima and Jamil, he realized the real reason that Larry was behaving uncharacteristically nonchalant about his pursuit of Salima. It wasn't that Larry was changing his game. It was that, for the first time in his life, Larry had met someone whom he didn't see as a game. It was easy to like a challenge when you'd never really been faced with one. Love didn't embolden you. It humbled you. And it brought the strongest and most confident of men to their knees.

*SubhaanAllah*, Jacob thought to himself as he saw the distress and irritation on Salima's face. *They're in love and have no idea what's happening to them.*

***

Deanna was blinking back tears when she turned her head to the right then the left as she sat on the floor next to Aliyah upon completing the evening prayer.

"We need to pray *'Ishaa* too," Aliyah said, her voice soft in the quiet of the apartment. "It came in before I got home. So we should combine."

Deanna nodded without looking in Aliyah's direction.

Without saying anything further, Aliyah stood and raised her hands as if in surrender, signaling the start of prayer. "*Allaahu'akbar,*" she said, her voice confident and firm as it resonated in the room.

On weakened legs, Deanna stood, wondering if she had the fortitude to hold herself together one more time. She hadn't heard Qur'an much since she was in jail, and she'd forgotten how much emotion the recitation could evoke. Her own reluctant mumblings during the occasional prayers she offered, she doubted counted as recitation at all. She'd never formally studied the rules for reciting Qur'an, so she had no idea if she was even pronouncing anything correctly. Standing next to Aliyah and hearing the clear, measured tone of *Al-Faatihah* made Deanna painfully aware that she was far from where she needed to be spiritually.

*"Then at least go to the masjid more often,"* Jacob had suggested while they were married. *"Study Qur'an or* tafseer *or something."*

*"I don't need to study Qur'an,"* Deanna had replied flippantly. *"I'm living it."*

Deanna winced at the memory. It was difficult to believe that she had spoken such haughty words. *What do you think of yourself now?* a voice taunted in her head.

"*Ameen*," Aliyah proclaimed, elongating the last part of the word, begging Allah to answer their prayer.

"*Ameen*," Deanna hurriedly mumbled after her, having been distracted by her thoughts. Feeling bad for her carelessness, Deanna resolved to focus better for the rest of prayer.

As Aliyah moved on to recite another part of the Qur'an, Deanna had no idea what she was listening to. So how could she concentrate? She was dumbfounded. Where did Aliyah learn all of this? Frantically, Deanna listened for any Arabic word she knew the meaning to. But she heard none.

Envy enflamed Deanna until she shifted in her place, aggravated that Aliyah felt the need to rub her religiousness in Deanna's face. It wasn't enough that she stole her husband. Now she had to act "holier than thou" too.

*Everything isn't about you,* the words of the self-help book came to her just then. *If you have a hard time maintaining close relationships, chances are, this is a lesson you still haven't learned. It's highly unlikely that your husband, wife, or friend wakes up with a mission to make your life miserable. So if their words or actions constantly make you angry, the problem is most likely with you. So change yourself, or get out of the relationship.*

"*Allaahu'akbar*," Aliyah said, eliciting a sigh of relief from Deanna as they finally bowed in *rukoo'*. Even if Aliyah wasn't trying to rub her Islamic knowledge in Deanna's face, couldn't she at least pick something short to recite?

It aggravated Deanna to no end when the imam would lead the prayer and choose the longest possible part of Qur'an to recite. That was partly why Deanna avoided the masjid so much. Everything there felt like one big "look at how religious I am" show. If you didn't dress a certain way or use all the latest, fanciest Arabic catch phrases, you were looked down upon and viewed as a bad Muslim.

And if that wasn't enough, you were tortured during prayer itself. Legs aching and mind wandering, all you could do was count down to the final *tasleem*, which was delayed so long that the end of prayer often felt like being set free after a prison sentence. And now Deanna was stuck there listening to Aliyah's supercilious extended recitation, and this agitated her for the rest of prayer.

"Did you have to recite *half* the Qur'an?" Deanna blurted after they turned their heads to the left, indicating the end of prayer.

A shadow of annoyance passed over Aliyah's face, but Aliyah did not respond or even look in Deanna's direction. Instead, she sat murmuring additional supplications, as if her mind was on more important things.

"You should do all that extra praying when you're by yourself," Deanna grumbled.

Seconds later, Aliyah's soft voice rose, and Deanna recognized the recitation as *Ayat al-Kursy*. She rolled her eyes and shook her head, disgusted that Aliyah would use Qur'an, of all things, to ignore her.

When Aliyah finished reciting, she stood and walked over to a small shelf, and Deanna's gaze followed her in annoyance. Glowering, Deanna watched as Aliyah removed a large book from the shelf then returned to her place next to Deanna on the floor.

"In the first *rak'ah* of *Maghrib*," Aliyah said, flipping through the pages of the book before lifting it toward Deanna, "I recited *Al-Humazah*." When Deanna glanced to the side, she saw that Aliyah was holding the Qur'an, which was opened to a section filled with short chapters. "In the second *rak'ah*, I recited *Al-Maa'oon*," she said, turning a page then placing her index finger on a *soorah* there. She turned to another page and pointed to it. "In the first *rak'ah* of *'Ishaa*, I recited *Al-Zalzalah*, and in the second *rak'ah*," she said, flipping a page again and placing a finger there, "I recited *Al-Bayyinah*." Aliyah set the Qur'an on Deanna's lap so she could see for herself. "These are some of the shortest chapters in the Qur'an."

*...And the people of the Scripture [Jews and Christians] differed not until after there came to them clear evidence. And they were commanded no more than this: To worship Allah, offering Him sincere devotion, being true [in faith]; to establish regular prayer; and to practice regular charity. And that is the right religion—*

Annoyed, Deanna closed the Qur'an and handed it back to Aliyah. "I wasn't asking for an Islamic studies class," Deanna said as Aliyah accepted the Qur'an and held it on her own lap. "I was just saying you should think about other people when you're leading prayer."

"I was," Aliyah said simply. "That's why I chose short *soorah*'s. I myself have trouble focusing when it feels like the person leading thinks they're on some Ramadan *Taraweeh* marathon or something."

Despite her sour mood, Deanna was unable to keep from chuckling at the analogy. "Well, that's what it felt like standing next to you."

Aliyah shrugged. "Maybe because I recite slow."

"Maybe..."

An awkward silence settled between them before Aliyah finally stood and returned the Qur'an to its place. She walked back over to where Deanna was sitting but sat on the couch instead of the floor.

"Where'd you learn to recite like that anyway?" Deanna said from where she remained on the prayer mat, her tone still carrying a tinge of annoyance.

"Most recently, Reem and Salima," Aliyah said. "But I've been studying Qur'an on and off since I became Muslim."

Deanna frowned. "I don't remember that."

"You came with me to a couple of classes when we were in college," Aliyah said.

Deanna's eyebrows rose doubtfully. "I did?"

"Yes," Aliyah said. "And you were pretty good, *mashaAllah*." Deanna grew silent, taken aback by the sincerity in Aliyah's voice. "The teacher used to say you were probably going to memorize Qur'an before the rest of us because you had such a good memory, *mashaAllah*."

"My memory isn't so great," Deanna muttered, but a half smile creased one corner of her mouth.

"It's almost photographic actually," Aliyah disagreed, no hint of sarcasm or resentment in her tone. "You'd read something once then recall it weeks later, word for word."

*Oh.* Deanna had forgotten that people considered that remarkable. "That's only for English books," she said. "I don't remember much from the Qur'an. I barely recognize the Arabic letters."

"Salima is starting weekend classes at the masjid after the winter break, *insha'Allah*," Aliyah said. "Maybe you can join."

"I don't think so." Deanna felt the knot in her stomach loosening itself and crawling back up her throat. She clamped her mouth shut and gritted her teeth until she was sure the threat of a scream had passed.

"Why not?" Aliyah's voice was hesitant, as if unsure she had the right to ask.

"I don't want all those sisters staring at me and talking about me behind my back." Aliyah was quiet, and Deanna sensed that Aliyah knew she was right. Aliyah herself had suffered the same. Deanna fought the flicker of guilt in realizing she was partly to blame for that.

"Then maybe Salima can teach you privately," Aliyah said, her tone thoughtful. "I'm sure she wouldn't mind. Maybe we could even study together."

Deanna's eyes widened as she looked at Aliyah in shocked disapproval. "You'd be willing to study with *me*?"

Aliyah shrugged. "Yes, why not?"

Deanna wrinkled her nose, feeling irritated with Aliyah all of a sudden. "Come on, Ally," she said, resorting to Aliyah's given name as she used to do sometimes. "Nobody's *that* forgiving. You must hate me at *least* as much as I hate you."

Aliyah's lips formed a thin line, and she pulled at a thread of her clothes. "I don't hate you, Deeja." Aliyah's voice was low, and Deanna thought she detected in it a tinge of hurt and offense. "And I don't think you hate me."

Deanna huffed. "Let's not pretend we don't know our history," she said. "*And* our present."

"I'm not," Aliyah said. "I just think *hate* is a strong word."

"Not if it's accurate."

Aliyah said nothing to that, and the implications of the silence sat like a bulky piece of unwanted furniture in the room. Neither of them denied it was there, yet neither of them attempted to move it.

The impasse seemed to stretch for several minutes and was interrupted only by the grumbling of Deanna's stomach and the simultaneous chiming and vibration of Aliyah's phone.

Immediately, Deanna thought of Jacob texting to check on Aliyah, and the infuriation she felt was so strong that she had to resist physically snatching Aliyah's phone. Instead, she pushed herself to a standing position, burrowing her fists into the carpet next to her. She bent over and yanked up her prayer mat and folded it in quick snaps of the heavy cloth. Firmly tucking the prayer mat under one arm, Deanna side-eyed Aliyah as she now folded the other prayer mat.

"That was Jacob, wasn't it?" Deanna said, glowering at Aliyah, furious accusation in her tone. It was all she could do to keep from boldly walking over to the couch and standing at Aliyah's shoulder.

"Yes," Aliyah said calmly. "He says the weather is getting worse, and they're forecasting a snowstorm that's supposed to last until three o'clock in the morning."

Deanna grunted, turning her back as she walked over to the small shelf and set the prayer mats there. "Then I guess I should get going," she said bitterly.

"He also said we should stay put," Aliyah added. "Because there are a lot of accidents out there, and the interstate is gridlocked."

Aliyah's use of the word *we* touched a soft space in Deanna's heart, but Deanna contorted her face, concealing her true feelings. "*We*?"

"Well, you, specifically," Aliyah clarified. "I wasn't planning on going anywhere anyway. He asked if I was willing to let you stay the night."

"How does he even know I'm here?" Deanna tone suggested that she was offended, but she was more pleasantly surprised than anything.

"I texted him before we prayed."

Deanna felt a lump in her throat. "What does he care if I get in an accident?"

Aliyah was silent for so long that Deanna thought she'd managed to annoy her. "Look, Deeja," Aliyah said finally. "No one's telling you what to do. If you want to go, I'm not going to try and stop you," she said. "It would just make him feel better if no one he cared about was out there in that storm right now."

"He doesn't care about me," Deanna muttered. But she was overcome with emotion at being referred to as someone Jacob cared about.

"And it would make me feel better too," Aliyah said sincerely. "The roads are all ice and snow, so it's better if you stay here tonight."

"You don't want me here."

"I don't want either of us here," Aliyah said. "I'd rather be at Salima's with my son."

Deanna huffed. Aliyah didn't say "and husband" but Deanna heard the implication.

The silence settled between them, and Deanna sensed another impasse. She wondered if Aliyah would ask her to leave outright since it was obvious she was just being hospitable to please Jacob.

"Deeja?" Aliyah said.

Deanna rolled her eyes knowingly. "I'm going *now*," she said as she walked toward the door.

"I'm not asking you to leave," Aliyah said. "We didn't even eat our gyros yet."

Folding her arms defiantly, Deanna halted her steps and turned around. "Gyros?" She pursed her lips in annoyance, but laughter tickled the back of her throat. She found the mention of gyros utterly ridiculous right then. "Girl, you're a trip," she said, a smirk on her face. "You can eat those gyros alone."

"I know. But I don't want to," Aliyah said, her tone serious. "And I won't be able to enjoy them if all I can think about is you being buried alive in a snowdrift somewhere."

Deanna burst out laughing. She had no idea why, but the vision of Aliyah munching on gyros while Deanna slowly died from hypothermia outside was hilarious.

Aliyah chuckled herself, apparently visualizing the same thing.

Recovering from laughter, Deanna shook her head, thoughts growing distant momentarily.

"Why did you come?" Aliyah asked after a thoughtful silence.

It took a moment for Deanna to register Aliyah's words. "What?" she said, regarding Aliyah with a question on her face.

"Today," Aliyah clarified. "Why'd you come?"

A twinge of embarrassment stabbed Deanna as she recalled waiting outside Aliyah's door for hours. Sighing, she walked over to the couch and sat on the far end opposite Aliyah. Deanna resumed folding her arms. "I don't know," she said, an edge of annoyance in her tone. "Does it matter?"

"To me it does," Aliyah said.

Deanna paused thoughtfully, and she felt a bitter taste in her mouth as she recalled her journal entry. *Apologize to Aliyah.*

"I came to apologize," Deanna grumbled finally, unable to look Aliyah in the eye. Deanna's stomach churned as she realized that she had spoken the dreaded words aloud. "I wanted to say I'm sorry," she added, the words nearly choking her, they were so difficult to form.

There was an extended silence, and Deanna sensed Aliyah's surprise. But she still couldn't bring herself to look at her.

"I'm trying to be a better person," Deanna mumbled.

## 35
## Reconciliation

"They have the problem that all good parents have. They don't see their children's scars or baggage. They only see everyone else's."

Salima felt herself growing upset at Jamil's statement. "Where is all of this coming from?" she said, her back to Jamil as she stood slicing carrots at a counter in the kitchen a Saturday evening in late December. She shook her head as the knife rhythmically hit the cutting board, her eyes on her task. "A few weeks ago, you were siding with them."

"*Siding* with them?" Jamil's voice rose in offense. "Do you really believe this is about taking sides? If there was even the *slightest* possibility that Larry is bad for you, I'd want you to know about it."

Salima halted the slicing and slammed the handle of the knife against the wooden cutting board before turning around and facing Jamil with her arms folded. "Oh, is that what that was about?" she said. "Your selfless brotherly concern? Then why didn't you drive up there yourself? Sending Jasmine to our parents' house was the worst thing you could've possibly done."

"I didn't *send* her there, Salima," Jamil said, his tone exhausted. "It was the only way to let you know about Larry without violating—"

"Attorney-client privilege," Salima said in unison with him, mockery in her tone as she nodded knowingly. "I know. I get it. Respect for your professional principles is the highest priority here," she said sarcastically. "But respect for *family* principles? That's negotiable."

"Well, apparently, I did *something* right," Jamil said. "You finally realized that Larry isn't good for you."

The fury that the statement ignited in Salima was so intense that she clenched her jaw and slowly turned back around toward the counter. She picked up the knife, and continued preparing the dinner salad in silence. For several minutes, the only sound that could be heard was the slow, steady chopping against the cutting board.

"Look, Salima," Jamil said, his tone softer and kinder this time. "I'm sorry if..."

Jamil's voice faded into the background of Salima's thoughts because she couldn't stand to listen anymore. Why did everyone keep saying that Larry wasn't good for her? Why did she believe it herself? And if he truly wasn't good for her, why couldn't her heart let go of him? Why was it so difficult to move on?

*"I don't know, Salima..."* Carletta had said doubtfully when Salima had asked her advice. *"I definitely think your parents have a point about the importance of marrying someone who was raised like you. But I don't know if I agree with the misogyny label for Larry's views. I could be wrong about this, but I'm getting to the point where I hate these labels. I used to call myself a feminist until I realized what it was doing to me. You get into this mental space where you find fault in almost everything and everyone, and for the stupidest things. Then you wake up*

*one day and find you've destroyed your life, and maybe other people's too, and you have no idea how you got there. But the worst part is what it does to you spiritually. I don't care what anybody says. In my opinion, if you really believe in these labels, you'll eventually find fault with religion and then God Himself, even if you never admit it out loud. So if you don't marry Larry, make sure it's because you truly believe he's not good for you or because he can't benefit your life or soul in a significant way. Not because his views fit into some feminist definition of sexist."*

Fear. The word settled upon Salima in accusation, and right away she recognized it as what was gripping her heart. It wasn't Larry or Jamil or her parents to blame for her apprehension. It was Salima herself. But she refused to absolve them completely. Larry could be more cognizant of the effects of his words. Jamil could be more concerned with more than his job. And Salima's parents could be less judgmental.

"You should have sent her to me," Salima said, cutting off Jamil midsentence as he was saying something she didn't even bother to process. She set down the knife and turned to face him again, this time with her hands on her hips. "If you really thought Jasmine had something important to say, you should've sent her to me," she said. "I'm right here in the city, and I'm the one you're trying to save. Why didn't you ask her to talk to me?"

"I did, but she—"

"Let me guess," Salima said with disinterest, putting up a hand. "She didn't want to. She said she wasn't, quote, *comfortable* talking to me."

"Well..."

"And you *fell* for that?" Salima coughed laughter.

An expression of frustration distorted Jamil's face. "Why do you do that?" he said. "Why do you always think any woman you don't like has some ulterior motive? First it was Muslimah. Now it's Jasmine. Maybe it's not just Larry who has a problem with women. Maybe you do too."

The defensive tone of Jamil's voice, the mention of Muslimah and Jasmine together, and the way his expression changed to distaste at the mention of Larry gave Salima the odd sensation that there was something her brother wasn't saying. "Wait a minute," she said as everything began to make sense. "You *like* Jasmine, don't you?"

His eyes slid to the side guiltily, but he managed to look defiant. "No," he said, but his tone was unconvincing. "But even if I did, why is that so horrible?"

"What about Muslimah?" Salima was asking out of pure curiosity and surprise, as she felt Muslimah was no better than Jasmine.

"What about her?" Jamil said with a defensive shrug.

"I thought you two were talking again."

"Who said we ever stopped?"

Salima nodded in sudden understanding, but it was more for herself than Jamil. She quietly turned back around and finished preparing dinner, knowing she would need to start as soon as possible looking for another place to stay. The signs had always been there, but it was only today that she saw them for what they were. Yes, there was that inkling of doubt, saying she could be wrong. Maybe Jamil was just being overly protective by encouraging Jasmine to talk to their parents. But her gut told her it was more complicated than that. He wasn't interested in saving Salima from a bad relationship. He was trying to destroy the good one she had.

But Jamil was right about one thing, Salima conceded. She did have a problem with women. It was why the vices of people like Deanna and Jasmine were so obvious to her, while she'd been completely blind to the vices of her own brother whom she lived with. But her blindness wasn't because she was sexist, misogynistic, or any other nonsense like that. It was because women were the only people she'd formed close, meaningful relationships with, such that she could have significant problems with them in the first place. With men she'd formed only one meaningful relationship, with Mikaeel, and he had been one of the good ones.

No, Jamil wasn't a bad person, Salima told herself. But he wasn't a good person either. He struggled with jealousy and resentment toward anyone who had what he felt he deserved. From childhood, he was extremely competitive and never liked being second best. There could be a thousand people behind him in a race, and he'd see only the solitary one who crossed the finish line ahead of him. But his gentle personality was the perfect mask—even if unintentional—for the frustrated disappointment that consumed him each day. And like so many people often did, Salima had interpreted her brother's unassuming personality as genuine humility and good character.

And she'd confused Larry's smug personality with arrogance and bad character.

Not many people knew Jamil was a lawyer, and it wasn't because he was humble about it. It was because he was ashamed about it. He wasn't a partner in the firm, and his name wasn't on the company plaque or stationery; so to him, that meant he wasn't a "real" lawyer.

"All I do is assist the name partners," he'd say whenever Salima asked him why he rarely mentioned his work. "When I become a *real* lawyer, I'll talk about it." He had a good salary and excellent benefits and was greatly valued at the firm, but that wasn't good enough.

Salima had always assumed Jamil's frustration was due to feeling he could do better for himself. But now she realized it was due to feeling others could do better for him.

"You're not perfect, you know," he'd often say to Salima. Usually, she'd laugh it off or say something lighthearted in return. Perhaps it was because he was her younger brother, but Salima rarely took his verbal jabs seriously.

"Can I ask you something?" Salima said, genuine curiosity in her tone. Her back was still to Jamil as she opened a cabinet and began removing dinner dishes.

"What?" There was an edge of impatience in Jamil's voice. But she sensed he didn't want to leave the conversation as they had. Even when he was a child, Jamil hated people thinking badly of him. So in order to avoid the possibility, either he'd say nothing and thus remain a mystery, or he'd over explain himself if he sensed someone's disapproval of him.

"Was the lawsuit inquiry the first time you and Jasmine talked?"

Several seconds passed in silence.

"No."

Salima nodded. In light of her recent realizations, she was not the least bit surprised by his answer. But she couldn't deny that she was deeply disappointed in her brother. "Did you contact her first, or did she contact you?"

There was a hesitant pause. "I don't remember," he said, but Salima sensed in his tone that he recalled more than he was willing to say.

"So you've been in touch for a while then, huh?" she said as she walked past him and set the stack of plates on the kitchen table.

Jamil shrugged. "We've been friends for a while."

"How'd you meet?"

"Through Larry."

*Of course.* She already knew that bit of information. That was how she herself had met Jasmine, the girlfriend of Jacob's brother. "After he became Muslim?"

Another hesitant pause. "I don't remember."

"Did you teach her about Islam?"

He shrugged again. "A bit..."

"Whose idea was it to discuss a lawsuit?"

Jamil walked over to the silverware drawer and removed the utensils they would need for dinner. "It's not what you think," he said in a low voice, an edge of defensiveness in his tone. "I didn't think she'd go through with it."

Salima's eyebrows rose. "So *you* suggested it?"

Jamil shook his head. "We were talking one day, and I told her that people sue for less than what she's been through." He carried the utensils to the kitchen table, avoiding her eyes. "I wasn't suggesting she actually take Larry to court."

Salima bit her lower lip as she arranged the plates on the table, trying not to reveal how upset she was at this revelation. "Is she going to go through with it?"

He shook his head again. "I don't think so."

They moved about the kitchen in silence for some time. "You wanted her to meet our parents," Salima said as she opened the refrigerator and peered inside. It wasn't a question, but she let the silence that followed suggest that it were. But Jamil didn't respond.

"And since you didn't want to say outright that it was because you liked her and wanted to marry her yourself," Salima continued, "you convinced her that it was because you were concerned about me."

Jamil still didn't respond.

Salima reached for a jug of homemade lemonade on the top shelf of the refrigerator and carefully lifted it with both hands. "Jasmine didn't want to make that drive. But you convinced her that it was the only way to keep me and Larry from getting married," she said. "But really, you just wanted her to meet Mom and Dad so they could bond somehow." She closed the refrigerator with her hip. "And what better way to do it than showing concern for their widowed daughter?"

Jamil said nothing as he now leaned against the counter next to the sink. But his expression suggested that he did not disagree.

Salima decided against mentioning that Jasmine's visit would also achieve the goal of making Salima look less admirable to their parents so that both she and Jamil could share the same parental scorn.

No, Jamil no longer cared about people thinking badly of him as much as he cared about people pitying him and thinking him weak. He'd always had somewhat of a savior complex when it came to women, but now he needed his sister and parents to think of him as a savior as well. He despised the sweet, helpless "little brother" image they had of him, so he was wedging a reputation for himself as a man.

"You can't save her," Salima said as she set the pitcher of lemonade on the table.

Jamil creased his forehead in confusion. "I can't save who?"

"Jasmine," Salima said. "She has to want to save herself."

Jamil coughed laughter, haughtiness in that sound. "I thought you didn't think she needed saving."

"I'm not talking about from Larry," Salima said. "I'm talking about from herself."

Jamil groaned and shook his head. "And you can't save *me*, Salima," he barked back. "Because I don't *want* to be saved."

He huffed. "You think you know why Muslimah and I got divorced, don't you?" he said, humored disappointment in his voice. "You think she got wrapped up in some crazy cult and some stupid sheikh said I wasn't good enough for her."

Salima furrowed her brows, taken aback by his words. "Wasn't it?"

Jamil chuckled and shook his head. "I was the one who introduced her to the sheikh in the first place."

Salima didn't know what to say. "But I thought…"

"I know what you thought." Jamil flipped his hand at her, impatience in his tone. "You and Mom and Dad have this fairytale view of Islam, like there are only two groups of Muslims. Us, and the rest of the people trying to lead us astray."

Stunned, Salima stared at her brother.

"I never believed we were right in the first place," he said. "How likely is it that *we're* the only ones on the right path?"

"I never said th—"

"You didn't have to," Jamil interjected. "You call people groupies and sectarian Muslims," he said bitterly. "As if *you* aren't part of a group or sect yourself."

"I'm not," Salima said defensively.

"You're part of the 'I have no *madh-hab* or group' sect."

"I don't think so," she said, miffed.

Jamil grinned as he brought a hand to his mouth. "Do you think *any* group *claims* to be breaking off into a sect?"

"Yes," she said firmly. "And you're very naïve if you believe every Muslim group is really trying to follow the Qur'an and Sunnah."

"*What*?" The amused expression on Jamil's face infuriated Salima.

She and her brother had had their share of arguments. But today felt different. There was a thick air of condescension in his tone, and she sensed that he was just getting started. It was as if he'd been waiting years for this moment, when he could tell her about herself.

"But I never said *we're* the only ones who are right," Salima said. "There are maybe millions of Muslims who believe we shouldn't be breaking up into sects."

"There you go again," Jamil said, extending his arm and pointing a finger at her, a smug grin still on his face. "You talk about other Muslims like they're the only ones with a problem."

"I never said that," Salima said. "But actions are by intention, and—"

"And you think other Muslims don't *intend* to do good?"

"—if you follow any teachings that you know aren't from the Prophet, *sallallaahu'alayhi wa sallam,* then you're *intending* to follow something other than the Sunnah."

"Well, I can assure you," Jamil said, mockery in his voice, "Muslimah and I were *intending* to follow the Sunnah."

Salima regarded Jamil, a curious expression on her face. "Why did you introduce her to the sheikh?"

Jamil shook his head, a smirk on his face. "The same reason anyone would introduce someone to a sheikh," he said. "Because he has a lot of knowledge."

"And because he's a *saint*?" Salima said, folding her arms as if in a challenge.

"*Wali,* saint, whatever," Jamil said. "It doesn't matter what you call him, but he sure has way more knowledge than *you.*" He grunted before adding, "*And* Mom and Dad."

"Is it time to eat yet?"

The small voice sounded so out of place that for a moment Salima had no idea where it had come from. It wasn't until Haroon pulled out a chair and sat down that she even remembered that he'd been upstairs the whole time.

"Yes, it is," Salima said softly, smiling down at him.

"I'll eat later," Jamil said gruffly then walked roughly past her.

Salima frowned after him, but she didn't say anything.

"Is Uncle Jamil sick?" Haroon asked, his innocent voice a sharp contrast to the argument moments before.

Salima was tempted to say, *"Yes he is."* But she knew that would be taking her anger too far. "I'm not sure, honey," she said finally. "But we can go ahead and eat."

***

Jacob leaned over and kissed Aliyah on the cheek then put his arm around her shoulder and pulled her close to him. It was late Saturday night and they sat on the couch of his living room, the boys having gone to bed a couple of hours before. Aliyah and Jacob were supposed to be watching a movie, but the sounds had quickly become background noise as they cuddled and chatted, reveling in each other's presence.

"I love you," Jacob murmured in her ear then playfully tugged at some of the two-strand twists at the back of her head.

"I love you too," Aliyah murmured back, unable to keep from grinning from how content she felt right then. Contentment permeated every part of her, even when she was not in Jacob's presence. She'd stayed married to Matt for more than ten years and had had one serious relationship as a teenager, but with neither of them did she feel internal contentment.

Before Jacob, Aliyah had always assumed that happiness was a fleeting, even if frequent, emotion in a good relationship, not part of the fabric of it. As a teenager, she had been giddy in her boyfriend's presence and, due to her low self-esteem, was happy to be desired at all. But after she and her boyfriend graduated from high school and went their separate ways, Aliyah realized that she'd been more in love with the idea of being in love than she'd been actually in love.

"You do?" Jacob teased, tickling Aliyah's side.

"Ye-es," she said, between bursts of giggles as she squirmed but was unable to wriggle free of him.

"Prove it," he said as he abruptly stopped tickling her and slipped an arm around her waist and pulled her close to him.

Aliyah smirked and started to ask what he meant, but he cut her off by kissing her softly on the lips. She relaxed as he leaned into her and kept kissing her, and she felt her heart racing in eagerness to be closer to him.

"I just need to make sure you're real," he whispered.

Aliyah opened her mouth to speak but her breath caught as he brought her hand to his lips and kissed it too. A second later he stood and scooped her off the couch and carried her up to his office, where he now kept a fold-out mattress.

*"We're going to make our own memories,"* Jacob had told Aliyah when he first showed it to her. *"Before marrying you, all I ever did in this room was work. It was the one place in the house that was only mine. I used to consider it my oasis,"* he told her. *"Now it really is."*

***

"Why did you keep saying no to me?" Jacob asked an hour later as they lay in the darkness of his home office, a streetlight outside the window creating a soft glow on their faces. "I mean, before we got married?" His head was propped up by a fist, his elbow in the fold-out mattress beneath them as his free hand toyed with the twists of Aliyah's air, his expression reflective.

Aliyah drew in a deep breath and exhaled, unsure how to answer the question. It was difficult to put into words. Her instinct was to say Deanna, but she now knew that wasn't fully true.

Going through a divorce had made the entire world seem like an unstable place. Nothing and no one was safe anymore. The possibility of someone genuinely caring for her, especially a man, was an experience she associated with fairytales and an eternal life after death. It didn't help that her own parents and siblings had abandoned her long before Matt did, so Aliyah was morose in the most visceral way. Burdened by feelings of worthlessness, she was afraid to trust again. It was too risky. Trust had only brought pain and abandonment. So it was safest to trust only herself.

And then there was the part of Aliyah that had believed what Deanna had said about her. Aliyah didn't know how to keep a man. She didn't know how to keep a marriage. She didn't even know how to keep her own family. *"If you can't find a way to have a good relationship with your own parents,"* Deanna would often say, *"then that says a lot about your Islam."* And perhaps it did say a lot about her Islam, Aliyah considered. It was a possibility that she didn't dismiss, even now.

"I was scared," Aliyah said finally, her voice low as she was lost in thought. "Marrying you went against everything I thought I believed."

Jacob was silent for so long that she feared that she'd offended him. "I know what you mean," he said finally. "I never thought I'd try to marry another wife, and I never thought I'd get a divorce."

Aliyah frowned thoughtfully as she looked toward him. "Really?"

He nodded as a reflective grin creased one corner of his mouth. "The Bivens are upstanding members of the community," he said, lighthearted sarcasm in his tone.

She coughed agreement. "Sounds like the Thomases."

He huffed and shook his head. "Sounds like the everybody, if you ask me," he said. "I don't think I've ever met a person who didn't at least at some point in their life imagine that their family was some remarkable gift to the world or an exception to all the corruption on earth." A shadow of sadness fell over his face. "Even the ones who come from the most miserable backgrounds."

Aliyah was quiet as she remembered the heartbreaking conversation that she and Deanna had had late into the night during the snowstorm. "Deanna told me about her cousin Bailey," she said, her tone heavy with sadness. "It makes me feel bad that I wasn't more patient with her."

Jacob sighed and dropped his fist to the bed and lay on his back, staring at the ceiling. "She told me after we got married." He spoke as if the memory still haunted him. "That's why I stayed so long."

Aliyah was quiet as she imagined the pain that Jacob must have gone through all those years. "You did the right thing."

Jacob exhaled in a single breath, unmasked self-reproach in that sound. "Did I?" Jacob's face was contorted in disagreement when he turned his head to look at

Aliyah. "I don't think so," he said, returning his gaze to the ceiling. "I should've never married her in the first place."

"You don't mean that…"

He shook his head, and Aliyah could see the firmness of his jawline in the dim light. "I do mean it," he said in a tone that suggested there was not a shred of doubt in his words. "And not because I think she was a horrible person," he said. "But because I think I was a horrible husband." He shook his head again. "She needed someone else. I just hope she finds him one day."

His tone was so regretful that it pained Aliyah to listen. "I didn't know anything about that kind of trauma," he said. "So I had no business trying to be her savior."

"But you didn't know until after you were married," Aliyah said softly, hoping her words would soothe him somehow.

"That's no excuse," Jacob said. "The signs were there long before then, clear as day."

Aliyah contorted her face in disapproval. "How?" she said. "You're not psychic."

"But my gut told me something was off from day one."

"Twenty-twenty hindsight," she said.

He placed one hand behind his head, his gaze still upwards. "Maybe," he muttered.

"Guilt and obligation get all of us, I think," Aliyah said reflectively. "It's hard to get away from because, like you told me before we got married, sometimes it's connected to pleasing Allah."

Jacob turned his head toward Aliyah, a curious smirk on his face. "*I* told you that?"

She smiled back at him. "Yes you did," she said. "Your exact words were, 'You have to be careful with that though. Guilty obligation isn't mutually exclusive to pleasing Allah.'"

"Hmm," he said thoughtfully. "I don't remember."

"You had stopped by my office and I started complaining about how my Islamic studies teachers had made me feel guilty instead of inspired, so I started doing things out of guilty obligation instead of trying to please Allah."

An expression of recollection passed over his face, and Aliyah smiled as she saw that his spirits had lifted. "Was that the day we were talking about that James Allen quote on your wall?" he said.

"*Adapted* quote to be exact," Aliyah said, a smile in her voice.

"We are anxious to improve our circumstances," Jacob recited, "but are unwilling to improve ourselves. We therefore remain bound."

"You have a good memory, *mashaAllah*," she teased, nudging him playfully with her elbow.

He chuckled. "It's really not that hard to remember, especially since I've read *As a Man Thinketh* a zillion times."

“Really? I thought I was the only nerd at the college.”

“Ha ha ha,” Jacob said, nudging her back.

“You think Dr. Warren would’ve really made me take it down if I’d left it as the original quote?” Aliyah said. “I went back and forth a few times before I decided it was safest to change *men* to *we*.”

Jacob shrugged. “I don’t know… She can surprise you sometimes, in a good way I mean. But I think your decision was wisest, especially since you were new there. The last thing you want to do is get on your supervisor’s bad side.”

Aliyah chuckled. “Too late for that.”

“Well…” Jacob said, humor in his tone, purposefully leaving his thought unfinished.

“Speaking of which,” Aliyah said, her voice rising cheerfully. “One of my atheist students had an epiphany.”

“What’s that?” Jacob said, looking at Aliyah, humored expectation in his voice.

“God exists!”

Jacob cackled in laughter.

“I know…” Aliyah said, laughter in her own voice.

“Did you tell her that God never ceased to exist, even when she was an atheist?”

“No,” Aliyah said, a smile in her voice. “I didn’t want to ruin her special moment.”

“*MashaAllah*,” Jacob said, his tone more subdued. “May Allah guide her.”

“Ameen.”

There was an extended silence, and Aliyah felt her limbs growing weak with exhaustion. She shifted her position so that she was lying with her back against Jacob, and he immediately wrapped his arms around her and pulled her close.

“I got the weirdest text yesterday,” Jacob said, a tinge of tiredness in his voice.

“What’s that?” Aliyah said as she settled comfortably in his arms.

“Deanna was saying that she thought the colors teal and black would work best for our theme colors,” he said.

“Oh yeah,” Aliyah said with a groan, remembering just then Deanna calling a week ago to say that she had decided to become proactive in getting beyond the past. “She calls herself helping plan our *waleemah*.”

“How did she even find out about it?”

Aliyah cringed in embarrassment. “I think it came up the night she stayed over.”

Jacob sighed, but Aliyah could tell he was more concerned than upset. “And you invited her?”

“No…”

“And you didn’t ask her to help plan it?”

“Of course not.”

“Then why would she text me something like that?”

"I think she considers this part of her healing process," Aliyah said, overcome with dread.

"Taking over our *waleemah*?" Jacob said in disbelief.

"I guess so..."

"And you're okay with that?"

Aliyah was quiet, unsure how to respond. In truth, she wasn't even sure she wanted Deanna there at all. But given that it would be an open invitation to the Muslim community, she didn't see how she could un-invite Deanna, especially since she was the mother of Aliyah's stepsons. "Not really," she said, embarrassment in her tone. "But I keep thinking, is it really such a bad thing, you know? I mean, what's the worst that could happen?"

Jacob huffed. "Trust me," he said. "That's not a question you want honestly answered in the context of Deanna."

There was a thoughtful pause. "She's seeing a psychiatrist now, isn't she?" Aliyah asked.

"Yes, finally," Jacob said, relief in his tone. "It was like pulling teeth to convince her that we couldn't start co-parenting counseling together until we did individual counseling on our own."

"*We*?" Aliyah repeated in confusion.

"Well," he said with a sigh, "you know how it is with her. She can't feel like she's the only one who needs help. So I told her I'd look into it too."

"And you really plan to?"

He was silent momentarily. "I'm thinking about it."

"But why?" Aliyah said, disapproval in her tone. "You're not mentally ill. She is."

"I never thought I was," Jacob said. "I just think it can help, you know..."

"With what?" Aliyah turned her head as far as she could.

"I have a lot of emotional baggage myself," he said.

"Don't we all?" she said. "That doesn't mean we need a psychiatrist. Some things we just have to give to Allah."

"And you think they're mutually exclusive?" he said doubtfully. "Allah sends down the disease, and He sends down the cure. And that's not just with physical diseases."

Aliyah sighed thoughtfully. "Just be careful..."

"Of what?"

"Some of these people have a God complex."

Jacob grunted agreement. "I know," he said. "That's why I'm dragging my feet. I've heard a lot of horror stories, especially from Muslims going to psychologists who were not understanding of Islam, to put it lightly."

"That's what I'm talking about," Aliyah said. "Everyone isn't qualified to advise us. They want to blame everything on our religion and try to convince us to leave Islam."

"Or suggest healing methods that contradict our faith," he said, "even if they're not doing it on purpose."

"Well, you won't see me going to one of them, *insha'Allah*," Aliyah said with conviction. "I don't trust a single one of them, even the Muslim ones."

"Are you serious?" Jacob sounded surprised.

"As a heart attack," Aliyah said. "Deanna was my introduction to Muslim mental health professionals, and I think I've heard enough for a lifetime."

A thoughtful silence followed. "You're going to let her help with the *waleemah*?" Jacob asked.

Aliyah sighed. "At this point, I don't think I have a choice."

"Don't do it unless you really want to."

"That's the thing," she said. "I don't know what I want. A part of me is scared to have her as an active part of my life again, especially for something so personal. But there's another part of me that's relieved and excited." She frowned self-consciously. "Does that make any sense?"

"It makes a lot of sense," Jacob said tentatively. "But I don't want you to do something you'll regret, especially on a day that should be about you."

"Do you mind if she's involved?"

"*Me*?" Jacob spoke as if the thought had never crossed his mind. "I don't mind either way, as long as you're happy." There was a brief pause as he seemed to be lost in thought. "I just fear this isn't going to end well," he said honestly.

"I know… I fear the same thing," Aliyah said. "But it's so refreshing to see her happy again."

"Again?" Jacob said, humor in his tone.

Aliyah chuckled self-consciously. "Well, it's refreshing to see her *happy*," she said. "And if I can be a part of making that happen, then I'm honored."

"As long as it's what you want to do," Jacob said, concern and doubt in his tone. "I mean, considering everything."

Aliyah nodded. "It is," she said sincerely. "It's not ideal," she admitted. "But I think we can make it work."

***

"Mashael!" Aliyah squealed into the phone Sunday morning as she held her cell phone between her shoulder and ear as she stood in front of the stove in Jacob's kitchen. She set down the spatula she had been using to tease the eggs then pulled the cell phone away from her ear. She turned to where Jacob stood at the counter dicing raw kale. "It's Mashael," she whispered, an excited grin on her face.

Jacob chuckled. "I heard," he joked. But Aliyah had already turned back around, picked up the spatula, and was engrossed in animated conversation, the phone back between her shoulder and ear. Jacob smiled to himself, pleased to see his wife happy.

“Is Sheldon with you?” he heard Aliyah say, hope in her voice. There was a brief pause. “Of course! We’re fixing breakfast now.” Another pause. “No, it’s no problem really…Great. *Insha’Allah*, we’ll see you soon.”

Aliyah set her phone on the kitchen table then walked back over to the stove. “Can you believe it?” she said, a smile in her voice as she shook her head, glancing at Jacob as she held the spatula in hand. “I almost didn’t answer.”

“So…” Jacob said in lighthearted teasing. “Are we having company?”

“Oh my God,” Aliyah said, apology in her tone. “Is it okay?”

Jacob laughed and shook his head. “I guess it is now, huh?”

“I’m sorry,” Aliyah said. “I was so excited, I didn’t even think to ask you first.”

“It’s okay, really,” Jacob said, and meaning it. “I’ll just wake up the boys so they can help me straighten up a bit.”

He set down the knife and gathered the chopped kale with both hands then walked it over to the stove and sprinkled it atop the scrambled eggs. “How far are they?”

“She said they’re about twenty minutes away.”

“From the city, or from here?”

“From h—” Aliyah’s eyes widened, leaving her response unfinished. She quickly dropped the spatula on the counter then hurried to the kitchen table to pick up her phone.

“What’s wrong?” Jacob said, concern in his voice.

“I think they’re on their way to my apartment,” Aliyah said, her forefinger quickly unlocking the screen and tapping the call log. “I forgot to tell her we’re here.”

As Aliyah walked out the kitchen with the phone to her ear to give Mashael the address, Jacob picked up the spatula. Folding the kale into the eggs, Jacob remembered the call he’d gotten from the realtor about the house. There was a family interested in buying and wanted to schedule a tour. Jacob had said he’d get back with them after he checked his schedule, but it had been two days, and he couldn’t bring himself to confirm a time.

Initially, selling the house seemed like the logical thing to do. This was a house he’d bought for him and Deanna, and he and Aliyah needed to start anew. It was even important for Younus and Thawab to have a fresh start, he’d decided. Having Aliyah as a stepmother in the same home in which their mother had lived would be confusing to them, he’d thought. But now he wasn’t so sure. Having Aliyah around, though only occasionally, had given life to the house in a way that Jacob had never imagined. Younus and Thawab laughed more, played more, and even talked more freely.

*“Divorce doesn’t have to be tragic,”* he remembered hearing a relationship expert say during a television interview. *“I’m still not sure why we prefer to believe it must be,”* she’d said, *“especially when there are so many more tragic stories from the homes of two people who would never even consider divorce.”* At the time, Jacob was still married to Deanna and didn’t give the expert’s words much

thought except to assume they were in reference to men and women who remained in abusive relationships.

"Why do we do that?" Aliyah had asked Jacob during a conversation one day. "Why do we put rules on ourselves that Allah doesn't? If Allah hates divorce, He hates even more for us to destroy our lives and souls," she'd said. "And that doesn't only happen when you're married to a monster."

*O Allah,* the Istikhaarah prayer said, *if you know this situation to be bad for me with regards to my religion, my life and my welfare in the life to come, then distance it from me, and distance me from it...*

"Does the *du'aa* say, 'O Allah, if you know this person to be abusive and horrible'?" Aliyah had asked rhetorically. "Then we shouldn't be saying it to ourselves when deciding what to do."

***

Aliyah had no idea why she was so ecstatic at the prospect of seeing Mashael. It wasn't like they had been particularly close or anything. But ever since the day Reem had said that Mashael had gone missing, there was a part of Aliyah that was genuinely worried about her. But when Jacob opened the front door, and Sheldon and Mashael stepped inside, hand-in-hand, faces beaming in the obvious signs of young love, Aliyah knew right away that she'd had no cause to worry. Mashael even looked better than when Aliyah had seen her last.

Dressed in wide-legged pants, a knee-length open sweater, and high-heel boots, Mashael showed no signs of stress, obvious or suppressed, and she exuded an aura of confidence and sophistication.

"You look good, *mashaAllah,*" Aliyah said after they exchanged salaams and Mashael and Sheldon removed their shoes.

"You guys relax and enjoy yourselves," Jacob said, a smile in his voice as he and Sheldon entered the living room behind Mashael. "And we'll serve *you.*"

"Ooooh," Mashael whispered as she squeezed Aliyah's arm playfully. "So romantic, *mashaAllah.*"

"I want to help too," Younus said, trailing behind his father into the kitchen, Thawab on his heels.

"I guess I don't have to ask if *you're* happy," Mashael teased as they settled on the couch next to each other.

"Look who's talking," Aliyah joked back, playfully nudging her.

Mashael grinned as she briefly turned her gaze toward the entrance to the kitchen where her husband had gone. "It's amazing, Aliyah," she whispered. "I still can't believe it's actually real."

Aliyah sighed, a grin on one side of her mouth. "I know what you mean..."

"We would've been stupid to give up something like this just because so many people disapproved."

Aliyah nodded emphatically. “It scares me to think what would’ve happened if my uncle didn’t practically trick me into getting married that day,” she said, laughter in her voice.

“That was so romantic, *wallah*,” Mashael said. “I was so happy for you.”

“I wish I could’ve been there for you,” Aliyah said.

“I know…” Mashael said, a sad but pleased smile lingering on her face. “But we really didn’t have much of a choice, you know?”

Aliyah moved her head in the beginning of a nod then realized she had no idea what she was agreeing with. “You couldn’t have invited at least a few of us?” she said in lighthearted teasing.

Mashael’s expression changed to one of self-conscious reflection. “No, I don’t think so.” She shook her head. “I didn’t want my family to be able to blame anyone. Arabs can be pretty hot-tempered, and they don’t forget easily,” she said. “They hold grudges for generations.”

Aliyah chuckled. “Who would even remember anything a hundred years later?”

“Arabs,” Mashael said, not a hint of sarcasm in her voice.

“But no one who is alive now will even be alive then,” Aliyah said in humored disbelief.

“But their children will be,” Mashael said. “My parents and grandparents and aunts and uncles have told us stories of our families’ problems with rival tribes that happened even before *their* generation,” she said. “And we’re not allowed to marry into those tribes even today.”

“What?” Aliyah said, laughter in her voice. “You’re kidding.”

Mashael shook her head, a solemn expression on her face. “I wish I were.”

Unsure what to say, Aliyah was silent, a half-smile of disbelief lingering on her face.

“Maybe now when you read the *seerah* of the Prophet, *sallallaahu’alayhi wa sallam*, you can really appreciate how remarkable his life and marriages were in his culture,” Mashael said good-naturedly. “I know I certainly can. What he did would be controversial in the Arab world even today.” She coughed laughter. “And we call ourselves modern.”

There was an extended pause. “I bet Reem was really relieved to know you’re okay,” Aliyah said, intentionally changing the subject.

“Reem?” Mashael said, creasing her forehead in confusion.

“She was afraid something might have happened to you.”

Mashael rolled her eyes knowingly. “*Tab’an*,” she said. “Why am I not surprised? Anything that doesn’t include the Muhammad family is a tragedy to her and my parents.”

Aliyah furrowed her brows. “You haven’t spoken to them?”

“No.” Mashael’s firm tone suggested that the answer should be obvious. “What do we have to talk about?”

"At least let them know you're okay." Aliyah had meant it as a friendly suggestion, but she heard the reprimand in her voice.

"They know I'm okay, Aliyah," Mashael said in a bored tone. "They just don't want me to think they do."

Aliyah drew her eyebrows together. "Why do you say that? I think they're really worried."

"Aliyah, *habeebti*," Mashael said, her voice sounding slightly condescending, but Aliyah could tell that Mashael didn't mean it that way, "my family has enough resources to find out anything about anybody they want, especially their own flesh and blood. Believe me, they *know* I'm okay."

"And Reem?" Aliyah said, sounding surprised. "You think she's pretending to be worried about you?"

Mashael lifted a shoulder in a shrug. "I don't know about Reem," she said honestly. "They probably don't say too much to her because they want her to track me down herself and guilt me back into keeping in touch." She sucked her teeth. "Or coming back home."

Aliyah was silent momentarily, unsure what to think. "You don't plan to keep in touch?"

"I know what you're thinking. *Silatur-rahm*," Mashael said.

"Well, keeping the ties of the womb is really important," Aliyah said, a tinge of defense in her voice.

Mashael offered Aliyah a weak smile. "Why don't you let me worry about that?" she said. "I'm not trying to cut ties with my family. I just need some time to myself for a while. I know some *shuyookh* would say even that's *haraam*." She shrugged nonchalantly. "But they're not living my life. I am."

Aliyah nodded. "I'm sorry. I just—"

"It's okay," Mashael said with a wave of her hand. "I'm just tired of everyone saying Allah will put me in Hellfire if I don't do every single thing my parents want." She shook her head. "I know most Muslims believe that. But I don't."

"Probably because of the high status of parents in Islam," Aliyah suggested.

"Maybe," Mashael said noncommittally. "But I think everyone has a high status in Islam. Parents don't just get free reign to stomp all over you for the rest of your life. I have the right to make *some* decisions on my own."

"That's true…"

"You have no idea how it feels to have someone try to control *everything* in your life," Mashael said, frustration in her tone. "I feel like I can't even breathe when I'm around them."

Hearing Mashael's complaints, Aliyah thought of her own family and saw her circumstance from a different perspective. Perhaps it was a hidden blessing that her parents had cut her off. She couldn't imagine how her life would be if they had tried to keep her close. She would probably be forced to do just what Mashael had done.

***

*Helping others is one of the most therapeutic things you can do*, the self-help book had said. *But start slow. You don't want to overwhelm yourself if being around people is painful for you. If you suffered abuse, neglect, or abandonment in childhood from someone you trusted, you'll likely have a hard time giving of yourself to others. You'll probably work to sabotage friendships and romantic relationships before they become too close, or you might avoid personal interactions altogether so that the opportunity never presents itself. Either way, this tendency can make your desire to help others an arduous task, especially if the person is a friend or loved one from a relationship you sabotaged in the past.*

Deanna lifted the bolt of teal polyester satin fabric and fought the surge of resentment as she placed it in the shopping cart next to the bolt of black fabric late Sunday morning. She wheeled the cart to the cutting table and waited for someone to come help her.

"Maybe you're right," Aliyah had said during the night Deanna stayed at her apartment and Deanna had mentioned that Matt didn't treat her like he should have. "But I honestly don't think it was his fault. I can't imagine how hard that was for him being married to me when he really wanted to be with someone else."

Perhaps Aliyah hadn't intended the comment to insult Jacob's marriage to Deanna, but Deanna had heard the accusation in Aliyah's words. But she reminded herself of what she'd read. *Everything isn't about you.*

"May I help you?" a fabric store worker said as he approached the cutting table.

***

"I'm pregnant."

Aliyah sucked in her breath and brought a hand to her mouth in surprise. "Are you serious?" she said.

Grinning, Mashael nodded, clearly proud of herself. "That's why I came today. I had to tell *somebody.*"

Aliyah thought of Reem and her family not knowing about a grandchild or niece or nephew about to come into the world, and it made her sad. But she kept her thoughts to herself. Like Mashael had said, the people with all the opinions about her life weren't the ones who had to live it.

A smile creased the sides of Aliyah's mouth. "Will you come to our *waleemah*?"

"*Tab'an*!" Mashael said. "I wouldn't miss it, *insha'Allah*. When is it?"

"In two weeks *insha'Allah*, at the masjid," Aliyah said. "I can text you the de—" The ringing of the doorbell interrupted her midsentence, and she immediately stood and creased her forehead as she walked toward the door.

"Are we expecting anyone?" Aliyah called out to Jacob as she passed the kitchen.

"Yes," he replied. "That's probably Larry."

When Aliyah opened the door, she saw Salima and Haroon standing opposite her. "*As-salamu'alikum*," Salima greeted as she and her son stepped inside. "Larry said we could meet him here. I hope it's okay."

"Yes, of course," Aliyah said, a confused smile on her face. "But I thought…"

"I know, I know," Salima said, waving her hand in embarrassment as she kneeled to take off Haroon's coat and boots. "I'll explain later *insha'Allah*."

"Well, I'm happy for the both of you," Aliyah beamed as she took Haroon's coat and hung it on the cast iron coat tree in the foyer. "I was really upset when you said you cut it off."

"I think you should save your congratulations then," Salima said as she unbuttoned her coat. "Today would be the first time we talked since everything fell apart."

"Really?" Aliyah said, helping Salima take off her coat then turning to hang it next to Haroon's.

"I texted him after *Fajr* to ask if we could talk, and I didn't hear back from him until about an hour ago," Salima said, disappointment in her voice. She kneeled to pull off her boots and aligned them next to her son's before standing and facing Aliyah again. "And all he said was that Jacob said it's fine for us to meet here." She gave Aliyah a tightlipped smile as she lifted her arms from her side then let them fall back down. "So here I am."

"Well, you're looking fly, *mashaAllah*," Aliyah teased as she gave Salima an approving once-over.

Salima smiled self-consciously as she placed the flat of her hand on her black pullover cashmere sweater with a large turtleneck and glanced down at her braided khaki wool skirt. "Thanks, *mashaAllah*."

"Where'd you get that black and khaki blend head wrap?" Aliyah said, admiring the way Salima had wrapped the cloth in a low turban style in the front and a cloth bun at the back.

"One of my Qur'an teachers bought it in Dubai and gave it to me as a gift," Salima said, lifting a palm to touch it gently. "It's actually really old, but you'd never—"

"Is that Salima, *wallah*?"

Salima stopped midsentence, apparently confused by the strange voice. But when she saw Mashael coming toward her with her arms outstretched for a hug, Salima grinned wide. "Mashael? What are *you* doing here?"

Mashael giggled as she drew Salima into a hug. "I'm pregnant and I couldn't keep the good news to myself."

"*MashaAllah*!" Salima exclaimed in excitement. "May Allah bless it to be an easy pregnancy and delivery, and may He give your child good health and strong *emaan* until they meet Him."

"*Ameen, yaa Rabb*!" Mashael said as they released each other.

"Is Reem here too?" Salima asked in anticipation.

Mashael gave Salima a playful pout. "No… Sorry. I'm only sharing the good news with my *real* family."

Salima chuckled and shook her head as they followed Aliyah to the couch. "Girl, you're a trip. You better call your *real* family and tell them the good news, too."

"I will, *insha'Allah*," Mashael said, and Aliyah sensed that Mashael wasn't comfortable opening up to Salima just yet.

The doorbell rang again just as the three of them settled on the couch. "I'll get that," Aliyah said, getting up immediately. "It's probably Larry."

"No," Salima said, standing up and placing a hand on Aliyah's arm to stop her. "Let me."

Cheeks going warm with embarrassment, Aliyah sat back down, realizing how awkward her enthusiasm must have sounded. She was sure that Salima knew the enthusiasm was connected to her excitement for Salima, but Aliyah sensed she should have known that she was the last person who should open the door at a time like this.

***

"You know, I had a bad feeling about the whole parent thing," Larry said from where he leaned against a wall opposite Salima in the hallway leading to Jacob's office. It was the only place that they could talk outside of earshot of the other guests without being completely alone.

Salima nodded humbly. "I'm sorry," she said, her voice subdued and her gaze lowered. "I guess I never saw that side of them before."

"Then there's a lot you don't know about them," he said, a reflective smirk creasing one side of his mouth.

Eyebrows drawn together, she looked up at him. "What do you mean?"

"No parents are completely hands-off, Salima. At least not ones who care."

He huffed and shook his head. "But I partly blame myself," he said.

"Why?" Salima said, pulling her head back in surprise.

"Because my gut told me that I should go to your parents myself," he said. "Alone." He shook his head again, clearly upset with himself. "But I called myself being respectful and trusting your judgment. After all, they're *your* parents." There was a tinge of sarcasm in his tone. "But something kept telling me, 'Larry, you know how narcissistic parents can be, especially when it comes to their daughters. They always think the worst of anyone they didn't pick out themselves.'"

Salima coughed laughter. "You know, Jamil said something similar," she reflected. "He said, 'They have the problem that all good parents have. They don't see their children's scars or baggage. They only see everyone else's.'"

There was an awkward pause, and Salima sensed that she'd said something wrong.

Larry grunted in disinterest. "Well, at least he's got *that* much right."

The sarcastic tone of Larry's voice made Salima wary, and she wondered if he'd found out about Jasmine's trip to her parents, and Jamil's involvement. "Why do you say it like that?" she said, careful to keep her tone neutral.

"You tell me," Larry shot back, his eyes fiery in accusation and hurt. "You're the one with all the secrets."

Salima winced at the harshness of his tone. "Did Jacob tell you about—"

"About what?" His voice rose challengingly. "Jasmine's little trip to your parents? Or Jamil backstabbing me?" He huffed and pushed himself off the wall as he shook his head in disbelief. "Or maybe there's something about *you* that Jacob might have told me?" he said, bitter sarcasm in his tone. "You know, since I'm in the dark about so much."

Larry contorted his face as if a thought had come to him suddenly. "And what did you want to talk to me about anyway?" His eyes were narrowed as he regarded her. "Why'd you suddenly feel the need to talk to me *today*?"

Cheeks aflame in embarrassment, Salima looked away and folded her arms. There was so much she wanted to say to Larry, but she had no idea where to begin, or even how to put her thoughts into words. She feared everything would come out wrong.

The past couple of weeks had been tortuous for Salima, and not only because she hadn't spoken to Larry and was deeply conflicted about the judiciousness of marrying him. This time period also represented a turning point in her relationship with her parents, and she didn't know how to make sense of it. She'd never disagreed with her parents on anything significant, at least not on anything that could affect her interactions with them in any significant way. But now she was beginning to see her parents in a different light, in a more conflicted light. But she had trouble letting go of her blind trust of them. Before this experience, she hadn't even realized she trusted them blindly at all.

Yet the argument with Jamil the day before uncovered wounds that she didn't even know were there. How was it that she had known her younger brother since he was a baby yet had never seen him until now? Maybe Jamil was right. Maybe she and her parents viewed the world through such a narrow lens that they couldn't process any differing outlook except that they felt compelled to view it with judgment and condescension. Salima had no idea who her own family was, she'd misjudged them so poorly.

And what if she exercising the same poor judgment with Larry? That was the question that had haunted her even before the argument with Jamil.

But it had taken her all the way until this morning to realize that she'd never know the answer to that question. And she was okay with that. *Marriage is an issue of the* ghayb, *the unseen,* she herself would often say. That was why seeking advice and making *Istikhaarah* were the best you could do after taking an honest look at who was in front of you, or at least at what you could see of them.

*"You're trying to play God,"* Carletta had told her. *"And you can't. What-if questions are useless, so just deal with what is."*

*"What if I don't know what is?"* Salima had said, inciting a fit of laughter from Carly.

*"Do you hear yourself?"* Carletta said. *"You said 'what if' again. Come on, Salima, what are you* really *afraid of here? That Larry is a bad person? Or that he's a good person that you're about to let go?"*

Salima nibbled at her lower lip and glanced up at Larry hesitantly. "I texted you..." The words got caught in her throat as she realized the enormity of what she was about to say.

If she hadn't known before, Salima knew with certainty right then. Carletta was right. What scared Salima most wasn't that Larry was a horrible person lurking behind a façade of goodness. It was that Larry was a sincere, goodhearted person that the world couldn't see because they were so distracted by the flaws that they could see. And Salima was afraid to be the person to show them.

"...because I wanted to..." She faltered, dropping her head in self-rebuke, frustrated that it was so difficult to get the words out.

"Because you wanted to *what*, Salima?" Larry said, impatient annoyance lacing his words.

Salima recited a silent prayer that Allah would guide her words and make this easy for her. "I'm sorry," she muttered, offering Larry a weak smile. "This isn't easy for me."

Larry folded his arms. "I'm here," he said, and it was obvious he was trying hard not to be brusque.

"Thank you," she mumbled gratefully, trying to gather her thoughts.

Salima had always been the golden child, not only in her family but also in the Muslim community. Her parents enrolled her in *hifdh* school when she was only five years old, and even there, amongst children from predominately Muslim and Arabic-speaking countries, she was the star. She not only memorized more quickly than the other children, she also recited with such proper pronunciation that she implemented the *Tajweed* rules with the ease and precision of one who'd formally studied them for years.

Students and their parents envied her. Her Qur'an teachers praised her. And from what her teachers said of her, Qur'an scholars oceans and continents away took a special interest in Salima, an interest that eventually led to her attaining her *ijaazah*, the honored certification that her style of recitation could be traced back to Prophet Muhammad himself.

Even when Salima had gone through her own spiritual crisis and removed her hijab, at some moments even coming close to giving up Islam, no one took notice. Because she was the golden girl, the pride of the African-American Muslim community, no one saw Salima as the flawed, sometimes broken human being that she was. It was a painful, terrifying, lonely experience, that invisibility. To have no one see you even as you stood at arm's length, to have no one hear you even as you spoke from your heart, to have no one see your tears even as they fell from your eyes.

*I know when the cruelty is coming,* Salima had said to herself once. *Right after the praise. I have no idea why, but many people feel you owe them for thinking well of you.*

"Because I need you," Salima said, the words dislodging themselves from her heart and settling, finally, upon her tongue. But she couldn't look at Larry as she spoke them. These were words she'd never even spoken to Mikaeel. Because there had been no occasion to.

Mikaeel, she knew now, was one of the people who had been blinded by his admiration of her. He often second-guessed himself in her presence, thinking her knowledge of Qur'an gave her a better understanding of everything else. He rarely openly disagreed with her, she realized in retrospect, probably because he didn't feel he had a right to. Even when she, in hotheaded female jealousy and insecurity, had insisted that he keep his own sister out of their home because of Salima's fear that polygamy was somehow contagious, he had acquiesced. But there was often this underlying frustration and resentment from him that would surface at the most inopportune times.

The last night she'd seen Mikaeel alive he had planned a surprise weekend trip for her and the children, as he loved spontaneity and surprises. When he announced the trip and told her to pack her things, she had to fight a wave of annoyance. He hadn't even taken time to research her schedule before making the plans. She'd been asked by a women's shelter to lead their Muslim residents in *Taraweeh* each night in Ramadan as part of an interfaith community service initiative.

*"But, Mickey,"* she said in as calm a tone as she could muster, *"you know Dr. Forester asked me to lead the Muslim prayers this Ramadan."*

*"Ramadan doesn't even start until Sunday or Monday,"* Mikaeel said, frustration in his tone.

*"But I have to spend this weekend reviewing my* hifdh, *Mickey,"* Salima said as if this should have been obvious.

A shadow of genuine confusion had come over Mikaeel's face then. *"Review your* hifdh*?"* he said. *"But you memorized the Qur'an when you were like eight years old."*

*"Nine,"* Salima corrected, trying to keep from getting upset. *"But I still have to review so I don't forget."*

*"You have to* review *your memorization?"* he said as if it was the oddest thing in the world.

*"Of course I do,"* Salima said, her face contorted at the ridiculousness of his statement. *"You know people who've memorized the Qur'an are constantly forgetting it."*

*"Yes, of course,"* he'd said. *"But I didn't know* you *needed to review. I thought it just came to you naturally."*

That was the first time that Salima realized that Mikaeel had never really seen her. It cut deep to realize that she had been married to her husband for nearly a decade and they had three children together, yet he still didn't see her as fully human. Even when he, upon her suggestion, went ahead with the trip and took their eldest two children and left her home with Haroon, who was nursing at the time, Salima had difficulty concentrating on the Qur'an. She just couldn't get his words out of her mind. It hurt that even after she'd explained herself, she could tell he resented her for ruining his weekend plans for the family.

*Too much admiration breeds contempt*, she'd written in her journal that night, furious at having to feel bad for being human. *It is better, I think,* she wrote, *to be understood.*

Larry coughed laughter, a grin of disbelief creasing one corner of his mouth. "Because you *need* me?"

"Yes," Salima said, feeling more confident in speaking her truth, even as she felt self-conscious and exposed.

"And why's that?" he said smugly.

"Because you see me, Larry." Salima heard the plea in her voice. But something inside her broke, and she didn't care if she sounded desperate and foolish, so long as he could hear her. "And I see you."

He huffed. "But not enough to be honest with me, huh?"

"I wasn't trying to be dishonest with you, Larry," she said. "I was really confused and didn't know what was right to say to you."

"How about the truth?"

"But what does that even mean, Larry? How can I tell the truth when I don't even know what it is?"

"Well, you knew our little friend Jasmine drove three hours to slander me. And you knew your brother Jamil was egging her on. Maybe you could've started with that."

"Larry, I know seeing clearly might come easy for you, but it takes time with other people."

"Other people?"

"Well, with me."

He nodded. "I can certainly agree with that."

"And I'm sorry," Salima said, and meaning it.

He huffed and shook his head. "Well, that's a good start," he said. "At least you know you're wrong."

"I do," she said, perhaps too eagerly.

There was an extended silence. "Is there anything else?" Larry said, impatience in his tone.

Salima hesitated momentarily, her heart racing in nervousness. "Just one more thing…"

"What now?" he said in exhausted impatience.

"I just wanted to ask you a quick question."

"Shoot," he said, gesturing for her to go ahead. "I'm listening."

"Will you marry me?" Salima cringed, realizing that the words had come out all wrong. But it was too late to take them back.

In any case, she wasn't sure she wanted to. Even if she could somehow find the right words for what she was trying to say, the meaning wouldn't change. She wanted to marry Larry, and there really weren't many politically correct ways to put it.

The silence fell between them, and it was as if a boulder hovered on a ledge above them, threatening to crush all hope. The threat extended for so long that the silence became like a stubborn impasse that neither could navigate, Salima because she'd already surrendered, and Larry because he refused to.

"I've been doing a lot of thinking myself," Larry said finally, and Salima was relieved to hear the annoyance gone from his voice and thoughtful reflection in its place. "And I realize that…" He pursed his lips as if finding difficulty formulating his thoughts. Salima held her breath, apprehensive about what he was about to say. "…I don't know if I like you all that much."

Salima opened her mouth to speak, but Larry turned abruptly and walked away. She heard his angry footsteps retreating down the stairs. Seconds later, the front door closed with a finality that was followed only by the boulder easing ever so furtively over the ledge.

## 36
## The Big Day

Pleased with herself, Deanna grinned as she stood in the dining hall of the masjid amidst the *waleemah* decorations. Shimmery teal tablecloths lay over each table, and shimmery black chair covers clothed each seat and were adorned by large teal bows, all Deanna's own handiwork. Teal and black helium balloon centerpieces sat atop each table and were accented with silver ribbon.

Deanna had pushed herself through her conflicting emotions and had done the interior design for the women's section of the wedding party for Aliyah and Jacob simply because it was a nice thing to do. The author of the self-help book was right, Deanna thought to herself. Selflessness was indeed therapeutic. Helping with the *waleemah* hadn't erased her feelings of resentment altogether, but it did help her realize that anger could only stunt her healing.

*But don't mistake therapy for healing*, the author had cautioned. *Just because something helps you in the path of healing doesn't mean it will ultimately heal you. More than anything, being a better person is a journey that has no final destination, except the journey itself.*

Deanna doubted her journey would ever lead her to fully forgive Jacob and Aliyah for what they had done, but she would be remiss to deny that she herself was in need of forgiveness.

"Well, what do you need me for?"

Deanna turned at the sound of a voice and saw Juwayriah standing near the entrance, hands on her hips as her gaze swept the length of the room. "It looks like you did everything yourself."

"We still need to lay out the napkins and silverware," Deanna said, nodding her head toward a large cardboard box on the floor near her feet. "And the cups and plates need to be put on each table so everyone can—"

"Why are you doing this?" Juwayriah interjected, disapproval in her tone, causing Deanna to stop mid-sentence.

Frowning in aggravation, Deanna rolled her eyes. The last thing she needed was someone criticizing her organizational skills an hour before the guests were scheduled to arrive. "Because it's easier than having everyone stand in line looking for the plates and cups."

Juwayriah flipped her hand dismissively. "I don't mean all this silly Martha Stewart stuff. I mean, *this*." She gestured a hand, moving it to indicate the span of the room. "It's too much. Aliyah doesn't deserve this."

Deanna's nose flared as she fought a wave of irritation and reached into the cardboard box. "Did I *say* Aliyah deserves this?" she said as she took out a package of black plates and tore into the plastic packaging. "I'm doing this for *me*."

Walking over to the box herself, Juwayriah lifted her upper lip in disapproval as she reached into the box and withdrew a large package of silver-gray napkins. "I hope you're joking, girl," she said as she ripped open the top and began laying out the napkins in front of the chairs of the nearest table. "How can celebrating someone stealing your husband help *you*?"

Right then Deanna was reminded of something her psychiatrist had said to her: *"I like that you want to remain friends with your husband's new wife, but I think it's too soon to be actively involved in anything that is a direct reminder of your pain."*

"Can you just shut up and set up the tables?" Deanna snapped, letting the loose plastic packaging from the plates drop back into the open cardboard box. "I asked you to come *help*, not tell me what to do."

"I'm not telling you what to do," Juwayriah retorted, wrinkling her nose. "I'm just asking a question. I really don't get what would possess you to do something like this."

Holding a stack of plates, Deanna glowered at her. "Look, are you going to help or what?"

"I *am* helping," Juwayriah said, slapping napkins on the table as she spoke. "I didn't know helping meant keeping my mouth shut. I'm only asking because I care about you."

"What's so wrong with doing a good thing?" Deanna said as she carefully placed a single plate in front of each seat at a table near her.

"You call this a *good* thing?" There was humored disbelief in Juwayriah's tone. "I don't see how your husband sleeping with your best friend could ever be good."

"We-are-divorced," Deanna said through gritted teeth, keeping her eyes on the plates she was arranging as she tried to keep calm.

"But you didn't *have* to be," Juwayriah said. "You should've never let Aliyah come in and sweep him up when you weren't looking."

Deanna halted her arrangements, a plate suspended midair as she turned to glare at Juwayriah. "You think I *let* this happen?"

"Of course you *let* it happen," Juwayriah said, not bothering to look at Deanna. "You are *way* better than Aliyah, but you're practically pushing Jacob to be with her."

Deanna opened her mouth to respond when she was overcome with an odd sense of *déjà vu*. It was if she were standing in Aliyah's apartment berating her for being so stupid as to have let Matt marry Nikki. Except, in the recollection, she found herself the recipient of her own tongue-lashing.

*"Stop trying, Ally, and do,"* Deanna had scolded her friend. *"I don't sit around saying I'm trying to stay married. I stay married... You look way better than Matt's new wife. There's no way he would've chosen her over you without you egging him on."*

Deanna hadn't suffered an involuntary screaming episode since she'd thrown herself into sewing tablecloths and chair covers and buying *waleemah* decorations. But right then, despondency settled over her as her legs weakened, and there was a restlessness clawing at the back of her throat.

*"When you feel the screaming about to happen,"* her psychiatrist had told her, *"separate yourself from the trigger immediately, and find a quiet place to sit where you can catch your breath."*

"I have to go," Deanna said suddenly, her voice clipped as she snatched up her purse from the seat of a chair and pulled the straps over her shoulder.

"Where do you think *you're* going?" Juwayriah's tone was merciless in its rebuke. "I didn't come all the way here to do this by myself."

"Nikki should be here any minute," Deanna said as she walked swiftly to the door, her back to Juwayriah.

"She better be," Juwayriah grumbled as Deanna pulled the door open and let it close behind her.

*Do not judge so that you will not be judged*, the Bible verses her mother often quoted resonated in her mind. *For in the way you judge, you will be judged.* The voice spoke in time with the pounding in her head. *And by your standard of measure, it will be measured to you.*

It did not escape Deanna the irony of being reminded of verses from the biblical chapter entitled Matthew, the same name of Aliyah's former husband, when only a moment before Deanna felt a sense of *déjà vu* at being Aliyah herself.

The cold air slapped Deanna's face and ripped into her arms, a harsh announcement that she'd left her coat in the masjid. But the keys to her car were in her purse, so she could sit in her car until the threat of a screaming episode passed. *You should've never let Aliyah come in and sweep him up when you weren't looking.* Deanna clamped her mouth shut, biting down rage as she pulled the car door open and lowered herself onto the ice-cold seat. She fumbled in the stiff cold as she pushed the key into the ignition and turned on the engine before pulling the driver's door closed.

*"Islam teaches us that God is the foundation of all our relationships, so when you understand this, life isn't so difficult..."* In her head, her own voice mocked her as the vent blew cold air in her face. *"Only people without a proper understanding of God and the sacred bond of marriage have serious problems in their lives and marriages."*

Then came the words, the lyrical invasion, falling upon her like an avalanche of rock, a stampeding reminder of the glumness of *qadr*, her own divinely decreed fate.

*Your tongue cannot stop* qadr. *But it can certainly complicate yours.*

***

Larry smiled into the full-length mirror affixed to the open door of the master bathroom of his home. "Well, what can I say?" he said, raising his voice as he smoothed down the lapels of his suit jacket with the flat of his hands. "I see you too."

He heard Salima's laughter from his mobile phone that lay on the counter near the sink. "But I didn't appreciate that, just so you know," her resonant tone crackled slightly through the speakerphone.

"I know you didn't," he said, humor in his tone. "But I didn't do it to earn brownie points. I really wasn't sure I liked you."

"Well..." Salima said, her tone sounding reflective. "I can't blame you for that."

"Oh, now don't get all self-flagellating on me," he teased. "You know my opinion of you wouldn't change how special you are."

"But it would change how special I *feel*."

"Then let's get married tonight," Larry said jokingly. "I'm sure that'll make you feel special again."

Salima laughed. "That would make for an interesting scandal," she said. "Qur'an teacher disappears with rumored womanizer. Last seen at her student's *waleemah*."

"Aw, come on," Larry said, picking up the mobile phone and carrying it away from his face as he walked into his room. "Why I got to be a womanizer?"

"I said *rumored*."

"And that makes it better?" he joked.

There was a thoughtful pause. "You sure your brother is up for this road trip next weekend?" Salima said, doubt in her voice as she changed the subject. "It feels like we're taking him away from his honeymoon."

Larry coughed laughter. "Honeymoon? With Aliyah eight weeks pregnant, I'd say they've already had their honeymoon."

"Aliyah's *pregnant*?"

Larry pinched his eyes closed and smacked a hand against his forehead in self-rebuke. "You didn't hear that," he said quickly.

"Aliyah's *pregnant*?" Salima said again, her voice rising in surprised disbelief. "But she didn't say anything about it."

"Like I said," Larry replied, speaking slowly as if coaching Salima, "you didn't hear it from me."

"Jacob told you?"

"Uh..." he said, humor in his tone. "Aliyah certainly didn't."

He heard Salima chuckle, as if laughing at herself. "I know. I'm sorry," she said. "I'm just...surprised."

"Why?" Larry said. "They're married."

"I know. It's just..." The speakerphone was silent for a few seconds. "Aliyah was really excited about finishing her doctorate and having her job pay for it and everything."

"Oh." Larry frowned thoughtfully. "Then maybe she can still do that," he said. "She has seven months before she has to worry about anything, right?"

Salima coughed laughter. "It's not that simple."

"I didn't say it was," Larry said. "I'm saying if she really wants to, she still can, and she has seven months lead time to worry about a baby."

"Okay, Larry," Salima said, laughter in her voice. "Whatever you say."

"But the subject only came up because Jacob was saying Aliyah might not be up for the drive," Larry said. "And we might have to bring the children along if she's not feeling well." He grunted. "And I figured you weren't up for asking Jamil."

"Not a chance," Salima said, her voice clipped. "I'm not even sure I'll let him know I'm going."

"You serious?" Larry said, chuckling. "You two have one little spat and all bets are off?"

"I don't consider it a little spat," Salima said, defensiveness in her tone. "Anyway, I'll still let him watch Haroon when I stay late at work."

"*Let* him?" Larry said, humored. "You say it like you're doing him a favor. He doesn't have to watch your son, you know."

"I know that," Salima said, voice tight. "But Haroon *is* his nephew."

"And your responsibility."

"I know," she muttered, seeming to let go of her offense a bit. "It's just hard to look at him the same."

"Why? Because he has his own mind?"

"Look who's talking. You're the one accusing him of stabbing you in the back."

"But he's not my brother," Larry said. "So I can think what I want." He shrugged. "At least until we're married."

"And he'll suddenly become an angel because you're married to me?"

"No. But he'll suddenly become family."

"And?"

"And I owe him mad respect for that."

Salima huffed. "Respect for what? Being born?"

"Look, Salima," Larry said, slight exhaustion in his voice. "I'm not going to lie. I'm not a big fan of Jamil right now. But he's a grown man, and Jasmine's a grown woman, so they can do whatever they want. He and Jasmine weren't in a relationship while I was with her, so I can't really say he stabbed me in the back." Larry grunted. "But I definitely don't appreciate him helping her jeopardize my chances with you."

"I think that was more about me than you," Salima said. "I think it was his way of letting me know he has opinions about my life just like I have opinions about his."

Larry set his mobile phone on the dresser then pulled open a drawer. "So he really joined that groupie thing you were telling me about?"

He heard Salima sigh through the speakerphone. "I don't know… We're not exactly on speaking terms right about now."

"It'll pass, *insha'Allah*," Larry said as he pulled out a neatly rolled pair of dark socks then closed the drawer. "Families go through stuff like this all the time."

"Not mine. This is new for us," Salima said, a tinge of sadness in her voice.

Larry chuckled, picking up the phone, the pair of socks in his other hand. "It was new for every family when it happened the first time," he said as he walked over to his bed and sat down on the edge. "Like I said, families go through stuff like this all the time. No one starts off knowing how to handle these sorts of problems. But no one escapes them."

"That's depressing," Salima said. "You'd hope *some* families stick together, no matter what."

"Salima, Salima, Salima." There was laughter in Larry's voice as he repeated her name and set the phone next to him then unrolled his socks. "There's so much you have to learn and so little time," he teased as he set down a sock then pulled on another, then picked up the other and put it on. "Sticking together doesn't mean you agree on everything," he said. "It means you're there for each other even when you hate each other's guts."

"I don't hate Jamil," Salima said tentatively, thoughtful reflection in her tone. "I just…don't understand him."

"And you don't have to," Larry said. "You think Jacob and I understand each other all the time? Or even our parents?"

"You all seem fine to me."

He coughed laughter. "Everybody *seems* fine, Salima."

There was an awkward pause before Larry heard Salima burst out laughing. An uncertain grin creased a corner of Larry's mouth. "Did I say something funny?"

"I'm sorry," Salima said in an apparent effort to gather her composure. "I just had a *déjà vu* moment."

Larry drew his eyebrows together. "About…"

"About me and Mikaeel."

At the mention of her late husband, Larry grew quiet. It made no sense to be jealous of a dead man, so he tried his best to remain levelheaded. "Really?" He hoped his voice sounded as genuinely curious as he intended.

"Yes." The carefree laughter in her voice quelled Larry's concerns, as she apparently hadn't picked up on his discomfort. "I used to always say somebody seemed nice." She spoke as if enjoying the memory. "And Mikaeel would say, 'Everybody *seems* nice, Salima. Come up with a better line.'"

Larry chuckled in an effort to encourage her relaxed mood. "I can't say he's wrong there."

"I probably would've said *Aliyah's* family seems nice if I didn't know any better."

He creased his forehead. "What's wrong with Aliyah's family?"

"What's *right* with it is a simpler question."

Larry felt uncomfortable with this shift in conversation. "You sure we're not breaking a friend code or something discussing her family like this?"

Salima was quiet momentarily. "I hope not," she said, a tinge of self-doubt in her tone. "She and I joke about swapping families all the time. Me so I can live my life without worrying about anyone's opinion, and her so she can know how it feels to have Muslim family besides her uncle."

"Isn't one of her brothers-in-law about to become Muslim?" Larry said. "I met him at Brother Benjamin's house."

"You mean Joseph?" Salima said, disapproval in her voice. "Cassie's husband?"

"Yes. Joseph," Larry said, remembering just then. "He went through a lot of trouble to meet his Muslim family. He and Jacob have been keeping in touch, I believe."

Salima huffed. "Not anymore, most likely."

"What makes you say that?"

"Last I heard, Joseph isn't interested in Islam anymore," Salima said.

"Really?"

"And apparently, he doesn't want anything to do with Aliyah, Jacob, or Benjamin," Salima said. "He even changed his cell number and everything."

The news disappointed Larry deeply. In some ways, Joseph had reminded Larry of himself before he became Muslim. He'd sensed Joseph's spiritual turmoil and keenness to find the truth despite the odds against him. "I'm sorry to hear that," Larry said sincerely, voice subdued.

"Aliyah thinks her mother might have threatened to take his job," Salima said, sadness in her tone. "And between that and Cassie threatening to divorce him, he probably felt he had no choice."

Larry's lips formed a thin line as he frowned thoughtfully. "That's a tough position to be in."

"I know…"

"This whole business of changing religions can be scary," Larry said, lost in thought. "No one wants to think everything they believed about life and God is wrong."

Salima was quiet for several seconds. "Maybe that's what Jamil is going through."

Larry drew his eyebrows together as he stood and walked out the room, carrying the phone inches from his face. "I thought you were both raised Muslim."

"We were. I just think Jamil thinks everything he learned from our parents is wrong."

"You think he's doubting Islam?" Larry's voice rose in concern as he walked down the hall and entered the living room.

"No, nothing like that," Salima said. "I just think he feels more comfortable with something specific he can hold on to."

Larry pulled his head back in surprise. "Other than *Islam*?"

"No," Salima said. "Other than our parents' generic, non-specific version of Islam."

"I thought we weren't supposed to have versions of Islam," Larry said.

"Well, that's what my parents and I believe," Salima said thoughtfully. "To us, there are only two goals when it comes to Islam. Follow truth, and avoid falsehood."

"Sounds about right to me."

"But it's easier said than done."

"What isn't?" Larry said as he set the phone on a table near the foyer next to his wallet and keys.

"I agree," Salima said. "But I think he feels it can be easier than we make it out to be."

"We as in you and your parents?" Larry said as he kneeled to put on his designer work boots.

"Yes."

He shrugged as he pulled on the laces of his boots and tied them. "Maybe it is."

"That's possible…" Salima said tentatively. "But to me, his solution is way more complicated than ours."

"What's his solution?" Larry said as he stood and opened the front closet.

"Commit to a single spiritual teacher and blindly follow him for the rest of your life."

Larry sucked in his breath in disapproval and concern as he removed his trench coat from a hanger.

"My thoughts exactly," Salima voice's crackled from the speakerphone. "I keep asking him, 'With so many different teachers and scholars out there, how can you settle on a single one?'"

"What does he say to that?" Larry said as he shrugged on his coat.

"He asks me the same thing," Salima said, defeat in her tone. "Except he says, 'How can you *not* settle on a single one?'"

Larry chuckled. "He has a point there," he said. "Leave it to the lawyer."

"But everyone has a *point*," Salima said. "My question is, where is yours pointing you to? I just don't see the safety in shutting your eyes to every source of religious knowledge out there except one random teacher," she said. "And then you don't even know whether or not your teacher will end up in Paradise?" She grunted. "No thank you."

Larry picked up the phone and took it off speakerphone then put it to his ear. "Can I play devil's advocate for a second?"

"As long as you don't mean it literally," Salima joked.

Larry chuckled as he lifted his wallet and put it in the pocket of his coat. "Isn't it sort of helter-skelter to distrust everybody, then learn from nobody?"

"I didn't say we should distrust everybody," Salima said, "and I didn't say we should learn from nobody. I'm saying it's impossible that the truth of Islam rests with a single person."

"Except the Prophet, peace be upon him," Larry added as he slid his keys off the table and walked to the front door and opened it.

"Well, with the Prophet, *sallallaahu'alayhi wa sallam*," Salima said, "that's a given."

"But he's no longer with us," Larry said as he stepped outside then pulled the front door closed. "So what do we do now?" he said as he turned the key in the lock, holding his phone between his shoulder and ear.

"Don't forget your *du'aa*," Salima said.

"What?" Larry said, thrown off by her words.

"The *du'aa* for exiting the house," she said.

"Oh…" Larry mentally scrambled for the words, the cold air stinging his face as he walked toward his car.

"*Bismillaah*," Salima said, reciting the *du'aa*. "*Tawakkaltu 'alallah, wa laa hawla wa laa quwwata illaa billaah*."

"*…illa billaah*," he repeated, stumbling over the words slightly.

There was a thoughtful pause. "But to answer your question," Salima said. "You make every day a time for study, *du'aa*, and *tawakkul*."

"You can't do that with a single teacher?" Larry said, ducking his chin to protect his face from the cold.

"You can do it with a single teacher, or a zillion teachers," Salima said simply. "How many teachers you have is irrelevant," she explained. "The point is, every day your focus should be on carefully assessing whether or not you are living a life pleasing to Allah and in line with the teachings of the Prophet, *sallallaahu'alayhi wa sallam*."

"And can't a teacher help you do that?" Larry said as he pointed his keychain remote toward his car and unlocked it.

"Of course. You're certainly not going to be able to do it on your own," Salima said. "That's why I say every day is a time for *study*," she said, emphasizing the last word. "But studying with humans is useless if you're not establishing a personal relationship with Allah separate from them."

In the car, Larry pulled the phone away from his face and pressed the speakerphone icon then set the phone in the compartment next to him. "Makes sense to me," he said as he put the key in the ignition and turned on the car. "But I have a hard time believing Jamil would disagree with you on that."

He heard Salima sigh. "My question to him is, what's so wrong with double checking what you're learning?" she said. "Why can't you talk to someone else to get another point of view, then pray *Istikhaarah* if you get confused?"

"What was his response?"

"If you commit to a single spiritual teacher, you won't get confused," Salima said, monotone.

"Okay," Larry said, laughter in his voice as he connected the wire of his earphones to his mobile then pushed an earbud into one ear. "I give up. I have no more comforting words for you. Your brother has officially lost his mind."

Salima laughed. "Thanks," she said. "You're no help."

"I'm sorry, Salima," Larry said, chuckling. "That's some far out sh, stuff," he quickly corrected himself. "You sure he graduated from law school? Because I can find a million holes in that logic."

"He graduated from law school, all right," she said, sadness in her words. "One of the top in his class. But I feel like people caught up in these groups pack away their brains when it comes to religion."

Larry coughed, humor in that sound. "Man," he said, returning to the topic of Jamil's argument, "that's like saying you'll never *feel* lost as long as you keep your eyes closed during the entire journey."

"Exactly," Salima said. "And then when the train stops, you just hope you're getting off at the right place."

"I tell you what," Larry said, glancing in the rearview mirror as he eased the car out of the parking space. "If I'm getting off at the wrong stop, it's going to be because I fought like hell to get off at the right one," he said with conviction, "not because I trusted some random person with a fancy name and title to get me where I needed while I slept the whole way."

"Muslimah used to say a spiritual teacher is never random," Salima said. "He's specifically chosen by Allah to guide you."

"So what do they say about all these different spiritual teachers teaching completely opposing and contradictory ideas?"

"That's exactly what I would ask her."

Larry smirked as he glanced down to shift the car from reverse to drive. "I think I'm afraid to ask what her answer was."

Salima chuckled. "That's why you have to find the one whom Allah sent especially for *you*," she answered.

"*What*?" Larry laughed out loud and smacked the steering wheel. "You've got to be kidding me."

"No joke."

"And what about avoiding Hellfire?" Larry asked.

"A true spiritual guide will never lead you to Hellfire," Salima recited monotone.

Larry was quiet momentarily as fear gripped him at the thought of going astray after Allah had guided him from disbelief to Islam. "Salima," he said quietly, "let's make a vow to never do that to each other."

"May Allah protect us."

"I mean, let's actually put it in writing."

There was a thoughtful pause. "I have no problem with that," she said.

"I just…" He sighed and pursed his lips as he tried to gather his thoughts. "I just don't want to be so scared to face Allah alone that I put the responsibility of my soul on someone else."

Salima was quiet momentarily. "I agree," she said. "But I do understand the temptation."

"I think we all do," Larry said. "That's why groups like this are so popular." He grunted. "In *every* religion."

Salima sighed. "I know..."

"I'm not going to lie." There was sad humor in Larry's tone. "Believing Jesus died for my sins felt really good."

Salima coughed laughter. "I can imagine."

"So I see where it can be addicting," Larry said, his eyes narrowed thoughtfully as he looked at the road in front of him. "It's terrifying reading all that stuff about the punishment of the grave and the torment of Hellfire."

"*Waqinaa 'adhaab al-qabr,*" Salima said. "*Waqinaa 'adhaab an-naar.*"

"*Ameen,*" Larry said, recognizing Salima's words as a supplication asking for protection for the dual torment of the grave and the Fire.

They were lost in thought for some time.

"But how would we word it?" Larry said.

"You mean the vow in our marriage contract?" Salima said.

"Yes."

She was quiet for some time. "Maybe we can say that we agree to establish our marriage on the clear, undisputed foundational principles of the Qur'an and Sunnah," she suggested. "And that any issue that is subject to differences of opinions amongst scholars and schools of thought, we will study the proofs for all of them, then make *Istikhaarah* before following any one."

Larry nodded. "I like that, *mashaAllah,*" he said. "And can we add that we'll never try to force each other to follow any human being completely except the Prophet, peace be upon him."

"Agreed," Salima said.

"And that we agree to never give complete allegiance to any ideology or group," he added, "except to Islam itself and to all our Muslim brothers and sisters?"

"And that we commit fully to following the truth," she added, "no matter where or from whom we learn it. And that we stay away from falsehood, no matter where we hear it or who teaches it."

Larry grinned, feeling pleased with the blessing that Allah was bestowing on him in his soon-to-be wife. "Can I add one more thing?" Larry said.

"Of course."

"That you teach me Qur'an every day," he said, "even it's only for five minutes."

"No problem," Salima said, and he could hear the smile in her voice. "I like that idea, *mashaAllah.*"

"With meaning and reflection," Larry added. "I don't want to just memorize the words."

He heard Salima laugh. "With all this," she said, "I'm not sure I'll even need a *mahr*. Marrying you is my marriage gift, *mashaAllah.*"

The grin on Larry's face spread wide. "And marrying you is my *life* gift," he said. "And I'll be honored to give you any *mahr* you desire, no matter how much it costs. Because marrying you is worth more than any dowry I could buy."

***

Jacob was standing in the hall outside the masjid prayer area overseeing the setup of the tables when he felt a buzzing in his pocket and heard a distant chiming sound. He reached into his pocket and pulled out his phone and saw a text message alert from Deanna. He groaned internally before unlocking his phone. *I need to change this passcode*, he thought to himself as he used his index finger to key in 0419.

*We need to talk*, her text message said. *It's really important. I'm outside.*

Jacob's first instinct was to ignore it. Deanna had a propensity for being dramatic, and Jacob wasn't in the mood for any Deanna drama right then. Guests would be arriving in about twenty minutes, and he and the brothers were already behind in getting everything set up. But he was relieved that at least Aliyah had a ride now. Aliyah was at her apartment with Ibrahim, Younus, and Thawab and had planned to drive to the masjid, but after he asked that she didn't, she'd texted to tell him that Salima agreed to pick her up.

*I'm inside*, he texted back. He was aggravated at the disruption, but he couldn't be sure that Deanna's concerns weren't related to the *waleemah* preparation since she had appointed herself as the event planner for the women's side.

*Can you just come outside? I'm in my car.*

Jacob clenched his jaw as he sent his reply. *No. I'm busy setting up.* Less than three seconds after he sent the message his phone rang, and he saw Deanna's name on the screen.

"What is it?" he said, speaking through gritted teeth as he put the phone to his ear.

"We need..." She sniffed. "…to talk." She sounded breathless, as if she'd been crying, but her voice was stern in insistence.

"Then talk," Jacob said. "I can't come outside."

He heard her huff in annoyance. "Can't you just give me *two* minutes?"

"I don't *have* two minutes, Deanna."

He heard her sniffling. "I gave you twelve years of my life," Deanna said, bitterness in her tone. "The least you can do is give me two stupid minutes."

He drew in a deep breath and exhaled, shaking his head as he turned his back to the brothers setting up the tables. This is what he'd feared when Deanna had volunteered to help. It seemed that nothing could go well with her except that she'd personally dismantle every single good she'd done. Everything with her was about keeping score instead of earning blessings.

"Not on the night of my *waleemah*," he said, unmoved. "So if what you say can't be said on the phone, then we'll have to talk another time."

The other line was silent for some time. "I'm going home, Jacob," she said finally. "I'm not staying for the *waleemah*."

Jacob heaved a sigh of relief, but he was careful to keep the relief out of his voice. "Why?" he said in obligatory annoyance. "Aren't you supposed to be setting up downstairs?"

"Juwayriah and Nikki are taking care of everything."

"Well, we appreciate everything you've done so far," Jacob said. "So *jazaakillaahukhairan*."

Deanna was silent for several seconds, and Jacob sensed she wasn't finished. "And I want you to know I'm fine with you and Aliyah," she said.

Jacob drew his eyebrows together, uncomfortable with Deanna's uncharacteristic kindness. "Well… thank you. I'm happy to hear that."

"So I want you to think about us."

Jacob's lips formed a thin line of annoyance. He should've known there was a caveat.

"And before you say anything," Deanna said, raising her voice, as if anticipating a refusal. "Just consider it, okay? I'm fine with being your second wife, even if we don't tell everybody just yet," she said. "You know, just like how you did with Aliyah."

Jacob's nose flared as he tucked in his lower lip to keep from speaking before he could calm the fury building inside him.

"Remember how you used to say men are the maintainers and protectors of all women?"

"Allah said that," he said with disinterest.

"Well, I…"

"Deanna, look," he said, unable to keep quiet any longer. "Let me just cut to the chase. I'm not going to marry you as a second, third, or even *fourth* wife." He huffed. "And even if a sheikh were to give a fatwa that the women whom our right hands possess could be anyone we chose," he said, "I would *never* choose you."

There was a voice inside Jacob's head telling him he was going too far. But in that moment, he was so infuriated with all he'd put up with that he wanted her games to end, once and for all. That she had the nerve to insert herself into his and Aliyah's life under the guise of supporting them only to try to snare him on the night of his *waleemah* was even more enraging. It wasn't enough that she practically stalked and trapped him before marriage, slandered the woman he wanted to marry, then made his life a living hell once she got him. Now she had to play the damsel in distress, trying to appeal to his Muslim male honor.

*No more,* he said to himself, just as he had after she'd slapped him for speaking his mind during their joint interview.

"I'm not asking for equal time," Deanna muttered angrily. "So what's the problem?"

"The *problem*?" Jacob said, lowering his voice out of fear he would start yelling. "What's *not* the problem, Deanna? Let's start there."

"We have two boys, and—"

"And?" he interjected challengingly.

"—the least we can do is stay together for them."

"Now you're trying to *guilt*-trip me?" He would have laughed if she weren't serious. "I don't believe in putting on faces for the world, Deanna. Been there, done that," he said. "Once upon a time I was stupid enough to believe that a miserable, destructive marriage was better than *any* type of divorce." He grunted. "For me *and* my children."

"But *Shaytaan* loves d—"

"But *Shaytaan*?" he interjected, before she could finish her sentence, humored disbelief in his tone. "Are you seriously going to sit here and tell me about what the chief devil likes?" He coughed laughter. "Let me tell you a little secret about our friend Iblis, Deanna," he said sarcastically. "Yes, he loves divorce. He loves destroying marriages and families and all that other stuff you learned at Sunday school." He paused then added, "In church *and* in the masjid." He huffed. "But you know what he loves to destroy more than all of that?"

Deanna was silent.

"Our souls," Jacob said. "You hear that? Our *souls*." He exhaled in annoyance and shook his head. "And being married to you was destroying my soul." He was quiet for several seconds as he let that sink in. "So if you can show me any verse in the Qur'an or hadith from the Prophet, *sallallaahu'alayhi wa sallam*, that says saving a marriage is more important than saving my soul, then I'm all yours."

Deanna was still silent.

"But for now, I have a *marriage* to celebrate," Jacob said, a taunt in his voice. "*As-salaamu'alaikum*," he said, disconnecting the call without even waiting for a reply.

***

"You sure I look okay?" Aliyah said, a lopsided smile on her face as she glanced down at herself uncertainly, pearl teardrops dangling from her ears. She was wearing a fitted cream sleeveless gown with pearl beading on the bodice and a matching short jacket that stopped just above her waist. Flat twists lay against the front of her head, and the back of her hair was swept up in pearl-beaded clip.

"You look amazing, *mashaAllah*," Salima said, grinning proudly at Aliyah from where she stood next to her in the women's bathroom across from the dining hall.

"Who's all here?" Aliyah said nervously.

"Everyone," Salima said. "Reem, Mashael, Nikki, Juway—"

"Reem *and* Mashael?" Aliyah said, excitement in her voice.

"Yes," Salima nodded. "Though I don't think Reem expected to see Mashael here."

"Oh, *mashaAllah*." Aliyah's heart raced, as she could hardly contain how ecstatic she felt. "I'm so happy they reconciled."

Aliyah shook her head then grabbed Salima's hands. "Can you believe it?" she said. "Everybody here to celebrate *my* marriage." She grinned. "To Jacob!"

"Well, Allah has certainly blessed you," Salima said. "*MashaAllah.* I would've never imagined things would turn out like this."

A sad smile lingered on Aliyah's face, and her eyes glistened as she let go of Salima's hands. "May Allah bless Deanna, truly," Aliyah said with a sigh. "I think with all she's done to help with my *waleemah*, I'm not upset with her anymore."

Salima nodded. "That's good, *mashaAllah.* I'm really happy for the both of you."

"I'll have to make sure I thank her personally," Aliyah said. "I mean, in front of everyone."

"I think she stepped out though…" Salima said, uncertainty in her tone. "When I was looking for her, Juwayriah said she had to run home or something."

Aliyah waved her hand dismissively. "That's fine. She probably just went home to change clothes," she said. "After all that setting up, she probably was sweaty."

"Probably," Salima agreed. "And you know Deanna has to look just right."

There was an extended silence as Aliyah smiled knowingly at Salima.

"What?" Salima said, laughter in her voice.

"So when's the big day for you and Larry?"

"Oh no," Salima said, chuckling and shaking her head as she grabbed Aliyah's hand and started for the exit. "Today is all about *you.*"

"But aren't you two driving up to talk to your parents next weekend?" Aliyah said.

Salima laughed. "I have no idea what you're talking about," she sang out as she guided Aliyah out the door.

A minute later, when Aliyah walked into the dining hall, the noise level rose as the sound of the daff filled the room, as did the ululating of several women. Aliyah laughed and danced along with the women, her cheeks hurting from how widely she was smiling from how happy she felt.

## 37
## Future Plans

The Sunday morning after her and Jacob's *waleemah*, Aliyah sat smiling to herself as she sat cross-legged on the fold-out mattress in Jacob's office where she and Jacob had slept the night before, Jacob having stepped out to take a phone call. The wedding party had turned out well, Aliyah reflected, and she was pleased that everyone seemed to have enjoyed themselves. Aliyah was a bit disappointed that Deanna did not end up returning to the *waleemah* and joining them. But Aliyah was grateful that she had remembered to make an announcement thanking Deanna for overseeing the decorations and part of the planning.

*Allah really blessed me by sending me Jacob*, Aliyah thought to herself. She wondered how her life would have turned out if she'd remained with Matt, or even with her high school boyfriend before Islam. Where would she be today if she'd believed all the faulty relationship advice she'd heard growing up? The vast majority of relationship guidance was rooted in focusing on the goodness of the person you were with instead of focusing on the goodness (or lack thereof) of your life and soul as a result of being with them. It wasn't until after she married Jacob that she realized the emotional and spiritual tragedy of viewing marriage from the outside in instead of the inside out.

*But God tells us to make decisions based upon the goodness a person or situation brings to our lives and souls.* Yet rare was the advisor—professional or religious—who advised taking an honest look within yourself and within your life before deciding on marriage or divorce. So much of their advice seemed to be rooted in emotional and spiritual manipulation instead of preserving your emotional and spiritual health. "If he's good to you, you have no reason to leave." Based on that advice, Aliyah should still be with Curtis, her high school boyfriend.

Ally and Curtis had discussed keeping in touch after graduation, but they both knew that their relationship wasn't meant to last beyond high school. Their conversation about "keeping in touch" itself was a sign that neither of them desired a long-term commitment. But what Aliyah found odd was that, until that conversation, she hadn't known that she felt that way. In the two years that she and Curtis were together, she'd honestly thought they would get married one day and have children, and she'd imagined that Curtis felt the same. But in the end, there was a silent agreement between them that this wasn't what either of them wanted.

Ironically, her experience with Matt ended up being similar to her experience with Curtis, even as she had matured enough to know that she wanted something deeper and more meaningful than her high school relationship. But whereas her low self-esteem and inexperience had made her excited to be with Curtis, her general loneliness and spiritual insecurity had made her excited to be with Matt, at least initially. In the beginning, the physical companionship alone was enough to make Aliyah content. But it wasn't a contentment that emanated from the heart. It was a contentment that emanated from the external security and sense of being needed that marriage offered, as all of her marital happiness stemmed from knowing she was in a "good marriage" to a "good man."

But neither that good marriage nor that good man had brought much goodness to her life and soul.

"It's *your* secret, man," Aliyah heard a crackling voice come from the speakerphone on Jacob's mobile as he returned to the room, cell phone in hand. "And you couldn't even keep it. So how do you expect me to?"

Jacob laughed. "It's all right, man," he said. "I'm sure she would've told Salima herself sooner or later."

"Tell Aliyah I'm sorry about that though," Larry's voice said.

"No problem," Jacob said, glancing toward Aliyah briefly. "But I'm still good for next Saturday, *insha'Allah*."

"Don't be dropping out on me, man," Larry said. "Salima might call off the whole trip if we have to drive there alone."

"Why doesn't she ask Jamil?" Jacob said, curiosity in his tone. "He might not mind spending the day with his parents."

Larry huffed. "Long story," he said. "But that's not an option. He doesn't even know we're going."

"Oh," Jacob said, as if remembering something just then. "Okay then, I'm good."

"All right, man," Larry said, humor in his tone. "You better be. You're not the only one who wants a good Muslim wife."

Jacob chuckled. "Okay, Larry," he said before giving the salaams and disconnecting the call.

"So Salima knows now, huh?" Aliyah said as she folded her arms, a knowing grin on her face.

"Larry sends his apologies," Jacob said, laughter in his voice as he sat behind Aliyah on the mattress then wrapped an arm around her to pull her close.

She leaned into him and turned to look up at him. "It's okay," she said. "I was going to tell her anyway. I just wanted to give it time."

There was a thoughtful pause, and Jacob kissed the top of her head. "How have you been feeling?" he said.

Aliyah shrugged. "Pretty good overall, *alhamdulillah*," she said. "But I've been feeling nauseated off and on." She chuckled self-consciously. "And I think my emotional rollercoaster is starting."

"Really?" Jacob sounded surprised.

She scooted up to release herself from his arms so she could sit at an angle to face him. "Last night I was so giddy, it was crazy," she said, chuckling. "I couldn't stop laughing and giggling." She coughed laughter. "I even got teary-eyed when I made the announcement about Deanna helping me plan the *waleemah*."

"Well, I'm not complaining," Jacob said, nudging her playfully. "You can come home wound up like that every night as far as I'm concerned."

Her cheeks grew warm, and she averted her gaze. "Don't count on it," she said with a hesitant grin. "It's just these pregnancy hormones coming in full force."

"You didn't feel them so much before?" he said, his tone more subdued.

She shook her head. "Not really. If it wasn't for my cycle not coming and me feeling just a bit off, I don't think I would've known at all."

"So I guess you won't be using birth control pills anymore," he joked.

Aliyah smiled. "I guess not," she said. "But I could've done something wrong since it's a new prescription."

There was an extended pause. "You sure you up to sticking it out at the college?" he asked, a tinge of concern in his voice.

Aliyah groaned. "Just when I restarted my doctorate," she complained good-naturedly.

"If you decide to resign," Jacob said, "I can pay for it myself."

She shook her head. "It's too much money. I don't think it's worth it."

"It is if it's something you really want to do."

"We have SAFE now," she said. "I'd rather we put money into that."

Jacob creased his forehead, a concerned expression on his face. "Is everything okay with Salima and Jamil?" he said. "I know they had a disagreement about Jasmine while I was there during the snowstorm. But I figured it was just normal sibling rivalry."

Aliyah frowned thoughtfully. "She hasn't talked about it much, but I know she's really bothered about Jamil getting involved with some cultish Muslims."

"Is it that *Khawaarij*-type group that says everyone's an innovator or disbeliever if they take pictures, listen to music, or don't go to their masjid?" Jacob said, disapproval in his voice.

Aliyah shook her head. "No, I don't think so," she said. "This group seems to be more into sheikh worship and sainthood and stuff like that."

A shadow of sadness passed over Jacob's face. "May Allah protect him and preserve him," he said. "It can get really confusing out there."

"*Ameen*," Aliyah muttered.

"I've always been a bit of a loner," Jacob said reflectively. "So groups were never really appealing to me, especially religious ones. But I know they're a huge *fitnah* for most people. No one wants to feel like they're going at it alone."

"But if you're Muslim, you're not going at it alone," Aliyah said. "You have Allah."

"Yes, but we all need tangible guidance and reassurance sometimes," Jacob said. "And if you can find a righteous, knowledgeable person you can trust, that's priceless."

"That's a big *if*," Aliyah said, caution in her tone. "How do you know if someone's righteous?" she said. "Or even knowledgeable, for that matter? *Shaytaan* has more knowledge than all of us. That doesn't mean we should follow him."

"But you studied Islam formally for many years," Jacob said. "Everyone hasn't had that opportunity. Most of us are so busy living our lives, it's a treat to even sit in front of a scholar once a year."

"But I didn't make *bai'ah* to any of my teachers," she said, slight defensiveness in her tone. "There's a big difference between benefiting from a scholar's knowledge of the Qur'an and Sunnah and turning him into some sort of demigod or intercessor between you and Allah." She huffed. "Or thinking he has some secret knowledge that even the Prophet, *sallallaahu'alayhi wa sallam*, didn't have."

Jacob's face contorted in worry. "Is that what Jamil is into?"

Aliyah lifted a shoulder in a shrug. "*Allahu'alam*," she said. "But it seems that way."

Jacob appeared to be overcome with sadness all of a sudden, and his gaze grew distant. "I'll keep him in my prayers," he muttered.

Aliyah nodded. "I will too, *insha'Allah*."

***

Holding her bathrobe closed with one hand, Salima stepped out of the bathroom as she pressed her cell phone against one ear. "Juwayriah," she said, her face twisted in confusion as she shook her head, "you have to slow down. I can't understand anything you're saying."

Salima had brought her phone with her to the bathroom because she had been expecting Larry to call back at any moment. She had turned up the ringer volume and set it on the sink counter before stepping into the shower, not wanting to miss his call. But when she heard the phone ring and parted the shower curtains, peering out to see Juwayriah's name on the mobile screen, she'd sighed in disappointment and resumed her shower. She could talk to Juwayriah later, she'd decided. When Juwayriah called a second time, seconds after her first call, Salima had become annoyed and stepped out the shower to send it directly to voicemail. She had been back in the shower for less than ten seconds when Juwayriah called a third time.

Though still a bit irritated at the repeated calls, Salima grew concerned and immediately shut off the water and stepped out the shower to answer the call. When she heard the desperate rambling of Juwayriah's voice, she didn't bother drying off and had merely used her free hand to put on her bathrobe and open the door to head to her room.

"Deanna *what*?" Salima said, halting her steps in the middle of the hallway as she narrowed her eyes, trying to make out what Juwayriah was saying. "She *passed out*?" Salima repeated, unsure if she'd heard Juwayriah correctly.

Slowly, Juwayriah's words began to make sense, and Salima's heart sank in dread. "You're at the hospital with her now?" Salima said, careful to keep her tone calm. She nodded as Juwayriah found her words, even as it was clear that Juwayriah was still a bit disoriented and understandably upset and confused.

"Look," Salima said finally. "Just text me the floor and the room number, and I'll call Jacob myself."

She calmly shook her head as Juwayriah began to ramble and complain again. "Don't worry about any of that," Salima said, speaking slowly and carefully. "I'll meet you there in about twenty minutes, *insha'Allah.* Then you can go home, and I'll take it from there, okay?"

Salima disconnected the call and immediately walked up to Jamil's door and pounded on it before opening it. Jamil was sitting at his desk in front of his computer, an expression of aggravation on his face, but Salima was only vaguely aware that he appeared to be in a video chat with someone.

"I need you to keep Haroon today," she said, not bothering to ask if it was okay. "Juwayriah just called to say Deanna is in the hospital and I need to get there right away."

"Juwayriah?" Jamil said, his face contorted in confusion.

"Apparently, Deanna spent the night at her house and—" Salima lifted a hand as if to stop herself. "Look, it's not important. But I have to get to the hospital right now."

"Why you? Doesn't she have a family?"

"I don't know why," Salima said, slight impatience in her voice, "but she listed me, Juwayriah, Jacob, and Aliyah as her family and emergency contact."

"*What*?" Jamil said, appearing even more confused than before.

"Just forget it," Salima said, waving her hand. "I just need you to stay with Haroon for a few hours."

"Whatever," Jamil said with a shrug, turning his attention back to the computer monitor. "I'm not going anywhere today anyway."

"Thank you," Salima said, pulling the door closed without waiting for a response.

***

Arms folded over the chest of her coat, Aliyah stood in the foyer of Jacob's home nibbling nervously at her lower lip as Jacob waited in the car for her with the engine running. He'd gone outside ten minutes before to warm up the car and put the hospital's address into the navigation system as they waited for Larry to arrive to stay with the children.

Salima didn't talk long when she'd called Jacob's phone and he'd answered on speakerphone, as she was on her way to the hospital herself. But from what Aliyah could gather, Deanna had passed out in the guest room of Juwayriah's home, where she had slept the night before. Apparently, that was where she had gone when she'd left the masjid last night, and she had waited hours outside of Juwayriah's house until she came home.

"I don't know..." Salima had said through the speakerphone, sounding exhausted after Aliyah had asked why Deanna didn't just stay at the masjid and go home with Juwayriah from there. "It probably just ended up being too much for her," Salima said, sadness in her voice.

Aliyah sensed Jacob's mood becoming somber with Salima's words, but she didn't have time to dwell on it because they were in such a hurry to get dressed and get to the hospital after they ended the call. But while he was putting on his coat to go outside and start the car, Aliyah did ask if he was okay.

"I'm fine," he'd said distractedly, avoiding her gaze as he opened the door and disappeared outside.

"Is Mommy sick or something?"

Aliyah started at the sound of a voice, and she turned to see Younus standing feet from her, his arms folded over his chest as he still wore his two-piece long pajamas. Aliyah opened her mouth to answer in the negative but decided against it. With Younus, he was probably asking more for confirmation than information.

"It seems that way." She pressed her lips together in a frown of empathy. "But *insha'Allah*, we'll find out soon."

Younus nodded thoughtfully. "So Uncle Larry's coming?"

"Yes," she said. "He should be here any minute, *insha'Allah*."

There was an awkward silence. "Aunty Aliyah?"

"Yes?"

"Is she going to be okay?"

Aliyah felt a wave of sadness at the question. "We're praying on it, Younus," she said. "And you should too."

He pursed his lips and nodded firmly in an apparent effort to appear emotionally stronger than he really was.

Aliyah started to say something reassuring when she heard the quick beep of a horn. "I think that means Uncle Larry just pulled up," she said with a sad smile, apology in her tone. "But hopefully, we won't be gone long."

She gave Younus the salaams, but before she could turn the door handle and open the door, she felt a thin body wrap around her and squeeze her tight. She let go of the door and held Younus in a warm embrace. For several seconds she held him, saying nothing. When the door opened and Larry stepped inside a second later, Younus jumped away from Aliyah and quickly wiped his face.

"*As-salaamu'alaikum*," Larry said, his tone solemn. "Jacob said to let you know he's ready to go."

Aliyah returned the salaams and nodded. "See you later, Younus," she said offering a gentle smile before stepping outside into the cold.

## 38
## Where's My Diagnosis?

"And Professor Thomas?"

Aliyah turned around just before she stepped into the hallway. "Yes?"

Dr. Warren had a pained expression on her face and the beginning of what looked like a poor attempt at a smile. "Thank you." She spoke as if the words were bitter on her tongue.

Aliyah creased her forehead in confusion. She started to respond in kind when she realized she had no idea what her supervisor was thanking her for. Had it been anyone else, Aliyah would have simply said, "You're welcome." But with Dr. Warren, even casual formalities could be mistaken for some unspoken agreement with some underhanded cause or another. And given that Aliyah had simply come to Dr. Warren's office for a signature that her graduate school required for some paperwork, there was nothing for the two of them to be agreeing on, underhanded or otherwise.

"For your work here, I mean," Dr. Warren clarified.

It was difficult to gauge from Dr. Warren's expression whether she was speaking sarcastically or in earnest, but Aliyah decided that since it was at least clear what was being ostensibly discussed, it was safe to resort to formalities.

"Thank you for having me," Aliyah said, realizing in that moment that she really was grateful to her supervisor for giving her the opportunity to work in the department. Since childhood Aliyah had an affinity for mathematics subjects, and she'd never imagined that she'd be appointed as a professor at a reputable college one day. That she was also trusted to teach computer science and networking courses was an additional honor.

"I know we've had a few misunderstandings." Dr. Warren spoke in a tone that suggested that she'd given this a lot of thought. "But I want you to know I'm pleased with what you've accomplished with our students." Her lips formed a thin line of disapproval, but Aliyah understood that her supervisor meant it as a pleasant expression. "I've received several positive reviews about your teaching, and the registrar's office has informed me that they're receiving specific requests from incoming students to have you as a professor."

A proud grin played at Aliyah's lips. "I'm happy to hear that," she said sincerely.

"We are too," Dr. Warren said, "given, as I'm sure you can imagine, that we aren't the most popular department in the school."

Aliyah nodded knowingly, a pleasant smile on her face. "Math and science usually aren't students' favorite subjects."

"Well, it looks like that tide is changing, even if just a bit." Dr. Warren gave a tightlipped smile again. "And you're partly to thank for that."

Aliyah was smiling to herself and turning back toward the door when Dr. Warren spoke again. "And Professor Thomas?" Aliyah turned to her supervisor.

"Let's meet first thing tomorrow morning. There are some department project ideas I want to run by you."

A smile still lingered on Aliyah's face when she returned to her office that Monday afternoon. But her expression became more pensive when she thought of Deanna still in the hospital. Perhaps it was a combination of the pregnancy and the stress of the situation the day before, but when Aliyah had arrived with Jacob at the hospital, she'd begun to feel nauseated and weak. She ended up sitting in a waiting area near the main entrance instead of accompanying him to Deanna's floor.

When Juwayriah was passing through the main lobby on her way out shortly after Aliyah had sat down, Juwayriah had done a double take upon seeing Aliyah. Aliyah immediately got to her feet and started to ask Juwayriah how Deanna was doing, but Juwayriah had contorted her face and lifted a palm to stop her before she could get the words out. "Don't speak to me," Juwayriah had said, not bothering to slow her steps and even look in Aliyah's direction as she spoke. "People like you disgust me." The automatic doors of the entrance slid open in a single motion, and seconds later, Juwayriah was lost in the rush of people exiting and entering.

Stunned into silence, Aliyah had sat dumbfounded, completely puzzled by Juwayriah's rude behavior. When Aliyah mentioned Juwayriah's behavior to Jacob later that afternoon on their way home, he'd brushed it off saying that everyone was stressed and had had a long day. Aliyah had thought it odd that Jacob showed no signs of shock or disturbance at Juwayriah's words. But when he'd explained that Deanna's condition was induced by stress and depression, his nonchalance began to make sense. Juwayriah was most likely blaming Aliyah for Deanna's condition, and Jacob was most likely blaming himself.

Aliyah's phone buzzed and chimed, and she immediately set her handbag on her desk and fished out her phone.

*Is it okay if Larry picks up Ibrahim? We need to talk.*

Aliyah creased her forehead in concern as she read Jacob's cryptic message, her thoughts flying immediately to Deanna. Something must have happened, she thought to herself in dread. Otherwise, why would Jacob need to talk to her without her son present? She imagined that Larry was picking up Younus and Thawab too.

*Yes*, Aliyah texted. She started to ask if everything was okay but decided against it. Clearly, whatever it was that Jacob needed to talk about couldn't be conveyed via text messaging. Otherwise, there would be no need for making elaborate arrangements with his brother.

*I'm on my way home now*, Jacob replied. *Meet me there.*

*Okay.*

***

As Aliyah drove to Jacob's house that cold January afternoon, the sun glinted off the snow, and she couldn't get Juwayriah's disgusted expression out of her mind. Part of Aliyah was offended by Juwayriah's behavior, but another part of her couldn't cast blame. After all, Juwayriah was one of Deanna's closest friends, perhaps Deanna's best friend since the falling out between Aliyah and Deanna. Most likely, during the night of the *waleemah*, Deanna and Juwayriah had spoken at length, and Aliyah imagined that Deanna had confided in Juwayriah about her lingering resentment toward Aliyah and Jacob. Though Deanna had gone through great lengths to make things better for herself and support Jacob's new situation, it was obvious that it would be a long time before she was fully healed.

With Deanna in the hospital, Aliyah felt an odd connection to her former best friend, and it tore at her heart to know that Deanna was hurting so deeply and that there was nothing Aliyah could do about it. Learning about what Deanna had suffered at only eight years old from her eighteen-year-old cousin was enough to make Aliyah forgive Deanna for everything.

*"Girl, you know I love you!"*

A lump developed in Aliyah's throat as she thought of Deanna's feisty warrior spirit that exuded positivity and confidence at every moment. Aliyah would have never imagined that it all was a mask concealing a wound that had festered for nearly three decades.

"I wasn't trying to steal him from you," Deanna had told Aliyah during the night of the snowstorm. "I really did think I was better for him."

"It's okay," Aliyah had said. "It's all in the past."

"Not for me," Deanna had said, a tinge of irritation in her voice. "Because now I lost everything."

"You didn't lose everything, Deeja," Aliyah told her. "You still have y—"

"My what?" Deanna had cut her off, meeting her eyes unblinking, as if in a dare.

"Well…" Aliyah had said, flustered. "Your health, your business, your—"

"I gave up my counseling business."

"But *why*?" Aliyah had no idea why this news had bothered her so much. "A lot of people benefit from you."

"Benefi*ted*," Deanna had said, emphasizing the last syllable with a roll of her eyes. "As in past tense. No one wants to hear relationship advice from some washed-up divorced woman who can't even keep her own marriage together."

"I disagree," Aliyah had said. "If anything, it makes you more relatable."

"I don't want to be relatable," Deanna had retorted. "I want to be *reliable*."

As Aliyah pulled into the driveway of Jacob's home, she had a sudden, intense craving for gyros followed by an intense desire for Deanna's company. What they'd had wasn't perfect, but it was reliable, Aliyah reflected. And now that Aliyah understood Deanna's struggles better, she felt confident that she could be more patient and compassionate with Deanna's overbearing tendencies. It was probably Deanna's only way of feeling needed after having lost so much.

***

"You know what I realized?" Reem said as she sat at the hospital bedside squeezing Deanna's limp hand, intravenous tubes snaking into her other one next to the IV pole where a clear fluid dripped slowly from a clear bag. "We're all going through the same thing. We just don't realize it." She glanced at Deanna lying still on her back, eyes closed and chest rising and falling in time with soft breaths.

"I never told you," Reem said, feeling oddly comfortable in the quiet room, even as she had no idea if Deanna was cognizant enough to hear any of her words. But Reem's *niqaab* was flipped back and lay over the top of her head so that her face was showing. "But I gave up one time too."

Reem's voice caught at the honesty of her words, and she exhaled a jagged breath, having not realized how difficult it would be to speak the truth aloud. "I was in high school and was in a lot of pain. You know the kind of pain that's hidden so well in plain sight that everybody sees it yet misses it at the same time?" Reem coughed laughter but tears sprung to her eyes instead. "That was me."

Reem paused thoughtfully. "You would've never recognized me, Deanna, I swear," she said, humor in her tone. "I looked like a punk rock Goth. I was far from the strict, veiled Qur'an teacher that you met." Reem wiped the moisture from her eyes with her free hand. "I had a pretty cool group of friends, and we were into a lot of stuff we had no business being involved in. But to tell you the truth, they were the best group of friends I ever had."

An awkward smile lingered on Reem's face as she reflected on the irony of those words. "They weren't Muslim," she said, a tinge of sadness in her voice. "But they had this raw honesty about them that made them see more clearly than most of the other students at our school. They didn't care what clothes you wore, or what car you drove, or even if you had a car at all. They didn't even care if you were into some pretty horrible things in your life. When we got together, we had only one mission, to make each other laugh and feel good for at least that moment."

Reem frowned and dropped her gaze as a painful memory returned to her suddenly. "I know that our friendship wasn't necessarily good," she said quietly. "But they were the ones who saved my life."

Reem sat in silence for some time as she allowed herself to go back to that day, and the more painful, unbearable days of her childhood. "I don't know what's hurting you," she said as tears brimmed her eyes. "But I think I have a pretty good idea." She drew in a deep breath and exhaled, offering Deanna a weak smile. "Because it's what's hurting me." She dropped her head again and held Deanna's hand in both of hers. "But giving up? It doesn't help anyone, and it only hurts the people who care about you," she said. "And the ones who don't care..." Reem's jaw quivered as she thought of her own flesh and blood, her father and half-brother. "…they'll go on not caring, no matter what you do."

***

Aliyah's stomach lurched as her eyes raced across the note penned in familiar handwriting that Jacob had reluctantly handed her. But she'd read only two lines when her eyes widened and she looked at Jacob in disbelief.

"What is this?" Her voice rose and her eyes glistened in fury as she shook the thin sheet of floral-trimmed stationery in front of Jacob's face from where she stood opposite him in the living room of his home.

"I have one too," Jacob said quietly, his expression pained as he folded his arms over his chest, lost in thought. "But I didn't read it."

"So this whole, quote, passing out ordeal was really an attempted *suicide*?" Aliyah nearly spat the word, she found it so repulsive.

Jacob frowned. "Yes."

Aliyah contorted her face and shook her head, unable to find the words for the disgust and disappointment she felt with Deanna right then.

"I didn't want to tell you last night because—"

"Oh, I'm glad you didn't." Aliyah's nose flared, and she shook her head again. "Sick and weak or not, I probably would've marched right up to that room and told her to go tell that sob story to someone else. *Wallahi*," Aliyah said, swearing by Allah, "I have no sympathy for people who use their death as a tool to punish and manipulate others." She wrinkled her nose. "That's the lowest and cruelest thing you could do, especially to people who care about you."

Jacob sighed. "Aliyah, I know how you feel, but—"

"No, Jacob," Aliyah said, snatching her arm away from his grip as he reached out to her, "you have *no* idea how I feel right now. And there's nothing, I mean absolutely *nothing*, you can tell me to make this excusable."

"It's definitely not excusable," he said quickly, a tinge of desperation in his voice, "but I think it's partly my fault."

Aliyah's eyes widened as she looked at him. "Are you really going to play right into her hands? This is why suicide is such a horrible sin. It mixes grief and guilt in the most sinister way." She grunted indignantly. "Not to mention *murder*."

"I'm not saying it's *completely* my fault," Jacob said. "But she was trying to talk to me Saturday night, and I…"

The self-reproaching way Jacob spoke squeezed Aliyah's heart and she had to look away from him to keep from becoming more enraged with Deanna. Aliyah could already tell from Jacob's solemn mood and body language that Deanna had tried to guilt him into taking her back, and he'd most likely responded in anger because he was annoyed at her bringing it up on the night of the *waleemah*. But Aliyah willed herself to keep quiet and listen, as she was already at her wit's end with Deanna, and she doubted there were enough words in the English language to exhaust what she felt about Deanna's unrelenting ruses to get what she wanted.

"…should've just tried to hear her out," Jacob said.

"What was she trying to say?" Aliyah said, careful to keep her voice level so that Jacob knew she was giving him her full attention.

"That I should consider marrying her as a second wife," he said as if speaking aloud to himself.

A wave of fury rose in Aliyah, but to keep calm, she silently recited the *isti'aadhah*, seeking refuge in Allah from *Shaytaan*. "But Jacob," Aliyah said, speaking as softly as she could manage, "how is that fair to you, or even me, for her to bring up something like that at that time?"

"I'm not saying it was fair," Jacob said tentatively. "I just think I could've handled it better."

Aliyah nodded. "Maybe you could have," she said. "But her decision to overdose on pills, or whatever she did, wasn't your fault."

"But she's been diagnosed with clinical depression, Aliyah," he said, his voice a plea. "I should've been mindful of that."

"She's been diagnosed with clinical *depression*?" Aliyah repeated, twisting her face in disapproval, unable to keep her composure any longer. "Labels and diagnoses are for getting *treatment*, Jacob, not for getting a free pass to treat people however you want."

"But I shouldn't have gotten so upset." Jacob folded in his lips and shook his head in self-rebuke, as if he hadn't heard a word Aliyah said. "Maybe it was what I said to her that made her snap. I could've at least said, 'I'll think about it' or something like that."

"Why?" Aliyah said, pulling her head back in disapproval. "So we can coax her back into the lion's den so she doesn't rip us to shreds? And what about when she comes back the next day to see what you've decided? And the next, and the next?" she said. "Do we keep leading her on?"

"I'm not saying we should lead her on. But…" He exhaled in a single breath, unable to find his words. "…if we know someone's been diagnosed with a mental illness, then we have a responsibility to treat them in a certain way."

"So where's *my* diagnosis?" Aliyah said challengingly.

Jacob's expression conveyed confusion when he met Aliyah's gaze. "I don't understand what you mean."

"Do you know how many times *I* felt like giving up?" she said, her eyes glistening in hurt. "How many times I wished Allah would take my soul so I didn't have to live another day on this earth, or even another hour? And do you know how many times I didn't even feel like getting out of bed? How many nights I cried myself to sleep? How many nights I couldn't even *go* to sleep?"

Jacob was silent, unsure what to say. But his concerned gaze mirrored the pain he saw in Aliyah's eyes.

"Do you know how it feels to have your own mother and father refuse to speak to you? To see you? Or even acknowledge you exist?" Aliyah said in anguish. "Do you know how it feels to get married to someone because the imam said you're a bad Muslim if you don't? And then lie down next to that person every night feeling obligated to give yourself to him because *Allah* said you have to?"

Her chin quivered, and she clenched her jaw to keep from breaking down. "Do you know how it feels to think your only purpose in life is to keep a man's body and food warm so that your Lord will give you warmth in Paradise? Or how it feels to walk around as only an empty shell of who you are so that your *husband* can be a whole person and live a full life?" Tears stung Aliyah's eyes, but she blinked them back, refusing to cry. "Or how it feels to believe that if you don't give up your *soul* for this man, you'll burn in Hell?"

Jacob's eyes widened slightly, as it was apparent he'd never known Aliyah had struggled with anything of this magnitude. He looked like he wanted to say something comforting but didn't know where to begin.

"And then to end up alone after even *that* falls apart?" Aliyah said, her voice breaking slightly and tears springing to her eyes despite her best efforts to fight them. "And to have your *only* friend say it's all your fault? And that you're a bad Muslim, a bad wife, and a bad friend? And that if you had the slightest good in you, you'd have a family and a husband and some self-respect?"

Aliyah wiped her eyes and shook her head, jaw clenched as her gaze grew distant momentarily. "So where's *my* diagnosis?" she said, frustration lacing her tone as she looked at Jacob, eyes full of confusion and hurt. "Where are all the professionals and community members rushing to my side, saying, 'Be patient with her. She's going through a lot'?"

Aliyah huffed, and her nose flared. "Instead, what do I get?" she asked rhetorically. "'People like you disgust me,'" she said, mocking the tone of Juwayriah's haughty voice. "Or I'm called a whore and a husband stealer when I've done nothing but stay in my home except to go to work, pay my bills, and pray to my Lord in the masjid."

She shook her head as if at a loss for words, her breaths audible. "So yes, I want to know, where is *my* diagnosis?" she said in fury. "Where is *my* label? Where is my right to patience and good treatment and to excuses and love?"

Fresh tears glistened in her eyes and hung there for a moment before slipping out and rounding her cheeks. But this time, she made no effort to stop them. "I don't know a human being alive who doesn't know pain," she said. A moment later she added, "*Intimately*."

Aliyah huffed and shook her head. "But somehow we think the only ones who deserve our compassion are the ones who cry the loudest and have the biggest tantrums and carve the victim label into their chests."

There was an extended silence as neither spoke for some time.

"When I was in high school," Aliyah said, her tone barely above a whisper, "a boy I knew committed suicide."

"I'm sorry," Jacob said, his tone regretful and sincere. "I didn't know."

"I think he's the reason I hate suicide so much." Aliyah spoke as if lost in thought, a look of distaste on her face. "When he died, he left a note saying who he didn't want at his funeral, and my boyfriend was on the list."

Aliyah coughed laughter, but it was to keep from becoming more upset. "And it wasn't like this boy was some angel. Yes, he was picked on and bullied, but he would bully and pick on people himself." She huffed. "And my boyfriend didn't even bother that boy, that's what's so crazy about what he did. That boy hated Curtis only because Curtis was openly Christian and didn't keep quiet about his beliefs. And that boy didn't keep quiet about his either," Aliyah said, voice clipped indignantly. "He would even call us Bible thumpers and stuff like that."

She shook her head, still troubled by the memory. "But all of a sudden when he killed himself, he became this hero. Even the principal and all the teachers played into the whole victim thing, and we had to write essays about accepting everyone for who they are and crap like that. And out of everyone who was on that list, it was Curtis who everyone whispered about, saying, 'I thought he was supposed to be all holy, but look at what he did to that poor boy.'"

"*SubhaanAllah*," Jacob said, speaking under his breath.

"And when I saw how sad and depressed Curtis became through all of that," Aliyah said, earnestness in her voice, "all I could think was, 'I pray to *God* that boy burns in Hell *forever*.'"

This time when Jacob reached out to Aliyah, she did not pull away, and she leaned into his chest, her shoulders shaking as she broke into sobs. With each cry, Aliyah grieved for the boy who'd senselessly taken his own life. She grieved for Curtis who'd suffered for a crime he didn't commit. She grieved for Deanna who'd given up on life and couldn't get beyond her pain. And she grieved for herself, the fragile girl who'd sustained wounds in every part of her, yet suffered in silence, thinking that is what it meant to be strong.

***

At her apartment, Aliyah remained in bed for the rest of the week, having called in sick to work each day. She would have no doctor's note to present to Dr. Warren when she returned, but Aliyah couldn't muster the energy to care. She had retreated into a quiet place inside herself, and the world around her became clamoring background noise to the numbness of her mind. Her limbs became like lead and her tongue thick in her mouth, and she found it difficult to move or speak. Prayer, food, and the need to bathe or relieve herself were all that inspired her to get out of the bed. But even then, her legs were too weak to stand for prayer, so she would pray sitting. And she could go an entire day without desiring a bite of food, so it was due only to concern for the health of the baby that forced her to put anything in her mouth.

When Jacob stopped by Tuesday after work to ask if Ibrahim should stay with him for a while, Aliyah had been lying curled up in bed facing the wall. When she heard him come in and shout the salaams, she was reminded that he had mentioned to her a couple of weeks before that he'd planned to make a copy of Ibrahim's apartment key. In the bed, Aliyah managed to respond to Jacob through moving her head ever so slightly in the beginning of a nod. But even that small gesture incited tears welling in her eyes, as she realized she was unable to take care of her own son.

"Don't be so hard on yourself," Jacob said when he'd come by Friday evening while she was still lying in bed. "It's only been a few days," he said, as if reading her mind. "No one can do it all. Everyone needs a bit of help sometimes."

Seeing the growing darkness beyond the curtains, Aliyah sat up in bed. "I need to pray *Maghrib*," she muttered.

"I do too," he said. "Let's pray together."

"Where are the boys?" Aliyah said, realizing the uncharacteristic quiet as she got out of bed.

"They're with Larry at my house," Jacob said.

Aliyah frowned as she dragged herself to the bathroom, feeling like a neglectful mother. She wondered if one day Larry would complain about all the childcare he was doing.

"And he doesn't mind, *mashaAllah*," she heard Jacob say just before the bathroom door clicked shut as she closed it.

After completing *wudhoo'*, Aliyah emerged from the bathroom with face and arms moist from ablution. She felt a flicker of energy as she pulled the one-piece floral garment over her head and found that she was strong enough to stand for prayer. But she still dragged her desk chair to the prayer mat that Jacob had laid out for her. During prayer, as she stood at an angle behind Jacob, Aliyah ended up needing the chair only once.

"How are you feeling?" Jacob asked once they'd finished their *adhkaar* and recitations after the sunset prayer. They were still sitting on the floor, and Jacob had turned to face her.

"*Alhamdulillah*," Aliyah said with a nod, surprised by the strength in her voice.

"You look better, *mashaAllah*," he said, offering her a weak smile.

She coughed laughter. "How did I look before?"

He grinned as he met her gaze. "And I see your sense of humor is coming back."

Aliyah smiled beside herself. "I guess the fog is clearing then, huh?"

"I guess so."

They were silent for some time, as each became lost in thought.

"I told Larry you probably wouldn't be able to make it this weekend," Jacob said.

Aliyah creased her forehead, a question on her face as she looked at Jacob. "What's happening this weekend?"

"Larry and Salima are driving up to talk to her parents."

*Oh.* Aliyah had forgotten about that. "Thank you," she muttered, but there was a pang of guilt at the thought of not being there for Salima.

A thoughtful silence followed. "But I think it would be good if you went," Jacob said.

Aliyah wrinkled her nose in uncertainty. "What if I get sick?"

"It's only three hours," Jacob said. "We could bring a sick bag or even pull over or go to a rest stop if we need to."

"I wouldn't want to ruin their trip like that," Aliyah said, but she heard the doubt in her own voice. Salima would be thrilled just to have the company, Aliyah knew, especially since without Aliyah, Salima would be the only female in the car.

"Well, we're leaving after *Fajr* tomorrow *insha'Allah*," Jacob said.

"Are you taking the boys?" Aliyah said.

Jacob frowned thoughtfully. "We were thinking to leave them with you if you didn't go."

"Oh yeah," Aliyah mumbled, remembering that she'd offered to keep them if Jamil couldn't.

"But Larry said Jamil came through at the last minute."

Aliyah brought her eyebrows together in confusion. "I thought he didn't know about the trip."

Jacob shrugged. "I guess he does now."

Aliyah nodded. "That's good, *mashaAllah*," she said. "I hated that whole standoff between him and Salima."

"Well, I doubt they've reconciled completely," Jacob said. "But at least they're getting back to behaving like family."

A wave of sadness came over Aliyah at the mention of the word *family*, and she found herself choked up and blinking back tears. Embarrassed, she averted her gaze and bit her lower lip, hoping Jacob would interpret her sudden shift in mood as pensiveness over Salima's situation.

"You heard anything from your parents or Cassie or anyone lately?" Jacob said after a few seconds of thoughtful silence, his tone soft with concern.

Aliyah's shoulders dropped, surrendering to her emotions as she realized there was no point in trying to shield Jacob from what she was feeling right then. "I got an email from my father a few days ago," she muttered.

There was a moment of stunned silence. "Your *father*?" Jacob's voice rose in surprise and concern.

Aliyah nodded as she pressed her lips together, unable to look directly at Jacob. "I was just lying in bed checking the messages on my phone when I saw it."

She felt Jacob staring at her, and she sensed in him a mixture of hope and curiosity. "This is progress, right?" Jacob said, a tinge of happiness in his voice. "You haven't heard from him since a few years after you became Muslim?"

"Him or anyone else," Aliyah said, melancholy in her tone. "Except my mother that day at Benjamin's house."

"Well, it's good he's making an effort to reach out," Jacob said, forced optimism in his voice.

Aliyah started to cough laughter, but it came out as a grunt. "If that's what you want to call it," she said.

Jacob was quiet momentarily. "What did he say?"

"It wasn't only to me," Aliyah clarified. "It was to my brothers and sisters too." She frowned as she met Jacob's gaze, her tone devoid of emotion. "He was telling us about a new non-profit program they're starting with disadvantaged youth, and he wanted our input and participation."

Jacob's eyebrows rose in pleasant surprise. "*MashaAllah*, that's good."

The beginning of a smirk creased one corner of Aliyah's mouth. "One of their programs received a government grant for a grassroots anti-terrorism initiative because the community is, quote, 'losing so many of our youth to Islamic groups.'"

A shadow of anger passed over Jacob's face.

"Apparently," Aliyah said, sarcasm in her tone, "it's become an epidemic in poor areas."

Jacob groaned knowingly. "In other words," he said, "too many black and brown people are becoming Muslim."

"Exactly," Aliyah said, rolling her eyes.

"That was subtle of him," Jacob said sarcastically.

Aliyah shook her head, realizing just then how much the email disturbed her. "But that's not the best part," she said.

Jacob chuckled. "There's more?"

"Guess who's just been appointed project manager?"

He glowered, as if mirroring how she herself was feeling right then. "Please tell me they didn't appoint *you*?"

Aliyah laughed and shook her head. "No, they didn't go *that* far, *alhamdulillah*," she said.

"*Alhamdulillah*," Jacob muttered, relief in his voice.

She offered Jacob a knowing smirk. "They appointed Joseph Daniels."

It took a second before an expression of recognition passed over Jacob's face. "Cassie's husband?" He sounded as if he was hoping he was wrong.

"Yes," Aliyah said, humor in her tone.

The despondency in Jacob's demeanor was so complete that Aliyah was taken aback momentarily. He seemed to withdraw so far into himself that for a fleeting moment, Aliyah wondered if she'd inadvertently said something deeply hurtful. His face was twisted in agonizing disappointment as he sat in pensive silence for some time.

"I'm really sorry to hear that," Jacob managed to say in a low voice a minute later.

"Me too," Aliyah said, but she sensed that her husband was more bothered by the news than she was.

A heavy silence hung between them for several seconds. "Be careful, Aliyah," Jacob said finally. "I don't want to lose you too."

She pulled her head back in surprise. "Lose me?" she said, confused.

"It just seems like we're losing so many Muslims these days." His tone was deeply pained and reflective.

Aliyah started to reassure him that she wasn't going anywhere but then realized he probably wasn't talking about losing her to a relationship fallout. "What do you mean?" she said.

He drew in a breath and exhaled, as if the topic was too weighty for words. "The other day I was reading about how a high percentage of converts to Islam end up becoming apostates," he said, lost in thought. "And I was thinking about how Muslims are always bragging about Islam being the fastest growing religion in the world, but no one wants to talk about how many people we lose every day."

His words reminded Aliyah of a conversation that she'd had with Salima some time ago. *"But how can someone leave Islam?"* Aliyah had said, and Salima had responded, *"If you understand how it feels to struggle in your faith, it's not too hard to understand giving up entirely."*

"But in the stories I read," he said, "a lot of people had experiences similar to yours."

Aliyah furrowed her brows. "*Apostates*?"

"Yes," Jacob said sadly. "Most of them were men and women who'd suffered spiritual and emotional abuse from Muslims they trusted."

Aliyah frowned thoughtfully. "I realize now that most of what I experienced from my family was emotional abuse," she said tentatively. "But I'm not sure that's what I'd call any of my experiences with Muslims."

"I agree that *abuse* is a strong term," he said, "but even if you take away the label and look at just the stories themselves, there are a lot of parallels between yours and theirs."

There was a thoughtful pause. "But that's still no excuse to leave Islam," Aliyah said. "No matter what anyone does to you, you shouldn't throw away your soul."

"Of course not," Jacob said. "But logic isn't what pushes someone to let go of their faith. It's the gradual and mostly imperceptible destruction of the spirit."

Aliyah was quiet, unsure what to say to that. She had never thought about spiritual crisis in that way.

"And by the time it reaches the level of *kufr*," he said, "your heart has sustained so many spiritual wounds that letting go actually feels freeing and therapeutic."

"*SubhaanAllah*," she muttered, at a loss for words.

There was an extended silence. "I felt like letting go myself sometimes," Jacob said, a reflective frown on his face.

Aliyah's eyebrows rose in surprise. "Really? I didn't know that."

He shrugged. "It's not something I like to talk about often," he said. "But feeling stuck in that marriage to Deanna almost made me resent God and religion."

Aliyah drew her eyebrows together, a confused expression on her face. "Why?"

"Because I felt it was a sin to divorce her," he said.

Aliyah didn't know what to say to that. She herself had come to think of divorce as a horrible sin.

"And I knew if I did, everyone would blame me for abandoning her and the children," Jacob said, "especially if I ended up marrying someone else."

Aliyah nodded in understanding. "So you felt like it was your God-given duty to stay?"

"Yes," he said, sounding relieved that someone understood. "And whenever I read the Qur'an, I'd feel so horrible because it was hard for me to fulfill everything Allah required men to do for their wives."

"But you provided for her well, *mashaAllah*," Aliyah said, hoping to make him feel better.

He shook his head. "I don't mean materially," he said. "That's the easy part. I mean being the leader of the household and being a helpmate to her spiritually and treating her with patience and kindness." He pursed his lips, as if overcome by a troublesome memory just then. "And correcting her if she becomes disobedient."

Aliyah was quiet, recalling when he'd come to ask her assistance in advising Deanna.

"Did I ever tell you about the passcode on my phone?" he said, looking at Aliyah with a half grin on his face.

She contorted her face in confusion, unsure about the reason for the sudden shift in subject. "No…"

"Zero four one nine," he said, coughing laughter. He shook his head as if enjoying a private joke.

For a second, Aliyah became concerned that he wasn't thinking clearly.

"That stands for *soorah four*, *ayah nineteen* in *An-Nisaa*," he said, a reflective smirk lingering on his face. "And live with them honorably," he said, reciting the English translation aloud. "If you dislike them, it may be that you dislike a thing and Allah brings through it a great deal of good."

*Oh.* Aliyah was overcome with weighty sadness as she realized the deep implication of the passcode comment. She could only imagine the emotional torment that Jacob was going through each day.

"I guess I should've used sixty-five two and three instead," he said, a tinge of humor in his tone. "Those are the two *ayah*'s that ended up saving my life." He grunted then added, "And my soul."

"*Soorah* sixty five?" Aliyah said, creasing her forehead. "That's *At-Talaaq*, isn't it?"

He nodded, a smile on his face. "The chapter about divorce."

"What do verses two and three say?" she said, humored curiosity in her tone.

"And whoever fears Allah and keeps his duty to him," Jacob said from memory, "He will make for him a way out. And He will provide for him from sources he could never imagine."

Aliyah nodded and smiled, recognizing the translation right away.

"And whoever puts his trust in Allah," Jacob finished, "then Allah is sufficient for him."

"That's so inspirational, *mashaAllah,*" Aliyah said. "I remember reading those verses during Ramadan and thinking how merciful Allah is, even when things don't work out in the way we think is best."

Jacob coughed laughter. "That's a far cry from the 'Allah will punish you if you divorce your wife' rhetoric I heard during Islamic talks all the time," he said. "They talked so much about how evil it was to follow your desires that I started to wonder if it was better if I didn't *have* desires, even for my wife."

"I know," Aliyah agreed, laughter in her voice. "That's how I felt when the imam was guilt-tripping me into marry Matt."

There was a thoughtful silence. "You know that's the definition of spiritual abuse, right?" Jacob said.

Aliyah's smile faded, and her gaze grew distantly momentarily. "I don't like calling people abusers," she said. "I'm just so sick of this victim culture, I don't want any part of it."

"I agree," Jacob said. "But recognizing the signs of abuse is not the same as calling someone an abuser. Anyone can fall into behavior that can be considered abusive."

"Then we need to find another way to describe it," she said, slight annoyance in her tone. "I'm tired of everyone acting like a victim. It's so tiresome."

"But understanding what you've gone through so you can heal is different from something like killing yourself and leaving a suicide note blaming other people for your problems."

"*That,*" Aliyah said, gesturing with her forefinger for emphasis, "I would call abuse, plain and simple."

"And you'd be right," Jacob said. "But using your death as a tool of emotional manipulation is not the only type of abuse."

Aliyah's nose flared in irritation as the topic reminded her of Deanna. "I tell you what," Aliyah said, firmness in her tone, "I'm glad they say she's going to fully recover, *insha'Allah.*"

"You mean Deanna?"

"Yes," Aliyah said, nodding emphatically.

"May Allah heal her," Jacob muttered.

"*Ameen,*" Aliyah said, raising her voice to underscore her agreement with the prayer. "And may she live to feel the regret for every single sin she inflicted upon herself and everyone else."

Jacob's lips formed a thin line, and Aliyah could tell he was uncomfortable with her supplication.

"You know the *du'aa* of the *madhloom* is answered, right?" Aliyah said.

Jacob creased his forehead, a question in his eyes. "The *madhloom*?"

"The one who's been wronged," she explained.

"Oh…" Jacob said.

"The Prophet, *sallallaahu'alyahi wa sallam*, said, 'And be wary of the supplication of the oppressed, for between it and Allah there is no barrier.'"

Jacob nodded hesitantly. "I've heard that before."

"Well, I made my *du'aa,*" Aliyah said, a triumphant smirk on her face, "and *insha'Allah,* Deanna will live a nice long life."

Jacob was quiet for some time. "I understand how you feel," he said tentatively. "But I guess I just don't feel so confident that I was wronged."

"I can understand that," Aliyah said sincerely. "When you were married to someone, it's hard to know who wronged whom more." She lifted a shoulder in a shrug. "But Deanna and I were just friends, and I *know* I didn't do anything to deserve that stupid suicide note."

Jacob frowned thoughtfully. "I don't think anyone ever *deserves* a suicide note," he said, a tinge of offense in his tone. "I'm just saying I'm not so sure that the hadith about the *madhloom* would apply to me."

Aliyah nodded. "I usually wouldn't either," she said. "But after all the hell Deanna put me through, I don't have any doubt left."

There was a thoughtful pause. "What did it say anyway?" Jacob said.

Aliyah drew her eyebrows together, a question on her face. "What did what say?"

"The note," he said. "I never read mine."

She shrugged. "I never read mine either," she said. "Except the first two lines," she added. "But that was enough."

Aliyah creased her forehead as a thought came to her suddenly. "Have you seen mine?" she said. "I couldn't find it the other day."

"I threw it away."

It took a few seconds for Aliyah to register what Jacob had said. "You threw it *away*?" she said, shock in her tone.

He nodded. "Mine too," he said. "But I shredded them first."

Aliyah blinked and shook her head as she tried to process what he was saying. "But…why?"

"Because I saw what it was doing to you," he said simply. "To the both of us actually. And after you told me about the boy in your high school and what his note did to Curtis…" He pursed his lips and shook his head. "…I knew the only way to stop the emotional abuse was to not give it an audience."

Aliyah was quiet as she digested what Jacob had done, and why. A part of her felt offended, but a bigger part was relieved. It was as if a huge burden had been lifted from her shoulders.

"And I figured since it was handwritten," he said, "there wouldn't be any other copies."

Aliyah moved her head in the beginning of a nod.

"Like you said, death doesn't turn someone into an angel," Jacob remarked. "And what we know of killing yourself, it's a major sin with a pretty severe punishment."

"That's true…"

"So the only way a person can take their own life is if they're blatantly disobeying Allah," he said, "or suffering from mental illness." He shrugged. "Either way, nothing they say in a suicide note should be given much weight." He shook his head, a frown forming at the sides of his mouth. "And the more I thought about it, the more I realized how even *reading* it could contribute to their punishment in the Hereafter."

Aliyah squinted her eyes in confusion. "How?"

"Because if they're not mentally ill," he said, "any emotional or psychological suffering their sin causes, especially intentionally, then they have to answer for that in front of Allah on the Day of Judgment."

"*SubhaanAllah*," she said. "I never thought about it like that."

"I didn't either," he said. "At least not until I saw how, even after all these years, you remember the pain that boy caused with his note." He paused thoughtfully.

"It's one thing to just kill yourself," Jacob said. "And that's bad enough. But to leave a note blaming people?" He shook his head, his expression pinched in distaste, as if words couldn't convey the weightiness of the issue. "*A'oodhubillaah*," he said, seeking refuge in Allah. "That's not a sin I'd want on *my* record."

"May Allah protect us," Aliyah muttered, terrified at the prospect of unjustly blaming someone for anything, even without a suicide attempt.

"*Ameen*," he said.

"This just made me think about all those people who kill themselves because people didn't accept their sinful lifestyle," she said reflectively.

"I know," Jacob agreed, nodding. "I was thinking the same thing."

"And then after they die," Aliyah said, "foundations and scholarships and other groups are established to support their cause."

"And they have to answer for every single person they influenced to support something wrong," Jacob added.

"That," Aliyah said, "on top of the sin of suicide." She shook her head. "*A'oodhubillaah*."

"Yes," Jacob said. "*A'oodhubillaah*."

# 39
# I Wish I Had a Family

"Excuse me for not standing," Aliyah said as she waddled to the front of the living room of her home, a palm resting on her swollen belly. She lowered herself onto the chair that Salima had placed in front of the women. "But carrying twins is breaking my back," she said, humor in her tone. She and Mashael exchanged knowing glances though Mashael was pregnant with only a girl while Aliyah's ultrasound had revealed that she was carrying both a boy and a girl. Reem stood next to Mashael, her veil flipped back, and smiled as she glanced at Mashael's protruding abdomen.

It was a Friday night in mid-May, and Aliyah was hosting Muslim Marriage Monologues in her home for the first time. After the lease on her apartment expired in February, she and Ibrahim had moved into Jacob's home. Because he had ultimately decided against selling, Jacob transferred his home into Aliyah's name as a fulfillment of her *mahr*, the dowry he had promised upon marriage. He then remodeled it based upon her ideas and directions.

The master bedroom was converted into an office suite with two offices side-by-side, one with a nameplate for Jacob and the other with a nameplate for Aliyah. The main entrance to the bedroom now led to a small hallway with the bathroom on the far end and the office doors along the hall. The master bathroom now displayed the simple sign *Restroom* on the door to add to the professional atmosphere. Jacob's former home office was now the master bedroom, and it was the only renovation for which Aliyah suppressed a tinge of guilt. Aliyah hadn't realized that the installation of a full bathroom into the room could be so complicated and costly.

When Jacob had offered to add a tennis court next to the basketball court outside, Aliyah declined, saying she'd rather save the money for whenever she returned to graduate school. It had been a difficult decision, but Aliyah never returned to work after the day she found out about Deanna's attempted suicide. The tragedy had made it difficult to readjust to what she'd previously experienced as the mundane normalcy of her life. It was as if her entire world shifted, and no matter how hard she tried, she couldn't place her feet on solid ground. Perhaps the pregnancy was exacerbating the emotional trial of the experience, but Aliyah had become almost obsessive with checking on Ibrahim and Younus and Thawab throughout the day and into the night to make sure they hadn't slipped and fallen or stopped breathing.

"Dr. Warren keeps asking about you," Jacob often teased when he returned home from work, but Aliyah would laugh if off, saying she was quite content as a stay-at-home mom. If given a choice, she would prefer the college environment over the primary school classroom, but Aliyah found it quite rewarding teaching the elementary curriculum to Ibrahim, Younus, and Thawab during their homeschooling sessions each day. They all now attended Qur'an school in the mornings and returned home in the early afternoon for their secular school lessons.

There were days that Aliyah felt sad about giving up the opportunity for tuition reimbursement for graduate school, but she didn't regret her decision. Like Jacob often reminded her, no one could do it all, and that was a difficult lesson for Aliyah to embrace fully. She had to decide what was most important, and she'd come to the conclusion that her physical and emotional health, as well as the connection between her and her sons, was the highest priority right then. She would likely have another opportunity for a job or graduate school, but she could never get the days, months, or years back with her family.

Fortunately, she and her former-atheist student Robin were now in regular contact, so that helped Aliyah feel connected to the part of her former position that she missed. And because she had officially resigned, she was free to talk to Robin unabated, and it seemed that Robin was close to accepting Islam.

Deanna remained an emotional trigger for Aliyah, so she avoided her former best friend as much as she could. Deanna visited Younus and Thawab once a month, but her visits were supervised. After Deanna's release from the hospital following her attempted suicide, she'd been in and out of psychiatric facilities and had on more than one occasion tried to physically attack Jacob and Aliyah and threatened to take the children.

When Deanna visited, Aliyah would remain upstairs in her office or in the bedroom, if she was home at all. It remained challenging emotionally and psychologically to keep her distance, however, since Aliyah still felt connected to Deanna in many ways. That Deanna seemed to be genuinely trying to be a better person made it that much more difficult not to give her another chance. But the relationship had become so toxic for Aliyah that the mere sight of Deanna or the sound of her voice incited a migraine and the onset of what felt like preterm labor. So she was forced to let go, even as her anger with Deanna about the suicide note had subsided and Aliyah was now more compassionate and understanding of Deanna's mental struggles.

"Today, I'm going to read something I wrote a while ago," Aliyah said. "But I ask you to forgive me in advance for its depressing tone," she said, a humored expression on her face. "I was in a really bad place at the time, and I had started journaling my thoughts, and this is what I wrote. But," she said, raising a forefinger as she offered them a weary smile, "I added a few lines at the end in hopes of making it a beneficial message." She drew in a deep breath and exhaled. "So here it goes."

Aliyah muttered "*Bismillaah*" as she glanced at the paper in her hand then said, "It's called, 'I Wish I Had a Family'...

I wish I had a family.
I hear families are there for you
No matter what.

I hear their blood is thicker than water
Their love is softer than rain
And that no matter what you're going through
That bond of the womb will take away your pain
I hear that mothers love their daughters
And daughters love their moms
And that nothing is strong enough
Or bad enough
To threaten or break that bond.
I hear that when a child falls
Mommy or Daddy comes to pick them up
I hear that when a child cries
Mommy or Daddy comes to cheer them up
I heard about something called brothers and sisters too
But I'm not sure if it's true
They say they're like your protectors and friends
And your advisors and supporters too
And if you hurt, they hurt,
Because that's what brothers and sisters do
But I think it's just a rumor
Or maybe just an old wives tale
Because the house I grew up in
Mommies didn't love their daughters,
And daughters just feared their moms
And it was only when someone wanted something from me
That I heard of the family bond
There was no Mommy or Daddy to pick me up when I fell
Because they were the ones who pushed me
There was no one to hurt when I hurt
Because they were the ones who caused my pain
There was no one to wipe my tears
To hear my cries
To even care I had a soul
And there was no brother or sister to protect me
Or to comfort me
Or advise me
Because compliance and obedience was my only role
But then one day
My life changed
And Allah guided me to His *deen*
Now I have a family, a faith family
And its bond is stronger than the one I dreamed
I have a Mommy and Daddy in every elder

A brother and sister in every shoulder touched in prayer
I have comforters and advisors
And protectors and supporters
And many friends I know will always be there
So my only hope for my faith family
Is that we cherish this bond with every breath
Because it's a bond that never breaks, bi'idhnillaah
Even after death

***

The lantern above the back door glowed as Deanna sat on a lounge chair on the balcony overlooking the backyard of her parents' home. The grass glistened in the darkness of night, and the book *YOU CAN BE A BETTER PERSON!* lay dog-eared on her lap. The notebook that she had been using to pen her thoughts sat atop the open book, remnants of paper entangled in the spiral wiring from where she'd ripped out pages she could no longer stomach reading. She had crumpled and tossed out the notes of apology to Aliyah that she'd written and scratched out then written again. But tonight, upon her psychiatrist's urging, she was writing notes of apology to herself.

"I wish that I had the strength and the courage to have faced my own demons so that I could have allowed someone to help me," former co-host of *The View*, Star Jones, had said in an interview with Oprah Winfrey that Deanna had watched on YouTube last week. The words had touched a part of Deanna that she didn't know was there. It was as if the words were spoken from her own heart, and she'd found herself getting choked up by the confession.

*Your tongue cannot stop qadr. But it can complicate yours.*

Deanna held her pen tight in her fist as she looked at the words she'd written in the first line of the letter of apology to herself. Bracing herself for what she knew she'd written beneath, she pressed her lips together as her eyes crawled to the next line.

*So I'm sorry, Janice, for not protecting you better.*

Deanna clenched her jaw and looked away from the paper. "For these letters of apology," her psychiatrist had said, "I need you to talk to Janice instead of Deanna. You cannot heal until you let Janice grieve, and Janice cannot grieve if you suppress her voice. Only when you let Janice express her anger freely and without censure can Deanna be free from pain. Healing cannot begin until you take an honest look at the wound."

*"Child, take your butt to the bathroom and put on some proper clothes and wash that crap off your face."* Deanna winced as she saw the loathing in her father's eyes as he looked at eight-year-old Janice proudly preparing for her "pretty lady" walk. She wore layers of fake jewelry, oversized heels, red lipstick, eye shadow, and foundation smeared childishly on her face.

*But it's not your fault, Niecey Meesy*, Deanna had written.

Upon seeing the silliness of her words, she shook her head and rolled her eyes. *"That's a stupid name,"* she said in her head.

Deanna flinched when she realized that these were the exact words Bailey had spoken to her that day. *"It's okay, Niecey Meesy,"* Janice had whispered to her alter ego in an effort to offset her offense. *"We'll think of a better name. You'll see."* Dr. Deanna J. Bivens, she was called now. Was this the better name that Janice wanted?

*I made a mistake Janice, and I'm sorry. I'm not apologizing for what Bailey did because that was his sin, not mine. I'm apologizing for what I did when I didn't let you cry or get angry and when I forced you to forgive before I helped you understand what you were forgiving.*

*"Forgive. Forgive. Forgive,"* Deanna heard her mother's voice in her mind. *"Good Christians love their enemies. So if you are showing any anger, then God is not happy with you."* Deanna's nose flared and she looked away from the page again. This whole exercise was beginning to feel like an utter waste of time. Deanna had half a mind to rip the pages of apology from the notebook, she felt so stupid reading her soppy words. Could she really take this letter seriously?

"Without censure, Deanna," her psychiatrist had reiterated. "Without censure. Don't criticize your words, and don't criticize Janice's pain. Both are coming from a place inside you that you've kept locked away for too long. Letters like these always sound awkward and humiliating at first," the woman said. "But that's only because your trauma has filled you with so much pain that you're ashamed to even look at or hear yourself with any honesty or compassion. But there's nothing shameful about listening to *anyone* with an open heart and mind, let alone yourself."

*Janice, the willingness to make mistakes is a part of emaan, part of our faith in God. So it's okay that we made a mistake in trying to forgive and run away, instead of face ourselves. It just means we're human and we need God that much more.*

Deanna wrinkled her nose, finding it difficult to believe that she'd written these pretentious words. She sounded like Aliyah.

*"You don't have to fix anything,"* Deanna heard Bailey's voice in her head as he looked hungrily at Janice. *"You're perfect just the way you are."*

Deanna frowned as she found herself agreeing with Bailey even as she wished there was some other voice she could hear say those words. *"Don't tell me you're almost pushing forty and you still haven't figured out what the hell is wrong with you?"* she heard Asher say to her, and she felt her heart soften toward her efforts of healing. Maybe writing the letter wasn't such a bad idea.

*Janice, don't let anger get the best of you,* Deanna hesitantly read her words. *We're all walking around with wounds, angry at the ones we think inflicted them. But we don't realize that our anger is only sharpening our own weapons to wound someone else.*

Deanna immediately thought of Jacob, and she felt sick to her stomach. How could she have not seen what she was doing to him?

*"Let me just cut to the chase."* She winced as she remembered Jacob's harsh words from the night of the *waleemah. "I'm not going to marry you as a second, third, or even fourth wife. And even if a sheikh were to give a fatwa that the women whom our right hands possess could be anyone we chose, I would never choose you."*

Fury rose in Deanna's chest. But she fought it, refusing to let Jacob's words offend her more than they already had.

*I'm sorry I never gave you a family,* Deanna read her words. *You don't know how much I wish I had one to give. We almost had one with Jacob, but I messed that up, and I'm working on getting it back. But Janice, I need you to know that my mother and father are not your family, and neither is Asher or Bailey. I used to think that the bonds of blood created unconditional love. But I realize now that the love that comes from family relations is merely a seed implanted in the heart of each person connected through blood. Just as with other seeds, there are some that lie in dry, untilled, unfertile land and ultimately wither away and die. That is the Michaels family, Janice. They never tilled or watered the soil. But the Bivens? Well, their seeds lie in moist, tilled, fertile land. That is why they are a family, and we're not.*

Deanna could feel her anger rising as she thought of Jacob divorcing her. "*He should not have given up on me!"* a voice cried in her mind.

*Don't expect people to never give up on you if you've already given up on yourself,* the words she'd written seemed to speak to her right then.

"Why don't you turn them into a book?" Jacob had asked when she told him about the letters she was going to write to herself. "It could be the beginning of restarting your counseling business. There are a lot of people who can relate to what you've gone through."

In the quiet of the night, Deanna lifted her gaze to the balcony's dark wood stairs that spiraled down to the grassy area enclosed by the fence that divided her parents' property from the neighbors, and she thought of the day her mother had fallen. A sharp pain stabbed her chest as she recalled that she was at least partly at fault for what had happened.

"You can also work with SAFE if you want to," Jacob had offered, referring to the non-profit organization that he and Aliyah had founded. Surviving Abuse and Family Estrangement. "And maybe we can even promote your new book."

Deanna frowned thoughtfully as her eyes lingered on the winding stairs. It was a tempting offer. But she was uncertain if she could handle being around Aliyah regularly.

"Maybe you can call it *You Can Have <u>You</u> All To Yourself,*" Jacob had joked. Deanna had laughed at his suggestion, but right then, as she held the notebook on her lap, the title didn't seem like such a bad idea.

*I gave up on you, Janice, and I shouldn't have. I'm sorry. I just didn't see the point of living anymore. But now I know that was such a stupid, selfish thing to do.* Deanna paused thoughtfully, wondering what would have happened if her suicide attempt had been successful.

When she'd gotten home from the hospital, Deanna had found a book on her bed, and she knew immediately that her mother had bought it for her. It was entitled *No Time to Say Goodbye: Surviving the Suicide of a Loved One* by Carla Fine. Initially, Deanna had only skimmed it, reluctantly reading a page or two. But after she found her depression getting the best of her, she decided that reading it couldn't hurt, especially after she was hospitalized a second time. And the story that resonated with her most was by a woman named Brenda who'd lost two friends, Faye and Maria, to suicide.

"I think Faye is at peace but I'm angry at Maria," Brenda said. "Yet, everyone who is left behind is devastated, no matter what. We all have big-time guilt that we could have done more. There was no sense of closure at either funeral, just a feeling that neither of them really cared about the rest of us…I really believe that suicide is an extremely selfish act."

BPD. In addition to "clinical depression," those were the three letters that the psychiatrist had used to sum up Deanna's condition. Borderline Personality Disorder. Deanna hated the label and wasn't fully convinced it was accurate. But she couldn't deny that her struggles ran parallel to others with the diagnosis. That many patients diagnosed with BPD had faced childhood traumas similar to Deanna's was unsettling. It was as if a bad family not only scarred you for life, but also took away the little quality of life you had left.

"For you," the psychiatrist had said, "I suggest bibliotherapy. What that basically means is using books as a means of healing. This form of treatment is not well-known, but I find it to be very beneficial, especially in patients who love to read."

After doing a brief internet search on the method, Deanna happened upon the organization Words Heal, Incorporated: Sadie Peterson Delaney Literary Collaborative, whose website suggested fiction books that people had found helpful in their healing. The one Deanna had chosen and was subsequently approved by her psychiatrist was *Trail of Broken Wings* by Sejal Badani.

"What he did to you can never be undone," the character Ranee said in the book. "But don't let it color your life. Don't let his actions or his way of living become your truth…You are your truth."

***

Jamil shook his head as a hesitant smile crept onto his lips. "I don't think I'm in a position to offer anyone relationship advice," he said from where he sat at the dining room table of Larry's home next to Sheldon and Matt and across from Jacob and Sayed. "But I send you nothing but love, man," Jamil said as he placed a hand over his heart and gestured his head toward Larry, who sat at the head of the table. "Because we're family now."

Larry smirked and nodded. "I appreciate that, man," he said sincerely. "For real."

"If you're not in a position to offer advice," Benjamin said, slight humor in his tone, "then none of us are. Some of my most powerful lessons came as a result of my mistakes."

Jamil chuckled self-consciously. "Now, I didn't say I made *mistakes*," he said. "I just don't think anyone's interested in hearing what I have to say."

"This is Larry's *halaal* bachelor party," Matt said jokingly. "I'm sure he wants to hear what we've all got to say. Otherwise, we wouldn't be here."

There was a ripple of laughter at the table. "Now, don't be getting me in trouble with the mullahs," Larry said, chuckling. "This isn't a bachelor party. I invited you here because Salima thought it was a good idea for the men to hang out too."

Jacob coughed laughter. "Then I guess you don't need my advice either, bro. You're already starting off on the right foot," he said. "Listening to your wife."

The men chuckled and nodded in agreement.

"I'll start," Benjamin said, clearing his throat. "Then we can go around the table and hear from everyone else."

Larry nodded approvingly. "I like that idea," he said. "Because I'm going to need some help here."

Benjamin grinned. "We all do, son," he said, "no matter how long we've been married."

Jacob and Sayed nodded in emphatic agreement.

"And one thing I think we men fall short on is courting our wives," Benjamin said. "We all know how to court *women*, but not our wives."

Larry narrowed his eyes and looked intently at Benjamin, curiosity piqued.

"But the most important courting period is after you've already won her affection," Benjamin said. "And if you want lasting *mutual* intimacy…" He raised his eyebrows to underscore his point. "…then it begins long before you're in the bedroom."

Sheldon creased his forehead and leaned his arms on the table, a question on his face. "What do you mean?"

"Talking to her, listening to her," Benjamin said. "Talking *with* her, spending time with her. Telling her she's beautiful." He shook his head. "And I don't mean foreplay. Women know when you're just saying something to get what you want. I'm talking about at random times," he said. "Like when she's in the middle of cooking or sending her a text when you're at work."

There was a thoughtful silence at the table.

"And give her a hug every day before you leave and every day as soon as you walk in the door. I don't care how long you've been married," he said. "That never gets old."

"Even if she's pissed at you?" Larry said in doubtful humor.

"*Especially* if she's pissed at you," Benjamin said, certainty in his voice. "And even if you're upset with her."

"But isn't that kind of disingenuous?" Larry said. "Like you're just going through the motions?"

Benjamin furrowed his brows. "Tell me something, son," he said as he regarded Larry. "Do you think you'll stop loving your wife every time you disagree with her?"

Larry chuckled. "Of course not."

"Then there's nothing disingenuous about showing affection when you're upset," Benjamin said. "You don't have to retract anything you said during the argument, or apologize for something you're not really sorry about," he clarified. "And you don't have to claim to agree with her on anything you genuinely disagree with. But you do need to let her know you love and care for her no matter what."

Larry nodded, indicating that he understood. "That makes sense."

"But what if the love dies?" Jacob said. Benjamin frowned, and Jacob could tell he didn't like the question. But Jacob really wanted to know. He doubted anything like that would happen with Aliyah. But it had happened with Deanna, and he didn't want it to ever happen again. "What do you do then?" Jacob heard a slight challenge in his own tone, but he had raised his voice only to emphasize the validity of the question.

"I'll tell you something I heard my sheikh say once," Benjamin said, compassion in his countenance as he looked at Jacob. "A marriage can survive without love, but not without mercy."

Jacob and the other men nodded, as if in deep reflection.

"*You* have a sheikh?" Jamil said, disbelieving humor in his tone as he looked at Benjamin.

Larry exhaled in a single breath, annoyance in that sound. "Can we not do this tonight, man?" He was looking at Jamil with an impatient plea on his face. Jacob tensed, having feared that Larry would bump heads with Jamil before the end of the night.

"I think it's good," Jamil said quickly. "I'm just surprised, that's all."

Benjamin squinted his eyes in confusion. "Why are you surprised?"

Jamil lifted a shoulder in a shrug. "Because Salima's always saying how we don't need a sheikh to understand Islam."

"That's *not* what she said," Larry said, raising his voice defensively. "She said we don't need to give *allegiance* to a sheikh in order to follow Islam. Everybody has to learn Islam from the people of knowledge," he said. "Even if you only learn from books, they're written by scholars."

"I think what we're trying to say is," Jacob said, his voice subdued in an attempt at a peaceful resolution, "everyone is responsible for their own soul, and you can't hand that responsibility over to anyone, no matter how knowledgeable they are. It's too dangerous," he said. "Learn Islam wherever you can find authentic information, but make Allah and His Messenger, *sallallaahu'alayhi wa sallam*, the only ultimate authorities in your religious life."

"What marriage advice do you have for us tonight?" Benjamin said, looking at Jamil in an obvious attempt to diffuse the situation.

Jamil contorted his face and waved his hand dismissively. "I don't h—"

"You sent your brother love earlier," Benjamin reminded him, his voice gentle but firm in letting Jamil know he wasn't going to wriggle his way out of this one. "So let's hear some of that love translated into *naseehah*," Benjamin said. "It's his right."

Jamil frowned, but it was apparent that he was affected by Benjamin's words.

"Tomorrow is your sister's *waleemah*," Benjamin continued, "and her husband invited us here tonight to hear our words of advice and support. Let's hear yours."

Silence permeated the room for several seconds.

"Don't hurt her, man," Jamil said finally, slight frustration in his voice. But he wasn't looking at Larry. "She's already been through hell, and it's not fair to put her through that again."

Larry nodded humbly. "I'll do my best, *insha'Allah*," he said, sincerity in his tone.

"And don't divorce her either," Jamil added, an intense expression on his face as he looked at Larry. "We lawyers know how to punish men who hurt women," he said, wry humor in his tone.

Jacob wanted to ask if they also punished women who hurt men, but he held his tongue. He didn't want to make tonight any tenser for his brother than it already was.

"I'd say play with the children and spend time with them whenever you can," Sheldon said, his lighthearted tone a sharp contrast to Jamil's. "I don't have any children yet," he said with a chuckle. "But that's something I always saw my father do, even when he was busy with the farm."

Larry nodded appreciatively, and Jacob sensed it wasn't only because of the advice itself. Sheldon's kind words had cut through the tension and revived the brotherly atmosphere.

"Don't lose yourself in your love for her," Jacob said, a half smile on his face as he looked at his younger brother. "I know it's hard when you've finally found the one. But you have to love yourself too, bro," he said. "And remember, she wants you to be the man of the house more than she wants you to be her man."

A proud smile creased the sides of Benjamin's mouth. "I second that," Benjamin said. "Being a kind and compassionate husband should never be at odds with you being the leader of the family."

"But that's a hard one for women nowadays," Matt said, a humored expression on his face as he shook his head. "You mention something like *leader* or *man of the house* and they run."

The men chuckled in agreement.

"They don't run," Benjamin said, a smile lingering on his face. "They *argue* with you," he said. "There's a difference."

"Not to me," Matt said in lighthearted humor.

"Then don't make it a point of conversation," Benjamin said simply. "Make it a fact of life. If we're living as real men who are leaders of our families, then we don't have to talk about our role. It'll just be a natural reflection of the culture we've created in our homes."

"I don't know…" Matt said, an uncertain grin on his face. "Women still don't like it."

"Then maybe those women are thinking of things in the context of abuse and oppression," Benjamin said. "But no woman wants a boy as a husband. She wants a man." He huffed, humor in that sound. "She'll try to get her way whenever she can," he said. "But she doesn't want someone she can push around. She respects you most when you stand firm on what you know is right, even if she disagrees from time to time."

Benjamin paused as he regarded Matt curiously. "What's *your* advice for us, son?"

Matt smiled self-consciously and shook his head. "I kind of feel like Jamil," he said. "I don't know what I can add."

"Anything," Benjamin said.

"Then I guess all I can say is stay prayerful, man," Matt said as he looked at Larry. "Like they say, a family that prays together stays together."

Larry nodded gratefully. "*Insha'Allah*," he added.

The men were quiet for some time, and a couple of them glanced in Sayed's direction.

"*Mabrook, akhi*," Sayed congratulated Larry. "*BaarakAllaahu laka wa baarak 'alayka wa jama'a baynakumaa feek khayr*," he added then translated. "May Allah bless you and shower His blessings upon you and join you both together in goodness."

"*Ameen*," the men uttered in unison.

"Thanks for the prayer, man," Larry said, humor in his tone. "But you still need to give me some advice."

Sayed chuckled. "I was getting to that," he said.

"Good," Larry said jokingly. "Because I know you're over there sitting on generations of sacred knowledge."

"We're all struggling in this world, *akhi*," Sayed said humbly. "But it's true that my people have had Islam in their country for centuries. And I think the only thing that makes us experts in is having made more mistakes."

"Then share with us what you've learned," Larry said. "I'm not trying to go into this reinventing the wheel. Share the knowledge."

Sayed nodded, a pleasant expression on his face. "I can only speak from my own opinion, not from any religious scholarship or authority. But I believe the most important advice for the practicing Muslim couple is to make Islam the foundation of your marriage." He paused before adding for emphasis, "Not your focus."

Everyone grew quiet in discomfort and uncertainty, and even Benjamin had a puzzled expression on his face. "You're going to have to explain that one for us," Benjamin said, chuckling. "I'm not following."

"Well, *tab'an*, if you're both practicing Muslims, Islam is most important to you, right?" Sayed said, nodding his head toward Larry.

"Yes, of course," Larry said with a nod.

"And this is your greatest strength, no doubt," Sayed said. "But it can also become your greatest weakness if you forget that marriage is more about focusing on getting to know the person you're with versus focusing on the Islamic ruling for this or that," he said. "I suppose it's like what Brother Benyameen was saying about the man being the leader. Islam isn't something you should have to talk about so much as live. When marriage becomes an argument about your Islamic rights, then you've lost the focus on getting to know each other as human beings. And now you're just two people on opposite ends of a religious debate." He shook his head. "I just don't think marriage should ever be like that. That's why I say Islam is the foundation, not your focus."

Benjamin nodded. "I think I understand what you're saying. But maybe the word you're looking for is *obsession* and not *focus*," he suggested.

"*Mumken*," Sayed said, nodding. "Maybe that is a better word."

"Because I think Islam *should* be our focus," Benjamin said. "But not something we obsess over to prove a point, or to guilt someone into doing what we want."

"*Aslan*," Sayed agreed.

"What I hear you saying," Jacob said to Sayed, "is that Islam should never be used as a tool of spiritual abuse or a shortcut to getting your way while ignoring the nuances of your relationship and the personality of the person you're married to."

"Exactly," Sayed said. "And if you're truly following Islam," he added, "your faith will bring peace to your marriage, not friction."

***

"I heard he's remarrying his ex-wife," Nikki said from where she held Bushra on her lap as she sat on the floor of Aliyah's living room amongst the other women. "Is that true?"

Salima shrugged. "That's what it looks like," she said non-committedly.

Aliyah sensed that Salima was uncomfortable with the shift in conversation. Salima had hoped that starting the night with poetry would liven up the evening and create a natural flow of conversation. She had told Aliyah that she was hoping for something that bonded the sisters and helped them offer each other advice on life and marriage.

Initially, Aliyah had offered to host a henna party that night. But Salima had declined, suggesting that Aliyah host Muslim Marriage Monologues instead. Because the reddish brown color didn't show up well against her complexion, Salima rarely wore henna and didn't want an entire sisters wedding party centered around something in which she herself found little interest. She'd said she tried the black henna once or twice but didn't feel comfortable dyeing the unnatural version into her skin.

"But I support my brother in whatever decision he makes," Salima said in an obligatory tone, and Aliyah wondered what she could say to change the subject seamlessly.

"Whatever happened to Jasmine though?" Nikki said. "Juwayriah said she was trying to get with Jamil now."

"I don't know," Salima said, exhaustion in her tone. "I haven't heard from her in a while. But Jasmine and Jamil are definitely *not* an item." She offered Nikki a tightlipped smile. "But you might want to ask Juwayriah since she seems to know more about this than I do," Salima said, and Aliyah heard the slight sarcasm in her words.

"Why don't we play Lessons Learned?" Aliyah said, her voice rising awkwardly as she tried to sound chipper.

"That doesn't sound like a game," Carletta said with a grunt. "Sounds like some type of confession."

Aliyah smiled at Carletta, grateful that she'd come tonight to support Salima even though she no longer participated in Muslim Marriage Monologues for whatever reason. "Well…" Aliyah said, relieved that they had moved on from discussing gossip about Jamil. "I guess you could call it that. But you're right. It's not a game. It's more like an icebreaker."

Carletta chuckled, her sonorous tone seeming to come from deep within her throat. "We've been here for two hours already," she said. "Don't you think it's a little late for that?"

"I like the idea," Salima said, enthusiasm in her voice. "If we're going to be here all night, I say let's do some bonding."

"This is a slumber party?" Nikki glanced at Aliyah in confusion.

Aliyah shook her head. "Only for whoever wants to stay," she said. "But Jacob is staying at Larry's tonight and Salima is staying here with me."

"Kalimah's flight arrives at eleven o'clock tonight," Salima clarified. "And she didn't want to miss my party, so we turned it into an all-nighter."

"Oh okay…" Nikki sounded relieved. "Because I have to get Bushra to bed soon."

"That's fine," Aliyah said. "But you're welcome to stay," she said. "We set up beds for the boys in the playroom, so it's no problem for you and Bushra to sleep in the empty bedroom."

Nikki wrinkled her nose and shook her head, but her expression remained pleasant. "Matt texted saying he should be here soon," she said. "But thanks."

"It's no problem," Aliyah said before turning her attention back to the group.

"I'll start," she said, offering a wide smile. "Here's a lesson I learned, and I guess it's something you probably already got from my poem. But family is a connection of the heart more than of the blood."

Tina nodded emphatically, the cloth of her veil creasing beneath her chin. "I agree one hundred percent. After I became Muslim, my mother is the only person who even bothers to talk to me."

Aliyah shook her head knowingly. "And my mother had pretty much forbidden everyone from talking to me."

"What are they so scared of?" Mashael frowned from the chair she sat on next to Aliyah's because their pregnancy made it difficult to sit on the floor and because the couch made it difficult to sit close to everyone. "Do they think all Muslims are terrorists or something?"

"I think they're just scared to face themselves," Tina said. "Lori and I were talking the other day, and she said something that really made me think."

At the mention of Lori, Aliyah felt happy for Tina. When Tina had shared her story at Muslim Marriage Monologues the year before about losing her best friend to polygyny, Tina and Lori were no longer in touch.

"She said that people fear the truth most," Tina continued. "And the closer that truth is to their heart, the less they can deal with it."

"Or they just have a guilty conscience," Carletta added. "When you learn about Islam, you *know* it's true," she said with emphasis. "And people don't like to be reminded of what they gave up when they rejected Islam."

"But some people are just ignorant," Nikki said, lighthearted disagreement in her tone. "And they're not trying to be mean or anything," she said. "When Matt became Muslim, I refused to have anything to do with him. But it wasn't because I felt guilty or scared. I just thought he'd lost his mind. I didn't know anything about Islam except what I'd seen on TV."

There was a thoughtful silence.

"But why didn't you research for yourself?" Mashael said in genuine curiosity. "You can't believe everything you hear on the news."

Nikki shrugged. "Why research something you already think you understand? It wasn't like I was consciously trying to be ignorant and Islamophobic," she said.

"I know, but…" Mashael's expression was troubled, and it was apparent that she was having a difficult time articulating what she was trying to say.

"But look at how you called it 'the news,'" Nikki said to Mashael. "Why?" she said challengingly. "It's not even something we think about. But those shows are not 'the news.' It's just what they call it."

"I second that," Carletta said, lifting her hand as if she were in church. "I'm a teacher, and I swear to you, the most ignorant people, from the students *and* the teachers, are the ones who sit in front of that television every day and night in the name of, quote, 'keeping up with what's happening in the world.'" She grunted.

"I'm beginning to believe you learn *more* about the world the *less* television you watch."

Some sisters huffed in agreement.

"I don't care what they call it," Carletta added with a shrug. "The news, a documentary, or a sitcom. It all has the same purpose," she said. "And there's a reason they call it all a *program*."

Salima nodded. "TV is definitely the plug-in drug," she said, "programming you to think and feel a certain way."

"*And* believe," Carletta added in agreement.

"But what's the solution?" Reem said, her voice conflicted. "We can't just sit around and be ignorant."

"I don't have a TV," Tina said, "and I haven't had one for almost two years. And I feel like I know more than I did before. I read books and interact with people," she said. "And I even feel less stressed, especially walking around with my face covered."

Tina shook her head. "I swear," she continued, "when I used to watch TV, I was always upset about all the crazy things they'd blame on Muslims, and I'd constantly feel judged." She shrugged. "Now I don't even think about it anymore. The only time I remember that most people think TV is real life is when I talk to Muslims about how scared they are for their safety. Or when some nutcase comes up to me and starts yelling at me to go back to my country."

"But it's important to at least know what other people are saying about us," Reem insisted, "even if it's not true."

Tina chuckled. "I think I have a pretty good idea," she said with humored conviction. "It's the same thing they were saying when I got rid of my TV two years ago." She lifted a shoulder in a shrug. "But I know many Muslims think it's more important to keep up with talking heads and anti-Muslim propaganda than they do with their prayers and Qur'an," she said in light sarcasm. "I'm just not one of them."

Reem frowned, and Aliyah could tell Reem took offense to Tina's words. "Knowing what's happening around you doesn't keep you from your prayers and Qur'an."

A smirk creased one side of Tina's mouth. "Like I said," Tina remarked, "I think you know what's happening around you by actually interacting with what's around you, not by listening to someone else tell you what's there." She lifted a shoulder in a shrug. "In my opinion, watching TV and obsessing over their so-called news distracts us from Allah and our spiritual responsibilities." She paused then added, "At least it does for me. If you think all of this Islamophobic media is good for you and your children, then more power to you. I just don't agree."

Reem looked as if she wanted to respond but decided against it.

"I'll tell you a lesson I learned," Salima said, her upbeat tone a sharp contrast to the slight friction of a moment before. "Or I should say, a lesson I'm *learning*," she clarified.

“Speak, girl,” Carletta said. “You always have some wise nuggets, *mashaAllah*.”

Salima laughed self-consciously. “Now I don’t want to share it,” she said jokingly. “People are going to expect something really profound.”

“The most powerful lessons are the simplest ones,” Carletta said. “So I’m listening.”

Salima pursed her lips. “It’s nothing groundbreaking,” she said apologetically. “But I’m learning to not compare myself to other Muslims.”

Carletta huffed in agreement. “Amen to that.”

“I guess I’m realizing there’s no point in trying to understand why they do what they do,” Salima said. “So I’m just making peace with the fact that not all Muslims experience Islam in the same way.” She coughed laughter. “They don’t even *believe* in it the same way.”

The women nodded, listening. “That’s so true,” Aliyah mumbled.

“To me, Islam is just about believing in Allah and doing what He commanded and staying away from what He’s forbidden.” Salima spoke as if lost in thought. “And if I die as a Muslim with all my sins forgiven,” she said, shaking her head to underscore how much this meant to her, “then I don’t care about anything else.”

The room was silent for several seconds, as the women seemed to be reflecting on what she’d just said.

Salima sighed. “But I’m learning that this isn’t what Islam means to everyone else,” she said, sadness in her tone. “I can’t even begin to understand what would make someone want something else from this faith.” She shrugged as if in reluctant humility. “But I’m learning that it’s not for me to understand,” she said. “They have their *qadr*, and I have mine. So I just have to focus on the path Allah put in front of me and not worry about why what other people see in front of them is so different, even though we call our faith by the same name.”

# 40
# His Only Wife

"Larry and Salima," Jacob sang out playfully after he recited the supplication for entering the home as he stepped into the foyer behind Aliyah and the boys. They had just returned from the *waleemah* Saturday night. "Who would've thought?" He smiled and shook his head before closing the door and turning the bolt.

Distracted, Aliyah frowned as the boys ran ahead of her and rushed downstairs to the playroom. "Ibrahim!" she shouted, frustration in her voice.

Jacob gently squeezed his wife's arm. "It's okay," he said. "It's not a school night."

Aliyah sighed as she rested a hand on her swollen belly. "But *I'm* tired," she said. "I can barely keep my eyes open."

"Then go on to bed," Jacob said, his voice soft in compassion as he gestured his head toward the stairs. "I'll make sure they shower and put on their pajamas."

Aliyah slapped a palm to her forehead, as if remembering something just then. "Oh my God," she said. "I don't think we packed Haroon's toothbrush."

"Do you need me to go back to Larry's?" Jacob said.

Aliyah shook her head. "It's okay," she said with a wave of her hand, exhaustion in her tone. She slipped off her shoes and stepped into the living room. "I only want to use the key again if we absolutely have to."

Jacob set his keys on the front table then kneeled to pull of his shoes. "Larry says to tell you thank you for offering to keep Haroon for the weekend," Jacob said as he aligned his and Aliyah's shoes on the rack.

"It's fine," Aliyah said, swaying slowly to the right and left as she waddled to the stairs. "It's the least we can do after all the times he's watched the boys for us," she said sincerely. "Besides, what's the point of him spending all weekend alone with Jamil when he can be with Ibrahim, Younus, and Thawab?"

"True." Jacob fell in step next to Aliyah and placed a hand on her back to guide her up the stairs.

They were silent as they took the steps one at a time, Aliyah gripping the banister with one hand.

"I'm really happy for them, *mashaAllah*," Aliyah said once they reached the hallway and started walking toward the newly renovated master bedroom.

"I am too," Jacob said, still walking in step with Aliyah, a hand on her lower back.

"And Reem's family too," Aliyah added. "I would've never thought her parents would offer to host an American's *waleemah* at their house."

Jacob chuckled. "You make it sound like we're contagious or something."

Aliyah chuckled too, hearing her words from her husband's perspective. "I just mean they aren't exactly the intercultural mingling type."

Jacob shrugged. "And we are?" he said skeptically.

Aliyah considered his question and was momentarily reminded of her and Benjamin's conversation about Americans' own struggles with cultural Islam. "I guess not…" she said, uncertainty in her voice.

Jacob reached ahead of Aliyah and opened their bedroom door. "I think it's only natural that people feel most comfortable around people they can relate to." He waited for her to enter then followed behind her.

Aliyah frowned as she made her way to the king-size bed they'd recently bought. "But her parents gave Mashael a really hard time about marrying Sheldon," she said.

"And your parents gave you a really hard time about everything," Jacob said with a shrug. "And my parents aren't exactly thrilled to have a divorced son in the family."

"But we're Muslim," Aliyah said.

"And we're also human," Jacob said, reiterating his point from an earlier conversation. "I can't imagine how I'd feel if our daughter wanted to run off with some boy from a strange country who wasn't even raised Muslim."

Aliyah's hand immediately went to her stomach as she felt a wave of protectiveness at the scenario. She had never thought about it like that. "I guess that would be kind of hard," she admitted.

"At the core, I think most parents just want what's best for their children," Jacob said.

Aliyah nodded as she lowered herself onto the edge of the bed and slowly let it receive her weight. "And what's safest," she added.

"Especially when it comes to their daughters," Jacob said as he sat next to Aliyah and gently rubbed her back with the flat of his hand. "It's human nature," he said. "You can't fault anyone for that."

Aliyah pursed her lips thoughtfully. "But isn't that just an excuse to shirk our responsibilities as Muslims?"

Jacob shook his head. "No," he said. "I'm sure it wasn't an easy decision for Reem's family to welcome a stranger into the family. But what's important is they did the right thing in the end," he said. "Allah is *Al-Ghafoor Ar-Raheem*, and we're all in need of His forgiveness and mercy."

Aliyah sighed. "That's true," she said. "*Astaghfirullah.*"

"But how are you and the babies?" Jacob said as he reached up and gently clamped Aliyah's shoulders with both hands.

Aliyah relaxed under his touch. "*Alhamdulillah,*" she said, slowly closing her eyes as his hands moved in the beginning of a massage on her shoulders.

"Have you thought of any names?" Jacob said.

Aliyah was silent for several seconds as she kept her eyes shut, wanting to delay thinking about anything other than Jacob's gentle touch. "Hmm…" she said finally. "I was thinking Ismail for the boy and maybe Juwayriah for the girl."

She heard Jacob chuckle. "Are you joking?" he said as he continued the massage.

Aliyah opened her eyes and offered him a smile. "No, I'm serious," she said. "You don't like the names?"

"Ismail is fine," he said tentatively. "I'm more than happy to have another son named after a prophet."

"But…" Aliyah said, egging him on, lighthearted teasing in her voice.

"But Juwayriah?" He wrinkled his nose and halted the massage as he regarded her, a disbelieving smile on his face. "You can't be serious."

Aliyah laughed out loud. "See?" she said. "That's exactly why I'm thinking to keep the name. You're thinking of the sister who's always starting *fitnah*, right?"

"It crossed my mind," Jacob said, a self-conscious grin on his face.

"Well, *I'm* thinking of Juwayriah bint Harith, the wife the Prophet, *sallallaahu'alayhi wa sallam*," Aliyah said with a grin. "May Allah be pleased with her." She shook her head. "And I refuse to let anyone pollute her legacy so much that I wouldn't want to name my own daughter after her."

Jacob nodded guiltily. "You have a point."

"Imagine if Muslims did that with the names Abdullah and Abdur-Rahman," Aliyah said good-naturedly. "Or even Muhammad and Ibrahim." She raised her eyebrows as she regarded Jacob. "And how many men do you know with those names who aren't living how they're supposed to?"

Jacob leaned over and kissed Aliyah on the cheek. "I stand corrected," he said with a smile, resuming the massage.

"Juwayriah bint Harith was one of the most beautiful wives of the Prophet," Aliyah said. "When Ayesha, *radhiyaAllaahu'anhaa*, first saw her, she was really jealous. And I want my daughter to be that beautiful," she said, "physically *and* spiritually."

"*Ameen*," Jacob said as he lowered a hand to rub Aliyah's lower back.

"But I'm still undecided," Aliyah said with a thoughtful frown. "I also like the name Asiya," she said.

Jacob raised his eyebrows in approval. "Now *that's* a powerful woman, *mashaAllah*," he said. "If our daughter can have *emaan* like the wife of Pharaoh, that would be a huge blessing."

"I know…" Aliyah agreed, a half smile on her face as she shook her head in agreement.

"My vote is for the name Asiya," Jacob said. "And not because of that sister named Juwayriah," he clarified, humor in his tone, as if anticipating Aliyah's disappointment. "But because Asiya was one of the four greatest women to ever live."

Aliyah nodded. "That's what I keep thinking," she said thoughtfully. "But I really like the name Juwayriah though."

"I like them both," Jacob said. "So I support whatever you decide."

There was a thoughtful pause. "What if we call her Asiya Juwayriah?" Aliyah said.

Jacob's lips formed a thin line as he considered the suggestion. "That's fine," he said tentatively. "But I prefer Asiya Jacob."

Aliyah laughed out loud. "Nice try," she said, rolling her eyes.

"I'm serious," he said, laughter in his voice. "But not because of me, but because that's the way children were named at the time of the Prophet, *sallallaahu'alayhi wa sallam*," he said. "Just like our Mother Juwayriah is known as the daughter of Harith, her father, I want our children to be known as the sons and daughters of Jacob."

Aliyah nodded, seeing his point. "It just sounds weird," she said, wrinkling her nose.

"It takes some getting used to," Jacob agreed. "But for tracing their lineage, I think it's best."

"I'll have to think about that one," Aliyah said honestly. "But I like the idea of following the tradition of the Prophet."

There was an extended pause as Jacob resumed massaging both of Aliyah's shoulders. Aliyah moaned, a relaxed smile creasing one side of her mouth.

"Well, since you're feeling charitable," Jacob said jokingly. "Deanna keeps asking if I'd take her as a second wife."

Aliyah rolled her eyes and smirked. "And she keeps texting me, saying I should encourage you since she's the mother of your children."

Jacob shook his head as if humored by a memory. "The irony..." he said, a smirk lingering on his face.

Aliyah grunted, laughter in that sound. "Tell me about it."

"She says I need to look at the bigger picture," Jacob said, his voice more serious though it carried a trace of humor.

"What?" Aliyah said, humored disbelief in her tone. "I *am* the bigger picture."

Jacob chuckled and shook his head. "I can't argue with that."

"Good," Aliyah said with a grin as Jacob released her shoulders. "Because I'm too tired and pregnant to think about Deanna right now. She had her chance."

Aliyah pushed herself to a standing position and walked toward the bathroom.

"But I feel sorry for her," Jacob said, his tone reflective. "I really wish there was something more we could do to help."

Aliyah drew in a deep breath and exhaled as she turned to face her husband in the open doorway of the bathroom. "I do too," she said sincerely. "But not enough to make her part of the family."

Jacob nodded. "I feel the same way," he said. "But I can't help feeling responsible for her though."

Aliyah was silent, unsure what to say.

"I just feel we as men can do better," he said, shaking his head in self-reproach. "There are so many single women out there fending for themselves."

"You can't save everybody," Aliyah said quietly.

"And I'm not trying to," Jacob said. "Even if I were to remarry Deanna, it wouldn't be a full marriage."

Aliyah was enflamed in jealous fury at the mere mention of the possibility. "What's that supposed to mean?" she said, realizing too late that her tone sounded more bitter than curious.

"She asked if we could do the Sawda bint Zam'ah arrangement," he said. "And I felt horrible saying no."

Aliyah wrinkled her nose, offended that Deanna was trying to play the martyr. "She offered to give up *all* her nights to me?" There was disbelief in her tone.

"Yes," Jacob said.

Aliyah lifted a shoulder in a shrug. "Then what's the point of getting married if there won't be any intimacy?"

Jacob was silent for some time as he seemed to be gathering his thoughts. "I think she just needs to feel like she has a family," he said finally. "And with me providing consistent financial and emotional maintenance, I think she'll feel like she's part of something again."

For a moment, Aliyah was moved and felt that it was something that Jacob should do, even if only for the blessings. But she quickly dismissed the thought. "She won't be satisfied with only that," Aliyah said finally. "At least not in the long run. If you marry her, she'll be compliant at first. But then over time, she'll start making more and more demands until you wonder how you got right back to where you started."

Jacob chuckled, a half smile on his face. "I keep thinking the same thing," he said.

"And keep thinking it," Aliyah said, huffing. "It's what'll most likely happen."

"But anyway, it's not something I'm seriously considering," Jacob said. "I don't think I could handle it anyway. Just talking to her is an emotional trigger for me," he said. "She needs someone who can appreciate who she's trying to be today. I'm still stuck in the past."

"Allah knows who's best for her," Aliyah said reflectively. "Let's just make *du'aa*."

"I am," Jacob said sincerely. "Every day."

Aliyah smirked. "Just make sure you specify that her husband should be someone other than *you*," she said. "I didn't sign up to be the other wife."

Smiling, Jacob stood and walked over to Aliyah then drew her into an embrace. "You have nothing to worry about, baby," he said, and she settled into his arms. "I'm just happy to have you as a wife at all, and *insha'Allah*, I'll be content if you're my only wife for the rest of my life."

**Also By Umm Zakiyyah**

*If I Should Speak*
*A Voice*
*Footsteps*
*Realities of Submission*
*Hearts We Lost*
*The Friendship Promise*
*Muslim Girl*

Order information available at ummzakiyyah.com/store

## About the Author

Daughter of American converts to Islam, Umm Zakiyyah (also known by her birth name Ruby Moore), writes about the interfaith struggles of Muslims and Christians, and the intercultural, spiritual, and moral struggles of Muslims in America. Her work has earned praise from writers, professors, and filmmakers and has been translated into multiple languages.

*To find out more about the author, visit ummzakiyyah.com or uzauthor.com, subscribe to her YouTube channel, follow her on Twitter, or join her Facebook page at facebook.com/ummzakiyyahpage*